TITLE: Novel 2 Murdered Father Malachi Martin's ANTICHRIST. Battle at Rose Fi ͞ ͭ ˡ ͦ Wales, 1250s A.D. Fictionalized.

BOOK TWO IN TRILOGY.

For Author only: Filename, search key words: Book1 wpu   This is Book 2 in the Trilogy.
For Author only: Constantly Up dated File Name:

Book Two in Trilogy. Book Two Title: Murdered Father Malachi Martin's Secrets about the AntiChrist and the Knights of the Sorrowful Lady. Battle at Rose Fire Castle, Wales. Around 1250s A.D.. Malachi Martin's Vatican Secrets in Fictionalized, Novel form. Just as did Murdered Father Malachi Martin.
By: Author-Publisher David Okey Cummings

Copyright Library of Congress Feb. 20, 2003 Author-Publisher David Okey Cummings
Copyright Library of Congress March 1, 2017 Author-Publisher David Okey Cummings
ISBN: 9781520752082 Imprint: Independently published

FORWARD:
WHO WAS MURDERED FATHER MALACHI MARTIN?
　　　Father Malachi Martin discovered that the purpose of globalism is war. War is the most profitable industry in history, in the world.
　　　Malachi's last book was an in-depth exposition. Exposition of the evils behind the international, corporate, globalist deep-state. The non-democratic European Union and anti democratic trade treaties like NAFTA. Also, the World Trade Organization and the Trans-Pacific Partnership. Plus the World Bank. In the Vatican's state department, Father Malachi discovered the purpose of trade agreements. International corporations designed international trade agreements upon corporate greed. To move wealth away from every country's middle class. To move manufacturing labor from democracies. From democracies to slave-like countries.

Slave-like such as China. To move the wealth into the hands of a few corporate owners, the globalist's deep-state.

Malachi termed the globalist deep-state as the home of the AntiChrist. An assassin murdered Malachi and stole the book Father Malachi had finished. The assassin emptied Malachi's apartment and stole his computer and papers.

Father Malachi discovered the dysfunction of non-democratic globalism. The dysfunction of appointing, not directly electing, representatives to the European Union. International corporations made sure that countries appointed European Union representatives. Free, open, secret ballots are the enemy of the European union. European Union representatives are not elected. Father Malachi discovered that the EU was and is the spawning ground for the AntiChrist. Before anyone else, Father Malachi discovered the cause of Britain's Brexit. The cause of Frances' probable Frexit. Discovered the historical democratic populism that is tearing down the globalist deep-state. The globalist foundation for the AntiChrist.

Malachi Brendan Martin (Irish: Maolsheachlainn Breandán Ó Máirtín; Born July 23, 1921; Murdered July 1999, New York); pseudonym: Michael Serafian.

My books contain Malachi Martin's most important and central secrets. Secrets about religion and politics. The AntiChrist's secrets to building a dictatorship, globalist deep-state.

Murdered Malachi worked as an exorcist. More important, as an assistant to the Vatican's Secretary of State. In the Vatican's consulate, the oldest continuous consulate in the world. Thus, Malachi Martin published both contemporary and ancient secrets. I have used these Vatican secrets in my books.

Old Father Malachi Martin was a devout Catholic Priest, a Vatican exorcist. He was about to publish his most damaging book of many. The most damaging of all. Damaging to the international globalists, revealing personal names, evil plans. Gaining him worldwide enemies. Then an assassin pushed the 78-year-old Catholic Priest down a flight of steps. In New York City. The assassin disappeared, disappeared with Malachi's books, papers and computer. Then the assassin cleaned out Malachi's apartment. The Devout Roman Catholic priest Exorcist died of a brain hemorrhage days later. In his many books, Father Malachi exposed the truth of religion and governments. Thus the Exorcist had gathered many worldwide enemies in every government, every religion. He exposed the existence of tangential, yet influential, Satanism in the Vatican. Malachi worked as an exorcist. Also, as an assistant to the Vatican's Secretary of State. The oldest consistent consulate in the world. Thus, Malachi Martin had access to contemporary and ancient secrets. I have used these Vatican secrets in my books.

As a multi linguist, ancient and modern languages, in the Vatican Malachi had access. Access both in face to face translation and to documents.

Malachi's last book was to be an in-depth exposition of globalism's structure of evil. Of the evil people behind the international, corporate, globalist deep-state. Someone unknown murdered him and stole the book Father Malachi had finished.

Father Malachi saw before anyone the dysfunction of non-democratic globalism. The cause of Brexit, probable Frexit, and the democratic populism. Democratic popularism that now tears down the invisible, globalist deep-state.

END THE FORWARD

-

-

-

CHAPTER, Year @ 1250s A.D., the place was the Black Mountains of Wales, Great Britain. Wolv's Red Fog Grows Denser. Over All England and Europe, Wales. The castle was the Pendragon Castle, Rose Fire, in Wales. The Holy Mary of the Child Jesus Castle.

THE AntiChrist's ROAR

On the seat of a bumping horse drawn wagon, six-year-old Warrick asked, "Mother. Why are we here? These Black Mountains are frightening and cold."

Beatrice Pentagon hugged her son with one arm and said, "Little Warrick. We will be safe when we find Father Malachi Martin. He is somewhere in Wales in the Black Mountains. We must find Father Malachi Martin. Malachi is the Vatican's strongest, most beloved and most hated, exorcist."

A roar shook the mountains and vibrated the castle. The roar was the phrase, "Father, you must forgive them. They know not what they do," echoed off the mountains.

Little Warrick bumped on the wooden seat and shouted, "What. What is that roar? It shakes the ground and scares the horses."

The tandem-horses in the wagon-train reared. Surprised, the driver pulled back on the reins and calmed the four horses. He cracked his whip over their heads so they would continue their run.

Seated beside the driver, six-year-old Warrick grasped his mother's arm. Through baby-teeth he said, "Mama. What is that horrible sound?"

The driver said, "Look around. We are in the dangerous red fog. Never let the red-fog hear you. Remember that the red-fog can climb up to you if it hears you. Never stop running if you are in the red-fog. If the horses stop running, the things in Wolv's red fog will catch us. Then they will eat us and eat the horses. That horrible growl is one of the AntiChrist's obsessions, Wolv's obsession. Wolv's red fog follows Wolv and his animal-head Skinwalkers wherever he goes. Wolv's Skinwalkers have animal heads and Skulls and Crossbones on their foreheads. The AntiChrist, Wolv, is very close."

Six-year-old Warrick said, "Why Jesus' words from the Cross, 'Father. Forgive them.'"

Then the driver said, "I see you know your bible. The monasteries ring the Sext bells. A thousand years ago Wolv nailed Jesus' hands and feet to the Cross. Nailed them at Sext bells, the zenith sun bells. Three hours later at Nones' bells Wolv rammed a Spear through Jesus' right side. Through Jesus' right side up through Jesus' heart. Those three hours and the Prime bells, the morning Resurrection bells, torture Wolv."

Beatrice Pendragon said, "Warrick. Do you remember the seven phrases Jesus said from the Cross?"

Between his milk teeth, little Warrick said, "My Father. Forgive them, for they know not what they do. Today you will be with me in paradise. Behold your son; behold your mother. My God, my God, why have you forsaken me? I thirst. It is finished. Father, into your hands I commit my spirit."

The driver said, "You are a good mother. You have taught your son in depth."

Beatrice said, "Warrick. Wolv howls from Sext bells to Nones bells. From the hour Wolv nailed Jesus to the Cross, zenith sun, to three hours later. To three hours later, when Wolv rammed a spear up in Jesus' s right side. Wolv howls those seven phrases wherever he is. Every day, those four hours terrify Wolv. He relives the Resurrection hour at sun up, Prime bells. The Resurrection hour tells Wolv that he cannot defeat Jesus. The three hours on the Cross make Wolv relive his guilt. Wolv's guilt for killing his childhood friend."

Little Warrick asked, "Childhood friend?"

Beatrice Pendragon said, "Yes. From Symon of Cyrene's writings, we know about Wolv. Wolv was Symon's half brother by Assassio. In Egypt, all age six. Wolv, Jesus, Symon of Cyrene, and a little girl, Pamia, played together. General Assassio, the general of Rome Assassins, was Wolv's father. King Herod of Jerusalem asked Rome to send General Assassio to find and kill Jesus. A scribe, Symon of Cyrene, wrote that Assassio tried to run over Jesus. Run over Jesus with a chariot. The soft road collapsed under the chariot. Yet, Assassio knew never to drive a chariot on that soft road. Assassio fell over a cliff to his death. Wolv's mother immediately died of a broken heart upon seeing Assassio's dead body. Since then, Wolv has claimed that Jesus murdered Assassio and his mother. Claimed that Jesus spooked Assassio's horses over the cliff. Thus, Wolv's hatred of Jesus began in Egypt."

Then Beatrice Pendragon said, "We are going to a castle. A Castle of the Sorrowful Lady's Knights. A castle of the Pendragon brothers, of my family line, the Symon of Cyrene Pendragons. If you ask, they will let you read in their library. They have ancient parchments that record that Wolv crucified Jesus. The parchments record that red-fog blotched out the sun this red-fog. Blotched out during the Crucifixion. Library-parchments record Wolv made a deal with Satan. A deal for many demons to possess Wolv. The powers of the demons keep Wolv alive. Yet the demons make him demented, obsessed, guilt-ridden. The demons keep him powerful and impossible to kill. Warriors have reported that they have dismembered him. Chopped him into many pieces, then they say that he heals."

Again the same roar, the same voice, different words, shook the mountains. This time with, "Today you will be with me in paradise."

Beatrice Pendragon said, "Fear not, my little son, Warrick. We will be safe when we find Father Malachi Martin."

The horses again reared. Quickly the driver cracked a whip over them to keep them running.

Six-year-old Warrick said, "Wolv is repeating the words Jesus said to the good thief."

The driver said, "Wolv is obsessed with all the words Jesus said. Wolv is the AntiChrist. Obsessed with everything Jesus did. Woman, you are this little boy's mother. You must hold tight to your son. The monster, the AntiChrist is near. Keep your son and yourself high. High out of Wolv's red fog. Never stop running in Wolv's red fog until you are above it. Also, Wolv has many slit-pupils in his eyes, snake-like slits. If you see them, grab your son and run. His Skinwalkers save heads of animals and Skulls and Crossbones on their foreheads."

Warrick said, "I am very hungry. Where is my father's castle?"

The driver nodded, "Many hours away. Sext bells will pass. Then three hours later Nones' bells will pass. When we arrive, we will hear supper bells, Vespers bells. Pray that the horses do not go lame. If we have to stop the Things in the red-fog will eat us. If we have to stop, you must not stop running in Wolv's red fog. Always remember that Wolv's red fog can climb. If Wolv's red fog hears you, it can climb up to you and kill you."

Sunset, revealed monasteries on mountainsides of the Black Mountains. High above Wolv's red fog, evening vespers bells called monks to prayer. To supper.

The driver said, "Here we are, safe. Your father's castle. High above Wolv's red fog. Those evening vespers' bells mean that sunset-prayers and supper are now. Find Father Malachi Martin and never, never stop running in Wolv's red fog. Remember that Wolv's red-fog can climb, if it hears you."

His mother said, "Two days travel without food, without stopping. Warrick. This is your father's castle. Father Malachi Martin is close."

The driver said, "Lady Beatrice Pendragon, it is a pleasure to serve you. Now I must stable the horses. Take your son in the castle. Your husband's servants will feed and bathe both of you."

Little Warrick licked his lips and said, "I smell roast boar."

His mother, Beatrice Pendragon, said, "Yes, and roast venison."

Warrick smiled as his mouth watered and his eyes sparkled.

Warrick said, "Mama, this strange pink castle is to be our new home."

Beatrice said, "Yes. Rose Fire. Your father's castle. Father Malachi Martin should be inside."

With little fingers and bare feet, Warrick crawled down from the merchant's wagon seat.

The little boy stood on the bailey's stone floor.

He pointed with his little finger and said, "Mama, look, like my father said. Daddy's castle does have pink-granite walls."

He looked up to see the flame-red-sky glisten on the red clay, tile-roofs.

His mother, Beatrice Pendragon, said, "The AntiChrist sieged us from my castle. We only have our torn clothes on our backs."

Barefoot, little Warrick ran across the bailey. To climb the Great Hall's steps, he put his hands on a step. Then he raised a knee onto the step. Next, he rolled onto his back. He rolled across the step. Warrick climbed and rolled up the cold, stone-steps. Behind him his mother smiled. She admired her child's determination.

She said, "Child, you have your father's determination, enough determination to create your own fate. You must stay close to me. This castle is dangerous."

Little Warrick looked up to her. Through his little baby-teeth and innocent smile, Warrick said, "Mother. You need not fear. I promise. I will protect you. Mother, I promise, I will protect you."

His mother smiled and took Warrick's hand.

A doorman opened the massive Great Hall door. A Black monk-like robe and hood hid all the features of the only doorman. The monk-like hood completely hid his face and neck.

Then with a wide smile, Warrick darted from his mother. On little legs, he ran through the Great Hall doors and across the Great Hall. Thirty torches on each parallel wall lit the pink granite Great Hall.

Then Warrick climbed into an empty chair, a chair beside his father's chair.

Warrick said, "Mama, where is Daddy. This is Daddy's castle."

His mother sat and pulled Warrick's chair over to her chair. She whispered, "Child, you must stay close to me. As I told you, this castle is dangerous."

As he stood in the chair to eat, Warrick waived his little hand. He said, "Mother, I will protect you from any danger. I promise. I will protect you from all dangers."

A black aura surrounded the doorman. Behind Warrick and Warrick's mother, the doorman pulled back his hood. Torchlights reflected off the doorman's multiple-pupil eyes. Little Warrick nor Warrick's mother realized that Wolv, the AntiChrist, was the doorman. They had no idea that the doorman was Wolv.

Behind them a black aura surrounded Wolv. Like a waterfall, Red-fog began to flow off him. Torch, oil lamp and candlelight glistened from Wolv's multiple-pupil-eyes.

Two days of no food. Now the sights and smells of all the food almost made the small boy dizzy. As he stood on a chair, he could barely reach the tall table. He reached with a small hand and grabbed a leg of chicken.

Behind six-year-old Warrick, the lord of the castle, Wolv scowled. He growled, "Orphans do not eat in this castle."

Red-fog poured off Wolv. The Red-fog covered the floor up to the table's top.

Warrick stood in his chair and turned around to Wolv.

With his baby-teeth clenched Warrick said, "I am not an orphan."

Warrick pointed to his mother. His mother beside him. "My mother sits beside me."

Wolv stuck a knife into Warrick's mother's back.

As Warrick looked at his mother, she slumped forward in her chair. The dagger-handle in the air.

Tiny Warrick said, "Mommy? Mommy?"

The AntiChrist raised his arm and backhanded Warrick.

The small boy and the chair flew across the hall. Warrick's head banged against the granite-wall and bounced off the floor. Blood ran from his nose and ear.

Wolv reached to shove the knife deeper into the back of Warrick's mother's back. Beatrice Pendragon's back.

Little Warrick gritted his tiny teeth. He jumped up, ran and plunged a table knife into the back of Wolv leg.

Then little Warrick pushed the knife completely into Wolv's leg, blade and hilt.

Wolv leaned back and howled. Pain froze him in place.

Then Little Warrick pulled the knife from his mother's back. With both his hands the six-year-old child, Warrick, plunged the knife into Wolv's stomach. Up to the hilt. He leaned and shoved the hilt into Wolv's stomach.

Tiny Warrick, then, made a mistake. Instead of running, he paused. He hit his chest with his tiny fist and shouted, "Like. Like my father, I am a warrior."

Wolv backhanded him against a granite wall.

This time Warrick did not get up.

Catholic Church Vigils bells announced midnight. Six-year-old Warrick woke on a straw bed. In a peasant's straw hut. An old, bald, bony man, Norwin Stoke, bent over him. Norwin unwrapped the death-shroud from around Warrick.

Norwin Stokes held the shroud. He said, "Little man. I thought that you were dead. On this knoll we are above Wolv's red fog. Wolv's red fog settles in the valleys. Beware Little Warrick, but we must be quiet. The red-fog can hear. If you make noise Wolv's red fog will climb mountainsides and eat you. The Things in Wolv's red fog can climb trees and castle-walls."

As Norwin rubbed his aged, bony hands together to warm them, he said, "Shear luck. I knew you and your mother because of luck alone. I was a knight for your father, before someone kidnaped him."

Suddenly something, or someone stepped on and snapped a limb in the forest. As quick as he could, Norwin put his hand over Warrick's mouth.

"Shhhhh," Norwin whispered. "No one must know that we are here."

For a several minutes, Norwin kept his hand over Warrick's mouth and did not move. He listened.

Then Norwin whispered, "Wolv tossed you out of the castle. He thought you were dead. He threw you into the buttery refuse-heap. Now that you are alive, I will fill the grave that I dug for you. Beware little man, we must make it look like I buried you."

Little Warrick jumped to his feet. Through his baby-teeth he shouted, "Mommy? Mommy?"

Norwin reached out and cupped Warrick's little mouth.

He said, "Little man, take my hand, you need to say goodby to your mother."

Little Warrick said, "Mommy said that we must find Father Malachi Martin."

Norwin said, "If you wish, we will find this Malachi Martin."

Norwin led Warrick from the hut. They walked along a ridge, through the forest. Atop a knoll, Norwin led Warrick to his mother's grave.

Old Norwin said, "Wolv murdered your mother because she had a claim on this lordship. For now Wolv thinks that you are dead. You are safe if he thinks that you are dead. Now kneel and say Paternosters for your mother."

Old Norwin looked at the trees to see if someone watched. He handed Warrick Paternoster prayer-beads.

Then Warrick pushed the prayer-beads away. Tears ran down his small cheeks. The tears dripped off his tiny chin. He knelt and gritted his baby-teeth. "God. I pray to you to give me the strength to kill Wolv. I pray to you to give me the strength to gain justice. Give me the strength to put Wolv in his grave."

Quickly Norwin clasped his hand over Warrick's mouth and looked around.

Norwin said, "Little man, you must be quiet. Wolv will kill you if he learns that you live. We must be very quiet. You must remember that no one can kill the AntiChrist. He even escapes from Hell. Escapes in the body of Satan worshipers. Satan worshipers offer their bodies and souls for Wolv to possess. So Wolv can escape Hell."

Norwin dragged a stone onto the mother's grave. With a broken dagger he chipped 'Beatrice Pendragon' into the stone. Next he filled the empty grave he had dug for Warrick. He pulled a similar stone on it. Again, with his broken dagger, Norwin chipped, 'Warrick Pendragon' on the second stone.

Old Norwin said, "Wolv will see your headstone beside your mother's headstone. Then Wolv will think that you are dead. Remember that you must never reveal yourself. Or Wolv will find you and kill you. You have a stronger claim than Wolv on his lordship, this castle."

In Norwin's straw hut, seven days later, Warrick yawned and stretched on a straw mat. He put his bare feet on the dirt-floor. He stood and stretched his small arms into the air. Norwin said, "Little Man, until today you have slept two days at a time. You needed the long hours of sleep."

The boy spun on one bare foot and said, "That noise, what is that noise?"

He peered out the hut's opening. "Norwin, a parade comes this way," the boy asked, "What, who comes in the parade?"

In the hut, old Norwin Stoke sat on a log. Rapidly, he reached over and grasped Warrick's arm. Quickly, he pulled Warrick over to himself. He said, "Warrick. You must not let anyone see you."

Then Norwin rubbed his old, bald head. He said, "The parade is the king's champion and his knights. They are here to siege Lord Wolv from this castle. The King's champion will fail, again. Then Wolv will again take his anger out on us, his peasants. Wolv will send his Hog-Head Skinwalkers and Things in the Red Fog to kill us. The Things in the Red Fog will eat even our bones. Unless we out run or climb above the red-fog, when it comes after us."

Warrick tightened his little fists and raised them to his bare chest. Then he gazed out at the mounted champion. The champion wore royal red and shining armor. As Warrick watched, he said, "I will create my own future."

Norwin smiled and said, "You are like your father. He too believed that he could create his own fate?"

From under a straw mat, Norwin pulled out his only treasure. A treasure wrapped in a deer-hide. The object was so heavy that he had could not lift it to his lap. While he unwrapped the enormous package, he said, "Little man, come back here and sit. I learned to read from this broken tome. Ancient parchments on the Roman Empire's war strategies and tactics. When others would not teach me to read, I stole this illustrated tome. I taught myself how to read. Knowledge is the only thing that I can give you. You must learn to read. If you learn to read, write and know your numbers, you can become a merchant-apprentice."

As his stomach growled, the boy asked, "Norwin. Do you have any more of that rabbit that you poached from Wolv's forest?"

A tear welled in Norwin's eye as he said, "I am sorry little man. You ate the last of it. We have nothing for you to eat."

Warrick leveled his jaw and stood straight. "Then I will learn to be hungry."

A tear ran down Norwin's cheek. He said, "Little Warrick, never have I seen anyone with your giant courage."

With gritted his milk-teeth, Warrick held his tiny fists to his chest. Then he said, "One day I will be the King's champion. I will be the Crown's greatest champion of all time. Then I will drive Wolv, his Red-Fog and his Skinwalkers from my mother's castle. I will kill Wolv and his Skinwalkers. I will also find a way to drive Wolv's red-fog from this land."

Bald, old Norwin Stoke smiled at the child's naivete. "Now that you are an orphan," the aged man said, "you are a peasant." Warrick, little man, I became a peasant when battle-wounds crippled me. Your father would have cared for me, but someone kidnaped, my lord, your father. You must understand, little man. Peasants can never become knights. Knights can become peasants, but peasants can never become knights."

Warrick gritted his baby-teeth and said, "No."

As Warrick stood barefoot and watched the cavalcade, he straightened his little back. He leveled his delicate jaw. He said, "Norwin."

A black aura filled the hut.

Outside the straw hut, a black aura surrounded Wolv. Wolv suddenly overturned Norwin's straw hut. A Boar's-Head Skinwalker hit Norwin with a spear-handle. The Skinwalker had the head of a boar, and a man's body. Norwin lay unconscious.

The AntiChrist, Wolv, reached down, and grasped Warrick's upper arms. He growled, "My huntsman spoke the truth. You live, but not for another hour."

Then Wolv lifted Warrick.

The AntiChrist held Warrick by the neck. Eye to eye to Wolv, little Warrick said, "Wolv. You should fear me, for one day, I will kill you."

Then Wolv threw his head back and guffawed. "I heard Old Norwin call you 'little man.' You do speak like a man. Look behind me, even the king's champion rides away now. Rides away in fear. I defeated him. As for you, 'pup', best to drown pups before they grow to bite. To the river, yes, I will throw you in the river now."

Wolv's iron-like grasp held little Warrick to Wolv's multiple-pupil-eyes. He carried Warrick to the river. He held six-year-old Warrick eye to eye.

Warrick gritted his milk-teeth. He put his tiny fist in Wolv's face. Little Warrick shouted. "Beware Wolv. You should fear me. I will become the English King's greatest champion. I will kill you."

Wolv stopped on the riverbank. A wide river in flood-stage with white-water rapids. He said, "First pup. You must live to become a champion. Now I will assure that you will not live."

With one hand, Wolv grasped Warrick's little legs.

Warrick plunged Norwin's long blessed paternoster-crucifix into Wolv's eye. Then Warrick twisted the crucifix. He broke it off in Wolv's eye socket. The dry blessed wood shattered inside Wolv's eye-socket.

Wolv howled and flung little Warrick out into the white water-rapids.

Black spiritual-fire of hate shot out of Wolv's multiple-pupil-eye.

The candle-keeper said, "Master. That was a blessed Crucifix. You nailed Jesus on the Cross. You must get out every splinter or your eye will be useless."

Wolv growled. He could not pull out all the crucifix-pieces.

Spiritual fire of hatred shot out of his bleeding eye, Wolv growled, "Now. Now a drowned pup can never return and harm me."

A Skinwalker with a bear-head pointed. He said, "My lord. You must look, the pup knows how to swim."

Wolv cupped his bleeding eye and shouted, "Shoot him with arrows. Kill him. He must die. Warrick is a Symon of Cyrene Pendragon. Every Cyrene-Pendragon must die."

The candle-keeper said, "We should have known that his father had taught him to swim." Mixed late Sext bells and early Nones bells rang. Wolv began to howl another of his Golgotha obsessions, "Behold your son. Behold your mother." The AntiChrist's howls shook the ground.

He fell to his knees and his eyes glazed black. He flung red froth in great globs from his gaping mouth.

Red-fog poured from Wolv's body. Globs of red froth poured from Wolv's huge mouth.

The candle-keeper said, "Master. You must stop shouting your Golgatha-Crucifixion obsession. These words that Jesus said to his Mother and his apostle John. Your obsessions distract you from battle."

Wolv did not stop howling. Wolv could not stop howling. The echo of his howling vibrated the ground, shook the mountains, vibrated the castle. Each echo sent waves over the white water-rapids.

Slowly Wolv gained his composure out of his obsessive-compulsive screaming.

Then as he held his wounded eye, he growled. "Yet. A child cannot swim in these rapids."

Wolv growled, "He said that he was going to find Father Malachi Martin. We must not allow the pup to find Father Malachi Martin."

"All of you," Wolv growled, "shoot arrows at him, the pup must not live."

A Skinwalker said, "The rapids have carried him beyond bow shot."

Surrounded by the black aura, Red-Fog poured off Wolv. Wolv roared, "I have a bad premonition about this pup. I command all you rotting Skinwalkers. Mount your warhorses. Race after him. Shoot him with your arrows. Ride. Ride. I order you to bring me Warrick's dead body. I will eat the pup for supper tonight."

-

-

-

CHAPTER,   The year, in the 1250's A.D.

THE SOUTHERN COAST OF WALES, WEST OF ENGLAND

The place is the southern Coast of Wales, West of England. Wales, a land of constant warring clans.

Wolv, at a Catholic church on Wales' Southern Coast, atop a rugged cliff. The storm winds churned the ocean into giant waves. Waves crashed against the cliffs below the church. Blood-red foam of the waves crashed two hundred feet into the air. Waves flooded the cliffs with red sea-foam. Fish, sea-otters, seals, sailors, all dead, scattered, dead upon the jagged cliffs. Blood-red sea-foam ran over their lifeless-bodies. Far below, on the shore, waves rocked wrecked ships back and forth. Sailors' bodies floated in the ocean. Sharks fought over the bodies.

Lightening cracked and thunder rolled across the fire-red sky. Wind snapped the tips of Wolv's black-cape. Wind wrapped his black cape around his feet. His cape's cowl flapped beside his many-independent-pupils-in-his-eyes. Each pupil in his eyes is a separate demon. The demons possess his body to keep him strong and alive.

Wolv grabbed his crippled eye and growled, "Candle-keeper. What is it that hurts my eye? I have not felt this pain in my eye. Not felt this pain for twenty years."

The candle-keeper held up his lantern. He held the lantern to Wolv's eye.

He said, "Master. Spiritual black-fire shoots out of your wounded eye. Also, black flame shoots from the wound on your leg and your belly wound. It can be only one thing. The pup Warrick you thought that you drowned over twenty years ago is here. He is alive. Warrick survived and has returned to kill you."

As red-fog poured off Wolv, Wolv said, "Satan's way of warning me. Warning me when my past enemies are close. The wounds on my body inflicted by my past enemies burn when they are near. I will cleave Warrick just as I cleave this church-door."

Wolv's rage shone through his body. His rage shone like spiritual fire. Spiritual red-yellow flames between black charcoal-briquettes. He raised his battle-ax. Then he crashed his ax through the Catholic Church's thick wooden door. Ocean-wind blew pieces of the wooden door. The wind carried the pieces down the jagged ocean-cliff.

THE RESURRECTION HOUR TORMENTS WOLV

The AntiChrist growled, "Candle-keeper! Is it a safe candle-hour? With the sky afire, I cannot know if it is night or day. Is it a safe-candle-hour?"

The candle-keeper held his candle-lantern high so Wolv could see.

Then the Candlekeeper said, "No, Master. No, the Prime candle-hour, the sunrise, is now. Hurry. Sunrise is Jesus' Resurrection hour. It is now. This is your most dangerous candle-hour. The hour when you relive Jesus' Resurrection."

Distant Prime bells began to ring, bells to announce the morning prayers. Prime bells to announce the Resurrection hour.

At the sound of the Prime bells, Wolv howled in terrifying pain. His eyes glazed over black. Then his howl caused the Black Mountains to vibrate. He turned into charcoal-black dust. As black dust he disappeared. Disappeared into the earth. The frozen earth.

As black dust, Wolv descended into the earth until he found a cavern. In the cavern Wolv solidified into his black-charcoal form.

Wolv's eyes, multiple-snake-pupils-slits, glazed over black, when his memories torment him. When his memories engulf and torture him.

In the cavern, Wolv trembled in fear and terror. He howled, "Jesus. You return from the dead to wreck vengeance. Vengeance upon me because I crucified you."

Deep in the earth he froze and remembered the morning of the Resurrection. Jesus' Resurrection that he witnessed in

Jerusalem. He stood with his Roman soldiers, sentries outside Jesus' Tomb. The ground shook and knocked them all to the ground. A great light bathed the area. Wolv put his hands over his eyes. Between his fingers he watched the enormous round stone that blocked Jesus' crypt move aside.

Wolv said, "No one is pushing that giant stone."

In his memory, Wolv stood. He pulled his sword from its sheath. Surrounded with blinding light, Jesus walked from the crypt clothed in light.

Wolv fell to his knees. In his memory he begged, "Jesus. I did not believe you when you said that you would rise from the dead. I saw you raise Jarius' daughter from the dead. Also, I saw you raise Lazarus from the dead. Now you use this knowledge to raise yourself from the dead. Please Jesus. Please give me this knowledge. Then I can raise my beloved Pamia from the dead."

Jesus turned to Wolv.

Jesus said, "My beloved childhood-friend. In Egypt, your half-brother Symon of Cyrene, Pamia and I were childhood-friends. We were happy and beloved friends. Yet, after you married Pamia, in your rages you abused Pamia. You caused her death when she did nothing but love you. You backhanded her off the Masada cliff. If you repent your sins and live in repentance, you will embrace Pamia in Heaven. As I told you before, Pamia is safe from you. She is in my Heavenly Father's arms."

Jesus disappeared.

In his Resurrection memory, Wolv hacked the ground with his sword. He wept, "Jesus. Give me Pamia."

In Wales, in the cavern, deep in the earth, Wolv's eyes were still glazed-over-black. His Resurrection memory began to fade. His growls of "Give me Pamia" shook the Black Mountains.

Wolv growled, "Never Jesus, never will I ask for forgiveness. I will never ask for forgiveness. I will rule the earth. Jesus, if you do not give me Pamia, I will kill all your followers. Jesus, get off my throne. You, Jesus, you sit on my throne."

Wolv's multi-pupil-eyes lost their black glaze. He came out of his powerful-Resurrection-memory. He said, "Surely. The Resurrection candle-hour has surely passed."

As charcoal-dust, Wolv rose through the solid earth.

On the earth' surface, Wolv solidified. He stood before the Wales Catholic Church. Wolv shouted, "Candle-keeper, is it a safe candle-hour?"

The candle-keeper ran up with his candle-lantern. As he held it over his head, he said, "Yes. The early Terce bells begin to ring."

Wolv growled, "By how much? How much past the Resurrection hour?"

The Candle-keeper said, "By almost one hour. You can hear the early Terce bells begin to ring. It is almost one candle-hour after Jesus' Resurrection. Almost one candle-hour after sunrise."

Wolv said, "Has anyone found Father Malachi Martin? We must find him and kill him?"

The Candlekeeper said, "No one, master."

Wolv said, "Find Malachi Martin and kill him."

Wolv stepped onto the blessed property. Blessed property of the Catholic Church.

The Candle-keeper said, "Stop. If you touch anything blessed, you burst into flame."

Then Wolv said, "I must have Pamia. Spiritual fire, spiritual flame never harms me. Physical flame can burn me to ash. Yet, the demons that possess me always heal me."

As his feet touched the church-floor, Wolv burst into red-yellow flame. All aflame, he continued to walk up the Catholic Church's center-aisle.

Wolv, the AntiChrist, walked up to the altar and grabbed the Tabernacle. He raised the Tabernacle over his head and crashed it onto the floor. The Consecrated Hosts in the chalice fell upon the floor.

The AntiChrist picked up a Consecrated host. He rested it in his palm. He said, "Jesus, you hide in this consecrated bread. I know that you are this bread. I can feel you in this bread. Feel you just as when we played as children. Children in Egypt. Feel you just as when I nailed your hands and feet to the Cross. Others need faith to know that the Eucharist is you. I know that the Eucharist, this Bread, is you. My curse is certitude that this Consecrated Bread is you. Satan does not need faith. Satan has knowledge, certitude. Jesus, I have Satan's knowledge, Satan's certitude. Satan knows the Consecrated Bread is you, Jesus."

Tears welled in Wolv's multiple-pupil-eyes as he said, "Jesus, please. Please raise Pamia from the dead. Please for me, please give me Pamia. I can smell Pamia's blood in every Symon Pendragon bride. Pamia's heritage in every Pendragon bride, but for centuries none of them have Pamia's soul. You force me to capture every Pendragon bride to test if they have Pamia's soul."

Wolv heard, "My beloved childhood-friend. You must ask for forgiveness. Confession to a Catholic priest. Ask for forgiveness of all your sins. You must live in constant repentance. Repentance of your sins. Confess each week to a Catholic priest. Then after you die, you can again embrace Pamia."

Wolv growled, "Never. Never will I repent." He burst into black-spiritual flames that did not burn the church. The black-spiritual flames filled the Catholic church, but did not burn the Church. The flames only burned Wolv.

Wolv, the AntiChrist, dropped the Eucharistic bread from his hands and ran from the church. As he stepped off the blessed ground, he no longer burst into flame.

The AntiChrist raised his hands to the sky as he growled, "Never. Never. Never will I ask for forgiveness."

Wolv asked, "Candle-keeper. Marian of Moray may have Pamia's soul. If she has Pamia's soul, she will recognize me. If she does not have Pamia's soul, I will kill and eat her."

The Candle-keeper said, "Master. No. Through eleven centuries you have thought that Pamia's soul is in Pendragon brides. Pamia's progeny through Pamia's daughter. Pamia's progeny that wed Cyrene-Pendragon brothers. You have never found Pamia's soul in Pamia's progeny. It always ends the same way. You capture Pamia's progeny. Then you find out that she is not Pamia reborn. Then in your rage you kill her. Remember. You told me that you killed Pamia in a rage. Your rage almost killed Pamia's daughter. When you saw that Pamia's daughter did not have Pamia's soul, you knocked her unconscious. Pamia's daughter by Pamia's first husband, a descendant of Able Pendragon. Able Pendragon two thousand years ago. Pamia's first husband, which you secretly murdered over a thousand-year ago."

Wolv's multiple-pupil-eyes glazed over black as his memories went back eleven centuries. Eleven centuries when Wolv, Jesus, Symon of Cyrene and Pamia were 32-years-old. In his memory he was not in Wales. In his memory he was on high, windswept Mount Masada. Mount Masada far outside Jerusalem. South of Jerusalem, east of the Dead Sea.

Still, in his memory, Wolv stood in his own Mount Masada Castle. His own, private, Masada Castle. On the highest Mount Masada cliffs. Mount Masada, the Jewish desert-fortress far outside Jerusalem. When Wolv was six-years-old, Wolv's father, Roman General Assassio, tried to kill Jesus. Tried to run Jesus over with a chariot. Instead, the road collapsed under General Assassio's heavy chariot. Assassio fell to his death. Wolv now had murdered his way into his father's original position, General of Rome's Assassins. The emperor of Rome gave many castles to his General of Assassins. As with his deceased-father, Wolv now possessed his father's many assassin's castle's. An assassin's Castle in every conquered Roman region.

In Wolv's memory, Wolv walked onto the Masada Castle balcony. He looked down the highest Mount Masada cliffs. He could see a thousand miles in every direction. Hundreds of miles, wind blew off the desert. Far off in the desert, whirlwinds picked up people and horses. The whirlwinds bashed them against rocks.

Still locked in his memory, Wolv took a drink of wine and said, "Pamia. My obedience to Rome won us many castles. A castle in each Roman empire province. All I have to do is obey Rome just as my father did. All I have to do is assassinate anyone the Emperor demands."

Pamia wept into her hands and walked onto a dangerous balcony.

The dangerous whirlwind drew close to Mount Masada. The wind blew her long hair and her ankle-length dress.

Wolv said, "Stop crying. You know that empires need assassins. The empire needs me. Always, the emperor rewards us."

Wolv said, "Pamia. You must step back into the castle. These balconies are too dangerous in this wind. Come back, come back off the balcony."

Wolv's castle extended over the highest Masada cliff. Desert-wind blew the curtains around the balcony.

Beloved Pamia held her hands over her face. She wept hard into her hands. Pamia continued to weep. She said, "We are friends with Jesus. Even childhood-friends. In Egypt. Mary and Joseph took him to Egypt. To keep King Herod from killing him. Now you are to kill Jesus. Now the Roman Emperor has sent us from Rome. He has ordered you to Crucify Jesus. You must resign your assassin-position."

Wolv growled, "Never. Jesus claims to be a king so the Emperor must crucify Jesus."

Pamia wept into her hands. She begged, "We must give up all the castles. Give up all the luxury. You must disobey the Emperor and protect Jesus."

Wolv growled, "Never. Never will I give up all this wealth. Never. Don't you remember how in Egypt Jesus spooked my father's chariot horses? The horses ran off a cliff, killing my father. My mother ran to my father's dead body. My mother died instantly of a broken heart. Jesus murdered my father and mother. Jesus spooked my father's horses so they ran off the cliff."

Pamia said, "I saw the soft road collapse under your father's heavy chariot. The road was only of soft-clay. Your father knew that the road was too narrow and too soft. The road had often collapsed under a single horse. I learned that King Herod asked Rome to send your father to kill Jesus. Your father was the general of Rome's assassins. Yes, your mother died instantly of a broken heart when she saw your father dead."

Wolv growled, "You dare blame my father's death on my own father's stupidity. Jesus spooked my father's horses over the cliff. I will happily crucify Jesus because he killed my father, and killed my mother."

Pamia wept harder and said, "Wolv. You know the truth. You know that I love Jesus."

In a blind rage, Wolv threw his cup against a wall.

Then Wolv yelled, "You love only me." In a blind, red-faced rage, Wolv backhanded Pamia across the face.

Pamia fell backwards over the railing.

Wolv caught her hand and shouted, "The tears on your hand. Your tears wet your hand and make it impossible to hold your hand. My love. Grab my hand with both your hands. Grab my hand with both your hands."

Too late, her small, tears-wet hand slid from Wolv's grasp.

Wolv watched as Pamia screamed and fell. She became smaller and smaller. The fall was eternity. She landed upon the jagged rocks. Rocks below the enormous Masada Cliffs.

Wolv growled and said, "She can yet live. I have seen Jesus bring the dead to life."

He called for his troops. He slid down a rope that dangled from the cliff-edge.

Below Mount Masada Wolv carried Pamia's crushed body to the horse stables.

General Wolv wept, "Pamia can yet live again."

Wolv held Pamia with one arm and mounted his fastest black stallion.

Back in Wales Wolv still stood silent with black-glazed eyes. As he relived how he murdered Pamia.

In his nightmarish-memory he galloped from Masada. Wolv galloped to the Jerusalem Temple.

Wolv dismounted with Pamia's dead body. He held her body across his arms as he ran into the Temple.

Jewish temple guards tried to stop him. General Wolv and his fellow assassins pulled their swords and killed the Temple guards.

As Wolv wept, he shouted, "Jesus. Jesus. Where are you?"

Jesus stood up in the Teacher's Chair.

With Pamia in his arms, Wolv ran up to Jesus and wept, "Pamia is dead. Jesus. You can raise her from the dead. I have seen you raise others from the dead. Please. Please raise Pamia from the dead."

Wolv wept. His tears landed on Pamia's body.

Jesus said, "Pamia is now forever safe from you. She is in my Heavenly Father's arms. You murdered her first husband. Since you married her, you have abused her. Pamia is now safe from you in my father's arms."

Christ turned and walked away with his apostles and many disciples and holy women.

In his memory Wolv fell. Fell to his knees. With Pamia's dead body. Her dead body across his arms.

Still in Wolv's nightmare, with eyes glazed black, on his knees he wept, "Jesus. Jesus. Come back and raise Pamia from the dead."

In Wales Wolv's multiple-pupil-snake-slit eyes lost the remembering-black-glaze.

In Wales he was on his knees. His arms out as if he were holding Pamia's dead body in his arms. Kneeling, Wolv wept, "Jesus. Jesus. Come back and raise Pamia from the dead."

In Wales, The Candle-keeper said, "Master. Master. Your memories cripple you more each time. Each century you grow worse."

Wolv growled, "Jesus. I will have my revenge on you. I will kill all your followers."

Then in Wales Wolv rode high into the Black Mountains. He entered a cave and rode back into a cathedral-like cave.

Within the cave Skinwalkers waited on hundreds of dead brides, all in rotten bridal gowns. All sat at a long supper table. The Hog-head Skinwalkers placed food and wine before the skeletons.

Wolv sat at the end of the table and said, "Pamia. Do you like the food and wine?"

A Skinwalker with a Tusked-Boar's-head bumped into Pamia's wax-covered skeleton. Pamia's wax-plaster-covered skull fell on the floor. The skin-colored plaster shattered.

Wolv picked up the wax-covered skull and screamed, "Jesus. Jesus. How can you torture me like this? Jesus, please end this torture. Please raise Pamia from the dead for me."

Pamia's skull, in Wolv's arms, said, "Beloved Wolv. You have only to ask Jesus for forgiveness of your sins. Then we can be in Heaven together."

Wolv's growl of "Never. Never will I ask for forgiveness. Never."

His repeated growls caused stones to fall from the ceiling of the cavern. Also, caused the Black Mountains to vibrate.

A Hog-head Skinwalker ran to Wolv. The Skinwalker used melted-wax to place Pamia's skull back upon her skeleton.

Then Wolv rode out of the cavern and out of the Black Mountains. He rode to his Skinwalker encampment.

Wolv growled to his endless mounted Skinwalkers. Each Skinwalker had a spear, a rotting head on the upraised point.

Wolv shouted, "We race to capture Marian of the Adam-Cyrene-Pendragons. To test if she has Pamia's soul. Marian is of Pamia's progeny, a progeny of Pamia's daughter. A progeny line over a thousand years old, the Adam-Pendragon line."

-

-

-

CHAPTER, Where, Oxford, England, North West of London, England., When, The Year About 1250s A.D. About Twenty Years had now passed since Norwin Stoke found child-Warrick.

Marian WARNED

Outside Oxford, England. From the bright sunshine, Sister Catherine dashed into Moray Manor's back door. In the buttery, she ran up to Marian. Exhausted, the nun collapsed unconscious on the buttery floor. The cooks screamed.

Marian knelt beside her. Sister Catherine quickly opened her eyes and rolled on her back. The nun raised her hands and cupped Marian's face.

On her back Sister Catherine said, "Quickly, close the door before the Red Fog enters. The Red Fog will kill everyone in the manor."

A roar of the words, 'My God, my God. Why have you forsaken me?' shook the large manor. Bricks fell from atop the manor's chimneys.

Marian asked, "What is that awful roar? How can it shake the manor and even the ground? What is that horrible smelling red-fog?"

Sister Catherine said, "Run. That roar is the AntiChrist, Wolv. His obsessions with the words that Jesus said from the Cross. The words that Jesus said from the cross when the AntiChrist crucified Jesus. No time for explanations, "Run Marian, run. The AntiChrist is after you."

Sister Catherine gasped. "Run while you have daylight. While the Nones' bells ring, run. In three hours the sun will begin to set at Vespers Bells. Run from the AntiChrist while you still have daylight."

Marian said, "But this is the Nones-Candle-hour of prayer. We must pray at this sacred hour. This is the Divine Mercy Hour. We must pray the Divine Mercy Chaplet given by Jesus to St Faustina. The third candle-hour after the Zenith sun. The Zenith sun is the Sext Bells when Wolv nailed Jesus to the Cross. Nones' bells are the hour that Jesus died. This is the hour that the AntiChrist rammed a spear into Jesus' right side. Up into his heart when Jesus hung on the cross. This is a sacred hour. My friend, we must pray."

Lady Brielle de Moray, Marian's mother and Nicola, Marian's seventeen-year-old sister, ran into the buttery. As Lady Brielle looked at the cooks she said, "Who screamed?"

Then Lady Brielle knelt. Brielle said, "Sister Catherine, why are you here, why on the floor?"

Then the nun reached up and cupped Marian's face with both hands. "Marian, you are in danger," Sister Catherine said. "Evil, the AntiChrist, is after you. I overheard someone in the confessional. The priest refused to forgive the unrepentant man's sins. I beg for God's forgiveness. It is a mortal sin to mention anything heard in a confessional. Do not make me explain. Evil, the AntiChrist, comes for you. You have only moments. Things called Skinwalkers may have followed me here."

Sister Catherine untied a leather bag from her waist belt. She held up the bag and said, "Marian. I stole these jewels from the nunnery chapel," the nun gasped. "Take them and flee, you must flee this minute. You must hide in some big city. Please, you must not make me explain."

Marian said, "You must. You must explain."

Sister Catharine begged, "The AntiChrist is after you. He rides here now to capture you. Run. He thinks that you are someone called Pamia. Pamia was his wife that he murdered a thousand years ago. When he finds out that you are not Pamia, he will murder you."

A TRAITOR

One of many cooks, Hiry, picked up an empty wine bottle. Hiry's eyes darted from Marian, Lady Brielle de Moray, and Nicola. Instantly, sweat of fear dripped from Hiry's chin and nose.

With the wine bottle, Hiry crept down into the wine cellar. Far back in the wine cellar's black shadows, Hiry struggled against the door. She could not lift the bar across the outside door.

Hiry whispered to herself, "I must break out of this door. I must tell Wolv that Marian is about to run, or Wolv will kill me."

With her bony hands, Hiry pushed up on one end of the bar. Dampness had swollen the wooden bar. Hiry could not budge the wedged beam.

She spoke aloud to herself, "I must. I must get out and tell Wolv Marian is about to run. Or, Wolv will kill me."

On the buttery floor, the nun gasped and said, "Run Marian, run. Take the jewels and run. Have Father bless all the weapons in the house. Have Father bless anything that you can use as a weapon. Satan's dominions and hierarchies of demons come for you. Find Father Malachi Martin."

As Marian knelt on the buttery floor, she took the jewelry bag. She tightened the bag's draw strings. Then she tied the drawstrings around her neck. Marian ran for the front door.

"No," Sister Catherine yelled. "They will see you from the front. The Nones bells, now the sun is three hours past its zenith. They will see you in the sunshine. You must run while you have daylight. Go upstairs. Upstairs, remember when we were children. You must go upstairs. Climb down the hidden down-spout that we used when we were children. Run and find Father Malachi Martin."

Then Marian did what she had done a thousand times as a child. She ran up the stairs. She entered her bed chambers. Hidden behind an enormous oak tree, she opened the window. Marian climbed out onto a ledge. A ledge behind the oak tree. In a niche hidden between the buttery and the great room. Marian slid down the long drain pipe. Then she ran through a dense apple orchard until she entered the stables. Her father's apple orchard was so dense that nobody could see her. Even in the Nones sunshine, no body could see through the orchard.

"Marian," the stable boy said. "I can see that fear tightens your face. What do you fear?"

"The race horse, I need the race horse?" Marian held the skirt of her gown and asked.

The stable boy pointed behind Marian. "Saddled, prepared for Nicola," he said.

"Good, good, I will ride," Marian said.

"This is Nicola's turn to ride," the stable boy said. "I just saddled and bridled the race horse for Nicola. She will be angry with me if you ride it now."

In a panic, Marian pulled a stool to the tall gelding.

The stableboy said, "This is your father's fastest race horse. His prize race horse."

Though Marian was in a long, royal-red gown, she nimbly stepped on the stool. Then she wrapped her left leg around the sidesaddle lady's-horn. Quickly she placed her right knee over her left ankle. She tightened her right knee on her left ankle. Then she tightened her thighs on the lady's horn.

A repetitive roar of 'I Thirst' caused her horse to rear. Each time the roar 'I Thirst' shook the barn and shook the ground.

The roar knocked the stableboy to his knees. He shouted, "That roar hurts my ears. If it does not stop, it will make the barn roof fall upon us. What is it?"

Marian pulled back on the race horse's reins to calm the horse.

The stableboy held his ears.

After a few minutes the roar stopped.

Her horse still reared on its hind legs.

She pulled the reins tight and said, "A Nun. A Nun said that the roar is the AntiChrist's obsession about Crucifying Jesus."

Marian said, "Stand and hold my horse's bridle to calm him."

He stood and held the bridle but the frightened horse still reared.

Marian pulled harder on the reins. She said, "Pull down on the bridle."

She said, "While Jesus hung on the Cross Jesus said, 'I Thirst.' The Knights of the Sorrowful Lady believe that the AntiChrist Crucified Jesus over a thousand-years-ago."

The stableboy said, "The horse will not calm."

Marian said, "Pull. Use all your weight to pull down on the bridle."

The stableboy said, "This AntiChrist must be ageless."

Marian said, "My horse will not calm unless you pull down on the bridle."

Still frightened, the horse continued to rear on its hind legs.

Then Marian said, "Ageless. Yes, the Knight's of the Sorrowful Lady believe."

Marian tightened on the reins.

As the stableboy struggled to control the horse, he said, "Believe what?"

She said, "Believe that the AntiChrist is over 1200 years old. Born when Jesus was born."   Then Marian said, "My friend told me to find a priest named Father Malachi Martin. He is an exorcist, a Vatican exorcist."

Marian pointed to the ground and said, "Look. The AntiChrist's Red Fog. The Things in Wolv's Reg Fog will eat you. When I leave, release the other horses to run away from the Red Fog. Then you climb to the hay loft to escape the Red Fog. You must remember that the red fog can hear you. The red fog can climb. If the things in the red fog hear you, they will climb up to you. Then the things will eat you. If you are in the red fog, never stop running. Always run or the Things in Wolv's red fog will eat you."

She said, "Release the gelding and step back."

He did.

Then Marian slapped the horse's hindquarters. The exceptionally long-legged racehorse shot through the stable. At breakneck speed, the horse ran through her father's immense oat and wheat fields. The horse jumped roof-thatch bundles prepared for peasants' homes.

Wolv was only yards away. Across the red clay road, Marian's enemy, Wolv, sat on his warhorse. He and his Skinwalkers hid behind tall field grass and apple trees. A black aura surrounded him, as if the light itself were afraid of him. The red fog and things in the red-fog cascaded off him. Wherever Wolv went, he made day into night, and night blacker. His hatred sucked in and destroyed the light. Wherever Wolv went, red-fog and things in the red-fog cascaded off him.

Soft, plowed soil of the oat and wheat fields muffled Marian's horse's gallop. Wolv could not hear Marian's horse. Apple trees hid any sight of her.

-

-

-

CHAPTER, Where, Oxford, England, Northwest of London, England, When 1250's A.D.

ON THE OTHER SIDE OF THE MOUNTAIN, Wolv's WORST ENEMY

On the other mountainside, in the bright sunshine, a young handsome warrior mounted. Grown Warrick Pendragon, son of Beatrice Pendragon.

Warrick said, "Father Malachi Martin. Where are you? Danger is about. Wolv's red-fog gathers on the ground."

Father Malachi said, "Here. Behind you on this wagon, with a student. We disguised ourselves as Druids. Call me Druod. I do not want others to know that I am a Catholic priest Exorcist. In the priesthood, some despise exorcism. These are scattered Catholic priests that will even kill exorcists. So that the AntiChrist can defeat Catholicism. They are Satan's Skinwalkers that lock churches so people cannot do Adoration. When you find a locked Catholic church, know that a Skinwalker priest is near. The first sign that the AntiChrist is ready for war is locked Catholic churches. Warrick, look at the ground. The AntiChrist's Red-Fog rolls in from the AntiChrist, Wolv. He is near. The church reports that the red-fog is all around the world."

Warrick said, "Yes. Father Malachi. Wolv's red-fog is thickening on the ground. This is Wolv's, the AntiChrist's, red-fog. You must take care because the red-fog is thickening, deepening."

Father Malachi said, "Warrick. You know that when it thickens, the Things in the red fog will eat everyone. Only Adoration of the Blessed Sacrament keeps away the red-fog. Many scattered evil priests in the Catholic Church have locked many church doors. Thus, few can do Adoration of the Blessed Sacrament. These evil catholic priests have sided with Satan. Some because they are lazy. Some because they do not believe in Jesus Real Presence in the Blessed Sacrament. A few because they want the AntiChrist to defeat Christianity."

Warrick said, "What can we do right now?"

Father Malachi said, "Warrick. My priest-exorcism students follow us by a few minutes with the Adoration-Confession wagon. Adoration from the Adoration wagon will drive away the AntiChrist's red-fog. Force the things in the red-fog and the red fog to descend into the earth. Be thankful that we can see the red-fog. Sometimes we cannot see the fog until it has already killed everyone. Warrick. You are my best priest, my best exorcism student. You are the world's only hope against the AntiChrist. The AntiChrist has made his home in Wales, among the rebellious Welsh. Red-fog means that Wolv is here. He changes location when he believes that he can find his dead wife, Pamia, reborn. Reborn in some Pendragon bride. Warrick, ride ahead, find this Pendragon bride and save her. Save the Pendragon bride. Ride ahead, ride like the wind and do the impossible, defeat the AntiChrist. Save the Pendragon bride. Warrick, you are the world's only hope."

Warrick eased the reins on his stallion. He touched his stallion's ribs, Zeus' ribs, with the heel of tall, blackened, leather boots. The huge horse began to canter. The young man tightened his thighs. His stallion broke into a fast gallop. He touched his heel to the horse's ribs again. The great, black stallion burst into the most dangerous and swiftest run, battlefield-attack speed. Behind him, the young warrior's black cape flagged in the wind. Flagged like great, black, eagle wings.

Thin red-fog swirled around his horse's hooves.

Full of youth and nervous energy, he and his stallion wanted to run. He tightened his thighs tighter around his horse. Then he relaxed the reins and leaned forward. Both horse and man felt the wonderful wind in their shiny, black manes. Man and horse were one. As he leaned forward, his long, black hair trailed in the wind. His black-leather cape attached to his shoulders flapped behind him. In happiness, he smiled and raised his hands over his head. Man and horse rejoiced in their youth, their strength, and the wind.

The stallion ran at the fastest, most dangerous speed. The horse had only one hoof on the ground at a time. Its ironclad hooves beat in a loud rhythm that pleased both man and horse. Both the young stallion and the young warrior were at the height of their strength. As the wind blew his hair back, he gazed up at the blue sky. He smiled as he raced around a wide turn.

Suddenly a slow wagon pulled into the road. It was piled high with roof-thatch bundles for peasants' homes.

-

-

-

CHAPTER, Where, Oxford, England, Northwest of London, England

THE TRAITOR

Back in the wine cellar, Hiry mumbled, "I must escape this cellar. Wolv will cleave me if I do not tell him that Marian has escaped." Tall, skeletal Hiry struggled against the heavy bar that held shut the vineyard door. After painful minutes, as Hiry pushed up, the bar moved. It came free in her hands. Then she dashed through the wine cellar's door out into the vineyard. She ran around the manor across the road. She saw Wolv on the other side of the road. He was behind tall field grass and apple trees. Hiry approached Wolv.

As Hiry looked up at Wolv mounted on his warhorse, she stepped backward. Wolv's black aura stunned her, frightened her.

Hiry said, "Lord Wolv, Marian knows. I am sure that she has escaped. Hurry. Marian knows. She has escaped."

The AntiChrist pointed to a few mounted Skinwalkers. "You four, I order you to run after Marian in that direction," Wolv growled. "You others, ride after Marian in the other direction. I promise to give a bucket of gold to the Skinwalker that brings her back. Alive."

Marian TRYING TO ESCAPE

On the hard packed red clay road, Marian heard hooves clatter behind her. She turned to see the four mounted Hogs-Head Skinwalkers with drawn swords chase her.

One yelled, "Catch her. Beat her so she cannot escape."

Marian had heard of Skinwalkers. She had heard that they ate people and possessed their bodies. The sight and words made her shake. She almost fell from the gelding.

Marian said, "My gelding will outrun them. I hope."

After a minute she looked back and said aloud, "Good. The gelding did run faster than their horses. I will race into Oxford. In Oxford perhaps I can find Father Malachi Martin."

Marian sighed in relief and spoke aloud, "They are far behind. I am free. Now I will run another fifteen minutes then slow to a gallop."

Quickly she disappeared from the sight of the Skinwalkers.

Marian smiled as she raced around a wide turn.

Suddenly a slow wagon pulled into the road. It was piled high with roof-thatch bundles for peasants' homes.

-

-

-

CHAPTER, Where, Oxford, England, Northwest of London, England , When, 1250s

Marian reined in too late. She saw a huge man, Warrick, in shiny black leathers, with black hair. Mounted on a humongous horse, he raced toward the wagon.

Warrick reined in too late. He saw a beautiful woman with long flowing blond hair racing toward the wagon. Marian. To avoid each other, both horses had to jump over a wooden fence. Over a wooden fence and down a mammoth granite cliff, an overhang. An overhang over a lake. Hawks nested in the road's ancient oak trees. The horses startled the hawks. They flew high above. Marian, the handsome warrior, Warrick, and their two horses fell off the cliff. They tumbled in the air.

Marian screamed, "I will fall forever."

From the top of the cliff, the lake looked small. To those who fished in the lake, the lake looked endless. The two horses, the young man, Warrick, and Marian splashed into the cold water.

Well trained, the warrior's stallion swam to the young man. He caught the stallion's saddle.

Marian popped to the surface and shouted, "I cannot swim in my gown. Help."

With his other long, thick, strong arm he reached out. He grabbed Marian around the waist. Then, with his arm around her waist, he lifted her to his chest.

Marian feared that he was just another murderous Skinwalker. She beat him with her fists on his chest.

Warrick laughed and said, "Hit me anywhere but my handsome face."

She demanded, "Let go of me. Cur, release me. Scoundrel. Let me go."

The young warrior commanded, "Obey me. Be quiet and hold to me. Obey me now." She beat his chest and said, "Let go of me."

He said, "As you request, my lady. Obey me, but if, you will not obey me."

He let go of her.

She sank.

-

-

-

CHAPTER, Where, Oxford, England, Northwest of London, England., When. 1250s A.D.

DROWNING

Then she bobbed to the top and gurgled, "Help, Oh God. Help. I cannot swim in my gown."

He again grabbed her waist and turned her to himself.

Now safely in his arms, she coughed and shouted, "You Scoundrel. You are an irresponsible fool. How could you let go of me? I cannot swim in my gown."

As she pulled her hair away from her face, she gasped.

"You . . . you fool," she shouted. "How could you have let go of me?"

"I cannot help you if you refuse the safety of my presence," he said. "Obey me."

As she gazed into his mesmerizing, emerald eyes, his stallion pulled them to shore. To shore and up on the dry bank. Water streamed from her gown. With her straight right arm and forefinger, she pointed at the young man.

Then she shouted, "You . . . you . . . you are an inane, mindless lunatic. How could you be so foolish as to ride so fast?"

The young man grinned wide. "You . . . you . . . you are an inane, mindless lunatic. How could you be so foolish as to ride so fast?"

A roar of 'It is finished' repeatedly filled the air. The roar shook the earth.

Each time the roar grew stronger and shook rocks off the cliff. The repeated roar caused waves on the lake.

Marian put her hands over her ears until the roar ended. Then Marian said, "Finally, a moment of peace."

Warrick said, "Wolv, the AntiChrist, is close. That is his roar of his obsessions. His obsessions of all of Jesus' words. Especially his obsessions of Jesus' words from the Cross. Wolv howls his Sext bells and his Nones' bells obsessions."

Warrick pointed to the other side of the lake. He shouted, "The Red-Fog is approaching from across the lake. The Red-Fog knows we are here. If you are in the red-fog do not stop running."

Then Warrick spun and pointed up the cliff. He said, "Look above, the Red-Fog is also flowing down the cliff.

Then Marian's scream echoed across the lake, off the hills and back to the cliff.

SKINWALKERS CATCH HER

Behind the young warrior she saw the four mounted Hog-head Skinwalkers.

The Skinwalkers shrieked, "Capture her. Tie her up for Wolv."

The four Skinwalkers galloped for her. Quickly, the young man lifted her in his arms. With her in his arms, he dashed behind a thicket of small thorn-trees. The mounted Hog-head Skinwalkers galloped inches from them.

"Woman, whoever you are, stay behind these trees. You are safer in these small trees. I will take you to London," he said.

With a peaceful look on his face, he jumped to his feet. He stood between her and the mounted Skinwalkers.

He searched for his sword belt for his blessed ax and blessed sword.

Then he shouted, "Woman, do you have a weapon? A weapon of any kind? Beside your tongue. All my weapons are on the lake shore, too far away."

Marian threw a hair pin to him.

Warrick caught it and said, "Oh, great."

Marian said, "You are so stupid that you lost your weapons."

He said, "So you are a beautiful dog that bites the hand that feeds you."

She said, "You are not only stupid. You are insulting, impudent and useless."

She flipped her blond hair and smiled. Then she said, "Beautiful? You said 'beautiful'?"

"Dog," Warrick said. "A beautiful dog."

She crossed her arms and stomped her foot.

The four mounted Skinwalkers turned their mounts to attach her again.

Warrick threw the hairpin. It stuck in a Skinwalker's eye.

Dressed in midnight, black leathers, the young man stood his ground.

He said, "Beautiful-dog, I promise to protect you. I promise to be your champion."

At clamoring Sext-Nones' bells, sunshine glinted off his emerald eyes. The sun glistened off his wet long black hair, and wet black leathers.

Without any weapons, the young man stood straight and tall with a level jaw.

He said, "You Skinwalkers bore me. I tire of you. Leave now and I will not kill you."

He crossed his arms in defiance. Then he shouted, "If you attack this woman, I will kill you. She needs a champion. I am her champion. I now defend her by Right of Holy Combat. Leave now. Let me take her to London, and I will let you live."

One Skinwalker guffawed and shouted, "You have no weapon."

He struck his chest and shouted, "I warn you. I am a weapon. Let us go in peace to London or I will kill you."

The thud of his chest echoed across the lake and off the mountains.

With his arm and finger pointed at them, he roared, "Beware, you should fear me. Leave now. Let us go in peace to London, or I will kill you."

The four mounted Skinwalkers burst into guffaws.

One mounted Skinwalker repeated, "Attack him, we can run him down with our horses. He has no weapons. He is only one, plus he is not on a horse. Run him down, then bind her. If she is not Pamia, we can eat her for supper"

She cringed and tried to hide behind a tree trunk. Then she panicked.

The young warrior glanced behind himself to see if she was in the small trees. She was not. She ran.

He barked a command to her, "Obey. Woman. Listen, I order you to run back into the trees, obey me, now, obey me. Obey."

His voice was so confident and commanding that she instinctively obeyed. As she shook in fear, she ran back to the trees behind her unnamed defender. The four Skinwalkers thundered down on him and frightened her.

Yet her champion's straight stance, determined face, and level jaw gave her confidence.

A Warthog-Skinwalker yelled, "Trample him. We can easily capture her. Then we will have Wolv's gold reward for her. If she is not Pamia, then we will eat her for supper."

With both hands, the young man ripped a young, tall, thorny tree from the ground. He rammed the tree's thorny branches into the first horse's face.

As the thorns punctured the horse's nose, the horse reared. Warrick pushed the branches harder into its face. As the horse reared in a panic, it fell backward. Then the horse's back smashed to the ground and crushed its rider.

The other three horses raced too fast to rein in. All three horses tripped and fell over the fallen horse. On their backs, the three horses flailed their feet in terror.

The tall warrior grinned, "I have crushed one of you. Leave now and I may let you live. Leave now and let us go to London."

His right eyebrow raised, as his right eyebrow always raised when he lied.

One of the three unhorsed Skinwalkers stood.

He shouted, "He only has a thin, thorn tree for a weapon. Cleave the tree and cleave him."

With their swords over their heads, the three unhorsed Skinwalkers attacked the young warrior.

The quick young man dashed forward and grabbed the first Skinwalker's sword hand.

"You will not have this woman," the young man shouted. He tightened his black-gloved hand around the rogue's sword hand and hilt.

With his other hand on the Skinwalker's throat, he forced the Skinwalker right and left. Thus, Lord Warrick blocked the other two on the narrow bank. The other two Skinwalkers could not run around the young champion to approach Marian. Her champion was too fast for them.

Then one Skinwalker yelled, "We should flee. I know this warrior. He is Lord Warrick, the Crown's greatest champion. We should flee. He is Lord Dread, Lord Warrick. God's Avenging Angel."

The Skinwalker that grappled with Warrick gritted his teeth. He growled, "Lord Warrick is just a myth. If it were true, with one hand he would squeeze and crush my sword hand."

With one hand, Warrick squeezed and crushed the Skinwalker's sword hand.

The Skinwalker's sword fell into the water and sunk beyond Warrick's reach.

With one hand Warrick crushed the Skinwalker's throat. The pain caused the Skinwalker to fall unconscious. Then the two other Skinwalkers attacked Warrick. Warrick lifted the Skinwalker's unconscious body and threw it at the other two.

Then the Skinwalker's limp body fell on the two. To throw the limp body aside, with his sword, one Skinwalker impaled the limp Skinwalker.

The weight of the impaled body pinned the two kidnappers to the ground. One kidnapper sat up, with the body on his legs.

Warrick grabbed a large stone. A Skinwalker tried to shove the impaled body from his own legs. Warrick threw the rock. The heavy granite-piece stuck in the Skinwalker's forehead. The impaled-Skinwalker pinned the other Skinwalker's legs to the ground. Then the Skinwalker with the rock in his forehead, fell on his back. A rock deep in his forehead.

Now the last Skinwalker sat on the ground. In a panic, he also tried to push the body off his legs.

Then Warrick reached down to his feet. He snatched the thorny tree that he had uprooted. He held the trunk, like a spear, trunk first, branches behind him.

Warrick said, "Surrender and I will let you live. Surrender and let me take this woman to London."

Again, Warrick raised his right eyebrow as he always does when he lies.

The Skinwalker said, "You cannot harm me with that tree."

Warrick said, "Skinwalker, this is your last chance. Ask mercy from Jesus. Otherwise, you force me to crush your head. Remember. I am Dread. God's Avenging Angel. Ask Jesus for mercy. Let me exorcize you of Wolv's demons."

The Skinwalker held up his hands and shouted, "You are Dread. Exorcize me. Yea. Jesus, have mercy on me. Forgive me my sins. Jesus, I Trust in you."

The Skinwalker breathed out black dust, demons.

Again the Skinwalker said the exorcism words, "Jesus, I Trust in. Forgive me my sins."

Then the Skinwalker turned into a Catholic priest in white collar and cassock.

As he sat on the ground he said, "I sold my soul to Satan. Hundreds of years ago, because I was afraid to be a martyr for Christ. I was a coward. Lilith would burn me to death if I did not give my soul to Satan. Lilith is powerful. Wherever she goes, she causes the unborn to die in the womb. Then to spread despair and horror, she digs up the stillborn children and eats them. "

Then Lord Warrick said, "Pull yourself from under the bodies. Take a Skinwalker horse. Ride to the nearest monastery. Pray that they accept you. If you do Adoration of the Blessed Sacrament continuously, Lilith will not find you."

The repetitive roar of 'Father. Into your hands I commit my spirit,' shook the earth.

The roar caused more rocks to fall from the cliff.

Warrick turned to search for the woman that he protected. He said, "Whoever you are, that constant roar means that the AntiChrist is after you. He is very near."

Marian raised the palms of her hands. She shrugged her shoulders and asked. "Why? I am nobody special? How did you turn that Skinwalker back into a Catholic priest?"

I and most of my brothers are Vatican Exorcists. We are Vatican exorcist priests. Priests of the secret Vatican Order, the Symon of Cyrene Sorrowful Lady's Knights. What you have seen you must tell to no one. Tell no one or King Edward will kill me, kill all the Sorrowful Lady's Knights. All kings have made a pact to kill Vatican exorcist knights. Only my brother Ross is not a Catholic priest. Not a priest of the Sorrowful Ladies Knights. Lady Bad Luck, I can only champion you if you tell no one."

Warrick paused to hold his head and said, "Lady Bad Luck. Your beauty does not make up for the trouble you are to me."

Warrick said "Lady Bad Luck. Whoever you are. We must race from here to London. The AntiChrist will send more Skinwalkers."

Warrick grabbed a sword and beheaded the dead Skinwalkers.

Marian asked, "Why behead them?"

"Beware," Warrick said. "Their heads look dead but they are not dead. Demons in them can still hear and talk with thoughts with the AntiChrist. Their thoughts are the AntiChrist's thoughts. The AntiChrist's thoughts are their thoughts."

Marian said, "You are crazy."

Warrick said, "Skinwalker's come back to life because they are demons."

Then he picked up the heads. He threw the four heads far out into the lake.

Then Warrick said, "Look. The headless Skinwalkers move. They begin to hunt for their heads. We must leave before their bodies find their heads in the lake."

Marian screamed as a headless Skinwalker grabbed her ankle. Warrick kick the Skinwalker's hand away.

Marian said, "Why do you want to take me to London?"

Lord Warrick said, "I cannot explain now. We must go and find Father Malachi Martin."

-

-

-

CHAPTER, Where, Oxford, England, Northwest of London, England., When: Around 1250s

SHE RAN FOR HER LIFE

Then Marian screamed, "Blood. Blood is dripping from your forehead."

With both hands, Warrick held his head.

He said, "One of them hit me with a mace. Bad luck. Lady Bad Luck blessed me."

Warrick looked at his blood on his hands. "Woman, whoever you are, maybe that is your name, Lady Bad Luck? Now, be quick. We must gallop from this place. Obey me."

Marian shouted, "You only want Wolv's gold. You killed them to get the gold for yourself."

As Warrick held his dizzy head with both hands, he spun in a circle. Spun to search for more Skinwalkers.

"Lady Bad Luck," Warrick said, "Whoever you are, quickly. Come to me and mount my horse with me, now, obey me."

As Marian walked backward, she said, "You only want to take me. To take me to Wolv for the gold."

"Obey me," Warrick commanded. "Wolv sent these four Skinwalkers to capture you. I am sure that he has sent more. You must obey me."

The swift death that he dealt to the Skinwalkers terrified her. Her wet gown clung to her legs. She lifted the gown's skirt to dash from Warrick.

Marian shouted, "I heard you speak those Monsters' language. You are just another murderous rogue. I know that you will give me to Wolv for the gold."

"King Edward also speaks Skinwalker language," Warrick. "Know thine enemy. Because Edward speaks Skinwalker, does that mean that he will trade you for Wolv's gold?"

As Marian walked backward, she said, "The king has done much worse."

Lord Warrick said, "We must find my brother's Adoration Wagon. Only Adoration of the Blessed Sacrament will keep the red-fog away. Whoever you are, mount Zeus with me. Quickly, we must gallop away with me from this dangerous place. Gallop away with me before the Red Fog eats you."

Marian turned to run only to step on her gown's hem. She fell. Then she stood. She struggled to run in the heavy, clinging gown.

Marian shouted, "Oh God, those monsters feared you. They called you 'Dread, God's Angel of Death.'"

He said, "Come to me. They exhausted you. You are cold, wet, and in a panic."

She said, "You are death. Even without weapons, you defeated four Skinwalkers in seconds. With a thorn tree."

He said, "And with a rock and with an appeal to repentance. With Exorcism. I am an exorcist under Father Malachi Martin, of the Vatican."

Then he said, "You are letting your fear run away with your thoughts."

She said, "Truly, the Skinwalkers are correct. Only an unarmed Angel of Death could defeat four mounted Skinwalkers. No unarmed human could defeat them. Even your black leathers and black hair looks like Death."

Warrick said, "Look. The Skinwalker bodies begin to stand. They are searching on the ground for their heads. The Red-Fog will soon be here and eat us. We must go. We must find my brother's Adoration wagon. Only Adoration of the Blessed Sacrament can keep away Wolv's red fog."

Again Marian stumbled over her wet gown and fell.

Warrick whistled for Zeus. The stallion galloped to him. Then Warrick jumped on Zeus and spurred the stallion toward Marian.

As she lay on the ground, she turned her head to see him. With him on its back, his huge war horse galloped at her.

"You want to trample me," she shouted.

Frightened, in a panic, she jumped to her feet and ran for her life.

-

-

-

CHAPTER, Where, Oxford, England, Northwest of London, England, When Around 1250s A.D.

THE KING'S CHAMPION TAKES ANY THAT WOMAN HE WANTS.

From the back of Zeus, at a slow smooth canter, Warrick reached down. With one huge arm he wrapped his arm around

Marian's waist. He whisked Marian up onto his horse. With both arms, he placed her side-saddle on his lap.

Warrick said, "The Skinwalker's have terrified you beyond reason."

She beat on his chest and shouted, "Let go of me."

Instead he held her with both his huge arms. He steered Zeus with his thick sinewy thighs. He spurred Zeus. Zeus burst into a run. Like great blasts of steam, Zeus' breath blew out of his nostrils.

Marian reached up to hit Warrick's face. He held her tight so she could not pummel his face.

Then Warrick and said, "You can hit me anywhere except on my handsome face."

She said, "You are a narcissist."

Warrick grinned and said, "The World's greatest warrior must have at least one fault."

"You must listen to me," he said, "tell me, why is Wolv after you?"

The sun was high. A few clouds drifted on the strange-fire-red sky. Unseasonable thunder, with no rain, rumbled and shook the earth. Lightening struck the center of the lake.

The crack of the lightening caused Marian to mash her eyes shut. She covered her ears. Then as she shivered and held her freezing shoulders, she shouted, "Let go of me."

Warrick held her tight and felt Marian shiver. The wind chilled her soaked, blond hair that reached to her waist. She held her shoulders and shivered and demanded, "Put me down. Let go of me."

Then he held her with one brawny arm. With the other arm, he pulled a tightly wrapped package from a saddle bag. With one hand, he unwrapped the oiled-leather-waterproof-package. A huge dry cloak identical to the one he wore fell out. The cloak had a warm, albino, deer-fur lining.

Zeus broke into a faster gait. With one hand, Warrick wrapped the cloak around Marian's shoulders.

Then Warrick laughed and said, "The Skinwalkers are wrong. You are too slender to make for a good supper." Warrick guffawed.

"You will not bind me with your cloak," Marian shouted. "I demand that you let me down, brut."

"Stop fighting, obey me. I command you to wrap this cloak around yourself." Warrick said, "Obey me."

"Command. Command," she shouted. "Let me go."

"Like when I let go," Warrick said. "Then you almost drowned?" As she pounded on his chest, her fists stopped as if they froze. Exhaustion and confusion calmed Marian. As she held her cold wet shoulders, she demanded, "Who are you? I demand to know who has kidnaped me."

"I am Lord Warrick Pendragon, King Edward's champion," he said. "You must be daft, do you have no ears? Did you not hear the Skinwalkers?"

Marian said, "Daft? No ears? Not only a rogue, you are an insulting, insolent varlet. By what right do you kidnap me?"

Warrick said, "The king's champion can take any woman he wants."

-

-

-

CHAPTER, Where, Oxford, England, Northwest of London, England, Around 1250s A.D.

TAKEN, BY HER HERO

She demanded, "You will not 'take' me. Stop and put me down."

Warrick said, "Where along the road should I leave you. Leave you so more Skinwalkers can find you? The Red Fog is not far behind us. The Things-in-the-Red-Fog will eat you."

His reply caused her to raise her eyebrows in confusion and anxiety. She hugged her cold shoulders. Her cold, wet gown chilled her until her teeth chattered. She crossed her legs and hugged her shoulders to warm herself. Her teeth chattered louder.

Then she pointed at him. Her eyebrows formed a sharp v of anger as she said, "You . . . you . . . you."

"Me . . . me . . . me . . . What?" Warrick asked.

Marian bounced as Zeus jumped over a log in the road. Lord Warrick tightly hugged her so she would not fall off. His face did not change from the expression of peaceful, confident determination. His eyebrows remained level. He had not a wrinkle on his bronze face.

He said, "We must find Father Malachi Martin and my brothers Adoration Wagon."

She was silent for a moment. Marian sighed in resignation. Her eyebrows raised level which wrinkled her forehead horizontally in confusion and anxiety. "How can I know that I can trust you?" she asked.

"You cannot," Warrick said.

"You will do with me as you wish?" She asked.

"As I wish," he replied.

"I am completely at your mercy?" Marian asked.

"Yes," he replied.

"So you have trapped me here," Marian said, "in your arms."

Warrick hugged her with both arms and said, "Yes, trapped in my arms. Obey everything that I say. Do everything that I want. Obey."

Fear, terror, and the chill of the lake water had wrecked her emotions.

Marian held her head up high and said, "Obey? I give orders. Never, never have I obeyed anyone."

Warrick said, "Listen. The AntiChrist's Golgotha-Crucifixion obsessions again. His roars."

The repetitive roar of 'Father. Into your hands I commit my spirit,' shook the ground.

Warrick's horse reared. A chimney of a nearby manor collapsed. With one hand Warrick held the reins. With the other arm he pulled Marian to himself.

Over his arm, he held the dry cloak. Heavy, warm, long, black and dry.

Then Warrick said, "What good does it do for me to fight to protect. You will now slowly die of the cold. Do you want to chill to death or do you want my extra cloak? Your teeth chatter so loud they will break."

She snatched the cloak from his arm and tied it around her neck. Then he lifted her and spread the cloak under her. Tightly, she wrapped it around herself. As she pulled it tight around herself, the deer-fur lining instantly warmed her. Warrick raised the cowl over her head.

Now that she was warmer, she looked up into his mystifying eyes. Marian thought, "Warrick's emerald eyes gather sunlight and glow."

Marian trembled in exhaustion and terror of the Skinwalkers.

She asked, "Why are you not shaking from the horror. You could have died a horrible death. How can you be so confident and peaceful? Your face has no expression. You are not even breathing hard? You even laugh."

Warrick said, "I was born into death dealing. I will die when God allows me to die."

Marian said, "You are wet. Yet, your skin is not cold. How? Steam pours off you and your horse."

"I will die when Jesus allows me to die. As to being warm, battle boils the blood." Said Warrick.

"That does not explain why you are so hot to the touch," she said.

Warrick said, "I suppose because I am about to take you."

Marian did not let him finish his sentence. She snapped, "Take me. No. Please. No."

"You are an impatient woman," Warrick said. "'Take' you home. I will again battle the AntiChrist. I am sure the AntiChrist is at your home."

As she misunderstood that he was jesting with her, she hit his chest. "Why are you so horrible? You jest about taking me at such a dangerous time." Marian asked?

"Jest? Yes, jest. That gives me an idea of how to strengthen Lady Bad Luck," Warrick thought. "I will tease her until she is angry. Anger will strengthen her if we must fight again. Better yet, I will tease her until she laughs, laughter will give her more strength."

He smiled and said words that he himself did not want to say. "First you must tell me. Why are you the most beautiful woman I have ever seen?"

Then Warrick remembered his broken heart.

He thought. "After my wife, Ogina, betrayed and murdered my knights, I made a solemn promise. I promised myself that I would never again call another woman beautiful."

Marian eyebrows formed an angry V. "Beautiful? Beautiful is a cad's word, a cad's flattery to seduce innocent women. You use a cad's phrase on me. You do intend to take me."

As he thought of his broken heart, he said, "No."

Then exhaustion caused Marian to say what she did not want to say. "No," she shouted. "No? Why not? Am I not beautiful enough for you to take me?"

Marian immediately thought, "What a stupid thing to say."

Warrick said, "You let your tongue slip. Perhaps you have revealed your most secret thoughts?"

Marian tightened his warm cloak around herself. "You are worse than a cad," she said.

The cloak's aroma stung her nose. She savored a biting aroma that she had cherished for all her twenty some years. The expensive bay-leaf aroma for meat. The aroma made her feel like she was in safe in her father's manor.

Then the ground again began to shake as Wolv roared, "Tiny Wolv. I will always love you." Repeatedly Wolv roared. Repeatedly the ground shook with each roar.

Marian asked, "What is that?"

Warrick said, "Lady Bad Luck. Secret Pendragon libraries have Symon of Cyrene's original ancient parchments. Symon eventually recorded that he, Jesus, Pamia and Wolv were six-years-old in Egypt. Symon wrote that other children tormented Wolv because he had a multiple-pupil eye. Jesus, Symon and Pamia loved Wolv. The other Egyptian children used to torment him. Dance around him. They would call Wolv ugly-eye. Jesus' mother, Holy Mary, would pick little Wolv up on her lap. She would hug him. Holy Mary told him that he was beautiful and intelligent. Holy Mary repeated to him every day, 'Little Wolv, I will always love you. Little Wolv, do not hate anyone.' Symon wrote that Wolv developed a deep love and devotion to Holy Mary. Symon later recorded that little Wolv always ran to Holy Mary. Always ran to Holy Mary when the other children tormented him. You now hear Wolv's Egyptian Holy Mary obsession. Though he loves Holy Mary, he still scourged and crucified her son, Jesus. Guilt causes Wolv to roar, 'Little Wolv, I will always love you.'"

"Wolv is a complicated soul," said Marian.

Then Warrick said, "Lady Bad Luck. The AntiChrist is complicated with ten thousand demons in him and unending hatred and guilt."

"My gelding, where is my gelding," Marian said. "My father loves that gelding."

"Behind us, the gelding gallops behind us," Warrick said. "Every horse knows where to find his sweet corn and oats. He will follow us."

Warrick said, "We must find my brother's Adoration wagon. Look at the ground. The red fog gathers thicker. Only Adoration of the Blessed Sacrament can keep Wolv's red fog away. If we stop running the things in the red fog will eat us. Wolv's Satan worshipers are everywhere. Satan Worshipers are calling the red-fog up out of Hell to help Wolv."

As he hugged her, he put his huge, rough, calloused hand on her hand. Warrick said, "Tell me, why does Wolv attack you?"

She pulled her hand back. She snapped, "Cad, I will not allow you to touch me."

This time he grasped the back of her hand. "You must answer me. How can I champion you if I do not know why Wolv chases you? I have sworn to protect you. Tell me. I need to know why Wolv attacks you."

His hand squeezed her hand to impress the importance. She was now too emotionally exhausted to protest. He had said the word 'protect' so often. So often that she began unconsciously to have confidence in him. Marian also felt safe because he did not let her slip from side to side. As Zeus raced, he hugged her tight. So tight, so firm, so warm that she felt physically safe, protected, and sheltered.

Zeus jumped over a mud puddle. To steady herself, with both hands, she suddenly grasped his wrist. Embarrassed, instantly she said, "Ohhh," and jerked her hands from his wrist. Her hands were smooth, delicate, beautiful, feminine. The touch of her hands and her beauty caused his lonely heart to jump.

Then his broken heart tormented him. In his mind's eyes he saw all his dead, betrayed knights. Betrayed by his treasonous wife, Ogina. The memory of his treacherous wife wiped away all tender feelings.

"Who is this Wolv," Marian asked? "I have not the slightest idea why he wants me."

"Wolv, I know Wolv very well," Warrick answered.

"Who exactly are you?" Marian asked.

"The line of Symon of Cyrene." Warrick said. "The leaders of the Sorrowful Lady's Knights are Symon's progeny. I told you. Lady Bad Luck, I am an exorcist priest of the secret Vatican Order. Symon of Cyrene founded The Knights of the Sorrowful Lady. Founded, vows of poverty, chastity and obedience to Jesus, Holy Mary and Saint Peter. Just after Wolv Crucified Jesus' Crucifixion and Jesus' Resurrection."

"Symon who?" Marian asked.

"The Cyrene, Symon, that helped Jesus carry the cross. From that day forward Symon dedicated his line to protect Christians. We are all Vatican priest exorcists. Symon of Cyrene was Wolv's half brother. General Assassio was the father of both Symon and Wolv, different mothers. Wolv was illegitimate. His biological mother was a prostitute. Syphilis drove her insane."

Marian said, "Is any more of this documented?"

Lord Warrick said, "Yes. Everything in hidden libraries. Symon himself wrote the original parchments. We keep the originals covered with wax and buried deep in sealed vaults. The Sorrowful Lady's Knights keep copies of these ancient parchments in secret libraries. Many copies all over the world. Copies in many languages. If enemies burn one library, we make more copies, more hidden libraries."

Marian reached up with both hands and tightened the deer-fur collar around her head

Zeus jumped a mud puddle. Marian almost fell.

Marian said, "You were supposed to hold onto me. I suppose you do want to throw me to the ground."

Warrick pulled her to himself and said, "It is a thought."

She said, "Tell me more of these curious facts about Wolv."

Warrick said, "Symon, Wolv, Jesus and Wolv's love, Pamia. All four were all born on the same day. Born at different places, but born on the same day. Wolv was illegitimate of General Assassio. A Cain-Cairo-Pendragon illegitimate progeny. General Assassio, was the General of Rome's assassins. General Assassio had sex with dancers and prostitutes throughout the Roman Empire. Yet, Symon's mother was the opposite of Wolv's biological mother. Symon's mother was married to General Assassio. She was graceful, majestic, even commanding. Symon's mother was an elegant Able-Cyrene-Pendragon, Egyptian. Two separate Pendragon lines exist. The Cairo-Cain-Pendragons and the Able-Cyrene-Pendragons. Opposite of Wolv's mother, Symon's mother ran her father's castle. A castle that protected a port of Cyrene, Egypt. Her parents did not tell their children that they were Able-Pendragons. Her parents hoped ignorance would protect them from the Cain-Pendragon killers. She did not know she was an Able-Cyrene-Pendragon until before fever killed her. Wolv's father, Assassio, did not know Symon's mother was an Able-Cyrene-Pendragon.

Unfortunately, Wolv's biological mother was of the Evil-Cairo, Egypt Cain Pendragon line. The Evil Pendragons. Wolv's biological mother was a dancer and prostitute. The prostitutes' disease, syphilis, made her insane. Wolv's father would have nothing to do with her or the babe, Wolv. In hatred Wolv's mother threw her own child, Wolv, into a well to drown him."

Marian said, "You feel sorry for the child Wolv."

Lord Warrick said, "Almost."

Zeus sped up his gait to a faster gallop, Warrick said, "Remember. This is a thousand years ago. A young waif of a girl dove into the well. She saved the child-Wolv. Though homeless, the waif cared for the child. Eventually the waif-girl by chance found Wolv's father, General Assassio. She approached him. Wolv's father pulled a sword to kill the waif and Assassio's misbegot son. His illicit son, Wolv, pulled a wooden toy dagger and stabbed Assassio in the hand. Stabbed hard enough to pierce the skin. Wolv's father threw his head back and guffawed. A thousand-years-ago, Rome's General of Assassins, Assassio, shouted that Wolv is a born killer. A natural assassin. Therefore, he would care for Wolv and the waif-adopted-mother.

General Assassio, Wolv's father, found the biological mother that threw Wolv into the well. To teach Wolv to be an assassin, he tied up Wolv's biological mother. He held the child-Wolv's hand and they together cut the throat of Wolv's biological. Both watched her beg and plead. Then they watched her bleed to death."

Marian said, "How old was Wolv? When he cut his biological mother's throat?"

Warrick said, "Symon's parchments read that Wolv was under six-years-old. In Egypt with Jesus, with Symon and with Pamia."

Marian said, "How is Wolv still alive?"

Warrick said, "How is Wolv still alive. Remember in the bible when Jesus met the demoniac of Gerasenes. Jesus exorcized a legion of demons from the possessed man. He threw the demons into a herd of two thousand pigs. A non biblical parchment reads that the herd was at least five thousand. When Jesus asked the name of the demons that possessed him, the Demons answered 'legion'. The size of a Roman legion. A Roman legion in a mayor Roman war could be 10,000 soldiers. We of the Sorrowful Lady's Knights believe that at least 10,000 demons possess Wolv. These 10,000 demons keep him alive. Heal him. Put him back together when someone dismembers him. I myself chopped him into pieces and fed him to sharks. Sharks off the coast of Wales. Three days later he crawled up out of the ocean, onto the beach. Then he turned into crows and flew away. We have dismembered him and burned him to ash. When the fire cools he always reassembles himself into his Roman General form. We can slow him by burying his body parts. We must bury them in different parts of the world. He always returns within a decade. I believe that Wolv will never die until he asks forgiveness for his sins. Just asking forgiveness, for his sins will exorcize the legion of demons. Then his body will fall into dust. Only then can Wolv be with his love, Pamia. I believe. Yes, one day Wolv's love for Pamia will cause him to ask Jesus for forgiveness. Love will save Wolv. In turn, love will save the world."

Marian said, "You are a romantic. You really believe love will save the world."

Warrick said, "Yes. One day."

Marian said, "Tell me more about Wolv's childhood. You sound like a silly romantic."

Warrick said, "Only one true romantic exists. Jesus. Jesus, love personified, came to earth to heal the sick, to heal us. We nailed him to a cross. Even from the cross he forgave us. Even now in Heaven he waits for us, even Wolv, to ask for forgiveness. Then enter Heaven for all eternity."

Marian said, "Tell me more about Wolv."

Warrick said, "I will continue to tell you the content of Symon's parchments. A thousand years ago, Wolv's father said to Wolv, 'Wolv. You must always kill your enemy. Your own biological mother tried to kill you. She tried to drown you in a well. Therefore, mother or not, she was your enemy. Always kill your enemy. Even if she is your biological mother. Odd though it is, a good assassin needs a protective mother. I will marry this waif that saved you from the well."

Then Warrick said, "Another of Symon's parchments recorded more of Assassio's words. Assassio said to Wolv, 'Your biological mother is from the evil Cain-side of the Pendragons. My side, I am from the evil-Cain-Cairo-Pendragons. Symon, your half-brother, Symon-of-Cyrene is from the compassionate Able-Cyrene-Pendragons. I am ashamed of Symon because he has a compassionate heart. For over a thousand years, the Cain-Pendragons have tried to kill the Able-Pendragons. You are to find someway to kill your half brother, Symon of the Cyrene-Pendragons.'"

Warrick continued to narrate.

Lord Warrick said, "Wolv, Jesus, Pamia and Wolv's half-brother Symon of Cyrene were in Egypt. They were all six-years-old when the road collapsed under Wolv's father's chariot. The chariot rolled down a cliff and crushed Wolf's father to death. Then Wolv's adopted mother, the waif that saved Wolv from the well, ran to Assassio. When she touched General Assassio's lifeless face, she died of a broken heart. She was Wolv's waif-adopted-mother of the stories that she died when she embraced Assassio's body."

Marian said, "This is all so complicated."

Warrick said, "According to Symon's own writings, Symon dedicated his line to protecting Christians. Carrying the Cross for Jesus fulfilled Symon's nature. Carrying the Cross for Jesus gave a purpose to Symon. Wolv crucified Jesus and dedicated himself to Satan, to killing Christians. Then, Wolv was at Jesus' tomb when Jesus Resurrected from the Dead at sunrise. At sunrise, at Prime bells. Jesus' Resurrection terrified Wolv. After the Resurrection, Wolv sold his soul to Satan to become the AntiChrist. Thousands of demons possess him to keep him alive. At Prime Wolv howls in disappointment that Jesus will not raise Pamia from the dead. This is why Wolv cannot stand the sunrise. I and my relatives are of the warrior line of Symon. Of Symon of the Adam-Cyrene-Pendragons. We battle the AntiChrist, Wolv. The AntiChrist from the Cain-Cairo-Pendragons. The AntiChrist's army is composed of fallen, possessed Catholic priests. Also, composed of possessed Cain-Cairo-Pendragons. Fallen Catholic-priests because they sold their souls to Satan rather than be martyrs. Rather than martyrs, they choose to be demon-possessed. The Sorrowful Lady's Knights are lead primarily by the Cyrene-Pendragon lineage. Wolv is constantly after Pamia's lineage to test if one of them has Pamia's soul. Half-brother against half-brother. Cain kills Able every day until the end of time. We must protect Pamia's lineage, Pamia's heirs."

Marian asked, "Why Pamia's heirs?"

"The Sorrowful Lady's Knights follow Pamia's lineage." Warrick said, "Why? Because our enemy, the AntiChrist hunts for them. We have records of every one of her line. They are many places in the world. Many are here in England."

"What happens to them if the AntiChrist finds them." Marian asked.

"He tests them to see if they have Pamia's soul." Warrick said. "They of course never do. Then, in a rage he always kills them. Just as his rage originally killed Pamia."

Warrick said, "Why follow Pamia's progeny? Wisdom of war policy, strategy of war, tactics of war. Simply because protecting Pamia's lineage is a way to know Wolv's location and plans."

Marian said, "This is too much information. Too extreme. A thousand years ago."

Warrick said, "A thousand years ago is just like yesterday for the Sorrowful Lady's Knights. Wolv Pendragon fought his half brother Symon Pendragon over a thousand years ago. Yet, Cain Pendragons fought Able Pendragons over two thousand years ago in Egypt. For over two thousand years the Cain Pendragons have battled the Able Pendragons."

Neither Warrick nor Marian knew it, but fate had bound them before their birth. From Warrick's conception, Jesus would not allow Warrick to find comfort in any other woman. Warrick was to find comfort only in Marian's arms. From Marian's conception, Jesus would not allow Marian to find comfort in any other man. Marian was to find comfort only in Warrick's arms. Lord Warrick Pendragon of the Able-Symon Pendragon line. Lady Marian of Moray also of the Able-Symon Pendragon line.

She secretly had liked the touch of his rough hand on her hand. With both hands she tightened the cloak around herself. She looked up at him and he down at her. Their eyes met in an unexpected, long, delicious gaze deep into each other's eyes. A gaze full of mystery and tension. Tension because their long gaze revealed to the other that they hungered for each other.

For Warrick her gaze brought back horrendous memories of his broken heart. Ogina had let the enemy into Warrick's castle. The enemy killed all Warrick's Knights of the Sorrowful Lady.

For Marian, his gaze was mysterious, unnerving. Mysterious and unnerving because she knew almost nothing about the only man that protected her. He was the most handsome, dashing, courageous man she had ever seen. Deep inside, somehow, without her knowledge, she had a vague feeling. She had a vague feeling that Warrick belonged to her.

Marian thought, "He held my hand as a lover would hold my hand. Why?"

Then her eyebrows formed a deep v in anger.

Marian thought, "I do not want him to touch me. What is it about him that forced me to stare into his eyes?"

Her eyebrows formed a deep v of anger again. *Marian though, "Why should I care about him? What spell has he put on me?"*

Warrick had woven a spell on her, the spell of championing her. Naive, Marian did not understand that maidens always helplessly fall in love with their champions.

Champions always know that they hold the hearts of their protected maidens in their hands. Maidens love their champions. It matters not whether the champions return the love. It matters not if they do not return the love. Also, it matters not if they steal the love.

Marian did not know that his gallantry had already conquered her heart.

He knew.

He had to decide what to do with her love.

Yet the memory of his broken heart caused him to suppress his want for Marian. His memory of Ogina, his traitorous wife, crushed any soft feelings for Marian. The memory of Ogina's military betrayal.

Some of her terror had already unconsciously subsided with his tenderness. Subsided with the familiar bay leaf aroma of his cloak.

Marian closed her eyes. She was too exhausted to recognize the effect of the aroma on her. The bay leaf aroma made her feel that she was in her comfortable kitchen. She closed her eyes. She unconsciously imagined she was in her father's manor. Imagined that she sat in a stuffed chair. A stuffed chair by the fireplace and inhaled the aroma of Vespers' bells supper. Then, she unconsciously sighed and licked her lips. Her tongue ran over the acidic lake water on her lips.

Marian spit and said, "Lake water in my mouth."

Again she realized her jeopardy. Fear and danger exhausted her. Her vision whirled in dizziness. She put her hand to her forehead and felt nauseous. Warrick felt her collapse backward unconscious into his arms.

Warrick said aloud, "Lady Bad Luck. Unconscious. Exhausted. Of course you are unconscious. You should not have stayed conscious this long."

He tightened his arms around her.

He said, "You are a strong woman to have been conscious this long. What with Skinwalkers and Red-Fog after you."

He shouted, "Awaken. Open your eyes. Your body is to limp. You will slide out of my grip. You must awaken."

Warrick lifted her with both arms and said, "Wake up. You almost slid off the horse."

She woke in confusion. She beat on his chest, "Let go of me."

The pungent bay leaf aroma of his leather cloak reminded her that she was safe. To feel safe, again she inhaled the strong, bay leaf. She felt the bay-leaf-aroma sting her nose.

While he hugged her, she tried to understand her contradictory feelings. Marian feared this strange, handsome, muscular warrior. A warrior that held her so tight. So tight that she knew that she could not escape. Then she feared the helplessness she felt in his arms. Yet she felt safe, and now warm, almost as if she were at home.

Marian kicked her feet to wrap the long cloak tighter around them.

Warrick commanded, "Stop kicking the cloak or you will confuse Zeus. Obey."

His command piqued her pride and made her angry.

She said, "Obey. For you everything is obedience, . . . to you. You have endlessly commanded me to do this or that. Do you command everybody?"

Warrick said, "Do you hear that roar, again." The AntiChrist is again roaring his obsession with Jesus' Crucifixion. Wolv's Sext and Nones Golgotha-Crucifixion obsessions.

Again, again, again the roar, 'Father. Forgive them. They know not what they do,' filled the air. It shook the earth.

The repetitious roar vibrated the earth and caused a barn to collapse.

Zeus reared.

Warrick commanded, "Obey me."

Warrick said, "That roar 'Father. Forgive them. They know not what they do,' is a warning. Wolv has decided to be your enemy. He will do anything to capture or kill you. Your only hope is to obey me. I was born to fight Wolv, the AntiChrist. I belong to the Simon of Cyrene-Pendragon line. The Knights of the Sorrowful Lady. The Able-Pendragon line of Cyrene-Pendragons. Wolv belongs to the Cain-Pendragon line of Cairo-Pendragons. Both lines of Egypt. Your only hope is to obey me. Wolv has ordered all the Skinwalkers, the Cain Pendragon line, to capture you."

She said, "Obey. For you everything is obedience, . . . to you. You have endlessly commanded me to do this or that. Do you command everybody?"

"Yes, sometimes I command all of England, in the King's absence," he said. "I am England's greatest champion, from India, Portugal, Russia to Scotland. When the King is elsewhere, all in England obey my blessed sword."

"I have goaded her pride," Warrick thought. "Perhaps I can goad her until she recognizes the humor in my words. Perhaps even make her smile. Yes, I will tease her until she smiles."

He smiled and lied, "Sometimes I even command the king." His right eyebrow raised as he lied. He always unconsciously raised his right eyebrow when he lied.

To put her at ease he said, "Sprite. Did you know that you are beautiful when you smile?"

Marian said, "Cad."

Warrick said, "I command you to smile. You are beautiful when you smile."

She hit his chest and smiled.

He said, "See. Everyone in England obeys me, and your beautiful smile."

Tears filled here eyes. She said, "We are in danger. Then you toy with me as if I were a child."

He said, "Lady Bad Luck. We are on a battlefield. On a battlefield, you are a child. Now smile so you can be beautiful and obey me."

Marian wept into her hands.

Warrick tightened his hugged on her.

Zeus galloped through the red-fog.

The sky was fire red. Lightening flashed in the distance. The lightening, of the rainless distant thunderstorm, highlighted his smile and his raised right eyebrow.

She put her nose into the air and shook her small fist in his face. "Again you treat me as if I were a fool," she snapped. "You endlessly order me about, then you jest that you will take me. Now you expect me to believe that you command the king. I am not a child nor a vassal. I manage a great estate. Stop ordering me about."

Warrick thought, "Now that she is angry, she is no longer frightened."

Warrick almost laughed at how futile, yet naively defiant her small feminine fist appeared.

He smiled and said, "By the way, did I hear you say 'Thank you?'"

She had not even thought of thanking him. "Impudence, you want me to thank you for insulting me? Infinite gall. You want me to thank you for ordering me about. Order me as if I were a vassal?"

He thought, "She must know that I jest. She can see my smile. Does she not know that I am only needling her? Anyway, since she is angry, she is stronger."

He smiled and said, "If I did stop ordering you about, you would have drowned. Or those Skinwalkers would have kidnaped or killed you. Or the cold would have chilled you to death. Obey and sit still and be quiet. Obey."

Warrick had teased her too much, but he did not realize it. She found no humor in his words.

She said, "Obey, obey, what arrogance you have."

He continued to tease her. He expected at some point for her to smile. Perhaps even to laugh, so he continued to tease her.

"You have the sharpest tongue that I have ever heard," Warrick said. "I just saved you from those Skinwalkers. Why are you so belligerent? You will be safe with me if you obey. Obey."

At the word, 'obey,' she almost slapped him. She wanted to show that Warrick was incorrect in demanding obedience. Yet she could think of nothing rational so she allowed emotion to twist her reason. She wrinkled her eyebrows in an inverted v of confusion and indignation.

Marian insincerely said, "If you. If you had not knocked me into the water, I could have outrun those Skinwalkers. Then you would not have had to fight them. I would not be chilled to the bone. Your foolishness caused all this terror."

She did not mean what she said.

Warrick understood that her words came from fear and exhaustion. He knew that she did not mean what she said.

He smiled and said, "So the danger you were in, now in, is, my fault."

Marian held her chin high, indignant that he used a commanding tone of voice. Her eyebrows wrinkled in an inverted v in confusion.

She looked up at him into his almost incandescent emerald eyes.

Marian thought, "How could I have said something so stupid, Warrick is my only protector? Since I have insulted him, he will have nothing to do with me again."

She raised her eyebrows in an inverted V of confusion.

Marian thought, "Why should I even want anything more to do with him? Why am I attracted to this hard, insulting, arrogant warrior?"

-

-

-

CHAPTER, Where, Oxford, England, Northwest of London, England, Year @ 1250s A.D.

DEMONS CHASING AFTER HER.

As she looked up at him, he gazed straight ahead. His emerald eyes fascinated her. She studied the curves of his chiseled granite-like face. Her eyes followed his wide mouth, the curve of his lips. Determination thinned his lips. Marian was a wreck. She was afraid of him. Yet she was warm, comfortable with him and angry with him. The quick death he gave to her enemies terrified her. Yet, she was relieved to be with him.

She looked up in his emerald eyes. He turned his head to search the horizon. Search the horizon for enemies.

Marian thought, "I sounded so stupid. I should have thanked him at least. Now it is too late. How wonderfully handsome he is. He wants to have nothing to do with me because of my sharp tongue. Why do I want to see him anymore? I have never wanted to see any man more than once."

Warrick said, "We must find my brothers' Adoration wagon. Or else a Catholic church where I can set up Adoration of the Blessed Sacrament. Only Adoration of the Blessed Sacrament can keep the red-fog away."

As the fire-red sky reflected off her blue eyes, Warrick looked down at her. *"How wonderfully beautiful she is," he thought. "After my murderous wife, Ogina, I am pleased she wants nothing to do with me. I am a rough, war-commander. I should have nothing to do with beauty."*

Zeus ran parallel to a split log fence. For her safety, Warrick tightened his steel-like arms around Marian's torso.

Marian pushed on his arm and said, "You dare touch my breasts?"

As Warrick held Marian tighter, in a run, Zeus raised his front legs. Zeus jumped and soared high over the split log fence.

Surprised, Marian grabbed Warrick's arm and snapped, "You should. . . ."

Zeus' front legs landed on the road. The jump had lifted Marian off Zeus' back.

She said, "Should have warned me. You should have warned me that we were about to jump the fence."

As Warrick reined Zeus, the stallion locked his legs. For a split second, Zeus skidded to a stop at an intersection. In the thick red fog.

Warrick smiled and said, "Prepare yourself, we are about to jump the fence."

Then Warrick prodded Zeus back into a gallop.

Marian said, "Ummmph, I do not appreciate your roguish humor."

"Which way do you want to go," Warrick asked?"

She pointed. "This way is at least four times longer, but it may be safer."

He said, "Good, my knights are coming down this road shortly. We will meet them ahead of us. Since you are so anxious that I release you, my knights will see you home."

Behind them Marian's gelding jumped the fence and followed them. Every day her gelding trotted through the fields back. Back to the barn for corn and oats. Out of habit, the gelding followed.

"She is so beautiful," Warrick thought. "She obviously does not want anything to do with me. Otherwise, she would not have insulted me. Thank God that she does not want anything to do with me. I do not want another murderous female near me. The king demanded that I marry one murderous woman. Constant

exorcism and war against Skinwalkers are my life. I do not want war in my household, again."

Warrick feasted his eyes on her beautiful face. He could not keep his eyes from her beautiful face.

Marian thought, "He is so handsome, so courageous. I want to see my champion again. Now he will ride out of my life. Why did I insult him?"

She did not realize how safe she felt. She knew that more Skinwalkers were close to her father's manor. Yet she felt safe in this supremely confident man's arms. She did not realize the reason she felt safe was that he carried her tenderly. So tenderly and securely she unconsciously felt that this mysterious warrior cherished her.

Warrick did cherish Marian.

"More Skinwalkers are outside my father's manor," she said.

Warrick spurred Zeus into an attack speed in the direction Marion pointed.

Warrick said, "I will let you off at a safe distance from the manor. Somewhere high above the red fog. When I let you off above the red-fog, do not make a sound. The red-fog will hear you, climb to you and eat you. If you end in the red-fog, never stop running. Climb into a barn loft or tree. Up ahead, I will destroy the Skinwalkers and come back for you."

Warrick looked down into her beautiful face.

He thought, "Her beauty is fascinating and fills me with warmth. I have had my fill of beautiful women. Yet, somehow I know that I will see her again. Beautiful women are a poison that men are destined to drink. The archbishop of Canterbury makes Catholic priests marry, if the king wishes. Catholic priests are the only educated people to administer the king's lordships."

Marian thought, "He is so handsome. He only thinks of me as a harpy. Now he will never want to see me again. He will put me down and the red-fog will eat me."

In the fire-red sky and sudden lightening, his forward-looking face showed only determination. Determination to find and defeat the enemy. Warrick's whole life had only one purpose. To find and to defeat Wolv and the Skinwalkers. He stared ahead.

Marian could not take her eyes away from his luminescence, emerald eyes.

Lord Warrick thought, *"Kissing such beautiful lips would be wonderful."*

Marian thought, *"If only I had the brazenness of a coquette. If only I were brazen enough to kiss this handsome warrior."*

Behind them the lightening of the rainless storm exploded a large oak tree.

Zeus reared. Marian lost her balance.

Lord Warrick hugged Marian tight. He had lifted her eye to eye. Accidentally, their lips touched. Then she slapped his face, lowered her head and . . . secretly smiled.

She said, "I slapped your face and you did not care. What sort of warrior are you?"

Warrick thought, "I must have Drayton and Morgan enforce our prayers. They must make sure that everyone does their hour of Perpetual Adoration. In the Adoration wagon. Perpetual Adoration of Jesus' Real Presence in the Blessed Sacrament. Make sure everyone does weekly confession. Together, Perpetual Adoration and weekly confessions repel the things in the red fog. Otherwise, the things in the red-fog will eat us."

Marian said, "You just spoke aloud about adoration, confession and red fog. That things in the red-fog will eat us."

Warrick said, "More bad luck for me. I spoke my thoughts aloud. I see no place to let you down. The thick red-fog covers the ground."

Marian said, "What will eat us?"

Warrick said, "Lady Bad Luck. Be not afraid of those that can harm the body. This is spiritual warfare with Satan's dominations and principalities. A hierarchy of evil, unholy demons. Similar to the hierarchy of Jesus' Holy angels. On earth, Wolv leads these evil dominations and unholy principalities. We Knights of the Sorrowful Lady fight the AntiChrist with Perpetual Adoration. Also, we fight with weekly confession. The AntiChrist's forces are Satan's dominations and principalities of demons. Fallen angels. Wolv brings up the red-fog from Hell when he tries to destroy the earth. At the time of the Crucifixion this exact red-fog covered the earth. Satan thought that he had conquered the earth at Jesus' death. Yet the light of Jesus'

Resurrection drove the red-fog back to Hell. This is why Wolv hates the Prime bells. He relives Satan's failure to conquer the earth. The things in the red-fog possess people and animals and make them into Skinwalkers. As demons they travel in the red-fog and either possess or eat people. The graces of Perpetual Adoration and Weekly confession drive the red-fog from us. Drive away from us anywhere we do Perpetual Adoration and weekly confession. Someone with us must always be doing his hour of Adoration. Someone in Adoration must always ask Jesus for graces. Always, someone must always ask. All of us must do weekly confession. Demons cannot possess a contrite heart that adores Jesus."

She quaked with passion and fear of this handsome man. A man that angered her and made her feel safe. A man whose talk of demons terrified her.

-

-

-

CHAPTER, Where, Oxford, England, Northwest of London, England, Year @ 1250s A.D.

NOTHING ROMANTIC EVER HAPPENS TO ME

Mounted on Zeus, Warrick asked, "Sprite, what is your name? Why do I tell you all this?"

Marian said, "You better explain more than this. I just saw you extinguish demons that began to stand and search for their heads. Also, I saw you turn a Skinwalker back into a Catholic priest. A catholic priest from hundreds of years ago. I should be more afraid of you than I am afraid of Skinwalkers. You are far stronger than Skinwalkers."

Warrick said, "I am stronger because of Adoration and weekly confession. Satan is a liar and a murderer. Satan lies to all those that join him. The Liar weakens all those that join him. Also, Satan murders all those that join him. Still, Satan worshipers are everywhere, in every town, in every city, in every village."

Warrick said, "I repeat, Lady Bad Luck, what is your name?"

Marian thought, "The Skinwalkers called him, Dread, God's Angel of Death. I do not want anyone with that name to know my name. I will lie."

Marian said, "You already called me Lady Bad Luck."

"So you want me to call you Bad Luck?"

"No." As she did when she lied, Marian unconsciously repeated and drew out her words. "My naaaame is . . . is . . . Taraaaaaaaaa."

Again the ground vibrated with Wolv's growl, "Tiny Wolv. I will always love you."

Zeus reared. Warrick hugged Marian and prodded Zeus back into run.

Wolv growled the phrase 'Tiny Wolv. I will always love you,' repeatedly. Each time the ground vibrated.

Warrick said, "Again that is Wolv's obsession with Holy Mary. In Egypt Wolv learned that Holy Mary is the Woman of Genesis. The Woman from the Book of Genesis that will crush Satan's head. Crush Satan's head at the end of time. This is one reason that the Resurrection hour, the Prime bell, terrifies Wolv. Though he crucified Jesus, Wolv failed to stop Jesus' Resurrection. Wolv knows that Holy Mary is destined to defeat Satan. Destined to defeat Wolv himself because Wolv serves Satan."

Marian said, "Too much information. I feel like I am in the middle of a hurricane."

Warrick said, "Just to kidnap you, Tara. You said your name is Tara. Wolv has his camp in Wales. Oxford is in the middle of England. Wales is hundreds of miles to the west, outside the borders of England. The AntiChrist has encamped in Wales. Why would the Skinwalkers come to the center of England, just to kidnap you?"

She indignantly said, "So you think that I am not important enough to kidnap?"

"If you wish, I will kidnap you," Warrick teased her. With her face hidden under the cowl, Marian's eyebrows formed an angry V. Then she smiled and raised her eyebrows in an inverted V of apprehensive approval.

She frowned and thought, "Kidnaped by my champion could be wonderful, exciting, romantic."

Then she raised her eyebrows and thought, "Foolish, dangerous . . . exotic, charming. Nothing romantic ever happens to me . . . or ever will. Nothing romantic ever happens to me."

-

-

-

CHAPTER, Where, Oxford, England, Northwest of London, England, Year @ 1250s A.D.

SAFE IF YOU ARE A VIRGIN

Marian asked, "Why did you fight for me?"

Warrick had his mind and eyes on the dangerous horizon. Thus, Warrick unconsciously spoke the truth, and revealed his future. "Because, I am your hero. I am here to save you."

Suddenly, Warrick unsheathed Dread.

He said, "Tara, danger may lurk ahead. From far down the road in front of us, I hear hoof beats."

Marian tightened her fists in terror and involuntarily held her breath.

He said, "Tara. You are safe. It is my first knight and brother, Lord Ross-The-Rake Pendragon. That is, you are safe from Ross-the-Rake if you are a virgin."

Marian breathed again. She sighed. She said, "Thank God." Then she said, "Virgin. Why virgin?"

Ross turned in the opposite direction to ride with Warrick.

Warrick asked, "Did you see any Skinwalkers? Any campfires along the road as you galloped toward us?"

Ross smiled and said, "Sorry, no. I regret to report that I had a peaceful ride. If they were there, they may have detected your knights coming down the road. If so, I am sure that they ran from them. Drayton, Morgan, and your knights are only a few minutes behind me."

Then Marian shouted, "Ross, the Rake? You give your brother the name of a sexual rogue, a sexual varlet. Well, Ross the Rake, I suppose you have a wife in every city."

Ross said, "Why should I marry when I only bed married women. Experienced older married women that appreciate me. At night their husbands are drunk and ignore their wives."

Warrick said, "Ross has only one flaw. He is a mighty knight, but Ross cannot turn away from a woman's wink."

Ross said, "I live in a sea of bodacious breasts and I swim. I swim until I have kissed all of them. Until the day I die, I will swim in a sea of breasts. I hope to drown in a sea of breasts."

Ross and Warrick guffawed.

Marian said, "Ross. You would like to live in a house of prostitution."

Ross guffawed and said, "Never. Since early manhood, older women have taught me. They taught me the art of love. Women love me and I love breasts. A sea of breasts and I swim."

Ross and Warrick guffawed.

Marian thought, "Horrible sexual rogues."

Warrick said, "Only Ross has the nickname 'The Rake.'"

Marian said, "Please change the topic."

Warrick said, "The rest of us Pendragons do not have Ross' genius for seduction. The rest of the Pendragons have a genius for war."

Marian asked, "Change the topic. Pendragon. That is the family name of the mythical King Arthur Pendragon. I suppose you claim to be part of the royal line of the Arthurian legend?"

Warrick laughed. He said, "Not myths. We have a Glamorgan Pendragon castle on Wales' southern coast, on the Swansea Peninsula. Within the Pendragon castle we have a great library of ancient tomes on myths. Many of those tomes trace the myth of King Arthur Pendragon to living Pendragon families. Of course none can verify any of the genealogies in the tomes."

-

-

-

-

CHAPTER, Oxford, England, Northwest of London, England, Year @ 1250s A.D.

SO YOU LIE

Warrick said, "Ross, did you find Father Malachi Martin?"

Ross said, "No."

Warrick asked, "Where is th Adoration wagon?"

Then Ross-The-Rake said, "Minutes away, with our half brothers."

Warrick said, "Ross. Satan worshipers are everywhere helping Wolv call his red-fog out of Hell."

Again the ground vibrated with Wolv's repeated growl, "Tiny Wolv. I will always love you."

Then Ross-the-Rake said, "Sprite. Over a thousand-years-ago, Symon of Cyrene wrote that Holy Mary comforted Wolv. Comforted Wolv on her lap when Egyptian children called him ugly-eye. Over a thousand years ago in Egypt. Guilt drives him insane that he still Crucified Holy Mary's Son. Symon of Cyrene recorded that Wolv deeply loves Holy Mary. Yet Wolv obeyed Rome and Crucified Holy Mary's Son, Jesus."

Then Wolv again vibrated the earth with the repeated, guilt-filled growl, "Beloved Mother. Get out of my head."

Marian said, "Why does Wolv call Holy Mary 'Beloved Mother?'"

Ross-The-Rake said, "Because Wolv is as crazy as a rabid dog. If Wolv howled an hour, he could destroy everything in a five-mile radius."

Marian said, "Warrick. You said, half brothers?"

Warrick said, "Same father, different mothers."

They continued to gallop toward Marian's manor in the red-fog.

On the road, Warrick put Dread back into the war-ax sheath.

Marian asked, "Ross is your first knight. What is a first knight?"

Lord Warrick said, "My first knight. Ross and Morgan are my co-captains of the knights, my half-brother Lord Morgan Pendragon. Morgan and Ross work as a team, as my first knights. Sometimes I think Morgan and Ross can read each others minds. My younger half-brother, Lord Drayton, is my captain of the archers. Morgan assumes my command if I am on patrol, or die. After Morgan then Ross takes command, then Lord Drayton, the captain of the archers. Drayton is self-conscious about his youth. We tease him about his young age. Yet no archer in England is better than Drayton."

Marian asked with an air of contempt, "Ross the Rake. Did you just ride from the village of Fost?"

Ross said, "Yes."

Marian said, "Warrick. Except the things in the red-fog, we have no need to ride hard. Ross the Rake. You yourself have already ridden by my father's manor."

Ross said, "I see that you have some contempt for my pleasures. From the tone of your voice."

Marian said, "How many young filles have you driven to heartbreak-suicide."

Lord Ross said, "None. I only drive older women to their 'little death.' I avoid young women like the plague."

They slowed to an easy lope.

Warrick said, "Ross. Where have you been? You have straw in your hair and on your shoulders."

Ross said, "Whenever I am here, Lady Lonanna and I meet for the 'little death'."

Marian glanced behind her to see Ross' blond hair down to his neck. Ross had gleaming blue eyes and oiled brown leathers.

She thought, "Ross is exactly the opposite of Warrick. Warrick has the blackest of moods. Even Ross' horse prances as if it were delighted. Zeus gallops as if it were in a charge into battle. The huge warhorse gallops steady, straight, firm, determined, as if in a black mood himself. Ross is so handsome, happy, and boyish. No wonder women love him."

Ross shook straw from his long blond hair

Marian asked, "Warrick, why do they call you Dread, God's Angel of Death."

Warrick said, "Tara. When you defeat an enemy, they never say that a weakling defeated them."

Warrick laughed. "They will always exaggerate."

Ross said, "Tara. I can assure you that Lord Warrick is no angel. He taught us to play off the bedouin superstitions. He taught us that it is not what you are that win wars. You win wars with what the enemy thinks you are. The bedouin raiders around Jerusalem and Egypt tell the legend that Warrick can fly. They even believe that he can come out of the ground any where. We spread the legend so that many bedouins would fear him and abandon their leaders."

Marian said, "So you lie?"

-

-

HOPEFULLY, THE ANTICHRIST KILLS ME, BEFORE MARRIAGE KILLS ME.

Marian looked up at him and said, "You spread lies about yourself?"

Warrick laughed and said, "Tara. Of course, to mislead and deceive the enemy. Every time I heard them call me 'Dread, God's Angel of Death,' I smiled. Their superstitious nature astonished me."

"When you fought those four Skinwalkers with no weapon," Marian said. "I can see how your enemies would call you God's Angel of Death."

Warrick and Ross laughed. Their laugh echoed off the hills.

Marian asked, "You laugh! Why? You could have died? You have death in the red-fog at our galloping horses' feet, and you laugh."

Again Warrick and Ross laughed. They spoke in almost unison, "Tara. We should have died hundreds of times."

"Tara. Knights that constantly practice for war," Ross said, "count the booty of their wins. Knights that constantly clank their ale mugs count the awesome lies that they must concoct. They must concoct great legends about the giants. Lies about giants and hellish specters that defeated them, . . . to save their pride."

Warrick said, "Tara. Greeks say, 'There is no shame if the gods defeat you. Shame on you if only a man defeats you.' Soon it will be our turn to clank ale mugs in the King's castles."

Ross said, "Yes, brother, we will have a bottomless tankard of ale someday. Bottomless after our last battle."

Again their laugher echoed off the hills.

Ross said, "Tara. The king never lets his Pendragon warriors retire from battle. As we wish, we are destined to die in battle."

"After our last battle, perhaps Heaven will have a great ale house," Warrick said.

They laughed with the enthusiasm of two young boys.

Warrick asked, "Tara, I have a letter from the king in my inside pocket. Pull it out and open it so I can read it."

She put her hand inside his black leather blouse. She ran her palm over his muscular chest. The hard muscles surprised her.

Again the earth shook with Wolv's repeated growls of, "Father. Forgive them, for they know not what they do."

Warrick said, "Wolv's Sext bells and Nones' bells obsessions. Wolv nailed Jesus to the cross at zenith sun, Sext bells. Three hours later Wolv ran a spear up through Jesus' Right side. Up through his right side into his heart, at Nones bells. Wolv will howl Jesus' seven phrases from the cross. Howl the seven phrases from zenith sun, Sext bells, to Nones bells."

Lord Warrick again looked down at her.

Lord Warrick thought, "I resent the control her beautiful face has over me. I feel peaceful and wonderful when I look at her beautiful countenance. Her beauty flows into my eyes and fills me to overflowing. My eyes are the portals and her beauty gushes in through them to saturate me. Her beauty saturates me with joy, happiness, well-being, desire, and hunger for her touch. I resent that she can control my emotions with her smile and beauty alone. Should I ask her if she would come with me on my duties? No, she has already told me that she dislikes me. I have already drunk my share of the poison called beauty."

Marian thought, "If only I were a coquette. Then, then I would ask him if he would just take me away. Yes, I wish that I had the forwardness of a coquette. His emerald eyes look through me as if he can read all my thoughts. How handsome he is. If I were a coquette, I would kiss him. Yet, he does not want to see me ever again after today."

As she searched for the letter, he hugged her tenderly, tighter, and galloped forward. Though she found and could see the letter, she continued to palm his chest. Black hair covered his chest. His chest muscles rippled with the rhythm of the horse. She had never touched such thick sensuous muscles that writhed under her palm.

She liked his warm skin pressed against her palm. Then she pulled her palm away. His still wet chest caused her palm to suck against his skin. The hard, warm feel of his chest excited her mind. Wonderful feelings very foreign to her. She pretended not to find the stiff sheepskin. Pretended just to continue to stroke her palm against his chest.

He said, "Tara. In my left inner pocket."

Marian elongated her words when she lied. She said, "You ride toooooo . . . tooooo fast. Your blouse is full of toooooo much wind. I cannot find it."

She continued to palm his chest. An irresistible power drove her hand down. Then she ran her hand down below his ribs, onto his rippled stomach. Then she felt the thick hair below his belly button.

He glanced down at her, she up at him.

He smiled.

She blushed.

With disappointment she realized her sensual search was over. She pulled the thick sheepskin from his inner pocket.

He asked, "Tara. Unwrap it so only I can see it."

Marian thought, "The king's seal, Warrick is important."

She broke the king's seal and unwrapped the short message. As the wind flapped the sheepskin, she held it so only he could read.

Warrick said, "The king writes of glorious news and inglorious news."

Ross said, "What is the glorious news?"

Warrick read aloud, "The king writes, 'My Champion, Lord Warrick. You are the world's only hope. Wolv has spread his deadly red-fog over all England and Europe. The same as when Wolv was Attila, from 434-453 A.D., the Hun. Attila, Wolv, as Attila, had reduced Europe to ashes, slaves and cannibalism. You know Wolv better than anyone in the world. You know that no one can kill Wolv. We can only slow him. We have an account of how one Pendragon slowed Wolv. Read and beware and learn. One of Attila's newest wives, Gudrun, was secretly of the Able Symon Cyrene Pendragons. She got him drunk and then stabbed him with Christian Blessed daggers. Gudrun shoved the daggers deep into his body to hide them. Also, she poured Blessed Extreme Unction oil down his throat. Then she rubbed the Blessed Extreme Unction oil over all his body. As always, contact with anything Blessed caused Wolv to burn in yellow-red flames. The spiritual flames did not burn him to ash. Pain from the blessed daggers caused him to be catatonic, as if dead. When the Huns saw him in ethereal flames, catatonic and dead-like, they buried him. The Huns did not know that he was the AntiChrist, demon-possessed. So when his Skinwalkers dug him up, he escaped his grave. The sight of Attila alive terrified the Huns. Thus, the Huns abandoned him. My champion, Warrick, you are the only warrior in the world that knows Wolv. Only you know how to slow him. Only you know how to trap him. Warrick, only you and the Able Symon Cyrene Pendragons are not afraid of him. Wolv is of the Cain Cairo Pendragons. You are of the Able Symon of Cyrene Pendragons. Your lines have battled each other over one two thousand years. Research your secret libraries, reach into your infinite courage, find a way to slow Wolv. Warrick of the Able Symon of Cyrene Pendragons, you are the world's only hope." King Edward.

Ross said, "You call that glorious news?"

Lord Warrick said, "Of course. What greater honor than to conquer the AntiChrist. Only the greatest champion can conquer the AntiChrist."

Ross said, "You do remember that the Huns killed Gudrun?"

Warrick said, "Gudrun was alone. I am with my brothers."

Lord Ross said, "What was in inglorious news?"

"Bad news, bad news, Ross," Warrick said. "The king commands me. He commands me to wed the third daughter of Lord and Lady Moray of Oxford. He commands me to marry an unnamed Lady of the Moray estate. She must be too ugly to give a name."

Shock cause Marian's hands to open. She lost her grip. Then she lost her balance and screamed, "Catch me."

Warrick tightened his hug of her.

Marian thought, "I am that third daughter of Lord Moray of Oxford. Finally I will marry."

Lady Marian's heart leapt for joy. She straightened her back and smiled. Marian thought, "From fifteen I managed my invalid father's great estate. I forever gave up on finding love. Every maiden dreams of marrying their champion."

Then instantly, it seemed as if Satan himself dragged her down to his Hades.

She frowned and bowed her head.

Then Marian thought, *"Oh God, I am foolish to be joyous. Now the king has bound me to a warrior. A bitter, cold, hard warrior. Now I must give up control over my father's estate, to a stranger. He is a stranger to me that could be brutal and foolish. He could be foolish enough to drive my wealthy estate into bankruptcy."*

Marian sighed in sad resignation. *She thought, "Warrick will be another drunken peacock lord. A drunken lord that will mistreat my family and bankrupt the Moray estate."*

Warrick said aloud, "I do not wish to marry, but it is my duty. Marriage is the quickest way for a knight to die. Wives are traitors. I will do my duty to my God and King. I will marry this third daughter of Lord Moray of Oxford. Ogina, my deceased first wife was a traitor. She caused the death of all my knights. Marriage is a poisonous snake that has already bit me. I do not wish the snake to bite me again. Marriage, I have come to hate marriage."

Marian thought, "Oh God, to what Hell has the king condemned Warrick and me. Cursed to marry a man that hates our marriage before he even knows me."

Ross said, "Warrick. You retreated into reason and logic. Yes, you became hard as granite. Ogina handed you and your knights over you to the enemy. So long ago. Surely, after such a long time, your wounds have healed."

"Ross. As you know, wounds are often not the problem," Warrick said. "Often the wound heals improperly. Then the scar, not the wound, cripples the patient. I will never trust another woman. Hopefully Wolv will kill me before I marry."

-

-

-

CHAPTER, Oxford, England, Northwest of London, England, Year @ 1250s A.D.

RECORDS OF ADORATION AND WEEKLY CONFESSION

Warrick's frown was deep. So deep that the corners of his mouth reached down to his chin. His deep frown pulled the skin on his cheeks tight.

Marian thought, "Lord Warrick has only two predominant moods, two expressions. One is a supreme, confident, tranquil mood even when he is in battle. The other is a quiet black mood. A mood with a deep frown, when he thinks of marriage. Our marriage will be horrible."

Ross knew that he had to change the subject quickly. Quickly, or Warrick would have one of his quiet black mood days.

Ross asked, "Who is riding with you all bundled in your cloak?"

Marian snapped, "Ross the Rake. I am Lady Bad Luck."

Warrick said, "Tara, you are a strange sprite. Why did you say 'Lady Bad Luck'? Your name is Tara."

Marian thought, "I do not want to marry a man that hates marriage."

Warrick looked down at Marian. He thought, "Tara is the most beautiful woman that I have ever seen. Even with all my bitterness, her beauty fills me. Her beauty fills me with a hunger that I have not felt for years. Beauty is poison that I will never again drink."

Zeus jumped a large puddle. Warrick tightly hugged her so that she would not fall.

Warrick thought, "Tara's beauty has bewitched me."

Marian thought, "Warrick's courage and handsomeness have bewitched me. Yet, he hates marriage. Warrick will bring only turmoil into our marriage. We will never be happy because he is so against marriage."

"Ross. Marriage to this third daughter of Lord Moray is horrible news," Warrick said.

The late after-Nones' sunshine reflected off Marian's tears.

Lord Warrick glanced down to Marian.

"Tara," he said. "Why do you have tears on your cheeks?"

Marian wiped her tears with the back of her hand. She stretched her words as she always does when she lied. She lied, "Just grit in myyyyy . . . myyyyy eyessss, eyesssss."

Inevitably again when she lied she repeated and drew out her words. "Jusssst gritttt."

Warrick heard the clatter of armor and looked ahead to see two other brothers.

Lord Warrick said, "My knights come. The world's best warriors. Tara, you are safe now. Look. Lord Morgan, my co-captain of my knights. Lord Drayton, my captain of my archers."

Warrick's knights and archers galloped behind Morgan and Drayton.

They split down the middle.

Ross, Warrick and Marians rode through the center of them. All the knights and archers turned in formation. On their warhorses they formed long lines behind Warrick and Ross.

Drayton turned and galloped beside Warrick.

Warrick said, "Drayton. Have you blessed all arrows, spears, other weapons and armor?"

Drayton said, "Yes. Lord Warrick. Brother, just as you have drilled us often every day."

Warrick said, "Where is the Adoration wagon?"

Drayton said, "With us. Look at the ground. Adoration of the Blessed Sacrament is already shoving away the red-fog."

Lord Warrick said, "Remember, we do not fight flesh and blood. We fight Satan's hierarchies and dominations of demons."

Also Drayton, "Have you made sure that everyone does their hour of Perpetual Adoration? In the Adoration wagon, Perpetual Adoration of Jesus' Real Presence in the Blessed Sacrament. Have you made sure everyone does weekly confession? Satan can easily conquer an arrogant heart. You know that only Adoration and weekly confession can keep the red-fog away. Never forget the army the red-fog ate in Regensburg, Germany. You saw the massacre with your own eyes. The red-fog ate every Regensburg soldier."

Drayton said, "Warrick. I have kept records of everyone's adoration times and weekly confessions."

-

-

-

CHAPTER, Oxford, England, Northwest of London, England, Year @ 1250s A.D.

KING ARTHUR PENDRAGON WAS NOT A MYTH.

From far away, on a knoll, Wolv's eyes glazed over black. Glazed black as his memories crippled him. He began to howl repeatedly, "Today you will be with me in paradise."

Red fog poured from Wolv. He spit out thick globs of red froth that cover him from mouth to feet.

The AntiChrist's repeated growls shook the earth and caused bricks to fall from chimneys.

Slowly Wolv came out of his Crucifixion obsession and his eyes lost the black glaze.

FAR AWAY.

Warrick said, "Tara. Wolv is very near. We can probably see Wolv."

From a knoll far away, Wolv watched Warrick's knights. He whispered, "Now that I finally find Marian, Warrick's army protects Marian. Where is my army of Skinwalkers? Lilith promised more Skinwalkers. I need my army to capture Marian. Where is my army? Every time I fight, I model my war on King Arthur. Centuries ago, I helped Mordred kill King Arthur Pendragon. Yet even with my army, Arthur destroyed my plans. With his last breath, he killed Mordred and Arthur dismembered me. When Arthur killed Mordred, Mordred's soldiers dispersed. I had no more allies. Arthur's knights shipped the pieces of my body to different oceans. Lilith took a hundred years to put me back together. I must assure that Warrick does not kill the leaders of my allies."

Beside Wolv, Swale said, "Wolv, King Arthur was only myth."

Wolv opened his palm and said, "A myth. Myths do not cleave you with Excalibur. Arthur ran Excalibur through my palm."

He flexed his palm in front of Swale and Gulum. "Arthur's spirit, his heart, was Excalibur's strength, the sword's holiness. King Arthur's spirit was Adoration of the Blessed Sacrament and weekly confession. We must kill all Adorationists. Shut the doors of all Adoration churches. You can still see the gash in my palm. Like Warrick, King Arthur had a strong, spiritual, contrite heart. Even after hundreds of years, my palm has yet fully to heal. Warrick is like Arthur. As a child, Warrick stabbed my eye. Just as with Arthur and my palm, my eye has yet to heal. To heal from tiny Warrick's stab. As a six-year-old, Warrick stabbed my eye with a Blessed Crucifix. He shattered it in my eye socket. Yes, Arthur was a real man that I destroyed. I deceived Lancelot into leaving France and sailing to England. I knew Arthur's weakness. As with Warrick, Arthur's heart, his resolve, was his strength. Long before Mordred's sword killed Arthur, a broken heart weakened Arthur. With a broken heart, Arthur lost his resolve, his concentration. I knew that Guinevere and Lancelot were too passionate, too beautiful. Too innocent to resist loving each other. Through Lancelot and Guinevere, I broke King Arthur's heart. In the same way, through Warrick's first marriage, I broke Warrick's heart. Warrick is already dead because his broken heart has made him too weak. Too distracted to survive battle against me."

"My lord, so Arthur's broken heart was his weakness," Gulum said. "Master Wolv. I know your weakness."

With a black aura around him, Wolv said, "I am timeless evil. Evil is timeless, eternal, invincible. Like evil, I am time, eternal, invincible. I have no weaknesses."

"My lord, we know that your strength is your weakness," Swale said. "You need people full of hate."

"Hate, yes, hate," Wolv said. "Yes, I do need people full of hate. I need people filled with perfect hate, people identical to you. Both of you, Swale, Gulum, do know me."

Then Wolv growled and slammed his fist against his thigh. "I will not allow Marian to escape from me," Wolv said. "A trap, I laid a perfect trap. Yet, my officers cannot follow a simple map."

A Tusked-Boar-Headed Skinwalker said, "Lord Wolv. If Warrick escapes, he will leave Oxford. With the king's army he will go into Wales. There he will lay siege to Rose Fire Castle. Warrick is King Edward's only hope. Edward's only top commander. Only commander with the ability to siege you out of Rose Fire, Builth Castle."

Lord Wolv said, "I want Marian, even if all my Skinwalkers die to capture her. I must test if she is Pamia."

Gulum said, "Master Wolv. Look at the ground. Warrick's Adoration wagon has driven away the red-fog. The Red Fog Things eat our enemies. We need the red-fog to defeat Warrick."

-

CHAPTER, Where, Oxford, England, Northwest of London, England, Year @ 1250s A.D.

TO HAVE A CHAMPION IS A CURSE

Marian thought, "Wise women have told me that to have a champion is a curse. A woman always falls in love with her champion. Most often that love remains unrequited. A champion rarely loves the woman he champions. I refuse to allow myself to love my champion. No man will take my heart only to abuse me."

Marian sighed, "Why should I deceive myself? I know that a maiden always falls in love with her champion. Too much, this is too much. My champion was too willing to give his life for me, too handsome, too strong. He has stolen my heart and destroyed my happiness in less than an hour."

Then Marian acted on her fiery impulse. She grinned. Her nose wrinkled. Her eyebrows formed a devilish v in anger. She pretended to slip from the horse. Lady Marian pretended accidentally to grab Warrick's thick, black, chest hair. Then she jerked out a fist full of his chest hair.

Warrick grimaced.

Marian repeated words and elongated them as she always did when she lied. "Oops, I am soooorry," she said. "I thought that I would fall. I just grabbed at the first . . . first thiiiiing that I could catch."

He looked at her and thought, "I. I am holding her so tight that she could not possibly slip. Why would she want to rip out my chest hair? Especially after I saved her from those monsters."

Tears again welled in her eyes. Warrick said, "Tara, I ask you again, why the tears? On the bank of the lake, I promised to champion you. My knights and I will eliminate all your troubles."

Marian jumped at the opportunity and, "To eliminate all my problems. I will hold you to that promise. More than you can now know, I will hold you to that promise."

Marian thought, "The Skinwalkers are a small problem. My marriage with this . . . this warrior will have many more problems."

Warrick thought, "Her troubles with these Skinwalkers will be over quickly. I will dispatch them. Then I will leave her at her home. Then, sadly, I will never again see her beautiful face."

Marian thought, "I will have troubles with Warrick while we are married."

Ross rode up closer to Warrick. Ross said, "The king always chooses a political marriage for his lords. In this way he torments his lords."

Warrick thought, "Marian's beauty is beyond description."

Again Ross said, "Warrick, did you not hear me? Your betrothed, did you forget already?"

Unconsciously, Warrick hugged Marian closer. She pushed away from him.

Warrick thought, "Any man would wish that he could have Tara's beauty with himself forever. Yet, yet, beauty is a snake that bites when you are weakest. Beauty kills."

Marian lowered her head and did not speak.

She thought, "If only Warrick were as honorable as he is heroic. If he were, he would be a wonderful husband. A wonderful lover."

"Warrick, come out of your daydream," Ross said. "I asked you about your betrothal?"

"Yes, as I said, the betrothal is bad news," Warrick said. "I can battle the enemy. I cannot battle a woman in my home."

Marian's heart dropped.

Marian thought, "To have a champion is a curse."

-

-

-

CHAPTER, Oxford, England, Northwest of London, England, Year @ 1250s A.D.

MARRIAGE IS A BATTLE.

She thought, "Warrick thinks that marriage is a battle."

She thought. "My tears, I cannot, I cannot let him see my tears."

She lowered her head and wiped her eyes with the back of her hand.

Ross said, "Warrick. We have good reason to believe in the Pendragon curse."

Warrick said, "Yes. The Pendragon curse, Wolv, caused Ogina to become a traitor. My love of her blinded me to her greed. Love of a spouse is the enemy's strongest weapon. She caused the death of all my knights and almost caused my death. Many of our cousins, uncles and aunts have miserable marriages."

Marian thought, "Just like Warrick's relatives, he and I will be miserable together."

Ross said, "Warrick. You believe the curse with the two criteria? First, that we cannot be happy in marriage until you find that, 'pure love.' The bride must give her life for her bridegroom. Second, each bridegroom must survive his individual trial by fire."

Warrick said, "Yes, Ross, and you have already taken all the women."

"I have not been so busy," Ross guffawed.

"Busier," Warrick shouted. "You take them two and three at a time."

Both guffawed.

Marian turned angry red and thought, "They laughed. Warrick wants me and two or three other women in my bed? I will have a terrible marriage."

Ross said, "So Warrick. Why are you drenched?"

"This sprite of a woman, Lady Bad Luck, defeated me," Warrick said.

Warrick said, "Tara, you seem to have the magic of Merlin himself. You dumped me into a lake. Yet, my first response was to fight your attackers. Not only did I fight for you. I also pledged to champion you against your enemies."

Ross and Warrick laughed.

Warrick said, "Tara. Perhaps your beauty has a magical enchantment."

Ross laughed and said, "Careful Warrick. You tread on dangerous words."

With his recollection, Marian could not help but have soft feelings for her champion. As he pulled her closer to himself, she leaned against him.

She thought, "I must not hope. Warrick is the same as all the others. What is the difference? My father will die soon. The

*king has engaged me to another drunken, adulterous lord. He will
have twenty mistresses. All the lords are the same, handsome or
not. All of them will drive my father's estate into bankruptcy."*

"Tara, what thoughts cause your tears," Warrick asked.

Marian lied, "Coooold, I am oooonly coold . . . coooooold."

She again repeated and drew out her words as always when
she lied.

Ross said, "So this sprite defeated you."

He told Ross what happened in the lake.

Ross said, "So you rewarded her for drowning you. The
reward was to fight unto death for her. Become her champion?"

Warrick decided to tease her and said, "Why? Yes? Tara,
you seemed to have bewitched me, do I defend a witch?"

Again Ross and Warrick laughed as if they were together
drinking ale in a tavern.

She leaned her head against him and asked, "Why do your
laugh? Right now you could be riding into many Skinwalker
henchmen. Why are you so casual? Do you have no fear of
death?"

Warrick wanted to tease Marian again. He said, "Tara, I
will die when I choose, not before."

*She thought, "I must marry a man of ridiculous pride and
pomposity."*

Ross asked Warrick, "Why were you running so fast
around that curve in the road?"

"Zeus wanted to expend his nervous energy. So did I,"
Warrick said.

"You have too much nervous energy," Ross said. "You
need to add a little pleasure to your life. Lay down that battle-ax
and lay a few women."

Marian's eyes grew round and white in embarrassment.
Her face reddened at Ross' words. She thought of the lords'
mistresses. Mistresses that strutted before the lords' own wives.
She remembered the king's tapestries of Biblical, Philistine, pagan
orgies. Pagan orgies to worship Astarte. They were the raucous
orgies. Orgies to ask Astarte to bless the Philistine's planting
season. The tapestries' orgies were so bacchanalia that she could
not tell which woman they entered. The tapestries hung in the
king's great hall. Even as an ignorant virginal adolescent she

would sit in fascination and look at them. The images had burned on her mind.

Warrick said, "Ross-The-Rake. You forget that your other brothers are Catholic priests. All with vows to the pope. Vows of poverty, chastity and obedience. We only marry if the king demands we marry."

-

-

-

CHAPTER, Where, Oxford, England, Northwest of London, England, Year @ 1250s A.D.

I MUST MARRY A CURSE

She thought, "So Warrick is a hypocritical Catholic priest. How many other women will Warrick want in our bed. I will trip any mistress as they walk down my manor's staircase."

Warrick said, "Ross-the-Rake. We must find Father Malachi Martin."

Warrick's silent thoughts turned to his traitorous wife. His frown dipped down to his chin. His mood and expression turned morbid and brooding.

Ross knew he was thinking about, Ogina, his murderess-deceased-wife. He quickly changed the subject.

"Back to the letter. The king's letter," Ross said. "Who again is the lucky bride. The bride that the Pendragon curse will bless?"

Marian thought, "Not only am I to marry an adulterous husband. I must also marry a curse."

Warrick said, "The king's sheepskin mentions no name. Just that she is the third daughter of Lord Moray of Oxford."

Ross decided to tease Warrick.

"Oh my God, I heard of her," Ross said. She has the face of a horse and dog hair all over her body."

Marian bit her lip to stop herself from blurting out. More tears flowed down her cheeks.

Lord Warrick said, "A horse face and hair all over her body. Ross, you should not multiply my bad news with ill omens."

Ross laughed and said, "A face like a horse and twelve feet tall."

To stop from shouting her protest, Marian bit her lip and clenched her fists.

Lord Warrick said, "God's sandals. I do not need the Pendragon curse, you Ross, are a curse. You have cursed my wife into becoming a twelve-foot tall hairy horse."

Ross laughed and said, "And six toes on her feet. Eight fingers on her hands. She also has only one eyebrow. It stretches from temple to temple, straight across her forehead."

Ross and Warrick guffawed. Warrick's laughter reverberated through his chest. She put her ear and palm to his chest. Just to feel his joy of laughter. Though she felt insulted, the infectious laughter caused her to smile, almost laugh.

Ross said, "You need a willing woman tonight. I know where many willing women sleep, not far away."

Warrick said, "Ross-the-Rake. You tempt an avowed Catholic priest, a Vatican exorcist."

Ross said, "Chastity is an unnatural state of life. God gave Eve to Adam for a purpose."

Warrick said, "Did God give many Eves to Adam?"

Then Ross said, "I can allow God this one little mistake."

Warrick and Ross guffawed.

Their bawdy words shocked Marian.

She thought, "Such immoral men? How can they say such ribald words in front of a woman? She looked up at Warrick and thought, "Oh God. No wonder women through themselves at Warrick. He is an incredibly handsome, sensual, passionate, sexy, and gallant man. My emotions are so contradictory toward him. His gallantry and handsomeness give me a wonderful warmth that I have never before felt. Yet, his words make me angry and suspect the worst from him. He is so handsome."

She gently, secretly put her palm on his chest.

Warrick replied, "Ross, all the willing women are married of course?"

"Of course they are all married," Ross laughed. "I never touch a virgin."

Again Marian's mouth dropped open with their bawdy words.

She thought, "My suspicions are true. Warrick does sleep with married women. My future husband is an adulterer. He just confirmed that he will doom me to live with mistresses."

"Ross, we must ride together to my doom," Warrick said. "I am to meet this third daughter of Lord Moray. A wife that is hairy, horse-faced, twelve feet tall. With one eyebrow, temple to temple, twelve toes, and sixteen fingers."

Ross asked, "And what do you want out of a marriage?"

Warrick said, "With the hairy horse with which you have cursed me?"

They laughed.

He pulled Marian closer to him so that she would not fall from Zeus.

Warrick said, "I want what of a wife? I want the impossible. I want an obedient, submissive wife. My dream is to do nothing but train servants and knights. She must serve me."

Ross asked, "So you believe that a woman duty is to serve a man?"

"Yes," Warrick replied.

Marian thought, "He will probably make me serve his mistresses."

Ross said, "The gossip is that the king is to give you a castle. A castle called Rose Fire that protects the lush, beautiful Wye Valley. In Wales' Black Mountains. Given for your loyal service. You only have to take it from the Skinwalkers. From Wolv."

Warrick thought, "The gossip betrays us to the enemy, the Skinwalkers. We head to the most beautiful castle in Great Britain. Rose Fire, in the Black Mountains in Wales. Wolv's thick red fog gathers in Wales Black Mountains. The red fog thickens all over the world. Then things in the fog will eat people. I must hurry. First, I must lay siege to Rose Fire to take it from the Skinwalkers. Traitors in the court know where I am going. I must disobey the king. I must lay siege to Rose Fire many weeks before the king has ordered me. The enemy knows the king's plans for me. Therefore, I must disobey the king and not follow his plans. Yes, I must spread lies. Lies that we travel to London."

Again, Warrick raised his right eyebrow as he always does when he lies.

Warrick lied, "Order the knights that we immediately go to London."

Ross held back for a moment. He ordered to knights to prepare for London.

Ross galloped back up beside Warrick.

"Brother, you are too quiet," Ross said. "You will have lots of fun. Married to a horse-face, tall-as-a-manor, eight-fingers and six-toed wife. Also, fighting Skinwalkers."

Warrick's frown became a laugh. He said, "Tara, you and your family have no worries now. If the enemy is around your manor, we will behead them. Behead them and burn their heads so they cannot come back to life."

Lord Morgan, Warrick's brother and captain of his knights said, "Warrick. All your knights are here."

"Good," Warrick replied. "We ride to the closest manor and search to exorcize Skinwalkers."

Warrick shouted, "Has anyone seen Father Malachi Martin?"

Morgan said, "No one. Father Malachi Martin must be exorcizing demons elsewhere."

Behind Warrick, his knights raised their blessed swords. They shouted, "To Protect the Innocent, to Serve Lord Warrick."

Marian studied Morgan's appearance. Morgan always carried a huge mace. He was as tall and strong as Warrick. His chestnut hair reflected the red sunset. A deep bronze complexion offset and highlighted his bright, green eyes.

Marian thought, "All four Pendragon brothers have high cheek bones. Their jaw muscles always flex when they talk. The four have granite-like strong chins and Warrick's devilish grin. They do not have an ounce of fat on them."

Morgan spotted Marian's long, light, golden hair.

"Morgan, brother, I see your devilish grin," Warrick said. "Ask your devilish question."

As he balanced his enormous mace across his arm, Morgan said, "What? Or who do you have bundled in your cloak?"

From under the large cowl, Marian quickly snapped, "Bad News. Lady Bad Luck." She said nothing else.

Morgan turned in his saddle and shouted, "Reque, Otan, water. You will find fresh water hanging on the Adoration-Confession wagon."

Warrick shouted, "Drayton. Make sure a knight is doing Adoration in the wagon always. Put them on hourly shifts. Only Adoration of the Blessed Sacrament can keep the red-fog away."

Marian asked, "Warrick. What is an Adoration, Confession wagon?"

Warrick said, "Lady Bad Luck. I told you that we are Vatican exorcists of the Sorrowful Lady. We take vows of poverty, chastity and obedience to the pope. We also take two more solemn vows to the pope. Two more solemn papal vows that give us our greater spiritual power. First. A papal solemn vow to do daily one hour of Adoration of the Blessed Sacrament. Secondly, we take a papal solemn vow to go to confession every week. Confession every week to live in contrition. Through Adoration and contrition, Jesus gives us enormous strength to fight the AntiChrist. The Sorrowful Lady's Knights are the Vatican's secret warriors against the AntiChrist."

Warrick paused and said, "Tara. To fight the AntiChrist, one of us, either priest or laity, must always do Adoration. Adoration of Jesus' Real Presence in the Blessed Sacrament. The AntiChrist sends his Skinwalkers to kill anyone doing Adoration. Many in the Catholic church ridicule Adoration as 'Tabernacle-hugging'. Those anti-Adorationists demand that anyone doing Adoration go earn money for the church. Greed drives their decisions. Jesus does not want grand buildings or expanding countries. Jesus wants contrite hearts in which he can live. I remember that the red-fog ate the king's army at York, England. We defeated Wolv in York only because we did Adoration and confession. The red-fog ate all others. We defeated Wolv because we drove the Adoration wagon onto the battlefield."

Reque, Morgan's squire, rode on a sorrel gelding in the back of the column. He pulled a goatskin full of water off the Adoration-Confession wagon. Then galloped beside the column to the column's head.

As Reque galloped to Morgan, Otan, Warrick's squire, picked up another goatskin of water. Otan reined in a white mare behind Warrick.

Then Reque reined in beside Lord Morgan. Morgan took the goatskin, turned it up and drank.

Reque asked, "Lord Warrick, may I speak?"

"Yes," Warrick said.

Then Reque asked, "Otan, how did Lord Warrick come to own you. Own you and the castle and lands in Germany."

Marian thought, "Warrick owns slaves. Slavery is so common in England. This century is supposed to be the glorious and enlightened Eleventh Century. The Carmelite nuns that educated me taught me to despise slavery . . . and slavers. Warrick owns slaves, so I will. Even against my volition, by law I will own slaves. I despise Warrick."

Instantly, Warrick frowned. Then Warrick reached into his blouse and pulled out a parchment. He silently handed it to Otan.

Reque persisted. "Then tell me how my lord gained possession of Otan. Possession of the vast castle and lands in Germany."

Warrick barked, "No."

Mounted on a war horse, Otan rolled the parchment open.

Otan silently read the king's handwritten words. '*To my Champion, Lord Warrick. You are the world's only hope. You must hurry into battle against Wolv, the AntiChrist. The AntiChrist's red fog thickens over all England and Europe. Soon the things in the red fog will begin to eat warriors and horses. Wolv's red fog can lay waste to all England and Europe. Exactly as Attila, the Hun, burned Europe and Asia. Remember your Vatican schooling where you learned that Wolv was Attila, the Hun. My Champion, Warrick, you are the world's only hope. Use all your knowledge and holiness to slow Wolv. Though no one can kill him."*

The words 'Warrick, you are the world's only hope' sent a chill up Otan's spine. His eye grew round with terror.

Warrick looked at Otan and said, "Otan. Your eyes are round with terror. Words should not terrorize you. Read the last line"

Otan silently read, "Also, upon your request, Lord Warrick. I, King Edward, declare Otan of Hern, Germany, to be a freeman.

The sudden, unexpected freedom choked Otan so hard that he could not talk. He gathered all his strength to keep tears from his eyes. Yet, tears filled his eyes. So no one saw, Otan quickly wiped his eyes with his sleeve. Then Otan stuffed the parchment into his blouse. As he genuinely smiled, he stood taller in his stirrups with his back straighter. With a level jaw, he put his vision on the horizon.

Otan thought, "Before Warrick, I had no hope. Now Lord Warrick has given me hope and a future."

Marian thought, "The Carmelite nuns taught me that slavery is an evil. Slavers breed their slaves. Breed them to sell the children of slaves. The Carmelites would say that Warrick is evil to have slaves."

Lord Morgan said, "Warrick. Why did you say no to Reque? I am sure that the story could help the morale of your warriors."

"No," Warrick repeated.

Marian touched Warrick's chest and said, "Do you really own slaves?"

Warrick glanced down at her with his brilliant emerald eyes.

He said, "Tara, you are not to question me."

Marian's eyebrows formed in a deep V of anger.

She whispered, "Warrick. How can you sleep with all those married women?"

Warrick snapped, "Tara. Who are you to question the king's champion?"

She thought quickly to find some reasoning. She said, "Not, who-am-I. Who are you? You are my champion. A champion is supposed to be virtuous."

Marian thought, "I must marry a curse."

-

-

-

CHAPTER, Where, Oxford, England, Northwest of London, England, Year @ 1250s A.D.

WHAT IF SHE THROWS AWAY HER PRAYER BEADS AND PREFERS YOUR BED.

"Tara. Your champion tells you to hold your tongue," Warrick snapped.

Marian whispered, "Almost every word from your mouth is an insult."

"All my weapons should be as sharp as your tongue," Warrick said. "Then my enemies would run when they even thought of me."

Reque asked again, "May we hear Otan's story?"

With his face straight ahead, Warrick snapped, "No, Reque. Now shut up and look around for enemies. Unless you want to be a stable boy, not a squire."

Warrick said, "Drayton. Check the records again. Make sure that everyone does their hour of Perpetual Adoration. In the Adoration wagon, Perpetual Adoration of Jesus' Real Presence in the Blessed Sacrament. Make sure everyone does weekly confession. Adoration and confession are our only defense against the things is the red-fog. Make sure everyone does their spiritual duty. If they fail, Wolv's Skinwalkers can eat us. Never forget the battle of Collioure, France. Wolv's red-fog ate all the other soldiers."

Drayton said, "Lord Warrick, my brother. As always, the records are up to the hour."

Marian startled at Warrick's brisk, biting manner. Then she again felt her contradictory feelings for Warrick. The pungent bay-lead oil aroma on his cloak stung her nose. The pungent aroma stung her lungs. That strange feeling of safety, protection, and confidence engulfed her. The feeling of safety permeated her with the sting of the aroma.

She thought, "In Warrick's arms I feel safe and protected, yet I fear him." She looked up in Warrick's face *and thought, "He is two people. One man snaps orders that others and I dare not disobey. Other, the other man carries an aura of supreme confidence, safety, and holds me tenderly."*

Reque asked again, "May we hear Otan's story?"

Lord Morgan grasped Reque's arm and pulled him close.

He whispered to Reque, "About how Warrick obtained possession of Otan. Gained possession of the huge German lands and castle. Warrick does not like to brag or give the appearance of bragging. He wants his knights, us, to live as he does, to fight today's wars. To practice for tomorrow's wars. Not to brag about yesterdays wars."

She pulled herself up to Warrick's face and asked with a low voice. "You sound so cruel and callous."

Warrick snapped, "Tara, you test my patience. Never test your champion's patience."

Warrick said, "Morgan. Make sure the column is some distance behind me. I wish to converse in private with Ross the Rake."

Morgan slowed his horse and said, "Yes, we will follow from a distance."

In a minute, ahead of his warriors, Warrick said, "Ross. You look pleased as a preening peacock. You know more about women than me. I do not have your social graces. All of my social graces are battlefield graces. You could charm your way into any woman's shift."

Marian thought, "He wants to charm his way into any woman's shift, oh God. With how many mistresses will I have to share him? Our bedroom will look worse than the Philistine orgy scenes in the king's tapestries."

"I am only at ease on the battlefield," Warrick said. "All I know is the battlefield. All I want to know is the battlefield. You should be the betrothed. I am already wed to the battlefield. What do I do with Lord Moray's third daughter?"

"I suppose that you could lock her in her keep," Ross said. "If you can find a keep tall enough."

Both laughed.

She thought, "They would even think of locking me in a castle keep?" Their conversation shocked Marian too deeply. She decided to act against her nature, to be quiet and listen.

Ross said, "Seriously, first speculate on what you hope the lady is like."

Warrick said, "I pray that she will be meek. Hopefully I must pull her away from her prayer beads to bed her. The king demands lords have children as heirs."

Marian put her finger tips on his hairy chest. She said something she thought she would never say to a man.

Marian said, "What if she throws away her prayer beads and prefers your bed?"

-

-

-

CHAPTER, Where, Oxford, England, Northwest of London, England, Year @ 1250s A.D.

TARA, SOMEDAY YOU WILL BW TROUBLE TO SOME MAN.

Ross and Warrick laughed. "Sprite, Tara, are you the voice of experience," Warrick asked?

Marian pulled the cowl over her head and said, "Nay."

Warrick said, "I know what I want at home. At home I want peace of mind and a quiet life."

Ross said, "What will you do if she is not meek. Not quiet, not peaceful, not obedient."

Warrick said, "If she is not another traitor. I hope she will be meek, quiet, peaceful, and obedient."

Marian snapped, "All women are not alike. She may not want to obey. She may not be quiet. Not be meek. What will you do if she does not obey?"

Warrick smiled down at her and said, "Tara. Sprite. Some day you will be trouble to some man."

Marian said, "Rein in here. This is my home, my father's estate."

At Marian's manor, Warrick reined in. Zeus reared. He held Marian tight.

Morgan galloped up to them.

"Morgan, I want you to take the knights," Warrick said. "Ride straight for a quarter mile from the manor. Then you must have the knights form a circle around the manor. A circle with that quarter mile radius. Have them slowly circle inward to the manor and subdue anyone they find. Exorcize any Skinwalkers. Behead any Skinwalkers that attack you. If you can, give them the opportunity to ask Jesus for forgiveness. If they ask Jesus for forgiveness, they will turn back into Catholic priests. Or turn back into whatever they originally were. Most are just peasant farmers that Lilith captured and threatened to kill. Otherwise, behead them. Then burn their heads so they cannot come back to life."

Warrick escorted Marian to the front door of her manor, the Moray manor. He did not know her real name. Thunder boomed as lightening ripped the sky. The lightening hit trees in the Moray estate's endless apple orchard.

Warrick thought, "Tara's beauty is phenomenal, singular, celestial. In the lightening, her skin glows. Glows like no other, like water lilies in the bright summer sun."

In the lightening, Lord Warrick's emerald eyes pierced Marian's emotions. His emerald eyes held her silent, breathless.

She thought, "He has the type of shoulders in my dreams. His long, black, hair down his neck is dazzling. Yet, I must marry a curse."

-

-

-

CHAPTER, Where, Oxford, England, Northwest of London, England, Year @ 1250s A.D.

HE SAID, "YOU LIED TO ME." SHE SAID, "I WILL NOT TAKE THE MARRIAGE VOWS."

Lord Warrick did not know it, but Marian's beautiful countenance would haunt him. He would see her beautiful face in his work. In rest, in dreams, in nightmares, in victories, in defeats. Her beauty had enslaved him for now, for ever.

As Marian looked up at him, she thought, "No one has ever fought for me. This adulterer championed me so quickly. He is so courageous, so gallant. So gallant that I could not help but fall in love with him. What kind of man must I marry; What kind of man is Warrick? He is a wonderful champion, but will he only become a roguish husband. A slaver. A breeder of slaves."

Warrick put his hands on her shoulders and said, "Tara, you are safe. I will leave knights at your estate to protect you and your family." Then Warrick turned and pulled a map from Zeus' saddlebag.

"When my knights come back," he said, "we must be on our way. You heard that I must travel to the Moray estate today."

She said, "I am the Moray estate. I am the hairy, horse-faced, twelve-foot tall daughter of Lord Moray of Oxford. I am not meek and I obey no one."

Then he looked at Marian and said, "You lied to me. You said that your name was Tara."

She said, "And you revealed yourself as an adulterer and a slaver. After our marriage, how many mistresses will you have?"

Warrick turned and looked around for Wolv. "Now I know why the Skinwalkers wanted to kidnap you," he said. "They wanted to capture or kill me."

"So I am not worth kidnaping," Marian snapped, "only you are worth capturing?

"They know the king's plans," Warrick said, "We must move very quickly. More of them could be waiting to attack us."

"So my question is not worth a reply," Marian asked? "You insult me by not answering my questions. In less than an hour you come into my world. You take my estate from me. I, Marian, made this estate into the largest, wealthiest lordship in central England. I command this lordship with hundreds of artisans and vassals. Now you take my wealth and independence from me. I say to Perdition with you. Perdition with the king that sent you. You will become a drunk and bankrupt my estate."

Warrick turned around and searched the horizon. He rubbed his chin and thought, "Wolv is out there, perhaps a mile away. He is watching us."

"You jested in the last hour that you are an adulterer," Marian snapped. "You said that you bedded many married women at a time. How many mistresses will you demand to be in our bed?"

Warrick continued to turn his head and squint to see the enemy. Warrick thought, "If I were Wolv, I would charge down from that high knoll. Yes, I expect an attack from that knoll. I will use the Carthage technique do defeat them, if we can defeat them."

Marian crossed her arms and snapped, "You will not even answer me."

Warrick raised his right eyebrow and said, "Go pack. Obey me. We go to London, to marry in the king's chapel."

Again, Warrick raised his right eyebrow as he always does when he lies.

Lord Warrick lied, "We ride to London."

She said, "Obey! Obey! Can you think of nothing but obedience? You do not want a wife. You want a servant."

He said, "Obey."

Again, Warrick raised his right eyebrow as he always does when he lies. He lied, "We ride to London to wed in the king's chapel. To live in a London castle."

She thought, "He will not even answer me. I want a husband that will kiss me. Hold me tenderly and caress me. I want a husband that will love me. What every maiden wants, a love of the heart. I want my husband to cherish me, and me alone. My dreams have always been of a champion like Warrick to love me. Yet, Warrick wants mistresses. Also, with my Carmelite training, can I love a knight that owns slaves?"

She looked up at him and spoke bluntly. "When I was fifteen, I began management of this estate. I have dragged the most powerful London lords to court and sued. Sued them successfully. In court, I won every time those lords tried to claim my estate. The law was in my favor so the king's judges always decided in my favor. Judges have even punished my opponents by putting their estates into my name. I can drag you before the king's judges also. Never will I let you abuse my family. Never will I let you bankrupt my father's estate. I will not say the marriage vows."

-

-

-

CHAPTER, Where, Oxford, England, Northwest of London, England, Year @ 1250s A.D.

TRAITORS AMONG US. SPIES, LIES AND TRAITORS. BAD LUCK.

Distant Vespers bells announced the waning of the supper-hour. The waning of the fire-red sun.

Marian's anger got the better of her.

She snapped, "You ignore me now. You will ignore me in the future."

She extended her finger and poked him in the belly. As a game she learned with her sister, she addressed him in the third-person. In anger she poked his belly with her straight forefinger. "Is Marian's champion able to predict the future," she asked?

Warrick grasped her finger. As he continued the third-person game, he said, "Of course not. Marian's champion cannot predict the future."

Warrick grasped her finger. With her other hand Marian poked another finger into his stomach. She continued to play the third person game. "Do you think that Marian's champion will always love and cherish Marian," Marian asked?

"Do you think that Marian will obey Lord Warrick," Warrick snapped?

Warrick grasped both her hands. Since he held both her hands, Marian kicked him in the chin.

Lord Warrick laughed. Then as Marian continued the game, she again addressed Warrick in the third person. "Are you sure that Marian's champion will love Marian and only Marian?"

Knee-deep grey fog obscured the ground. Warrick played the third-person game. He said, "As always, Warrick will do his duty."

With a long finger Warrick continued the game. He smiled and gently poked Marian's shoulder. He said, "Will Marian always be obedient to Lord Warrick?"

At the manor door, Warrick could not know Wolv's location.

Far beyond Warrick's knights, Wolv sat on his warhorse.

Hidden on the far knoll, in the apple orchard, Wolv gritted his teeth. Gritted his teeth in hatred. In hatred of Warrick. Of Warrick touching Marian. Spittle dripped from Wolv's mouth.

He said, "I will torture Warrick for touching Marian. Marian is mine. Marian is Pamia."

They were within Wolv's vision. Outside the manor door, Marian cupped Warrick's stubble cheeks with her delicate hands. As she looked into his emerald eyes, she snapped. "Marian will NOT obey Lord Warrick. Or anyone."

Warrick threw his head back and laughed. So loud that it echoed off the hills. His guffaws sounded like a thunder clap to her.

In the long, apple orchard, with the black aura around him, Wolv heard their laughter. In jealously he growled between his gritted teeth, "Warrick dares to touch Marian, my Pamia."

Wolv growled and drew his sword. In irrational rage he swung his sword.

Suddenly Wolv's Holy Mary obsession overcame him. His multi pupil eyes glazed black, as his memory went back to Egypt. He remembered in Egypt when he was six-years-old. His memories froze him. As if he were dead. The children gathered around him and called him ugly-eye. At six-tears-old, one of his eyes had multiple-pupils from birth. Little Jesus led his Mother, Mary to Wolv. Mary picked up Wolv and took him to her small shelter. A shelter over the entrance of a cave. A clean cave Mary, Joseph and Jesus used in Egypt. Clean cave with a secret fresh water well behind it. A well that healed diseases because little Jesus blessed it. Mary placed Wolv on her lap and said, "Tiny Wolv I will always love you. Always remember. You are beautiful to God. Always remember. You are beautiful to me. Never hate."

The earth shook as Wolv repeatedly howled in his obsession. "Tiny Wolv I will always love you. You must always remember that you are beautiful to God. Wolv, always remember. To me you are beautiful."

Red-fog poured off Wolv. Hatred and rage caused Wolv to slobber great globs of red foam. The thick red foam ran down his chest and covered his chest to his feet. He spit great globs of red foam around himself.

His repeated howl was so powerful that it shook bricks off nearby manors.

Wolv's repetitious howl seemed endless. Slowly Wolv came out of his obsession. Slowly his eyes lost the black glaze.

In a rage, Wolv swung his sword in a wide circle. Then Wolv turned his head to see that he had beheaded a Skinwalker. Also, beheaded a warhorse.

IN THE MANOR

At the manor door, Warrick pulled his blessed sword and held Marian tight. He said, "Wolv's growl causes even the Manor to shake. His curse on the land is endless. Soon the Red-Fog will return. Only our Adoration wagon keeps the red-fog away."

Grey fog reached to their knees. At the manor door, Marian said, "Maybe. Maybe we really can be happy together."

Warrick said, "If you obey."

She said, "How many men are inside you? I know of two. One man inside you is my champion. The other man inside you is a slaver, an adulterer. Will both men inside you want me?"

Warrick thought, "I am not a slaver."

He should have told her that he was not a slaver. Yet, he never apologized or explained.

She again kicked his chin. "Listen to me. You must swear on your honor that both will want me. Both love me and love my family."

Warrick laughed and said, "It is my duty that both want you. I promise on the honor of my knighthood to fulfill my duty. Remember. You must obey me."

She said, "I fear that you are nothing but duty, orders, and obedience. You are only a warrior. All black leather, and as hard and cold as your battle ax. I fear that you may have no soft human emotions. With which one of you will I live? Will I discover a heart in you or just duty? Is your heart hardened and unemotional. Full of bitter duty, the result of too many wars and your traitorous wife?"

The mention of his traitorous wife caused Warrick to close his eyes. His jaws bulged as he ground his teeth. In anger at his first wife Warrick snapped, "Talk. Talk does nothing but slow us. We must pack and leave for London. Now it is time for you to obey. Go pack."

Marian raised her eyebrows and said, "Obey. Obey. My God, all you talk about is obedience."

Warrick snapped, "Now go to your chambers and pack, we must leave tonight."

He raised his right eyebrow and lied, "Marian. We go to wed in the king's chapel and live in a London castle."

Warrick raised his right eyebrow as he always did when he lied, he repeated, "Tonight. Tonight, we leave for London, where we are to wed in the king's own chapel. Go pack. We leave tonight."

Marian gazed at him and said, "You commanded me again. In the same harsh way you command your knights."

Angry with him, she crossed her arms and turned her back. Her black, leather cloak extended from her head to drag on the ground. When she turned to him, the cloak bellowed and sent eddies in the ground fog. Like slow ocean waves, the fog at their knees undulated. Then suddenly Marian opened her eyes wide. She smiled and her eyes sparkled.

She spun around to him and shouted, "You said London, London? The king allows only a few to use his own chapel?"

Again Warrick lied, "The king has given us a castle just outside London."

Marian clasped her hands and her eyes lit up like two blue stars. "London, we are to live in a castle near London? Life in London is wonderful."

As Warrick gazed into her eyes, he thought, "My lies. My lies about the king's chapel and London will deeply hurt Marian. Yet I must mislead any spies. Spies, lies, and traitors, the world is only spies, lies, and traitors."

His brow furrowed and his eyebrows formed a sharp V. He snapped, "Obey. Go. Now."

Marian thought, "He expects the same quick obedience from me. The same quick obedience that he expects from his knights. I hope that I eventually find that he has softness in him."

Marian said, "London is a wonderful place to live. From the castle, we would have access to all of London."

Warrick thought, "I hope. I dearly hope that everyone here believes that we are headed for London to wed. Instead we go to Wales."

Happy at the thought of living in a London castle, Marian turned. She walked quickly into the manor's great hall. From across the great hall, she saw her mother. Lady Brielle de Moray and Sister Catherine.

From the buttery, Nicola, Marian's little sister, shouted "Marian."

Marian's little sister dashed from the buttery with her arms out to hug Marian. A family friend, Father Bumpus, with a wrapped foot, hobbled behind Nicola. The four of them looked at her with simultaneous joy and terror. While Marian ran to them, they ran to her and hugged her. Tears ran down their cheeks.

Behind Marian the grey, ground fog oozed through the door. The roaring fireplace's draft pulled the fog across the floor.

Like an upside down whirlpool, the draft sucked the fog up the chimney.

Marian hugged and kissed them and said, "All is well. We have a protector, a great knight. He promised to be my champion and . . . my husband."

Her mother said, "What? In just over an hour you galloped away with kidnappers after you. We thought that you might be dead. Now you return wet as a drowned rat and say that you have a husband? A champion?"

Marian turned and pointed at Lord Warrick's back. Lord Warrick stood in the open doorway and barked orders.

From outside, Wolv growled, "Tiny Wolv, I will always love you."

Lady Brielle covered her ears and said, "What is that awful growl? It has shaken the manor most of the day."

Marian said, "Mother. I cannot explain now. Just cover your ears. The growl will fade away."

Slowly Wolv came out of his Holy Mary, Egypt, obsession. The growl faded away.

Lady Brielle said, "Marian. A champion?"

Marian pointed at Warrick's back and said, "Him, Lord Warrick. A man as hard as his steel ax. The king's champion. My betrothed and my champion."

As Warrick shouted orders, the grey ground fog rolled beside him. Through the manor's door. The chimney continued to suck the thick grey fog off the floor, up the chimney.

Warrick shouted, "Morgan. Drayton. Again. Make sure that everyone does their hour of Perpetual Adoration. In the Adoration wagon, Perpetual Adoration of Jesus' Real Presence in the Blessed Sacrament. Make sure everyone does weekly confession. Remember, only adoration and confession keep the red fog away. Otherwise, the demons in the red-for will eat us. They will eat those around us. Bring me the names of anyone that has skipped their Adoration or weekly confession. Contemplate the bones of the army of Tallinn, Estonia after the red-fog ate them. Morgan. Drayton. You saw the red-fog eat them. You heard their helpless screams."

Morgan said, "Yes my Lord Warrick. Brother, as you command."

Warrick shouted, "Drayton. Morgan. Have a knight guide the Adoration wagon in front of the manor. Or else Wolv's red-fog will eat us."

A knight was doing Adoration of the Blessed Sacrament within the Adoration wagon. Another knight prodded its horses to pull the Adoration wagon to the manor's door.

IN THE MANOR

Lady Brielle said, "Lord Warrick is only a legend, a myth. Everyone says that he is dead, just myth."

Marian said, "Then you are looking at the back of a tall, strong, handsome myth. A myth that orders many knights. He is fearsome, frightening. I think that his emerald eyes can burn through his enemies. Lord Warrick promised to be my champion."

Lady Brielle said, "Marian. It is bad luck to have a champion."

"Funny," Marian said. "That is what he called me, Lady Bad Luck."

"You just do not go out and in one hour betroth yourself," her mother said.

Marian said, "By order of the King we go to London tonight. We are to prepare to marry in the king's very own chapel. With my champion, Lord Warrick.

In the buttery, tall, bony Hiry thought, "London. They leave for London tonight? I must tell Wolv."

Again Hiry, the traitor, descended the steps into the wine cellar. She ran through the length of the wine cellar. Then she exited out the cellar's vineyard entrance. Out into the black night and grey, ground fog. To avoid the knights, Hiry crawled through the vineyard in the thick grey ground fog.

ANOTHER TRAITOR.

From another room, the royal court's busiest tart, Lady Blanche, ran into the great room. Then she shouted, "Lord Warrick. Someone said Lord Warrick is here. Where is Lord Warrick?"

No one knew that Lady Blanche was Wolv's genius spy.

Unbeknownst to Marian and Warrick, Blanche constantly, secretly, bounced royal court beds until they broke. She bounced men until they broke.

She fed Wolv information until Wolv conquered many Welsh castles.

In bed with court members, she learned secrets. Secrets that she sold to Wolv. Blanche sold England's secrets to all of England's enemies.

With both hands she held up her gown's skirt and dashed across the room.

"Warrick," Blanche yelled.

In the doorway Warrick turned to Blanch. She jumped. He caught her.

In Warrick's arms, Blanche hugged his neck. With her feet off the floor, he had no choice but to catch her. Fake tears ran down her face as she hugged him.

Blanche said, "Everyone said that you were dead. The archbishop even said a funeral mass for you."

Blanche hugged Warrick tight about the neck. Warrick swung her in a circle. Her skirt swished the grey fog in wide eddies.

Warrick hugged her and said, "Blanch. You have always been a trustworthy and faithful friend. The most beloved of the king's court."

Blanche thought, "Before the sunrise's Prime bells, I will have Warrick. Yes, before the night is over. I will seduce Warrick and have access to his wealth. My charms can separate any man from his gold. The king has given Warrick one of Wolv's Wales castles to conquer. I will help Wolv, then Wolv will give me that castle."

Lady Brielle said, "Marian, you can trust Blanche. She is more virtuous than a nun."

Marian said, "Mother. Why has the king blessed me with his court's most helpful lady, Lady Blanche?"

Lady Brielle said, "She just arrived with her wagons in the last half hour. Blanche has a papyrus with her. The papyrus says that Blanche is to go with you wherever you go. She is to be your aid and confidant."

Then Lady Brielle opened a drawer and pulled out another papyrus. She said, "We received this confirmation a month ago. Lady Ada, another court lady in waiting, delivered it. I forgot to tell you."

Lady Brielle handed her daughter the papyrus.

"Mother, the queen herself orders Blanche bound to my service," Marian said.

"Marian, daughter," Brielle said. "Marian, in less than an hour you are betrothed to the king's champion."

Lady Marian laced her fingers with her mother's fingers. "Happily, we go to London tonight to prepare to marry. We will marry in the king's very own chapel."

Marian said. "Mother. I am lucky to have Blanche to help me."

Lady Marian gazed at Warrick's back. He stood in the strange grey fog to his knees. In his deep voice, he shouted orders. Orders to his knights on how to pack large wagons.

Lady Brielle said, "How could this happen so quickly?"

Sister Catherine said, "I can feel it. I can always feel it. Marian, Lord Warrick is your destiny. You are Lord Warrick's destiny."

In the doorway, Blanche smiled. She again hugged Warrick.

Blanche said, "My lord, I am so happy that you are alive."

Warrick said, "Morgan. Drayton. Ross. Satan worshipers are everywhere. We must hurry. Satan worshipers are near and listen to everything we say."

Blanche thought, "For years I have deceived everyone. Everyone thinks that I am virtuous. Whatever evil I must do, I will do to gain Warrick's wealth. I will help Wolv defeat Warrick, then Wolv will give me Warrick's castle."

-

-

-

CHAPTER, Where, Oxford, England, Northwest of London, England, Year @ 1250s A.D.

A BETRAYED-ANGRY-BRIDE-TO-BE. HER WEDDING ON A BATTLE FIELD.

Thunder of a rainless storm rolled across the sky. Then lightening bolts turned the grey ground fog fluorescent. Lightening bolts made the ground-fog glow yellow for a few seconds.

Blanche thought, "I must cause so much trouble for Marian that Marian leaves Warrick."

Hiry was across the road. On hands and knees, hidden in the ground fog.

Hiry said, "Lord Wolv, Hiry, I am Hiry. You must set ambushes between here and London. Warrick and Marian leave for London tonight."

The AntiChrist, Wolv, said, "Hiry, stand, let me see you."

Tall, skeletal Hiry stood. "If you are wrong, Hiry," Wolv growled. "You will suffer. How can you be sure?"

Then Hiry said, "Please my lord. I am never absolutely positive about anything. I heard Marian say exactly those words. Marian said that they go to London tonight by the king's order."

"My lord," Gulum said. "We should take the precaution and put ambushes between here and London."

"Lord Wolv," Hiry said. "Now, I must return to the manor before Lady Brielle misses me."

As Hiry crawled on her hands and knees in the thick fog, Wolv said, "Gulum. We have much more time than we need to prepare for Warrick's siege. Warrick's siege of Rose Fire. After five weeks we will begin to stock Rose Fire Castle with provisions."

AT THE MANOR

At the manor, Reque led a mounted, ugly, but wealthy merchant. He led the hunchback merchant up to Blanche and Warrick. A robber's sword had split his face and it had healed wrongly. The grotesque merchant dismounted. The most expensive finery hung from the merchant's shoulders. Gold and silver thread and white deer fur.

He bowed and said, "Lady Blanche. I heard in the king's court that you would be here today. I had to come."

Blanche smiled and took the wealthy merchant's arm. She lifted her scarlet gown with her other hand. Quickly, she walked far away from Warrick into the orchard. Blanche did not want Warrick to hear her lies. Her lies that she was to tell the merchant. The merchant, Fragate Schaaner, walked with Blanche, Wolv's Spy. He led his horse. Out in the orchard, away from Warrick, the merchant held a bejeweled box. He then opened the jeweled, gold and silver inlaid wooden box. The waning red-pink sunset sparkled on diamonds and rubies.

He said, "Lady Blanche, I bring these jewels as a gift for you. I want you to spend many days with me. Then I can prove to you that I can be a wonderful husband for you. I would be in Heaven if I could wake each morning to your seductive face."

Blanche's greed made her smile. She reached out and took the box of precious stones. As she always as she lied, she traced a circle. Traced a circle with the tip of her shoe. She smiled. She lied, "I know where you live. Go home. I will go to your manor tonight."

Blanche thought, "Fragate Schaaner is an ocean merchant. If I married him, I would always be on ocean ships. I hate voyages because I am always seasick."

The merchant mounted his horse. He turned to Blanche and said, "My lady. You are the most seductive woman on earth."

For a brief moment, Blanche's greed was now satisfied. She held the box of jewels and gold.

She said, "Go now." Blanche slapped the horse's rump. With Blanche's slap on the horse's rump, Fragate's horse reared. His horse bolted away through the orchard. The horse's legs swirled the ground fog in wide eddies. The merchant almost fell.

Blanche carried the box back to Warrick. She placed it on the door stoop beside Warrick.

Blanche hugged Warrick.

Warrick put his hands on Blanche's shoulders and pushed her away. He commanded, "Blanche, go pack, now."

Blanche's eyes grew wide in surprise that Warrick had rejected her attentions. She backed up from Warrick.

She bowed her head and said, "Yes. My Lord."

Blanche thought, "For Warrick's rejection of me, I will watch Wolv kill Warrick."

Then she picked up the box of the merchant's jewels. With her other hand she lifted the skirt of her gown. To hide her angry frown from Warrick, she lowered her head.

Blanche thought, "I will drive Marian from Warrick. Warrick is the king's wealthiest lord. I will not quit until I have Warrick's wealth. If I help Wolv defeat Warrick, Wolv will give me Warrick's castle."

Warrick turned his head and saw more of his knights. From patrol around the manor, they rode up in a great clomping of spiked hooves. Warhorses' blessed armor clanked and clunked. Knights shouted. Horses grunted and whinnied. Leather squealed against leather. Warhorses reared. Knights' blessed armor clanked as they walked.

Warrick shouted, "Everyone. Dressed in your blessed armor. Carry your blessed weapons."

Lord Drayton walked up to Warrick at the open door. He carried his blessed bow in one hand. His other hand on the hilt of his blessed sword.

Drayton smiled and said, "Brother, the area is safe. Safe for a quarter mile radius from the manor. We can hear Wolv's roar, but he is keeping away."

Again Warrick shouted, "Everyone. Dress in your blessed armor. Carry your blessed weapons. Put blessed armor on all the horses."

THE ANTICHRIST FAR AWAY ON A KNOLL

Far away, on a knoll, Lord Wolv, the AntiChrist, turned up a goatskin of wine. His drunken bloodshot eyes glowered as he bared his teeth in a growl. He tightened his fist.

Red-Fog flowed off Wolv. Wolv shouted, "Swale, where is my Skinwalker army? I must have my army to capture Marian. I must have my army to kill Warrick, so I can capture Marian."

IN THE MANOR

At the manor, Warrick ordered, "Pack everything that Lady Brielle de Moray shows you." Then Warrick lied, "We leave immediately to marry in the king's chapel in London."

Warrick's knights obeyed instantly.

Then Warrick shouted again, "Everyone dress in your blessed armor. Dress your horses in blessed armor. Carry your blessed weapons."

Warrick thought, "I hope. Hope the deception about the wedding in London will mislead Wolv. Mislead Wolv about the route and when we will arrive at our destination, Rose Fire. Rose Fire, never have I seen so many spires. So many rose-colored keeps. Rose Fire, a towering pink granite castle on a mountainside. Builth Castle, Rose Fire, has the highest spires in the British Isles. The castle's glazed red, roof-tiles reflect the sun like rose-red fire. I will drive Wolv from Rose Fire and, as my duty demands. I will give Rose Fire to Marian. As to spies, I know that Wolv's spies are here in Marian's manor."

The grey fog swirled around his feet up to his knees. Lord Warrick walked into the manor. With his arms out he pointed and snapped orders to his knights. He walked as if he owned it. He did own it, with the king's order of marriage.

A rotund priest, put his crutches under his arms. The priest hobbled up to Warrick.

He said, "I am Father Bumpus, a long time friend of Lord Moray. Sister Catherine told me what happened. I deeply appreciate your protection of Marian and her family."

Lord Morgan lead Warrick's other knights up to the door. Ross entered with them in. Without a word, they packed and carried trunks of items. They carried and stacked the trunks on a long line of wood-covered wagons.

Warrick turned to Marian and snapped. "Marian. I told you to go to your chambers and pack. Go. Quickly. Go now. You must obey."

She pointed her finger at him. Her eyebrows formed an angry V. Then she raised her eyebrows in confusion and resignation.

She thought, "I almost told Warrick to get out of my manor. The manor now belongs to Warrick."

Marian did not understand why he demanded instant obedience. She did not yet comprehend that Satan was everywhere.

Then Marian said, "Why are you so demanding? Your words are insulting, insensitive, and oafish."

Warrick thought, "I have not been around a woman, . . . of honor . . . for years. I did not intend to insult her or bully her. I need to learn how to treat a wife."

Marian snapped, "Now you will not talk to me. You insult me with your silence."

Warrick thought, "Marian thinks that we are moving to London. She expects peaceful London with beautiful safe gardens. Gardens and streets where we can safely stroll. We are in truth headed for a battlefield. A beautiful castle that we must surround with a battlefield."

-
-
-

CHAPTER, Where, Oxford, England, Northwest of London, England, Year @ 1250s A.D.

THE RED-FOG HIDES SKINWALKERS

Warrick snapped, "Marian, you must do as I order, now."

Warrick turned to his knights. The strange grey fog continued to pour onto the great hall's floor. When he turned, his cape and legs twirled the grey fog. The rare dry storm continued. In the night blackness, lightening exploded trees. Many put their hands over their ears to protect them from the loud thunder.

With both hands, Marian pulled up the skirt of her gown. Then she turned her head to Warrick and said, "Ummmph."

She grasped a trencher candle-holder with a lit candle. She put her nose in the air. Lake water dripped from her gown. She strode up the spiral stairs to her chambers. At the top of the stairs she stopped and turned to look down.

"Ummmph," she shouted. "Warrick. No one has told me to go to my room since I was a toddler. You act like you own my manor."

"I do," Warrick said.

Warrick looked up at her he said, "I do own your manor. By royal order, as your betrothed, I do now own your manor. Also, by the same order, I own you. Now, as my ward, do as I say. I order you to pack your room. Now."

Atop the stairs Marian said, "Warrick, you are a beast."

Then she turned and ran through her chamber door. She placed the trencher-candle holder onto a table.

THE TRUE BEAST

Wolv sat on his horse a full mile from the manor. Suddenly his eyes again glazed over as his obsessive memories conquered him.

Again Wolv memories went back to Egypt when he was six-years-old. In his memories his eyes remained glazed over black.

As a six-year-old, he sat crying on Holy Mary's lap. Little Wolv could see the blue glow that surrounded Holy Mary.

Holy Mary said, "Little Wolv. I will always love you. Do not hate anyone. Little Wolv, I will always love you."

Wolv could not stop his repetitious roar. 'Little Wolv. I will always love you. Do not hate anyone; always will I love you.'

His obsessive-compulsive roar shook the earth like an earth quake. Haystacks fell sideways.

Upstairs in the manor Collette, Marian's handmaiden, grasped Marian in a tight hug. Collette shook in terror. Terror made Collette's eyes round, and white. Collette said. "What is this horror? That roar will collapse the manor on us."

Marian hugged Collette and said, "Fear not. We have the king's greatest champion protecting us."

As Marian hugged Collette, "See. The roar is only temporary. I saw Lord Warrick defeat four hell-demons, Skinwalkers, with only a small thorn tree."

Marian's handmaiden Collette said, "Marian. You still have some civilized pleasures. I have prepared a bath for you."

While Marian stood, Collette pulled the wet, heavy clothes from Marian. Then Marian sat in her huge half barrel warm bath.

She sighed, "The king has tossed away our lives as we know them. Mother, father, Nicola, you, all the other servants. We are all now a warlord's chattel. We are now the chattels of a warlord that loves war, and loves nothing else."

Collette lit sandalwood incense. The incense's aroma filled the room. Collette then tossed a handful of dried rose buds upon Marian's bed.

Marian sat in a half-barrel tub and bathed. Collette poured warm water over Marian's hair. She washed Marian's hair with lavender oil scented soap. After she toweled Marian's hair, Collette put drops of lavender oil in her palms. She rubbed the oil on Marian's hair. Marian bathed as Collette brushed Marian's waist long hair. Other servants packed Marian's chambers. Marian quickly dressed.

Warrick ran up the stairs to Marian's bed chamber.

Warrick ordered. "Hurry. Pack."

Marian pushed on his chest and shouted, "Warrick. You order your hairy and horse-faced bride to hurry."

She pushed him again, "You order your twelve-feet-tall bride to hurry."

Again she pushed him and said, "You order your bride with twelve toes to hurry."

Again she pushed him, "You order your bride with sixteen fingers to hurry."

"You order, order, order" she pushed him again.

He crashed backward through her bedroom window and fell from the third story.

Marian screamed "I have killed my bridegroom."

She heard Warrick shout, "Not yet. Lady Hairy, horse-faced. A twelve-feet-tall, twelve-toed, sixteen-fingered bride. Not dead yet."

She looked out the broken window to see Warrick had landed on a bush.

He looked up and said, "Not dead yet. Lady Angry. Lady Bad Luck. Though that, was an adequate try. Worthy of the slyest traitors. Worthy of demon Lilith herself."

Warrick's brothers ran around the manor.

Warrick said, "Brothers. Marian is innocent, impetuous and impulsive. She does not see the dangers around her. She innocently pushed me through the glass of the third story window."

Then Warrick said, "Shades of Ogina. I hope Marian innocently pushed me."

Drayton, Morgan and Ross all said in unison, "Lady Bad Luck."

They said together, "Knock on the wood of the Crucifix." Then they knuckled Warrick's head as if it consisted of wood.

Warrick said, "I will need a wooden head to survive Marian."

Marian ran out.

Warrick held out his hand and said, "I suppose. Suppose now you want to push me down that well. Go back to you chambers and pack. Try not to kill anyone."

Dejected, with her head down, Marian returned to her bed chambers. She finished packing and dressing.

Fully dressed Marian walked down the stairs inside the manor.

At the sight of Marian, Warrick's mouth fell open and his eyes grew round. Lady Marian wore an open, royal-red fox cloak that hung to the floor. Her blond hair cascaded down her shoulders and back. Under the open, royal red fox cloak, she wore a matching royal-red satin gown. Glowing fog surrounded her legs up to her knees. The fireplace flashed bright red off her gown and cloak. Her red gown highlighted the fireplace's flickering reflection on her blue eyes. Fireplace reflections also highlighted her cameo skin from her face to her neck. Around her hips she wore a gold chain. On the end of the gold chain, between her thighs, a dagger hung. Rubies encrusted the dagger's handle and sheath. Between her upper thighs, the dazzling ruby reflections captured everyone's eyes. Her gown flowed on the curves of her breasts, her narrow waist. Her gown clung to her thighs as she walked. From both sides her long blond hair circled her breasts. As she walked across the room, all eyes were on her. Everyone's eyes went from her cameo face then to the bejeweled dagger.

Warrick thought, "Marian's beauty is . . . is . . . beyond words. She is delicious."

Then Warrick whispered to Drayton, "Would you please tell me what to do now?"

Drayton said, "You must have forgotten everything you knew about women. Walk over to her, kiss her hand. Then put her arm across your forearm."

Warrick whispered, "Drayton. Somehow, without her pushing me out a window?"

Warrick kissed her hand and placed her hand on his forearm. Everyone's jaws hung open in astonishment at Marian's beauty.

With Marian's hand on his arm, Warrick gathered his senses.

"Father Bumpus, you leave tonight with us for your new assignment," Warrick said.

Marian stepped over to Father Bumpus and hugged him. "Wonderful, you will be with us," she said.

The priest straightened and asked, "To where?"

Warrick said, "To wherever I say."

Bumpus asked again, "To where?"

As Warrick unconsciously raised his right eyebrow, he lied, "London."

Warrick interrupted and said, "Drayton. Morgan. Unceasingly assure me that everyone does their hour of Perpetual Adoration. In the Adoration wagon, Perpetual Adoration of Jesus' Real Presence in the Blessed Sacrament. Unceasingly assure me that everyone does their weekly confession. You both have seen Wolv's red-fog eat armies. Armies that did not do adoration and weekly confession. Bring me the names of anyone that has not done adoration or weekly confession. Our only defense is Adoration and confession to keep Wolv's red fog away. Away from us and those that we protect. Stay focused. Always remember the cries of Carcassonne, France as the red-fog ate the soldiers and citizens. We are in great danger. Keep that vision in your mind. Remember their screams of horror."

Then Bumpus protested, "The archbishop assigned me to this comfortable Oxford parish. By what authority do you reassign me?"

"By the privileges and rights of the king's champion. The archbishop has assigned you to me," Warrick snapped.

Bumpus's mouth fell open. Surprise rounded his eyes into great white orbs. On his crutches, he hobbled back away from Warrick.

"Yes, you have the privileges and rights of the king's champion," Bumpus said. "From this time forward I will go with you. From where do we go after London?"

As with the deception about London, Warrick's right eyebrow raised. He lied, "We will stay in London. Marian and I will wed in London and live in a castle outside London. You with us."

Marian said, "Yet, I overheard Ross. He said we will go to a castle in Wales. A castle now held by Skinwalkers."

Then Warrick put his fists on his hips and raised his right eyebrow and lied. He said, "Ross mentioned that you were hairy and horse-faced. Twelve-feet-tall, with twelve toes, and sixteen fingers. Can you believe Ross, the Rake?"

While Marian stood in the great room, with fog to her shins. She smiled, clasped her hands and said, "Joy. Off to London we go. With a bridegroom that hates marriage."

Warrick thought, "The deception about London and the location of our wedding will hurt Marian. She may not trust me again. Her distrust of me could cause her death." Again Warrick unknowingly raised his right eyebrow. He lied, "Yes, the king has given us a wonderful castle outside London. We will wed in the king's own chapel."

With both arms, Marian hugged Father Bumpus' arm. Marian said, "Father, you are to live in a castle with us, near London. Wonderful, we will wed in the king's own chapel."

Marian held Father Bumpus' arm and said, "With you, Father Bumpus. London will not be so strange. So strange for my little sister Nicola. You are a piece of Oxford coming with us."

Bumpus sighed and said, "Bad luck for me. This means you will always be with me. You will stop me from eating pork and drinking wine."

Marian shook her finger at Bumpus' face and said, "No, no. No wine and pork. You already have sores on your foot from the gout. Wine and pork bring the gout."

Father Bumpus said, "Wine and pork bring happiness."

Warrick and Ross laughed. Then Warrick raised his right eyebrow. He lied, "Father. In London you can have all the wine and pork that you can eat."

Father Bumpus then said, "Yes my lord. Then it is good that I go with you."

Marian said, "No, Warrick, no wine and no pork. Look at the gout wrapping on his foot. Everyone knows that too much wine and pork cause the gout."

Bumpus held his head low then Bumpus glanced at Warrick and winked. Then he raised his eyebrows and waited for Lord Warrick's reply.

As Warrick unconsciously raised his right eyebrow, Warrick winked back.

Then, suddenly, a strange chill filled the room. A cold wind circled the room and swirled the fog on the floor. Whirlwinds blew out the fire in the fireplace. The whirlwind blew out all the candles.

Marian ran over to Warrick. She hugged his arm and said, "What evil is this?"

Warrick said, "Wolv is near. Wolv is about to call upon Satan. His presence can block out the sun. His presence can extinguish all light. Lilith travels in the darkness."

He motioned to the servants and said, "Quickly. Restart the fireplace. Relight the candles. In moments Lilith will engulf us. In moments Wolv's evil will engulf us. Hurry with the lights. Wolv's obsessions can extinguish all light."

On a knoll, far from the manor, Wolv sat on his warhorse. His eyes glazed black as his memory went back to Egypt. When Wolv was six-years-old, Egyptian children danced around him. They called him ugly-eye because he was born with a multiple pupil eye.

With his eyes-glazed-black, still as a corpse, Wolv sat on his horse. In reality, outside Oxford, England. In tormented memory, in Egypt, as a six-year-old, sitting on Holy Mary's lap.

Holy Mary said, "Little Wolv. I will always love you."

Wolv repeatedly growled, "Little Wolv, I will always love you."

Wolv's eyes remained glazed over black as his memories captured him.

Then Wolv's eyes lost their black glaze. He continued repeatedly to growl, "Little Wolv, I will always love you."

To stop his obsessive repetition, Wolv growled, "Holy Mary, get out of my head." Then Wolv stabbed himself in the leg with a dagger. He pulled the dagger out and shouted, "Jesus. I will kill all your followers."

Wolv, the AntiChrist, growled, "Warrick, Warrick. I know that you can hear me. Warrick. I renew my curse on the Symon of Cyrene Pendragon line. Warrick, again. Now I renew my curse on your Pendragon line."

Again, Wolv's eyes again glazed over black as he called upon Satan. The AntiChrist repeatedly shouted, "Satan. Satan. Hear me. Put Legions of demons within me. I renew my curse on Symon of Cyrene's progeny. I renew the curse that 'Only-burning-love-can-defeat-burning-hatred.' The progeny of Symon must endure burning fire to keep their loves. I renew the curse that their brides must give their lives for their loves."

Wolv's repeated growl, repeated call upon Satan, was like an earthquake.

All could hear and feel Wolv's repeated growl for miles in all directions. The repeated growl shook bricks from chimneys and collapsed barns.

The growls grew louder and spread darkness into Marian's manor. Then Wolv's darkness caused the relit fireplace and relit candles to fade. To fade as of they were embers.

Warrick shouted, "Servants. Everyone. Run. Light more candles. Light torches. Wolv's blackness can hide Skinwalkers. Lilith can hide in the blackness. Hurry. In moments Wolv's darkness will engulf us. In moments Wolv's evil Skinwalkers will engulf us. Hurry. Throw coal oil on the fire place."

They built the fire to a roar. Yet the encroaching blackness made the fire as if an ember. All was black except the ember-like-glow of candles and the fireplace.

The earthquake of Wolv's obsessive compulsive repetition of his curse faded. As the roar faded the blackness faded. As the roar faded, the candles and fireplace burned brightly.

Then far off on a knoll, Wolv roared, "Holy Mary. Get out of my head. Get out of my head."

Warrick said, "Marian. You have just lived through the easiest part. The easiest part of Wolv Curse on Symon's progeny. Wolv's curse spreads darkness. In that darkness Wolv's Skinwalkers can travel unseen. The thick red-fog also hides Skinwalkers from us."

-

-

-

CHAPTER, Where, Oxford, England, Northwest of London, England, Year @ 1250s A.D.

DAUGHTER, BE CAREFUL FOR WHAT YOU PRAY. YOU PRAYED FOR A CHAMPION. NOW YOU HAVE PRAYED US INTO A CURSE.

Late midnight Vigils' bells mixed with early Matins bells. Vigils' bells, midnight, the beginning of the three Witches hours. The Three Witches hours when Lilith, the supreme witch, is strongest.

Early Matins' bells, before three hours after midnight. Matins church bells called monks, nuns and priests to prayers. Early Matins bells, confusing, normally three hours after midnight, Matin's prayers.

Lady Brielle whispered to Marian. "Marian. Your pride and your compassion will destroy Lord Warrick. You must control your pride and compassion. Your pride will deprive him of your love. Marian. Your compassion will pull him out of battle. You both must understand that some loves must be. Some battles must be. No matter what, some loves must be. No matter what, some battles must be."

Lord Morgan walked over to Warrick.

Morgan said, "Warrick. Remember the Pendragon curse. Your first wife was not meant for you. You must remember the words of the curse. 'Only burning love can defeat burning hatred' if you are to protect Marian. Marian must remember that she must give her life for you. Just like Able Pendragon's wife blocked Cain Pendragon's arrow with her own chest."

Marian overheard Morgan. She snapped, "I must give my life for Warrick, what nonsense is this?"

Morgan said, "Remember, Warrick. Remember Wolv's curse on the Able-Symon-of-Cyrene Pendragon line. 'Only burning love can defeat burning hatred.' You must endure fire for Marian. Also, she must give her life for you."

Drayton had his bow on his back, the bowstring across his chest. Drayton said, "Marian. You just had your first experience with the curse on our family. Wolv placed a curse on his stepbrother's progeny. Us, the progeny of the Cyrene Pendragons. Pendragons go back a thousand years before Christ. Our line of Pendragons originally separated over the love of a woman, in Cairo Egypt. In Cairo, Egypt over a thousand years before Christ. Cain and Able Pendragon, brothers, both loved the same woman. She chose Able. Able Pendragon wed her. Able had a daughter by her. Then Able had a family celebration for his daughter's birth."

Morgan continued the narration, "Cain went to the celebration of Able's daughter. Cain's goal was to kill Able then kidnap the wife of Able. He hid behind trees and bushes. At the celebration, Cain Pendragon tried to kill Able. Jealously overcame Cain. Cain shot an arrow at Able. Able's betrothed jumped in front of the arrow. The arrow pierced her chest. Able's betrothed died in Able's arms."

Ross sais, "Yes. Marian. Cain Pendragon had wanted to kill Able Pendragon so he could have Able's wife. Cain became enraged that he had killed his own love. Enraged, Cain shouted a murder-curse on all Able's progeny. A murder-curse that Cain Pendragon's would always seek out and murder Able Pendragons. Then, Cain called upon Lilith so he could breed with Lilith. To breed a line of Skinwalkers to murder Able's line. A murder-curse that Cain's progeny of Skinwalkers would wage an eternal war against Able's progeny. Wherever Lilith flies, Lilith kills children in the womb. Lilith spreads the curse of stillborn birth. Lilith, like Satan and Wolv, they hate innocence; they hate innocent lives in the womb. Always Lilith returns, digs the stillborn from their graves, and eats them."

Warrick continued, "Marian. Cain's progeny of Lilith's Skinwalkers has always warred against Abel's progeny. To escape Cain, Able took his daughter to Cyrene, Egypt. Yet Cain-Pendragon's progeny continued to kill Abel's progeny. They were half a country apart. Cain cursed his own progeny eternally to hate Able's progeny. His brother's progeny."

Ross said, "Marian. Cain called upon the demon Lilith and slept with her. Thus, from Lilith, Cain bred an army of demons. Cain bred Skinwalkers. Wolv has Lilith's blood. Lilith's demons possess every Cain-Pendragon-progeny. This is why we must behead every Skinwalker and burn their heads. We can also exorcize them if they accept exorcism. If they do not accept exorcism, we must behead them. Or else they can find their heads and heal."

Drayton said, "Marian. Beware. Also, Lilith is a shape shifter. She follows us. Lilith can be with us in any form. She is loyal to her Skinwalkers. Lilith will leave us alone only when we defeat Wolv. The Skinwalkers are the Lilith-Cain progeny. They can possess anybody, especially fallen, unrepentant Catholic priests. If a Skinwalker-Catholic priest asks Jesus for mercy, he turns back into the Catholic priest."

Morgan said, "Marian. This is why we try to give Skinwalkers the chance to ask Jesus for mercy. Asking Jesus for mercy, exorcizes them."

Marian asked, "How do you know all this?"

Morgan said, "Marian. A thousand years before Jesus, Able Pendragon began our writing-culture. Able-Pendragons write everything in multiple copies of papyrus and sheepskin. Why write all this down? Able-Pendragons must know our enemy. We have piles of documents, papyrus and sheepskin, in secret libraries. Able-Pendragon was the first to start the multiple libraries. He wrote everything. Then battle-crippled Able-Pendragon's became scribes. Also, Symon of Cyrene wrote everything down. The Pendragons have kept war-plan libraries by necessity. From the time of Cain's Lilith-murder-curse."

Ross said, "A thousand years after this Cain-Able Brother curse began, then. Then Wolv put a new curse on the Able-Cyrene-Pendragons. Because Symon of Cyrene, Wolv's half-brother, did two things. First, Symon helped Jesus carry Jesus' Cross. Symon of Cyrene Pendragon was a descendant of Able-Pendragon-of-Cyrene."

Morgan sais, "On Golgotha, Symon of Cyrene helped take Jesus' body down from the Cross. Symon placed Jesus' body on Holy Mary's lap. Holy Mary wept over her dead son's body, on Golgotha.

Ross said, "On Golgotha, Wolv pulled his sword to dismember Jesus. Wolv thought that if he dismembered Jesus that Jesus could not resurrect."

Drayton said, "The second reason for the curse, Symon knew Wolv's evil intentions. Then Symon pushed Wolv off the Golgotha mount. The two of them rolled together down the mount. Quickly, Symon took Wolv's sword from Wolv."

Ross continued to narrate, "Wolv said, 'Symon. Jesus claimed to raise from the dead in three days. He can never rise from the dead if, not. Not if I chop his body into pieces."

Morgan narrated, "Symon said, 'Foolish Wolv. If Jesus does rise from the dead, then. Then you will have another chance to beg Jesus. To beg Jesus to raise Pamia from the dead.' Symon then tossed Wolv's sword far down off the Golgotha mount."

Drayton continued the history of the Crucifixion-Cyrene Pendragon Curse. "Many yards away on the steepest side of Golgotha, Wolv stood. Wolv shouted, 'Satan. Satan. Hear me. Take my soul if you must. Put a Legion of Demons in me. I place a curse on Symon's progeny. I place the curse that Only-burning-love-can-defeat-burning-hatred. The Symon's progeny must endure burning fire to keep their loves. I place the curse that their brides must give their lives for their loves.'"

Marian said, "Drayton, a kidnaping and a curse in the same day."

Marian turned to Warrick. She asked, "Warrick. You and your kin are serious about the love curse?"

Warrick only looked at her and nodded.

Lady Brielle walked across the hall and said, "We must pack much More." Then she stopped and turned so quickly that her gown's skirt twisted about her.

As her gown twisted back and forth, it flipped the fog on the floor. "Lord Warrick," Brielle snapped. "Did I hear you correctly? I hope that you do not have a cursed family?"

Warrick said, " I will leave some priest-knights here in the manor with you. They will set up Perpetual Adoration of the Blessed Sacrament. Adoration of Jesus's Real Presence in the Blessed Sacrament. Perpetual Adoration and Weekly Confession will protect you from Wolv's red-fog. Wolv knows that Adoration of the Blessed Sacrament defeats him and Lilith. Adoration of the Blessed Sacrament weakens Skinwalkers."

Lady Brielle said, "Lord Warrick. You mentioned a curse?"

Lord Warrick said, "Yes, Wolv is the curse. Cain Pendragon, Wolv's Cairo ancestors, put a murder-curse on our family tree. Over two thousand years ago. A murder-curse. Also, Wolv put a further curse on the Symon family tree. At the time of Jesus' Crucifixion, over a thousand years ago. Wolv's curse is a marriage curse, a much more complicated curse."

Lady Brielle spun and pointed her arm and forefinger at Marian. "My daughter." Brielle snapped. "I told you to be careful for what you pray. I told you not to pray for a champion. You prayed this family right into a curse."

Lady Brielle paused for a moment and said, "Warrick. Somehow I feel that I lost a few moments. Nicola, Sister Catherine, Father Bumpus and I were in the great room. Then on our feet, we awakened in the buttery."

Warrick said, "Do not ask me to explain. The lost time was part of the curse. Lost time is one effect of Lilith. Wherever Lilith goes, her presence kills lives in the womb. I fear that Lilith is among us. Lilith hates innocence. Especially, Lilith hates the innocence of lives in the womb."

A female servant, Atant, fell to the floor and screamed in birth pangs. She gave birth on the floor. Another servant wrapped the child in a towel and screamed, "The child is dead. Cold. Lifeless."

Warrick said, "Atant. You are in terrible grief. You must cremate your still born child. Lilith always returns, digs up the graves of the children she kills, and eats them. This is evil's way. In this way, Lilith spreads hatred, evil, and despair."

Warrick, being a priest, gave the still born child last rites. In tears, Atant wrapped her dead child in a towel. She placed the dead body in the fire place. In the blaze, the tiny dead body disintegrated to ash almost instantly.

Warrick shouted, "Drayton. Morgan. Do you hear that scream? That was Lilith's scream. She screams that she cannot eat the dead child. We are in great danger. The demon Lilith is here. Make sure that everyone does their hour of Perpetual Adoration. Check that someone is in the Adoration Wagon doing Adoration now. Otherwise, Lilith could not be here. In the Adoration wagon, Perpetual Adoration of Jesus' Real Presence in the Blessed Sacrament. Now. Never tire of this warning. Make sure everyone does weekly confession or die at Lilith's hands. Forget at your peril. Only Adoration and weekly confession can keep the red-fog away. Morgan, order a knight into the Adoration wagon now, to do Adoration. Remember the screams of the San Gimignano, Italy army as Wolv's red-fog ate them. Lilith lifted them up into the air and ate them whole."

As Warrick pointed at a trunk for two knights to lift, he said, "Lady Brielle." He unconsciously raised his right eyebrow. "After we have prepared our London castle, I will call for you to join us."

Warrick said. "Lady Brielle. Remember I will set up three priest-knights to do Perpetual Adoration of the Blessed Sacrament. Here in your manor to protect you. You also must participate in Perpetual Adoration and weekly confession. Later, you can help Marian plan her wedding. Until then I will leave knights here to protect you."

Lady Brielle stepped over to Marian. Then she hugged her and said, "Marian. You will have a London castle. Also, have a wedding in the king's own chapel. These are the dreams of every woman."

Warrick did not know how disappointed and betrayed Marian would feel. His lie would crush her heart. He did not know the lie would make her think she could not trust him.

WOLV FAR OFF ON A KNOLL

From far off, on a high knoll, Wolv said, "Swale, Gulum. My spy says that Warrick will go to Rose Fire in many more weeks. He goes first to London. Where is my army? Lilith promised me a Skinwalker army. The king has ordered Warrick to siege Rose Fire. Yet not for many more weeks. He goes to London. We must gather my Skinwalkers. We must lay ambushes between here and London."

Wolv growled, "Where are my Skinwalkers?"

Gulum said, "Lilith must have led them off to spread chaos."

-

-

-

CHAPTER, Where, Oxford, England, Northwest of London, England, Year @ 1250s A.D.

YOU HAVE THAT POISON OF BEAUTY, TO OVERFLOWING

Lord Warrick thought, "Wolv does not expect us to arrive for many weeks. I know Wolv. The AntiChrist will spend weeks in drunkenness before he prepares for our siege."

Inside the manor, Lady Brielle said, "Lord Warrick. Please take Nicola. She is only in her late teens. She needs the security a father can offer. You are now the closest person to a father that she will have. Upstairs, her father reclines on his deathbed. Nicola is much wiser than her age. Nicola is younger than Marian, yet Nicola advises Marian. On money matters and on matters of human nature."

"I will take Nicola," Warrick said. "Marian will need a family member."

Marian said, "I have much more to pack."

Nicola and Marian ran up the stairs to their chambers. They laughed like two children.

Marian said, "Nicola, you are coming with us to London. We will have such fun."

Nicola said, "Marian, everything is going to be wonderful. We are going to London. Your wedding will be glorious. In the largest, most splendid chapel in all England."

Then Sister Catherine leaned over to Marian. She put her hand to her mouth. The nun whispered into Marian's ear, "Marian. I heard someone say. Say that you were going to the rebellious territory of Wales."

Marian said, "That would be a terrible fate. The Skinwalkers and Welsh clans have reduced much of Wales to rubble. To ash and rubble."

Lady Brielle said, "Marian. You will ruin that gown on the trip. Go to your bed chambers. Find a shift and gown with heavier linen, something warmer. Something tougher."

Warrick said, "Otan, come with me and find my clean set of leathers."

In the barn Otan poured buckets of cold water over Warrick.

Warrick smoothed his hair with both hands and said, "Good. The lake was muddy."

Then Warrick dressed in a clean set of black leggings, boots, blouse, and cowled-cloak. Now bathed and in clean leathers, Warrick walked back to the manor.

Warrick yelled, "Everyone, put on your blessed armor."

Lord Warrick said, "Otan. I want you to prepare my blessed armor. Before the morn Prime bells, I expect Wolv to attack us. Also, rinse my leathers. Dry them over the fireplace." Remember. At Prime, sunrise, Wolv is helpless. Helpless because of his Resurrection obsession. He will hide in the earth to try to escape reliving Jesus' Resurrection. To try to escape Jesus' refusing to raise Pamia from the dead for him. Helpless, but we still cannot kill him."

With twice the stride of most men, Warrick's feet swirled the ground fog. Swirled the grey ground fog in long lines of quick eddies. The grey ground fog oozed through the open manor door. Warrick walked into the great room. Then he bounded up the spiral staircase to Marian's chambers.

Without a thought, Warrick opened the bedchamber door.

Naked, as she turned to Warrick, Marian held a gown in front of herself. She pointed her finger at the door and shouted, "Out, out."

As a warrior, with only the thoughts of a warrior, Warrick ignored her complaints. "Marian, you were supposed to be downstairs, dressed, ready to travel."

Warrick commanded. "Now, dress. We leave in minutes."

She held a gown before her naked body. Marian again shouted, "Out, out."

Instead Warrick said, "Dress. Now. Obey. We have little time. Obey."

In a warrior's haste and impatience, he grasped a shift from the bed. Then he raised it over Marian's head. "Put your arms through the sleeves, now."

He lowered the bunched shift to her forehead. The bedchamber fireplace reflected on her creamy face.

Marian said, "Warrick. Are you going to stand there and gawk at me until my arms fall?"

Warrick's memory went back to Ogina's betrayal. To Ogina's betrayal of his knights, leaving his first castle unlocked.

Warrick frowned down to his chin. He turned his back to Marian.

Marian said, "Your frown tells me you have bad memories. Memories of your first wife?"

With his back to Marian Warrick said, "I once drank the poison of beauty."

"You," Marian said, "You say that I am beautiful?"

Warrick said, "Yes. You have that poison of beauty, to overflowing."

Nicola banged on the door. She demanded, "Marian. Unlock the door, unlock the door. The knights are here to carry your chests."

Ross knuckled the door and shouted through the door. "Warrick. We have your blessed armor. Don your blessed armor so we can hurry."

Behind Warrick's back, Marian pulled her tight shift down. Then she pulled her gown over her head. She smoothed it on her waist and hips.

Warrick turned around and helped her pull on her tall boots.

Marian said, "Memories of your first wife haunt you."

Warrick answered like a warrior that understood nothing about women.

He did not answer, *but thought, "Marian. Yes, Marian is the most beautiful woman I have ever seen. Again beauty conquers me. Again beauty distracted me from the enemy. The enemy is near. Again I allow beauty to draw my attention away from the enemy. I risk drinking the poison of beauty."*

Marian said, "You will not answer me? I am not a waif that you can just ignore."

Warrick thought, "Beauty distracted me one fatal time. Beauty will not distract me again."

Marian snapped, "I can see that I am not important enough to you. Not important enough for you to answer me."

She wiggled her hips and pulled down on her gown. Thus, she adjusted her gown.

She said, "Warrick. Silence? I suppose that you will always treat me as if I do not exist."

As Warrick unlocked the door he thought, "Wolv is close. Ross knows that Wolv is close. These few minutes with Marian could have been a fatal distraction."

Otan and Reque stood in the hallway with Warrick's blessed armor and blessed armor padding. With Ross, many knights, all in blessed armor, entered Marian's bed chamber. They carried her chests to wagons outside the manor. She had wooden chests all over the floor. Chests filled with her gowns and other clothing.

In the hallway, through the open door, Warrick turned to watch Marian.

Warrick thought, "Marian's beauty is addictive."

Reque and Otan strapped blessed armor on Warrick. Marian looked through the doorway into Warrick's emerald eyes.

His silence angered her. Yet, his emerald eyes mesmerized her. She did not even realize that she was staring at him. She felt her passions rise, feelings that no one else could cause her to feel. Her feelings of anger dissipated. Lady Marian was completely unfamiliar with these feelings. Marian picked up his now-cleaned extra black cloak from her bed. She placed his cloak to her nose. Unconsciously she breathed deep of its bay leaf aroma. The bay-leaf gave her the deepest feelings of well-being that overwhelmed her. With the bay leaf aroma, she felt as if nothing could harm her.

While she gazed into his eyes, she felt that he would fulfill all her dreams.

Warrick watched the candle flames and fireplace reflect from Marian's eyes. He thought, "Yes. Marian's beauty is magical. Marian's beauty is addictive."

Now in his blessed armor, Warrick said, "Otan. Reque. I want you to carry this last trunk from Marian's bedchamber."

As Reque and Otan carried the trunk downstairs, Warrick stepped back into Marian's bedchamber.

Marian realized that she stared into Warrick's emerald eyes. She lowered her head and looked sideways at him.

"I feel as if you can read my thoughts," Marian said.

He smiled and said, "Of course I can. You are passionate. Obstinate, independent, exacting, demanding, and compassionate, to a fault. Your compassion can cause our deaths."

Warrick said, "You want passion. Yet you do not know what passion is. You are as innocent as a new born child."

Marian said, "How can you know?"

Warrick said, "Your eyes. I see everything in the honesty of your eyes. I can see everything about you. Thoughts, hopes, dreams, schemes. You have never harmed anyone. You have no guilt in you. Otherwise, you would look away when I look at you."

She felt violated and said, "Ohhh. How can you just read my mind, my most intimate thoughts?"

She crossed her arms and turned her back to him. Then she secretly smiled, pleased that he was in her bed chamber.

He thought, "You are so beautiful that knights would wag war to see your smile."

Marian said, "You just said that I was so beautiful. So beautiful that knights would wage war to see my smile."

Warrick said, "So. You read my mind?"

Marian said, "No. You spoke aloud."

"Now we must hurry," Warrick commanded.

Lady Marian said, "We are mad to travel this early in the morning. Nicola cannot go outside with the darkness, lightening and thunder. I heard the very late midnight Vigils bells and very early matins' bells. The time is perhaps three hours after midnight. Freezing, the temperature is freezing.

Warrick said, "Marian, we must steal away like shadows in the night."

He stepped over to her. Instinctively, her eyes grew round and white as she stepped backward.

Warrick said, "Marian. You have the eyes of a frightened child. I frightened you?"

She looked up and said, "Warrior. You are a warrior, a war lord. I fear anyone that glories in wars."

Lord Warrick said, "We must hurry."

Marian's eyebrows formed and angry V as she said, "Oh. You are insufferable, so controlling."

Lord Warrick stepped into the hallway. "We must hurry, obey."

He closed the door. Marian made a fist and hit the door. Her eyebrows formed an angry V. She said, "Oh, how he controls me."

Nicola opened the door from the solar and jumped on the bed.

"Lord Warrick is beautiful," Nicola said. "He is everything that you prayed for in a spouse. Also, a warrior."

Marian said, "You were listening?"

Nicola said, "Yes, of course I was listening. I heard every word."

Marian said, "You are such a devil. Yes, Nicola, he is beautiful. I so hope he is beautiful inside and out. You are such a pixie! Truly, tell me the truth, what did you hear?"

Nicola clapped and said, "Every Oh and Ah. What did he do to you to make your cheeks so pink?"

Marian said, "One day he will do everything in the troubadours songs."

"Oh! None of that is true," Nicola laughed.

With her palms on her breasts, Marian leaned forward. She said, "Nicola. I hope that the troubadour songs are true."

Then with both hands, Marian grasped Nicola's hands. "Nicola," Marian said. "Imagine the fun. We are to live in a London castle with the king's champion. We are so lucky to wed and live in London."

DOWNSTAIRS IN MORAY MANOR'S GREAT HALL

Then Marian ran downstairs into the great hall. The grey fog, to her knees on the great hall floor, swirled around her cloak. With a white gloved hand, Marian grasped her mother's forearm. Then she pulled her aside. "Mother," Marian whispered. "Lord Warrick frightens me to the point that I cannot think."

Lady Brielle said, "You prayed to wed a man like him. Did you forget that you scorned all other suitors? You put your nose in the air to them. You flipped the back of your hand to the best suitors. Marian, you rejected all the best suitors of Oxford and London."

Marian said, "Mother. You saw them. Those men wore silk ruffles and primmed their hair like expensive prostitutes."

Brielle snapped, "Marian. Tell me, how do you know what an expensive prostitute does?"

"Mother," Marian said. "Both you and I have been to London. Anyway, I wish to talk about the other suitors. Though the king approved of them, they had bankrupted their estates. They would have bankrupted us. I wanted a warrior which the king admired. I wanted a warrior that all other warriors admired and followed. Then I wanted to wrap his will around my little finger. In my imagination, I wanted him romantically to kneel at my feet. I want him to ask for my hand. Also, I wanted him to write poetry for me. Instead I fear that I will dissolve in his unbending will. He seems to only want my obedience."

Marian thought, "And wanted him to want my body."

Lady Brielle said, "Daughter, you have a wish for a warlord. You did not know for what you prayed. You asked God for a man like Warrick. Especially Lord Warrick, the king's champion."

Marian said, "I did not know that a warrior like him was so hard. When I was fifteen years old, I prayed for a knight. I prayed for a warrior that all knights admired. Now I have that knight. Not just a knight, I have the king's most demanding warlord. The king's champion. I am helpless and overwhelmed in his arms."

"You are sometimes a foolish daughter," Brielle said. "You prayed to have a man like him. Now you have him. The greatest lesson of life is to be careful for what you pray. Now you will have one central duty, to obey him. You found it easy to disobey your father, but this is a warlord. Be very careful, Marian, you must be obedient to him. Be obedient to him or he will lock you in your chambers. Lock you in your chambers and leave you there."

-

-

-

CHAPTER, Where, Oxford, England, Northwest of London, England, Year @ 1250s A.D.

THE ANTICHRIST ATTACKS. BOAR'S-HEAD SKINWALKERS SURROUND HER.

Marian's eyes grew round with surprise and she said, "No, mother. I will not obey Lord Warrick. I go where I will, do what I will, see what I will."

Lady Brielle said, "Yes, you are foolish. You prayed for your dream to come true. It has come true. Now you must learn to live with reality. Quickly, you must finish packing and be off to London."

"At least we are going to London," Marian said. "London is a civilized place and not some godforsaken, war-torn, uncivilized place like Wales."

Lady Brielle said, "The king allows only a few to wed in his own chapel. To live in a castle in London is a fairy tale come true."

Matins' bells announced that they had three hours before sunrise.

Warrick said, "Hurry. Matins' bells. It is three hours past midnight-Vigil bells. Three hours before sunrise, Prime bells. We must hurry. We must leave under the cover of night."

Warrick's knights worked in the apple orchard, in night's darkest hours. The three hours before dawn's Prime bells. The knights tightened the ropes on the wagons. Each knight carried a tar-torch. Blackest night. Grey ground fog up to their knees. Warrick's armored knights loaded the last trunks.

Moray servants had quickly dried Warrick's leathers before the fireplace. Otan walked across the room. Ground fog swirled up to his knees. At the fireplace, Otan gathered Warrick's cleaned leathers.

Warrick said, "Drayton. Again. Make sure that everyone does their hour of Perpetual Adoration. Remind everyone of the urgency. In the Adoration wagon, Perpetual Adoration of Jesus' Real Presence in the Blessed Sacrament. Make sure everyone does weekly confession. We are in the greatest danger. Remember every moment that only Adoration and weekly confession can keep the red-fog away. Remember the army you saw eaten in the Bruges, Belgium battle against Wolv. Wolv sent his red-fog out into the valley. The things in the red-fog ate them. We survived because we did Perpetual Adoration and weekly confession. We survived because we took the Adoration wagon in with us."

OUTSIDE

Outside, Warrick wore with his primary, black, leather cloak. Clasped on his shoulders and around his neck. Warrick carried a torch. Again a distant Matins bell rang.

Lord Warrick said, "Hurry. Matins Bells tell us that the Prime Bells sun will soon be upon us. We must hurry or the enemy will see us leave. Be quick for we have only three hours before sunrise, Prime bells."

The night-ground-fog grew so thick that no one could see their feet. Warrick long strides made him walk as fast as most men run. Warrick's legs churned the fog into whirlpool eddies. He carried his cleaned cloak in his other arm. The cloak was the cloak that he gave Marian after she fell into the lake. As he folded the cloak, he opened a saddlebag to store it.

In the knee-deep fog, Marian ran to Warrick. She snatched Warrick's extra black, bay-leaf-aroma-cloak from his hands.

"Mine," Marian said.

She took off her royal-red, fox cloak. Then she clasped Warrick's long black cloak around her neck. Then she inhaled the bay leaf aroma. Unconsciously she felt the comfort, the peace of her manor. The aroma made her unknowingly feel safe. The safety she felt after Warrick saved her from the four Skinwalkers at the lake. Her feeling of safety in that cloak overwhelmed all her other emotions. Then she stuffed the royal-red, fox cloak into Warrick's saddlebag.

With Warrick's black cloak around her, Marian took the reins of her gelding.

She looked at Warrick and said, "Well? Warrick. Obey me."

Warrick smiled.

With his iron gauntlets Warrick grasped Marian's slender waist and lifted her onto her gelding.

Marian wrapped her left leg around the lady's horn. Then she locked her left ankle under her right knee.

Warrick put his gauntlets on Zeus' saddle. With one leap, Warrick did what only the strongest knights could do. In the enormous weight of full, shiny armor, he jumped and landed in Zeus' saddle. Zeus stood as if a feather landed in the saddle. Marian and Warrick repeatedly trotted the cavalcade's length of wagons to supervise the loading. As Zeus trotted, the great horse blasted breath from his large nostrils. Zeus' hot, moist opaque breath eddied behind him. Behind Zeus as if it were smoke from a fire deep inside his lungs.

TRAITOR.

Blanche stood in the fog, beside her personal wagon and servants.

A knight walked over to Blanche. With his gauntlet, he took her hand and lifted it to his lips.

He kissed her hand and said, "Lady Blanche. May I say how angelic and lovely you are."

"Not now. Go, go away," Blanche snapped.

She turned her head and pushed him away.

Blanche thought, "I know this knight. This knight is landless."

MARIAN ON HER GELDING

Marian's gelding pranced beside Zeus in the ground fog.

Marian said, "Warrick. I am so excited to see London. What fun Nicola will have in London."

Warrick did not reply to her remark.

Instead Warrick thought, "to protect Marian, time is my most effective ally. Marian will not trust me again for lying to her. She is too happy about the wedding and life in London."

Drayton reined in and said, "Warrick. Everything is packed for the trip to London."

THE ANTICHRIST ON A KNOLL FAR AWAY

Wolv sat on his warhorse. Atop a high knoll in the dark and ground fog. His warhorse nervously pranced in place.

Wolv's effort to hold his original Roman general handsome form exhausted him. To maintain that form, Wolv had to fight his nature. Exhausted, Wolv changed from his Roman general handsome form to a dusty, crumbly charcoal form. His eyes and the eyes of his horse became full of red-yellow flame. Spiritual hate-filled flame that did not turn him to ash. His mount also changed into the same crumbly charcoal consistency. Also, with eyes of red-yellow flame.

A Boar's head Skinwalker rode up to Wolv and growled. "My lord. Part of your army is now hidden in the valley behind you. We await your orders."

Wolv swung his sword and cleaved the Skinwalker's head. "Swale. Tell the army that I behead Skinwalkers that cannot read a map. This time you must pick officers that can read maps."

Wolv's horse reared. "Now we must capture Marian. Marian is from Pamia's progeny by Pamia's first husband. I must test if she has Pamia's soul. If yes, she lives with me. If not, I will kill her. We must change Marian's destiny. I want you to capture her, for me and me alone."

A naive mercenary said, "My lord. Our Welsh partners paid us only to kill Warrick, not to capture Marian. Marian is only supposed to be bait to catch Warrick."

Wolv swung his sword at the mercenary. The mercenary was too far away. He spurred his horse to its fastest speed. He turned his head to see if anyone was following him.

Wolv said, "I will not tolerate questions."

He pointed to his Skinwalkers and said, "The two of you. Run him down, kill him."

ON ZEUS

Zeus reared as he detected the noise of Wolv's men. On Zeus, Warrick turned to the noise and saw Wolv's red, fire eyes. Eyes of eternal, spiritual hatred. Physical fire could temporarily harm Wolv, even turn him to ash. Yet, the demons that possessed him always healed him from physical fire. The pain of physical fire could keep him from changing form. Pain could keep Wolv from escaping, temporarily.

ATTACK

Wolv yelled, "We have four times the number of Warrick's knights. Attack, capture Marian. Show no mercy, attack, and bring Marian to me, alive. I must test Marian to see if she is Pamia."

CIRCLE MARIAN, PROTECT MARIAN.

Warrick shouted his command, "Circle Marian."

Lord Warrick's knights mounted.

Lord Warrick thought, "That is the voice of my worst enemy. Wolv. That wraith deceived my wife, Ogina, into treason against me. He turned my wife into a traitor. His Skinwalkers killed Ogina. How will he defeat me this time?"

WOLV ON THE KNOLL

Far away on the knoll, Wolv thought, "I was too long. I was too long in my original form for too long. I used too much energy to keep my Roman general form. Now I am too weak to fight."

MARIAN WITH WARRICK

Warrick held the reins of Marian's gelding. Zeus reared and galloped toward the wagons. Then Warrick unsheathed blessed Dread.

He said, "Marian. My duty is to protect you. I was foolish to put you on a horse without any armor."

A mass of Skinwalkers, in Boar's-Head shape helms, charged down the knoll at Marian. They all shouted, "Capture Marian."

Warrick's knight's mounted. Again he yelled "Circle Marian."

His knights obeyed and formed their warhorses into a circle around Marian to protect her. Warrick on Zeus took the front of the circle.

Warrick turned to Marian and said, "Forgive me for putting you into such danger. I should have put you in the warm, armored wagon."

Marian smelled the aroma of his cloak around her. The aroma made her irrationally feel like no one could harm her. Like no one could harm her while she was with Warrick. The aroma made her fell that Warrick was invincible, invulnerable.

All armored with Boar's-Head shape helms, Skinwalkers galloped faster down the knoll. They shouted in hellish voices, "Capture Marian."

Warrick realized that the enemy attacked from only one direction.

He yelled, "Prepare for Scipio Africanus' Carthage Tactics."

The back of the circle behind Marian divided. His mounted knights formed a long line in front of Marian. A long line before and parallel to the wagons.

Warrick shouted another command. "Drayton, Archers. Now."

From behind his knights, his archers shot into the Skinwalkers. Many horses of the Skinwalkers fell under the hail of blessed arrows.

Then Warrick said, "Forgive me Marian. I have no time to put you into the safety of the armored wagon."

Warrick said, "Drayton. Remember my realistic obsession. Make sure that everyone does their hour of Perpetual Adoration. In the Adoration wagon, Perpetual Adoration of Jesus' Real Presence in the Blessed Sacrament. To motivate you, contemplate what you saw in Toledo, Spain. We slowed Wolv, but his red-fog ate Toledo's army. Remember the helpless screams of women and children."

Drayton said, "Brother. My lord, Warrick. We follow your every word. We know that you are the world's only hope in stopping the AntiChrist."

Marian said, "Warrick. When I am with you, I feel safe. Your oafish commands insult me, but I feel safe from the enemy."

The aroma of his cloak clasped to her shoulders filled the air around her.

Warrick raised his blessed sword and yelled, "Scipio Africanus' Tactics. Attack."

All mounted, he and his knights charged up the knoll.

In the grey, ground fog and night blackness, another nunnery rang Matins bells.

The two armies crashed. Horses groaned and fell. Men cried in pain. Beheaded Skinwalkers screamed. Weapons clanged on armor.

From blessed Dread, concentric circles of wet red droplets arced and reflected the torch lights.

Warrick swung his war ax with one arm and his blessed sword with the other. Then Warrick yelled his most critical battle formation, "Now, now. You must use the Carthage, Scipio Africanus Tactics. They are four times our number. Use the Carthage, Scipio Africanus tactics, now. Now."

Morgan, Ross, and Lord Warrick's mounted knights surrounded the mounted enemy.

Warrick had only one fourth of Wolv's warriors. Yet, Warrick had trained his knights better than any other knights.

As did Scipio Africanus, Warrick's knights forced the Skinwalkers into a tight, crowded circle. The enemy tried to charge from the circle. Instead, their horses stumbled upon each other.

Warrick's warhorses, from trained habit, held the circle tight. They blocked them and pushed in. Warrick constantly trained his warhorses to block. To block and herd the enemy's horses into a circle. He trained them so well that they now instinctively blocked the enemy mounts. His warhorses instinctively herded the enemy's horses into a tighter, chaotic, deadly circle.

Since Warrick's knights surrounded the Skinwalkers, they kept most Skinwalkers trapped inside the circle. Skinwalkers trapped inside could not battle the knights on the edge of the circle.

The Skinwalkers and mercenaries shouted, "Capture Marian. Remember Wolv's promised Gold."

Warrick's knights would not allow any of the Skinwalkers to break out of the circle.

Then Warrick yelled, "Drayton. Light your blessed arrows and shoot now."

From outside the circle, Warrick's archers shot flaming arrows inside the circle. The pine-tar-flaming blessed arrows pierced the Skinwalkers and their horses. Packed tightly together, when the flaming arrows pierced the horses, the horses panicked and reared. The flaming pine-tar-arrows landed on the ground. Enemy horses stepped on the burning tar. Tar fires burned the enemies' horses. The burning tar stuck to their hooves, tails and manes. They reared and flailed their front legs. After they reared, the horses tried to lower their legs. Instead, their front legs landed on the back of other enemy horses. Skinwalkers' own horses kicked the Skinwalkers to the ground. Then the burning horses slipped on the enemy's own armor and fell. Inside the circle, Skinwalker horses trampled horses, Skinwalker horses trampled Skinwalkers.

The Skinwalkers did not realize that Warrick's knights had trapped them. Greed made the Skinwalkers irrational. They yelled, "Capture Marian, remember the buckets of gold Wolv promised."

Warrick had trained his armored war horses much better than the Skinwalkers' horses. Morgan and Ross guided Warrick's knights. They stood firm. Knights pushed their shielded-horses around the circle. Blessed shields covered the horses. With blessed axes and blessed swords they cleaved the panicked enemy near them. Their warhorses shoved the enemy's untrained mounts and warriors tight. Tighter into the cramped compressed interior of the circle. Just as Warrick had planned. His knights had practiced countless times. The enemy's horses continued to rear on their hind legs. The enemy's horses threw their riders. Enemy horses trampled fallen horses and fallen Skinwalkers.

Warrick yelled, "Now. Throw the flaming-pin-tar torches."

Drayton's archers threw thick flaming-pine-tar torches into the center of the circle. Panicked Skinwalkers dropped their weapons to control their rearing horses. Pine tar burned on enemy horses and Skinwalkers.

Warrick had trained his armored warhorses to clash head to head. To shove side to side with the enemy horses. Under such tight pushing, with the flaming torches falling on them, the enemy horses reared. They fell backward. To the Skinwalkers' dismay, their own horses trampled them to death.

On the edge of the circle, Warrick and his knights swung their weapons with accuracy. The knights cleaved, faster and harder than the Skinwalkers.

-

-

-

CHAPTER,   Where: Now in Hereford Town, Wales, The Wye Valley, Insight of Rose Fire Castle Year @ 1250s A.D.

WHERE IS FATHER MALACHI MARTIN. NEVER AGAIN WILL I TRUST A WIFE.

Warrick's yelled, "Do not penetrate the circle. Do not penetrate the circle. For Marian, Knights. You must follow my commands, squeeze them tight. Do not penetrate the circle. Let none escape. Give no quarter, ask for no quarter."

Marian irrationally and mysteriously felt safe behind Warrick. She wrapped his extra leather cloak around herself. Deeply she breathed of the bay leaf aroma.

From atop the distant knoll, Wolv watched the battle and foresaw the outcome.

Wolv thought, "I am too weak from maintaining my Roman general form. Too weak to join the battle."

Then Wolv said to the Skinwalkers with him, "I cannot capture Marian here. We must create ambushes along Warrick's way to London."

Then Lord Wolv and his remaining Skinwalkers galloped south, toward London, to set up ambushes. To create ambushes on the way to London.

AT THE KNIGHT'S CAVALCADE.

At the cavalcade, Wolv's Skinwalkers burned like a bonfire. They screamed and lay on the ground, dying. Still in a panic, in flames, the Skinwalkers' own horses reared and trampled them.

Warrick's knights raised their weapons and shouted, "Victory. The victory for Lady Marian, the lady Lord Warrick."

BLANCHE THE TRAITOR IN HER WAGON

Inside her warm wagon, alone, Blanche gritted her teeth in anger. Anger that the cheers were for Marian, not for her. Anger that her master, Wolv, had lost the battle.

Then Blanche walked from her wagon and approached Marian's servants.

Blanche thought, "I must plant discord between Marian and Warrick."

Blanche saw Marian's youngest handmaiden, Neeve, at the corner of a wagon. Neeve was the most frightened, the most naive of servants. Quickly, Blanche walked up behind her and said, "Neeve. Do not look around."

With wide, round, white, frightened eyes, Neeve said, "Why? Who are you?"

At the back of the servant, Blanche said, "Who? I am someone that can send you back to poverty if you turn around. You must not look at me."

Behind the frightened handmaiden, Blanche whispered. "Tell Marian that she needs immediately to care for the wounded. They need her excellent healing arts. Tell Marian that Warrick will not care for the wounded. The wounded need Marian's skills."

Neeve asked, "Why can I not see you?"

Blanche said, "No."

Again the handmaiden said, "Why can I not know who are you?"

Blanche said, "Neeve. If you turn and see me, I will send you back. Back to your dirt-floor straw hut. Tell Marian's handmaidens that Marian needs to treat the wounded. You must tell her handmaidens that Warrick always lets the wounded die on the battlefield. You are to tell Marian's handmaidens that the wounded now need Marian's healing skills. Tell all of Marian's handmaiden's what I said. Now. Go. If you tell anyone who you think I am, I will have. I will have Marian expel you from her service. Then you will again live in a straw, dirt-floor hut."

Neeve knew that the alternative to serving Marian was extreme poverty as a vassal. Immediately, the naive, frightened handmaiden told all of Marian's servants and other handmaidens.

Blanche, Wolv's slyest spy, had successfully planted the lie in the servant's thoughts. She knew that Warrick always did the honorable thing. Blanche knew that Warrick always administered aid to the wounded. Enemy and allied wounded alike.

MARIAN'S DANGEROUS COMPASSION

On the back of her gelding, Marian's nature dominated her. Her compassion quashed her caution.

Marian said, "Look, the wounded will bleed to death. I must help them. I am a healer. My mother trained me in the healing arts."

Marian dismounted. Warrick shouted, "Marian. Forget the wounded."

Zeus reared as if to celebrate victory. In his shiny blessed armor, Warrick dismounted, then he lifted Marian off the ground. He carried her and ran with her to the armored wagon.

She said, "We are safe? I must tend to the wounded."

Warrick said, "No Marian. Another attack could come from any direction at anytime."

Warrick placed Marian into the wagon with Nicola and Collette. Then he slammed the iron door shut.

The servant, Neeve, that Blanche had deceived, entered the comfortable wagon.

Marian said, "Nicola. Neeve. Lord Warrick does not care for the wounded. He told me to 'Forget about the wounded.' An honorable knight cares for all the wounded. Warrick is a dishonorable man."

The naive, frightened servant, Neeve, said, "Yes my lady. I have heard that Lord Warrick does not care about the wounded."

Neeve believed the lie that Warrick did not help the wounded. Now Marian believed the lie. This would taint Marian's understanding of Warrick and build a wall between them.

Outside Marian's wagon, Warrick turned to his squires and pages.

EXORCISM OF THE SKINWALKERS.

Lord Warrick yelled, "Skinwalkers, if you want to live, chant, 'Jesus, have mercy on me. Jesus, forgive me my sins.'" Again Warrick yelled, "You must let me exorcize Satan's demons from you. If you wish to remain Skinwalkers, we must cut off your heads. Then burn your heads to ash. With your heads burned, you cannot come back to life."

The Skinwalkers began to chant repeatedly, "Jesus. Have mercy on me. Jesus, forgive me my sins."

The Skinwalkers fell to their sides. Long demons as charcoal-black-dust ran from their mouths. The charcoal-black-dust disappeared into the earth.

Two Skinwalkers shouted, "Never. Never will we ask for forgiveness of our sins. We will kill you and take Marian."

They stood to attack Warrick.

Warrick swung his battle ax, Dread, and decapitated both of them. Then he threw their heads upon a burning pile. He put burning torches upon them to burn them to ash.

One burning head screamed, "Exorcize me. Please exorcize me. I do not want to burn in hell. Forgive me my sins, Jesus. Lilith possessed me centuries ago."

The Skinwalker head changed into a young, redheaded teenager and said, "Warrick. You have saved my soul. He died."

The other exorcized Skinwalkers said in unison, "Warrick. You have saved our souls."

Warrick said, "Look at you. You have changed back into Catholic priests. Many monasteries exist around Oxford. Lilith's demons have possessed all of you for many centuries. Go and find monasteries that will let you do Perpetual Adoration and weekly confession. Only Perpetual Adoration and weekly confession can protect you from Lilith. Without being in Perpetual Adoration and weekly confession, Lilith will smell you out. Do not let Lilith find you. Lilith's demons have possessed you for centuries. Her demons know the smell of your souls."

The now exorcized Catholic priests stood and limped from battle wounds.

Warrick commanded. "Pages. Squires. Tend to the wounded as I have trained you. Lady Brielle will have bandages and salves."

TO ESCAPE ANOTHER ATTACK

Lord Warrick said, "Morgan. Quickly. You must lead the wagon-column at a fast trot. Go now, we will follow."

Inside the embellished and richly padded armored wagons, Nicola said, "Marian. What did you see?"

Marian looked at Neeve with big surprised eyes and an open mouth. She said, "The wounded need me. My lord said, 'Forget the wounded.' He intends to let them bleed to death on the battlefield."

Marian's servant Neeve said, "Yes. Lord Warrick has no mercy."

Nicola said, "Marian. Do not let your compassion get out of control. It is not safe out there."

Marian said, "Warrick lives in Hell. War harasses him, and now I find that he has no mercy in him. I feared that he would have no tenderness in him. Now I find that he has no mercy in him."

OUTSIDE THE MANOR ON THE BATTLEFIELD.

Warrick said, "Drayton. Be tireless. Make sure that everyone does their hour of Perpetual Adoration. In the Adoration wagon, Perpetual Adoration of Jesus' Real Presence in the Blessed Sacrament. Again, bring the names to me of anyone that has not done their spiritual duty."

Outside the wagon on the road, Warrick pointed to a trusted knight.

Lord Warrick said, "Tell the pages and squires to bring the enemy's wounded to me. Take our wounded knights into the manor. Behead the dead Skinwalkers so they cannot come back to life. Burn their heads to ash or they will come back to life. Remember, they are Lilith's demons, spawn of Cain Pendragon."

An exorcized Catholic priest asked, "What is this land? What is the year?"

Warrick said, "This is England. The eleventh century."

With wide eyes of terror, the priest said, "Lilith possessed me in the year 200. I did not want to die as a martyr at Wolv's hand. I was a coward, so I asked Lilith to possess me, to keep me alive."

Warrick said, "As I told the others. Find a monastery. Live in Perpetual Adoration of the Blessed Sacrament. Go to weekly Confession. Beware. Lilith will come after you. Stay on blessed ground or she will find you."

Warrick pointed, "Monasteries are in that direction. Run. Lilith has the smell of your soul. She will follow you. Go. Run to the monasteries."

In his long black cassock, the priest ran like the wind.

Warrick walked among the wounded Skinwalkers. He beheaded the dead enemy Skinwalkers and threw their heads into the bonfire.

With the wagon on the run, Marian pushed the wagon's door open. She said, "I am a healer. I must go out and help the wounded."

Nicola caught Marian by the shoulders and said, "Oh no! You do not. Control your compassion. If you step outside this warm, armored wagon, the enemy could still capture you."

Nicola pulled Marian backward, then she shut and clasped the door. The wagon rumbled on the cobblestones as the column gained a fast trot.

Outside the moving cavalcade, Warrick lied. He raised his right eyebrow and said, "We must quickly arrive in London."

Warrick thought, "We must arrive at Wales Rose Fire castle weeks before Wolv expects us. Wolv will create ambushes on the roads to London. When his ambushes do not catch us, he will ride to Rose Fire. Hopefully Wolv will think that he simply missed us. That we still went to London for a wedding. Hopefully, Wolv will wait for us to leave London to ambush us around London. Therefore, I hope that he will wait weeks to reinforce Rose Fire. His horses carry nothing but their riders. Therefore, so he will still arrive at Rose Fire before we will. Our horses pull heavy wagons. We must travel by slow, rough back roads to avoid him, to bypass other ambushes. The wagons slow us, so Wolv will arrive at Rose Fire before us. Wolv will arrive before us. Yet, we will arrive weeks before they reinforce Rose Fire for our siege. The king ordered me to siege the castle later. I must disobey him and go weeks earlier. We must hurry. I can tell no one where we are going. We must not rest until we arrive. If any spy does ask, they must believe we left for the London wedding."

Warrick knelt beside a wounded Skinwalker and asked, "How many. How many are you in total?"

The Skinwalker rolled from his chest to his back. Warrick opened the Skinwalker's boar-helm visor. The Skinwalker gasped.

"Wolv has a remaining handful with him. Lilith will give him thousands of Skinwalkers. He will hire thousands of mercenaries more. He wanted Marian so desperately that he expended us in this foolish battle."

The Skinwalker coughed and said, "I told Wolv to wait to capture Marian. Tried . . . I tried to tell him that your knights were too well trained. Impossible, Wolv is impossible to advise. Told Wolv that your war horses would herd us into a tight circle. Not listen. Wolv would not listen when. When I told him that we could not defeat you hand to hand. Swale had better plans to attack you on a bridge. On a bridge and separate you and Marian from your knights. Foolish, Wolv could not wait. Ever since Wolv saw Marian, he could not control himself. She reminds him of his wife. We know that he murdered his wife, Pamia. His insanity is his wife that he himself murdered. We know the story from his blind rages. He often rages that he knocked Pamia off a cliff of Masada. Because she said a thousand years ago that she loved Jesus. When they were childhood friends in Egypt. An insane jealous rage."

The Skinwalker coughed and rolled to his side. He said, "Also, many of his mercenaries deserted him. Deserted him when they learned that they were to attack you, Lord Warrick. They were afraid of you. Insanity for Marian blinded Wolv. He attacked too soon."

Warrick thought, "Wolv was originally here to kill me. To prevent me from recapturing Rose Fire. Now his only motivation, his only goal, is to capture Marian."

IN THE MOVING WAGON
In the moving wagon Marian held her hands to her cheeks. "Nicola, my lord does not care for the wounded," Marian said. "He just lets them die."

Nicola said, "Marian, your compassion could drive you to foolishness. Let Lord Warrick do as he wills. You commanded a great peaceful estate, but."

Marian interrupted, "I commanded lords of Oxford and London. They had to pay me to sell through my many shops, taverns, and inns."

As the wagon rumbled, Nicola shook her finger and said, "Marian. You must leave Warrick alone. You must let him run the battlefield, before, during, and after the battles."

BACK AT THE BATTLEFIELD.

Back at the manor, out on the battlefield, Warrick asked the wounded Skinwalker. "Tell me More."

As he coughed, he said, "When Wolv. When Wolv heard that you were in England, he called his army." The wounded Skinwalker coughed again, "But it took him too long to gather his army. Everyone thought that you would not arrive at Moray Manor for weeks. We expected you to spend many days drinking ale and sleeping in stews with prostitutes. Unfortunately for us, you were dutiful and loyal to the king. You acted too fast."

Warrick asked, "Where will Wolv go now?"

As the Skinwalker grimaced, he whispered, "He will ride directly to Wales. He fights the English with David of Gwynedd and Wales' self declared Prince, Llewellyn."

Warrick asked, "Do any of the other wounded here know Wolv's destination?"

As the wounded Skinwalker sighed, he said, "None that are alive. Wolv is very secretive. He will not ride immediately to Rose Fire Castle. He has no wagons to pull, so he will arrive at Rose Fire before you. After your wedding in London, he will prepare Rose Fire for your siege. I was his. . . ."

The Skinwalker ceased to breathe as his head fell to one side.

Warrick said, "With your last breath, save your soul. If you are a Catholic priest, you should ask Jesus for mercy."

The Skinwalker spit at Warrick and said, "I stay with Satan."

Warrick beheaded the dead Skinwalker and threw the head on the bonfire.

Lord Warrick thought, "Our destination, Rose Fire, is not a secret. Yet we can be there so early that we can outwit Wolv. We can arrive before the enemy is prepared for us. With no wagons to pull, the AntiChrist will arrive before us. I know that he will wait for weeks to strengthen Rose Fire for the siege."

The last of the column of wagons sped beside them at a swift trot.

Lord Warrick said, "Ross, all depends on speed. We must not rest until we camp at our destination."

Drayton put his bow over his shoulder. He said, "Why must we go so quickly to London? Our real destination is not London?"

Warrick pulled off his shiny helm. His right eyebrow raised as he said, "Of course. Our destination is London. Where Marian and I will marry and live."

Warrick said, "Drayton. Check again. Make sure that everyone does their hour of Perpetual Adoration. In the Adoration wagon, Perpetual Adoration of Jesus' Real Presence in the Blessed Sacrament. Also, their weekly confession."

Warrick put his helm back on and flipped up the visor.

Drayton whispered, "Morgan, we know better. We know that the king would never send his champion, Warrick, to London. To grow fat and lazy in a London castle. The king always sends his best warriors to rebellions and wars."

Warrick thought, "Our only hope is speed. They may already be laying to ambush us on our way to Rose Fire. We must race to the castle by near-impassable back-roads. The rough roads will destroy many of our wagons and cripple many horses. At least Wolv may believe that I will spend weeks in London to wed there."

Warrick said, "Drayton. Do not question the king's orders. We go to London."

Warrick called a trusted knight to himself. "You will and manage The Moray manor and businesses. Tell everyone that we leave to wed and to live in London. Take three priest-knights and set up Perpetual Adoration and weekly confession. Perpetual Adoration will keep the red-fog from returning to Moray Manor."

Warrick thought, "Wolv has only one goal: to have Marian. He wants to test if Marian has Pamia's soul. Marian will find no peace until I do the impossible, defeat Wolv."

Ross looked at the wide battlefield. He said, "With this victory, word will spread. Word will spread that you will kill anyone that interferes with the Moray estate. They will end under blessed Dread."

Warrick said, "Yes, Marian's parents are safe. Not even Wolv would expend more Skinwalkers to conquer Lady Brielle's estate."

INSIDE THE WARM WAGON

Inside the warm wagon, as it rumbled and bumped, Marian said, "Nicola. I am to marry a man who has no mercy in him. He orders me about as impersonally as if I were one of his knights." The servant, which Blanche had deceived, repeated, "Yes, Lord Warrick has no mercy. He does not care for the enemy's wounded."

IN THE TRAITOR'S WAGON

In Blanche's wagon where no one could see her, Blanche grinned. She thought, "I have planted in Marian's thoughts the first of many lies. My lies will divide Marian and Warrick. Warrick never explains. He never apologizes. Lord Warrick will never tell Marian his pages and squires tend to the enemy wounded. Never, Warrick never explains. In fact, he rarely explains even to his brothers Drayton, Morgan, or Ross-the-Rake. They know simply to obey. Marian will believe that Warrick did not treat the wounded. He is not accustomed to explaining, or apologizing. Warrick expects only instant and unquestioning obedience from his knights, . . . and from Marian. Marian does not understand that Warrick never explains and never apologizes."

Blanche was alone in her four-horse wagon as it rambled over the rocks. Blanche grinned and showed her teeth.

"First I must drive Marian away from Warrick," Blanche thought, "Then. Then I will have Warrick and his wealth."

Greed made Blanche's eyes sparkle. Greed caused her to palm the back of her hands endlessly. Blanche smiled and reclined into the deep pillows.

She thought, "I have put a permanent divide between them. I will cause much more trouble between the two of them. In the end, Warrick's wealth and power will be mine."

THE KNIGHTS FOLLOW THE CAVALCADE

Warrick and his knights mounted and caught up with the cavalcade. Beside the wagons, they traveled west. With little rest for men or horses, from Oxford, England to Wales' border.

For centuries the Pendragons had bred their warhorses to have endless energy at a gallop. The weaker wagon-horses slowed.

At farms they purchased fresh wagons-horses when their own wagon horses were too tired.

Days upon days they did not stop to eat properly or sleep. They did not stop to rest.

Warrick refused to stop a night for any reason except to purchase new wagon-horses.

At a gallop, Morgan placed his great mace across his shoulder. He rode beside Warrick. Morgan said, "Warrick. Lack of sleep does not bother your knights or the war horses. Yet Marian, Nicola, and her handmaids are sick from lack of sleep."

Warrick said, "We will have time to sleep very soon."

INSIDE THE WAGON

Inside the wagon, the wagon's iron-banded wheels bounced on rocks.

Marian said, "Nicola. When we stop to purchase new wagon horses, I use my Sextant. I read the stars. We are miles and miles north of London. We are going to the chaotic, war-torn Wales. The Wales clans are in rebellion against England. Warrick did not trust me even with the place of our wedding. He lied. He said that we were to be wed in the king's chapel. Live in a castle in London. My lord lies so easily to me. I am only a pawn, an expendable pawn in his war games. He feels he cannot trust me even with our wedding plans. Never will he trust me."

Nicola said, "Marian. Yes. It is a great disappointment for a bride. For her betrothed to lie about their wedding."

ON ZEUS

Zeus galloped outside the warm wagon. On Zeus, Warrick pointed his war ax and said, "Look ahead. Morgan, do you see smoke?"

Morgan said, "Yes, I see smoke, too much smoke. We have trouble ahead."

Warrick pointed Dread and said, "That river is the Wye River. We are deep in Wales. The smoke is from the town of Hereford. Someone is burning the town. Follow me but do not go faster than the wagons can travel."

Lord Warrick sped Zeus to a faster gallop. Then he saw many Boar's-Head Skinwalkers rape, pillage and fire the town. The Boar's-Head Skinwalkers stabbed merchants and raped their wives. They tied their children to sell for slaves. Warrick gave out a war hoop that made all the Skinwalkers turn to him. His war yell caused the Skinwalkers' jaws to hang open. The Skinwalkers eyes grew round and white with terror. Terror froze them in place. They stood with wide eyes of fear.

In full, bright, shiny blessed armor, Warrick, with Dread, bore down on them. He spurred Zeus to a war charge. The Skinwalkers released their captives and turned to fight Warrick. All the captives ran into the forest. Many Skinwalkers shouted, "Lord Warrick. Lord Warrick rides to fight us. The myth lives. Run. Dread, God's Avenging Angel, rides to kill us. Run."

Many Skinwalkers ran into the forests around Hereford.

One Skinwalker turned with his sword and said, "Stop. Marian is with Warrick. Wolv will give us a bucket of gold to the man that captures Marian. Look. Warrick is only one. We can kill him and capture Marian for Wolv."

Lord Warrick held his battle ax, blessed Dread, by the end of the handle. A Skinwalker threw a long chain. The long chain wrapped around Zeus' front legs. Zeus tripped and fell head long onto the cobblestone road. Lord Warrick flew head first onto the cobblestones. He rolled and stopped on his back. Dread landed too far away for him to reach.

Many Skinwalkers hacked at his armor. One shouted, "Kill Warrick and then we can capture Marian. Then Wolv will give us the gold.

Warrick pulled his blessed, narrow dagger and plunged it into a Skinwalkers ankle.

One Skinwalker shouted, "Warrick is dead. Now the gold is mine."

Another turned to him and shouted, "No, the gold is mine."

Greed overcame their reason. They cleaved each other for the gold. Skinwalkers fought each other. Then all the Skinwalkers turned to see their worst nightmare. Their greed had caused them to kill each other. Warrick had rolled to Dread. Now Warrick held Dread and growled.

Four Skinwalkers shouted in unison. "Run, Warrick is on his feet, run."

The four ran into the forest. Then another Skinwalker shouted, "Stop. We are many. Warrick is only one."

The chain dropped from Zeus' legs.

Warrick held Dread with both hands and spun like a whirlwind. Dread beheaded Skinwalkers. As Warrick had trained Zeus, Zeus lowered his armored head. He trampled Skinwalkers.

Arrows clunked into Warrick's armor and fell to the road. Zeus turned. He did as Warrick had trained him. Zeus charged through the Skinwalker archers.

Wet red blood arced off Dread. High in the air, red droplets flickered in the glare of the town's yellow-red flames.

Warrick shouted, "Surrender or die."

A Skinwalker yelled, "He is only one. Remember. Wolv will give a bucket of gold to the one that captures Marian. Kill Warrick and find Marian. Remember the bucket of gold."

They rushed him. Lord Warrick swung Dread. Dread threw huge, concentric circles of wet red droplets. Long circles of wet, red, blood droplets splashed on the charred buildings and cobblestones. The enemy fell lifeless. In full armor, Zeus reared and neighed. He pranced around Warrick as he always did to celebrate justice's victory.

Warrick's knights rode into the town. Ross' warhorse pranced over to Warrick.

Warrick sheathed Dread.

From atop his warhorse, Ross, said, "Brother. My Lord Warrick. My God, you alone. You alone slaughtered all these Skinwalkers. You cannot continue to drive your knights as hard as you drive yourself. Warrick, my brother, you will break us all."

Lord Warrick did not answer Ross.

Instead Warrick said, "Ross. Order my knights to search every building for Skinwalkers. If they surrender, offer them exorcism. If the Skinwalkers do not surrender, behead them and burn their heads."

Morgan said, "Warrick. Listen. From the Wye Valley monasteries, early Vespers bells call monks to sup and to pray. Soon dusk will cover us. We do not have many more hours of sunlight."

Within moments Ross dismounted and walked to Warrick.

He put his gauntlet on Warrick's armor shoulder and said, "Hereford. Hereford is free of Skinwalkers. In the inn several Skinwalkers must have drunk too much ale. They must have killed each other in a stupid fight."

Warrick's knights shouted three times, "Victory to Lord Warrick and Lady Marian. To protect Lady Marian, to serve Lord Warrick."

Warrick raised his hand and made a circle. Immediately, his knights surrounded the city to guard against another attack.

A weaver and his daughter wept and walked over to Lord Warrick.

The weaver said, "How can we thank you. They were about to slaughter us all and burn all of Hereford. Many of us have small amounts of gold. Would you accept our gold in thanks, as a reward?"

Lord Warrick lifted his visor and said, "Our reward is your safety. We ask for nothing. We ask only to see you safe. Our reward is your safety."

Warrick knelt beside the long line of manacled children.

"I will have no slaves in my lordship," Warrick growled.

With his gauntlets, Warrick grasped the children's neck manacles. He used his dagger as a wedge to force open dozens of neck manacles.

Then he said, "Children, where are your homes?"

The eldest boy pointed, "Look. Our homes, our parents are ashes. The Skinwalkers murdered our parents."

Warrick reached into his purse and pulled out gold pieces. Then he shouted, "Reque."

Reque ran to Warrick.

Warrick said, "Reque. Down the mountain, the Skinwalkers did not burn the nunnery below the town. Give this gold to the nunnery to house, clothe, and feed these orphans. This is enough gold to care for the children for many years."

In the blizzard, Reque and the orphans ran down the mountain to Hereford's nunnery.

Ross said, "Morgan, did you see the monasteries and nunneries, so many."

Morgan said, "Monastic orders cover the Wye Valley. I saw walled fields for the Knights Templars, Augustinians, Franciscans, Benedictines, and Dominicans Mendicant."

A knight asked, "The Knights Templars protected the pilgrimage routes to Jerusalem. Why would the Knights Templars have a monastery in Wales?"

Ross said, "Why? To recruit more warrior monks, retired wounded and old knights."

Morgan said, "I have never seen so many religious orders in one place. As we rode through the valley, I recognized four other religious order emblems. The orders were Carmelites, Cistercians, Carthusians, and Celestine."

"From here they look like small walled towns," Ross said.

Lord Morgan said, "They are bigger than many towns. Ross. Why do you think that the Skinwalkers have not attacked the religious orders?"

Ross said, "Wait until the Skinwalkers have destroyed all other food sources. Then they will destroy the walled churches, monasteries, and nunneries."

"Why does the valley have so many religious orders," Morgan asked?

"War. War drives people to seek sanctuary," Ross said. "The decades of the Skinwalkers and the Welsh/English wars drove people to seek sanctuary. The Religious orders give them sanctuary. Then the orders purchase farmland to feed the protected. Most nuns and monks were war widows, war orphans, and the wounded."

Morgan said, "I hope that the valley's cacophony of canonical bells let us sleep. They ring every three hours. The bells are constant in the day. They will ring from Vespers-supper, Compline-bedtime, midnight-Vigils, Matins prayers and sunrise Prime bells. After Prime they start again with Terce, Sext, Nones, Vespers and then Compline again. Every three hours. No one will sleep in Rose Fire."

Otan ran up to Warrick, "My lord," Otan said. "I found a live Skinwalker. You can question him." Then Otan pointed to a wounded Skinwalker on the ground.

"He is the only enemy alive," Otan said.

Marian stepped from her armored wagon. She said, "Why are we here? Where are we going? My God, what happened here?"

Marian dashed to the wounded townspeople. She tore her gown into long shreds for bandages.

The Supper Vespers' bells of Hereford's nunnery echoed off the mountains.

Lord Warrick demanded, "Marian, you can hear the early supper Vespers bells. Soon the sun will begin to set. You know that you are not safe here, climb back into the wagon."

Lady Marian whispered, "No. Warrick. You lied to me about wedding and our London castle. Now I cannot trust that you will care for the wounded. You are a man of lies and no mercy. Even . . . you even have slaves. An honorable knight would help the enemy's wounded."

Warrick thought, "Slaves? Lies? No mercy? I can see the future now. I must lock Marian in her keep. Otherwise, Marian will constantly insult me before my knights."

Marian pointed to Lord Warrick's knights.

Then she commanded, "Knights. Help me, now." She tried to command them. Just as she had commanded everyone on her father's huge estate.

Marian demanded, "Knights. Carry the wounded into the tavern and bandage their injuries."

She spoke from compassion.

Warrick said, "Your motivation witless compassion and excess pride."

Warrick did not understand that she was a commander of her father's huge estate. The knights did not understand that she was accustomed to others obeying her. They did not understand that she obeyed no one. Her father's estate was so large that Oxford and London lords had to obey her.

Of course the knights did not move. They only looked at Warrick and waited for a command.

He said to the knights, "No."

Marian walked up to Warrick and whispered, "You are heartless."

Warrick said, "Knighthood's greatest sin is disobedience of their lord. Like my knights, your greatest sin in war is to disobey me, your lord."

Drayton whispered into her ear, "Marian, we will only obey Lord Warrick. He has trained us well. By his wits alone he has kept us alive and together. We know in and out of battle our lives depend on our obedience to him. Obedience to Warrick and only to him."

Marian said, "Warrick. Obedience, obedience, obedience, is there nothing but obedience?"

Drayton whispered in her ear, "Marian. For a knight, obedience brings all good things."

She bent down and grasped a wounded woman by the shoulders. The weaver carried the woman's legs. One by one, Marian helped the town's people carry the wounded into the tavern.

Marian whispered into Warrick's ear, "Why are we here? Where are we going? Why all the secrecy? My lord, can you not confide in me? You would not tell us the truth about my wedding in London. Then why should you tell me the truth now. You feel that you cannot trust even your own betrothed?"

Warrick thought of his first betrothed, Ogina, a traitor. He thought, "No, I cannot trust my betrothed."

She walked out into the town's road and asked, "My lord. You do not trust me? Warrick, you should trust me and tell me where we are going. Why do you insult me with your silence?"

Warrick did not answer her.

He thought, "Another valley monastery rings their supper Vespers' bells. We have precious few hours of light. I must question the Skinwalker."

Marian did not see that all the Skinwalkers, but for one, were silent . . . forever, decapitated. All their heads in a bonfire.

Warrick knelt to the only live, wounded Skinwalker. He pulled off the Skinwalker's rusty Boar's-Head helm. Lord Warrick asked, "Tell me what you know about Wolv."

The wounded Skinwalker said, "Wolv led the siege of Rose Fire. Wolv commanded the siege that captured Rose Fire from England. We were going to Rose Fire to fight with Wolv. Until . . . until . . . we had the bad luck to fight . . . you."

Warrick said, "Speak the words that exorcize you of Lilith's demons. Ask Jesus for mercy."

The Skinwalker said, "Jesus. Have mercy on me."

As the Skinwalker lay on the floor, demons came out of his mouth. Out of his mouth, as a long line of black dust. He turned back into a Catholic priest."

The priest said, "Lilith threatened to kill me if I did not join her. She captured me in the year 500 A.D. Over five hundred years ago Lilith held me over a fire to burn me alive. Lilith's presence killed every unborn child in the city. That night every pregnancy ended in a stillbirth. Lilith is powerful. She came back to that city and dug up every stillborn child and ate them. Christian martyrdom terrified me so I joined her. She possessed me with her Skinwalker demons. I am dying, but you have saved my soul."

The Catholic priest's head fell to the side. He ceased to breathe.

Marian shouted, "Warrick. Why will you not answer me? You purposefully ignore me to insult me, to denigrate me?"

She grasped a wounded townsman's shoulders and helped carry him into the tavern.

Warrick shouted, "Ross-the-Rake. Morgan. Drayton. Have you seen Father Malachi Martin? We need Father Malachi Martin to defeat the AntiChrist."

Morgan said, "No one has seen him. No one knows the location of Father Malachi."

Marian returned to the road and said, "Warrick. You are supposed at least to talk to me."

Warrick thought, "I confided in my wife, Ogina. Ogina used my trust, my love, to blind me to her traitorous plans. Never again will I trust a wife. Wolv killed Ogina though she helped him."

With his visor raised, Lord Warrick only glanced at Marian.

Lord Warrick thought, "Never again will I trust a wife."

-

-

-

CHAPTER, Where, Now in Wales, Hereford Town, Rose Fire Castle in Wales, Year @ 1250s A.D.

DANGEROUS CLIFFS. MARIAN'S EVEN MORE NAIVE DANGEROUS COMPASSION.

Lord Warrick stood in the road. Silent, with unblinking eyes.

He thought, "Marian's enemies. Marian's enemies can be behind any rock, any tree, hidden in any shadow."

Ross instinctively walked up to him. "Do you sense an ambush?"

Lord Warrick gazed straight ahead, "Yes, Ross. Listen. Monks in another monastery ring their supper Vespers bells. In very few hours the dangers of the night will be upon us. I see too many shadows on the road ahead. We must ride by that cliff. A cliff above the road and a cliff below the road."

Ross said, "We could go back to Leominster and use the oxcart roads."

Warrick said, "We would be days behind. Many of Wolv's Skinwalkers escaped into the forest. We only have a short time before he knows that we are here. Skinwalkers talk by thought with Wolv and Lilith. Hopefully Wolv is drunk and does not hear his Skinwalkers, or Lilith."

Ross said, "If we do not give the wagon-horses a rest, they may die."

Lord Warrick waved to his knights, "Purchase whatever fresh horses the town's people will sell."

Warrick then shouted, "Drayton."

With his bow in his right hand, Drayton ran over to Warrick. Drayton snapped, "Brother, Lord Warrick, at your command."

Warrick said, "Climb the mountain far above the cliffs. When you are there, start signal fires at the mountain top. You must take your archers with you. Shoot anyone with a weapon. Be sure to run straight up the mountain. Light a signal fire when you reach the top. Turn toward the cliff only when you are high on the mountain. Otherwise, you will be below the enemy. Run, you must be quick. Remember. Light a signal fire when you reach the top."

Drayton and his archers ran and disappeared into the trees above the cliff. High in the Black Mountains, a blizzard began. Across the Wye Valley, red fog circled the black Mountains like a great slow tornado.

Warrick said, "On this side of the cliffs, this blizzard is not good. The snow will block our vision. Also, the snow clouds will bring in an early dark night. No moonlight. No starlight. We need daylight to race through the dangerous cliffs. The weather in the Black Mountains is very strange."

Warrick said, "Drayton. Morgan. Make sure that everyone does their hour of Perpetual Adoration. In the Adoration wagon, Perpetual Adoration of Jesus' Real Presence in the Blessed Sacrament. Assure me that everyone has done their weekly confession. Both of you fought as red-fog massacred the Prague army. The Prague General thought the AntiChrist was just a man. Then the red-fog turned into a tornado and ate them. The red-fog left no bones, no blood. Red-fog ate their horses. Contemplate the screams of Prague you heard and remember. Only Adoration and weekly confessions protect us from the things in the red-fog."

The weaver said, "Strange. Yes. Very strange, with summer in the Wye valley. I have seen snow cover the mysterious Black Mountains. High up there in the mountains, around Rose Fire, snow will freeze the ground. Blizzards could blow for several more weeks."

Inside the tavern, Marian tore strips from her long gown for bandages. Wounded townspeople bled all around her. She walked into the road. The blizzard-driven snow collected on her blond hair. She ran her hand on her hair.

Marian said, "Warrick. We need bandages."

As she walked, her beautiful, long legs showed through her shredded gown. Then, she turned to walk back into the tavern. Warrick took off his gauntlets and mail gloves. He grabbed Marian by the waist and lifted her into the armored wagon.

He said, "Marian. You are mine by order of the king. My duty is to protect you and your duty is to obey me. Stay in this warm, armored wagon with Nicola and your handmaidens. Collette and Neeve. The wagon is luxurious. My pages lined the walls, floor and ceiling with sheep's skin with the thickest wool. Marian. Dressed in your torn gown in this vespers' cold, you will die of the vapors. The thick wool covers the wagon's interior. You have the softest, down pillows. You even have Collette's collection of incenses and dried rose-pedal-throwings and scented candles. No weapon can penetrate the iron plate on this wagon."

From the mountainside, a Skinwalker crossbow arrow swished in the air. It pierced a joint of the armored wagon.

Inside the wagon, Marian touched the tip of the arrow. It pierced her finger. She said, "Warrick. You were saying?"

Marian ignored the danger. Her compassion gave her courage. She grabbed a bag of unguents. Then she jumped out the wagon door. She squatted to her hands and knees, and darted between Lord Warrick's armored legs. Then she ran back into the tavern and wrapped wounds.

Warrick said, "Morgan. Marian's excess pride overwhelms her caution and reason. Her naive compassion endangers all of us."

Morgan said, "Warrick. Marian is not the problem. Time is our problem. The Wye River valley has so many monasteries and nunneries. Again I hear another Vespers bell that reminds me. Reminds that we must race around those cliffs before nightfall. Because they sound like home, usually canonical bells comfort me. Now they only remind me that we must hurry before sundown. The blizzard and snow clouds will soon bring in night hours before the Compline bells. I hear early Cistercian Compline bells which are three hours before midnight, Vigils bells. Midnight Vigils bells, when the Queen of Witches, Lilith is strongest."

INSIDE THE TAVERN

Inside the tavern, Marian took a large knife from a chopping block. She gave it to the tavern owner. She commanded, "Heat this knife. Then you must cauterize all the wounds that bleed. If you find any arrow heads in them, tell me. We will take them out."

Marian spoke with such force that the owner stiffened like a soldier at attention. Then he said a quick, compliant, "Yes, my lady."

Warrick said, "Morgan, the snow will do a good thing for us. The snow will muffle the sound of our wagon wheels and horses."

Marian's impetuous compassion drove her, in her shredded gown. Marian ran from the tavern's safety to her wagon. She asked, "My lord, when will we stop this endless travel? Nicola is seventeen-years-old, but she is delicate. She must sleep sometime?"

Lord Warrick heard. He chose not to answer.

Warrick strained his eyes to find the enemy. He thought, "Skinwalkers could be behind buildings. The enemy could be in trees, behind rocks. In the tall snow-blown grasses. In snowdrifts, in the shadows."

Marian said, "So, you prefer to insult me. You want to insult me with your silence. What have I done that I deserve an insult? What can I do to undo it? Tell me. What did I do to make you lie to me about our London wedding? Why, O God, have you no mercy in you?"

Warrick thought, "How can we defend ourselves from an ambush on the cliffs?"

Marian glanced behind Warrick to see three small children. Seven-year-old triplets stood barefoot in the snow. Half-frozen, two boys and a little girl. Ice clung to the frayed ends of their ripped clothes. In the places where their clothes were not frozen, they smoldered. All three had snow-covered hair as red and bright as the brightest Vespers sun. Ash covered them.

The two tiny boys bared their baby teeth in a growl. The two boys pointed two broken spear points at Warrick. In unison the two said, "Stay back, we will defend our sister."

In snow, in bare feet, their sister sang to an imaginary doll. A doll that she cradled in her arms.

Otan whispered, "Lord Warrick, in Germany I saw this many times. The small girl is in a world in her mind. She may never come out."

Then the weaver walked over and pointed, "Look. That was their parents' bakery, now burned. The two charred bodies at the center of the bakery. In the ashes are their parents. Hours before you arrived, the triplets watched Wolv murder their parents. Now the triplets have no one."

Morgan said, "Another Vespers bell tolls."

Ross said, "Perhaps the monasteries and nunneries are calling for help from each other."

Morgan said, "I see no smoke in the Wye River valley. Perhaps the tradition here is for them not to toll their canonical bells simultaneously."

Lord Warrick thought, "Drayton's archers . . . where are Drayton's archers?"

Warrick said, "Otan. The triplets are too small for the nunnery. In the nunnery, the other children will not understand the tiny girl. Children can be cruel. They will unintentionally torment the little girl. We must take the three to Rose Fire. The tiny girl will only survive in Rose Fire's hospitaler. We will keep the three together since the two boys will protect their sister."

Marian did not hear Warrick say that he would take the triplets to Rose Fire.

Marian put her hands on her hips, elbows out. She squinted her eyes in determination.   Then Marian snapped, "Lord Merciless. Who will care for the triplets?"

The weaver said, "No one in this village will take them into their home. The tree spirits curse anyone that cares for war orphans. No one in this village will take them into their home."

Morgan said, "Tree spirits. You are druids."

-

-

-

CHAPTER, Where: Now in Wales, Hereford Town to Rose Fire Castle, Wales, Year @ 1250s A.D.

MEMORIES OF HIS FIRST WIFE'S DEATH CRIPPLE HIM. THIS HORRIFIC MEMORY.

Warrick whispered into Otan's ear, "I do not use my own enclosed wagon. Put the triplets in my wagon. Then I want you to put Marian's handmaiden, Collette, in my wagon. Collette can care for the triplets."

Marian did not hear Warrick tell Otan to help the triplets. So she impetuously stepped in front of Otan to approach the triplets. Incredulous that the town would not care for them, Marian shouted, "No one. Not one of you will help these three children? They are freezing. They have ice on their clothing."

Then Marian turned to Warrick. She jabbed her finger at him and said, "And I already know about you. I know that you will not help them."

The two small boys again raised their spear points, this time at Marian. "Stay away," they shouted. "We will defend our sister."

Otan whispered into Warrick's ear, "My lord, should I let Marian care for the triplets?"   Warrick sighed and whispered, "Do I have a choice. Yes, if she is able."

Marian ripped off what was left of her gown. She grabbed their spears and tossed their spears points aside. Then she threw her torn gown over the two boys. Like cats in a sack, the boys struggled. Then she stood clad only in her torn shift, torn to her hip. She held both boys and took them to her warm wagon.

Marian's eyebrows formed an angry V. She commanded a knight, "Grab the little girl."

The knight did not move but only said, "My lord, what shall I do. I cannot obey Lady Marian."

Warrick said, "You are not to obey her."

Warrick pointed to page and said, "Put the fille-child in the wagon. Also, make sure the thick wool sheepskins are tight to the walls, ceiling, and floor. I want you to take more pillows from the storage wagons. Put them into Marian's wagon."

Then Warrick said, "Morgan. Make sure that the Adoration wagon is in the middle of the wagon cavalcade. Otherwise, Wolv's red-fog will eat us."

Warrick put his gauntlets around his face to block the snow. He stared through the blizzard. He stared up the mountainside and searched for Drayton.

Lord Warrick thought, "I have brought Marian into too much danger. Drayton's archers must climb higher than the enemy archers. Otherwise, Marian will be in great danger. We cannot return or Wolv will have time to prepare for the siege. If Drayton's archers do not find Wolv's archers, we cannot go forward to Rose Fire. I was so foolish to bring Marian into such a dangerous territory."

The boys fought until the page placed their sister between them in the wagon. Then the boys saw food, a ham. With ash-covered hands, both boys tore into the ham. The triplets sat beside

Marian's sister, Nicola. Both boys placed food into their sister's mouth. She would chew and swallow what they put in her mouth. Yet, she would sing and cradle an imaginary doll in her arms. She did not reach for food herself.

As she stood at the wagon door, Marian turned to Collette, her handmaiden. "Collette. You are to care for these three."

Marian asked, "Tell me your names?" One boy said, "I am Luchas, my brother is Samuel, and our sister is Greta. I name this ham, delicious, delicious ham."

In the comfortable wagon, as he ate ham, Luchas said, "Wolv did this. I saw Wolv's face. His fire eyes and crumbly black skin, when he killed my parents."

On the wagon's plush floor, the seven-year-old boy stood. He tightened his tiny fist and spoke through his gritted baby teeth. "I will have revenge on Wolv."

Warrick remembered his own childhood under Wolv's boot. "You remind me of someone," Warrick said.

"How old are you, Luchas," Marian asked?

"Seven," Luchas said.

Marian said, "How can a seven-year-old get revenge on Lord Wolv." On the wagon's down pillows, Luchas crawled up to Marian's ear.

He whispered into her ear, "Because . . . I am a thief. . . . A thief can go anywhere."

A knight asked, "My lord. The war-orphan curse, a curse will be upon us if we take in war orphans? It is well known that they weaken knights' resolve to dispatch the enemy in wars. The knights feel sorry for the enemy's children that will be left orphans. Then the knights hesitate a second to strike a fatal blow. They hesitate just long enough for the enemy to land the first blow. We must."

"Forget the orphan-curse, you are a heartless creature," Marian interrupted him. With a long straight arm and forefinger, she pointed at the knight. Her eyebrows formed an angry V as she commanded. "We will take the three orphans with us. You, the one that worries about the orphan curse. You will yourself personally assure their safety."

The knight whispered to another knight, "I was about. About to say that we must take the children to Hereford's nunnery."

Through Warrick's lifted visor, Marian saw Warrick's face, red with anger.

Marian thought, "His emerald eyes look like that will shoot flame and burn me."

The other knights, including Lord Ross, saw Warrick's red face. They stepped back out of the reach of Lord Warrick's powerful arms. All the other knights moved with some effort in their blessed armor. Warrick's blessed armor was thicker, heavier. Yet he moved in it as easily as other men wore a leather blouse. Warrick stepped between Marian and the knight. Then Warrick grasped Marian's upper arm. He led her into the tavern's safety and warmth. Inside where he thought the other knights would not hear.

He led Marian into the warm tavern. He thought, "Marian is in danger. Where are Drayton's archers? Have they cleared Wolv's archers from the cliffs?"

NEVER CONFUSE MY NIGHTS WITH COMMANDS

Warrick demanded, "Marian. You must never confuse my knights with commands. Confusion kills knights. Only a warlord commands knights. Confusion kills knights. You must also always honor their battlefield superstitions. Marian, warlords understand the power of battlefield superstitions. I have defeated huge armies because I have used their superstitions against them. Outside Jerusalem, I once tossed butchered hogs onto a battlefield during the night. The dead hogs caused Moslems to retreat. They believed that Allah would curse them if they touched pork. Some knights will spend many sleepless nights perfecting designs on their blessed armor. Only because they have had victory with those designs. Knights will obsess over a color of cloth to tie to their armor into battle. War twists warriors' minds. Respecting their superstitions is one element that keeps their spirits high. Confusion kills knights."

Warrick's strong tone and angry red face shocked Marian. She stood and looked at him. Fear made her open her eyes until they were round and white.

OUTSIDE ON THE ROAD

In the road, outside the tavern, Morgan put his enormous mace across his armored arms. He said, "Ross. Marian understands nothing about knights and battlefields."

INSIDE THE TAVERN

Inside the warm tavern, to keep from crying, Marian raised her chin. She crossed her arms. Then she rolled her eyes back as if Warrick bored her.

"Look at yourself, your excess pride is dangerous on the battlefield," Warrick said. "You roll your eyes back like a spoiled brat. I should have left you in Oxford. In fact, when I can, I will send you back to Oxford."

Warrick thought, "And then retrieve Marian after the battle."

He should have told her. Told her that after the battle, he would retrieve her from Oxford to Rose Fire. He did not tell her.

Marian thought, "The worst shame on a woman is for her betrothed to reject her. No one will wed me if Warrick sends me back to my parents. If only I could take back my words. I am about to cry. No, I must not cry because I will show weakness. My champion, my groom does not want me."

To keep from crying, she rolled her eyes upward. She held her nose high to hide her sadness.

OUTSIDE ON THE ROAD

Another knight whispered to another knight. "Lady Marian is making it harder and harder for us to protect her."

The knight he whispered to said, "No matter what happens. We remain loyal to Lord Warrick. He wants her protected, so we will protect Marian. We will protect Marian with our lives."

INSIDE THE TAVERN

Though inside the tavern, Marian heard their whispers. Her tears filled her eyes when she heard, "So we will protect Marian. Protect her with our lives."

Quickly, she turned her back to Warrick. With her sleeve, she wiped her eyes before anyone could notice.

Marian thought, "As a child, I had daydreams of knights protecting me. Handsome, armored knights. I dreamed that their shiny armor reflected the sun during the day. Reflected the moon at night. Now my dream has come true. Yet, I have thrown my dream away. Warrick has rejected me."

With her nose held high, Marian walked from the tavern. She stepped into the wagon. She held the door open. Nicola whispered into her ear, "Marian. You still cannot control your temper."

Warrick thought, "To protect Marian, Drayton must notify me. Why has Drayton taken so long to notify me? Where are the signal fires?"

IN THE ROAD

In the road, Lord Warrick whispered, "Ross. What is the probability that Marian will ever obey me?"

With the door open, Marian snapped, "My lord. I heard that. I am not a knight. Not an archer nor a foot soldier. I am to be your wife."

"Marian, my army could defeat any enemy," Warrick said. "If they had weapons as sharp as your tongue."

Ross whispered, "Warrick, the Pendragon curse?"

"Yes," Warrick said.

As she sat on the pillows, in the wagon, Marian said, "I heard that too. Yes, we have too many curses? The curse of a London wedding that will not be. The orphan-curse. Pendragon curses. Battlefield superstition curses. We have curses, what more could a bride ask from a spouse."

FINALLY IN THE WAGON

On her knees, inside the wagon, Marian reached forward, grabbed the door handle. Then she slammed the wagon's iron door shut and locked it. Marian reclined on her back and put her head on Nicola's lap.

She said, "I do not understand Warrick. It seems that everything I do is wrong. He risks his life for me as my champion. Then lies to me about a glorious London wedding. How could he lie about living in London? How could he lie about our London wedding?"

Nicola said, "Marian. I love to read military history. History books record that military deception is very important. The method is to spread false rumors to mislead the enemy."

Marian said, "So our marriage is to be a false rumor. A pawn to deceive the enemy."

Nicola brushed Marian's hair as Marian wiped her tears.

OUTSIDE THE WAGON

Outside the wagon on the road Morgan said, "Triplets. Warrick. You have triplets even before you are wed."

Warrick said, "Yes, I have become an orphanage administrator."

Warrick walked up to the knight that mentioned the orphan-curse. "Do not worry about the orphan-curse," Warrick raised his right eyebrow and said. "Good luck comes from training an orphan to be a page. They can play with the pages and learn their duties. Thus, we can turn a curse into a blessing."

Again Warrick unconsciously raised his right eyebrow and said, "As to the seven-year-old girl. She will become a patient in our infirmarian. Her presence in the infirmarian, the hospitaler, will cancel the orphan-curse. In the infirmarian, blessed objects will surround her and thus cancel the curse. We have solved the problem of the orphan-curse. I want you to go and tell the other knights the solution."

Ross said, "Sending the triplets to the nearest nunnery would be easier."

Warrick said, "The girl will not survive an ordinary orphanage. Ross. I had already decided to take them into Rose Fire. She spoke so fast that I could not tell her. What am I going to do with a woman with so much stubborn pride?"

The blizzard piled snow on the back of the horses and the wagons.

Lord Warrick grasped a knight's arm. "Order the knights to knock the ice from their armor, wagons and horses. The weight will slow us."

Quickly, the knight said, "Yes, my lord." He ran to do Warrick's bidding.

Warrick thought, "Where are Drayton's signal-fires? We must race when Drayton signals that he has cleared the cliffs of

Wolv's archers. I am usually not this foolish. Why was I so foolish to put Marian into such danger?"

Lord Warrick stared at Rose Fire Castle, high in the Black Mountains. Thick red fog circled Rose Fire.

Then the weaver covered his eyes with both hands. He pointed up in the Black Mountains to Rose Fire. "You are not going up to that castle are you," the weaver asked? "My lord, the castle is full of demons, Skinwalkers. Some have seen the Dragon Lilith above Rose Fire. The devil himself possesses Rose Fire. Some have seen Lilith breathe fire. Wolv has impaled live people on flag poles to terrify everyone."

From inside the wagon, Marian said, "Nicola. That was the voice of the weaver. Maybe we are under orders to go to Rose Fire?"

Nicola said, "Marian, how bad are the Black Mountains?"

Marian slid open a visor in the wagon and said, "Warrick. Can you confide in me yet? Are we going to Rose Fire?"

Warrick thought, "Where is Marian's enemy? Marian's enemies are very close. The red fog surrounds Rose Fire."

He walked up to Lord Ross and said, "Ross. From where will the enemy attack?"

Ross said, "Marian had opened the wagon's visor. She said something to you."

Lord Warrick thought, "Where, where, where is Marian's enemy?"

"Ross. The enemy fears us right now because we are unfamiliar to them," Warrick said. "Ross. We can be certain that they will attack after dark."

Lord Ross said, "Brother, may I speak plainly?"

Warrick said, "Ross. I know that enemy archers are on the cliffs, between Rose Fire and us. Why has Drayton not notified us," Warrick said?

"Brother, I repeat," Ross said. "May I speak plainly?"

Warrick said, "No, do not distract me."

"Warrick. We have a moment for distraction," Ross said. "Brother, your mood is as black as your hair and as hard as your armor. We have a moment to breathe now. You must talk to Marian."

Lord Warrick turned and snapped, "Marian. I command you to close the wagon's visor before an arrow enters it."

Inside the wagon, Marian closed the wagon's visor. Then she reclined beside Nicola. As both lay on the thick down pillows, Marian rested her head on Nicola's stomach.

Marian asked, "Please Nicola, would you play with my hair. You always calm me when you play with my hair."

Nicola finger-combed Marian's blond hair. Marian put her arm across Nicola's waist and said, "Little sister, I love you."

"I love you too, Marian," Nicola said. She continued to finger-comb Marian's hair.

Collette sat on her own feet. She pulled Nicola's long chestnut hair from under Nicola's head. While Collette brushed Nicola's hair, Nicola twirled locks of Marian's hair around her forefinger.

"Men that I want will never love me," Marian said.

"Marian," Nicola said. "I have seen Lord Warrick's eyes when he has time to watch you. Your beauty rivets his eyes on you. His duty to protect you and your beauty will affect him. They cause him to see you as his beautiful possession. Then his possessiveness and your beauty will cause him to love you. Beware Marian. You are not prepared for Lord Warrick's intense love, the king's most accomplished champion. His love will devour your reason and melt your will."

Marian asked, "Nicola, you are younger than me. How do you know these things?"

Nicola braided Marian's hair and said, "You were busy with our father's estate. So busy that you never saw where I rode the gelding."

Marian tickled Nicola's knee and said, "You . . . did you? You are only seventeen."

Nicola laughed and said, "I know much more about love than you."

OUTSIDE THE WAGON

Outside the wagon, Ross said, "Warrick. I meant for you to talk to Marian. Not snap off her head."

Warrick thought, "Rose Fire is on a mountain side. I must find a way to siege the castle."

Ross said, "I know that your intention was to protect Marian. Yet, I know something about women."

Warrick snapped, "You should. You have slept with all of them."

"Warrick, listen to me," Ross said. "Marian thinks that you intend to insult and belittle her."

"Ridiculous," Warrick snapped.

Lord Warrick thought, "Ridiculous. My only concern is Marian's safety. Now Marian's safety depends upon Drayton's archers."

"Lord Warrick. Your remark 'ridiculous' is exactly what I mean," Ross said. "We know that you are a battlefield genius. We know that if we obey you, your commands will protect us. Protect us from even our own foolishness. Your warriors know that if we obey you that we are an unbeatable military. Marian does not know. You have never lost a war. Never lost a battle. Never lost a fight. My God, Warrick. Since childhood you have never even lost a chess game. Marian does not know. You have always defeated your opponents. Because you always practiced more, trained more, and studied more. Even without your knights, you tricked, therefore defeated your wife's murderous allies. Every squire in England and the Continent studies how you defeated them with fire. Warrick. We know that you have more determination than any other. You must understand that Marian does not know. One loss, you have only lost once, your heart. Wolv turned Ogina into a traitor and killed Ogina. Brother, your first wife broke your heart. You lost your heart. I fear that she broke your heart into too many pieces. You have blocked Marian from your mind. Because, because deep inside you think Marian will also be a traitor. Marian is only inexperienced."

"Ross," Warrick snapped, "Order the knights to mount. Order them to ride a hundred yards into the forests around the town."

"Brother," Ross said. "Warrick. Listen, you have not heard a word that I said."

"Ross, Go, you are to do as I command," Warrick snapped.

"Yes, my brother," Ross said.

Warrick said, "Wolv burned Ogina."

Ross stopped. He said, "Warrick. I did not know."

Beside Ross, Warrick bent over and threw-up his last meal.

With his gauntlets on his knees, Warrick said, "Traitor or not. Ogina did not deserve to burn. Oh God, Ross, I had a duty to protect Ogina. I could not reach Ogina as she burned."

Warrick again regurgitated.

Then he straightened his back and put his gauntlets over his ears. He gritted his teeth, held his ears, and leaned his head back. "Ross. Every day, all day, Ogina's screams shatter my soul into pieces. She screamed that I forgive her and for me to help her. I could not fight my way to her. Endlessly she screamed for forgiveness. Oh God, forgive me, she screamed for forgiveness for me to help her. I had not trained hard enough. Not trained long enough. I was not strong enough. If I had trained harder, longer, night and day. Then smoke would not have overcome me. Then I could have carried her through the flames. Trial by fire, I failed my trial by fire, Ross. Oh God, I failed. She did not deserve to burn. Her screams have tormented me day and night. I found the scrolls of Ancient Greek fire. I used Greek Fire. Wolv threw her into the Greek fire. She threw a bucket of water over her head. I yelled to her not to use water. She poured the water over her head. The water only caused the Greek Fire on her to spread faster. Greek fire burns water. As she stood and screamed, she turned into a torch. The secret of Greek Fire will die with me. That day I burned the ancient Greek scrolls of how to make Greek fire."

"Warrick," Ross said. "Brother. You have secretly carried this horrible burden. Secretly carried this nightmare, by yourself for all these years?"

Ross thought, "Warrick does not deserve this burden of guilt. Ogina was the most wicked of women."

Warrick lowered his hands from his ears. He snapped, "Ross, why do you delay? Go, do as I commanded, now."

"Immediately," Ross said.

Then Ross' eyes grew round as he thought, "How can Warrick so quickly? So quickly suppress this horrific memory."

Warrick shouted, "We must find Father Malachi Martin. He is supposed to be here with us. Look for him. We need Father Malachi Martin because the Black Mountains are full of Satan worshipers."

-

-

-

CHAPTER,   Where: Now in Hereford Wales, The Wye River Valley, across from Rose Fire Castle, Year @ 1250s A.D.

THE BLACK MOUNTAINS FULL OF SATAN WORSHIPERS
Inside the wagon, with her head on Nicola's stomach, Marian turned on her other side. Nicola lay on her back. This way, with her head on Nicola's stomach, Marian could see Nicola's tilted face.

Marian said, "From Oxford to Hereford, Warrick has said almost nothing to me," Marian said. "His knights do not speak to me. He does not read the works of the ancient Arabs and Greek philosophers. Warrick and I have nothing in common."

Collette brushed rose oils into Nicola's hair. Nicola continued to braid Marian's hair.

Marian said, "Warrick is a huge, brooding man. Always dressed in black leathers and black padding and cold, polished armor. He lied about our London wedding. I do not understand him. He never sleeps. Warrick gallops on that huge warhorse, Zeus, or else he sharpens his battle ax, Dread."

OUTSIDE THE WAGON
Outside Marian's wagon, on the cobblestone road, Warrick said, "Morgan. Have you seen any signal-fires? From the mountainside that Drayton has tried to contact us?"

Morgan shook his head 'No'.

Warrick though, "I cannot protect Marian if Drayton. Cannot unless Drayton defeats the archers above the cliffs."

Warrick said, "Morgan. Tell the knights to stop knocking the snow from their armor, wagons, and horses. The snow's weight will slow us. Yet, in this blizzard the snow will also camouflage us. Go. Now. Go. You must tell everyone to leave the snow and ice on everything. We need camouflage more than we need speed. Especially if Drayton does eliminate Wolv's archers on the cliffs."

INSIDE THE WARM WAGON

Inside the warm wagon, Nicola brushed Marian's hair. She said, "I am younger than you, only seventeen. Nevertheless, I am so much wiser. Lord Warrick has military reasons for saying that we were headed for London."

Marian said, "His purpose is to prepare me for a marriage of frustration and disappointments."

Nicola said, "It is one of a woman's worst disappointments. I know. He does not understand your need for him to cherish you. Yet, I see in his eyes that your beauty has captured him. You do not understand his warlord thinking and emotions. If you both are patient, you will come to love each other. Remember, what I told you. A knight's instinct to protect always turns into possessiveness, then into love. For now, he is constantly trying to predict a Skinwalker attack upon you. For now he is trying to protect you. Marian, you have never been in an area at war. The enemy can be around the next bend in the road. They can drop from the trees. Or they could shoot arrows at us from places we cannot see. This is why Lord Warrick's knights now constantly wear blessed armor. I read war history. Our father has a wonderful library. This road is the key to the defense of the Wye River valley."

OUTSIDE THE WAGON

Outside the wagon, Lord Warrick said, "Morgan. We must buy supplies. Buy anything and everything the village has to sell."

INSIDE THE WAGON

Inside the wagon, Marian said, "Nicola. How can Lord Warrick bring you into such a place? A place full of war and superstitious ignorance?"

An arrow thudded into the building beside Lord Warrick.

-

-

-

CHAPTER, Now in Wales, Hereford Wales to Rose Fire Castle, Wales, Year @ 1250s A.D.

RACE AROUND THE DANGEROUS CLIFFS. THE SIEGE BEGINS.

Warrick pulled the arrow from the wall and opened a note wrapped around it.

He shouted, "Drayton's note says to ride hard. Now. Ross! Morgan! Everyone! Mount your warhorses. We must move. Mount the wagons. This note says that Drayton's archers have slain many enemy archers. Drayton's archers will give us cover. Now while we have daylight to see the road, we must ride fast. Now. We must ride now. Ride while the blizzard camouflages us. Ride now while the snow muffles our wagons and horses."

Warrick mounted Zeus. Zeus reared. Then Warrick shouted, "Morgan. I want you to lead everyone through the pass. Now! Gallop quickly between the upper and lower cliffs."

Zeus reared and pranced in place. Warrick's cavalcade thundered beside him. Warrick shouted, "Faster, faster, we have only a few minutes of daylight."

Lord Warrick pointed to a group of his pages. "Now we know that the enemy will not attack the town. Gather the wounded. Bind their wounds then follow us."

Warrick galloped behind his cavalcade.

As he galloped Warrick thought, "The snow is so deep. Deep enough snow that I cannot hear the horses' hooves or the wagon wheels. Good. Good. The deep snow does muffle the horse's spiked hooves and wagon wheels. The blizzard and snow on the wagons, horses, and knights camouflage them."

Warrick said, "Ross, I hear the thud of arrows."

Ross said, "Warrick. You must look up at the top of the cliff. I can see Skinwalkers fall from the top of the cliff. Drayton is shooting Wolv's archers."

"Ross. No one has attacked the cavalcade," Warrick said.

Ross said, "Look along the road. At least a hundred Skinwalker archers lay with blessed arrows in their backs."

Warrick said, "The blizzard is too thick for anyone in Rose Fire to see us."

While Morgan led them, they raced around the cliffs. They came to open fields on both sides of the road. Now the cavalcade's full length had open fields on both sides. Morgan raised his hand and gave the signal to slow the cavalcade to a gallop. Then in the west the sun suddenly lowered behind the Black Mountains. In the Black Mountains' shadows, no moon, no stars. In a blizzard, black night engulfed them. Red fog came up to their ankles. Their Adoration wagon chased away the red-fog.

Morgan turned, raised his hand and shouted, "Hold. Stop. We must wait for the archers. They are on foot."

Ross galloped the length of the cavalcade. His warhorse pranced in place beside Morgan's warhorse. Morgan's warhorse raised his head high. Then to the ground as it blasted the air with its steamy breath.

Ross said, "Morgan. Warrick will be with us in a minute. He could not have timed racing around the cliffs at a better time. On the cliff's other side we had the daylight we needed to see the road. Now we have the night, so Wolv cannot see us."

Morgan said, "I thank God that Warrick is a military genius."

Ross said, "Morgan. Listen. I hear another Wye Valley church toll for Vespers prayers."

Morgan said, "Nobody in the valley will know the correct time of day. The churches, monasteries, and nunneries do not coordinate their canonical hours."

Ross pointed and said, "Morgan, you must hold longer. Look at the other end of the cavalcade. I can see Drayton and his archers mount their horses."

Drayton galloped up to Lord Warrick.

Drayton said, "The archers were Wolv's Skinwalkers. They will never bother us again. One Skinwalker said Wolv arrived before us and is in the castle. He said Wolv rode all the way to London expecting the London wedding. He refused exorcism so I decapitated him. We burned their heads. Before he died, he also said that Wolv is totally unprepared for a siege."

Warrick said, "Do you believe him?"

Drayton said, "We will wait and see. Skinwalkers are so arrogant that they often say the truth."

Warrick said, "Wolv rode here faster than us because he had no wagons to pull."

Drayton said, "The night and blizzard hide us from Wolv's view. We are lucky the deep snow muffles the horses' hooves and wagon wheels."

Lord Warrick said, "Morgan. Never cease Perpetual Adoration. Make sure that everyone does their hour of Perpetual Adoration. In the Adoration wagon, Perpetual Adoration of Jesus' Real Presence in the Blessed Sacrament. Make sure everyone does weekly confession. Contemplate the screams you have heard of all those that the red-fog has eaten. Never let yourself forget, only Adoration and weekly confession can keep the red-fog away."

The column continued at a determined gallop.

The Adoration wagon destroyed the red-fog.

Ross pointed, "Warrick. Far in the distance. High on the red-fog-covered Black Mountains, that is your castle. Even in this blackest night, Rose Fire glows. During the day the sun gives the castle the color of flaming rose pedals."

As he turned to his brothers, Warrick said, "Ross. Drayton. Morgan. I want you to ride beside me, so that I can talk to you."

His brothers reined in parallel to him.

Ross said, "No one has even sounded Rose Fire's warning bells."

Warrick said, "I know Wolv and his Skinwalkers. If they have not seen or heard us by now, they are all drunk. The Skinwalkers talk with Wolv by thought. Wolv is probably too drunk to listen to their thoughts. Drunk in the castle's great hall. So we are safe enough for Marian to step from her warm wagon. Otan, I want you to find Marian's mail and blessed armor. Dress Marian in her mail and blessed armor."

Squire Otan reined back on his warhorse. His horse pivoted on its hind legs. Then he galloped to the back of the cavalcade. Within a minute, Otan and the blacksmith rode up to Marian's warm, armored wagon.

Otan rapped the iron wagon door with his knuckles.

Marian slid open the wagon's visor slot and snapped, "Warrick. What do you want to chide me for now?"

"Lord Warrick is not here," Otan said. "My lord wants you to dress in your mail and blessed armor. Then he wants you to mount a warhorse and ride beside him."

The smith said, "My lady, I have not yet finished your personal mail and armor. For now, you can wear this squire armor."

They strapped the warm padding, mail and armor on her torso, arms, head and legs.

Otan and the smith helped Marian, in full armor, mount a warhorse. They placed a cowled white-rabbit fur cloak on her. Then they clasped it down the front.

Otan held the reins and led Marian's warhorse to Warrick. Lord Warrick turned to her and looked deep into her eyes. Their eyes locked on one another. Even with all their conflict, her heart skipped a beat in expectation. She felt as if his gaze entered her eyes and flowed down into her body. She felt as if he could read her every thought.

Under Warrick's lifted, visor, a smile formed on his lips.

Lady Marian felt her cheeks redden and grow hotter.

With lust in their eyes, suitors had looked at her. She had never returned the same gaze. No man had ever made her feel so full. Marian could not pull her eyes away from his. Also, she did not know the source within herself of these feelings. He was the mystery of her future. His mysterious emerald eyes seemed to pierce through her body. Pierce her soul. Marian could not lower her gaze away from this mysterious man. She felt as if he read her mind. Her thoughts were her sacred secret hiding places, her fantasies, her secret treasures. Now she felt he could invade all her secrets with one look. Now she resented his overwhelming handsomeness. Resented those piercing emerald eyes, because they robbed her of her privacy. Simultaneously she resented and loved his piercing emerald eyes. They invaded her privacy. Yet they filled her with a passion she had never known. Also, she savored the unfamiliar hot tingle as her heart raced.

Warrick thought, "Marian's beauty burns into my mind. I will see her beauty and smell her lilac and apple-blossom fragrance in my dreams."

As she stared at Warrick's handsomeness she suddenly thought, "I am with strangers. None of these men know Nicola or me. I do not know one of them. Can I trust them, no, I do not know them? So I cannot trust them? Anyway, Warrick will send me back in shame which will ruin my life. No other lord will ever want me. Never want me when they learn that another lord rejected me and sent me home."

Marian looked down. Her eyes near closed. The corners of her mouth drooped in sadness. Even her shoulders slightly lowered from her normal, proud, straight-back.

Warrick said, "Marian. In this blizzard your enemy cannot see or hear us. You are safe, even this close to the castle. Inside the castle your enemies are drunk and asleep."

Marian did not look up. Warrick commanded, "Marian, You must look at me. You are sad and ill at ease. In this hostile land with strangers, you are unsure of yourself. "

He became serious. He said, "Look at me. Marian."

Back, moonless, starless night.

Marian turned her blue eyes to meet his emerald eyes. As she frowned, she raised her eyebrows in an inverted V of confusion.

He said, "Marian, who is your champion?"

Marian smiled. She said, "You are, my lord."

Warrick said, "I want you to know that I will always be your champion."

Lady Marian did not look up.

Warrick said, "You are still sad. Apparently Marian, you do not know. Do not know what it means to have a champion. Do you?"

Marian continued to frown, her chin to her chest. She looked at the mane of her horse.

"Champions have the duty to protect their charges, "Warrick said. "The duty to guarantee . . . their happiness."

As they rode, then Marian smiled, and her eyes twinkled. Then she looked at him and said, "Guarantee my happiness?"

"Of course," Warrick said.

Marian grinned and said, "So your duty to champion me gives me power over you."

"Of course," Warrick smiled and said.

She raised her nose and snapped, "I have power over you."

Then she frowned and lowered her head, "Power over you, if I obey you. Or you will lock me in my keep?"

"Locked in your keep of course," Warrick said.

Marian snapped, "For years my father has been bed ridden. I served as the lord of his massive lordship. I commanded his knights, farmers, blacksmiths, and stonemasons. Alone, I developed a granite quarry on land that I purchased. As a tall, determined woman, I ran his vineyards, orchards, and smokehouses. While other young women braided their hair and waited for husbands, I created businesses. I created and managed taverns, warehouses and stores from London to Oxford. Alone, I created and managed lumber mills. My workers sold lumber from

Norway to Italy. By myself, I also created and ran smelters and sold iron bars for construction. My smelters manufactured and sold copper nails to every shipyard in England and Europe. Originally my father had only orchards and vineyards. Alone, alone I created the iron and copper smelters, the granite quarry. By myself I managed the smokehouses, taverns, warehouses, and stores from London to Oxford. I created the lumber mills. Alone, I wrote shipbuilders all over Europe and sold them lumber and copper nails. I suppose that you will take this all away from me."

"Of course," Warrick said. "Lady, I, I, I, I. Can you refer to yourself more times?"

" I, I, I, I, I, I, I, I, I, I." Marian snapped.

Warrick said, "Lady 'I, I, I, I, I, I.' You need to come close to me. I, I, I, I have much to tell you, you, you. Now that we are at Rose Fire."

Lord Warrick reached out and with his gauntlet, he grasped her horse's reins. He pulled her warhorse beside Zeus.

Then he flipped her visor shut.

Warrick said, "Marian. Now, we will know that an arrow will not hit your disobedient little head."

Marian said, "I cannot turn my disobedient little head, or lift my disobedient little arms."

Warrick threw his head back and guffawed. His laughter pierced the blizzard and echoed off the Black Mountains.

Morgan said, "More laughter as loud as that will tell Wolv that we are here."

Marian leaned over to Warrick and whispered, "So . . . the great Lord Warrick also makes mistakes."

"Of course I, I, I, I, I make mistakes." With his visor up, Warrick smiled.

Warrick commanded, "Morgan. Keep the cavalcade moving at a trot. We must not stop until we encamp on the knoll opposite Rose Fire."

Morgan said, "Yes my brother. As always, your word is my command."

Marian raised her visor. She smiled.

Warrick said, "Marian. Even in the darkest night, your face beams. Beams like the last pink rays of a sunset. Your face is as beautiful as your tongue is sharp."

Warrick smiled.

She said, "I do not understand you. I will never understand you. In the same breath you raise me to the joys of Heaven and insult me."

Warrick said, "Now I can confide in you. You will become the Lady of Rose Fire. The Lady over a wide and rich land, the Wye Valley. The Wye lordship is much larger than the Moray lordship. First we must siege Wolv out of the castle. This is why I could not tell you until now. Also, I had to be careful that the enemy did not know our destination. This is why I had to tell everyone that we were going to London. To London for our wedding. You need to understand and immediately to grow in knowledge and wisdom."

Marian raised her head and said, "Huuuu, you think you are wiser than I."

"The correct English is 'than me'," Warrick said.

Marian said, "Oooooooo. Will you never stop your insults?"

Warrick said, "Wolv has rebelled against the English king. He has captured Rose Fire. We go to take it from the Skinwalkers and make it our home. I could not tell you until now, but secret Skinwalkers also advise the king himself. I had to come here without the king's knowledge. His treasonous war planners would have betrayed us."

Marian asked, "That is why we left Oxford like thieves in the night."

Warrick said, "Yes. Marian. We had to leave Oxford unbeknownst to anyone in the king's court."

On the back of her warhorse, Marian said, "You call the king a traitor?"

Warrick said, "No. Skinwalkers are in the king's war planning chamber. They can take any form, any human, any animal. Spies have the king's confidence and friendship. Convincing the king that a spy is close to his heart is difficult. He is excessively loyal to his advisors, unless betrayal is very evident."

Marian thought, "I will always remember. Remember that Warrick treated our marriage as a war planning pawn."

THE BATTLEFIELD KNOLL

In the blinding blizzard and black night, Warrick pointed to a knoll. His cavalcade climbed to the level top of the knoll. Under cover of the moonless night, Lord Warrick silently camped on the high rock knoll. The knoll was safe distance from Rose Fire. Also, the knoll matched in height and width of Rose Fire's rock knoll foundation.

On back of Zeus, Warrick commanded to his knights, squire, and pages, "Now. You must take buckets to the mountain stream beside us. On the knoll's sides, I want you now to pour hundreds of buckets of water. You must pour water over the knoll's sides every night all night."

Warrick said, "Drayton. You must search for Father Malachi Martin. Father Malachi is supposed to be here."

Then Warrick said, "Otan, where are you?"

From behind Warrick, on his own warhorse, Otan snapped, "Here."

On Zeus, Warrick twisted backward and said, "Find Morgan, Now."

Through the blizzard, Morgan said, "Here. Warrick, what is your command?"

"Morgan, take the many tents out of the extra wagons. You must raise hundreds of extra tents," Warrick commanded. "Now. "While the blizzard hides us in the darkness and the snow muffles our noise. We must trick Wolv. We must trick Wolv to think that we have over a thousand warriors. After you put up the tents, you must light many more campfires. One campfire for every twenty-five tents. I want Wolv to howl in panic when he sees us. We must make him believe that we would defeat him if his Skinwalkers attacked us. Otherwise he would storm from the castle and defeat us. Hopefully he will wait and expect us to storm Rose Fire's battlements. I need Wolv to keep his Skinwalkers and mercenaries in the castle. In the castle until they consume all their firewood and food. Then hunger and cold will drive his Skinwalkers into madness when they do attack us. Wolv must believe that we have more than a thousand warriors. Also, I repeat. Order all the squires and pages to pour buckets of water over this knoll's sides."

Warrick thought, "If the water freezes, protecting Marian will be easier."

As Marian rode her warhorse, it broke through the hard packed snow. It sunk to its knees.

"Why pour water everywhere," Marian asked?

Warrick reached down from Zeus and grasped the bridle of Marian's horse. He snapped, "Marian. Never question me. You are only to obey. Everyone is to obey. Never ask why."

Marian's eyebrows formed an angry V as she snapped, "Why? Why? Why? . . . Why? Whyyyyy? Whyyyyyyyy?"

Marian's horse raised its legs high to walk in the deep snow. She said, "Why? Why, why, why must you always insult me?"

Warrick said, "Why, whyyyyyy, whyyyyyyyyyy must beauty always be obstinate and disobedient?"

With her hands on the reins, Marian said, "Obey. Obey. Obedience. You only think about obedience. Hummmmmmmphta."

Warrick thought, "I must make the battlefield safe for Marian."

For many minutes, Warrick stood in his stirrups and pointed to his many warriors. He ordered them to their duties. While Warrick directed the camp's construction, Marian sighed and calmed.

Warrick ordered, "Drayton. Put the Adoration wagon in the middle of the camp to drive off the red-fog. Never stop Adoration in the wagon. Bring me records of everyone that did not do Adoration or weekly confession."

Marian said, "Never have I seen such a beautiful castle. It glows even on this moonless night. In the blinding blizzard, the pink granite walls gleam as bright as a full moon. Never have I seen so many spires and so tall. The king gave you this . . . this beautiful castle?"

Warrick said, "No, to you and me. The king gave this beautiful castle to you and me. I had hoped for Rose Fire. No other castle in England is as majestic. Rose Fire's beauty is legendary. Legendary for inspiring honor, courage, and chivalry."

Marian said, "I am to live in a fairytale-like castle?"

Warrick ordered, "Throw buckets of water over the knoll's sides. More."

Warrick said, "Yes. Marian. Many say that it is the most beautiful castle in perhaps the known world."

Zeus reared to a noise on the mountainside. Warrick turned to the noise. He squinted and strained his eyes to see into the forest above him.

"Ross, one man comes," Warrick shouted "You must alert the others."

An old man in antlers walked from under the trees.

Lord Warrick said, "Druod. Finally, Father Malachi Martin, you arrived. Did you see the Skinwalkers enter Rose Fire?"

Father Malachi said, "Of course, Warrick."

Warrick said, "Malachi. Stay disguised as a druid. Fewer people will want to kill you."

Warrick asked, "How many are there in the castle?"

Father Malachi said, "Many more times than the castle can support."

Lord Warrick asked, "How many exactly does he have?"

"My lord, Wolv leads them," said Malachi. He pulled his deer-skull-hat down on his head. Then he tightened the deer hides around his shoulders.

His deer hides blew in the blizzard. Father Malachi Martin said, "Lord Warrick. Wolv is very crafty. He may have a thousand Skinwalkers and five hundred warhorses. The AntiChrist may have as few as five hundred Skinwalkers and a hundred horses. No matter which, they have too many in Rose Fire. They will soon fight among themselves for food and warm places to sleep. I can hear the horses kick and bite each other for room in the stables."

Father Malachi tightened his deer hides and said. "They are hexed with drunkenness and gluttony. My lord, I am too weak. Too frozen."

Warrick led Father Malachi beside a blazing campfire. He said, "Old Friend. Warm yourself."

Lord Warrick said, "Reque. Find thick cloaks. Throw them over him and his antlers. Otherwise, he will freeze. Bring him a hot bowl of deer stew. Then dress Father Malachi in armor padding and blessed armor, under his druid disguise."

As Warrick turned, he said, "Otan. Order the other squires and pages to put the pine-tar caldrons on the campfires."

Otan said, "Yes, my lord." He ran to the pages and other squires.

Warrick turned to Drayton and pointed to Rose Fire's far side. "Drayton. On the other side of the castle. You must put twenty archers high in the forest. I want you to station them out of bow shot from the castle. On Rose Fire's other side, you must put them along that mountain stream. Station them behind trees. They are to shoot any Skinwalker from the castle that goes to it for water. Rose Fire has two mountain streams, one on each side. If we keep the Skinwalkers from both streams, thirst will push them into madness. Rose Fire's seepage well cannot supply water for everyone in the castle."

Warrick reached up and lifted Marian by the waist from her war horse. He placed her on the ground beside himself.

She stood beside Warrick. Then Marian said, "My lord. They have plenty of water. They have a well."

Marian held the reins of her warhorse. Then Warrick opened his saddlebag. He rolled out old diagrams of Rose Fire.

He pointed at the diagrams and said, "Marian. Look at the capacity of the seepage well. By these records it takes one week for the well to refill. They do not have enough water, nor food nor hay for the Skinwalkers. The horses do not have enough hay in the castle. The Skinwalkers will eat each other before they starve."

Lord Warrick put his hands on his hips, "We arrived much sooner than they expected. Wolv has spies in the king's court. The king ordered me to come here in two months or later. So Wolv knew, therefore he has obviously waited to prepare the castle for the siege. They expected a siege in warmer weather. Warmer weather when they would not be concerned with firewood for warmth. As to weather, the valley is springtime. Yet, here, high in the mountains, we have our strongest ally, Wales' coldest mountain weather. Mountains so tall they create their own weather. We are deep in show. They expected to be able to stock up with water from the two mountain streams. Now that shallow seepage well will not supply enough water. I am positive that they do not have enough firewood for a snowfall-weather siege. They probably do not have enough food stored either. That is why we will defeat Wolv and his Skinwalkers."

Marian asked, "Are you not concerned that you disobeyed the king? You came here at least two months before he commanded."

Warrick said, "Marian. King Edward loves victory more than blind obedience. He expects his generals to take the initiative."

Drayton and his twenty archers walked up to Warrick. Drayton said, "Warrick. We are ready per your commands."

Warrick said, "I will repeat." While Warrick pointed to the mountain stream on Rose Fire's other side, he said, "Drayton. I repeat. Station twenty archers in three shifts. Station them on the far side of that mountain stream. We now have the cover of darkness. Dress them in extra sheepskins so they will not become frostbitten. White sheepskin will camouflage them. They are to shoot and decapitate any Skinwalker that comes for water. Also, shoot and behead any Skinwalker that goes out to hunt. I repeat. Tell your archers always to stay behind thick trees. The enemy's horses will collapse from thirst. Then they will shoot all their arrows to try to kill your archers."

He looked at Marian's beautiful face.

He thought, "Her beauty magically affects me. Just as Ogina's beauty also distracted me. Beauty is a poison that I must again drink."

Warrick shouted, "Throw buckets of water over the knoll's sides. More."

-

-

-

CHAPTER, Now on the Knoll Across From Rose Fire, Wales, Year @ 1250s A.D.

THE TRAITOR

Marian raised her visor. Her bright sexy innocent eyes filled his vision. Her long eye lashes brushed the air. High arched eyebrows and eyelashes framed her beautiful blue eyes. He wanted to reach out and touch her cameo forehead. Touch her gently curved jaw, ruby lips, and her straight nose. When he had a reprieve from war, her beauty would enchant him. Her beauty filled him with happiness and well being. If they could stay together, her beauty would conquer him.

He thought, "Why did the king betroth her to me? The image of her face stalks my mind. Marian's beauty enters my vision and incapacitates me at the most inopportune time."

To come back to reality, he blinked his eyes.

He took Marian's arm. Then he walked her to a large campfire.

He said, "Marian. Listen. Hear the ruckus from the castle. They have so many mounted Skinwalkers that they have too many horses in their stables. The horses have so little room that they are unable to separate themselves. They bite and kick each other for room and for hay. This will work to our advantage. When they attack us, their horses will already have wounded and exhausted each other."

Marian asked, "We prepare to attack in the morn, at Prime bells?"

Warrick said, "No. They have many more Skinwalkers than we do. Also, from the sound of their stables, many more horses."

He pointed, "See. The horses have trampled the snow and torn the grass in all directions. In all directions toward the drawbridge. Only hundreds of war horses could churn so much grass into mud. Besides, with this snowstorm, snow should be on the ground when they attack us. Now, in a charge, the snow and the freezing weather would be our enemy. We would have to charge through the snow, down this slope. Then run across the ravine. Then charge up the other ravine-slope and across their practice field. We would slip and slide on the snow. By the time we got to Rose Fire we would be too tired. The castle is on a large stone knoll. We cannot breach or climb it without great loss of life. The moat is deep and freezing. If our warriors fall into it, they will simply freeze."

Marian said, "My lord, may I have my leave to go back to the wagon?"

Warrick said, "Of course. Why do you ask?"

Marian looked around to make sure nobody could hear them.

She said, "Because, my lord, I do not understand you. As my champion, twice in one day you fought unto the death to protect me. I love the part of you that is my champion. As my betrothed warlord, you are merciless. I find that you leave the wounded on the battlefield to bleed to death. You insult me with your silence. You even lied about the place of our wedding and where we would live. With your own words you said that you had many trollops in bed at once."

She put her hands on his chest.

She said, "I love you as my champion. I wish to live with you as my champion. Yet, I fear the warlord in you. The part of you that is the warlord is heartless, insulting, lying, and . . . and . . . unfaithful."

Warrick thought, "She completely misunderstands the honor of a warlord. An honorable warlord would do none of those things. After my first wife murdered my command, I swore never again. I swore I would never again hope for happiness. I want only the honor that comes from duty."

Then Warrick said exactly the wrong words. He should have told her that she was beautiful.

Instead, he said, "Marian. I am one person. My actions define me. Your champion, your betrothed, and your warlord are all the same. Me."

Marian incorrectly thought, "With his own words Warrick confirms. Confirms that he insults me, is heartless, a liar, and unfaithful. My champion has my heart, forever in his unfaithful hands."

Lady Marian lowered her head in disappointment.

Marian walked back to her wagon.

THE TRAITOR

The traitor Lady Blanche walked over to Warrick.

To deceive Warrick about her nature she said, "My lord. You will need to put more fur lining in Marian's wagon. More fur lining and more hot stones. Marian and Nicola are not accustomed to such cold."

Warrick said, "Compassionate Blanche. You are always ready to help everyone. You will be a great help to Marian. Blanche, you must go back to your wagon."

Blanche lowered her head so Warrick could not see her scowl. Her eyebrows formed an angry V. She walked back to her warm, luxurious wagon.

THE CHAMPION'S THOUGHTS
"I want Marian," Warrick thought, "my betrothed. I want Blanche to go away."

Warrick ordered, "Throw buckets of water over the knoll's sides. More."

TO SEDUCE A HEART BROKEN WARRIOR
Inside Marian's wagon Nicola brushed Marian's hair.

Nicola said, "Marian. I heard everything that you and Warrick said to each other. You know very little about Warrick. You need just to be quiet with him. Just spend a long time looking into his eyes and say nothing. Just walking up to him and hold his hand."

Marian paused for a moment and said, "Nicola, you are only seventeen. How do you know of such things?"

Nicola laughed, "Because . . ." Nicola rolled her eyes upward and to the side as she laughed.

Marian said, "Nicola. You are such a petulant little prodigy. Where did you get your wisdom about romance?"

Nicola brushed Marian's hair in long gentle strokes, "I have beaus. I read the Arabic love stories. Also, I watch women like you make fools of themselves."

Marian pushed herself from her sister and said, "Go away."

Collette said, "Nicola is seventeen-years-old going on forty-five-years-old. Marian. You know that the King's ladies-in-waiting ask Nicola for advice about love."

Marian rolled her lower lip out in a pout. She again rested her head on her sister's lap. Nicola again brushed Marian's hair in long strokes.

Nicola said, "The Arabian love stories. They tell that the beginning of love is in the eyes. Love begins in long lonely looks. They say, 'Come hither. You frighten me, but I want you to come hither. I want to taste your kisses and lose myself in your embraces.' This is why the Arabians make their women cover their eyes. Your power is in your eyes not in your words."

Marian said, "My lord's power is in his emerald eyes. He can see through me, all my secrets. He can peer down into the depths of my soul. His emerald eyes take away that last place of privacy, my thoughts. He can see what I think about. What I know and do not know. Sometimes I think his emerald eyes are the Devil's eyes. Sometime I think they are the eyes of an angel."

Nicola put wine and venison before Marian.

She said, "Sister. You need to eat first. Then make your eyes soft, a soft face, with a slight smile. Look into his eyes. Then make your eyes say, 'Come hither.'"

Marian said, "What! What! Where did you learn such language?"

Nicola said, "Arabian poetry and love stories, like I said. I have many beaus in Oxford."

Marian said, "Who else have you told this?"

Nicola said, "Do you remember Dally. She was our homely supervisor of servants that left us. Left us to marry that rich, handsome Duke? I taught her the look."

Marian said, "Nicola. Our father was really upset with you because she left. Dally ran the household."

Then Nicola said, "Yes, Dally was unbecoming. Yet, I taught her the come-hither-look. All she needed was the trap. The trap of the 'Come-Hither' look and she got her man. I taught her how to be charming. How to flirt, to praise everything a man does and says. She already knew how to pretend to obey. Charm will capture a good man's heart. Then, after your charms trap him in marriage, you can be disobedient."

They laughed and giggled.

Marian ate venison then drank wine from a bottle. The three of them drank too much.

The triplets slept in a corner.

Look into my eyes and think, "What is in Warrick's mind."

Collette began to laugh. They giggled like they did when they were in their father's house. All the worries were outside the warm wagon's walls. They were safe and comfortable inside.

Their giggles seemed uncontrollable. Marian spilt wine.

Lord Warrick's warriors were doing their duties. So they could not hear the laughter from Marian's wagon.

Warrick, Ross, Morgan, and Drayton stood beside the wagon.

The laughter from within the wagon pierced the night.

Drayton held his bow to his chest. He asked, "What in God's feet is going on in there?"

They heard the three young women talk in unison and laugh and giggle.

Their laughter infected those outside the wagon. Ross, Drayton and Morgan laughed and looked at Warrick. Lord Warrick smiled. His smile grew wider. He began to laugh. The four warriors roared in infectious laughter.

Warrick ordered, "Throw buckets of water over the knoll's sides. More."

-

-

-

CHAPTER, Now on the Knoll Across From Rose Fire, in Wales' Black Mountains, Year @ 1250s A.D.

THE LADY'S SMILES KILL ME, OR A SNAP OF HER SHARP TONGUE.

IN ROSE FIRE

Inside Rose Fire, Wolv heard Warrick's laughter echo off the Black Mountains. Wolv's black aura radiated from him. Red fog and things in the red fog poured from him. The red fog and shapeless-things in the red fog filled Rose Fire.

Gulum said, "Lord Wolv, Warrick and his knights are in high spirits. His knights will be hard to battle."

The AntiChrist ground his teeth. He growled, "I will have Marian. Even if I must walk over the bodies of all my Skinwalkers."

OUT ON THE BATTLEFIELD

Out on the battlefield, Warrick said, "Otan. Order the squires and pages to put more pine tar into the caldrons. You must assure that the tar boils always."

Then Otan snapped, "Yes my lord." Like a rabbit, Otan ran to do as commanded.

Then Warrick turned and asked, "Ross. May I ask you for some personal advice?"

Ross said, "Yes, but it must be a question that only a 'cuckolder' can answer. Questions that only Ross the Rake can answer."

The four of them laughed.

Warrick said. "Ross. I no longer want nor know how to romance a wife. The snake, marriage, bit me once. I do not want another dose of poison."

Warrick looked up in the sky and sighed. "The king demands that I marry Marian. By his order I am supposed to love her, whatever love means. Love, . . . Ogina guaranteed that I do not want, nor know how, to love a wife. I just want Marian to be obedient. Obedience, I do not know how to seduce her into obedience?"

Ross said, "Warrick. Nor do I. Yet. I do know how to seduce. However, I do not know how to romance for marriage. I only want eyes that wink and warm, wet thighs."

Morgan leaned on his mace and said, "Ross, I am a Catholic priest. Yet, more talk like that and I will want your women."

The four laughed.

Warrick asked, "How do I seduce her into obedience?"

Ross said, "You must accept the advice of a rascal and a rake."

Warrick said, "Yes."

They laughed.

Ross said, "Warrick. If you want a woman's wet thighs, first see a smile on her eyes. If you want a woman naked in your bath, first seduce her to laugh."

Ross paused and said, "Warrick. I can tell you how to get into her shift. No one can tell you how to make her obedient."

Drayton tested his bow and said, "Ross. Every page knows that."

Morgan took off his gauntlet and glove. He said, "Warrick. You have two curses. First, warriors make very lousy husbands. Second the family curse, the Pendragon curse. Marriage is always bad luck for warriors."

Warrick said, "Yes, bad luck."

Drayton unsheathed his blessed sword. He put his foot up on a stump and rested his sword across his knee. Then he ran a sandstone along its length to sharpen it.

Drayton said, "Warrick. Never respond with anger to her angry remarks. We uprooted her from everything that she has known. Marian ran the largest, most efficient, wealthiest lordship in all of Oxford and London. She commanded hundreds of vassals, and here she feels like a vassal. She thinks that you wish only to marry her because the king ordered it. To her, a marriage-nest is like that vast Oxford estate she managed. She is an extraordinary woman."

Drayton smiled at Warrick and said, "Perhaps. Perhaps she is more than you can handle."

Warrick said, "I have defeated many Skinwalkers by myself. Yet Marian can slay me. Slay me with but a smile or a snap of her sharp tongue."

His three brothers laughed.

Ross said, "When women marry, they nest. No two women nest the same. Some brides nest only in their private chambers. Some brides demand that the whole castle's interior become their nest. Marian is headstrong. She will demand the most, that the whole lordship, will become her nest. Marian will make the whole Wye Valley lordship her nest. Unlike other brides, Marian will build many enterprises in the Wye Valley. I can give you no guidance about Marian. Marian is just the opposite of my women. My women are already married and want an intriguing tryst. She is the type of woman that I absolutely avoid. Because, because she will love once and only once. Beware Warrick. She will never obey. In Moray, she has tasted independence. Marian wants a life of independence, disobedience and romance. You may conquer her enemies, but you will never conquer her disobedience. I know nothing about women like Marian."

Morgan said, "Ross. For a man that knows nothing about virtuous women, you just gave a long lecture. You should marry Marian, not Warrick."

Ross raised his hands over his head and said, "Oh God no. I would have to give up all the women that I already have, oh no."

The four brothers guffawed.

Ross said, "Anyway, no man can conquer Marian's disobedience."

Warrick said, "To honor the king's command, I must conquer my wish not to marry. Perhaps, . . . hopefully, . . . she does not want to marry. Yet, our duty is to marry and be faithful administrators for the king."

Morgan put the heavy end of his huge mace on the ground. He rested his wrists on the hilt. He said, "Brother, you should not be angry with her anymore. She acts according to her nature and is only trying to do right. She will learn how to administer Rose Fire with you."

"Marian must learn quickly," Warrick said. "We are in dangerous surroundings. You can hear that she is drunk now."

Warrick said, "Drayton. Morgan. Again, Check. Assure me that everyone does their hour of Perpetual Adoration. In the Adoration wagon, Perpetual Adoration of Jesus' Real Presence in the Blessed Sacrament. Make sure everyone does weekly confession. We all saw the Gothenburg, Germany disaster. The Gothenburg army refused to do adoration or confession. The red-fog turned all of them into Skinwalkers. Then we fought the Skinwalkers for seventy-two straight hours. We had to behead them and burn their heads in a great bonfire. The king's never learn that only Adoration and weekly confession can defeat Wolv's dominions. Kings never learn that this is a spiritual war against the AntiChrist. Only King Arthur set up Perpetual Adoration and weekly confession."

Ross said, "Warrick. You did a terrible error. You used the announcement of her wedding to deceive the enemy. Even I know that every girl dreams her whole life about her wedding day. Marian believes that you treated her wedding as a chess pawn. Warrick . . . you have spent no quiet time with her. You need time when you do not talk. Time when you only walk together."

Drayton laughed and said, "Ross, you lied. Expert, you are an expert on women like Marian."

Ross said, "I am an expert in avoiding women like Marian. I avoid women whose heart can be broken. Women like Marian want one and only one special man."

Warrick said, "I feel like the three of you are bludgeoning me. Do you believe that I have done at least one thing right with her? You are saying that all my actions with Marian have been wrong? God's shoes, I was correct to swear off happiness. Marriage will only offer misery. The closest that I can ever come to happiness is the honor of duty. She has pushed me out of one window. She will probably accidentally drown me in a well."

Ross laughed, "Warrick. You are in a trap. A trap that I can always sense and avoid. You are to wed a virgin that will only love once. I can always see this in a woman's eye. I avoid these women like I avoid manacles and prison. My only search is for married women that . . . first wink at me. Marian needs to learn about you. You need to learn about Marian. Marian and you need to be together, quiet, for many months."

Warrick said, "'Quiet-together,' that will never be. With Marian's sharp tongue, we will never have quiet time together."

Warrick shouted, "Throw buckets of water over the knoll's sides. More."

Then Warrick said no more. He walked over to a tent and sat on a stool. From his blouse he took out a piece of deer-hide parchment and wrote.

Lord Warrick, I am Your Faithful Warrior, to My Monarch, King Edward. Wolv has many spies in your military and court. Please let no one else read this dispatch.

For the glory of your Majesty, we lay siege to Rose Fire. Forgive me for preparing this siege without your knowledge. Your Majesty, please do not tell even the most trusted. You have traitors in your court. Traitors that have your ears. We battle to rededicate our lives for your glory and honor. I beseech you to send five hundred of your best knights immediately. Please do not tell even your most trusted aids. Do not tell any of your military leaders. You must tell each knight face to face. Then have each leave immediately when you tell each.

Beware my King. Wolv's red-fog grows thicker. Wolv grows stronger. He spreads red-fog throughout the world. The Dragon Lilith has gathered many demons. They strengthen Wolv. Wolv pours red-fog from himself and it grows thicker. Beware of the things in the red fog that eat warriors and horses. Do not go out at night. Stay high in your castles, high out of the red-fog.

I am your faithful champion, Lord Warrick of Able Symon Cyrene Pendragons.

-

-

-

CHAPTER, Now on the Knoll Across From Rose Fire, in Wales, Year @ 1250s A.D.

THE LYING TRAITOR, BLACK CATS AND CURSES

Then Warrick folded and sealed the deerskin parchment with wax. He stamped the seal of his ring in the wax. He waved to a knight, "Deliver this directly to the king's hand. No other is to touch this letter. Do not rest until the king has it in his hand. Kill anyone that takes it from you. It is of the upmost urgency. Return with the king's answer before the full moon. If before the full moon, then I will build a manor for you. Remember. Kill anyone that takes this parchment from you."

The knight said, "Manor? My lord, I will fly."

Warrick thought, "Marian is in danger."

Otan knocked on Marian's wagon door to bring her roasted venison. A feral black cat had wandered into the encampment. Barefoot, Marian jumped from the wagon and picked up the cat. She carried it into her wagon. That night the black cat gave birth to a litter of black kittens.

ORDERS THROUGHOUT THE NIGHT

Warrick ordered, "Throw buckets of water over the knoll's sides. More."

INSIDE ROSE FIRE

Inside Rose Fire's Great Hall Wolv screamed. "You, Candlekeeper. Is it a safe candle hour?"

The Candlekeeper ran up with his candle-lantern over his head. He screamed, "Forgive me Master. I hear the Prime bells. This is not a safe candle hour. This is Jesus' Resurrection hour. You must hide in the earth as you always do at the Resurrection hour. You are weakest at the Resurrection hour."

Wolv screamed. His eyes glazed black as his memories captured him. He pulled his sword and split the candle keeper down the middle, head to groin.

Then Wolv turned into black dust, carbon, charcoal dust. As black-dust he disappeared into the cracks between the stones. The stones under his feet. As black carbon dust he sank deeper and deeper into the earth. Finally, very deep into the earth he came to a ledge beside an underground lake.

He stopped on the ledge. His eyes glazed black. His eyes always glaze black whenever his memories captured him.

In his memory Wolv stood in Jerusalem beside the huge stone that blocked Jesus' tomb.

In his memory, the earth shook. Shook so hard that Wolv fell to his hands and knees.

On the ledge beside the underground lake Wolv also fell to his hands and knees.

In memory only, Wolv looked up to see the huge round stone move by itself.

Jesus, like a great light, stepped from the tomb.

On his knees, Wolv wept. "Jesus. I saw you raise people from the dead. Please. Please raise Pamia from the dead for me, please."

Jesus said, "My Beloved childhood playmate. In a jealous rage you knocked Pamia off the Masada cliffs. You killed Pamia. Now Pamia is safe from you in My Father's arms. Just ask for forgiveness for your sins. Then one day you will see Pamia in Heaven."

Wolv growled, "Never. Never will I ask for forgiveness. I serve Satan."

On his knees beside the underground lake, Wolv growled "I serve Satan." Louder and louder and louder, Wolv growled "I serve Satan." So loud that rocks dropped from the cavern roof.

Red fog poured for Wolv's body. He slobbered great globs of red foam that covered him from chin to knees. Red-foam born of rage and hatred.

Father Malachi Martin walked over to Warrick and said, "Wolv's Resurrection obsessions."

Warrick said, "Yes Father Malachi. Ross. Hear Wolv scream. 'I serve Satan' repeatedly. Wolv is in the middle of his Prime hour Resurrection obsession."

Then Warrick pointed at Rose Fire. He said, "There, look. Wolv's screams make stones fall from Rose Fire's battlements. The earth moves like an earthquake."

Deep in the earth, in the cavern, Wolv's eyes lost the black glaze. Again he had the multi pupil eyes of demon-possession. A legion of thousands of demons.

Wolv turned back into black-dust and rose through the rock. He appeared again in Rose Fire's Great Hall.

Wolv growled, "Candle keep. Is it a safe canonical hour?"

A Hog-Head Skinwalker stood far away from Wolv. He said, "Master Wolv. Your Candle keeper lies cleaved from head to groin. You killed him. Yes. It is a safe candle hour. Early Terce bells ring from the many valley monasteries. Monasteries have ceased to ring Prime bells. The Resurrection hour is past by one or two candle hours."

Wolv growled, "You are not the new candle keeper. Keep me informed about safe candle hours or I will cleave you too."

OUT IN CAMP

Out in Warrick's camp, Warrick said, "The ground ceases to quake. Wolv has recovered from his Resurrection obsession."

Morgan said, "If only we could catch Wolv in his weaknesses, his Resurrection obsession."

Warrick said, "Morgan. One knight long ago caught Wolv in his Resurrection-Prime obsession. Then that one knight dismembered Wolv. The knight shipped his body parts to different oceans. It took Lilith a hundred years to find the parts and put Wolv back together. The earth was safe from the AntiChrist for those one hundred years."

Ross asked, "Warrick. Who was that knight?"

Lord Warrick said, "King Arthur, with his last dying strength, cleaved Wolv. Then Arthur's knights obeyed Arthur. They boxed the pieces and sailed them to different oceans. One piece per ship. King Arthur's holiness gave him the strength to cleave Wolv."

Morgan said, "Warrick. Some knights say that you are King Arthur reborn."

Warrick said, "Morgan. Careful what you say. If King Edward heard that rumor, he would send a thousand assassins to kill me. A thousand assassins to kill all the Pendragons."

Warrick ordered, "Throw buckets of water over the knoll's sides. More."

Very early Terce bells echoed off the mountains.

Warrick again ordered, "Throw buckets of water over the knoll's sides. More."

Marian opened the wagon door at a page's knock.

THE DEVIL, THE DEVIL, THE DEVIL WILL KILL US.

The page screamed, "The devil is here. We are all going to die."

Knights rushed to the warm wagon, "Where is the enemy?" They repeated in unison.

"There," the page screamed and pointed at the black cat, "There, a soul from Perdition."

A knight wrapped his gauntlet around the cat's torso and picked it up. The knight said, "We will dispatch this evil demon of Satan with haste." With the cat in his gauntlet, he turned to walk away.

Barefoot, in only her shift, Marian dashed from her wagon. In the snow Marian raced after him. She grabbed the black cat from the knight, "It is just a cat. Look."

She held it to her open mouth, "The cat does not steal my breath. Look."

She gazed in the cat's eyes, "Look. It does not steal my soul through its eyes. Black cats bring good providence, not bad providence. Cats chase away rats. According to the ancient Arab texts, the plague happens where rats run free. Cats are good omens according to the Egyptians. Good luck, . . . cats are good luck. I had hundreds of cats on my father's estate. They kept rats and other rodents from our barns. The rodents would have eaten and infested our stores of grain and corn. You can trust my judgement. Cats ate vermin. Thus, I had fewer ill servants than other lordships. Other lordships from Oxford to London. I make my decisions based upon facts and results. The other lords based their decisions upon superstitions. They killed off their cats in the belief that cats were devils and witches. Then the rats overran their manors. Their servants and vassals caught the Black Death. Now their manors are bankrupt. My judgement created Moray into the most profitable lordship in Oxford-London. Nobody knows why, but rats bring the plague. Cats eat rats. Cats are necessary."

In only her shift, Lady Marian held the cat and spun on her bare feet.

Then Marian banged her head on an iron bar used to rotate whole roasted venison.

She crumbled unconscious. She opened her eyes. Then she saw the same knight walk to the edge of the camp.

He had his sword in one hand and the black mother cat in the other. She ran to the knight and pulled the cat away.

The knight holding the cat said, "My lady. The knot on your forehead proves black cats bring diabolic humors and damnation."

Lady Marian held the cat to her lips. Then she said to the cat, "You are safe now."

Marian stepped back into her warm armored wagon. She closed the door.

THE TRAITOR'S TRAPS

From inside her wagon, Blanche heard Marian's every word. In her wagon, she dressed in her boots and warm cloak.

Blanche thought, "Now is my opportunity to drive Marian away from Warrick. I understand battlefield superstition. Marian does not."

Blanche stepped from her warm, armored wagon. She pulled, Coors, a naive, new, male servant behind her wagon.

Blanche said, "Coors, you must tell no one that I spoke to you. If you tell anyone, I will have Warrick banish you from his service."

The young, homeless boy had lived in hunger until Warrick hired him. Fear caused Coors' eyes to grow round and white. Tears of fear flowed down Coors' cheeks. He said, "Yes my lady, I promise that I will tell no one."

He looked down at his first shoes he ever wore. Shoes Warrick had given him. Coors pulled the first cloak he ever owned tight around his shoulders. Warrick had also given him the cloak.

Blanche compounded Marian's trouble with Warrick with another lie. She said, "Coors, you must listen carefully. To save us from Lady Marian, you must tell every page what Marian will do."

Blanche always did two things when she lied. Always, she smiled and formed an imaginary circle with her shoe's toe. She said, "Lady Marian said that to protect the cats she will find a witch. She said that she would pay the witch to curse everyone. Curse everyone including the knights and squires, to protect her cats. The curse will be horrible. You must tell the other pages and servants. Marian will curse everyone to protect her cats."

Coors stepped back in wide-eyed surprise and said, "Lady Marian said this?"

Blanche lied to frighten the boy, "Yes, Coors. If you tell anyone that I told you, I will have Warrick banish you. He will banish you back to starvation. He will take away your shoes and cloak. You will freeze. The squires and knights must wear a red-green sash over their shoulder. The red-green sash will ward off Marian's curse. All knights must carry Holy Water to defend against Marian's curse."

Coors was young, homeless with no relatives or friends to help him. The young servant shook from fear and said, "Yes, Lady Blanche. I will tell no one that you told me. Marian is horrible to curse us."

Coors believed Blanche's lie. He ran and told every servant and page Blanche's deception.

Blanche walked to Marian's wagon and knocked.

Nicola opened the door and said, "Lady Blanche. We are always happy to see you."

Blanche climbed in and sat beside Marian. Then Blanche began to brush Marian's hair.

OUTSIDE THE WAGON

Warrick ordered, "Pages. Squires. Knights. Throw buckets of water over the knoll's sides. More."

-

-

-

CHAPTER, Now on the Knoll Across From Rose Fire, Wales, Year @ 1250s A.D.

IN A SATANIC RAGE

From Wye Valley monasteries a cacophony of late Terce canonical bells rang.

Wolv looked from Rose Fire's battlement. He snarled and his eyes squinted in rage. Then he roared, "Warrick. I know that you can hear me. You disobeyed the king and came to siege Rose Fire weeks early. While we are warm in Rose Fire, you will freeze in your tents."

ON THE BATTLEFIELD

Warrick was across the deep ravine between himself and Rose Fire. On the knoll's top, Warrick turned to his knights. He held his index finger on his lips.

Then he whispered, "Otan. Run. Tell everyone not to respond to Wolv. Thus our silence will insult him and cause him to rage. His rage will then make him irrational and easier to defeat."

IN A RAGE

Wolv shouted in rage, "Warrick. You insult me with your silence. For this insult I will spike your head on Rose Fire's highest spire."

Wolv turned to his Skinwalkers in the Rose Fire bailey and said, "Gulum. Soon it will be so cold that wood will freeze and become brittle."

Wolv turned to another Skinwalker and ordered, "Magoott. Order everyone to keep their weapons, especially their bows, under their capes. Otherwise, the bows will freeze. Then when the archers pull them, the tension will break the bows."

Lord Wolv then turned to Gulum and said, "Warrick. Warrick has never fought in weather so cold that wood freezes. If he tries to storm the castle battlements, we will easily defeat him. If he delays his attack on Rose Fire, cold will freeze him."

Gulum prudently stepped backward beyond Wolv's reach. Then Gulum said, "My lord. Unlike us, Warrick has access to all the forests for firewood. He and his knights can stay warm until warmer weather. We are the ones with limited supplies of firewood."

As Wolv drew his sword, he growled, "Never contradict me." He swung it in Gulum's direction, but Gulum knew Wolv's raging temper.

Wolv said, "You were wise to stand beyond my reach."

Then Gulum said, "My lord. If you kill me, you will lose a brother in pure hate. You weaken when you are away from those that hate, that feed your hate. A plant bathes and grows in the sun's rays. You grow stronger in the black rays of pure hatred. Pure hatred that beams from Swale and me."

Wolv growled, "If I did not need hate. If I did not need your hate and Swale's hate, I would cleave you. We will wait in Rose Fire while Warrick's knights freeze. Then we will attack them and pry their weapons from their frozen hands."

"My lord, we. We are the ones that will freeze," Gulum said, "not them."

"Beware Gulum," Wolv growled. "I need to consume your hate to stay strong. Yet, anger me, and I will cleave you. Our fellowship in hatred will not save your life."

Then Wolv's eyes glazed over black and he fell to his knees. In Wolv's memory he was six years old, in Egypt, born with a multiple-pupil-eye. Egyptian children, strangers, gathered around him and chanted, "Ugly Eye, Ugly Eye."

In his Egyptian memory, Holy Mary walked over to Wolv. She picked up little Wolv and seated him on her lap. Holy Mary said, "Wolv, you are beautiful and intelligent. Little Wolv, I will always love you."

On his knees, eyes' glazed over black, Wolv growled repeatedly, "Little Wolv. I will always love you."

Wolv's growls caused blocks to fall from Rose Fire's battlement merlons.

Then Wolv's eyes lost their black glaze and Wolv shouted repeatedly, "Holy Mary. Get out of my head. Holy Mary, get out of my head."

-

-

-

CHAPTER, Now on the Knoll Across From Rose Fire, Wales, the Wye River Valley, Year @ 1250s A.D.

A SUCCESSFUL TRAITOR

Marian opened the wagon door. To the midmorning late Terce and very early Sext-bells.

UNENDING GUILT

At the Sext bells, Wolv fell to his knees and held his head. Again Wolv's eyes glazed over black. His memories went back to zenith sun, Crucifixion on Golgotha.

Symon of Cyrene put the Cross down on Golgotha. At zenith sun Wolv grasped Jesus' hands and feel and nailed them to the Cross. With each hand and foot, Wolv paused and whispered into Jesus' ear. "Jesus. Raise Pamia from the dead and I will end your torture. Give me Pamia and I will end this torture. Just raise Pamia from the dead and I will let you escape."

Jesus did not reply.

Roman soldiers tied rope to the cross and raised it. It thudded into a hole. Then the Roman soldiers pounded wedges at the cross' base to steady it.

Then Jesus, as he hung on the Cross said, "Father. Forgive them, for they know not they do."

Wolv's obsessions took him over. With eyes glazed over black and on his knees, Wolv began repeatedly to howl, "Father. Forgive them, for they know not what they do."

He foamed at the mouth from madness, hatred and rage. Great globs of bright red-foam flowed from his mouth and covered his front. Red fog poured from his body.

Slowly Wolv's guilt driven obsessions faded and his eyes lost their black glaze.

Wolv howled, "Jesus. Get out of my head. Jesus, stop torturing me."

OUTSIDE ROSE FIRE

Marian said, "That horrid growl again."

Nicola said, "The monster Wolv. Wolv's Golgotha obsessions. At Sext, zenith sun, Wolv nailed Jesus to the Cross."

Marian said, "Wolv's own choices torment him."

Nicola said, "He has only to ask Jesus for mercy and his torment will end."

TELLING TIME BY CANONICAL BELLS IN WYE
VALLEY. TAKE A GUESS.

Lady Marian said, "Nicola. Can you tell the hour by the canonical bells?"

Then Nicola said, "All the religious orders have their own prayer schedules. The Terce bells are usually three hours after sunrise. Yet, I also hear Sext bells that are usually at zenith sun. Zenith sun, six hours after Prime, when Wolv nailed Jesus to the Cross. Sext bells are three hours before Jesus died on the Cross at Nones' Bells.

"So take a guess," Nicola. "How many hours is it past sunrise-Prime bells in Wye Valley?"

Nicola said, "Terce. Usually Terce-bells are three hours after sunrise-Prime. Early Sext is about four hours after Prime-sunrise. The early Sext bells now peals. We are about four hours after Prime-sunrise. In normal canonical hours. Jesus will carry his Cross two more hours to Mount Golgotha. Symon of Cyrene will help Jesus carry the cross to Golgotha's top. Then atop Golgotha, at normal Sext, Wolv nails Jesus to the Cross. Normal Sext bells are at Zenith sun."

NO REST FOR THE ANTICHRIST

Inside Rose Fire Wolv growled. "Candlekeeper. Is it a safe hour? I again hear Sext bells."

From a safe distance from Wolv the Candle keep said. "No. An unsafe hour approaches. Six canonical hours from Prime, normal Sext bells. When you nailed Jesus to the Cross. Your Crucifixion obsessions are about to overtake you. I can hear distant Sext bells now. You know that you must go talk to Jesus now."

The Wye Valley Sext bells echoed off the Black Mountains.

Wolv growled, "When will this torture end?"

Against his will Wolv walked into Rose Fire's Catholic chapel. Inside the Chapel, Wolv stepped on blessed ground. Contact with blessed ground caused Wolv to burn into spiritual red-yellow flame. He walked up the center aisle to the altar. Then he crashed the tabernacle open on the stone floor. Then Wolv picked up a consecrated Host of unleaven bread. Upon contact with the Consecrated Host, the spiritual flames rose higher off

Wolv. He held the flat, round bread in his hands and wept. Red-yellow spiritual flames rose high off him up to the chapel roof. Wolv's spiritual flames never caused anything material to burn.

Wolv held the bread and said, "Jesus. I do not need faith to know that you are this bread. I do not need faith to know that this bread is the Holy Trinity. Like Satan, I have the same certitude as does Satan. My curse is that I know. Certitude, I saw you raise people from the dead. Curse this certitude; I can feel you in this bread. The same as when we held hands and played as children in Egypt. You in this bread, I can feel you in this bread. The same as when I held your hands and feet. When I nailed you to the cross. Please, please raise Pamia from the dead. Please, my heart is so empty. Jesus, please, I need Pamia. I saw you raise people from the dead."

In Wolv's heart Wolv heard, "My Beloved Childhood Friend. One day your love of Pamia will save your soul. Love will save the world. You have only to aks me for forgiveness. Love will save the world."

Then Wolv burned in black flame. The spiritual black flames reached the chapel's roof. Wolv's spiritual flames never burned anything but himself. He repeatedly growled, "Never, never will I ask you for forgiveness. Never, never will I ask for forgiveness for I serve Satan."

In Wolv's obsessions he fell to his knees as his pain became unbearable. He growled, "Love will save the world. Love will save the world." Jesus' words to Wolv.

Red fog poured off Wolv. Madness born of rage and hatred caused Wolv's mouth to foam. Red-foam from his mouth, and cover him.

Wolv's red-yellow nor his black flame burned Rose Fire. Yet, his black flame rose above Rose Fire Castle. From outside the castle looked like it burned, yet it did not burn.

OUTSIDE ROSE FIRE

Warrick said, "Another earthquake. Always at Prime bells when Jesus rose from the dead. Always at Sext and Nones bells. Sext bells when Wolv nailed Jesus to the Cross. The Nones bells, when Wolv speared Jesus' right side up through Jesus' heart. When Wolv speared Jesus and watched Jesus bleed to death on the

Cross. Jesus' blood poured down upon Wolv when Wolv pulled the spear from Jesus' side."

Ross pointed to Rose Fire and said, "Look. Again Wolv's growl knocks stones from Rose Fire's battlements."

Drayton said, "I have never heard Wolv's scream that 'Love will save the world'."

Warrick said, "I have. I have battled Wolv often, all over Europe. For Wolv his love for Pamia is worse that a thousand deaths. Also, Wolv's guilt that he killed Pamia is worse than a thousand hells. If Wolv repents, Wolv will become the greatest Catholic saint. Image Judas Iscariot's sainthood if he had asked Jesus for mercy on Golgotha. Asked for mercy while Jesus hung on the cross. Instead Judas Iscariot hanged himself from shame; Judas Iscariot chose to go to Hell by suicide."

A SUCCESSFUL TRAITOR

In Warrick's camp, amid mixed Terce and Sext bells, Marian carried her black cat. In show, out on the battlefield, across the deep ravine from Rose Fire Castle.

She turned to the wagon's open door and said, "Nicola! Look! Each knight wears a beautiful red and green sash. A sash over their right shoulder to their left hip."

Nicola said, "That is . . . not . . . good. The sash is to protect them from witches, demons, and curses."

Warrick ordered, "Throw buckets of water over the knoll's sides. More."

At the sight of Marian and her cat, all the knights' eyes grew round. A chorus of 'Ooooooooooooos' rose.

The knights bowed low and backed out of Marian's sight.

Marian said, "Nicola, why did the knights back away from me?"

Marian noticed that Father Bumpus blessed water. Then Father Bumpus poured it into a knight's flask. Another knight walked up and another. Each to have his small flask filled with holy water. They tied the flasks to their sword belts.

She said, "Nicola. Not only do they wear red and green sashes, they have flasks of Holy Water. They carry the flasks on their sword belts."

Nicola said, "Both are defenses against a witch's threat."

Marian said, "Why?"

Nicola said, "Marian, they are very superstitious. The stress of battle causes many superstitions.

Marian reentered the wagon and pulled the wagon door shut. She said, "Nicola, these men are impossible to understand. Warrick is the hardest to understand. When I lived in Oxford, suitors sat at my feet. They sang to me and begged for my kisses. Those suitors despaired if I did not smile at them. I could bend their will and I knew their intentions and thoughts."

Nicola said, "Would you have married any of them."

Marian said, "No, they were like corn mush. Runny with no flavor, with no will of their own. I wanted a strong man, a knight that would fight for me, protect me."

Nicola said, "Then why do you fight with Lord Warrick?"

Marian gazed off into the distance and did not hear Nicola. Marian said, "These knights and Lord Warrick. When will I understand them?"

"Never," Nicola said.

Nicola tickled Marian, then they laughed like two youngsters.

SOME SERIOUS EXPLAINING

Outside, Father Malachi Martin, Druod, stood. In Antlers and deer hides he knocked on the wagon door.

Marian unlatched it.

Father Malachi pulled it open and said, "My lady. You have some serious explaining."

Lord Warrick opened the door wider.

Lady Marian looked up to see a red-faced enormous Lord Warrick. In his red face, his emerald eyes glared. Warrick held his helm and helm mail under his arm. Exasperation formed his eyebrows into a deep angry V. Then his mouth formed a hard deep frown down to his jaw bone.

Warrick remembered his traitorous Wife. He said, "Marian, Like Ogina, you insist on killing us all. You are about to curse my knights. They have followed me into battles through which no man should have lived. Then you, with a simple sentence, a simple threat of a curse. You make them afraid for their souls.

From fear of you my knights have asked to seek allegiance to another lord."

Warrick ordered, "Throw buckets of water over the knoll's sides. More."

Marian said, "I did not."

Warrick raised his hand to cut off her words. Marian had tried to say that she had no thought of cursing his knights.

"I must act immediately. Now or my knights will leave me," Warrick said, "all but my brothers."

Marian thought, "I am too inexperienced to be on a battlefield. I do not understand knights or knighthood. I do not understand warriors. Warrick should not have brought me here until after he captured Rose Fire."

To calm his temper, Warrick held his breath and paused for a moment. The confusing Terce and Sext bells continued to ring.

Warrick said, "With a curse to protect your cats, you try to destroy my men. The very men that have sworn to die for you. To die for you if evil comes to one of your fingers."

The words, 'Die for you,' pounded in Marian's head like a great hammer. Hammered in her head as she remembered how Warrick fought for her. Fought for Marian the day they first met.

Then Warrick pointed to the center of the camp.

He said, "You get down there right now and apologize. You tell them that you will not hire a witch to curse them. To curse them to protect your cats."

His voice echoed off the Black Mountains. Marian saw the red-anger of Lord Warrick. The anger of a war lord when anything threatened those he protected or his command.

The king's champion roared against her, "Now."

Marian bowed her head in fear and held her fingers over her mouth. Then she ran into the camp's center. She wiped tears from her eyes.

Lord Warrick said, "Now. Now, in the middle of the camp. Stand here and do it. Now! Shout it so all can hear, before all my knights return to London."

Marian looked up to see most of Warrick's knight's mounted. They held the reins of the warhorses, ready to return to London.

She looked up at him. "Warrick. I did not say that I would curse."

Warrick raised his hand to cut off her words. "Now," he shouted, "Now."

INSIDE ROSE FIRE

From Rose Fire's outer wall battlement Wolv turned to a Skinwalker. "Warrick's knight's look as if they are about to leave."

The AntiChrist said. "Quickly. Order all the Skinwalkers to attack out the drawbridge when they leave. Tell them to capture Marian. No one can have her but me. A bucket of gold to the man that carries her to me, . . . alive."

ON THE BATTLEFIELD

Out on the battlefield knoll, Warrick said, "Marian, you must apologize now. Apologize now before they leave for London and I have no knights to protect you. My knights requested that I allow the king to assign them to another lord. They want another lord with a lady that will not harass them with curses." Warrick sighed and said, "Marian. You have destroyed my lordship with a few simple words."

Marian looked at Warrick and said, "I did not."

Again Warrick raised his hand to cut off her words.

Warrick shouted, "Pages. Squires. Throw buckets of water over the knoll's sides. More."

Warrick said, "Now, before my knights ride away."

To keep his knights from immediately riding away, Marian shouted through her frightened tears. She shouted an apology for what she had not done.

She shouted, "I am sorry. Sorry that I threaten you with a witch's curse. I did not mean you harm. I will never do you harm. Please forgive me and do not leave my lord's service."

Stern angry looks bore down upon her from everywhere in the camp. Because of her apology everyone incorrectly thought that Marian had planned to curse Warrick's knights. All the knights, squires, and pages blamed Marian.

Then Marian shouted, "Knights. Search, discover who propagated this false, evil gossip. Discover him or her. A water bucket of Moray Manor gold to anyone. To anyone that finds the source of this gossip."

A FRIGHTENED TRAITOR

Inside the wagon Blanche's eyes grew round and white with terror. Terror shook Blanche like a leaf in the wind.

Silence roared like thunder.

Marian again shouted, "A water-bucket of Moray Manor gold. Gold to anyone that finds the source of this gossip. Enough Gold to buy a London manor."

Inside the wagon Blanche shook in terror.

She thought, "If Warrick discovers that I propagated the rumor, he could kill me."

Morgan raised his huge mace and shouted. "That is the proper way for the Lady of Moray Manor to respond. Marian. We will find the source of this gossip."

Ross shouted, "Marian is an honorable Lady. All dismount."

Then Warrick's knights dismounted and went about their duties.

Nicola walked up to Marian and said, "Marian. They will not take off their red/green sashes. Also, they will keep the flasks of holy water on their belts."

With her cat in one hand, Marian grasped her cloak. She raised her cloak so she would not step on it. Then with Nicola, Marian ran back into the wagon.

Inside the wagon she sighed, "I do not understand these men, these warriors. I have no friends, no scholars to converse with but you. I am lost in a land that I know not."

Again Warrick ordered, "Everyone. Throw buckets of water over the knoll's sides. More."

In the wagon, as she stroked the black cat, Marian said, "Nicola. I did not threaten or plan to curse Warrick's knights."

Nicola said, "Marian, fear and apprehension easily spread gossip."

Drayton used a stone to sharpen his blessed arrows. He walked over to Warrick. Drayton said, "Warrick. Calm down or that blood vessel on your forehead will explode. Slowly, I will walk the camp and investigate. I will tell everyone that Marian did not say that she would curse us. I am certain that talk of this curse is only gossip. A woman as successful as Marian in managing the Moray lordship is wise. She would never threaten to curse your knights."

First Drayton tapped on Marian's wagon. Marion opened the door. Drayton asked, "Marian, may I speak with you."

"Yes," Marian replied. "If you do not mind talking to a walking curse."

Drayton grinned and continued to sharpen his blessed arrows. Marian stepped from the wagon.

She said, "I did not."

Drayton raised his hand, the one with the sharpening stone. He whispered, "Marian, I know that you did not threaten to curse anyone. Yet, it does not matter whether you were about to curse us or not. What matters is that you now ignore the rumor. Battlefields are strange places with stranger rumors. I will tell everyone that you did not plan nor were about to curse anyone. I will say that it was just a rumor. That you courageously apologized only to end the curse's foreboding. You can look courageous. Because I will stress to everyone that you courageously took the blame. A lady of a castle would act as if this never occurred. If you ignore the rumor, it will confirm that it was only a rumor. A lady never reacts to rumors. Remember. Act as if it never occurred. Then everyone will think you are courageous to take the undeserved blame."

Marian whispered, "So you would lie, just as Warrick lied?"

Drayton dropped a blessed arrow into his quiver. He smiled. He whispered, "Of course, my lady. Lies, rather than the truth, conquer the enemy."

Marian said, "Do you believe that I would put a curse on Warrick's knights?"

Drayton said, "Of course not. You are an honorable, successful woman. You should not be anxious. Warrick is not the only one here sworn to protect you. Ross, Morgan, and I are also here. We have no battlefield superstitions to weaken us."

Drayton looked at the sky and said, "However. I must have an eagle embossed on my blessed armor. Also, we never fight on a day when the sky is red in the morning. We try never to fight on a barren battlefield. Also, we never fight on a day when eagles fly low over the battlefield."

Marian's mouth fell open. Her eyes grew round in surprise. She raised her eyebrows. She said, "You are superstitious."

-

-

-

CHAPTER, Where: Wales on the Knoll Across From Rose Fire, Year @ 1250s A.D.

PLANS TO SEND HIS BRIDE AWAY.
Drayton laughed, "My lady, you need to learn to laugh. That was a joke. Also, avoid Warrick for today. His mood is as black as his leathers."

Drayton continued to sharpen blessed arrows.

Marian sighed and entered her wagon.

OUTSIDE THE WAGON
Outside the wagon, Lord Warrick paced back and forth on the battlefield's edge. The edge that faced Rose Fire. He could not expel, from his mind, the image of Marian, motionless, lifeless. Lifeless never to love or move again. The image of Ogina in his arms burned to ash. Marian, dead because his knights were not there to protect her. His knights were not there. All because Marian had driven away his knights with a threatened curse.

He tried to preoccupy himself in war practice. He unsheathed blessed Dread and practiced battle-axe moves.

As he practiced, he whispered, "Mother. Forgive me. I failed you. I did not stop Wolv from killing you."

Then Warrick ordered, "Everyone. More water. Throw buckets of water over the knoll's sides. More."

As he practiced, he thought, "I have taken Marian to a battlefield. I am a fool. Now she will cause herself and all my knights to die."

Warrick said, "Drayton. Morgan. Marian is in great danger. Again. Make sure that everyone does their hour of Perpetual Adoration. In the Adoration wagon, Perpetual Adoration of Jesus' Real Presence in the Blessed Sacrament. Make sure everyone does weekly confession. Write down who does and does not do adoration and confession. Remember the horrible battle around Mont-Saint-Michel, France. Wolv's red-fog ate the king's militia.

Lilith sat in the battlefield and ate the French soldiers alive. Never stop contemplating the horror. Only adoration and weekly confession can keep the AntiChrist's red-fog away. Lilith, Wolv and the Skinwalkers all need the thick red-fog."

Terce and Sext bells rose from the valley. Warrick practiced with his ax. His muscles bulged against his leathers.

From a safe distance behind Warrick, Ross said, "Warrick. You need to calm yourself. From under your armor, I can hear your muscles rip your black leathers."

Warrick thought, "I can have no hope against the Pendragon curse. Marian will eventually drive away my knights and leave herself with no protection."

Then Warrick walked to his tent and sat at a table for a long time.

TO SEND HER AWAY

He sat, with his back straight, his gauntlets on the table. He thought, "I was a fool. Yes, I was a fool to bring Marian to a battlefield. Marian should not even be in Wales. Her inexperience will eventually cause the death of all my knights, and herself. Today her inexperience placed everyone in deadly jeopardy."

As he sat at a table in his tent, he took out a parchment. He wrote.

To My King and Sovereign, I most graciously have a request. For many days, I have been with Lady Marian of Moray, Oxford. She is in great danger here in Wales. She needs temporary protection far from Rose Fire Castle. For her safety, I request that you send one hundred of your best knights. Knights to return Marian to Oxford. Please assign her to the temporary protection of Oxford's Lord Protllyy. When all is safe, I will retrieve her from Oxford. Only after I have driven Wolv from Rose Fire. Also, beware. Wolv grows stronger by the day. The red-for grows denser, thicker. Soon the things in the red-fog will eat people. Eat people everywhere if we do not weaken Wolv."

Lord Warrick of the Able, Symon of Cyrene Pendragon Line. I am your Loyal Champion until death in battle.

He folded and sealed the parchment with wax. Then he pressed the seal on his ring into the wax.

Warrick thought, "I find a woman whose beauty beguiles me. Then fate will not allow us to be together."

He waved to a squire, "Do you know the back roads to London? Directly to the king's palace?"

The squire said, "Yes, my lord, I know the roads."

As he sat at his table, Warrick said, "Take another squire with you. I want you to deliver this to the king. To the king's hand and only to the king's hand. Go by the back trails to avoid any trouble. Wolv's Skinwalkers prowl the main roads. Therefore you must ride hard and overtake the knight that I just sent. If you return before the full moon, then you can take your knighthood tests."

With the parchment, the two squires mounted. They spurred their horses into a full run, down the twisted mountain road.

Warrick ordered, "Throw buckets of water over the knoll's sides. More."

-

-

-

CHAPTER, Now Wales on the Knoll Across From Rose Fire, Year @ 1250s A.D.

AN AVALANCHE BURIES HER CHAMPION.

INSIDE THE WAGON

Inside Marian's wagon Marian asked, "Nicola. What is the canonical hour?"

Nicola said, "Now the sunset-Vespers bells ring. The bells have moved from late morning Terce. Then Sext's zenith sun bells when Wolv nailed Jesus to the Cross. Then Nones bells when Wolv speared Jesus' heart on the Cross. Now the sunset-supper Vespers bells ring. Vespers' bells now call monks and nuns to prayer and supper."

OUTSIDE THE WAGON

The sun lowered behind the Black Mountains. Wolv's red fog circled the Black Mountain's peaks.

Ross said, "Marian has hidden all day."

"Yes, Ross," Warrick said. "From morning Terce bells, through Sext's zenith sun. Then to Nones, and now supper Vespers bells. Marian has stayed in the wagon."

Ross said, "The eve came on us quickly and the snow has stopped. We can now see the night sky. Beautiful, the full moon and stars reflect off the snow. We can better see the enemy."

"Also, the enemy can better see us," Ross said.

Morgan said, "Look. Rose Fire glows like a pink, marble beacon in the night. Brighter than the moon reflects off the snow."

Drayton said, "Brothers. Can you feel the warm air?"

Morgan turned to the south and said, "Warm air will form fog. Fog will hide the enemy."

Ross said, "I smell sea salt."

"Yes," Warrick said. "Near impossible. This unseasonable warm, ocean air blew from the south, halfway across Wales."

Otan pointed to the Wye Valley and said, "Look. The cold is turning the warm air into a thick grey fog."

Within fifteen minutes, another monastery rang their late Vespers bells. A thick, opaque, grey fog filled the Wye Valley. The cold quickly turned the warm air into opaque, ground fog. Opaque fog disquieted and alarmed the knights. All the knights jumped to their feet. They held up their blessed shields and blessed swords. Up to their knees, the grey, ground fog covered the battleground and the knoll. Reflections, the full moon reflected off the grey fog. Just like the moon reflects off the ocean. In the knee-deep grey fog and snow, Warrick paced the battleground. He read diagrams of Rose Fire.

Then Warrick said, "Everyone. Throw buckets of water on this knoll's sides. All sides. I command you to ignore the fog. Pour buckets of water over this knoll's sides. Every night. All night. Now."

His knights jumped to do his command.

Ross said, "The ground and snow are so cold. So cold that the warm air does not melt the snow."

In the knee-deep fog, Warrick paced a deep trough in the snow. The dry snow crunched under his blessed armored boots.

His squire, Otan, walked up to him and said, "My lord, did you hear. Drayton learned that Marian did not put a curse on anyone to protect her cats. The threatened curse was only another rampant battlefield rumor. Marian did not plan or threaten to curse anyone. She apologized to end the curse's foreboding. To prevent your knights from leaving. She bravely took the blame and the scorn to save your command. Marian courageously took the blame. Lady Marian has courage. She only needs experience."

Warrick said, "Battlefields are strange places where strange rumors become reality."

Then Warrick said, "Compline Bells. Only three or four hours to midnight - Vigils bells. Vigil bells that begin the Witches' three hours until Matins bells. Lilith, the Queen of witches, is strongest in the three Witches' hours."

Warrick ordered, "Everyone. Throw buckets of water over the knoll's sides. More."

Morgan said, "The midnight-Vigils hour. The hour when the Catholic church prays that Satan prowls. Prowls like a lion looking for someone to devour. The dreaded midnight hour, The Witches hour."

Ross said, "Beware. Many of our knights think they see witches in the air at Vigils - midnight Hour. The Vigils - midnight bells will spook some knights."

Warrick said, "Now Compline bells are three hours from midnight -Vigils. These early Compline bells are four candle hours from midnight-Vigils. Reque. To decrease Vigils-fears tell the knights to wear their red-green sashes and holy Water flasks."

Reque ran to do as ordered.

Ross said, "Thank God we are still in early Compline bells."

ATTACK FROM THE MOUNTAIN

As early Compline bells rang, arrows struck the ground around Warrick's feet.

Lord Warrick pointed up the mountain.

Morgan shouted, "The arrows came from high on the mountain."

Ross said, "Yes. Where we thought, the snow was too deep and dangerous for anyone. We were wrong."

In full armor and on foot Warrick called four knights to himself.

He said, "Brothers, I want you to stay here. Ross, I want you to take command until I return. Morgan, I want you to assure that not one guard daydreams. Drayton, space your archers around the champ. You must tell them to put blessed arrows in their bows, ready to fight. I want you to tell them not to wait for the command to shoot."

Warrick ordered, "Pages. Squires. Throw buckets of water over the knoll's sides. More."

Warrick led the four other knights up the mountain side. He wore his heavy blessed armor as if it were a satin blouse.

As they climbed the mountain, the other four knights struggled under their blessed armor's weight.

Lady Marian heard the commotion. In her white, deer-fur cloak, she stepped from her wagon.

Instantly, Drayton put his blessed shield in front of her.

Marian asked, "Where is my lord?"

Drayton put an arrow in his bow. He said, "My lady, he is high on the mountain, in danger. In a battle with unknown numbers. He could fall into a deep crevasse and perish. Or he could freeze in deep snow."

Early and then late Compline bells rang. Compline bells called Nuns and Priests and parishioners to bedtime prayers.

Not warriors.

Then Marian heard swords clash. Men yelled. Skinwalkers scream. Then quiet. Windless, breathless, quiet. Marian grew dizzy as she held her breath.

Marian said, "What was that rumble? Why is Warrick so quiet? No swords now clash. No one yells from high on the mountain. Is Warrick still alive?"

Drayton tightened his bowstring. He said, "The rumble was an avalanche. We will know if Warrick lives when someone returns."

Marian said, "We must go up and find Warrick."

Ross said, "Not in the night. Not unless more arrows hit the camp. We would never find Warrick in the night."

Agonizing hours dragged on. The moon moved across the sky behind sparse snow clouds.

Hours passed.

Late Compline bells ceased. Three more candle hours passed. Then valley Vigils-bells rang.

Marian said, "Since childhood I have always feared Vigils bells. The stories of Satan going about as a lion always terrified me. Now I have seen demons for myself."

Ross said, "Since battling the AntiChrist, I also dreaded the Witches hour of midnight-Vigils-bells."

THE-RAKE-CRUSHED

Morgan said, "Ross. What is that sheepskin under your breast plate?"

Ross said, "An unread letter from Lord Birmingham. I have yet to read."

Ross pulled the letter from behind his breastplate.

Lord Ross said, "Morgan. Blood covers the letter."

The Rake, Ross, read.

Suddenly Ross fell to his knees. He began to weep.

Morgan put his hand on Ross' helm and said, "What? What news makes you weep? How horrible can it be?"

On his knees, with a great flow of tears, Ross said, "My dalliances. My bedding of Lord Birmingham's daughter caused her suicide. She looked much older and wore a wedding ring, I thought. I thought she was a worldly woman. The blood on the parchment is his daughter's blood. I thought wrong. She was unmarried. She was a virgin. Birmingham's daughter learned that I was only playing with her affections. I had no idea that she was a virgin. Loved me, she loved me. Death, she jumped off his manor to her death. Pregnant, she was pregnant with my child. This also contains her suicide note. Avoided, I have avoided women like Marian for years. Now my dalliance has caused a suicide. A suicide of a woman like Marian. Not only have I caused her suicide, Catholics go to Hell if they commit suicide. She was pregnant with my child. I did not know that she was a virgin."

Ross rolled open another sheepskin and read. "The Archbishop of Canterbury. He says that the circumstances are unique. Given the holy life that Lady Innocence lead. That I can live austere penance and earn her way out of Hell. A life of painful fasting and prayer and fighting the AntiChrist. My fasting, my prayer and my fighting the AntiChrist can earn her release from Hell."

Morgan said, "Prayer can begin now. Yet, for now, as your co-first knight, I order you to eat to stay strong. Fasting can cause your weakness and thus cause Marian's death. Pull out your Rosary and pray for Birmingham's daughter now. Live among us as a Knight Templar. Follow the Rule of the Knights Templars. Take vows of poverty, chastity and obedience. Then you might earn Lady Birmingham's freedom from Hell."

On his knees, Ross said, "Her name was Innocence. Lady Innocence of Birmingham Lordship."

Father Bumpus walked up and said, "What? What in the name of all that is holy is wrong with Ross, the Rake."

Morgan explained.

On his knees, Ross said, "Father Bumpus. You are England's Provincial of the Knights Templar. Morgan explained the disaster that I caused upon Lady Innocence. Hear and accept my vows of poverty, chastity and obedience to you."

So then Morgan explained everything.

Father Bumpus laid his hands on Ross' helm. He accepted Ross' vows into the Knight's Templar Order.

Then Father Bumpus ordered, "Rise. Ross Templar of the Knights Templars. Rise and prepare to kill Wolv and to kill Skinwalkers. I change your name from Ross, the Rake, to Ross Templar Constantine. Rise and earn your lover's way out of Hell."

Ross Templar Constantine tried to stand but his knees were frozen to the ground.

Morgan pulled Ross to his feet and said, "Now. Ross Templar. Obey you Templar Provincial superior and prepare to kill Skinwalkers. When Prime-sunrise bells ring and the sun rises, we go to find Warrick's frozen body. For now black night is our enemy. We are still in the Vigils-midnight witches-hours."

MATINS' BELLS.

Three more candle hours had passed during Ross' agony, time for Matins bells.

Then Matin bells announced prayers three hours after midnight.

In the black night suddenly one of Warrick's knights stumbled down the mountain side. He rolled in the snow to the camp's edge.

Ross Templar and Morgan carried the knight beside a fire. The ice on his blessed armor began to melt.

Drayton pulled on the knight's helm. Ice held the knight's helm tight. Drayton took out his sword and tapped the hilt on the helm's ice. As the ice fell away, Drayton pulled the helm off.

Ross Templar knelt beside the knight and asked, "Lord Warrick. Where is he?"

On his back by the fire, the near frozen knight shivered. His face was blue. His teeth chattered. Thick ice on his blessed armor melted in the campfire's heat.

As his teeth chattered, he said, "Lord Ross. Lord Warrick ran up the mountain like a deer and killed the Skinwalker archers. He beheaded them and threw their heads into a deep ravine. Then the snow collapsed under him. He fell out of sight into a deep crevasse. Terrible, . . . , terrible, then an avalanche swept him off a cliff. We looked down the cliff. No one could survive such a fall. Another avalanche piled hundreds of feet of snow where Lord Warrick fell. The three knights that went with me sank out of sight in the deep snow. I dug for them and Warrick until I could no longer use my arms. Lord Warrick is dead."

-

-

-

CHAPTER, Now Wales on the Knoll Across From Rose Fire, Year @ 1250s A.D.

AVALANCHES AND MORE AVALANCHE.

EARLY PRIME BELLS

In the dark for two hours Warrick's remaining knights and archers paced the camp. Early Prime bells announced monastery prayers five hours after midnight. Three knights rolled in the snow down the mountain. In the darkness they rolled to a stop at the camp's edge. Otan and the other squires dragged the three frostbitten knights over to the fire.

Morgan said, "What of Warrick, where is Warrick?"

The knight lay on the ground. Then he hit his own gauntlet on his own helm. With a dagger's hilt, Morgan hit the ice on the helm. As the ice fell away, Morgan pulled the knight's helm from his head.

The knight gasped, "Suffocated . . . the ice almost suffocated me."

Morgan repeated, "What of Lord Warrick?"

Morgan lowered his head to the frozen knight's mouth to hear his whispers.

The knight whispered, "The snow collapsed under my lord. He fell an ungodly distance into a ravine. Then an avalanche filled the ravine. We searched. We searched until, until we."

The knight fell silent and breathed out for the last time. Without motion, unfocused eyes, his eyes stared.

Morgan said, "He froze in his attempt to find his lord."

Then Morgan closed the knight's eyes.

Morgan said, "Ross-Templar, Drayton. These four knights are of Warrick's most faithful and wisest. If they say that Warrick is dead, Warrick is dead."

News of the confirmation of Lord Warrick's death spread throughout the camp. Tears ran down the cheeks of Warrick's eldest and most loyal knights.

TEARS

Again very early Prime bells faintly greeted the sunrise.

Marian thought, "Now. Now that I no longer have my champion, I realize how much I loved him. I need my champion's smile. I will never love another, only my champion, Lord Warrick. Now I would even welcome Warrick's anger, my champion's anger."

Warrick's senior knights had fought with him to Persia and back. They stood with bowed heads. Marian wept. She leaned against the wagon. Shock made her dizzy. She stepped back into the wagon.

INSIDE ROSE FIRE

Inside Rose Fire Wolv growled, "Candlekeeper. Is it a safe hour?"

The Hog-Head Skinwalker held the Candle lantern high. He said, "No my Lord. You hear the faint early Prime-sunrise bells. It is Jesus' Resurrection hour. This is the hour King Arthur defeated you. Jesus' Resurrection hour."

Wolv growled and split the Candlekeeper from head to groin.

Then Wolv obeyed his obsessions. First Wolv's eyes glazed over black as his obsessive memories conquered him. He turned into black dust and disappeared into the cracks of the stone floor.

Again he sank deep into the earth. Sank until he reached the shelf beside an underground lake. Luminescent mushrooms lit up the underground cavern.

At the underground lake, in his memory, Wolv watched. In his memory, Wolv again watched the huge stone at Jesus' tomb roll aside. Roll aside with no one visible pushing it.

Wolv looked up, in his memory, to see Jesus emerging as bright as the sun. Wolv repeatedly begged, "Please Jesus, please raise Pamia from the dead for me, please."

In his memory Wolv watched Jesus disappear.

Rage and hatred caused Wolv to foam at the mouth. Great globs of red-foam poured from his mouth.

Then Wolv growled, "Pamia, Pamia."

OUTSIDE ROSE FIRE

Outside Rose Fire, in Warrick's camp, Morgan said, "Wolv's Prime-sunrise obsessions caused another earthquake. The AntiChrist's growls of 'Pamia, Pamia' shakes the ground."

Ross Templar said, "Wolv's Resurrection obsessions are his strongest obsessions. Listen. The earthquake has caused another avalanche. This second avalanche will surely bury Warrick now."

In weak morn sunlight, Warrick's knights searched the mountain for Warrick.

NEAR FROZEN.

High in the mountain, deep in a crevasse, buried in snow, Warrick opened his eyes.

Unable to move, near frozen, Warrick said, "Who are you?"

A figure in bright light said, "King Arthur."

King Arthur knelt and put a cup to Warrick's lips.

Arthur said, "Drink. Drink from the Holy Grail. Marian and you have a great part to play in the world's future."

Arthur put his hand behind Warrick's head and said, "Drink More."

Then Arthur reached up. Warrick saw St. Michael, The Archangel. The Archangel gave his own ethereal sword to Arthur.

Arthur lowered the glowing sword lengthways into Warrick's body.

Arthus said, "Warrick. Now you have Excalibur. Now you are Excalibur until your death."

King Arthur said, "Now. Get up off your butt and save the world. Get off your butt and save Marian. Wolv's obsessions have loosened the snow. Now get up and move before you freeze to death. Save Marian. Wolv's obsessions caused another avalanche. The snow atop you is gone. You are free."

Warrick gritted his teeth and slowly began to break the encrusted snow from himself.

Lord Warrick thought, "My arms and legs do not work. I will freeze before I get to the fire in the camp."

KNIGHTS SEARCHING.

As the sun rose, Warrick's knights searched the mountain for Warrick.

Far below, Warrick's camp, an hour later, more late Prime and early Terce bells rang. The later Prime and early Terce bells announced the higher morn sun.

In the wagon, with tears in her eyes, Marian grasped Nicola's hands.

CHEERS

Marian said, "I hear cheers. The knights are cheering."

Marian flung open the wagon door to see Lord Warrick. He staggered from the mountain's trees. Thick ice clung all over his blessed armor. In only her shift and barefoot, she ran to him faster than the others. Then into his arms, she jumped and grasped him around his helm. The impact knocked ice off his armor. He put one arm under her bottom to hold her. Then with his other hand he sheathed Dread.

His men shouted, "Only Lord Warrick. Only Lord Warrick."

Warrick flipped up his visor and shouted, "Back to your posts. You are not rogues, back to your duties. All of you, I command you to return to your posts."

Otan held Warrick's Pendragon banner high above his head. Otan shouted in joy, "My lord. Always the commander. We can be sure that Warrick is healthy when he barks orders at us."

Late Prime and early Terce bells celebrated the bright morn. Marian hugged Warrick's helm. Then Warrick pulled off his helm, mail cowl and skull pads.

She kissed his face and said, "When. When I thought that I lost you, I knew that I loved you."

"Marian," Warrick snapped. "You should be in your wagon."

Then he turned and shouted, "Ross. Morgan. Drayton. An attack can come from any time. I command you to run back to your posts. Enemy or ally, someone is on the mountain. Someone woke me, ally, or enemy, I know not."

Warrick ordered, "Throw buckets of water over the knoll's sides. More."

While Marian clung to his neck, Warrick said, "Marian, you are in danger out here. You are supposed to be in your wagon. You are a foolish, foolish girl. Marian, you dressed yourself in only your shift. The vapors will be the death of you, and barefoot. On this battlefield, you will cut your feet on old broken weapons."

Marian hugged his snow-covered neck and said, "I just told you that I love you."

As Marian hugged Warrick's neck, Warrick carried her with one arm under her bottom.

Warrick said, "Morgan. We must hurry. Drayton! I want you to devise three shifts of two archers each. The three shifts are to take turns guarding where we were high on the mountain. I want you to gather the bows and arrows from the vanquished enemy. Bless them so they spiritually burn the Skinwalkers and Wolv. Order the archers to allow no one above or below them. Someone is on that mountain. Someone that woke me."

Warrick pointed at Ross and said, "Ross-the-Rake. You disobeyed me. You improperly allowed Marian out of her wagon. Why? The Skinwalkers could attach us now? If any harm came to Marian, I would lose my honor in the king's eyes."

Marian sat on Warrick's iron-covered forearm and hugged his neck.

NO LOVE.

Marian thought, "Warrick. Warrick did not say that he loves me in return. He is my champion, but he does not love me."

Warrick opened the wagon's iron door. He glanced around to assure that his knights were at their duties. With Marian in his arms, Warrick turned to a noise on the mountain. He squinted to find the enemy. Without a word, as if Marian were a feather, he placed Marian into the wagon. Then he banged the door shut.

Warrick said, "Ross. I want you to keep your eyes on the tree line. Someone . . . something followed me down the mountain. I met someone when I was under the avalanche. Someone woke me before I could freeze. Even now I can barely lift my arms from the cold."

Morgan walked up to Warrick and said, "Lord Warrick. I must tell you about Ross, the Rake. He is now Ross Templar Constantine. He caused the suicide of Lady Innocence of Birmingham."

Warrick ordered, "Throw buckets of water over the knoll's sides. More."

Morgan explained Ross' complete metanoia, a complete change of heart.

Morgan said, "In a flash Ross, the Rake, changed to Ross Templar Constantine. Almost like Saul became St Paul when Jesus knocked Saul off his horse."

Warrick said, "Everyone knew that Lady Innocence was a virgin. Everyone knew that she was going to be a nun?"

Lord Morgan said, "Not Ross, the Rake. Lady Innocence's beauty beguiled him. He thought she was older and worldly. Later she found that she was pregnant and she thought that Ross abandoned her. She jumped from atop her father's manor to her death."

Warrick said, "The Pendragon curses. Now Ross will have Ogina-like nightmares and horrors in his daydreams. Like the two-thousand-year-old tragedy of Able Pendragon' bride. His brother Cain accidentally killed her trying to kill Able. Wolv Pendragon, himself, a Pendragon, has a Pamia Pendragon nightmare. In Wolv's rage, Wolv knocked Pamia to her death off the Masada cliffs. Pendragon men are cursed never to find love."

Morgan said, "Now Ross. Once the happiest of us all, once the most joyful, has his nightmare."

Warrick sighed and said, "Ross Templar Constantine Pendragon. Ross' joy is gone forever."

From across the battlefield Ross Templar said, "Yes Lord Warrick. You called for me? I am here beside the blacksmith." Ross stood beside the camp blacksmith.

Warrick walked over and said, "What is this?"

Ross said, "He is forging the weight of my sins. A heavy Rosary of iron chain and balls."

Warrick ordered, "Throw buckets of water over the knoll's sides. More."

The blacksmith said, "A Rosary of twenty decades. A rosary of thick chain and thicker iron balls. If Lord Ross is not praying, he can throw it to trip a horse. Or swing it to behead a demon Skinwalker. It weights twice Morgan's mace."

Warrick said, "The iron Rosary will be as heavy as my battle ax, Dread."

Ross Templar said, "Heavier. I will wear it over my shoulder and pray it always, for Lady Innocence. The Rosaries' weight is part of my penance."

INSIDE THE WAGON

Inside the warm wagon, Marian said, "I told Warrick that I loved him. Then he only told me to get back into the wagon."

Nicola said, "Marian. Listen, the late Prime and early Terce bells seem to celebrate Warrick's return."

Marian snapped, "Celebrate. I wanted to celebrate. I told Warrick that I loved him. All he did was order me to stay in this wagon. He had not one tender word for me. The monks and nuns must obey the bells as if the bells are commands. Just like the monks and nuns obey commands, I must obey Warrick's commands. He is only command. He is as hard as his blessed armor. Obey the commands, commands, commands, obey the bells, bells, bells. My world will be only obedience, with no love, with no tenderness."

Marian rolled on her side and pulled white rabbit and white fox coverlets over herself.

Collette wanted to change the subject. She said, "My Lady. The Wye Valley has too many religious orders with too many bells."

Nicola also wanted to change the subject. She said, "Yes Collette. Each order rings its eight canonical bells at different times. Therefore, we never know the correct time. I can barely sleep for all the continuous bells at night."

OUTSIDE THE WAGON.

Warrick ordered, "Throw buckets of water over the knoll's sides. More. Throw move water on the snow."

IN THE WAGON

As little Luchas sat in the corner, he said, "Stop making fun of my home. I love the Wye Valley's bells."

Beside Lucas, little Samuel said, "Yea, the valley is my home. Stop talking badly about my home."

Marian sighed and said, "Who else wants to chide me. Two small children chided me and Warrick chided me."

"Marian, I have a solution," Nicola said. As Nicola opened the wagon door, she yelled, "Reque."

Reque ran up to the wagon. He slipped and fell on his butt. With a red face, as he sat in the snow, Reque looked up at Nicola.

"Yes my lady," Reque said.

Nicola said, "Reque, I want you to bring Marian's special mail."

Reque jumped to his feet and ran as fast as a rabbit.

Marian said, "All the knights, squires, and pages refuse to obey me. Yet, Reque jumps when you speak. Why?"

Inside the wagon, as Nicola winked at Marian, she said, "Marian. If I flirt with a squire or page, they will do anything for me."

Marian's eyes grew wide and round with astonishment.

She said, "Nicola, No. You. . . you do not trade favors, do you?"

Warrick again ordered, "Throw buckets of water over the knoll's sides. More. Now while it is snowing."

Nicola winked and laughed. "If I blow a kiss to a young squire, he will do anything for me."

Again Nicola laughed.

Reque again skidded to a stop at the wagon door. He carried the chain-mail the blacksmith had made specifically to highlight Marian's curves. Inside the wagon, Collette brushed lavender oil into Marian's hair. Then she dressed Marian in her warm padding. Collette tied the mail over the padding. Her mail highlighted her slender legs, delicate waist, and large breasts.

OUTSIDE THE WAGON
Reque held Marian's hand as she stepped outside the wagon. He put her cowl padding and cowl mail on her head. Then he opened a wooden chest. He pulled out a great cowled cloak of white squirrel. Then he wrapped the cloak around her. Reque held it so she could push her arms through the sleeves. He pulled it tight around her shoulders. Then he clasped it from her neck to her feet. Squire Reque pulled the white squirrel cowl over her head.

Reque said, "My lady. The white cloak will protect you from the cold. Also, make you hard to see in the snow."

As Reque stepped back from her, he said, "My lady, you. You are so beautiful. Lord Warrick is a very lucky bridegroom."

Marian thought, "Not according to Warrick."

From the open wagon door, Nicola said, "Marian. You must now go hold Warrick's hand, walk with him everywhere he goes. Just hold his hand and go where he goes. I want you to remember the look and thoughts that I taught Dally. For God's sakes Marian, do not say anything. Do not utter a word. Do not argue with him."

Mid-morn Terce bells filled the valley and echoed off the Black Mountains.

Warrick thought aloud, "The red fog atop the Black Mountains grows darker each day. Lilith and Wolv grow stronger each day. Soon Lilith will kill every unborn child in the Wye Valley. Lilith is growing stronger."

Lord Warrick walked over to the edge of the deep ravine and studied Rose Fire.

Marian walked over to him.

Warrick said, "In your mail, I am not so worried that arrows will harm you. You can stay outside the wagon for a few minutes."

Nicola's advice, 'Do-not-argue-with-him' bounced around in Marian's mind.

Warrick ordered, "Throw buckets of water over the knoll's sides. More. Now while it snows."

Marian thought, "I will do as Nicola and Collette had said." She looked into Lord Warrick's emerald eyes.

Then she thought, "I will be silent and listen to Warrick."

Warrick shouted, "Morgan. Someone in the Adoration wagon is asleep. Look at Rose Fire's castle. Wolv's red fog approaches. Awaken the Adorationist. Now before the red fog reaches us and eats us."

Morgan ran to the Adoration wagon. He grabbed the sleeping knight and pulled his from the wagon. Then Morgan grabbed another knight and said, "You. Now. Begin faithful Adoration so your Adoration can push back the red fog."

In the wagon, the knight knelt. He began to read the Adoration prayers before a Monstrance.

Morgan pointed at Rose Fire and shouted, "The knight's Adoration is sincere. The red fog retreats."

Warrick shouted, "Morgan. Put the knight that fell asleep in Adoration on latrine duty."

Marian put her arm around Warrick's arm and drew up close to him. She said nothing. For hours she simply held his arm. Marian said nothing, and walked wherever he walked. Lady Marian listened to all he said to everybody.

HER HONOR DEFENDED.

A huge knight walked over to Warrick and said, "Warrick. We cannot obey a lord married to a prostitute. The lords of Oxford and London call Marian a prostitute. We cannot obey you if you marry her."

Warrick said, "Are you ready to pay with your life for that insult? I will fight you now. Pull your weapons."

Morgan ran up and said, "Warrick. You have not recovered from nearly being frozen. Your arms and legs are weak. Let me defend Marian's honor."

Warrick said, "No. This is my duty. Marian is my charge. He has challenged my command."

The knight, twice as tall as Warrick, pulled his sword and shield.

Warrick pulled his sword but he could not lift it. He held his shield before him.

The huge knight attacked and knocked Warrick's shield away from Warrick.

Warrick fell at the knight's feet.

The knight raised his sword to cleave Warrick.

Marian screamed.

Warrick ran his dagger into the knight's arch of his foot.

Then the huge knight roared in pain. Then Warrick twisted the dagger.

Lord Warrick grabbed the huge knight's stabbed foot and lifted it.

The enormous knight screamed in agony and fell forward.

Warrick pulled the dagger from the knight's foot and put it to the knight's throat.

"Surrender. Apologize to Marian and ride out of my employ forever, or die here," Warrick said.

The huge knight said, "I surrender. Lady Marina, I apologize."

Warrick said, "Marian. By right of combat I have saved your honor."

The huge knight with the wounded foot again apologized to Marian. He limped, mounted his horse and rode back to Oxford.

Marian said, "Warrick. I was sure he would kill you."

Warrick said, "Marian. Have confidence in me. I trained him. I knew how he fights. Because he is huge, he always knocks his opponent to the ground. Marian, I let him knock me down so I could stab his foot. Armor does not well protect the arch of the foot. Yes, I knew he would surrender when I grabbed his stabbed foot. Nothing hurts as much as a wounded foot. Achilles' heel. Remember that only an arrow in Achilles' heel defeated him. Though, the rest of Achilles' body was invulnerable."

Marian hugged Warrick and she wept.

Warrick asked, "Marian. Why would he call you a prostitute?"

Still Marian wept. She said, "Warrick. When a woman defeats a lord in court, they call women horrible names. I defeated many Oxford and London lords in court. They have called me Satan's concubine because I outsmarted them."

Warrick said, "Come with me. Let us continue to outsmart them."

Then with Marian, Warrick carried long scrolls of architect drawings of Rose Fire. Constantly, he studied them constantly. He carried and opened scrolls of battlefield drawings. Drawings that showed every inch of the ground around the castle. From them he studied every rock, boulder, and all the varied angles of the ground.

Then Warrick ran his finger along a drawing and said, "An underground river with lakes. This is an old druid drawing of an underground river under Rose Fire. Long ago, druids explored these Black Mountain underground rivers and lakes. The underground rivers feed the Wye river."

Then for a long time he looked into Marian's eyes.

"Warrick. When you gazed into my eyes," Marian said. "I felt like you are reading my most private thoughts. You. . . . I feel like you take away all my privacy with just your gaze."

"Of course," Warrick said. "I know all your secrets, because I can read your thoughts. Your eyes tell me everything about you."

As she held his arm, she said, "Ooooooooo."

With her small fist, she hit his upper arm. Warrick smiled and remembered Morgan's advice, "Do not react. Do not respond to Marian with anger when she is angry."

Then Warrick jerked his head to Rose Fire. A roar came from Rose Fire's bailey, a great fire. The drawbridge dropped. Warrick yelled, "Hold your positions, you must maintain the circle around the camp. I do not want anyone to leave your positions. You must maintain the circle around the camp."

All his knights grabbed their weapons and took up battle positions.

Warrick ordered, "Pages. Squires. Continue to throw buckets of water over the knoll's sides. More."

ATTACK

Suddenly many Skinwalkers descended from the trees and snow on the mountain above.

Warrick yelled, "The fire in the castle is a diversion."

Marian held her back straight and her jaw level. She had an overabundance of courage.

She said, "My champion, I feel safe with you."

With his long arm, Lord Warrick pointed at the Skinwalkers ran down the mountain.

He yelled, "Waaaaaaaait. Waaaaaait. Waaaaaaaait. Continue to Waaaaaaaaait. Now."

Warrick bellowed, "NOW."

Lord Warrick's knights pulled on ropes buried in the snow.

A clamor of Terce prayer bells filled the valley and echoed off the Black Mountains.

The knights had attached the ropes to attached parallel rows of blessed spears. As they pulled on the ropes, the blessed spears broke up out of the snow. The knights pulled the parallel rows of spears into a slanted position. The spears pointed up the mountain. They had planted the blessed spears' butts in the frozen ground.

At the sight of the spears pointed at them, the Skinwalkers screamed. They slid on the snow. They tried to stop their charge down the mountainside. Instead they screamed in terror as they slid on the snow.

Terce-prayer-bells continued to call monks and nuns to prayer. Attacking Skinwalkers screamed and slid on the snow. As they slid, they impaled themselves on the blessed spear points.

Suddenly, the camp was then . . . silent.

Warrick ordered, "Squires. Pages. Throw buckets of water over the knoll's sides. More."

The valley's Terce prayer bells faded into echoes.

Lady Marian said, "The wounded?"

He turned her to face Rose Fire and said, "The wounded are not your concern."

She thought, "My champion does not care for the wounded. He is heartless. Will he be a heartless husband?"

Lord Warrick hugged her. "The attack is over," he said. His right eyebrow raised as it did when he lied. Warrick said, "We were never in any danger."

Lord Warrick took Marian back to her warm wagon and put her into it.

OUTSIDE THE WAGON

Then Warrick said, "Morgan, Drayton. Exorcize the Skinwalkers."

Warrick walked over to the wounded Skinwalkers and said, "Chant 'Jesus. Have mercy on me' if you want to cease being Skinwalkers."

Most of the Skinwalkers chanted, "Jesus. Have mercy on me."

Long lines of black, charcoal dust came out of their mouths. They changed back into Catholic priests, possessed by Lilith hundreds of years ago. Possessed because they did not want Lilith to burn them to death.

With spears through them the Catholic priests said, "Warrick. Father Malachi Martin. You have saved our souls." With many spears in each exorcized Catholic priest, they bleed and died.

Warrick walked over to the Skinwalkers that refused exorcism. He asked, "For you, do you wish to remain Skinwalkers?"

They spit at him and said, "We serve Satan, on earth and in Hell."

Warrick decapitated them and threw their heads into the campfires.

INSIDE THE WAGON.

Marian opened the wagon door and stepped out into the snow.

She sighed and put the question of wounded warriors from her mind. Then she walked out over to Warrick.

Marian said, "I can see that all the wounded are dead."

Warrick said, "They chose to fight me, so they chose to die. Most with saved souls. A few with doomed souls."

She said, "You are calm, like the sunrise's reflection on a glassy ocean. What horror have you seen to be so calm? Battle calms you?"

Warrick said, "Yes, Marian. Battle is my art, and art calms the soul."

He hugged her tight to his iron-covered chest. His right eyebrow unconsciously raised as he lied to reassure her. "Marian, I have defeated greater armies than Wolv's with fewer men."

Warrick said, "These overlapping late Prime, Terce and early Sext bells. They make it impossible to tell time."

Marian said, "You are calm. How?"

He lifted her chin and said, "Marian. You must be calm and confident. You must without question leave all the decisions on all matters to me?"

Warrick ordered, "Throw buckets of water over the knoll's sides. More."

Drayton overheard Marian's worry and spoke the truth, "You can be confident with Warrick. When Warrick is present, he has never lost a war. Warrick has never lost a battle. He has never lost a fight. He has never lost a joust. Even since childhood Warrick has never lost a chess match."

Drayton spoke the truth, except that Warrick had lost in love, his broken heart.

Then to comfort her, Drayton rubbed his stiff neck as he did when he lied. "Marian, we will easily defeat Wolv in this battle."

With that lie his neck became stiffer, as it always did when he lied. He leaned his head side to side to limber and stretch his cramped neck muscles.

In Wye Valley, distant, faint early Sext bells announced the coming zenith sun. The zenith sun when Wolv nailed Jesus to the Cross.

Ross Templar frowned and glanced to the left as he did when he lied. "Yes, my lady, we will easily defeat Wolv."

INSIDE ROSE FIRE

Inside Rose Fire Wolv growled, "Candlekeeper. Is it a safe hour?"

A hog-head Skinwalker with huge tusks said, "The Sext hour is close. The hour when you nailed Jesus to the Cross approaches. The Sext hour is never a safe hour for you."

Wolv walked into the Rose Fire chapel. As he stepped on Holy Ground, he burst into spiritual red-yellow flame. He walked up the aisle and picked up a consecrated Host from a broken Tabernacle.

Wolv looked at the host in his hand and said, "Jesus. As always. Certitude is my curse. As always, I can feel your presence in this Consecrated bread. The same as when I nailed you to the cross. Your hands and feet to the Cross, I feel you."

Wolv fell to his knees and begged, "Please Jesus. Raise Pamia from the dead for me. Please, Jesus."

On his knees, Wolv growled, "Pamia, Pamia."

OUTSIDE ROSE FIRE

Outside Rose Fire, on Warrick's battle field, Ross-Templar said, "Again. Wolv's Sext bells obsessions. He screams 'Pamia. Pamia."

Drayton pointed to Rose Fire's spires and said, "Again Wolv's obsessions cause an earthquake. Stones fall from Rose Fire's spires. Hell could not be more painful for Wolv than living with his obsessions."

Warrick ordered, "Throw buckets of water over the knoll's sides. More. Now while it is snowing."

Lord Warrick thought, "I was foolish to bring Marian here before I captured Rose Fire. Now Wolv might capture Marian. To test if Marian has Pamia's soul."

Lord Warrick said, "Again. Drayton. Morgan. Make sure that everyone does their hour of Perpetual Adoration. In the Adoration wagon. Remember, Perpetual Adoration of Jesus' Real Presence in the Blessed Sacrament. Make sure everyone does weekly confession. We do not want a repeat of Carcassonne, France. Where the king did not believe us. The red-fog ate the heads of the king's militia. The red-fog has eaten armies all over England and Europe. Wherever Wolv decides to conquer, we first always must part his red-fog. We can only slow him with adoration and weekly confession. Keep your focus that only Adoration and weekly confession will part the red-fog."

-
-

-

CHAPTER, Now Wales on the Knoll Across From Rose Fire, Year @ 1250s A.D.

THE BATTLE APPROACHES

On the battle field, Ross-Templar shouted, "Morgan. Drayton. Look at Rose Fire's chimneys. No more smoke comes from their chimneys. Wolv and his Skinwalkers have run out of firewood."

Warrick walked up with Marian and said, "Listen. Their horses no longer fight. Their houses are out of hay. The horses are too weak to fight for space. The seepage-well probably is also dry."

On the battlefield, Warrick ran his gauntlet down Marian's back.

Warrick said, "Soon Wolv must attack out of Rose Fire. He needs to gain drinking water and firewood. Soon the dead and blood will cover the battle field."

She hugged him tight and said, "My lord. I feel so safe in your arms."

"It fulfills me to hold you safe," Warrick said. Soft, and safe and warm."

He looked down into her blue eyes. As her beauty overpowered him, he dropped his gauntlets and gloves. While he looked into her beautiful eyes, he forgot. He forgot that he was in the middle of his battle camp. His heart beat faster. Into the snow, he dropped his helm and mail cowl and helm padding. Then he pulled back the cowl of her white fur coat. He exposed the mail on her beautiful blond hair. Then he lifted the mail cowl off her head. With his bare hands, he cupped her long blond hair up out of her coat. The wind blew her hair like the autumn wind. Just like the autumn wind blows the golden leaves on a tall oak. Warrick palmed her beautiful blond hair. He did not know what passed between them. Suddenly he felt a great warmth wrap around them. He felt as if this irresistible warmth pulled them together. Pull so hard that they became one person, one body. Her beauty was his opiate. His warrior's expression never showed his happiness. Yet, his happiness soared when he simply saw her smile. Warrick had an unchanging stoic, Spartan expression. He hungered for her beautiful body. Hidden behind his motionless Spartan countenance, he hungered for her every word. Both felt the same irresistible overwhelming feelings. These feelings excited and frightened her. Neither wanted to need another this powerfully. They hungered for each other's touch, smile, and presence. This hunger had grown stronger with each day. The hunger made them dependent upon the other. Marian had never had an irresistible eternal love. She did now. A maiden always loves her champion, forever, in true love. She had no choice.

Lord Warrick's emerald eyes and his long black hair mesmerized her. Warrick's long black hair wafted in the blizzard. His bronze features contrasted against the sparkling snow-covered mountains. Her eyes traced his granite-chiseled like cheek bones. Traced his jaw and his jaw muscles bulge. His emerald eyes fascinated her.

Warrick automatically ordered, "Throw buckets of water over the knoll's sides. More. Now while it is still snowing."

As he breathed harder, he felt like a predator about to jump on her. Warrick felt like a predator with no morals, just raw satiation to ravage her.

She felt his innate aggression, the fast beat of his breath. She feared and craved the feeling that he would pounce on her and take her.

Then the blizzard engulfed them like an impenetrable flock of swirling white doves. The snow storm was like a sea, a blanket, of white that descended upon them. They could not see more than a foot. The storm gave them the privacy that they needed for that moment.

The sun had risen higher, closer to its zenith.

SEXT BELLS. INSIDE ROSE FIRE.

Sext bells echoed off the Black Mountains.

Inside Rose Fire, at the sound of Sext bells, Wolv again fell to his knees. His eyes glazed over black. Then Wolv's Golgotha obsessions overcame him.

In Wolv's memory, he stood on Golgotha. Holy Mary and St John the Apostle stood many yards away. The good thief, Dismas, on Jesus' right. The wicked thief, Gestas, on Jesus' left.

Gestas said from his cross, "Jesus. If you are truly God, save yourself and save us."

Dismas said, "You should have fear of God. We justly deserve our punishment, but this man is innocent."

Dismas turned his head to Jesus and said, "Jesus. Remember me when you come into your kingdom."

Jesus said, "Today, you will be with me in Paradise."

Repeatedly Wolv growled, "Today you will be with me in paradise." His growls shook the Black Mountains.

Rage and hatred caused Wolv to foam at the mouth. Globs of red foam flowed from his mouth and covered him from mouth to feet.

On his knees in Rose Fire, slowly Wolv's eyes lost their black glaze.

On his knees, Wolv growled, "Jesus. Leave me alone. Stop torturing me."

OUTSIDE ROSE FIRE

Warrick said, "Wolv Sext obsessions. Jesus words to the Good Thief."

Warrick turned his back to the blizzard to protect Marian from the wind driven snow. Snow built up on his black hair and black cloak. The black-cloak that hung from the shoulders of his blessed armor.

Then he thought, "If I stay near Marian, I will soon need her. If I stay near her longer, I will soon need her smiles to be happy. I do not want happiness. All I want is the satisfaction that I have done my duty."

Marian thought, "I wish that Warrick would tell me if he needs me. His face is so expressionless. I wish he would tell me if I make him happy."

Warrick would only speak with actions, not words. Warriors would speak with actions. Yet he should have told Marian that her smile made him happy. Marian needed to hear these tender words.

She hugged him tight and said, "My lord. The safety in your arms sometimes feels like a jail. When I am in your arms, I feel that I cannot control my fate. Sometimes I hate the feeling of safety in your arms because I cannot control it. Is this the dreaded Pendragon-lineage curse?"

Warrick said, "Pendragon marriages are always tragic. The lucky Pendragons have at least short marriages, though tragic. They are the lucky ones. The unlucky are dead, or prisoners of the king's enemies. Or even the king's prisoners."

Marian said, "So the curse dooms you dead? Curses doom me to be a nag and a miser, at best?"

Warrick ordered, "Throw buckets of water over the knoll's sides. More. Now while we still have the blizzard."

Warrick said, "At best. As the story goes. Written history has recorded the curse's damage for more than a thousand years."

She said, "My lord. Will we ever be happy together?"

"Happy? Me?" Warrick asked. "Marian. I never expect happiness. Fate would never allow me to be happy. The closest that I come to happiness is my duty to protect you.

Marian thought, "Love, what about love?"

"Duty," Marian said. "You just kissed me. Did you kiss me because it is your duty to kiss me? I want you to tell me the truth. Did you kiss me because of duty? The truth, why did you kiss me?"

Marian thought, "I hope he says that he kissed me because of love for me?"

As the blizzard became a light snow, Warrick whispered, "The truth? I protect you because my duty demands that I protect you. In truth, I kissed you because I cannot resist your beauty."

As she looked up into his eyes she thought, "I am. I am to have a loveless marriage. He only kissed me for how I look. He did not kiss me for love of me. My champion protects me, but my bridegroom does not love me."

A tear filled her eye.

Late Sext and early Nones bells echoed off the Black Mountains.

Warrick ordered, "Throw buckets of water over the knoll's sides. More."

CRUCIFIXION OBSESSIONS.

Inside Rose Fire Wolv growled, "Candlekeeper. Is it a safe hour?"

A Hog-Head Skinwalker stepped far away from Wolv and said, "No. Master. Your obsession with Jesus' death on the Cross approaches. When you speared Jesus up through his right side, then through his heart. Can you not hear the distant and faint early Nones Bells? Nones' bells three hours after the Zenith sun. In your obsessions, you are about to kill Jesus on the Cross."

OUTSIDE ROSE FIRE

Outside Rose Fire Warrick ordered, "Throw buckets of water over the knoll's sides. More."

INSIDE ROSE FIRE

The Nones bells grew louder. Then Wolv's Golgotha obsessions again captured him. Against his will Wolv again walked into the Chapel. As he stepped on the blessed stones, he burst into red-yellow flame. He picked up a Consecrated Host.

Again he spoke to the round piece of consecrated bread and said, "Jesus. Again I feel your hands and feet as I nailed you to the cross. Release me from this curse of Certitude. That I know that you are in every Catholic tabernacle. Certitude that I know that you are this consecrated bread. Jesus, please raise Pamia from the dead for me."

In his mind Wolv heard, "My Beloved childhood friend. You have only to ask me for forgiveness for your sins."

Wolv growled, "Never. Never will I ask for forgiveness. Never. Jesus, I go to kill your followers. I go to obey my father, Satan. To kill Christians."

Repeatedly Wolv growled, "Give me Pamia. Raise Pamia from the dead for me."

Red fog poured from Wolv. His rage and hatred caused his to foam from the mouth. Red-foam poured from his mouth, down him, onto the floor.

Black flames burst from him and plumes of black smoke. His spiritual flames did not burn Rose Fire. The black flames rose high above Rose Fire.

ON THE BATTLEFIELD.

Out on the battlefield Drayton said, "Wolv's Nones-bells obsessions caused another earthquake. Again, he has caused another avalanche high above us."

OBSESSIONS WITH A CORPSE.

In Rose Fire, Wolv stood and burst into black crows. In the blizzard the crows flew high into the Black Mountains. High in the Black Mountains, Wolv flew into the mouth of a huge cavern.

He flew over a long table. A long table with many dead brides on both sides. All sat. All dead brides in wedding gowns. Skeletons, all skeletons. Hundreds of dead Adam-Symon-Pendragon brides. The brides' skulls on the table or floor.

The crows came together and formed Wolv in his original Roman General form.

He sat at the head of the table. Beside Pamia's one-thousand year-old corpse. Wax and painted-plaster-made Pamia's corpse look as if she were alive.

Wolv, in his original Roman form sat at the table's head and said, "Pamia. I have ordered the Skinwalkers to give you the best venison and wine. How is the wine?"

Skinwalkers served food and wine to all the corpses.

Then Wolv said, "I see that you are not hungry or thirsty."

Wolv growled, "Bring Pamia better venison, better ale."

Then Wolv stood and said, "Pamia, my Skinwalkers will take good care of you."

Then Wolv burst into a flock of crows and flew back to Rose Fire Castle.

OUTSIDE ROSE FIRE ON THE BATTLEFIELD

A hundred paces closer to Rose Fire, many arrows thudded into the frozen ground.

Lord Warrick said, "Wolv attacks. Marian, into the wagon, you are safer in the wagon. You must not come out until I call for you."

Warrick and his knights grabbed their weapons and blessed shields.

Warrick ordered, "Throw buckets of water over the knoll's sides. More. Now while it snows."

Warrick shouted, "Ready for an attack."

Again, Warrick ordered, "Throw buckets of water over the knoll's sides. More."

As Warrick paced the camp, he kept his eyes on the mountain and Rose Fire. He paced while cacophonies of extremely late Sext and Nones bells waxed and waned.

IN ROSE FIRE

As crows, Wolv flew into Rose Fire. With the Nones bells Wolv's obsessions again shook the Black Mountain range. He growled, "My God, my God, why have you forsaken me?"

OUTSIDE ROSE FIRE
Everyone stopped and waited for the quaking to end.

ON ROSE FIRE'S BAILEY FLOOR.
Slowly Wolv came out of his obsession.

ON THE BATTLEFIELD.
Lord Warrick paced to peer around the trees. Eastward shadows lengthened.

Warrick said, "Drayton, the sun is well past its zenith. We are deep into the day's wane. The trees' long eastward shadows show that we are close to the Compline bells. Order all the knights to return to their daily duties. Begin the Compline prayers and meals. Wolv's archers shot those arrows from desperation. They will not attack now. They will attack soon."

Warrick shouted, "Otan. Keep the squires and pages throwing water on the knoll's sides. Continue with the water."

While Warrick paced, he read and reread war maps. The latest Nones bells rang along with Vespers and even early Compline bells. Warrick paced and studied Rose Fire's original architectural plans. He paced for hours. The eastward shadows grew longer. The day darkened. Then the early Vespers bells announced the red sunset and time to sup. Slowly the red sunset bathed the Black Mountains and valley in a pink hue.

Warrick said, "These canonical bells are very confusing. No wonder they torment Wolv. Wolv never knows when it is a safe hour for him. I never know when it is the proper time."

Warrick thought, "I forgot Marian. She has waited in the wagon to Nones and then to Vespers bells. Marian has a sharp tongue. This wait will only sharpen her tongue."

Lord Warrick knocked on the wagon's iron door.

Through the door Warrick said, "Marian. The immediate danger is over. You can come out if you wear your mail and white fur cloak."

The Black Mountain shadows of dusk settled over the camp and Rose Fire. Marian stepped from the wagon.

She snapped, "You forgot me. You forgot me. The camp was safe hours ago and you forgot to come and get me."

She put her fists on her hips, elbows out as she frowned up at him. Her eyebrows formed an angry V. Then she said, "I am just a forgettable tryst for you."

Warrick said, "Marian. Wolv is preparing to attack. I can hear the rattle of the Skinwalker weapons. They prepare to raid the Valley for food, water and horse feed."

As dusk grew darker, the Vespers bells filled the valley. She glared up at his handsome face.

LADY HUNGRY EYES

Lord Warrick said, "Marian. Lady Hungry Eyes, you look at me with hungry eyes. Continue to look at me with hungry eyes and I might not defeat the enemy. Lady Hungry Eyes."

"What, my anger frightens you," Marian leaned forward. She placed her fists on her hips.

Warrick said, "Sometimes you are a silly woman. Your anger would never frighten me."

"Silly? Silly? Ohhhhhhh, how could I forget, nothing frightens you," Marian said.

Warrick shouted again, "Pages. Squires. Faster. Continue to throw buckets of water over the knoll's sides. More."

"Marian. Beauty frightens me," Warrick said. "Beauty distracts me. Poison, beauty is a poison that kills knights."

With her fists on her hips, her eyebrows formed an angry V, she blurted, "Again. You insult me. This time you say that I am silly and beautiful just to insult . . . to insult?"

Surprise made Marian's mouth fall open.

She asked, "You fear my beauty? I am beautiful? . . . You said that I am beautiful?"

Still with her fists on her hips she leaned forward and looked up. Then she raised her eyebrows in confusion, "Beautiful . . . you . . . you said that I am beautiful?"

With round eyes and raised eyebrows of surprise, Marian clasped her hands behind her back. As she smiled, she stared up into his emerald eyes.

Marian said, "You said that I am beautiful?"

His stoic, handsome face and emerald eyes enthralled her.

After a few minutes, Warrick said, "Lady Hungry Eyes. I told you. Continue to look at me with hungry eyes and I may not defeat the enemy."

-

-

-

CHAPTER, Now Wales on the Knoll Across From Rose Fire, Year @ 1250s A.D.

THE WORLD'S ONLY HOPE.

Embarrassed, she blinked and she lied, "Hunnnnger? I have no hunnnnnnnnger in my eyes. Me? Looooooking? I was only loooooking because you were staaaaring at me."

Warrick smiled and mimicked Marian's pronunciation, "Lyyyyyyying, hunnnnnnnnger, staaaaring."

Warrick ordered, "Ross-Templar. Morgan. Make the squires and pages run. They must throw more buckets of water over the knoll's sides. More. Now in this blizzard."

Marian turned her back to him and crossed her arms.

Again Warrick ordered, "Throw more buckets of water over the knoll's sides. More."

She thought, "Now he knows when I tell a lie. He can read my mind. When he looks into my eyes, he sees everything, my most private thoughts. My thoughts were my final retreat. My thoughts were my hiding place. The 'place' where I could hide away from the world. Now, with Warrick I have no privacy. Now, now I must change the topic. Yes, I will change the topic so he can no longer read my mind."

Warrick ordered, "Drayton. Order half your archers to throw buckets of water over the knoll's sides. More."

Marian turned to Warrick. With her arms defiantly crossed on her breasts, she pointed. Pointed across the deep crevasse between them and Rose Fire.

Lady Marian asked, "Warrick. Have you changed your tactics to conquer such a strong castle?"

Warrick ignored Marian and ordered, "Morgan. No one is to sit beside the fire. Make everyone throw water over the knoll's sides. More."

The Vespers bells continued as the dusk grew darker.

Marian said, "You ignore me."

Warrick said, "Yes. Lady Hungry Eyes. I ignore you."

He said, "How will I conquer the castle? Have I changed my tactics? I have already told you. I will repeat if only to calm you."

Warrick ordered, "Everyone run. Quickly. Throw buckets of water over the knoll's sides. More."

Marian crossed her arms and said, "Your insults are never ending. Now I am not only silly. Now I also have a fevered mind that you must calm."

Warrick said, "Lady Fevered Mind. Good, you finally agree with me about something. Lady Beautiful Eyes."

With her arms crossed she twisted her head and torso to Warrick and said, "Oooooooooooooooooooooo."

A long line of squires, pages and knights continuously tossed water over the knoll's sides.

Then she smiled and glanced back at him, "Lady Beautiful Eyes. Beautiful?"

Warrick said, "Faster. Faster with the water. Run faster with the water."

Warrick smiled and said, "Lady Silly, Lady Upset, . . . and Lady Beautiful."

Marian turned to him. As she smiled, with her arms still crossed, she said, "Have you changed your tactics? Rose Fire is impregnable. How will you conquer such an impenetrable castle?"

Warrick said, "I will conquer it when I do not conquer it. I know some of Wolv's greatest weaknesses. He needs the Skinwalkers with him because he needs people full of hate. His arrogance and drunkenness spawn his overconfidence and impatience. Wolv thinks that he is safe and secure behind Rose Fire's battlements. Deception, . . . I have deceived Wolv, so he is wrong. He is not safe nor secure. Wolv does not know that we have trapped him and his Skinwalkers. Trapped him within Rose Fire. Snow storms in the Black Mountains last so long. So long that they will soon burn all of their fire wood. When you have too many warriors in a castle, they will soon empty the buttery. I know from the old architectural drawings that they only have a shallow well. The well will run dry with so many drinking from it. War horses are very thirsty. More important, on this knoll, we have no castle walls. No walls to keep us from hunting for meat and gathering water. Plus, we have a forest of fire wood to stay warm. We have only to wait while those in Rose Fire run out. Run out of firewood, food and water. Listen now, again, from the clamor in the stables. Their horses fight each other for stable room. Wolv has too many horses and too many Skinwalkers. As the horses fight each other for space, they will exhaust themselves. Wound each other. Wolv expects us to attack the castle. Instead we will wait for Wolv's Skinwalkers to grow irrational. Irrational from starvation and thirst."

Wye Valley Vespers bells continued to ring and call everyone to prayer and sup.

Warrick ordered, "Otan. Don't slip again with the water. We do not want slippery ice in the camp. Just water over the knoll's sides. More. Do not stop."

Marian said, "We need more knights. Why did not more knights come with us?"

"No time," Warrick said. "Wolv's Skinwalkers have surrounded nine fortifications. Chester, Knighton, Newton, Hope, Flint, Rhuddlan, Conway, Beaumaris, and even Artpool. England's knights are defending those nine castles. Rose Fire is Wolv's strongest foothold. The Skinwalkers want the fortifications from Bristol to Liverpool. We had to make any show of force. Any show at Rose Fire, in the middle of the Wolv's territory. If we can recapture Rose Fire, England will have a foothold. A foothold in the center of the AntiChrist's Skinwalker rebellion.

Then to comfort Marian, Warrick lied, "More knights. More knights will come to join us in a few days."

Marian said, "I saw your right eyebrow raise. We are so few against so many? Wolv's Skinwalkers will kill us."

Morgan whispered to Ross, "Ross-Templar. Marian again breached battlefield superstitions and etiquette."

Ross-Templar whispered, "Yes, Morgan. In front of Warrick's men, Marian has questioned his ability."

Lord Warrick sighed and glanced up at the sky.

He thought, "Why? Marian breaches my battlefield authority. Still, why do I want Marian here with me? Because . . . because, . . . I want my eyes, my soul, to drink in her ravishing beauty. I want to dive into her blue eyes and swim in her. Morgan told me not to be angry with her. Yes, I will follow Morgan's advice. Now I will not react to her with anger."

Warrick ordered, "Steady with the buckets, only toss water over the knoll's sides. More."

Father Malachi Martin, in Antlers and deer hides, walked up behind Marian. Malachi wore armor and chain-mail under his druid disguise. He said, "My lady. Lord Warrick is not overconfident."

Snow flakes dropped through Father Malachi's druid antlers and settled on his deer hides.

Marian stepped forward and turned to Malachi.

Reque slipped with a bucket of water. Lord Warrick picked him up and said, "Be careful. We want no ice in the camp."

Marian said, "Father Malachi, how do you know?"

Father Malachi Martin said, "Marian. Lord Warrick is our only hope against the AntiChrist. My lady, Lord Warrick is not overconfident. Overconfidence comes from self indulgence, sloth, and weakness. Confidence comes from strict discipline, constant hard training, and planning. Lord Warrick has long years of experience. My lord knows what causes the enemy to charge in irrational and self-destructive rage. That is his plan now."

Later Vespers bells rang. A small slice of the dusk sun sent rays onto the Black Mountains. Thicker red-fog circled the top of the Black Mountains.

Marian had a pink-sun glow on her white, fur, cowled cloak. Lady Marian said, "So few against so many?"

Warrick ordered, "Morgan. Order them faster with the water."

Malachi Martin said, "My lady. You should not worry. You must trust my lord."

Warrick ordered, "Faster. We must prepare the battle field."

Ross Templar said, "The buckets are exhausting some knights."

Lord Warrick said, "Better exhausted than dead."

Morgan rested his huge mace in his crossed arms. He said, "We have studied accurate maps of the terrain. The weather, this blowing snow, the freezing nights, and the mountains will defeat Wolv. Let me give you an example. Once in Spain Warrick and I had a pack of starved wild dogs after us. Far too many wild dogs for us to fight. The dogs would have harmed our horses' legs. We had no armor or mail. Therefore, Warrick decided to ride faster for a deep ravine. We had the near starved wild dogs at their fastest speed. Our horses jumped the ravine. As we had ciphered, the dogs ran so fast that they could not stop. The dogs tried to jump after us and fell to their deaths."

Marian asked, "My lord, you are going to turn these murders into irrational wild dogs? These vultures are clever. They prey on the weak with murder and rape and arson. Wild dogs cannot reason. These murders are smart. Many are the most clever of men."

Early valley Compline bells called monks and nuns to prayer and bedtime.

Warrick ordered, "Do not tire. Faster. Throw more water over the knoll's sides. More."

Lord Warrick sighed to hold back his anger. Anger that anyone would question him before battle in his knight's view.

He replied, "In starvation, frost bite and thirst, men quickly throw reason aside. They become just like half-starved dogs."

More Compline bells rose from the Wye Valley and echoed off the mountains and hills.

Lady Marian's fear welled up in her, "What about Nicola?"

Marian thought, "O Great Lord Warrick. Lord of Arrogance and Overconfidence, never to become the lord of Rose Fire. Warrick is going to get us all killed."

Marian said, "I want Nicola and the triplets, warm, in my father's Oxford manor."

Warrick quipped, "You had your chance to stay in Oxford. You had many suitors in Oxford that you could have married?"

As Marian crossed her arms and raised her nose she said, "Yes, many."

Late Compline bells announced that Vigils hour was two hours away. Vigils-hours, Midnight, the Witches' three hours. When the Queen of Witches, Lilith, was strongest.

Marian thought, "None of them. Not my other suitors would have brought Nicola to such a dangerous place."

He teased her by saying, "You had your opportunity to marry one of them. You could have married none and bedded all of them."

Ross-Templar, Morgan, and Drayton laughed at that remark. The three knew that they should leave Marian and Warrick alone. They motioned to the other knights to walk backward away from Marian and Warrick. Warrick's knights did their duties beyond Warrick's voice.

They ran in a great circle with water buckets. Water streamed over the knoll's sides.

Marian said, "Lord Warrick. Lord Thickheadedness. You and your brothers insult me. Your brothers just laughed at me."

She started to walk back to the wagon. He wrapped his muscled, steel-plated arms around her. Then he said, "I merely expose your lost opportunities."

In the Wye valley, Compline bells began to fade.

Warrick said, "The Vigils-bells will begin. Midnight, the witches' hours approach. The three hours between midnight Vigils and Matins bells are the three witches' hours. The three hours when Lilith is strongest."

While she struggled to shove his arms away, she remembered her mother's words. *"Be careful for what you pray; you may get it."*

She shoved against his arms and said, "You hold me against my will."

As he hugged her, she turned to him.

She said, "The aura of safety, of security and of warmth around you frightens me. I feel safe against my will. It is as if you have an unnatural power over me."

She smelled the strong aroma of bay leaf on him. As in her Oxford manor, the bay leaf made her feel safe, protected, even loved. The bay leaf unconsciously made her feel her father's love in his Oxford manor. Bay leaf spice permeated her father's buttery. Thus, the bay-leaf aroma had caused Marian to feel her father's love. Lady Marian had smelled bay leaf in her father's manor since childhood.

He smiled and said, "I like you in my arms where you are safe. You are my charge by order of the king. You will always be safe in my arms. This is my nature, my training, to protect you, Marian."

His training to protect the innocent was ingrained in him. Ingrained so deeply that it welled in him. His will to protect her overpowered his anger at her quips.

His smile, and not angry frown, surprised her.

Marian said, "Warrick. You smile, you usually react in anger and frown to everything that I say. Why not now? You act like you enjoy my banter."

Warrick said, "Marian. It could be a spicy flavor that I have begun to savor."

She caught his gaze.

Then she thought, "The king could have given us an assignment in Oxford. The king has enemies in Oxford. The king has enemies everywhere."

Marian said, "My lord. I have no training to suit Nicola or me for these conflicts."

Warrick teased her, "You finally realize that. Just obey me and you will be safe."

He pulled her close to him and said, "Marian. You are safe here. I and my knights will try to allow for your quips and jabs. We will try not to breathe fire when you cause trouble."

His protective predisposition overwhelmed all his other emotions. As they stood, all he wanted to do to Marian was to hug her. He tightly hugged her.

Warrick's smiths forged new weapons and blessed armor. The pounding of their hammers echoed off the mountains.

His warriors continued to throw water over the knoll's sides. Unusual grey fog froze in the air and fell like fine snow. The snow crunched under their feet.

Warrick said, "Strong Vigils bells. Vigils' bells announce midnight. The three hours of Witches begin."

Vigils' bells rose from the valley and echoed off the Black Mountains. Vigil's bells of the midnight three hours of Witches. Warrick pointed to the top of the Black Mountains. He said, "The red-fog circles the peaks. The demon Lilith is in that red-fog. She is gathering reinforcements for Wolv."

Warrick hugged Marian.

Warrick pointed above Rose Fire and said, "Marian. See the small amount of smoke above the castle?"

Marian said, "Yes."

As the snow fell, the snow clouds blocked out the full moon and stars.

Lord Warrick said, "Morgan. Ross Templar. Drayton. Come to me."

They stood beside Warrick.

Warrick pointed at Rose Fire, "Look at Rose Fire's chimneys. Only the smoke of embers. They have burned their tables, chairs, even the stables' wood. They have little firewood. The pink granite walls have chilled. Wolv freezes. Within hours, Wolv's Skinwalkers will thunder across Rose Fire's drawbridge and attack us."

A knight thundered up the road to Warrick's camp. He dismounted. A page took the reins of his warhorse. He handed Warrick a scroll sealed with the king's wax seal.

Warrick asked, "How did you get back so fast?"

The knight's horse fell to the ground, dead.

Beside the horse, the knight collapsed unconscious.

Ross Templar shouted, "Morgan. Drayton. Come, I need you to come here and help me carry him to the fire. He may have ridden himself to death."

While Morgan, Ross-Templar, and Drayton carried the knight, Warrick broke the seal. He read in ancient Greek.

Lord Warrick,

I consulted with Sir Colne. My champion, you are the world's only hope. We came to the sad conclusion that I could spare no knights. Wolv's red fog grows thicker in London. When the red-fog settles, it has eaten people. Or, the red-fog turned them into Skinwalkers. As instructed, your knight handed your message to me and only to me. The only other one to read it was Sir Colne. Then Sir Colne, burned it in my brazier. I will search for the viper in my court. My champion, beware that the red-fog grows thicker over the world. My champion, you must slow the AntiChrist. You are the world's only hope.

King Edward

Warrick thought, "The king is blind, Colne is the viper in his court."

Then Warrick crumbled the parchment and threw it into a camp fire.

Warrick whispered, "Father Malachi. The king will not send us reinforcements. Marian is in great danger."

Father Malachi cast his eyes down and said, "Warrick. I have been in worse battles with demons. With fewer knights."

Lord Warrick whispered, "Malachi. You always cast your eyes down when you lie."

Father Malachi said, "All is not lost. Look around. A constant blizzard has covered the Black Mountains. As we need, the snow is deep. The ground is frozen as hard as granite."

Vigils' bells echoed off the Black Mountains. A hundred paces nearer Rose Fire a cloud of arrows thudded into the ground.

Marian shouted, "We are under attack."

Father Malachi said, "Marian. No, not yet. Panicked Skinwalkers within the castle shot the arrows in a desperate attempt to harm us."

Warrick said, "Marian. Their bows are not powerful enough to reach us."

He led Marian to the armored wagon and said, "Stay inside. The time of the attack is close."

Lord Warrick said, "Drayton. Morgan. Ceaselessly make sure that everyone does their hour of Perpetual Adoration. In the Adoration wagon. Perpetual Adoration facing Jesus' Real Presence in the Blessed Sacrament. Make sure everyone does weekly confession. Remember the disaster of the army of Edinburgh, Scotland. The Scots would not listen. They refused to do Adoration and confession. Like so many others they thought Wolv was just a man. Remember, the red-fog ate the Scots skin and left them alive. Stay focused. Adoration and confession keep the red-fog away. Edinburgh, Scotland buried their army in mass graves. Without their skin, no one could identify the bodies."

Lord Warrick said, "Ross-Templar. Have each hold two buckets."

Warrick commanded. "I want you to gather more water from the mountain stream behind us. At night all night. I want everyone to continue to pour buckets of water down the knoll's sides. The water will freeze."

INSIDE THE WAGON.
Inside the armored wagon, Marian and her sister, Nicola, lay side by side. They pulled thick wool-covered sheepskin blankets over themselves.

Nicola said, "By the look on your face, you are dreaming of Lord Warrick again."

Marian said, "Yes, he is a handsome man. Handsome like a desert lion with a black mane is handsome. His sharp stone-like features are not boyish. He is a consummate warrior. He is the consummate warlord."

Nicola replied, "Yes, his dark, brooding, emerald eyes are always serious."

Marian said, "Those emerald eyes. How did he ever get such bright emerald eyes? I am obsessed with those eyes. When he looks at me, I get goose flesh. My blood tingles in places I am ashamed to mention."

They giggled.

Nicola said, "Listen to the valley. The clamor of the late midnight Vigils bells must awaken everyone."

Marian said, "It is so warm with these hot stones wrapped in leather. The knights are generous with their time. Outside we would freeze."

Her seventeen-year-old sister did not laugh but said, "No. You must not say such a thing. You could curse us to freeze. Hurry, knock on wood to drive away the evil Druid spirits."

They gently knuckled each other's heads to tease the other. Teased that they had wooden heads and laughed.

Marian said, "The Church says that 'knock on wood' means to knock on the Crucifix. To knock on the Crucifix as a prayer."

Nicola again knocked on Marian's head.

Marian leaned beyond Nicola's reach. Then she clapped her hands and laughed.

Marian said, "Listen to the clamor of the Vigils bells."

Nicola said, "I hear early Matins bells. We are half way through the three midnight Witches hours."

OUTSIDE THE WAGON

Lady Marian dressed in her padding, mail and white-squirrel cowled cloak. Then she dangled her legs from the wagon door.

She said, "My lord, is it safe to step from the wagon?"

Warrick said, "Marian, are you ill? Did I hear the impossible? You asked for my recommendation? Now I know that you are ill."

As Marian dangled her legs from the wagon door, she crossed her arms. She said, "Humphhhhhh."

She rolled her lower lip out in a pout.

Warrick said, "You should pull your lip back before it freezes."

As she dangled her legs, with crossed arms, she hung her head and said, "Warrick. Can I ever win over you?"

"Think carefully Marian, if you won, what would you win," Warrick asked?

Marian put her hands to her forehead. She said, "You . . . you . . . you give me a headache. May I step from the wagon?"

"You . . . you . . . you and your pretty head. You may come over here and have headaches," Warrick teased her.

"Thank God," Nicola shouted.

In the wagon, behind Marian, Nicola put her feet to Marian's back. With both feet she pushed Marion from the wagon.

As Marian fell on her bottom in the deep snow, Nicola shouted, "Reque. Reque. We need more hot stones to warm the wagon. Marian held the door open long enough to freeze us."

Warrick reached down and grasped Marian's hands. He pulled Marian to her feet. Then she brushed the snow from her bottom. Reque and other squires carried hot stones from the campfires. They put the stones in the wagon's braziers.

Marian said, "We will have a wonderful wedding. I will bless our marriage with the best thyme-honey mead for passion. Also, I will fill the chapel with yellow and white crocuses. To bless us with cheer and gladness."

Warrick said, "Yes, Marian. I will find the best thyme honey for your wedding mead. Also, as you wish, I will fill the chapel with rare yellow and white crocuses."

Marian walked with Warrick. She said, "I want to build a large infirmarian within the bailey."

INSIDE ROSE FIRE

Inside Rose Fire, on the bailey floor Wolv howled, "Holy Mary. Get out of my head."

Wolv eyes glazed over black and he fell to his knees. In memory he was back in Egypt as a six-year-old. Children circled him and chanted, "Ugly Eyes." He wept.

In his Egyptian memory, Holy Mary walked over to tiny Wolv. She picked up Wolv and carried him to a stone chair. A chair that six-year-old prodigy, Jesus, used to advise politicians and spiritual leaders. Six-year-old prodigy Jesus solved business disputes and counseled marriages.

Holy Mary seated Wolv on her lap and said, "Wolv, you are beautiful and intelligent. Do not hate anyone. Tiny Wolv. I will always love you."

Wolv knelt on the Rose Fire Bailey floor and repeatedly roared, "Tiny Wolv. I will always love you."

Wolv's repeated roars caused an avalanche. Stones fell from the Rose Fire merlons.

The black glaze on Wolv's eyes cleared and he said, "Holy Mary. Please stop torturing me. Holy Mary. Get out of my head."

OUTSIDE ROSE FIRE

Warrick said, "Wolv's obsessions again. With each century Wolv's obsessions grow worse."

Marian said, "Finally this obsession now fades away."

Warrick asked, "Marian, what is so magical about your particular infirmarian."

Lady Marian said, "My lord, my patients live to go home to their families? If I may ask, what is so magical about what you say?"

Warrick said, "My soldiers live to go home to their families, my enemies do not."

Marian said, "How can we ever be happy when your only concerns are enemies?"

Lord Warrick raised his hand to stop her sentence and said, "Happy or not. Your concern is to obey me. You will obey me, because it is your duty. I will marry you and protect you because it is my duty."

Marian said, "My lord, will you come to love me?"

As Warrick thought of his first wife, Ogina, the traitor, he said, "Duty. It is my duty to protect you?"

Lady Marian said, "Just duty? We are to have a loveless marriage?"

Warrick turned to a noise from Rose Fire.

Marian returned to the interior of her iron-plated wagon. On the wagon floor, she rolled on her back on thick pillows and said, "Nicola. I am to have a loveless marriage. Duty, Warrick only wants duty."

As the early Matins bells rang, Marian fell asleep.

BURNING SOMETHING IN THE CASTLE

Ross-Templar shouted, "Hurry Warrick. Wolv is burning something in the castle. He is planning something."

IN THE WAGON

Marian woke. She sat up and thought, "I told Warrick often that I loved him. Why did he not say that he loved me? He did the same thing on the battlefield. I told him that I loved him then. He only told me to climb back into the armored wagon. Does Warrick really love me or am I his play thing?"

-

-

-

CHAPTER, Now Wales on the Knoll Across From Rose Fire, Year @ 1250s A.D.

SOON THE ATTACK.

INSIDE ROSE FIRE. RESURRECTION HOUR OBSESSION.

Inside Rose Fire, in the Great Hall, Wolv roared, "Candlekeeper. Is it a safe hour?"

A Hog-head-Tusked Skinwalker shouted from across the room. "Lord Wolv. Can you not hear the early, faint Wye Valley Prime Bells? They mix with the extremely late Matins bells. Your Resurrection obsession hour is about to defeat you."

As always in his obsession, Wolv's eyes glazed black. He again turned into black-dust and sank into the cracks in the Great Hall floor.

Wolv sank into the earth through an underground river and waterfall. He continued to sink until he again solidified on a shelf beside an underground lake.

In his original Roman General uniform, with black-glazed eyes, he watched Jesus' Resurrection. In Wolv's memory, the earth quaked so hard Wolv fell to his knees.

Wolv's obsessions defeated him as he said, "Jesus. I watched as you raised people from the dead. You love Pamia. I love Pamia. Please raise Pamia from the dead for me."

Suddenly, Pamia stood beside Jesus.

Pamia took Wolv's hand and said, "My love. You have only to ask Jesus for forgiveness. Then we can eventually be together in Heaven."

Wolv growled, "Jesus. Jesus, you torture me with Pamia's presence. Know, you know I serve Satan. You know that I will never ask for forgiveness."

'   Wolv howled, "Jesus, please raise Pamia from the dead for me."

Rage caused Wolv to foam at the mouth. Red foam, born of rage and hatred, streamed from his mouth and covered the floor.

OUTSIDE ROSE FIRE

Outside Rose Fire, the sunrise Prime bells rang in the valley.

Inside her wagon, Marian dressed in her warm padding, boots, and mail. Then she dressed in her thick, white, fur cloak. Now dressed and camouflaged in the white cowled cloak, she stepped from her wagon. She walked over to Warrick.

With his hand on his blessed sword's hilt, he said, "Marian. Look above the outer wall battlement. You see no more smoke above Rose Fire."

Warrick pointed and said, "Marian. You can see no smoke even over the sloped-inner wall battlement, the talus wall. Look higher and you will see no smoke from Wolv's keep. If they had any firewood, smoke would come from Wolv's keep. Wolv has no firewood to cook in the buttery or to heat the castle. I know that they have burned furniture, the stables, anything they could break and burn. Yes, I was right to come here two months early. Two months early when the mountains were still frozen. Now when we are warm around our campfires, they freeze. They have already used up the stores of food. With certainty, I know that they have emptied all the water from the well. They have sent many runners to fill buckets at the mountain stream. The mountain streams on Rose Fire's far side. Drayton's archers are along the mountain stream on Rose Fire's far side. Drayton's blessed arrows stick out of their runners' headless bodies. His archers have assured that the runners did not return. Rose Fire has little water. I told you. When Rose Fire seepage well is emptied, the well takes a week to refill. Now that they have no water, they and their horses are beginning to wither. Wolv knows that if he does not attack us soon that he must surrender. Wolv never surrenders."

Morning Prime Bells rang all over the Wye Valley. The red morning-sun cast off long shadows. Long shadows from east to west. The red sun reflected pink off the snow.

Marian said, "Your warriors still run to throw water over the knoll's sides."

Warrick said, "All night, every night."

Lady Marian said, "They look exhausted."

Lord Warrick said, "Better exhausted than dead."

Marian crossed her arms, impatient that Nicola was not yet as safe as she wished. She whispered into his ear. So those on the battlefield would not hear her impertinent question.

"Warrick. I am impatient that Nicola is not safe," Marian said. "You may be the Lord of Ice and Snow. Yet, Nicola cannot live in that wagon forever. Nicola needs to eat more than dried venison."

As Warrick smiled, he whispered, "Marian. Soon Nicola will eat honey and sweet bread. Then you will eat your impatience, Lady of Sharp Tongues. Now take my arm, follow me, listen and learn."

She wrapped her arm around his arm.

Warrick said, "Marian. Listen. Wolv's Resurrection obsession. These Prime Bells mean that Wolv's Resurrection obsession will soon end. Then in the Terse Bells Wolv will attack us."

Strong Prime bells echoed off the Black Mountains.

Wolv's growls of 'Jesus, please raise Pamia from the dead' shook the earth.

Lord Warrick said, "Marian. Listen. The AntiChrist's growls caused another avalanche. He will attack after he recovers from the exhaustion of his Resurrection obsession. In about two hours after this obsession."

From the mountain they heard a loud thunderclap. Then the long splinter of wood.

Warrick said, "Marian. Listen. The only time that I have heard that noise is the collapse. The collapse of the great Thames River wooden bridge."

Warrick shouted, "Drayton. Ross-Templar. Morgan. What was that loud noise on the mountain?"

Drayton said, "I do not know? Will they attack us from above?"

Morgan said, "Impossible. Now the snow is too deep even for horses up there. Ross-Templar. What was that noise on the mountain?"

Ross-Templar said, "I have wisdom from unlikely places. I bedded a lady from the Scottish Highlands from Moray Firth. She said."

Morgan said, "Your forays into other husband's bedrooms. They have something to do with this battle?"

Ross-Templar hung his head in shame. He said, "As I said. Wisdom comes from unlikely places. As we lay in the hay, she told me of winters in the Scotland Highlands. She said that the Scotland Highlands could be so cold. So cold that the trees freeze, burst, split and fall."

Warrick said, "Never have I known colder weather. Trees freeze and burst, yes? That is the only thing that could cause such distinct noises."

Warrick turned to Drayton and said, "Drayton. Make sure that the long bows and cross bows are dry. We do not want them also to freeze."

As Marian walked with Warrick, she kept her arm twined on his forearm. She held him close and paced with him. Warrick paced and memorized different architectural vellums of Rose Fire.

Father Malachi Martin walked over and said, "Warrick. We must be very watchful. The Black Mountains are full of Satan worshipers."

Through the day and night they heard two sounds. Canonical bells echoed in the Black Mountains. Trees continuously exploded high on the mountains.

Prime sunrise bells rang, trees exploded.

Midmorning, Terce bells rang, trees exploded.

The sun climbed to its zenith as Sext zenith-sun bells rang, trees exploded.

CRUCIFIXION OBSESSIONS.

In Rose Fire, on the bailey floor, Wolv fell to his knees. Again his eyes glazed over black as his memory went back to the Crucifixion.

In his memory he looked up at Jesus on the Cross. Jesus said, "I thirst."

A Roman soldier put a sponge on a spear. He held it up to Jesus' mouth.

Then Wolv's obsessions rumbled the Black Mountains as he growled repeatedly. 'I thirst.' Each growl shook the mountains.

Red fog poured off Wolv. Wolv's rage was now so great that he blew red and yellow from his mouth.

Slowly Wolv came out of his obsessions and his eyes lost their black-glaze.

OUTSIDE ROSE FIRE

Warrick said, "At Sext bells Wolv nailed Jesus to the cross. From Sext bells to Nones bells, Wolv yells his Golgotha obsessions. Some believe Jesus asked for water. Others believe Jesus thirsted to save souls."

Warrick said, "Wolv's Sext-Nones bells' obsessions are not finished. Remember. At Sext Bells Wolv nailed Jesus to the Cross. Three hours later, at Nones bells, Wolv rammed a spear up Jesus' right side. Up though Jesus' heart. Just wait and listen and learn about Wolv"

Warrick said, "Listen for Wolv. Distant early Sext Bells continue to ring, Sext bells, the Zenith sun bells. Early Sext Bells when Jesus carried the Cross. Zenith sun Sext bells when Wolv nailed Jesus to the Cross.

In Rose Fire, Wolv stood in Rose Fire's great hall. His eyes glazed black as his memory went back to Jesus carrying the Cross.

In his memory, Wolv whipped Jesus as Jesus carried the Cross. Jesus fell. Jesus tripped over his own ankle-length robe. Wolv grabbed Symon's arm, Symon, Wolv's own half-brother. He growled, "Symon. Carry the cross or Jesus will not live to be Crucified. We must humiliate Jesus with Crucifixion. Rome demands that we Crucify Jesus. Rome demands that Jesus die on the Cross."

In Wolv's memory, Symon of Cyrene, Wolv's half brother, shouldered the cross. He put Jesus' arm around his neck. Symon stood and staggered forward.

In Rose Fire, captured by guilt-ridden memory, Wolv's eyes remained glazed black.

In Wolv's memory, Wolv continued to whip Jesus and whispered into Jesus' ear. "Raise Pamia from the dead for me. Only then will I end this torture."

Symon carried the Cross atop Golgotha.

Wolv remembered, atop Golgotha, that Symon put the cross on the ground. Then Wolv's Roman soldiers pushed Symon away from Jesus.

Then Wolv relived nailing Jesus' hands and feet to the Cross. With each nail, Wolv whispered into Jesus' ear. "Raise Pamia from the dead for me and this torture will end."

Within his memory, Wolv whispered between greeted teeth. "Three hours on the Cross. Still Jesus refuses to raise Pamia from the dead."

Wolv shouted, "Break their legs. Break their legs."

Wolv growled and grabbed a long spear. Then Wolv mounted a horse and rode up to Jesus on the cross. Wolv thrust the spear up into Jesus' right ribs, up into Jesus' heart. Then Wolv pulled out the spear. An impossible amount of blood and water gushed from Jesus' right side. Gushed onto Wolv.

Still, in Wolv's memory, on Golgotha, Symon helped take Jesus' body down from the Cross.

Gently, Symon placed Jesus' body on Holy Mary's lap. Holy Mary wept over her dead son's body.

Wolv stood on Golgotha. The other Roman soldiers marched away from Golgotha. Their work ended with the deaths of the two thieves and Jesus' death.

Beside Symon, Wolv pulled his sword.

Symon said, "Wolv. I know you. I will not allow you to dismember Jesus."

Symon pushed Wolv off the Golgotha mount. The two of them rolled together down the mount. Then Symon snatched Wolv's sword from Wolv.

Memory still captured Wolv. In Rose Fire's great hall, Wolv's eyes remained glazed over black.

Symon said, "Enough Wolv. I know your evil. You are evil, I repeat. I will not allow you to dismember Jesus."

Wolv said, "Symon. Jesus claimed to raise himself from the dead in three days. If I chop his body into pieces, he can never rise from the dead."

Then Symon said, "Wolv. If Jesus does rise from the dead, then you will have another chance. Another chance to beg Jesus to raise Pamia from the dead."

Symon turned and threw Wolv's sword far down off the Golgotha mount.

In Wolv's memory, Symon and Wolv were many yards below Golgotha's height. On the steep side of Golgotha. In memory only, Wolv stood on the steep side of Golgotha.

In reality Wolv stood in Rose Fire's great hall in Wales.

With his eyes glazed-over black, Wolv shouted, 'Symon. I curse you and your progeny. Satan. Satan. Hear me. Take my soul if you must. Put a Legion of demons within me. I place a curse on my half-brother's progeny, Symon of Cyrene Pendragon. I place a curse on the Adam Pendragons. The curse that 'Only-burning-love-can-defeat-burning-hatred.' The progeny of Symon must endure burning fire to keep their loves. I place the curse that their brides must give their lives for their loves."

Inside Rose Fire, Wolv stood, still in his black-glazed-eyed memory.

Wolv's repeated growl was like an earthquake. "Satan. Satan. Hear me. Hear me, take my soul if you must. I curse, place a curse on Symon of Cyrene's progeny. The curse of burning love, 'Only-burning-love-can-defeat-burning-hatred.' Symon's progeny must endure burning fire to keep their loves. Their brides must give their lives for their husbands."

All could hear and feel Wolv's repeated growl for miles in all directions. The repeated growl shook bricks from chimneys and collapsed barns.

The growls grew louder and spread darkness. Then Wolv's darkness caused the campfires and torches to fade. To fade as of they were embers.

Warrick shouted, "Everyone. Run. Light more torches. Throw more wood on the fires. Wolv's blackness can hide Skinwalkers. Hurry. In moments Wolv's darkness will engulf us. In moments Wolv's evil Skinwalkers will engulf us. Hurry. Throw more wood on the campfires."

They built the fire to a roar. Yet the encroaching blackness made the campfires as if an ember. All was black except the ember-like-glow of torches and campfires.

The earthquake of Wolv's obsessive compulsive roar faded. As the roar faded the blackness faded. As the roar faded, the torches and campfires burned brightly.

Warrick said, "Marian. You have just lived through the easiest part. The easiest part of Wolv's Curse on Symon's progeny. Wolv's curse spreads darkness. In that darkness Wolv's Skinwalkers can travel unseen.

NONES' BELLS

Early afternoon midday Nones bells rang, high on the mountains, trees exploded.

Warrick said, "Marian. Listen. At Nones bells Jesus died in the Cross. Listen and you will hear Wolv's Nones-obsessions."

INSIDE ROSE FIRE

Inside Rose Fire's Great Hall, as the Nones bells rang, Wolv fell to his knees. Wolv's Eyes glazed over black as his memories captured him. In Wolv's memories he was back a thousand years ago, on Golgotha, Jerusalem. Watching, as Jesus dies on the cross for three hours.

In his memories Wolv looked up at Jesus in the cross. Jesus said, "Father, into your hands I commend my spirit."

On his knees, in Rose Fire, Wolv repeatedly growled, "Father. Into your hands I commend my spirit."

Continuously he growled, "Father, into your hands I commend my spirit."

Wolv's growls shook the earth. His growls again caused stones to fall from Rose Fire's battlement merlons.

OUT ON THE BATTLEFIELD

Marian said, "Those were Jesus' last words on the Cross."

Warrick said, "Jesus' last words. Just before Wolv rammed a spear up through Jesus' right side, up through Jesus' heart. Wolv has such a blessing and a curse to have heard them. I often ponder on Judas Iscariot. Judas Iscariot would have been the Catholic Church's greatest saint of repentance. If only, on Golgotha, Judas would have asked forgiveness from Jesus. Instead, in despair, Judas Iscariot hung himself. He chose to go to Hell. Greatest repentance, Wolv still has the chance to be the greatest saint of repentance. If only Wolv would ask Jesus for mercy. A greater saint than Mary Magdalen."

Supper, Vespers bells, rang, trees exploded.

Warrick yelled, "Everyone. Throw water over the side of the knoll. More."

Compline, bedtime, bells, rang, trees exploded.

Again, Warrick yelled, "Everyone. Throw water over the side of the knoll. More."

Warrick said, "Marian. You should go sleep. The midnight witches hours will soon be upon us. Vigils' bells will soon announce Lilith's strongest three hours of the night. The Witches hours that begin at midnight Vigils bells and end at Marin's bells."

Marian said, "Warrick. Sleep. Impossible. The AntiChrist is about to attack. I jump at every sound. Exploding trees are constant. Like a constant roar. No one in the camp can sleep."

Midnight Vigils bells, the Witches hours began, trees exploded.

"Be ceaseless," Warrick yelled, "Everyone. Throw water over the side of the knoll. More. Now while it is snowing."

Warrick and Marian walked. They studied maps.

Then Matin's bells rang, the end of the three hours of Witches, trees exploded.

Marian and Warrick walked and studied maps.

"Never stop, we must prepare for battle," Warrick yelled, "Everyone. Throw water over the side of the knoll. More."

Very early Prime bells again announced that sunrise was close, trees exploded.

Marian said, "Finally early Prime bells. Finally, the sun will rise. No one in the camp has slept."

As the cold exploded trees high on the mountains, Warrick walked over to his brother. "Ross-Templar, we have little time before the full sunrise's strongest Prime bells."

Warrick said. "The time of deception is over. We must sharpen our weapons. Our many decoy tents have made Wolv think we are many more than we are. Therefore Wolv has delayed his attack until the Skinwalkers are now desperate, hungry, and thirsty. They will attach us in irrational madness after sunrise. During midmorning Terce bells. After Wolv's Prime-bells Resurrection obsession."

In her mail and white squirrel cloak, Marian hugged Warrick's arm. She smiled up at him.

Warrick said, "Marian. I know that you are frightened beyond your reason. Thank you for having the courage to come out here with me, this last night. Your beautiful face reminds me why I fight."

Marian only smiled as she paced back and forth with Warrick. Their path was long. No one in the camp had slept.

Warrick walked to each group of knights and said, "Be prepared for the battle. Battle at Terce bells, at full light."

Then Warrick turned and said, "Where is Otan?"

From the camp's center, Otan stood. "I want you to order the pages to saddle and bridle the horses."

Warrick shouted. "The pages must ready the horses for battle. When the Terce bells ring in the full morning light, Wolv will attack. He will order his Skinwalkers to storm out of the castle. Wolv's Skinwalkers will rumble across the drawbridge and down into the deep ravine. Then they will climb this knoll to attack us."

Suddenly a blizzard and blinded them.

Warrick shouted, "Everyone, you must throw wood onto the campfires. We need bonfires to boil the pine tar in the caldrons.

We need bonfires to give us light if we must battle in the dark blizzard."

They piled wood onto the campfires. The long line of bonfires flashed red and yellow on the falling snow.

Then as the bonfires reflected yellow-pink from Rose Fire's pink granite walls, Warrick shouted, "Enough. I want you to stop putting wood on the fire. That is enough wood, the fires are high enough. We can now see through the blizzard."

Marian was so jittery and nervous. So nervous that she did not realize that lack of sleep had exhausted her.

Reque walked to Warrick and said, "My lord. You are not tired. You are never tired."

Warrick ignored Reque's words.

Otan whispered, "Reque, you must not disturb Warrick before a battle. His mind whizzes with war contingencies."

Squire Reque whispered, "Incredible, Otan. Lord Warrick never tires."

"Yes, Reque," Otan said, "since King Edward made Warrick a war lord. Every night since then Warrick paces long lonely hours."

Then Reque whispered, "When does Warrick sleep?"

"Reque. If Lord Warrick does sleep," Otan whispered, "he never sleeps at night. I see him pace and practice with Blessed Dread every night. Even as we sleep. Many of us think that he never sleeps, that he does not need to sleep. The knights whisper that Warrick's nightmares keep him awake. Nightmares filled with sorrow and undeserved guilt."

Suddenly the cold exploded dozens of trees high on the mountain.

Warrick said, "The darkest and coldest time is just before the Prime bells. The cold froze those trees until their sap expanded and burst the trees open."

Morgan said, "Prime bells. First light. Three hours after Prime, Terce Bells will signal full morning light."

Ross-Templar turned to the mountain and pointed, "What is that?"

Warrick said, "Grey fog that will work against us. We will not see the enemy as they attack us. We may have to battle in this grey fog."

The grey fog oozed up from the Wye Valley. Up the mountain and covered them up to their knees.

Lord Warrick shouted, "Quickly. I want everyone to throw more wood on the bonfires. We must burn this grey fog off the battlefield. Morgan, get Holy Water. Throw Holy Water on the ground, on everyone, everything. This grey fog is not natural. Lilith could hide in the grey fog. Skinwalkers could hide in the grey fog."

Warrick shouted, "Knights, squires, pages, servants. Throw more buckets of water over the knoll's sides. Now. Now, while we still have falling snow even in this strange grey fog."

The sun peaked over the eastern horizon. This morn's sun threw red sunbeams onto the Black Mountains. Slowly the red sunbeams crept from the mountain peaks and down the mountain sides.

Fire-red sun rays brightened the mountains' snow and green pine trees. Red-pink sun rays bathed the Wye Valley's normal grey fog. Pink sun's rays reflected off the grey fog like sun reflects off a smooth lake. The grey fog had filled the Wye Valley. Thick grey fog was like a lake of slow translucent, glowing waves.

RESURRECTION TORTURE.

In Rose Fire Wolv heard distant prime bells and growled, "Why torture me Jesus?"

The Candlekeeper ran over and said, "Master Wolv. It is not a safe candle hour. The Resurrection hour is open you."

Wolv growled, "You were supposed to tell me before the bells."

Wolv swung his sword and decapitated the Skinwalker. Then he said, "After you heal your head back on your shoulders, remember. Tell me before the canonical bell. Next time I will burn your head in the andiron. Now you are lucky that I have no wood to burn in the andiron."

Wolv turned into black, pure charcoal dust. As dust, he disappeared down into the cracks of Rose Fire's floor.

As charcoal dust, Wolv sunk deeper and deeper into the earth, through rocks. Through under ground rivers. Down in underground white water rapids.

He came to rest in an underground cavern.

With Wolv's eyes glazed over black, Wolv saw with his heart. In his tormented memory, in great light, Wolv watched Jesus walk from his tomb. Wolv held up his hand because the light hurt his eyes.

Again, as with every morning, Wolv begged, "Jesus. Jesus, please raise Pamia from the dead for me. Please. My heart is so empty without her."

Jesus did not look at him.

Pamia leaned down and took Wolv's hand. Pamia said, "My love. It is so simple. Just ask Jesus forgiveness for your sins, then we can be together in Heaven."

Wolv growled, "Never, never will I ask for forgiveness. Jesus, get off the Heavenly Throne. Satan is supposed to rule heaven, not you. Nor the Holy Spirit and nor the Heavenly Father. Never will I ask for forgiveness."

The AntiChrist, Wolv, beat his chest and growled, "I serve Satan. Pamia, Pamia, Pamia."

Wolv's rage caused red and yellow fire to shoot from his mouth. His fire filled the underground cavern.

Again Wolv's growls of 'Pamia' shook the Black Mountains.

Slowly Wolv's Resurrection obsession faded. Slowly his eyes lost their black glaze. Then Wolv changed into carbon dust. As pure carbon dust, he rose back through the earth.

He rose from the cracks on Rose Fire's floor. On Rose Fire's floor, Wolv formed into his original Roman General form.

Wolv screamed, "Jesus. Stop torturing me."

-

-

-

CHAPTER, Where: Now on the Knoll Across From Rose Fire, Wales, When: Around 1250s A.D.

ATTACK

Wye Valley Terce bells rang. Rose Fire's drawbridge crashed down and shook the earth. Around the drawbridge the ground fog swirled. Just like Lord Warrick had predicted, Wolv's Skinwalkers attacked.

Boar's-Head Skinwalkers, mounted. Skinwalkers in black rusted armor rumbled across the drawbridge. On armored horses, the Skinwalkers screamed unintelligible, insane war cries. The ground fog swirled around their galloping horses.

Marian said, "Now their archers will shoot us."

Warrick said, "No. As I predicted, they have used all their arrows."

Then Morgan yelled "Shields. Raise your shields." A cloud of enemy arrows descended upon the camp.

The arrows bounced off their blessed shields. Then another cloud of fewer arrows fell upon them. Another cloud of even fewer arrows fell, then fewer, then no more arrows.

Morgan said, "Look at their quivers, their quivers are empty. The enemy had used all their arrows.

Marian said, "Any more predictions, Warrick?"

Warrick said, "One prediction is true. Listen to them, as I expected. Hunger, thirst and cold have driven them insane."

"Longbows," Warrick shouted, "longbows. Dip you arrows in the boiling tar."

All of Warrick's warriors picked up long bows. All their blessed arrows stuck out of many cauldrons of boiling tar.

Marian watched Lord Warrick straighten his back and level his jaw. He planted his feet firmly in the snow.

Warrick was unafraid as Skinwalkers in full armor galloped toward them.

Wolv screamed in Skinwalker language, "Warrick has few men. Attack. Slaughter them. A bucket of gold to the Skinwalker that brings Marian alive to me."

Marian shook in fear. She realized that she was the Skinwalkers purpose, the focus, of attack.

Warrick stepped in front of Marian. He raised his right eyebrow as he lied, "Fear not Marian. We have defeated greater armies with fewer men."

Saliva dripped off the Skinwalkers' helms as they charged from the castle. They charged down into the ravine and up Warrick's side of the ravine. As their horses climbed Warrick's knoll, their hooves slipped on the ice. The ice Warrick had formed with the buckets of water. Then the boar's head Skinwalkers' horses fell on their sides. Skinwalkers on hands and knees climbed the icy knoll. On hands and knees, they slid on the ice back down into the ravine. With their axes and swords, the Skinwalkers began to chop away the ice.

Marian watched Lord Warrick. His calm expression did not change. He did not flinch. Nor did he have a line or wrinkle of worry on his face. She pulled on Lord Warrick's arm, "We are so few and they are uncountable."

Warrick did not glance at Marian.

She said, "My lord. Your confidence means that you are either crazy or a wizard. A wizard that can see the future. Or else you are in a guild with the devil."

He grinned and decided to tease her with a lie. He intentionally raised his right eyebrow to show her that he lied, "The last two."

Marian said, "And I am crazy to stay here with you."

The sight of the multitude of Skinwalkers made Marian tremble with terror. Terror she had never known.

Yet she held her back straight and her chin level.

She thought, "No. I will not go into the wagon. I will not give the enemy the satisfaction to know that I am afraid."

Lord Warrick's knights and squires did not have a worry line on their faces. He pulled a blessed-arrow out of the cauldron of boiling tar. On the end was a thick wad of cloth and fur soaked in boiling tar. The tar was liquid as water. He touched the tip to the fire. The tar burst into flame. Then he pulled back on his long bow.

It broke.

All his warriors' bows broke.

Warrick's knights looked at Marian. They thought that she had placed the curse on them. In truth, the cold had cracked hairline breaks in the bows. Just as the cold had burst trees.

On Rose Fire's drawbridge, Wolv roared, "Warrick's defense has failed. Attack. Their long bows have broken. Slaughter them. I will give a bucket of gold to the man that captures Marian alive."

Marian said, "The Skinwalkers can climb on the slippery ice. Warrick. You cannot stop them."

Warrick calmly dropped his bow.

He shouted, "Crossbows."

Squires tightly cranked the crossbows.

The wooden cross bows broke. The cold had also frozen the moisture in the wood and formed hairline cracks.

Marian said, "Now we will die."

-

-

-

CHAPTER, Now Wales on the Knoll Across From Rose Fire, Year @ 1250s A.D.

NOW WE WILL DIE

Warrick calmly dropped his broken crossbow.

He said, "Only iron cross bows would work in this extreme cold. We have no iron cross bows."

Warrick thought, "I should have known to warm the bows beside the fire. I should have known when I heard the mountain's trees freeze and burst. I and my knights have never fought in such cold. We should have stored the cross and long bows in chests. In chests beside the fires to keep them warm. I would never have imagined that the cold could freeze our bows."

Warrick's knights again looked at Marian. Their eyebrows formed the shape of angry vs.

Ross-Templar whispered, "Morgan. They suspect that Marian cursed them to break the cross and long bows."

Drayton whispered, "Yes, Ross-Templar. Many of Warrick's knights fear that Marian has cursed them. Cursed them to protect her cats."

NOW WE CAN BE AFRAID

As Warrick looked at the angry Vs of his knight's eyebrows, he thought, "Now. We can be afraid."

Warrick yelled, "Raise the fixed blessed spears."

His knights pulled on ropes that popped up the rows of blessed spears. Spears to impale the Skinwalkers. Skinwalkers in the hundreds climbed the icy knoll. They hacked their way through the blessed spears.

Warrick yelled, "Javelins and the water buckets."

Squires brought up bundles of javelins. They had tied bundles of cloth and animal pelts on the javelins' points.

"Water," Warrick yelled. "Pages. I want you to throw water over the knoll's sides. Now. Now."

From the mountain stream behind them the pages filled buckets. They threw water down the ice-covered slope. With the water on the ice, the ice was even slipperier. The Skinwalkers still climbed, but slower.

From Rose Fire's drawbridge, Wolv roared, "Everyone. I will give a fortune if you bring Marian alive to me."

Wolv thought, "I drank ale and wine. Ale and wine weakened me, so I cannot join the fight."

Swale yelled, "Warrick's defense has failed. His long bows and crossbows broke. Attack. Slaughter them."

Warrick's knights dipped the javelins' cloth ends into boiling tar caldrons. Then they lit the ends in the bonfires. With all their strength, they threw the javelins down the slope. Then the javelins bounced off the Skinwalkers' armor. The Skinwalkers' laughter at Warrick echoed off the Red-Fog-covered Black Mountains.

Marian's heart beat faster. She wanted to run, but she held her chin high. Warrick's knights saw her courage in the face of disaster.

Otan whispered, "Reque. Look, Marian stands firm, she does have courage."

A javelin glanced off a mounted Skinwalkers's thick boar's head visor. As he sat on his warhorse, he laughed at Warrick.

Then the Skinwalker cried in pain and panic.

Reque yelled, "Look. The burning tar on the blessed spear's cloth ran into the cracks. Ran into the cracks of the Skinwalker's helm. The pads under his helm burn."

As the Skinwalker dropped his weapons, he howled in panic. He pulled off his helm and mail cowl. With his gauntlets, he clawed at the flaming pine tar on his face. He jumped from his warhorse. Then he buried his face in the snow to extinguish the fire. The snow did not extinguish the flaming pine tar.

Warrick thought, "Thank God one type of weapon worked today."

Warrick's knights threw hundreds of burning-tar javelins. Burning tar dripped from the rags and animal pelts on the javelin's tips.

The javelins glanced off the boar-helm Skinwalkers' armor. Yet, the tar splashed and ran into their armor's joints. On Skinwalker after Skinwalker, tar ran like flaming water into their armor and burned them. Within seconds mounted Skinwalkers and foot Skinwalkers grasped at their armor to take it off. Horses and Skinwalkers lost their balance. They slid against the feet of other Skinwalkers and horses.

Still, many enemy Skinwalkers dug their axes and swords into the ice. On hands and knees they climbed up the ice-covered knoll. They scrambled like dogs, mad from hunger and thirst.

As Warrick had planned, the Skinwalkers and horses slipped on the thick ice. Slipped back down into the ravine.

Previously, under the cover of night, his warriors had poured water over the knoll. Each bucket of water froze until they had covered the slope with solid ice. The snow had hidden the thick ice from the attackers.

Marian thought, "I am frightened to the point of dizziness. I refuse, yes. I refuse to give the enemy the satisfaction to know that I am afraid."

Though her stomach turned and fear shook her, she kept her chin high. She kept her back straight.

All the knights and squires had absolute confidence in Lord Warrick. They had often used this fire-javelin technique. The enemy's rage terrified the new pages. They knew that if they ran in fear, Warrick would reject them. Warrick would send them back to their parents in shame. The new pages stood and trembled.

A page shouted, "Look at Lady Marian. She does not run. She is not afraid."

Marian thought, "He is a silly page. Where would I run?"

Warrick's knights continued to throw burning blessed spears down the slope at the enemy.

Marian heard a squire whisper to Warrick, "We do not have enough boiling tar."

As her eyes grew round in fear, she kept her back straight. She kept her jaw level.

Below in the ravine, the boar-helm Skinwalkers tossed away their armor. They took off their iron mail and their burning padding. In a great mass, they slid together at the bottom of the ravine. They walked and fell upon each other. The burning tar on them spread to other Skinwalkers. Soon all the Skinwalkers became a stumbling mass of flames. A mass of flames and madness as they tried to climb the ice-covered knoll.

The burning tar on the blessed spears splattered like great yellow and red raindrops. Splattered onto the enemy's armor and horses.

The Skinwalkers' horses became their worse enemy. As the tar burned the horses, they reared. Their horses fell on their riders and crushed them. All their horses were on fire. Now the panicked horses were Warrick's most effective weapons. In red and yellow steams, the tar ran into the divisions of the enemies' armor. More Skinwalkers slid to the ravine's bottom.

In the ravine, the Skinwalkers took off their armor, padding and burning clothing. They rolled in the snow to extinguish the tar-fire on their skin. If they extinguished it, they touched another Skinwalker and again burst into flames. Skinwalkers and horses slid down the knoll's icy slope. Horses rolled into the ravine and crushed the enemy. In but a few moments uncountable numbers of men and horses lay atop one another. All on fire. Horses and men stomped on one another in the deep rocky ravine below the knoll. Fire spread from clothing to clothing. Men and horses rolled in the snow. They fought only to take off their armor. To put out the fire in their padding.

Lord Warrick shouted, "Skinwalkers. Yield or burn to ash. You must take off your armor and mail, throw down your weapons and yield. Burn your weapons in a pile.

No one in the ravine replied.

Otan turned to Warrick and whispered, "My lord. We have no more spears nor boiling tar. If the Skinwalkers knew, they might regroup and attack. This time they would defeat us."

Lord Warrick smiled and whispered, "Otan. Then it is important that we not tell them."

Lord Warrick yelled a lie, "Surrender. Surrender we will use more tar and burn you like a funeral pyre."

Then Warrick pointed at the road and said, "Look at the road. A thousand monks stand on the road. Each with a pitchfork. A hundred mounted Knight-Templars, all in full blessed armor, lead the monks. If I raise my hand, they will slaughter you. All the monks of the valley's monasteries have answered my request.

You already burn. Do you want to end on the wrong end of a pitchfork?"

Morgan whispered into Warrick's ear, "Warrick. I know that you have over one hundred mounted Knights-Templar. Yet, age has broken them. Yes, the Knights Templars are each in blessed armor, in full colors, with lances high. Yet, Warrick. They are all frail, aged, sick, and exhausted."

Warrick whispered, "Morgan. Like I told Otan, then do not tell the Skinwalkers."

Morgan said, "But, but."

Warrick said, "Morgan. Look at their pride. After lifelong, sever injury, the aged Knights-Templars sit tall in their saddles."

Morgan said, "But all the monks are aged or sick, or untrained. Wolv's Skinwalkers would kill every one of them."

Lord Warrick said, "All the monks know the risk. All the monks know that they are helpless. Yet, to deceive Wolv, all the monks are willing to die to destroy Wolv."

To encourage his Skinwalkers, Wolv shouted, "Those monks. They are untrained."

From the road, a Knights Templar shouted, "Wolv. You and your Skinwalkers have proven to us that you are not men. You have proven to us that you are rabid dogs. Monks have all the training they need to kill rabid dogs."

Warrick shouted, "Skinwalkers. You heard the monks reply. The monks will kill you because, they know you are Skinwalkers, not people. Surrender to me if you want to live."

From the ravine, as pine-tar burned on his chest, another Skinwalker screamed, "Surrender. We surrender."

Beside Rose Fire, Wolv lifted a crossbow from under his cloak. Where he had kept it warm. With the warm, bendable crossbow he shot. He shot the back of the Skinwalker that shouted the surrender.

Then Wolv growled, "I will shoot anyone that surrenders."

Warrick yelled, "Which is the most painful death? An arrow or fire? Wolv cannot shoot all of you. Throw your weapons and burning armor pads into a large pile. Or else we will burn you all. Then I will wave to the monks to finish you."

Many Skinwalkers panicked and shouted, "We surrender."

As the flames panicked the Skinwalkers, they obeyed Warrick. They threw their burning armor pads and weapons into a pile. In the armor pad's flames, the weapon's wooden handles burst into flame.

On Rose Fire's drawbridge, Wolv sat on his warhorse and shouted, "Fools. Warrick has no more weapons. Pick up your axes and swords. Use them to climb. I order you to break the ice on the slope and climb. You are many. Warrick has few knights. The monks are untrained or retired. You can defeat the monks. You can defeat Warrick. I will kill any Skinwalker that surrenders."

Wolv's men turned to him.

They whispered to each other, "Wolv is a coward. Wolv did not lead us in a charge up the slope. Lord Wolv is a coward. Lord Warrick, God's Avenging Angel, stands and fights with courage. Even Marian stands unafraid."

Another Skinwalker whispered, "Why should we die for Wolv. When Wolv will not fight with us?"

Wolv thought, "They call me a coward. I could have fought with them if I had not drunk ale and wine. Ale and wine weaken me."

Wolv shot his few arrows into the backs of some Skinwalkers that surrendered. This only caused his warriors to hate Wolv more.

As Warrick's tactics demoralized the huge Skinwalkers army, the Skinwalkers shouted, "We surrender."

Every one of them stripped off all their armor and mail. They threw their weapons onto the burning pile. They all stood with no weapons in their hands, no armor, and little clothes.

Warrick turned to Marian and said, "Wolv is correct. If the Skinwalkers had used their weapons to climb the slope, they could defeat us. We are so few and have no more tar. They are so many. Marian, now you must remember your first lesson. You first of many lessons about how to survive in this rebellious land. As always in war, the victor is the best liar. We defeated them because we demoralized them. We demoralized them because they falsely believe that we defeated them. In minutes their pile of weapons will burn to ashes, then they cannot defeat us."

Marian could see how quickly the battle had ended. She stood stunned and exhausted. The tall flaming pile of the

Skinwalkers' weapons collapsed upon itself. The collapse sent a great cloud of black smoke and sparks into the air.

Warrick said, "I was waiting for the fire's collapse. Their weapons' wooden handles are now in ashes. The iron weapons are too hot for the enemy to touch."

Then Warrick turned to his brothers and said, "We have deceived the enemy. Victory is now ours."

Warrick waved to the monks to return to the valley. A Templar waved his aged arm. As quiet as fog moves, the monks disappeared into the valley's morn fog.

Warrick's knights chanted, "Victory for Lady Marian. Rose Fire for Lady Marian, the Wye Valley for Lady Marian."

They chanted this and held their blessed axes and blessed swords high in the air.

With her thumb, Marian quickly wiped tears from her eyes and said, "Warrick. Why do they chant for me?"

"Marian, my knights are the most honorable of warriors," Warrick said. "These knights have been with me in wars all over the known world. If you allow them, they will honor and even love you. You are the lady of their lord."

"Love me," Marian asked? "Yes Marian," Warrick answered, "love you and die for you."

"I . . . I do not understand," Marian said, "love. Warrick. Will you come to love me?"

Warrick thought of his dead, traitorous wife, Ogina, and changed the subject. "Marian. The flames of the pile of Skinwalkers weapons leap high into the air. The wooden handles of the Skinwalkers axes and maces crackle and pop. Their weapons now glow red-hot, too hot to touch."

"You did not say that you will come to love me," Marian said.

AntiChrist's TRUE FORM

Suddenly Wolv changed form into a charcoal, dust cloud and eyes of red flame.

Warrick pointed at Wolv's flame eyes and said, "Marian. Look, on the battlement. Quickly look at the true nature of your enemy."

"God, please help us. What is that monster," Marian asked?

As a charcoal, dust cloud and eyes full of flame, Wolv said, "Swale. Gulum. For now we must retreat. We will find another way to capture Marian. We will find another way to kill off the Able Cyrene Pendragon line. To kill off the Able Cyrene Pendragon line and thus conquer the world for Satan."

From a cloud of charcoal dust, Wolv burst into a flock of crows. As crows in flight all the crows shouted in unison, "Lord Warrick. I will return and spike your head on my pike. Marian, I will have you to test if you are Pamia."

Behind the crows, Swale and Gulum's warhorses crushed cobble stones under their spiked horseshoes. They spurred their horses in the direction deeper into Wales, to the land of Gwynedd.

Lord Warrick pointed to three knights that had served him to Persia and back. To three of his most trusted and loyal knights, he said, "Ride hard. Got to the king. Tell him we have taken Rose Fire. Tell the king that the battle caused no harm Rose Fire."

On their warhorses, the three knights thundered down the snow-covered mountain road.

Marian asked, "My lord, why are those other knights staring at me? They look so angry."

Warrick waved many knights toward the rocky crevasse between the two knolls. They charged down to gather the prisoners.

Warrick said, "Marian. Why do those knights look at you with anger? Do you want the truth?"

Marian said, "My lord, tell me."

Warrick said, "Marian, this is only a temporary victory. You will be the Lady of a great castle, Rose Fire. Often enemies will siege it. During a siege you must have silent courage. You must not panic. This could cause the servants and even some warriors to panic. Today you showed that great courage. However, they still have a suspicion that you cursed them. They suspect that your curse caused our long bows and crossbows to break. This suspicion will never go away. In their eyes, in their suspicion, you could be an evil omen. An omen of future doom. I know now that the extreme cold caused the wooden bows to break. The cold froze the wooden bows. Just as the cold froze and burst the trees on the mountain. I will explain to them the effect of the extreme cold on wood. I know that you did not threaten to curse them to protect the cats. Battle-hardened knights can be a very superstitious group."

THE EDGE OF CHAOS
Warrick sighed and continued, "Marian. You are now living on the edge of chaos. You are living on a battlefield in a rebellious land. This is not a jousting match. You will find no safe streets. We have no safe highways. We have no safe gardens in which to walk. Marian, we can take no midnight strolls in the forest. This is the edge of peaceful civilization. The king sent us to Rose Fire to capture and hold it. To conquer these murderers. The king sent me to dispense his justice. You must quickly grow in wisdom and judgement. During a siege often most knights will be off on patrol. I may be elsewhere. Your example today and in the future will give courage to Rose Fire's defenders. Today you kept a straight back, with no tears and with no visible fear. Often your quiet, courageous example alone, I repeat, alone, will determine victory or defeat. You will become the lady of Rose Fire. You are not to command my knights. Yet, in my absence you must give a courageous example. This is why I brought you here to see this siege. You must see that you can defeat any enemy with courage, deception and intelligence."

Marian was too exhausted. She had not had confidence in Lord Warrick and said, "I was so frightened. I am still frightened."

Then she held out her hand, "Look Warrick. My hands shake like poplar-tree leaves in the wind. My heart beats so fast that it will jump out my throat."

Marian's doubts and fears bubbled to the surface as she said, "We were so few. Luck. It had to be just luck. Luck that they did not slay us, luck, not your judgement or skill. Impossible, it is impossible that you could be so intelligent."

On Warrick's bronze face, anger formed furrows on his forehead. His eyebrows formed in a sharp angry V. Then Knights and many squires around Warrick stepped back in fear. They knew Marian's words would anger any war lord. His emerald eyes grew brighter than the sun that peeked through the snow clouds.

Warrick said, "Marian. If a knight insulted me as you did, I would banish him, or worse. By law, I could even execute him."

She held her hands in front of her face. Thinking he would backhand her with his gauntlet.

Marian asked, "You will hit me?"

He said, "God's feet! Woman, I would never hit you. You are my charge. Wolv backhanded Pamia off Mount Masada. She fell to her death. Wolv is evil. I am not evil."

Marian said, "Spite did not cause me to speak. Terror made me speak, terror for Nicola and the others in the wagon. I find it impossible that you could have calculated such an easy victory."

Father Malachi Martin walked over and said, "Lord Warrick did calculate this victory. Though, it is only a temporary victory. Warrick calculated every detail of this victory. You need to come to have confidence in my lord. As much confidence as I have in him. The AntiChrist will return and defeat us often before we vanquish him. Lord Warrick is the world's only hope."

The rest of Warrick's knights continued their duties. They left Marian and Warrick alone in the deep snow.

He dropped one gauntlet and the mail glove under the gauntlet. Then he pulled off his helm. With his bare hand, he put his bare finger tip on her chin. He raised her chin.

Warrick said, "Marian. Always believe, you must always know, that I would never hit you. I am your champion. I will always be your champion."

Her chin quivered.

She said, "I thought you were about to hit me. Just as you hit an enemy."

He threw off his other gauntlet and mail glove. Then he put his huge calloused hands on her cheeks.

He said, "I would never hit you. The king has given you to me to possess and protect."

Marian said, "What then do I do when you are so angry with me?"

Warrick said, "I do not know."

Marian lowered her eyes and said, "Warrick. Maybe you will just lock me in my chambers."

Warrick threw back his head and laughed.

He said, "Yes. I will lock you in your personal keep. The lady of Rose Fire has her own keep."

Then he pointed to Rose Fire and said, "Yes. I will lock you in one of the twelve keep towers."

She lowered her head and looked up at him through her eyebrows.

She said, "Of course, you would not. You would never lock me in my chambers. Would you?"

He said, "Of course not. I would never lock you in your keep."

She pointed at his right eyebrow and said, "Hahhh. I saw your right eyebrow raise. You always raise your right eyebrow when you lie."

He pressed her against his blessed armor. Marian turned her head sideways away from him.

With his finger tip on her chin, he turned her face to him. As she looked up into his eyes, he smiled.

As he smiled, she thought, "Though he is angry with me. He still smiles at me. Perhaps I can trust him when he is angry with me."

As her fear of him lessened, she smiled back at him.

Then he turned his head to a noise. He waved his arm to signal his knights to search Rose Fire for more Skinwalkers. He looked at Rose Fire, and he waved signals to his knights.

She looked up at his eyes.

Their eyes met.

Warrick thought, "Marian's innocent eyes tell me that she trusts me. Her innocent eyes tell me that she will offer to me whatever I want. The problem? I do not know what I want."

Marian felt wanton to look so long into a man's eyes. She could smell his male musk and his bay leaf fragrance. Marian liked it.

She lied, "I do not like the . . . the baaaaaaaay-leaf smell you use. The bay leaf is toooooooooo biting."

-

-

-

CHAPTER, Now Wales on the Knoll Across From Rose Fire, Year @ 1250s A.D.

EXORCISM. A TEMPORARY VICTORY ON THE EDGE OF CHAOS.

He said, "You do know that you streeeeeeeeetch your words when you lie?"

The bay leaf aroma was the scent that she most enjoyed about her champion. When she smelled it, she knew that she was safe.

He smiled and said, "You will become accustomed to the smell of bay leaf. Accustomed because you will have time to . . . practice."

She quipped, "Yes, you do need praaaaactice."

He smiled.

Warrick said, "Drayton. Morgan. Bring me the records of everyone doing Adoration and confession. Make sure that everyone does their hour of Perpetual Adoration. In the Adoration wagon. I ceaselessly repeat, Perpetual Adoration of Jesus' Real Presence in the Blessed Sacrament. Make sure everyone does weekly confession. Reflect on the battle in Siena, Italy. Wolv's red-fog entered Siena's army buildings at night and ate Siena's soldiers. Then the red-fog ate all those in the city sleeping on their home's first floor. Always contemplate these horrors. Only Adoration and confession keep the red-fog away."

ASK JESUS FOR MERCY.

Warrick said, "Morgan. Assure that the Skinwalkers have an opportunity to ask Jesus for mercy."

Morgan went down among the burned, helpless Skinwalkers. He shouted, "Chant with me. 'Jesus. Have mercy on me'."

All of the helpless, burned Skinwalkers chanted. "Jesus. Have mercy on me."

The demons that possessed them came out of their mouths like black dust. The black dust disappeared into the earth.

All the Skinwalkers turned into Catholic priests. Possessed centuries ago from fear of martyrdom. Martyrdom by fire by Wolv and Lilith.

They shouted in unison, "Lord Warrick. You have saved our souls. Warrick, saved, you have saved our souls."

Warrick said, "Drayton. Move the Adoration-confession wagon into Rose Fire. Set up Adoration and confession in the

Rose Fire chapel. Make sure that everyone does their hour of Perpetual Adoration. Give me a daily written report of everyone's adoration time and time of confession. Find others to do Adoration in the wagon. Perpetual Adoration of Jesus' Real Presence in the Blessed Sacrament. In the wagon and in the chapel. Make sure everyone does weekly confession. Wolv sends in spies to kill Adorationists. Keep Adoration in the wagon in the bailey. Also, Adoration in the Chapel. Wolv will send spies to kill Adorationists. Therefore, keep Adoration in the chapel and the wagon. Repeat to yourself that Adoration and confession keep the red-fog away. We are in the greatest danger. We live on the edge of chaos."

Father Malachi Martin said, "Warrick. I will go to Rose Fire to prepare the infirmarian. May I have wagons to carry the wounded? Warrick. Of course you know that this is only a temporary victory?"

Lord Warrick said, "Father Malachi. You know that you can always take what you need. Put the enemy wounded outside the castle walls in tents. Do not use the Adoration wagon. Yes, all the knights know that this is only a temporary victory."

Marian's eyes grew round in surprise. She leaned back and held her hands to her chest.

She said, "You do succor the enemy wounded."

Lord Warrick said, "Of course, but only if a Skinwalker asks Jesus for mercy. Otherwise, he chooses to remain possessed. Then we must behead the Skinwalkers. It is the honorable action to succor the enemy wounded."

Marian said, "Who spread these two invidious rumors. One rumor was that I would curse your knights. The other rumor was that you let the enemy's wounded bleed to death. Bleed to death on the battlefield. Who would spread such rumors?"

Warrick said, "Rumors and gossip on the battlefield are common. Remember that my knights will always be wary that you still might curse them."

Marian looked at the castle.

A MYTHICAL CASTLE

She said, "Rose Fire is like a castle out of myth. The most beautiful castle that I have ever seen. The castle glows like a bright pink torch in the clouds. Do the clouds always float around Rose Fire's twelve tall keeps?"

"Yes," Warrick said. "Rose Fire is so high that clouds always linger around the twelve keeps. The castle has six keeps on the outer wall. Six keeps on the inner wall. That slope on the inner wall is a talus. A talus keeps the enemy away from the base of the wall. I have never seen such beautiful keeps."

Marian said, "Never have I seen such a beautiful castle."

Warrick said, "Many also call Rose Fire 'The Fire in the Sky.'"

Marian said, "My lord. I want to help Father Malachi in the infirmarian."

Warrick said, "No. You are not to go near the enemy's wounded. This is only a temporary victory. You must stay away from the wounded."

Marian incorrectly thought, "Still my lord has a problem with mercy."

Lord Warrick knew that the enemy's wounded often faked injury. That they harmed their helpers then escaped. For now Marian was too inexperienced to know that wounded enemies were dangerous.

Warrick pointed to a keep. He said, "The tallest keep is for you and Nicola. Your keep is the most beautiful. Since Edward sent Blanche, Blanche must have a chamber off your solar. To put her elsewhere would insult the king."

As Warrick approached Rose Fire Marian asked, "Warrick. Why are you so somber? You should be happy, joyful, because you just had a wonderful victory. Your frown dips to your jawbone."

A WALK BACK INTO SORROW.

Warrick did not answer. As he walked toward Rose Fire, he turned and walked deep into the forest. Marian had to run to keep up with him. Ross-Templar, Morgan, and Drayton followed Warrick. They searched the dark forest for signs of the enemy. Ross-Templar held his blessed-sword. Morgan held his enormous mace at the ready. Drayton held his blessed-sword.

Lord Warrick walked with long, fast steps.

Then Ross-Templar ran up to Marian and put his hand on her shoulder. "Marian. Do not keep up with Warrick. Stay with us. You must let Warrick walk where he will. Right now Warrick does not, cannot, hear you."

Deep into the forest Warrick walked up a small knoll in a clearing. He wore shiny blessed armor and a long black cloak tied to his shoulders. Warrick knelt on one knee.

With his bare hand Warrick brushed snow aside until he read "Beatrice Pendragon." He grew weak, bowed his head, and had to put his elbow on one knee. He grew weaker and put his other hand onto his mother's grave to steady himself.

"Mother," Warrick said, "I am so sorry that I did not protect you. Mother. I failed. I failed you."

Morning Benedictine Terce bells began and ended. Warrick did not move.

Warrick did not take his hand from his mother's rough headstone.

Carmelite Terce bells also began and ended. Again Warrick did not move.

Carthusian, then Franciscan Terce bells began and ended. Lord Warrick did not move.

As he knelt, the sun climbed and morning shadows decreased in length.

Marian reached for Warrick.

Morgan grasped her arm and put his finger over his lips. Then Morgan shook his head 'No' so Marian would not disturb Warrick.

The Augustinian tubular Terce bells began and ended. Still, Warrick did not move.

With his head bowed Warrick again whispered, "Mother. I am so sorry that I did not protect you. Mother. I failed. I failed you. We just had a temporary victory over Wolv. Mother, I so love you. Mother, sorry, I am so sorry that I failed you."

"You . . . you were just a . . . little man," said an old voice. An old voice that choked on happiness.

-

-

-

CHAPTER, Defeated Wolv, Wales on the Knoll Across From Rose Fire, Warrick's Mother's Grave, Year @ 1250s A.D.

OLD VOICE CHOKED ON HAPPINESS
Warrick looked up to see a smiling old peasant in rags. Warrick said, "You are Norwin, Norwin?"

"Yes little man," Norwin said.

Warrick stood. With his one arm, Norwin embraced Warrick. Then Warrick embraced his only father-figure. His father-figure, though Norwin had been with Warrick for only a few days.

"You will freeze," Warrick said. "You only wear rags. We just had a temporary victory. Wolv will return, better prepared."

Lord Warrick pulled off his fur-lined, cowled cloak. He put it on Norwin's thread bare shoulders.

Norwin said, "Your mother would be so proud of you if she could see you."

Ross-Templar said, "Warrick. You must hurry. We all know the knights' superstitions. They believe that they must ritually parade into the castle within a set time. A castle that they have just captured. The late Terce bells have ended. We must parade into Rose Fire before the bells of Sext finish. Quickly, we must parade before the zenith-sun wanes westward. Now, while our zenith-sun shadows are directly under us. Hurry. The last Sext bells, the Cistercian bells, will begin and end soon."

They ran to begin the parade. Within moments, with pennant colors triumphantly high, Lord Warrick led. Led his warriors and Marian over Rose Fire's drawbridge.

On a white mare beside Warrick, as he rode Zeus, Marian said, "Warrick. You never mentioned Norwin."

Norwin rode a warhorse beside Warrick.

Beside Warrick said, "Norwin. I thought that you were dead."

"Part of me is dead," Norwin said as he pointed to his empty sleeve.

Norwin said, "Warrick. I also thought that you were dead."

"Part of me is dead. In my mother's grave, also in my wife's grave," Warrick said. He paused and thought of his mother's grave. Then Warrick also thought of his traitorous wife. He closed his eyes and sighed as guilt tightened his stomach. Guilt lowered his shoulders and bowed his head.

Warrick thought, "Though my wife was a traitor. Yet, she did not deserve to burn to death. I did love Ogina. Yes, I did love Ogina."

Norwin said, "I understand that part of you died. When Wolv killed your mother, I could see that your joy died."

Norwin pointed at Marian. He whispered, "Warrick. I see the way this beautiful lady looks at you. She intends to resurrect your joy."

Then Norwin said, "When you were six years old Wolv threw you in the river. Only a warrior could have survived those freezing rapids. I was sure that you drowned."

Sext bells echoed throughout the Wye Valley.

SEXT BELLS OBSESSIONS.

High in the Red-Fog-Covered Black Mountains in a cave Wolv fell to his knees.

Wolv yelled, "Sext bells. Jesus. Leave me alone."

Wolv's eyes glazed over black as his memories again entrapped him.

In his memories, Wolv stood on Golgotha, outside Jerusalem, as Jesus hung on the Cross.

Jesus looked down at St John the Apostle. St John had his arm around Holy Mary's shoulders.

Jesus looked at his mother and said, "Woman, behold your son." Then Jesus looked at St John and said, "Behold, your mother."

Entrapped in obsessive memory, Wolv repeatedly growled, "Behold your son. Behold your mother."

As always, Wolv's growls shook th mountains.

Rage, hatred and anger exploded from his mouth as flames and filled the cavern. His spiritual flames only burned him, nothing else.

TEMPORARY VICTORY

Everyone stood silent as Wolv's growls shook the earth.

Warrick said, "Wolv shakes the Black Mountains range. Now with the words that Jesus told Holy Mary and John, the Apostle."

Morgan mentioned, "Ross-Templar, Drayton, do you not hear the Sext chimes and bells? We must enter Rose Fire before the last Sext's bells end, the Cistercian bells. Otherwise, we will not have met the knight's one hour, parade superstition. Our shadows grow eastward even now. Warrick raised his hand to break the parade into a trot.

As they circled the parade in Rose Fire's bailey Morgan whispered, "Drayton. The Cistercian Sext bells have ended. The tail-end of the parade has yet to cross the drawbridge."

Drayton's warhorse reared. Drayton reined back and petted his warhorse's neck. The horse calmed.

BAD LUCK OMEN

Drayton whispered, "Yes Morgan. Bad luck. We did not finish the parade ceremony within the hour, bad luck. Therefore, some knights will believe an enemy will drive us from Rose Fire."

In the bailey, both Warrick and Marian were on warhorses.

Warrick turned. "Marian. I have sent word to the king that we have captured Rose Fire. Now, Marian. You must prepare Rose Fire for the comforts of the king and his court. They will soon be here for our wedding. While the king is here, we will use Nicola's chambers. The Queen's ladies in waiting will use the solar, Blanche's chambers and the servant's quarters. The king and queen will use our chambers."

Marian said, "I will need help? We will need thyme-honey mead to bless our marriage with passion. Also, we will need yellow and white crocuses to bless our marriage. To bless our marriage with cheer and gladness."

Warrick dismounted. Then he reached up and grasped Marian's waist. She held his upper arms as he lifted her off her white mare.

As Warrick lowered her to the bailey floor, he said, "I promise. I promise that I will provide the thyme-honey mead and the yellow and white crocuses. I always honor my promises."

Warrick said, "About the preparation for the king's visit and our wedding. All you need to do is ask. I want you to avoid the wounded. They are the enemy. They could still harm you."

ILL-ADVISED COMPASSION

As usual, Marian's compassion overrode Warrick's command.

She walked on the bailey floor toward the wounded to help them.

As he turned, Warrick saw her with pages treating the enemy wounded.

He ran to Marian and threw her on his shoulder.

Warrick said, "Marian. I told you to obey for a reason. You are not to treat the enemy wounded."

With her over his shoulder he bounded into the Great Hall. Then five steps at a time, he climbed the tallest keep's spiral stairs, Marian's keep.

She said, "I suppose that you are going to beat me for disobeying."

Warrick laughed and said, "It is a thought. No, but I am thinking of a more pleasant punishment. The pleasant punishment may also be a way to celebrate our capture of Rose Fire."

With Marian in Warrick's arms, Marian hugged his neck with both arms. With his black leather boot, Warrick pushed open the door to Marian's bedchamber.

Warrick said, "Good. My squires and pages have already furnished your chambers."

Marian said, "How? Wolv burned all the wood. He even burned the wood of the stables."

Lord Warrick said, "Gifts. Grateful monasteries, nunneries and even peasants have refurbished the castle. With material and labor. Wye Valley laborers have almost completed the stables. Look. You have a bed, chairs, torches, tables, candles, and a roaring andiron."

She laughed as he tossed her on her back onto the thick goose-down bed. She laughed, then she jumped up and ran for the solar door. He unclasped his black cloak and threw it like a net. His cloak fell over her head. She stopped to throw it off. From behind her, he wrapped his strong arms around her. Under his cloak, she laughed and trembled from excitement.

He pulled his cloak off her. He hugged her tight.

Marian threw her head back in laughter and said, "Wonderful punishment?"

Warrick laughed and said, "Yes, and one day, it will be awesome. For now, remember, this is only a temporary victory. Celebration and lasting joy must wait until the impossible, until we have subdued Wolv. At least like King Arthur subdued Wolv."

SATAN WORSHIPERS

Outside Marian's chambers, Father Malachi Martin said, "Warrick. Danger is near. The drums of Satan's worshipers. They call demons, witches, warlocks and Skinwalkers from around the world. Warrick, make sure Perpetual Adoration is set up in Rose Fire's Chapel."

Warrick yelled out Marian's chamber door, "Morgan. Hear those drums?"

From the bailey floor Morgan shouted up at Marian's keep, "Yes, Lord Warrick. I hear the drums."

Warrick said, "Morgan. Those are Lilith and Wolv's drums of Satan worshipers. You can hear the screams of children. They are throwing their own children into fires. Into fires, sacrifices to Satan. Satan worshipers are calling demons, witches, warlocks and Skinwalkers worldwide. This is only a temporary victory. Wolv is amassing Satan's forces. Look to the peaks of the Black Mountains. The Red-Fog that surrounds the Black Mountain peaks is as thick as a lake. Completely opaque. Morgan, make sure Perpetual Adoration is set up in Rose Fire's Chapel. If that red-fog comes down here, it will eat us all as we sleep."

EGYPTIAN TORMENTS.

High in the Black Mountains, in a huge cavern, Wolv sat beside Pamia's corpse. A thousand-year-old corpse covered in wax and plaster to look exactly like Pamia. Like Pamia when she was alive.

Wolv seated himself beside Pamia's corpse and said, "My love. Is the cavern warm enough? I can have my Skinwalkers put more wood into the andiron."

Then Wolv howled, "Not now Holy Mary, not now, not when I am with Pamia."

Wolv fell from his chair to his knees and growled, "Not now Holy Mary."

Wolv eyes glazed over black as they always do when his memories capture him.

In his memories he was in Egypt. Egyptian children surrounded him chanting, "Ugly Eye."

Six-year-old Jesus took six-year-old Wolv's hand and led him to Holy Mary. The child Wolv wept. Holy Mary picked up Wolv and seated Wolv on her lap. She said, "Wolv. You are beautiful and intelligent. Little Wolv, I will always love you."

Wolv began repeatedly to howl Mary's words, "Little Wolv, I will always love you."

Wolv shook the Black Mountains with each howl.

Flames of his anger and rage and hatred burst from his mouth. Blasted as black flames from his mouth. Black spiritual flames that filled the air, but burned nothing but himself.

Slowly Wolv's Holy Mary obsession faded and his eyes lost their black glaze.

Wolv stood and raised his fists into the air and growled, "Holy Mary. Leave me alone. Leave me alone. Get your son, Jesus, off my throne."

Then Wolv saw that his howls had caused the skull of Pamia's corpse to fall. The skull shattered on the floor. The AntiChrist wept into his hands and shouted, "Jesus, Jesus. Give Pamia to me. Over a thousand years ago I saw you raise people from the dead. Please raise Pamia from the dead for me."

Wolv howled, "Pamia, Pamia."

INSIDE ROSE FIRE

Warrick said, "Wolv has no rest. Also, Wolv will give us no rest. His howls will continue to vibrate the Black Mountains and Rose Fire. Continue until we somehow contain him. Perhaps the way King Arthur contained him."

In Marian's chamber, Lord Warrick tossed his cloak across a chair.

Ross-Templar was correct. Marian's beauty did restore Warrick joy.

He said, "Your beauty is irresistible. I am like a stone. A stone that helplessly rolls down a mountainside. Then splashes into the lake of your beauty. Like bees need honey, like grass needs sunshine, I need your beauty."

Marian's beauty would capture Warrick's heart. Marian's love would save Warrick's soul.

She watched in fascination as his muscles moved and flexed under his leathers. She had never seen such thick defined lean muscles.

"Your beauty takes me into another world," Warrick said. "I want to dive into your eyes and swim."

On the walls, their shadows danced in the candle and torch light and andiron flames. Yellow-red candle and torch light reflected off his tanned face.

She hugged him and breathed deep of his pungent bay leaf fragrance. He traced his scarred, calloused fingertip along her cameo forehead. Chills ran up and down her spine. He traced his finger across her eyebrow. Then down her high cheek bone.

TRAITOR AT WORK
Blanche was in the solar, with her ear to Marian's door. Blanche thought, "I cannot allow Warrick to leave Marian with his child. I want Warrick's riches and lands."

NOT EVEN A KISS
Warrick said, "You are 'Lady Beautiful'. More beautiful than even Rose Fire Castle in the Prime red sun."

He held her head to kiss her.

A page knocked on the door, then he shouted through the door. "My lord, we need you outside the outer wall battlement. Hurry my lord. A huge load of stones fell from the top of the castle wall. Someone cut the ropes."

Marian said, "My lord, I order you; I command you to come back here when you finish.

Warrick said, "No kiss for now."

With his hand on the door he laughed. He said, "My bride that I must obey?"

She laughed and said, "Yes, your bride that you must obey. Come back here and finish that kiss."

She wagged her finger at him.

She said, "You will learn that obedience has its rewards."

Warrick laughed and ran out the door.

Blanche stood at the solar door at Marian's chambers. With a smile, she held a small dagger. Then she hid the dagger under her breasts. The dagger that she had used to cut the pulley rope.

Marian waited. She fell asleep.

-

-

-

CHAPTER, In Rose Fire Castle, Wales, Builth Castle, Wales, Year @ 1250s A.D.

THE WAR JUST BEGUN

Very early Prime bells woke Marian.

As she lay in the bed, she said, "Where are you?"

Collette said, "Here, my lady."

"No, not you, Collette," Marian said. "Where is Lord Warrick? Collette, why are you here?"

Collette said, "My lady. I have always entered your room at the Prime bells. To bathe and dress you."

"Yes, yes of course, Collette, but where is Lord Warrick," Marian asked?

"My lady, many believe that Lord Warrick does not sleep," Collette said. "At the Prime bells, when I entered your solar I saw him in the bailey. In his black leathers, he practiced with his huge battle ax. The ax everyone calls Blessed Dread. A battlement guard told me that Warrick practices all night. He said that some believe that Warrick is not human because he never tires."

Marian said, "Warrick must be human. I am to marry him."

Collette tossed a handful of dried rose pedals onto the floor to perfume the room. She lit lavender incense. Servants carried buckets of warm water and poured them into a half barrel tub. As the servants bathed and dressed Marian, Collette brushed Marian's hair with lavender oil.

Minutes later, dressed in her white, rabbit-fur, cowled cloak, Marian saw Warrick on the battlement. He had his black-gloved hands on a tall merlon. With his back straight, he stood on the battlement's walkway. He put his foot up on a crenelation between two merlons. The mountain wind blew his long black hair to one side. He looked out over the grey-fog-covered Wye Valley.

Warrick turned at the creak of the keep's battlement level door, Marian's door. Warrick saw Marian. Then he smiled and waved her to him. She walked to him. The stiff cold wind parted her cloak's white rabbit fur in chaotic lines.

To keep Marian warm he wrapped his long strong arms around her. "Marian, look out over the valley, all that you see is yours. Of course, after we do the impossible, subdue Wolv."

With her back snug against Warrick, she said, "You mean 'yours.' The king's law does not allow women to own property. You have many tomes written about Wolv in many ancient languages. I have been reading them. You have hundreds of tomes the Able Pendragons have written about Wolv Pendragon. I will read everything in every ancient language. Together we will find Wolv's unknown weaknesses. You have wagons of ancient tomes on Wolv."

"Marian, what is a lord without a lady," Warrick asked?

Marian smiled. Prime bells rose from under the blanket of fog that covered the valley. They stood on the outer battlement. Together they watched the Prime red sun peek over the eastern horizon.

"This is my favorite part of the day," Marian said. "The moon still shines as the red sun rises. The sunrise's yellow-red rays are like birth. A renewed birth of hope and all good things."

Then Prime bells of many monasteries rose from the valley. Night turned to Prime break of fast. The shadows of the Black Mountain trees stretch westward.

"Look at the valley," Warrick said. "Every Prime we will watch the sunrise. Watch the sun reflect red and yellow off the Wye Valley's sea of grey fog."

From behind Marian, Warrick tightly hugged her. In her champion's arms, Marian was so happy that she had no need to speak. She ran her hands along the back of his huge hands. She felt warm, joyful.

Prime bells echoed off the Black Mountains.

Warrick pointed at the peaks of the Black Mountains and said, "Marian. We are still in terrible danger. Look at the thick red-fog atop the Black Mountains. The red-fog grows thicker each day as Wolv amasses more Skinwalkers, more demons. More Things-in-the-Red-Fog."

HIGH IN THE BLACK MOUNTAINS IN RED-FOG
Wolv flew as black crows above a Black Mountain peak. The sound of Prime bells caused the crows to collapse to the snow.
In unison the crows screamed, "Jesus. Stop torturing me. Holy Mary, leave me alone."
The crows walked to one point. They formed into Wolv's original Roman general form and his horse. At the sound of the prime bells Wolv fell from his horse. His eyes glazed over black. He turned into charcoal dust and descended into the earth.
Wolv descended quickly through underground waterfalls and underground lakes. Beside an underground lake, Wolv took on his original Roman General form.
Wolv howled, "Not again. Jesus, leave me alone."
In obsessive agony, Wolv fell to his knees. As with every morning, Wolv looked up to see, in his memory, Jesus. Jesus, bright as the sun, walked from his Jerusalem tomb.
On his knees, Wolv begged, "Jesus, raise Pamia from the dead for me."
In his memory he watched. Jesus did not look at him. Then Jesus disappeared.
Wolv's growls of 'Jesus, raise Pamia from the dead for me' shook the earth.
Wolv's anger and hatred came out of him. Out as red foam from his mouth, born of hate, rage and anger.
As midmorning Terce Bells rang, Wolv came out of his Prime bells Resurrection obsession.
He turned into charcoal dust, a form of pure carbon. Then he ascended through the earth to the Black Mountains' peak.

IN ROSE FIRE
Everyone in Rose Fire stood still until Wolv's Resurrection obsession ended.
Then the smells of break of fast wafted about the castle. The aromas were roast beef, stewed pork, hot bread, apple jellies. Jams heated to boiling, and hot apple cider. While the cold wind flagged

Marian's hair, she turned around to Warrick. Marian ran her hands under his cloak. Then she ran her hands along his huge chest muscles. She hugged him.

"I filled, full, fulfilled, because I know that my champion loves me," she said.

Marian said, "I know that my champion loves me, does my bridegroom love me?"

Warrick thought of his traitorous wife, Ogina. Marian looked up at Warrick.

She said, "Warrick. Your face is now drawn and as hard as stone. Ogina? You think of Ogina, your traitorous wife? Your smile has turned to a frown. Every time I mention our future marriage, you withdrawal from me somewhere inside your grief. You become so quiet when I mention marriage."

With a frown, Warrick said, "Marian, I am an honorable man. I always do my duty."

Also with a frown, Marian said, "Warrick. I do not want to be a lord's 'duty'."

Warrick said nothing.

Marian thought, "He embraced when he championed me. He hugs me now. His hugs always tell me that somewhere inside him he loves me."

Marian laced her fingers with Warrick's. Then she turned and watched the Wye valley.

Amid Terce bells, morning sunbeams made the Wye Valley grey-fog glow. Cook fires and torch light shone from homes in the valley. Yellow and red torches reflected off the castle's pink granite battlements. The sun spread its rays. Rose Fire's guards stuffed the torches into sand buckets to extinguished them.

The morning sun camouflaged the full moon. The orange-pink sun beams reflected pink off the red clay road up the mountain sides.

Marian pointed, "Look, who is coming to Rose Fire?"

More Prime bells rang.

Warrick said, "I cannot see them through the grey fog. Yet, I hear the clink of armor and the clomp of horses. Therefore, I would say that they are King Edward's knights. Too few and too late."

UNEXPECTED LINE OF WAGONS

Marian said, "Through the grey fog I can now see a long line of wagons."

Warrick waved a guard to himself.

The guard marched up to Warrick and clicked his heels.

Lord Warrick said, "Find Lord Ross-Templar, Drayton, and Morgan. I want them to take a squad of knights and inspect the entourage."

-

-

-

CHAPTER, Now in Rose Fire Castle, Wales, Year @ 1250s A.D.

MY CHAMPION DOES NOT WANT ME. THE ENEMY ATTACKS ALWAYS.

ROSE-FIRE-CASTLE IS FULL OF DEMONS. THEY DID NOT EXORCIZE THE ANIMALS.

On the drawbridge, within a short time, Ross-Templar shouted up from outside the battlement. "Warrick. Lord Thetford leads the forty knights you requested."

Upon the battlement, Warrick shouted, "Ross-Templar. I had requested far more than forty."

Thetford shouted from outside the castle, "Lord Warrick. We are too late with the knights of course. We also have architects, masons, and other artisans to refurbish Rose Fire."

From the drawbridge Drayton hollered, "Warrick. They are all faithful subjects of the king."

Warrick stepped back and waved his hand and said, "Let them in. Raise the portcullis gate."

Slowly two husky archers pulled on the great wooden pulleys of portcullis machinery. They raised the thick iron grate. Iron ground against iron. Ropes squealed and wood pulleys creaked. The cavalcade of horses and wagons rode across the drawbridge. Then into Rose Fire's bailey.

TRAITOR. ON BAILEY FLOOR.

Blanche flew down the outer-wall battlement steps and jumped into Lord Thetford's arms. Thetford was a man of the king's court that Blanche had not yet bedded. She hugged him to

fake that she liked him. Blanche had deceived Thetford to think
that she like him. Lord Thetford laughed and hugged her. Then he
extended his arm to Blanche. Blanche twined her arm on his, and
he walked with her.

ON THE BATTLEMENT
Marian held Warrick's arm and walked to Marian's
chamber. They stood at the top of the keep steps. Then Marian
walked into her chambers to change her gown. Warrick sat in
Marian's solar on a bench. He pulled his boot off. As he turned
his boot upside down, a stone dropped from inside to his hand.
Behind them Thetford and Blanche had also climbed the
steps to the solar. Lord Thetford walked over to Warrick.
Thetford said, "The king sent this parchment to you."
Thetford handed the parchment to Warrick.
As Warrick sat with the stone in his hand, he broke the
kings' wax seal. He unrolled the parchment and read:
Lord Warrick.
You are the world's only hope to slow the AntiChrist. As to
Lady Marian. My consideration about your betrothal was that
Marian was the fairest child of England's lords. You are my
greatest champion. You are England's greatest champion.
Marian is England's fairest maiden. I gave England's treasure,
England's fairest maiden, to England's greatest champion. So that
she would have the greatest protection. I will not honor your
request to send Marian back to Oxford. Nor will I honor your
request to assign Marian to the protection of another lord. Also,
the red-fog grows thicker in London. Grows thicker across all
England. The red-fog gathers in the low lands. Where the red-fog
gathers, the things in the red-fog are eating people. My guards
can already see shapeless things move in the red-fog. Whatever
you are to do to conquer Wolv, you must do it soon. Inside or
outside Rose Fire, both Wolv and the demon Lilith are too strong.
My champion, you are the world's only hope. You must not allow
Wolv to gather the strength he had as Attila, the Hun. Slow him,
you are the world's only hope."
King Edward
As Lord Warrick sighed, he thought, "The king's reply is
too late. I have already conquered Rose Fire. I have not

conquered Wolv, only displaced him. His Skinwalkers will grow stronger in the Black Mountain caverns. For now, Marian is temporarily safe within Rose Fire's walls. No need temporarily to put Marian under the protection of Oxford's Lord Protllyy."

Someone shouted from the bailey, "Lord Warrick. Come quick. A lance impaled a squire."

A TRAITOR'S SUCCESS

Blanche wanted to read the parchment. For the moment, she needed Thetford and Warrick to leave the solar. She feigned compassion for the injured squire. She insisted, "Quickly, my lords. Both of you must go and help the squire. He needs your battle-wound knowledge."

Lord Warrick tossed the velum parchment onto a table with many blank, velum parchments. Thetford and Warrick ran down Marian's keep-spiral steps. Blanche wanted to obtain any information to use to chase Marian away from Warrick. Any information to help Wolv conquer Warrick. She opened the parchment and read it. Blanche, just as Marian, would misunderstand the parchment. Neither Marian nor Blanche would, or could, understand the truth. The truth that Warrick had wanted to send Marian to Oxford only temporarily. Only temporarily until Warrick had driven Wolv from Rose Fire.

Blanche incorrectly thought, "Wonderful. This parchment is Warrick's official rejection of Marian. If Marian reads this parchment, the rejection will break her heart. This parchment will break her heart so much that she will never marry Warrick. With Marian out of my way, then. Then I can get the king to betroth me to Warrick. I will have Warrick's wealth, social status and Rose Fire. Then I can betray Warrick to Wolv. Then Wolv will give me Rose Fire. Wolv always rewards royal traitors."

ON THE PRACTICE FIELD

Marian, Collette, and Nicola ran behind Warrick down the keep steps. They ran out onto the practice field. Warrick's black cloak waved like a flag behind him.

THE TRAITOR.

Up in the keep's solar, a wicked smile grew wider on Blanche's face. She waited until all had left Marian's chambers. Then she snuck in and put the parchment on Marian's bed.

AFFECT OF THE TRAITOR.
In a minute, Marian and Collette dashed up the keep steps to Marian's bedchamber. Marian said, "Faster, faster. We need unguents."

In the neat bedchamber they lifted and emptied trunks on the floor. Then, on their knees, they threw clothes in the air. To find unguents for the injured squire. Marian pulled open a cabinet and threw its contents on the bed. She knelt on the bed and pushed her hands through the heap.

With both hands, Marian pulled an unguent's pouch from under candles and incense pouches. Marian said, "Hurry, Collette. You must run these balms to my lord."

Late Prime and early Terce bells rang. Marian saw the parchment on her bed.

She read it. Her mouth fell open. The sentence, *'Nor will I assign Marian to another lord,'* burned her. She did not know that Warrick had meant for Lord Protllyy temporarily to protect her.

The phrase tore her heart into pieces.

She thought, "Warrick does not want to marry me. He has rejected me and wants to send me home to Oxford in shame. My champion wants to send me to another lord. My bridegroom, my champion has rejected me."

All the blood ran from her face. She tore the parchment into shreds and burned it in her brazier. Then she sat on the bed and wept into her palms.

In Marian's brazier the parchment burst into a yellow blaze of tall flames. Flames and white smoke.

Nicola heard the commotion and ran into the room. Nicola said, "Marian, Marian. Why are you weeping?"

She hugged her sister. Tears ran down Marian's cheeks and soaked Nicola's arm.

ON THE PRACTICE FIELD

With the squire, Lord Warrick said, "You. Hold this on his wound to stop the blood flow. I can hear Marian weep. I fear that someone has attacked Marian."

He and his brothers dashed across the bailey, into the great hall. Five steps at a time, they ran up the keep steps. Their cloaks flew behind them like great black wings.

Warrick rushed into the room with Blessed Dread held high to cleave any enemy. With blessed swords drawn, Lord Ross-Templar, Drayton, and Morgan ran up behind him.

INSIDE THE BEDCHAMBER.

Inside the bed chamber, Nicola said, "My lord. I do not know what causes Marian to cry so hard. A blessed sword or Blessed Dread cannot vanquish the cause."

He held Blessed Dread's handle and then he rested its point on the stone floor. As Warrick knelt by her bed, he said, "What, what?"

He touched her. She violently rolled over to the other side of the bed, "My lord. Would you please go? Please My lord, would you leave me? Please."

Lord Warrick said, "Marian. I will honor your wishes and leave you alone, for a few minutes."

Marian's brow wrinkled with anger in a deep V. She shouted, "For an eternity of minutes, until the world's last days."

He stood stunned, "What happened? You were so happy. We are to wed."

She said, "Not if I can help it. Never will I end like Onslow and my older sister Louise. He ignores her, treats her with scorn, mocks her, and sleeps with mistresses. Like you will, he humiliates her in the presence of England's royalty."

Anger reddened Warrick's bronze face and brightened his emerald eyes.

Marian cried, "Earl of fiery emerald eyes. You are the lords of the angry face, red as the Vesper's sunset. You can burn me with the flames from those emerald eyes. Even . . . you can cleave me like you cleave an enemy knight on the battlefield. I will not marry you. I would rather that you cleave me with Blessed Dread than marry you."

Morgan whispered, "Warrick. I see no enemy here. If we do not hurry, the squire will bleed to death."

Warrick stood and said, "I will be back."

Marian shouted, "No, no. Never enter my chambers again, never!"

As Terce bells rang, Warrick lowered his head and sighed. Then he ran his long muscular fingers through his hair. He sighed. Then Warrick closed the chamber door. Quickly, he ran back to the wounded squire out on the battlefield.

In the bed chamber, Marian wept.

The Franciscan Terce bells faded. She tiptoed and peered out an arrow-slot to see Warrick on the battlefield.

She said, "Nicola. Warrick is now my lost love, my lost champion, my lost joy."

Nicola said, "Marian, what in the name of God's Robe is wrong with you? My lord's actions prove that he loves you."

Marian pointed to the brazier. "Nicola. Those parchment ashes prove that Warrick asked the king to send me another lord. Warrick asked the king to assign me to another lord. He asked the king to betroth me to another lord. He has no love for me. Now I know why he made sure that I remained a virgin. Now I know why he does not sleep with me at night. I know why he pretends to be busy. He wanted another man to wed me, any other man but himself. Now . . . now I know why he could so easily lie about our wedding in London."

From her chambers, through the arrow notch, Marian watched Warrick.

Marian said, "Nicola. I had dreamed of the love that might have been. I still love him because he fought for me. Requited or painfully unrequited, a maiden always loves her champion. A maiden's champion always steals the maiden's heart. Nicola, . . . you should have seen Lord Warrick beside the lake. How magnificent he was when he stood in the sunshine before those mounted Skinwalkers. He stood without his weapon, without his horse, without his blessed shield. In the face of sure death, he could have run and abandoned me. Instead he uprooted a small thorn tree for a useless weapon. The mounted Skinwalkers guffawed at him. They said, 'Englishman, we will let you run away. We only want the woman.' Warrick put that small thorn-tree across his palms as if it were a mace. With a straight back he said, 'I declare myself to be this unknown lady's champion. If you attempt to touch this woman, I will kill you.' My heart jumped at the sight of his bronze skin. As he moved, his long black hair swished around his head. My heart broke for him to see his raw, foolish courage before certain death. I remember that the rogues laughed and said 'He has no weapon.' With supreme illogical, confidence, Warrick pointed his long arm and finger at them. His warning rippled the shore's lake water and vibrated leaves on trees. He shouted. 'I am a weapon.' The only weapon that Warrick had was his faith in God. On their warhorses the Skinwalkers attacked him to trample him. Suddenly he looked like a defenseless child that tried to act like a little man. He looked so little as if he helplessly fought giant mounted ogres, for me. The mounted Skinwalkers attacked. Through tears, I almost laughed at his whimsical, self-confidence. Though I feared him, I suddenly loved him. Then I feared Warrick more because I realized. I realized that I would, that I did, love him. I feared him because I knew from that moment that I would love that stranger. Love my champion, forever. As the rogues attacked, I closed my eyes. Then, when I opened my eyes all the Skinwalkers lay at Warrick's feet."

Marian paused and turned to her sister. She wiped the streaks of tears on her cheeks.

"Warrick does not want me," she said as she sobbed into her palms. "He does not want me. I must find a way to escape this humiliation."

ON THE PRACTICE FIELD.

Out on the practice ground, the squire lay unconscious. Marian heard Warrick's loud angry commands.

Warrick pointed at the injured squire and said, "Otan. I want you to carry him into the infirmarian. You must find Father Malachi Martin. Do not jostle the injured squire or he will begin to bleed again."

Warrick shouted, "Who told the squire to practice without armor?"

A knight raised his hand. Warrick marched over to him. Then he smashed his huge black-gloved fist against the knight's closed visor. Though in a closed helm, the knight fell unconscious.

Lord Warrick said, "Ross-Templar. When he wakes, send him away to serve another lord."

Morgan turned to all the knights and shouted, "Take this as a warning. Lord Warrick will not allow fools in his service."

IN HER BED CHAMBERS.

In her chambers, on her bed, Marian wept, "Warrick only played with me. What a wicked liar he is. Lord Ross was honest with women. All he wanted was a wild night with three or four of them. He tells them that when he first meets them. He was honest. Warrick. Warrick is the worst of all men; he stole my heart. I will never get over this. Nicola, do not let anyone steal your heart. You must run away from anyone like Warrick. Or else, you will end in the hands of an Onslow, like Warrick."

Marian wept into her palms and sniffled. "Nicola, I know what is happening. He thinks that I will marry him. Then he can have mistresses here in Rose Fire, just like Onslow. Warrick and his mistresses have never known or seen the likes of me. No mistress, no trollop, has ever met the equal of my anger's fury."

ATTACK

On the practice field Warrick shouted, "There, on the tree line, Skinwalkers."

Arrows landed at Warrick's feet. He shouted, "Everyone into Rose Fire. Now! Now! We do not know how many attack us."

At Warrick's orders, everyone retreated into Rose Fire.

ATOP THE BATTLEMENT.

Then from the top of the battlement, Warrick watched the tree line.

Morgan said, "Wolv's Skinwalkers are retreating up the mountain."

While the Dominican Terce bells rang, Warrick said, "Drayton. I want you to take a few archers and follow them. Do not engage them. You must dress your archers in white fur to camouflage them in the snow. I only want you to follow them, count Wolv's Skinwalkers. Then come back. Do not engage them. We will go back to the practice field."

Warrick said, "We must expect attacks each week. Every day. Every canonical bells.

ON THE PRACTICE FIELD.

Out on the practice field, Warrick said, "Morgan. Why in the world would Marian reject me? Why was she angry with me? What came over her? Has the Devil possessed her? I thought that she was happy?"

Morgan said, "I do not understand women. They are a mystery."

Warrick paused for a moment.

Lord Warrick thought, "Marian's beauty intoxicates me. I must learn why she is angry with me."

He should have told Marian of his feelings for her. Yet he was sure that she understood his warlord's actions. That his actions proved his devotion to protect her. He did not express his softer emotions. Also, he had told his traitorous wife, Ogina, that he loved her. His wife had manipulated his love to murder his knights. She succeeded. Then he remembered his wife's attempt to murder him, while they made love. Ogina attempted to shove a dagger in Warrick's back.

In her chambers, Marian said, "Nicola. Warrick never loved me."

Out on the practice field, Warrick thought, "Love is a dagger in the back. I fear that I will love Marian. No, I fear that I might already love Marian. She is too beautiful. A knight's, a champion's dilemma has three inevitable stages. First the champion protects his beautiful charge. Then, if the champion stays with his charge, the champion takes jealous possession of her. Third is the dagger in the heart. As always, fate causes him to love his possession. She is now my beautiful possession. Love blinded me once to a traitor. Love will not blind me again. Yet, Marian's beauty conquers me. Marian's beauty blinds me. Soon Marian's beauty will conquer me. Then I will have no choice but to love Marian. I must never again allow my blindness to endanger my knights."

DOOR OF THE GREAT HALL.
Warrick said, "Morgan. Come with me to check our armory off the great hall."

Morgan said, "Warrick. We will soon need many more weapons."

In the door of the great hall, Blanche overheard Morgan.

Morgan said, "Warrick. After you wed, Marian will have access to all your lands and wealth."

"Yes Morgan, of course," Warrick said, "I expect Marian to spend as she wishes. Marian will have all my wealth and lands. She will also have the social status and riches of Rose Fire."

Morgan turned and said, "Blanche. Your face is green, why are you green?"

"Yes, Blanche, why are you green?" Warrick asked, "and why do you grind your teeth?"

Blanche turned her head away from Warrick and Morgan. She thought, "How stupid of me. I should have turned my head. They saw my greed, my envy and my anger."

Blanche lied as she traced a circle with her toe. She lied, "I think I ate a bit of rancid rabbit."

Blanche walked away.

Morgan said, "Warrick. I do not know why Marian is angry with you. You have respect and honor for her."

IN HER BEDCHAMBERS.
In her chambers, Marian said, "Nicola. Warrick has such contempt for me. He has treated me with disrespect and dishonor. He will dress my children and me in rags and shower wealth on his mistresses."

TRAITOR.
Blanche had her back to Warrick and Morgan. The thought of Marian with Warrick's wealth, gagged Blanche. She coughed and almost lost her last meal.

BED CHAMBER
In Marian's chambers she said, "Nicola. I want you to look out the window at the sky. Strange black, storm clouds have gathered over the Wye Valley. Storm clouds form over the valley

just as black storm clouds form over my marriage. My lightening will obliterate Warrick's mistresses."

Nicola said, "Marian. Warrick is not dishonorable."

Marian said, "He is dishonorable. He may be dishonorable, but he is my dishonorable champion. I cannot stop my love for my dishonorable champion."

In Marian's chambers, Nicola sat on Marian's bed.

Nicola said, "You need to go talk to Lord Warrick about the parchment. You must not let your pride ruin the obvious love between the two of you. You have too much pride."

-

-

-

CHAPTER, Now in Rose Fire Castle, Wales, Year @ 1250s A.D.

EXCESS PRIDE.

In her chambers, as she paced with her arms crossed, Marian shouted, "My pride? My pride? Lord Warrick is the one that lied about the London marriage. Warrick is the one that wrote the king to send me away. You ask me about my pride? Never would I give him the satisfaction that I am still in love with him. Lord Warrick would only laugh at me and send me home in shame. He will demand that he have mistresses after our marriage."

From the field Warrick ran up the bailey's stairs to the outer wall battlement. He stood in the shadows between a keep and guard tower. He put a foot on a crenel. Then he leaned forward and put his hands on a merlon. Hidden in the shadows, he did not move.

High midmorning. The last Terce bells, the Cistercian Order's bells, rang and faded. Lord Warrick was like a silent hawk that waits for the enemy to show itself. Warrick did not move.

Hours later Sext bells announced that the sun's zenith was near.

Warrick said, "Morgan. As always, make sure that everyone does their hour of Perpetual Adoration. Either in the wagon or the chapel. Perpetual Adoration of Jesus' Real Presence in the Blessed Sacrament. Make sure everyone does weekly confession. Ponder Wolv's defeat of York's English army. The duke of York refused to have his soldiers do Adoration and confession. They spent their time in York's famous brothels. The Things-in-Wolv's red-fog had possessed the prostitutes. The things-in-the red-fog possessed many of York's soldiers. Then the prostitutes turned into Skinwalkers and ate many of York's soldiers. Then the possessed soldiers turned into Skinwalkers. Skinwalkers can take any form, women, children, men, animals. That day the duke of York lost his whole army. Remember. We had to fight those Skinwalkers for three days. Most of the prostitutes asked Jesus for Mercy. Thus, we exorcized their demons. Some of them refused, remained deadly Skinwalkers, and fought us. Fought us until we had to behead them. Days of battle. Remember how many of them turned into monstrous snakes as they fought us? York's soldiers could have won if the soldiers had done Adoration and confession. Never take your thoughts away that Adoration and weekly confessions keep the red-fog away. We do not fight flesh and blood. We fight dominions and hierarchies of Satan, of the AntiChrist."

     SEXT OBSESSIONS.
     High in the Black Mountains, thick red fog poured from Wolv. Shapeless things in Wolv's red fog moved. As Sext bells rang in the Wye Valley, Wolv fell off his horse. He fell into the snow.
     On his knees again he shouted, "Jesus, leave me alone." His eyes glazed over black.
     In his memory he looked up to see Jesus on the Cross. As Jesus hung on the cross, Jesus said, "My God. My God, why have you forsaken me?"
     Atop the Black Mountains, Wolv growled repeatedly, "My God, my God. Why have you forsaken me?"
     Wolv's growls shook the Black Mountains.
     As he growled, black-red flame erupted from his mouth. The black-red flame covered the sky from horizon to horizon. Red-fog and Things-in-the-red-fog constantly poured from him.
     Slowly Wolv came out of his obsession.

     IN ROSE FIRE
     Everyone waited until Wolv's growls ended.

Nicola said, "Marian. Wolv's growls will one day collapse Rose Fire."

They walked to the Great Hall to eat the midday meal. Warrick was not in the Great Hall.

On the battlement, without a shadow to hide in, Warrick stepped into a guard tower. He watched the forest line through the arrow slots. Silent as a lion that waits to ambush prey, he watched the forest.

Hours later, the sun waned far beyond the zenith. The trees now had long eastward shadows.   The Nones bells began.

NONES OBSESSIONS.

From high in the Black Mountains, red fog continued to pour off Wolv. Things in the red-fog came out of him. From the red-fog, shapeless red-things flew out over England and Wales and Europe.

Wolv heard the Nones bells. His memories caused him to fall off his horse.

On his knees, Wolv growled, "Jesus. Do not torture me. Jesus, stop torturing me."

Wolv's eyes glazed over black as his memories captured him again. In his memories he looked at Jesus on the Cross. Jesus said, "It is finished. Father, into your hands I commit my spirit."

On the cross, Jesus' knees collapsed to the right side and his arms elongated. He no longer supported himself.

In Wolv's memory, he mounted a horse, took a spear and rode up to Jesus. Wolv rammed the spear up through Jesus' right side, up into and through Jesus' heart.

Then Wolv pulled out the spear. An impossible amount of blood and water poured out of Jesus' side. From Jesus' side out onto Wolv and the ground.

Atop the Black Mountains, in the snow, on his knees, Wolv growled, "It is finished. Father, into your hands I commit my spirit."

He growled repeatedly.

Born of rage and hatred and anger, black-red flame erupted from Wolv's mouth. The black-red flame covered the sky.

Everyone in Rose Fire was quiet as Wolv's obsessions shook the Black Mountains.

Slowly Wolv quieted.

IN ROSE FIRE
From the early Franciscan to the late Cistercian Nones bells, Warrick did not move. He did not eat. Warrick watched the mountain's tree line.

Then Warrick saw deer and white rabbits run from the tree line. His knights shot the deer and rabbits with arrows.

Pages ran over the draw bridge to drag the deer and rabbits into the castle. The pages tied long ropes to the hooves of the deer. *Warrick thought, "Something I expected has frightened them. Frightened the deer and rabbits from the woods. Something evil."*

Unseen Skinwalkers shot arrows at the pages.

The pages quickly ran across the drawbridge. From the safety of the castle they pulled the several deer into the castle.

The Nones bells had ended. Hours of long westward shadows began.

Shadows had lengthened into early dusk. Morgan and Ross-Templar climbed the bailey stairs up to the outer wall battlement.

Benedictine Vespers bells called the Benedictine monks to prayer and supper.

Morgan and Ross-Templar walked over to Warrick.

Shadows hid the three brothers on the battlement.

Morgan held his giant mace with one hand and rested it over his shoulder. He said, "Warrick. Today has been a long, long day. Rose Fire is secure for the night."

The sun set behind the Black Mountains. Thicker red-fog circled the peaks of the Black Mountains. More red-fog poured from Lilith and Wolv. In the red-fog, red wraiths, things in the fog, came out of Lilith and Wolv. The red things in the fog flew out over Wales, Scotland, Ireland, England and Europe.

Cooking fires glowed from the valley's thatch-roof homes.

Augustinian, Knights Templar, Benedictine and Carthusian Vespers bells echoed in the valley.

DRAYTON'S RETURN
Warrick pointed with his long arm and said, "Ross-Templar, Morgan. Look. Drayton and his archers are in danger. Drayton has returned. You must look at the tree line."

Ross-Templar said, "Yes, finally. From Terce to Vespers. Drayton was in the mountains, near the whole day. Morgan and I feared that Wolv had killed him."

In their white fur camouflage cloaks, Drayton and his archers ran. Ran from the tree line across the practice field.

Skinwalker arrows landed around them.

Lord Drayton and his archers ran faster.

Warrick commanded, "Lower the drawbridge and raise the portcullis."

Guards in the guardhouse above the drawbridge turned huge spools of ropes. Guards lowered the drawbridge and raised the portcullis. Ropes squealed. The great wooden drums creaked. Drayton and his archers dove for the partially lowered drawbridge. They caught the edge, pulled themselves up and rolled down the drawbridge.

ON THE BATTLEMENT

With Drayton's archers safe in the castle, Warrick shouted, "Guards. Close the drawbridge."

Drayton and his archers ran up the battlement steps to Warrick.

Drayton said, "Warrick. We followed Wolv's Skinwalkers up the mountainside. At a high point on the mountain, fresh snow had covered their footprints. For two canonical hours we could still see them higher on the mountain. As they climbed, they entered a mountain top blizzard. The mountain top blizzard hid them. We lost them. They were twenty Skinwalkers, a scout party."

Warrick turned from Drayton and said, "Ross-Templar. Wolv wants Marian. He is high on the mountainside where he can look down into the castle. Ross-Templar, Morgan, is the castle secure? Are Knights doing Adoration?"

Morgan said, "Yes, the castle is secure. Yes, faithful knights do Adoration."

Lord Ross-Templar put a hand on his blessed sword's hilt.

With his other hand Ross-Templar said the Rosary on the giant Rosary. The giant Rosary he now always kept over his shoulder.

Lord Warrick said, "You never cease to say Rosaries. To say Rosaries for lady Innocence's soul."

Lord Ross-Templar said, "I will never cease until Holy Mary gets permission from Jesus. Permission from Jesus to let me descend into Hell and carry Lady Innocence into Heaven."

Ross said, "As to the castle's security. I checked all the guards and I told them their orders and duties."

The cold Vesper's wind flagged Ross' neck-length, blond hair.

Morgan said, "Warrick. I have secured all gates."

Warrick said, "Yes, good. Morgan, the guards must be alert to keep Wolv's Skinwalkers away from Marian."

While Warrick turned, he said, "Drayton. Take your archers to the buttery. They need to eat then sleep. Tired archers cannot protect Marian."

Drayton turned to his first archer and said, "You heard Warrick. I want you to do as Warrick ordered."

Drayton's First Archer ran down the outer battlement's bailey steps into the bailey. He led the other archers into the Great Hall to sup.

Morgan said, "Warrick. The guards have lit all the wall torches and oil lamps for the night."

Drayton said, "Warrick. Listen. Why do the Carthusian monks ring their Compline tubular bells so early? The hour is not yet Compline."

"Drayton," Warrick said, "The early Carthusian Compline bells are calling other monasteries to an emergency. If the Carthusians want our help, they will ring the bells in groups of three."

Morgan said, "Warrick. I smell a familiar stench in the air. Sulfur."

Drayton said, "Morgan, that is Wolv's stink, sulfur."

"Yes, Drayton," Warrick said, "Wolv is close enough to smell. We must stay attentive to protect Marian."

Warrick cleared his throat and said, "As to Marian, brothers, I have a question. What should I do about Marian's anger? I went up to her chambers. She would only cry and refuse to see or talk to me."

Morgan said, "My brother, you are lost. The Pendragon curse has caught you. All you can do is wait and hope."

Ross-Templar put his hand on the hilt of his blessed sword. He said, "Warrick. All the stonemasons and other artisans are within the castle, safe. Well fed and asleep."

Warrick turned to Ross-Templar.

Warrick poked Ross-Templar in the chest and said, "Ross. You know more about women than me. Why will Marian not tell me the reason that she is so upset?"

"I know, knew, how to seduce women, plural," Ross-Templar said. "I do not know how to live with women. If I did Lady, Innocence would not have jumped off her father's manor."

Morgan said, "Ross-Templar. How . . . can you believe that you . . . do not understand women. Your smile alone . . . breaks their hearts."

Ross said, "My smile is a curse."

Drayton said, "Yes, Ross-Templar. Yet you can still advise Warrick. You know women better than you know your own hands."

"Ross-Templar," Warrick said, "how can I protect Marian. She will not even talk to me? Everything I do is for Marian."

IN HER BED CHAMBERS.

In her chambers, as she sat on the bed, Marian said, "Nicola. Lord Warrick has no thoughts of me."

As the sun set, Marian watched Warrick through her open chamber door. The open keep door to the battlement. She watched Warrick and his brothers laugh on the outer wall battlement.

As Marian pointed, she said, "Nicola. There they are, in the eve, Morgan, Warrick, Ross-Templar and Drayton. I am sure that they are trading stories on conquering women. The four of them could set up a school on how to humiliate women. Ross-Templar and Warrick will bed two, three, and four women at a time. I am sure that Drayton and Morgan are the same. Warrick will never again give me a thought."

ON THE BATTLEMENT.

On the battlement, with his long arm, Warrick pointed out over the Wye Valley.

"Brothers, what do you see out there," Warrick asked?

Morgan rested the point of his long iron mace on the outer wall battlement. He said, "Warrick. Fog. I see the Vesper's sun, red hues, strange storm clouds, stranger lightening. Lightening with no rain, the Wye River."

Warrick said, "I see none of those. All I see is Marian's face, the face of my charge. How can a man do his duties when all he sees is his beloved's face? The face of his stubborn, disobedient, angry, insolent, insulting, beautiful charge?"

Drayton ran his fingers along his bow string. He said, "The champion's-quandary has ensnared you. First you protect her. Then you naturally want jealously to possess her, then the trap, love. Many ladies have used the 'champions' dilemma'. Used the champion's dilemma to ensnare the man that they want to marry."

Morgan said, "Warrick. You can go about your duties. You can because one of your duties is now to ponder. To ponder the face of your impudent, stubborn, disobedient, angry, insolent, insulting, beautiful charge."

Drayton said, "Warrick. Your duty to protect Marian has naturally become an obsession. An obsession to do everything for her safety. I can see that her beauty has caught your eye too often."

Ross-Templar said, "Female beauty. A man can drown in a woman's eyes. As he drowns, he will feel no responsibility, only pleasure. Now my responsibility tortures me."

Morgan said, "The boyish, poet-lover's tongue gives words of wisdom and responsibility."

Warrick said, "I do not need the words of a happy, boyish lover. I need the wisdom of an experienced father or grandfather."

Morgan said, "Only God knows where our grandfathers are. We know that someone kidnaped our father. Long ago, when we had to stand on chairs to eat at the table."

From the bailey floor old Norwin shouted, "Warrick. Though I was in the buttery, I could hear you and your brothers."

Warrick said, "So, I spoke of a father."

Norwin shouted, "Warrick. Come down here and help me climb these steep steps."

Warrick descended the steps. He wrapped his arm around old Norwin's waist. Then, Warrick helped Norwin hobble up to the battlement walkway.

Old Norwin said, "I never thought that I would see the Wye Valley from here. This is God's view. In the daylight I can see for hundreds of miles. Yet this is not why I came into the bailey. I heard you talk about Marian, Warrick. You must just do your duty. If you protect Marian as the king trained you, Marian will come to understand you. Even begin to obey you. You must focus on Rose Fire's preparation for when Wolv will siege Rose Fire. Wolv will not retreat, he will not stop until he possesses Marian. Wolv believes Marian is Pamia. Remember that obsessions are Wolv. Wolv is an obsession."

Late Vespers and early Compline bells rang.

Lord Warrick said, "Brothers. The three of you should go to bed. Then I will again check the guards. I want you, Norwin, to come with me to your warm buttery. In the buttery you are close to food and warmth."

Norwin said, "No Warrick. Now that I have seen this view, I want to stay at the battlement level. I cannot climb the keep or bailey steps to the battlement. So I want to sleep at the battlement level."

Lord Warrick took Norwin's arm, he said, "Good. You can take a chamber off Marian's solar. A chamber next to Nicola. Perhaps at some serendipitous time you can talk to Marian for me. This keep is not as warm as your buttery chamber."

In a chamber off Marian's solar, old, frail Norwin lay. He snored on a goose-down mattress. As Norwin snored, Warrick pulled a heavy, rabbit-fur coverlet over Norwin.

Warrick's brothers walked to their own keep's chambers. Each brother had their own keep tower.

Warrick walked around Rose Fire's exterior battlement bailey. Then he walked around the talus battlement inner bailey. As he walked, he wrapped the battlement torches with more pine tar-soaked hides. He lit the torches. Then he put more oil into the guardhouses' oil lamps. Compline bells rang and he again checked the guards.

Lord Warrick walked upon a guard, asleep, standing.

He grabbed the guard by the breast plate and growled, "You. You are supposed to protect Marian. By right I have the authority to run you through right now."

From the guard tower Warrick threw a rope over the outer battlement into the moat. He pushed the guard to the rope.

"By right I could throw you over the battlement. Instead, I will allow you to climb down this rope and leave. I never again want to see your face. Marian needs my guards to be awake, to be ready to fight for her."

Then he shed his armor so he could swim the moat. The guard slid down the rope. The guard ran to the Wye valley and disappeared into the gathering grey-red fog.

Then in the bailey, Warrick began his night-training regime. As the night progressed, grey fog filled the bailey. In the grey fog, all night, Warrick practiced with his blessed sword and blessed Dread.

Every few minutes, Warrick whispered, "Mother. Forgive me. I failed you. I did not stop Wolv from killing you. Mother. Forgive me."

Warrick did not notice the Vigils midnight, Witches hours' bells.

Warrick did not notice that the red-fog tried to descend the mountain. Adoration of the Blessed Sacrament drove the red-fog away. Warrick also did not notice a great dragon. A great dragon flying high above Rose Fire, the dragon Lilith.

Nor did he notice the Matins bells that ended the three hours of Witches.

The pre sunrise early Prime bells did not attract his attention.

Then after three hours, the red sun broke over the eastern horizon. The red-pink sun bathed the valley's grey-fog in a pink hue. Prime bells echoed off the Black Mountains. Pink-sun rays glowed on Rose Fire's walls.

He had practiced from Compline to Prime bells. As the loudest prime bells sounded, Warrick stopped his practice. He stood in the bailey and inhaled.

He thought, "Mother, I am sorry that I failed you. Forgive me my mother. Marian. Oh Marian. How will I respond to Marian today?"

Then he ran his fingers through his long, black hair. Fog droplets had accumulated on him in the night. The droplets ran in streams down his black leathers. His muscles were hot from exercise. Steam rose from his black leathers just like his breath condensed. The steam rose from him like steam rises from a warm lake. A warm lake when the air is colder than the lake.

The Prime's pink glow grew brighter. A chaos of Prime bells awakened the Wye Valley.

RESURRECTION OBSESSIONS.

High above in the Black Mountains, as crows, Wolv ate a live disobedient Skinwalker.

Then the Skinwalker screamed in agony.

Wolv howled, "Jesus. Go away from me. Not again. Not again. Every morning, every Prime you torture me. Sext, you torture me. Nones, you torture me. Holy Mary tortures me."

Wolv changed from crows to his original Roman general form. His eyes glazed over black as his memories captured him. On the Black Mountain peak, in the snow, Wolv changed into black, pure, carbon dust. As dust, Wolv descended into the snow, then into the earth.

Descended through underground lakes, underground rivers, descended over underground waterfalls. Then Wolv stopped in a hug cavern, lighted with glowing mold and glowing mushrooms. Luminescent mold, luminescent mushrooms.

On the cavern's floor, eyes glazed lack, Wolv changed from dust to his Roman form.

Wolv fell to his knees and growled, "Please Jesus, not again."

In Wolv's memory, the ground shook. Wolv saw the huge stone over Jesus' tomb move aside. In his mind, Wolv saw Jesus, bright as the sun. Jesus stepped from the tomb, in Jerusalem.

On his knees, Wolv begged, "Jesus, please raise Pamia from the dead for me."

Jesus did not answer.

Pamia appeared beside Jesus. Then Pamia knelt and took Wolv's hand. She said, "My love. You have only to renounce Satan's Kingdom on earth and Hell. Then ask Jesus for forgiveness for your sins."

Wolv said, "Pamia. Satan has given me castles all over the earth. You must leave Jesus, Pamia, leave Jesus and come live with me."

In glowing blue, Holy Mary appeared beside Pamia and said, "Little Wolv. I will always love you."

Then Jesus, Pamia and Holy Mary disappeared.

Wolv howled, "Never, never will I give up Satan's castles, never. The castles are mine. All over the world."

Then Wolv repeatedly growled, "Jesus, please raise Pamia from the dead for me."

As always, Wolv's growls shook the Black Mountains.

Rage, anger and hatred caused black-red flames to erupt from Wolv's mouth. The spiritual flames filled the cavern, but burned nothing except Wolv.

At Terce bells, Wolv's eyes lost their black glaze. He changed into pure carbon dust and rose up through the earth. Atop the Black Mountains Wolv changed into black crows and flew to his wedding-reception cavern.

Deep in the wedding-reception cavern, Wolv sat beside Pamia's corpse. He said, "See beloved Pamia. Jesus did raise you from the dead for me. For here you sit. I did not have to ask for forgiveness nor give up my castles."

INSIDE ROSE FIRE

On the bailey floor Warrick said, "Morgan. Wolv's Resurrection obsessions were stronger this morning."

Morgan said, "One day, I expect him to collapse Rose Fire with his howls alone."

IN HER BEDCHAMBER

From the buttery, the smells of the break of fast wafted up to Nicola's chambers. Late Prime and early Terse bells mixed. Aromas of hot apple cider, fresh bread, and roasted pork woke Nicola. She smiled, licked her lips and jumped from bed. She wore only her long white shift. On bare feet she ran on the frozen pink marble floors. Across the solar, into Marian's chambers. Then she jumped into Marian's warm bed. Quickly Nicola rolled like a cocoon into Marian's white rabbit blankets.

Nicola said, "Wonderful. Your bed is still warm in the spot where you slept."

As Marian sat on the bed's edge, she did not answer Nicola.

With a firebrand from the andiron, Collette lit a block of clove incense.

Streams of incense smoke drifted in the chamber's circular eddy drafts.

Marian picked up an andiron firebrand. With the firebrand she lit candles and oil lamps on the walls of her chambers.

Then Marian sat on the edge of the bed. Collette rubbed a drop of lavender oil on her own fingers. Collette then ran her perfumed-fingers through Marian's waist length hair. Marian sat on the edge of the bed. Collette folded her legs under herself and sat on her legs. Then Collette picked up a boar's hair brush. She brushed the lavender oil into Marian's blond hair.

The servant, Collette smiled and said, "My Lady Marian. Your hair glows like gold in the sun."

Nicola asked, "Why are you dressed even before the end of Prime bells? You have no sunrise duties."

While Marian turned her head to Nicola, Marian's eyebrows formed an angry V. With a deep frown she said, "Nicola. If I must marry Warrick, I will learn his plan for his love life. No, he does not have a love life. He only has a sex, an orgy, life. I will find out his plans for his sex life. Then I will put a stop to them. The king said that I belonged to Warrick. I cannot escape my marriage to him. Yet, I will not allow him to bed another woman. I will follow Warrick everywhere he goes. Then drive away his mistresses and trysts."

Already dressed in her gown, Marian stood. She pulled on her white-squirrel, cowled cloak. She ran from her chambers. Then Marian bounded down her keep steps into the Great Hall. As she walked from the Great Hall out into the bailey, cold fog engulfed her. She looked in every direction for Warrick.

As she walked in the fog, she asked a stonemason, "Where is Lord Warrick?"

The mason pointed to another keep. He said, "My lady. Lord Warrick may be in his Black Mood keep or with the carpenters."

Marian asked, "What do you mean, 'The Black Mood keep?'"

"Black Mood Keep," said the stonemason. "The name we give to Lord Warrick's war and castle planning keep."

Then the stonemason pointed and said, "I see him there. With the carpenters, over there, in the smoke house. Directing the construction of that huge smoke house attached to the inner wall battlement."

Marian watched. Carpenters put water-soaked apple firewood into an andiron full of hot coals. Sweet-smelling smoke rose to fill the large smokehouse. From the buttery, the cooks walked with sides of beef, venison, and wild pork. The buttery servants hung the meat from large hooks on the smokehouse ceiling.

Warrick grasped a cook's elbow. He said, "I will send the archers out for fresh venison. Assure that the smokehouse's andiron smoker never goes out. If the smoke ceases, the meat will spoil, and you will not enjoy your fate."

In the bailey, Nicola walked up to Marian.

Marian said, "Nicola. I did not give you permission to wear my black squirrel cloak."

Nicola said, "Me? Marian, I did not give you permission to wear my white-squirrel, cowled cloak."

Marian said, "Nicola. Warrick has a life without me. I will do the same. I am going to build a life of my own. By law I must marry Warrick but I am going to be independent. Now I will use all the skills that I used to manage my father's estate."

Then Marian crossed her arms and walked over to the carpenters. With her eyebrows in an angry V, arms crossed, she commanded. "Two water wheels, I demand that you build two water wheels. You will build them outside the castle, on that stream above that large boulder. Start now. Wine press. I want a wine press beside the outer wall outside the moat. You must also build a brewery. One water wheel is to run a saw mill, the other to run an iron-smelter."

Marian turned to some servants. Then Marian commanded, "The ground has begun to thaw. I want you to go to my solar. Collette will show you a trunk of seeds for fruit trees. You must bring the seeds to me. I will show you how and where to plant them. Why do you stand here? Run. Now." Marian shouted.

At Marian's shout, the servant's eyes grew round and white in fear. They ran to obey her.

Marian turned, "Nicola. I will have many more businesses. Just as I had on her father's estate. My businesses will consume my time. Therefore, I will never again think about Warrick. We will find copper, gold, silver, coal and iron ore in the Black Mountains. We will ground flower and cornmeal. I will spend the day with the architects on waterwheel drawings. I will be so busy that I will never see the Lord of Orgies."

IN THE MOUNTAINS

Wolv circled the Black Mountains as a huge flock of crows. Crows within the thick red-fog. Lilith took the form of a Red Dragon and circled with him. Red-fog and things in the red-fog oozed from both of them. The red shapeless things in the red fog flew out all over the world.

Then as crows, Wolv flew to seat himself beside Pamia's corpse. He said, "Pamia, you look exceptionally beautiful this morning."

IN ROSE FIRE

Marian said, "Nicola. One day I fear Wolv's obsessions will crumble Rose Fire."

Nicola said, "Marian. I talked to the stone masons. They said the original stone masons built Rose Fire to withstand earth quakes. The Black Mountains are growing. They have earthquakes about every fifty or seventy years. The Black Mountain range has underground rivers that cause the mountains to collapse."

Nicola said, "Marian, your smile just turned to a frown. You look like you will slay someone today?"

Marian snapped, "Only Warrick. He wrote the king to give me to another lord. Nicola, what is all the commotion in the bailey?"

Nicola said, "Excitement. The archbishop has sent his exorcist to exorcize demons from Rose Fire. The exorcist was to drive out any devils or demons brought in by Skinwalkers curses."

Both dressed in royal blue gowns. Marian wore her full-length white squirrel cloak. Nicola wore a red-fox, full-length cloak. Both pulled their cowls over their head.

They walked down the keep's spiral staircase. Through the great hall, out the inner portcullis to the outer bailey.

"That exorcist priest," Nicola whispered, "Look at his nose. His nose is so hooked that a child could swing from his nose."

The king's exorcist stepped from an enclosed wagon. The sun glistened on his bald head.

Fat Father Bumpus bowed to the exorcist.

He said, "Father. Father. You can sleep in my chambers off the chapel. I will sleep in the servant's quarters."

Next morning, at early Prime bells, all followed the exorcist room to room. Behind the exorcist, Nicola whispered, "Marian. This is so tiresome. Must we follow this priest to every chamber of the castle?"

The exorcist turned to them and said, "Shhhhhhhhhhhhhhhussssssss. This takes several quiet days. We must hear the demons and devils when the holy water lands on them. The Skinwalkers could have called on many demons to possess the castle."

The exorcist threw Holy Water onto a dog. It turned into a Hog-Head Skinwalker and threw Marian into a bag.

Warrick beheaded the Skinwalker and threw its head into a blazing andiron.

Then the Skinwalkers head screamed as black dust ran from its mouth. All the black dust descended into cracks in the floor.

Then the exorcist said, "Lady Marian. Every day you must receive Holy Communion. Every day you must sprinkle Holy Water throughout Rose Fire. I can sense that Wolv is deep under this castle. He spends much time on a shelf beside an underground lake. Especially during his Resurrection-Prime obsessions. Holy Water can keep his demons from coming up through the ground."

Again the exorcist threw Holy Water. This time on a dog.

It burst into a giant flying Skinwalker. It rose into the air and said, "Little Warrick. We meet again."

Warrick threw Blessed Dread into the air and beheaded the flying Skinwalker.

It fell to the floor. The Skinwalker's head said, "Little Warrick. One day I will kill you. Marian. Wolv will have you."

Warrick picked up the head and threw it into the blazing andiron. Again a long line of black dust came out of the Skinwalkers mouth. The black dust disappeared into the cracks of the floor and descended into the earth.

The exorcist said, "Possibly, thousands of demons possess Rose Fire."

-

-

-

CHAPTER, In Rose Fore, Wales, Year @ 1250s A.D.

GIVE ME TO ANOTHER LORD

That evening, at Vespers bells, Marian had to sit beside the exorcist at supper.

In the huge andiron, in the middle of the room, large oak logs burned clean. Clean with little smoke. The smoke drifted up and out through planned holes in the very high ceiling. Flames boiled the logs' sap. Logs cracked open and whistled. Sparks spun and shattered into smaller yellow sparks. Shattered against the tall circular mail-curtain that surrounded the fire.

The king's parchment to refuse to assign Marian to another lord, saddened Marian too much. As she frowned, she also still felt betrayed about the expectation of a London wedding. As she frowned, she lowered her head.

Marian walked across the great hall. When Marian reached the steps of her keep, Warrick walked behind her.

At the bottom of the keep steps, Warrick asked, "Marian. You must tell me why you insist on addressing me formally as 'Lord'. You called me Warrick before you lost your mind."

Marian snapped, "Lost my mind, lost my mind?"

THE KING'S EXORCIST LEAVES

Prime bells rang in the fog-covered Wye River Valley, in Rose Fire.

On the bailey floor, in his black leathers, Warrick walked up to the exorcist. He held out his hand. He said, "Take this pouch of gold pieces, they will buy you easier travel."

Before the Terce bells, the exorcist had gathered his entourage in the bailey. He climbed into his wagon. Within a minute the exorcist's long retinue galloped over the drawbridge. Then the retinue raced down the mountain's red clay and rock road.

LOVER'S QUARREL.

From the hallway outside the chapel, Warrick said, "Marian. I want you to walk with me to the battlement. We must talk."

Marian crossed her arms and slowly followed Warrick to the battlement.

As he stood on the battlement, in the mountain wind, he turned to Marian.

On the battlement, Warrick called a knight to himself. He commanded, "Take our fastest steed to the king. You must hand this parchment directly to Colne's hand. Make haste. You must not stop to sleep. You must eat on horseback. I want you to purchase fresh horses rather than let your horse rest. Remember. I order you to deliver the parchment directly to Colne's hand. Colne's hand. No one else but Colne, the king's treasurer."

Warrick gave the knight a small leather pouch of gold pieces. "Return with Colne's answer before the next Saint's Feast Day and I will reward you. I will buy a farm for you in the valley. Go. Now. Give the parchment only to Colne."

The knight's eyes grew round with surprise. "A manor?" he asked.

Warrick replied, "Yes, a manor, you deserve to be a landed knight. You have been faithful to me for many years."

Seven steps at a time, the knight ran down the battlement steps. With a wide smile, he ran across the outer bailey to the stables.

With her eyebrows in an angry V, Marian grasped Warrick's elbow; she pulled him to herself.

She whispered so no one else could hear her impudence. "Warrick. Oh my great lord of cold hearts and hardheadedness, that was a lie."

Warrick thought, "I must plant falsehoods into Colne's mind. Colne works for Wolv. He is a Skinwalker."

Lord Warrick misunderstood Marian. He said, "The knight will have his manor."

Lord Warrick remembered what Drayton had told him not to be angry with Marian.

Lord Warrick smiled, "Marian. As to lies, you need to learn the first law of administration. The first to reach the king's ear is the first believed."

Marian thought, "Warrick tells lies all the time."

She whispered again so she would not insult Warrick before his knights. "Oh, Great Lord of hardheartedness."

Warrick ran his fingers through his hair when women flustered him. As he ran his fingers through his long hair, he said, "More insults. I am about to lock you in your keep for your insults."

Marian braced her fists on her hips, her elbows out. With her eyebrows in an angry V, she leaned forward.

She crossed her arms, raised her chin, and snapped, "Hummmmmmmph."

Marian turned her back to him. Marian marched up the spiral stairs. She entered her bedchamber and remained alone in her chambers for the day and night.

The next Prime bells, Marian woke from a nightmare. She had dreamed about her older sister's marriage. Now she thought Warrick treated her the same way. The abuse Onslow did to her older sister.

Warrick knocked on her chamber door.

Collette lit clove incense with an andiron firebrand. Marian motioned for Collette to open the chamber door.

While Collette opened the door, Marian turned to see him. She said, "Lord Warrick. The king may have given me to you, yet you will not break me. You will not destroy me like the brut Onslow destroyed my older sister, Louise."

Warrick said, "I am not Onslow."

While Marian and Warrick tussled with words, Collette ran from Marian's bedchamber into the solar.

Marian said, "My lord, I know your secrets. By law I am now your chattel, but you will not crush me. I will not allow an oaf like you to beat me into obedience. You are identical to Onslow, an oaf. I know that you will drink too much wine and mead. You will treat me as if I were a vassal. I will not obey. Fight you, fight you with every breath, every step, every word. You will not crush me. Lord of oafs, I know that you will want me to bear your heirs. Then you will demand that I do the duties of Rose Fire's lady. Then, just like my brother-in-law, you will bed endless mistresses. Like Onslow, you will pay no attention to me or our children. If I must, I will wed you. Yet, but know right now that you are a clod. Like Onslow. You will have no thyme-honey mead for passion. No yellow and white crocuses to gladden our wedding."

Warrick said, "Marian. How could you say that all in one breath? Every word is wrong, but I have decided to have infinite patience with you."

Marian said, "My lord. You will not make fun of me or make me the butt of your jokes."

Marian stood in her shift. Lord Warrick took her gently by the upper arms. He said, "It is your duty to obey. Do you not understand? I must fight the Skinwalkers. I have no time to fight you. You must be completely obedient."

He held her gently by the upper arms.

Her eyes followed the curve of Warrick's eye brows.

She thought, "His handsome face is, so delicious, so close. Yet he deprives me of his kisses with his unfaithful ways. If only he would be faithful, tender and kiss me. If only he could somehow show me. Show me that life with him will not be an endless argument. He has not a tender thought of me."

Warrick thought, "How can I protect Marian if she will not obey me? Marian is so beautiful."

The pain of her champion not kissing her was more than she could bear. She turned her head to the side and closed her eyes. He held her lightly by the upper arms.

Warrick said, "Marian. You are like a naive, untamed, wild, young mare. A mare that runs in the mountains unaware of danger."

Marian's eyebrows formed an even deeper V of anger.

She said, "Lord Warrick. You want a tame mare? I suggest that you wed a horse. You can wed a horse, or perhaps a twelve-foot tall woman with a hairy horse-face."

-

-

-

CHAPTER, Where: In Rose Fire Castle, Wales, When: About 1250s A.D.

NEVER LOVED. NEVER HAPPY.

As he held her upper arms, Marian said, "Am I one of your knights?"

She looked away as he held her upper arms.

Then she accidentally spoke from her heart, "Am I one of your knights. Or, am I your love?"

Warrick spoke and showed that he had no understanding of Marian's emotions.

As he gripped her upper arms, Marian turned her head to the side.

Warrick said, "Marian. You must understand. I must, I will, honor my duty to protect you. You also must learn. We are in dangerous lands. The time will come that only your courageous example will bolster the knights around you. Inexperienced knights. If you bolt, the inexperienced knights around you will bolt. Then Wolv will capture you. If you hold firm, though you are terrified, your inexperienced knights will hold firm. Then the victory will be yours."

She turned her head away and thought, "I asked him if I am his love. He only talks of my protection."

She said, "My lord, you understand nothing about women."

As Warrick held her upper arms, he pulled her closer to him.

He said, "Is that why you are angry with me. Understanding, because I do not understand women?"

Marian did not answer. As he pulled her nearer, she kept her head to the side. A tear filled her eye and wetted her cheek.

Marian said, "I understand that I and my sister are your chattels. I will not allow you to treat Nicola like a chattel."

Warrick said, "Is our life to be a constant argument? I was a fool to have thought I could have a happy life with you."

Marian thought, "Yes. You planned to give me away to another lord. Why would you have expected to be happy with me? I should ask him about the parchment. Cannot, and I cannot tell him about the parchment. My champion does not want me."

Her tears streamed onto her cheeks. Her tears dripped off her nose and chin. His handsome face attracted her. Against her will, she gazed up into his emerald eyes. She found that they hypnotized and enchanted her.

She thought, "How I hate that his handsome face could offer such promises of kisses. Yet Lord Warrick only offers me betrayal. A future of adultery, ruthless commands and anger."

She thought again, "If only he were faithful, gentle, tender. If only he kissed me as I have dreamed."

Marian said, "You are only anger, demands, duty, and battle fury. I love you as my champion in you. Yet, I cannot trust you as my betrothed."

Marian thought, "All he knows is battle and carousing with loose women."

He held her upper arms and pulled her closer.

Lady Marian again looked to one side. Black thunder clouds formed over the Wye Valley.

Both looked at the sky as thunder rumbled in the valley.

They gazed at each other's eyes. Both gasped as lightening highlighted each other's mesmerizing eyes.

His handsomeness mesmerized her.

Her beauty held him. Now was his opportunity to tell her that she was beautiful.

He did not. Actions, not words, were how he expressed his emotions, his thoughts.

As tears streamed down her cheeks, she again turned her head to the side.

He put a big, calloused hand behind her head and turned her face to him.

A fury of lightening and thunder broke upon them.

He wrapped his arms around her back and crushed her against his chest. She melted in his arms.

Marian thought, "I do love my champion."

Then she pushed against his chest and thought, "Yet, my champion does not want me."

She pushed against his chest. Yet, his huge arms held her tight to his chest.

Marian said, "You are about to take me by force?"

Warrick said, "The king's champion can take any woman he wants."

Marian thought, "Please, please, take me. Take me so that I may pretend. Pretend that you love me at least for a moment.

Lady Marian sighed then *she thought, "No, no, I do not want to pretend."*

On the outer wall battlement, as she pushed against his chest, he released her.

While Warrick lowered his arms from around her, he asked, "Marian. Will we ever be happy together? What has possessed you?"

Marian said, "You. You have possessed me."

She hugged herself to stay warm. Then she walked to the keep's battlement door. She walked through it and opened the door to her chambers. As Marian held the door, from a distance across the battlement walkway Warrick repeated, "Marian. Will we ever be happy together?"

Marian turned to him. She raised her chin and said, "Never."

-

-

-

CHAPTER, Where: Rose Fire Castle, Wales., When: Around 1250s A.D.

HER UNBENDING PRIDE

Then Marian stepped into her bedchamber and closed the door behind herself.

Ross-Templar, Drayton, and Morgan had walked up to the battlement steps. Morgan held his great mace over his folded arms. He said, "The three of us heard your . . . words. As your brother, may I say something?"

Warrick said, "Yes? I want you to tell me anything that can help."

Morgan said, "Whatever is happening, whatever the problem, it is too much for her. She may foolishly try to return to her mother on her own. You cannot protect her if she hates you or fears you."

Warrick said, "What is wrong with Marian?"

Inside Marian's bedchamber, Marian said, "Nicola. What businesses do we know enough about to try?"

Nicola said, "Why?"

Marian said, "I must be independent of Lord Warrick, and I must preoccupy my mind. If I think about my lord, my reason flies away like a startled bird. Besides, the Skinwalkers destroyed the town. We must preoccupy ourselves with helping the town's people. Also, we need gold to purchase supplies for the infirmarian."

Nicola said, "You know more about business than me, why do you ask me?"

Marian said, "Please, Nicola. I am too emotional to think. You must help me think of something, anything other than Lord Warrick."

Nicola said, "When you call Warrick, 'Lord' you create a wider gulf. A wider gulf between yourself and Warrick. Every time you call him 'Lord Warrick your contempt for him shows on your face."

Marian crossed her arms and turned her back. "Will you help me think or will you not?"

"Yes. In Oxford," Nicola said, "you managed our father's iron ore smelter. You could set up a smelter. You could make nails for the town."

Marian said, "Yes, the blacksmith can help us set up a smelter."

Nicola said, "Marian, father had a water wheel that powered a saw mill." Then Nicola pointed and said, "Marian. The plans to build a water wheel are in that chest. With the waterwheel sawmill, we can cut lumber for the town. Our father made charcoal and sold it. We know how. Many villagers have bee hives. With the honey, we can brew mead for sale. We have our mother's strain of yeast that makes such sweet, fluffy bread. We brought much of that yeast. With the yeast and the honey we can raise the bread, and sell it. Our father also made his own wine."

Marian said, "Yes, also, I used to boil pine sap until it became pine tar."

Nicola said, "We cannot use our own names. The law of England does not allow women to own businesses without the king's permission. We can ask Warrick to ask permission."

Marian said, "No. I cannot talk to my lord without boiling over. Boiling over like a pot left on an andiron."

Nicola said, "Then be naughty. You can make up a name. Put a fictitious name on the request to the king."

Marian laughed.

On a stiff deer skin, Marian then wrote a lie to the king of England.

To Your Majesty, King Edward, I, Lady Marian of Moray, humbly request a Royal Favor.
Merchant Bailey Donjon requests permission to form businesses around Rose Fire Castle. He wishes to produce iron, lumber, charcoal, honey, mead, wine, bakery-buttery, and pine tar. He also wishes to construct water wheels. An accident damaged Merchant Bailey Donjon's hand. Therefore, I write this request for him.

I am Your Servant, Lady Marian Moray de Oxford, for Merchant Bailey Donjon.

Nicola peered over Marian's shoulder. She asked, "Marian. I hope that a Merchant Bailey Donjon does not exist? You are lying to the king."

Marian said, "Yes, we will be in trouble if he does exist. Yet, we must use a false name. If the king would say 'no' to me, as Marian, I would have no chance. Royal law does not allow women to own property or own businesses."

Nicola laughed and said, "Marian. Royal law does allow a woman to own one business, one property. Women can own a stew of loose women."

Marian laughed. She said, "That would make Warrick very happy."

Then Marian said, "Nicola. If I write for a fictitious person, I can always ask the king again. Again with another fictitious name."

Marian opened the lid of a chest. The strong aroma of camphor oil, rubbed into the wooden chest's interior, filled the chamber.

Nicola said, "Wheeeh, the camphor burns my eyes."

She waved her hand before her face to wave away the strong aroma. "That chest will have no insects with that strong oil."

Marian then pulled a large, ancient, Syrian tome from the chest. On her knees, she reached down into the chest. She pulled out a wide deer-hide leather wrap. She folded back the soft-deerskin. With the deerskin open, Marian showed Nicola two brilliant, ornate daggers.

Marian said, "Lift them, Damascus steel daggers. They are heavy and indestructible. I am going to make steel harder, better than this."

Nicola sat on the floor. She took the daggers and said, "Do not joke with me."

Then while Marian opened the tome she said, "I do not jest. I know how, it is all here in this tome."

She turned many brittle, papyrus-like pages and pointed.

She said, "Right here. These Syrian Arabic words tell how to use the highest temperature crucible-smelting. The tome also tells how to make and use the hottest-blistering smithing with quick-cooling. I think that we can make the hardest steel in England. Lord Warrick has England's most learned blacksmiths."

Nicola said, "You stole this tome from the monastery outside Oxford?"

Marian said, "Yes, I stole this tome and many, many more. A copy. They made copies. Those Benedictine monks had the tomes for centuries. They do not have enough monks to translate all their collected ancient tomes. I hid under a cowled monk's robe and walked into the monastery's library. I could live in that enormous Oxford library."

Nicola said, "Father said that some Benedictines wanted to open the Oxford monastery. To open the Oxford Monastery and library as a college."

Marian frowned and lowered her gaze to the floor.

Nicola said, "Sister, Marian. You suddenly changed from a smile to a frown. Now you are thinking about Warrick. Your pride is a wall between you and Warrick. You must talk to him. Enough foolishness. I have seen enough of your hurtful pride. Wait no longer. Now is the time that you must tell him about the parchment. You must tell him that you love him."

As Marian knelt beside the chest, she crossed her arms and frowned. She shouted, "Nicola, never, never will I admit to him that I love him. So he can humiliate me again."

Nicola said, "You are unbending. Marian, you are creating your own heartache."

Marian said, "Me? Me? You think that I am creating my own heartache? Nicola, you do not understand. If I ask Lord Warrick about the parchment, he will confirm my worst fear. He will confirm that he wants me gone. Or worse, that he wants mistresses in bed with him and me."

ON THE BATTLEMENT.

In the wind on the outer battlement, *Warrick though, "I cannot. I cannot protect Marian if she hates me. Why, why would Marian hate me. I do everything for her protection."*

-

-

-

CHAPTER, Where: Rose Fire Castle, Wales, Year @ 1250s A.D.

A BUTTERY THIEF

Vespers' bells. In the Great Hall, the rotund buttery master cook ran to Warrick's supper chair. He leaned down between Marian and Warrick and said, "My lady. Lord Warrick. Most of the honey is gone. I can find a little salt. Someone has stolen most of the honey and salt. We need salt to cure the meat in the smoke house."

No one knew that this thief would help determine Marian's destiny.

Marian and Warrick walked into the buttery and searched with the cook.

The cook turned to Warrick and said, "My lord. Terrible, terrible, we have a thief of food."

With crossed arms and her eyebrows in an angry V, Marian gazed up at Warrick.

She said, "We also have a thief of hearts."

Warrick ran his fingers through his hair as he did when a woman befuddled him.

VIGILS BELLS THAT NIGHT.

Later that night, midnight, Vigils bells from the valley overpowered all other sounds.

Marian put the triplets to bed. She decided to find out the identity of the thief. As she walked in the shadows to the buttery, she bumped into Warrick.

Warrick whispered, "Marian, be quiet."

Marian whispered, "You be quiet."

Warrick said, "If you continue with this obstinacy I will lock you in your keep."

Then in frustration over Marian, Warrick ran his hand through his hair. Marian had now left Warrick in a complete emotional quagmire. They waited in the shadows of the buttery.

Ross-Templar, Drayton, and Morgan waited in the Great Hall's dark corners.

Then Marian and Warrick saw a small figure creep into the buttery.

Marian's survival would one day depend on that small unknown thief.

Lord Warrick put his hand over Marian's mouth and whispered, "Say nothing."

The figure reached into the shelves that held the salt and honey. Whoever it was, he or she, was tiny. Then the thief carried two bags out of the buttery. He or she crept through the shadows. The shadows along the Great Hall's walls and almost stepped on Drayton's boots.

Ross-Templar, Drayton, Morgan, Warrick and Marian followed.

The diminutive individual climbed the steps to the outer wall battlement. Then squeezed through a wide arrow slot. Warrick, Ross-Templar, Drayton, Morgan, and Marian held their breath.

Surprise rounded their eyes when they saw the petite figure disappear over the outer battlement. They thought the tiny figure fell to his death. The five of them ran to the battlement. They looked over the side to see the thief. Then the dwarf-like rogue shoved his tiny fingertips and toes into very small cracks. Cracks between the pink granite stone.

Warrick whispered, "Brothers. The thief climbs like a fly."

Marian whispered, "And the 'fly' has infinite courage to climb without a rope."

Quickly, the minuscule figure climbed hundreds of feet down Rose Fire's exterior battlement. The thief was so small he sat on a plank in the moat. He paddled with his hands to cross the moat. Once on the other side of the moat, he or she ran from the castle.

Warrick tied a rope to a battlement merlon and threw it over the side. He climbed down the battlement. Faithful knights followed Warrick. Then Warrick walked on a thin, secret plank an inch under the moat water. He followed the gnomish thief. The figure jumped bareback, without a bridle, onto an old mare. A mare Lord Warrick had put out to retire in pasture.

Not just the thief, fate had also tied this old mare to Marian's future destiny.

With long silent strides, Warrick ran down a dangerous shortcut. He jumped down cliffs and then waited far down on the mountain road. Warrick's knights followed Warrick. The bantam thief held tight to the mare's mane. On the mare, he rubbed his or her heels into the mare's back. The thief had frightened the old mare. So the mare obediently, loyally ran faster than it could sustain. As the mare obediently ran, the old horse wheezed. Then the mare ran around a turn. At the turn, Warrick reached up and grabbed the small thief.

Warrick said, "Luchas, you are a thief?"

In Warrick's arms, for a second Luchas struggled. Then Luchas looked around at the other knights and knew he could not escape.

He lowered his head and sighed in resignation.

Luchas said, "Yes, my lord. I have always been a thief."

Warrick put Luchas on the ground and knelt beside him. He asked, "Why?"

Little Luchas said, "My lord, in the infirmarian. Greta just dances in circles and sings to her imaginary doll. Whatever I steal I sell in Hereford and hide the gold for Greta."

Warrick said, "You do not need to worry about Greta. Come with me."

Drayton, Ross-Templar and Morgan lowered the drawbridge. With Warrick's three brothers around her to protect her, Marian ran across the drawbridge.

Marian grabbed Luchas from Lord Warrick.

Warrick turned to his knights and said, "Knights. Make sure that everyone does their hour of Perpetual Adoration in Rose Fire's Chapel. Or else in the Adoration wagon. Give me the names of all those that have done adoration and confession. Perpetual Adoration of Jesus' Real Presence in the Blessed Sacrament. Make sure everyone does weekly confession. Knights, take a lesson from our battle in Colmar, France. Remember the sight when we rode into the city too late to expel the red-fog. The red-fog had eaten or changed every man, woman and child into Skinwalkers. With our adoration and confessions, we drove Wolv away. Only after he had killed nearly everyone and burned the town. Let every lost battle against Wolv be a lesson. Only Adoration and confession keep the red-fog away. Only Adoration and confession can defeat Satan's dominations and hierarchies."

In Marian's arms, Luchas, only seven years old cried, "My lord. Please do not beat me."

Warrick said, "Should I beat you?"

In Marian's arms, Luchas said, "Yes my lord, I have done wrong."

Marian hugged Luchas and shouted, "Lord Warrick. You would not beat a child, would you?"

Warrick said, "Marian. Why must you call me 'lord?' You should call me Warrick."

Quickly, Marian turned her head away from Warrick.

Warrick ran his fingers through his black hair.

Lord Warrick asked, "Marian. When will you say why you are angry with me?"

In Marian's arms, Luchas struggled to push her away. Because Marian tightly held him, Luchas stopped his attempt to escape Marian's arms.

Then Luchas held his hands before his face and said, "My lord. You are about to beat me?"

Warrick said, "Perhaps we."

Marian interrupted Warrick, "I will not allow you to beat this child."

Warrick ignored Marian. Then Warrick repeated, "Perhaps, . . . perhaps we can come up with an alternative to a beating."

He said, "Luchas, you have a choice, which do you want? You rode the mare without saddle or bridle. You could help to train the pages to ride bareback or."

Luchas clapped his small seven-year-old hands and said, "Horses, horses, horses."

Lord Warrick said, "You must not ride the old mare. She will obediently run until she bursts her weak heart. She deserves a long retirement."

Marian held Luchas' hand and said, "You will steal no more?"

Luchas said, "Yes, I will not steal again. No more stealing, my lady, no more stealing."

Warrick said, "Luchas, say it without that sly smile."

Little Luchas grinned up at Marian.

Marian squeezed his hand and said, "Luchas. I do not like the thoughts that must be behind your grin."

Luchas again grinned up at Marian.

Lord Warrick clapped his hands and said, "Luchas. You must go to bed, now."

Everyone else, but Warrick went to bed.

All night Warrick practiced with Blessed Dread in the bailey.

As he practiced, he whispered, "Mother. Forgive me. Forgive me that I did not stop Wolv from killing you."

Warrick did not notice the dragon, Lilith, flying high above Rose Fire. Also, Warrick did not notice the red-fog trying to come down the mountain. Adoration of the Blessed Sacrament blocked the red-fog.

The guards whispered that Warrick was not human because he never seemed to sleep.

-

-

CHAPTER, Now in Rose Fire, Wales, Year @ 1250s A.D.

SHE WEPT INTO HER HANDS. A WARRIOR WITH A
BROKEN HEART.
The next day after break of fast, the valley Terce bells rang.
Warrick stood on the outer wall battlement. From the battlement,
Warrick waved his arms to give formation commands. Formation
commands to his mounted knights on the practice field. With each
wave of his arms, his knights galloped and changed direction and
changed weapons. Then Warrick waved his arms to command to
his archers. They formed lines and shot arrows into different
directions. For a moment, on the other side of Rose Fire, Warrick
turned to Marian's keep. He watched Marian through her open
chamber door.
Then he watched the cloud or red-fog over the Black
Mountains grow thicker. Grow more opaque.
She and Nicola played chess on Marian's bed. They
laughed together as if they were two little filles. They had joy on
their faces as they tickled and teased each other.
Drayton, Ross-Templar and Morgan walked up the
battlement steps to Warrick.
Warrick pointed to the red fog over the mountains and said,
"Drayton. Look. We can see red Things in the fog leave the
mountains and fly toward England. They are going out to possess
people, to turn people into Skinwalkers."
Drayton held his longbow and said, "Warrick. Skinwalkers
will attack here soon enough. The flying Things in the fog possess
people that do not do Adoration-of-the-Blessed-Sacrament.
Warrick, now come with us. The stone cutters need you to choose
the design for arrow slots."
Lord Warrick did not hear. He watched Marian.
*"Marian is so beautiful," Warrick thought. "Marian's
obstinance makes it harder for me to protect her."*
Morgan put the point of his mace on the battlement
walkway. Then he rested his palms on the handle.
He said, "Warrick. You are too involved in watching Marian
and Nicola play chess and laugh. Did you not hear what Drayton
said? The stone cutters want you."

Then Warrick turned and said, "Brothers. Why are you here?"

Ross-Templar leaned against a battlement merlon and crossed his ankles.

Ross smiled and said, "For a purpose that will obviously have to wait."

Within her chambers, Marian turned. She looked through the open door. Marian saw Warrick on the battlement walkway as Warrick looked at her.

DO YOU STILL WANT YOUR CHAMPION?

Nicola saw Warrick. She said, "Marian, do you still want Warrick? You still love Warrick?"

Marian said, "Yes, I love the oaf, my wild boar, my champion. I want to escape this confusion. Yet, the enemy Skinwalkers surrounds us. What kind of champion asks the king to send his betrothed away in shame? How can he be my champion and reject me?"

Nicola said, "Then you should go tell him about the parchment. Clear up the confusion."

With her fists on her hips, Nicola stood with her elbows out. She stood and leaned forward. Nicola said, "Marian, I have had enough of your foolishness. If you do not tell Warrick about the parchment, I will."

Marian jumped to her feet and grabbed Nicola's shoulders.

She said, "You must never tell Warrick, never. I fear the worst. He will confirm that he wants to send me home in shame. Or else he will say that he wants mistresses."

More valley Terce bells reminded the servants to work faster. Faster for time would soon rob them of their morning.

Nicola hugged Marian and said, "Stop your tears, I will not mention anything to Warrick. You will be the one to tell him."

Nicola and Marian sat on the bed.

With the back of her hands, Marian wiped her tears. They were quiet for a moment.

TO SEDUCE A KNIGHT'S HEART.

Nicola said, "I know a way that you can make him obsess about you."

Marian said, "Impossible, he is obsessed with mistresses."

"Marian," Nicola said. "You are so silly. Warrick has no mistresses. I know men like Warrick. All he talks about is how to protect you, just protect, protect, protect. Otherwise he would not have fought for you when you first met. He is obsessive about protecting his royal charges. He cannot allow evil to befall you. Otherwise, he would lose his honor in the king's eyes. He is obsessive about his honor and thus your protection. Therefore, we can make him worry even more about you. Marian, follow my advice, you will bedevil him until you are his only thought."

"How? You jest." Marian said.

Nicola said, "I do not jest. In Oxford I stole many young knights' hearts. Stolen with the bedevilment that I will teach you."

Marian said, "Nicola. You were wicked to lead young knights into the belief that you loved them."

Nicola said, "Marian. I needed practice for when I find the lord that I want to marry. Then I will trap him with the web I will teach you. First you will shadow him everywhere for days. He will become obsessive about looking up and seeing you. He will expect to see you everywhere he is. Thus, know that you are safe."

Marian said, "Impossible."

Nicola said, "No. My bedevilment succeeds every time. Remember that I used it on many young knights. They all eventually begged our father for my hand."

Marian said, "Nicola. I did not know. Sister. You are wicked. You are a wicked, wicked young lady. Now be quick, teach me this wickedness."

Nicola said, "Marian. It is Warrick's duty to protect you. Warrick will do his duty because he is an honorable man. Just glance behind you and look at him, gazing at you. Even if he had tried to give you away to another lord. Glance around at his concentrated expression on you. Lord Warrick is obsessed with protecting you. You are his royal charge, Lord Warrick's only royal charge. A knight forever forfeits his honor if he cannot protect his charge. The king would not trust that weak, useless knight again. Remember that Warrick has lost one charge, Ogina."

Nicola said, "The king demanded that he protect and marry you. In that parchment, the king demanded that you remain his charge. He will not offend the king. Look at him. He is already unable to go away from you or approach you. Marian, you are Warrick's destiny. Warrick is your destiny."

Marian said, "Nicola, you are a silly girl. You will find no destiny to find a lover. Every woman will end with an Onslow, just like my older sister."

Nicola said, "You need to listen to me. If you will not tell him about the parchment, then. Then you need to tease him with your smile. He does not understand a smile. He does not understand joy. The tragedy of his first marriage harmed him too deep. Warrick has fought too many wars. You misunderstand him. He is a warrior with a broken heart."

Marian said, "You are only seventeen, where did you get this wisdom."

Nicola said, "Unlike you, I listen, and shut my mouth, and watch my lover's eyes."

Marian laughed. She said, "Oh. Nicola, you are such a wicked, little imp."

Then Marian put her hands on Nicola's shoulders. She shoved Nicola backward onto the bed."

Nicola said, "You first need to shadow him everywhere he goes. Always be in his line of sight. For Heavens sake, Marian, you must always smile. He is already obsessive about protecting you. He will become obsessive about having you with him. Since he will always see you, safe with him. After some days, Warrick will be like a fish on a hook. Then you will go somewhere out of his sight. He will be afraid for you and run after you. You do not have to say you love him. Just always smile and be directly in his line of sight. Never, never argue with him."

Out on the outer wall battlement, in the stiff breeze, Warrick said, "Brothers. My fear is for Marian. Marian is so up set that she may try to leave Rose Fire. If I go to Marian, she will only reject me."

Ross-Templar put his hand on the hilt of his blessed sword. He said, "Yes Warrick. She is in ill humor."

Amid Terce bells of many monasteries and churches, Warrick asked, "Brothers. What is it that Marian has over me?"

Ross-Templar sat on a battlement crenel. He said, "I see the change in your face. In battle I learned to read your expressions. To take direction from them even before you spoke.

For years, until you met Marian, you had only the clenched jaw of a warrior."

Ross-Templar glanced at Marian. He said, "Warrick. Before the two of you began fighting, her smile caused your clenched jaw to relax. Now I think that Marian and Nicola are conjuring up another mischief. This time, Warrick, you are the victim."

Warrick pulled Ross from the crenel. An arrow hit the merlon beside where Ross had been.

Warrick said, "Careful Ross. Never sit in a crenel."

Drayton noticed a movement on the tree line. From the height of Rose Fire's battlement he fired his crossbow. The arrow stuck into a camouflaged Skinwalker.

Warrick said, "Skinwalkers are in the tree line with powerful crossbows. We must make the field around Rose Fire safe for Marian. Drayton. Put a line of twenty camouflaged archers higher than the tree line. Three groups of twenty on eight hour shifts, night and day. Shoot and exorcize any Skinwalkers. If they refuse exorcism, behead them. We must make the field around Rose Fire safe for Marian."

Then Ross-Templar stood behind a merlon. Another arrow hit the merlon.

Again Drayton noticed movement in the treelike. He used his crossbow and shot another arrow. It stuck in another Skinwalker. Then the tree line broke into activity as the Skinwalkers retreated up the mountain. Up the mountain to try to run beyond Drayton's crossbow accuracy.

Drayton loosed another arrow and downed another Skinwalker. Then another.

Drayton said, "The Skinwalkers are now out of range. They will not return today."

Warrick said, "Drayton. Tonight. Start your patrol above the tree line after dark. In the dark descend the back of the castle with ropes. We will retrieve you with the same ropes."

Then Ross-Templar grinned and poked his finger into Warrick's chest. He said, "I know. Warrick. Marian conquered you the moment she broke the surface of that lake. The moment you saw her beauty. Now she thinks that she has to change you. From what into what I do not know. I know that her smile is dangerous to a man like me. If the king gave me a charge with a smile like hers, that smile. That smile would destroy me. Marian's smile is not a lusty smile. Her smile is of confused and innocent love. I avoided these smiles anywhere I went. Her eyes are wide and open, filled with confusion, hurt, and innocence. I tried never to bed innocent women. Many women love once and only once. They will never love again if their first love is lost. Marian will only love one man, . . . you. I wanted women who loved men as easily as they laugh. Before Innocence, I wanted women that batted their eyes with that romp-with-me-in-the-hay smile. My kind of woman would laugh, wink and look behind her. Behind her to make sure that I am following her. My women did not want my faithfulness or my heart. They wanted laughter and a night of passion."

Warrick rested his hand on the sheath of Blessed Dread. He said, "Ross. We always knew what kind of women you once wanted. Before Innocence, you wanted many, many, many at once."

Warrick said, "Brothers."

Drayton raised his hand and said, "Warrick. We know what you are about to ask. Why did Marian's mood change toward you? The three of us do not know. Marian's behavior baffles us as much as you."

Warrick crossed his huge muscular arms. He said, "Did the three of you come here to needle me about another purpose?"

Drayton held his longbow across his shoulder. Then he said, "I need the new designs for the moat. Morgan needs the new calvary-war plans you designed last night. Ross-Templar needs to know which granite pits to quarry. The best granite pit is close to enemy lands. Also, the stone masons want to know which design you want for the arrow slots."

Warrick said, "Drayton. As to the arrow slots and moat, the Krak-des-Chevaliers design is the best design. You will find all your other answers in my Black Mood Keep. I wrote everything on the vellum on my table. The granite pit, we have no choice. Ross-Templar, you must take knights and archers with the wagons to the granite pit. We must quarry the pit that has the hardest granite, the pink granite. The quarry-pit close to enemy lands."

Drayton, Morgan, and Ross-Templar walked to the Black Mood keep to find the designs. Out on the battlement, the wind blew Warrick's hair and flagged his long black cloak.

Then Warrick thought, "Impossible to protect Marian if she does not trust me. She will not obey me and thus do foolish actions."

Warrick's mood turned even more sour. He frowned and put his huge calloused hands on the battlement merlon. Warrick leaned his head back and breathed in the cold mountain air. From the Rose Fire battlement, Warrick gazed over the great Wye River Valley. He saw so far away that mountains and valleys appeared as blue haze. If he concentrated, he could see more mountain ranges. Ranges on the far side of the blue haze. Marian's hatred of him befuddled him so much that he unknowingly pulled off his glove. Lord Warrick ran his fingers through his hair.

Then Warrick turned to the clatter and scape of boots. He glanced into the bailey and saw his three brothers. From the Black Mood Keep, Drayton, Ross-Templar and Morgan marched across the bailey floor. With long strides his brothers bounded up the battlement steps to Warrick.

With the zenith sun near, a monastery chimed and rang Sext prayer bells.

Morgan said, "The monasteries, nunneries, and churches seem to compete. To compete on who can make the best musical bells."

Ross-Templar said, "Wolv is about to make a din. His Sext bell's hour's obsession. The hour Wolv nailed Jesus to the Cross."

RED-FOG AND THINGS IN THE FOG SURROUNDED THE MOUNTAIN PEAKS IN A GREAT DARK SWIRL.

On the Black Mountain peak, Wolv again fell to his knees, in snow. He relived how he Crucified Jesus. With his eyes glazed black, he relived pounding nails in Jesus' hands and feet.

The cross lay flat on Golgotha ground. Jesus lay flat on the cross. Wolv relived pounding nails into his boyhood-friend's feet and hands.

With eyes glazed black, Wolv, in his memory, whispered into Jesus' ear, "Jesus. Raise Pamia from the dead for me. Then all this will end."

As Jesus lay on the cross on his back, Jesus said nothing. Wolv commanded to the Roman soldiers, "Raise the crosses."

Wolv relived the raising of the Cross. How the cross thudded into a deep rock hole. Then Wolv relived how Roman soldiers pounded wedges to steady the Cross.

On his knees, in the snow, Wolv held his head, with his eyes glazed black. He repeatedly howled three of Jesus' words from the Cross. "It is finished."

Each time he howled the words 'It is finished', the Black Mountains quaked.

Black-red flames shot from Wolv's mouth and covered the sky from horizon to horizon.

Slowly Wolv came out of his obsession. Slowly Wolv's eyes lost their black glaze.

Wolv stood in the snow. With his fists to the sky, Wolv shouted, "Jesus. Leave me alone."

BELOW IN ROSE FIRE.

Ross-Templar said, "Now that is a din. I welcome the music of the canonical bells. We always know the danger of Wolv is near."

Ross-Templar wanted to brighten Warrick's mood. He brought up a topic that always caused them to laugh, their tournament foibles. The four of them stood on the battlement and laughed. They laughed about their own joust foibles when their opponents' lances unhorsed them. Their laughter echoed off the mountains and out over the Great Wye River Valley.

HIGH IN THE BLACK MOUNTAINS

High on the mountain Swale stood beside Wolv as Wolv gazed down upon Rose Fire. Wolv said, "I will have Marian."

Swale said, "I can hear the Cyrene-Pendragon's laughter. Lord Wolv, their spirits are high. With their spirits so high they will be hard to defeat."

Wolv said, "I burned Jerusalem and murdered everyone in it. Also, I can burn Rose Fire and murder everyone in it."

IN ROSE FIRE. TEARS,

As Marian watched Warrick, her eyes began to tear. Inside her Rose Fire bedchambers, on her bed, Marian wiped her tears.

She said, "Nicola, I want you to look at all four brothers. They are joking about their mistresses."

Nicola said, "Marian. We cannot hear them. You must remember when you first met Warrick. You were unknown to him, yet he instinctively fought unto death for you. A knight so honorable that he fought unto death for an unknown lady. That knight would never cuckold his royally betrothed bride."

Out on the battlement, Warrick and his brothers continued to guffaw. To guffaw about their joust foibles, in England and Europe.

Marian said, "The Pendragon brothers do not want women, they want trollops. On the first day with them, I heard them. Ross-Templar, Drayton, Morgan and Warrick all laugh about bedding married women."

Nicola said, "Are you sure that it was Warrick that bedded them. Perhaps it was just Ross before he met lady Innocence? Perhaps only Drayton or Morgan that said that they slept with married women?"

Marian lowered her head in sadness. She traced the edge of the chess board with her finger. She said, "They all laughed about sleeping with married women."

Nicola said, "Maybe they were only laughing. Men laugh about many things. Women laugh about bedding married men."

Marian said, "Ross still had straw in his hair. He had bedded Lady Avon in a barn."

"Not Lady Avon," Nicola said, "she is so proper."

Marian said, "And Ross-Templar is so boyish and charming."

Nicola said, "On the opposite, Warrick is as hard as steel. Marian, most often Warrick's temperament is as black as his leathers. Warrick has nothing boyish or charming about him."

Lady Marian said, "Nicola, Warrick's charm is his courage, his handsomeness. You did not see Warrick when he fought for me and stole my heart."

Nicola said, "You told me. You gave him your heart when he fought for you."

THE CHAMPION STOLE HER HEART.
Marian said, "I did not give my heart. Nicola. Against my will, he stole my heart and I can never get it back."

OBSESSIONS AGAIN.
Marian said, "Listen. Again Wolv's obsessions shake the mountains."
Atop the Black Mountains, thick red fog poured from Wolv's body. He fell to his knees and growled, "Holy Mary. Get out of my head. Holy Mary, go away. Get out of my head."
Again Wolv's eyes glazed over black and he saw himself in his Egyptian memory. He was six years old, crying on Holy Mary's lap. Crying because Egyptian children called him Ugly Eye, for his multiple-pupil eye.
In his memory, Holy Mary, surrounded by a blue aura, hugged Wolv. She said, "Little Wolv. I will always love you."
On the mountain top, in the snow, Wolv repeatedly howled, "Little Wolv. I will always love you."
Again, born of rage, hatred and anger, black-red flame spewed from Wolv's mouth. The black-red flame filled the sky.
His growls shook the mountains.
Slowly Wolv's eyes lost their black glaze. He stood and raised his fists to the sky and growled, "Holy Mary. Go away. Leave me alone."

STOLE MY HEART. IN ROSE FIRE.
Marian looked out the window and said, "Nicola. My tomes record that the black-red flames come from Wolv's mouth. When his rage incapacitates him."
Teenage Nicola said, "Marian. Back to the parchment. The parchment agitates and confuses you now. You must trust Warrick. Marian. Obviously you do not know the truth about Warrick."
Marian said, "Know the truth. How can you still doubt me?"
Then Marian crossed her arms, raised her chin, and turned her back to Nicola.
Nicola said, "Treat Lord Warrick as an honorable man. If you trust him, you will find him to be an honorable man. He wrote the parchment for an honorable unknown reason."

Marian's confused and aching heart made her say, "Nicola. Lord Warrick wrote the parchment because he wants only trollops. He rejected me and wants to send me to Oxford in shame. No other lord would ever marry me if he knew another lord had rejected me."

Nicola said, "Not so, Marian. A man that fights unto death for you, he will not. He will not sleep with other women. I am sure that he does not sleep with other women. Warrick had an honorable reason to ask the king to wed you to another lord."

ON THE BATTLEMENT WALKWAY.

Out on the battlement walkway, Warrick said, "Drayton. Go now out on the practice field and instruct the archers."

Warrick turned to Morgan and said, "Also, Morgan. Instruct the knights and squires in jousting on the practice field. Make sure that Luchas teaches pages how to ride bareback."

Without a word, Drayton and Morgan walked down the battlement steps and across the bailey. They walked across the open drawbridge and out onto the practice field.

From far across the battlement, Warrick looked at Marian as Marian sat on her bed.

She tried to smile at him.

Ross-Templar said, "Warrick. You look like someone hypnotized you. I can see that Marian's beauty has mesmerized you. Duty and beauty weave an escapable web. That used to be my fear, my greatest fear. A web of beauty and duty around me. Now a web of guilt and duty to pray entraps me. A web of guilt over Innocent's suicide."

Warrick said, "Marian's anger and disobedience befuddle me and endangers her. I have seen this behavior before. She will soon do something desperate and dangerous to herself."

In her chambers, Marian said, "Warrick is so handsome. His bronze complexion frames his emerald eyes. Sunlight reflects off his long black hair. I wish that I did not love him. I am so confused. Warrick does not know that he has conquered me."

Out on the battlement, Ross-Templar said, "Warrick. You do not know it, but Marian has conquered you."

IN THE BEDCHAMBER.

Nicola said, "Go to him, walk to him. He is under the command of the king to love you. With your smile alone, something has changed in him. Smile always, do not argue with him, just go, now. I want you to take his arm. Press his arm to your breast, and you must not argue with him. Remember that your smile, your presence, will conquer him. Look out on the battlement, see how Warrick watches you. If you have trouble with your pride or anger or sorrow, remember. Remember what I told you. His honor and duty plus your smile and constant presence will conquer him."

Marian stood and dressed in her white-squirrel, cowled cloak. She clasped her gloved-hands behind her back, and she smiled and walked to Warrick. Her smile magically affected Warrick.

ON THE BATTLEMENT

He smiled.

Ross-Templar whispered, "Marian approaches. I take my leave. Now is the time for you and Marian to be alone. Warrick. Do as Drayton said, 'do not react with anger to Marian's anger'. We do not know what has upset her."

The nunneries' Sext bells rang while the zenith sun began to wane to the west. The trees' westward shadows changed to eastward shadows.

As she walked to him, Marian looked down in sadness. In her cowled, white, squirrel cloak, she held her hands behind her back. She slowly ambled over to him. Then as she glanced up into his emerald eyes, she forced her lips to smile. When she stepped beside him, she took his arm and pressed it against her breast. As they walked, she looked up at him. She saw the softer features of a man with a smile. She stopped. His emerald eyes and gaze on her face made her raise her chin. He was peaceful. Then she realized a terrible contradiction. That she felt safer today with him that she had ever felt.

Lady Marian thought, "I cannot stop or control my love for my unfaithful champion."

With a thumb, he wiped her tears and said, "What fills your eyes with tears? What is wrong? Tell me. Is there another enemy that I must defeat? Tell me what to do?"

The thought that he was her beloved champion, yet unfaithful betrothed infuriated her.

Yet, she remembered Nicola's words. *'You will conquer him with his honor and duty plus your smile and presence.'*

Otan walked up to Warrick and said, "My lord. Those many knights on the road from distant lordships want to serve the King's Champion. They say that they will serve without pay. That they will live in tents outside the castle walls."

Warrick said, "Tell them that if they prove worthy, that they may enter my service."

Marian said, "These knights are the sons of great lords. They could train in the king's own court. Why do they come to serve you without pay, without a place to sleep?"

Warrick looked out over the Wye Valley and said, "Marian. Because they know the truth, I am the best."

Marian said, "I suppose that."

She did not say what she thought, "I suppose that your words should impress me."

Instead she cut off her words. She did as Nicola said. She held her tongue and smiled. Her smile smoothed the sharp edges of Warrick's war-hardened bronze countenance.

As he looked down into her beautiful eyes, she could not look at him. Her broken heart was too painful. Marian closed her eyes and turned her head away. He gently grasped her upper arms and pulled her to him. Then she turned her head to the other side. A tear ran down her cheek.

Marian thought, "I am so angry and I hunger for my champion's kisses. I want my champion's kisses and I want to escape from my betrothed."

Yet sadness filled her eyes with tears.

In the far distance, later Sext bells announced that the sun had waned further westward. The eastward shadows grew longer.

Her beauty trapped him into an uncontrollable urge to possess her in every way. He wanted her and only her. He wanted to build this castle in the sun around her. Around her to protect and possess her forever.

Marian thought, *"If I must share Warrick with other women, can I?"* She thought, *"I need him, I love him. I can, if I must, . . . I can share him with other women?"*

Warrick thought, "I want Marian's beauty and Marian's beauty alone."

Lord Warrick could have solved so many problems if he would just tell her. Tell her that her beauty had conquered him. Yet actions, not words, were how he expressed his emotions. He did not know that he might wait until it was too late. Because of his traitorous first wife, Ogina, Warrick did not understand. Did not understand a good woman's need of tender assurance?

Lady Marian did not realize that all his actions were for her. She thought that his actions were only the hard, dutiful actions of a warlord. In her mind's eye she saw him kissing another woman, in another woman's bed. She tried to accept what she thought she had to accept. Herself and other women, and Warrick in the same bed. Large tears welled in her eyes. Then her tears flowed down her cheeks. She did not know whether to flee from him. Or try to charm him as Nicola told her. Marian's confusion overwhelmed her. Lady Marian could not accept that another woman would bed him. Marian wanted to flee Rose Fire.

SHE WEPT.

Then Lady Marian sat on an outer wall, in a battlement crenelation. Marian wept into her hands. She wanted Warrick to cherish her, and only her. True love. Marian wanted a marriage of true love.

Even later distant Sext bells rang. Warrick squatted so he could look her in the face as she sat. He gently grasped her shoulders. He said, "Marian, what is wrong. Why do you weep? What has happened?"

IN THE BLACK MOUNTAINS.

High in the Black Mountains, Wolv's Sext obsessions again overcame him.

In the snow Wolv fell from his horse. On his knees, his eyes glazed over black.

In his tortured memories he looked up at Jesus on the Cross. Jesus said, "Father, into your hands I commit my spirit."

Wolv repeatedly roared his obsession, "Father, into your hands I commit my spirit."

Wolv's roars quaked, quaked the Black Mountain range.

Again Wolv's hatred and rage erupted from his mouth as black-red flames. Black-red flames that filled the sky. Lilith, as a dragon, flew around in the flames.

Slowly Wolv came out of his obsession. His eyes lost their black glaze. The flames blocked out all light until the wind blew away the smoke.

WITHIN ROSE FIRE.

Lord Warrick said, "Marian. You can hear and feel the AntiChrist is close. He will give us no peace."

Marian was too troubled even to feel Wolv rumble the earth.

She thought, "Why does Warrick not say. Say that he either loves me or does not want me? He does not know how to love."

Warrick said, "Marian. I am your champion. Why will you not tell me what is wrong?"

Marian said nothing. She wept.

Nicola ran out onto the battlement. In front of Warrick, Nicola said, "Marian. You must tell him about . . ."

Marian shouted, "No, no."

She knew Nicola was about to mention the parchment.

IN THE BEDCHAMBERS.

Marian jumped to her feet and grabbed her little sister's arm. She pulled her back to her chambers.

Then Marian slammed the door and said, "Nicola. You must never tell my lord about the parchment. Never ask him about the parchment. I fear the most horrible of answers. He will only confirm that he wants me gone. He will confirm that I have two choices. The first choice will be to return to mother in shame. The second choice will be to marry him. Yet be equivalent to one of his many mistresses."

Warrick pushed on the door and said, "Marian."

Marian had not locked the door. It swung open at his touch.

As Warrick said, "Marian. Your beauty has defeated me."

UNABLE TO HEAR

Marian could not hear Warrick. Cries of pain from the training field were too loud. Warhorses had crashed and knights cried in pain.

Warrick knew immediately the cause. Two armored warhorses in practice had clashed head to head. Lord Warrick knew that a horse had fallen on knights.

Marian did not understand the importance of the clash. Marian thought it was just a loud guffaw, a loud laugh. Only a battle warrior knew that sound of pain.

Warrick ran from Marian's chambers to the practice field.

Marian could hear his hard boots clatter on the granite, spiral steps.

Lady Marian wept. Then with both hands she grabbed her glass figurines. Lady Marian threw them through the open door against the stairwell wall.

Shattered glass rained down upon Warrick and settled in his hair.

He muttered, "I tell Marian that her beauty has conquered me. Her response is to throw her glass figurines at me. I do not understand women, because they are not understandable."

She said, "Never again will a man play me for a fool."

Rapidly, she threw more of her glass figurines.

More glass rained down onto Warrick's hair.

Extremely late Sext bells rang. Warrick ran across Rose Fire's drawbridge onto the practice field. The sun was now far beyond the zenith.

Morgan had cleaned and bound the two knights' wounds. Morgan said, "Warrick. The knights had no broken bones, just cuts and bruises."

IN HER BED CHAMBER.

In her keep, Marian peered out the arrow slit of her chambers. She did not see the two wounded knights.

Marian said, "Nicola. Warrick makes me furious. The king engaged me to a cad, a trickster, an oaf, a cruel oaf."

ON THE PRACTICE FIELD.

Out on the practice field, Warrick stood and looked high up at her chamber window. He saw her in the arrow slot as she gazed down at him.

In the bed chamber, Nicola said, "Look at Warrick out on the practice field. The two of you must talk to each other. Both of you must speak to the other from the heart."

From the practice field, Warrick looked up at her.

He thought, "What did I do to make her smile at me on the battlement? What did I do to make her weep? What did I do to make her so angry? So angry that she threw her glass figurines at me?"

Nicola peered out the window. She said, "Marian, you are a silly fool. Look at him. Warrick is beautiful. The sun flashes off his black hair and his black leathers. He stands in his black cloak, black leathers and mail. Stands like the king's champion that he is. See how he looks up at you. Can you not see the devotion in his eyes? Look at how his men obey him because they admire him."

Marian said, "Nicola, you are foolish. They obey him because they fear him, just as you should fear him."

Nicola said, "Marian, you should . . ."

Marian flushed bright red and said, "I should? I should? He seduces married women. He has no respect for marriage and will have no respect for our marriage. The first day that I met him I overheard him guffaw with his brothers. Guffaw about their adulterous affairs."

Marian did not realize that it was only Ross that had bedded married women.

Marian's eyes narrowed in concentration and determination. For a moment she again became the strong administrator of her father's estate.

She said, "Nicola, I will find a way to tame this lion. I will not allow him to send me to my father's estate in shame."

Nicola said, "Good. Now you are talking like the courageous woman that ran the huge Oxford estate. Now, Marian. Run down there and be with him as he takes care of that fallen squire. Be with him, smile at him, and you will control him. Your smile and your constant presence will conquer him."

She thought, "My smile, my presence, and. . . ."

Then in her mind's eye she saw herself in bed with him, with another woman. She remembered the parchment. The thought of mistresses and the parchment defeated her. She lost her determination.

Marian said, "No. Nicola, I will never find love with Lord Warrick. I want his whole heart or I will have nothing. So, I will have nothing. I will preoccupy my mind with other things."

Nicola said, "Marian, you are hopelessly confused."

Marian said, "Nicola. I will spend my time at the smelter the blacksmiths built for me. Must preoccupy my mind with something other than Warrick?"

The valley's early Nones bells began to ring.

The mountains began to rumble.

ON THE PRACTICE FIELD

Warrick said, "Listen. Wolv is near. His Nones obsessions when he was on Golgotha with Jesus. The AntiChrist repeatedly screams, 'Father. Forgive them, for they know not what they do.'"

Warrick said, "Look. At the sky, the AntiChrist's hate and rage filled the sky with black-and red flames. His smoke blocks out all light from the sky. We will have light again, when the wind blows the smoke away.

Everyone froze until Wolv's screams stopped rumbling the mountains.

Then everyone turned to the Great Hall to eat their Nones' meal. Marian sat beside Warrick's chair. The tall chair at the head of the enormous horseshoe-shaped table. In a rush, Warrick and his brothers marched into the Great Hall.

Warrick thought, "We are in trouble. The new granite shattered under the stonemason's chisels. We must find a new quarry, immediately. We need to study the geography maps now."

In a run, each brother grasped a trencher of venison and an ale tankard. Then they rushed to the Black Mood Keep. Behind the brothers, the fat stone masons huffed and sprinted. Sprinted to catch up with the brothers. In a run, the brothers and masons disappeared. Disappeared up the spiral steps of the Black Mood Keep.

Marian sat beside Warrick's empty chair.

She thought, "He ignores me. He walks beside me and does not speak a word to me. I am correct. Warrick wished to send me away."

Warrick should have stopped and explained to Marian. Disappointment caused Marian to leave the table. She climbed the spiral keep steps to her chamber.

Hours after the Nones bells, Warrick had urgent duties to fortify Rose Fire. He walked out of the Great Hall, into the bailey. Then he climbed the bailey stairs up to the outer battlement's walkway.

THE LADY OUTSIDE ROSE FIRE.

From the battlement, Warrick looked down. He saw Marian walk over Rose Fire's drawbridge. She walked out to her new smelter. From the battlement, Warrick pointed to six mounted armored knights. All outside the castle hidden in the trees. Then he pointed to Marian. From a distance the six mounted knights kept a safe circle around Marian.

He had put the six knights outside Rose Fire to protect Marian. To protect Marian when she was beyond the castle walls.

Morgan, Ross-Templar, and Drayton walked up the battlement steps. They walked over to Warrick.

Morgan rested his huge mace on the battlement and held the handle. He said, "Warrick. The stone masons need you. You must pick the size of the tiles for the moat border."

Warrick thought, "Marian is so beautiful. Why is she so angry with me? Why does she not understand? That all my actions are for her happiness, my royal charge's happiness?"

Outside Rose Fire's walls, Marian turned. She saw Warrick on the battlement.

She thought, "Warrick is so handsome. He will only reject me if I tell him that I love him. He has already rejected me with the parchment."

Morgan repeated, "The stone masons need you. To pick the size of the moat's border tiles."

Warrick thought, "How is it possible? Possible that Marian does not understand that she is the reason for all my actions?"

-

-

CHAPTER, Now in Rose Fire, Wales. Temporarily Driven Wolv from Rose Fire, Year @ 1250s A.D.

ROSS-TEMPLAR TRIES TO INTERVENE.

Morgan put his hand on Warrick's shoulder. He repeated, "The stone masons want you to choose. Choose the size of the moat's border tiles."

Warrick turned and said, "Morgan, why do you pester me?"

Morgan said, "I had a question that obviously must wait. I can see that you are worried about Marian again?"

Lord Warrick said, "Why?"

Drayton said, "Warrick. You are gazing at her so hard. Lightening could strike you and you would not notice?"

Warrick said, "Brothers. Did you ask everyone what is wrong with Marian?"

Ross-Templar said, "We asked everyone. No one could tell me her problem. She is a mystery to everyone."

Warrick gave a hand signal to the six knights to hide. To hide from Marian's view in order not to antagonize her.

Lord Warrick said, "Nicola knows something. Did you ask her?"

Drayton adjusted his bow on his shoulder. He said, "Nicola knows, but she will say nothing."

Ross-Templar noticed Warrick's hand signals. He said, "Marian does not realize that six knights are protecting her?"

Warrick said, "No. I think that she would only be angry with me if she knew. She would say that I give her no freedom."

Ross-Templar said, "I have seen a woman act like Marian one other time. That woman fled on horseback away from her bridegroom."

Morgan said, "Warrick. You let her build the smelter? It preoccupied your smiths and stonemasons?"

Lord Warrick said, "Yes. They built it in three days. Hopefully Marian will piddle with the smelter and forget whatever bothers her."

Morgan put his mace over his shoulder. He said, "Which tiles do you want to line the moat?"

Lord Warrick said, "Morgan, you decide. You are well trained. I am guiding other construction. I must spend time figuring why Marian is so angry with me. How can I protect her if she runs from me?"

Ross-Templar said, "And she may run from Rose Fire, into Wolv's hands."

Warrick said, "Marian does not understand the danger that surrounds her."

FROM THE BATTLEMENT

From the battlement, Warrick put his palms on a merlon and watched Marian.

He thought, "She seems not even to know that I protect her."

From the blacksmith's smelter, Marian looked up at Warrick and caught Warrick's gaze.

She thought, "He is so handsome, and he has rejected me."

She could not overcome the disappointment caused by the parchment.

Marian thought, "Nicola is wrong. My smile will not affect Warrick. Warrick already tried to give me to another lord."

Marian sighed and thought, "I must find a way to leave. As a rejected bride, I will live in shame. I would rather live with my mother in shame. Absolutely, I cannot marry a man with mistresses, even my champion? True love, I want true love."

Love for her champion broke her heart. Warm tears streamed down her cheeks.

At the smelter, Marian thought, "Plaything, I am only my champion's play thing. His toy, like his mistresses will be, or probably already are. How many mistresses does he already have?"

Within the blacksmith's shop, the rotund grimy smith asked, "My lady. Why do you cry?"

Marian said, "It is just the smelter smoke in my eyes."

He asked, "I have never known a lady that wanted to build a smelter. Why do you want a smelter?"

Marian wiped her tears with her palm. She said, "I must be busy or I will go insane."

The smith said, "You could do something else, knitting perhaps."

Marian said, "Wolv's Skinwalkers burned the town of Hereford. Hereford is in need of nails and lumber, not knitted floor mats."

The smith said, "My lady. I know that compassion motivates you. You saw the ashes of the town. Please reconsider. The Skinwalkers could capture you anywhere outside the walls of Rose Fire."

Marian ignored the smith's plea and said, "Did you do as I ordered?"

Then the smith said, "Yes, my lady. I constructed the two furnaces and the tools as you directed. They are as hot as you requested. I placed the iron scraps in the clay crucible. Then I put the lid on the crucible."

Marian read from the ancient arabic tome and told the smith. "Now, pull the mortar plate. This will direct the lower fire's flames up. Up through the spaced, clay-tiles. The tiles under the second fire. We must preheat the spaced tiles that support the second fire."

The smith warned, "My lady, the furnace will suck in air too fast. It will melt the ovens."

Marian pointed to a page of the tome. She said, "Not according to this ancient arabic passage. Now do as I say. I want you to pull the mortar plate. The tome says that the circulated flames are safe. It will preheat the tiles to a safe, steady glow. The hot tiles will then suck in more fresh air. Then the hot tiles will pre heat the air. The preheated air before it burns the charcoal piled upon the tiles. I trust the tome, which says that this process is safe. You must do as I say."

Then the smith said, "But my lady, it is dangerous, it is."

Marian said, "Do it. Pull the lever. Do it. Pull the mortar plate."

He pulled the mortar plate. The lower fire's flames circulated up through the spaced tiles.

Suddenly, the flames blew through the cracks in the clay oven. Warrick noticed the flames flare through the cracks. With a wave of his arm, he ordered his six mounted knights. Ordered them to pull Marian to safety.

The smith ran from the smelter. From outside the smelter, he said, "Run my lady, run." Confident, Marian turned a leaf of the tome. She read.

The smelter chimney roared. Everyone in the castle ran to the battlement to see the source of the roar.

Marian stood at the smelter door. She said, "Hear that roar. That is the draft of the second fire's chimney. We will soon have iron nails to rebuilt Hereford."

The smith said, "My lady. I would not have believed it. You designed a new type of iron smelter."

Marian said, "Not new. This Damascus velum tome is more than a thousand years old."

From atop the battlement, Warrick sighed in relief as the smelter began to function properly. He waved his knights back to their distant positions.

Marian said, "I want you to feed the higher fire down through the chimney. You must close the furnace door and drop charcoal and coal down the chimney. For now you must attach the bellows to the waterwheel."

The smith did as Marian had ordered. As the waterwheel moved the bellows up and down, the smith said, "My lady. I have never seen an iron smelter so white hot."

Marian said, "Feed the two fires until tomorrow at Nones bells. The other smiths can relieve you during the dark Compline, midnight-Vigils, Matins and Prime hours. By tomorrow we may have much harder steel and nails. Hereford's survivors need nails to rebuild the town. The other waterwheel will become a sawmill."

Marian walked back into Rose Fire, across the castle's drawbridge. She noticed Warrick up on the outer wall battlement. He looked down at her.

She stopped and looked at him.

She thought, "God, I love him. I wish that he loved me, but he secretly despises me."

Up on the battlement walkway, Warrick thought, "Marian's beauty brings me pleasure. Pleasure that I have never known. Yet, Marian despises me, why?"

IN HER BEDCHAMBERS

As Vespers bells rang, Collette bathed Marian in Marian's chambers.

Then Marian walked down the spiral stairs to the Great Hall's enormous table. Lady Marian sat at the head of the table to sup, beside Warrick's chair.

Warrick was in a rush to prepare Rose Fire for possible siege. Therefore, Warrick ate in his Black Mood Keep. With his brothers, they studied war and castle construction. Warrick had not explained why he did not eat meals with her.

Marian thought, "Warrick insults me again with his absence at meals. Everyone in the castle sees that Warrick does not sit beside me. They believe that Warrick despises me."

IN HIS CHAMBERS, COMPLINE BELLS.

During the late evening Marian retired to her chambers. Compline bells called the valley's religious orders to prayer and bed. Then Marian cracked the door to her chamber. So she could watch Warrick on the battlement. She blew out the candles in her bed chamber. So Warrick could not see her.

THROUGH THE NIGHT, HE PRACTICED.

In the fog, in cold black night, Warrick practiced with axes and blessed swords. Practiced on the battlement walkway.

As he practiced Warrick whispered, "I am sorry, mother. Sorry that I failed to protect you from Wolv. Sorry that I had not practiced enough to protect you."

TEMPLAR TRIES TO INTERVENE.

Ross-Templar knocked on the solar door to Marina's chambers.

Collette opened the peep-view and said, "Marian. Lord Ross-Templar knocks on your door."

Marian said, "Enter."

Collette unlocked the door. Lord Ross-Templar rested his hand on the hilt of his blessed sword. He pushed the door open and asked, "Marian, may I speak?"

Marian said, "Ross-Templar, you are never at a loss for words, yes. You may speak."

Lord Ross-Templar said, "Marian. I do not know what is happening between you and Lord Warrick. Yet, Marian. I want you to know that you are the center of all his though. When Warrick builds, he builds for you. When Warrick practices, he practices for you. You need to know. Every action of Warrick, every thought of Warrick, is for your protection."

Marian said, "I . . . I . . . I read. . . ." Then the parchment saddened Marian, so she grew silent.

Ross-Templar said, "Marian. I can tell that you were about to tell me. Tell me why you are so angry with Warrick. You must tell him before your emotions fester and you do something dangerous."

Marian looked away to the side, as if to ignore Ross.

Ross-Templar said, "Marian. I have been with Warrick as a brother and warrior. I know him. You can be assured that he will do his duty as to you."

Lady Marian said, "Brides are only to receive duty?"

Ross-Templar said, "Duty is the highest honor that a knight can bestow. I wanted to tell you how important you are to Warrick."

Marian thought, "Important to Warrick. Important enough to give to another lord."

Lord Ross-Templar said, "Marian, I have other duties, leave, I must."

Then Ross-Templar stepped into the solar. He pulled the door closed behind himself.

-

-

-

CHAPTER, Not Safe in Rose Fire, Year @ 1250s A.D.

THE TRAITOR, AGAIN, AND AGAIN.
Compline bells announced bed time. In the dark, knights and artisans walked across the drawbridge into Rose Fire's bailey.

EVIL CREPT.
Before Warrick ordered the drawbridge raised for the night, Blanche crept out. Out to do evil to Marian's new smelter. Out to undo Wolv's orders to weaken Rose Fire.

Blanche approached a thatcher. She said, "The lady of the castle said that she needed a thatch roof. A thatch-roof on the smelter. Lady Marian said that rain would crack the hot furnace. You must start tonight, she needs it immediately, work through the night."

Blanche walked to the water wheel. Her eyes narrowed in concentrated evil. She looked around to assure that no one saw her. Then she widened the trough gate that let water pour onto the water wheel. Blanche let in too much water. The excess water rushed in and overflowed the waterwheel's cups.

Blanche thought, "Too much water on the wheel will make the wheel turn too fast. The old bellows attached to the waterwheel will blow sparks. The sparks will catch the thatch roof on fire. Warrick will blame Marian for the fire. Then he will send her back to Oxford. Rose Fire and Warrick's wealth will be mine. Then I will betray Warrick to Wolv. Wolv will reward me with Rose Fire Castle."

Blanche had a wide satisfied grin. She raised her gown's skirt with both hands and walked back into Rose Fire.

As the thatcher put his ladder to the smelter's wall, the smith said, "Stop. A thatch-roof will catch fire too easily. That is why smith shops do not have roofs."

A bundle of thatches on his shoulder, the thatcher looked down from his ladder. He said, "The lady of the castle ordered it."

The smith said, "If my lady ordered it, put the thatch on. Yet, smith shops never have thatch roofs because of fires."

The next day at Sext bells, the sun was at its zenith. Warrick stood on the battlement.

IN THE BLACK MOUNTAINS. IN A HURRICANE OF RED-FOG.

High in the Black Mountains, Wolv's Sext bells Crucifixion obsessions overcame him. Wolv's eyes glazed over black.

He fell to his knees and begged, "Jesus, please leave me alone. Jesus, please stop this torture."

In his memories Wolv was back on Golgotha Mount at the Crucifixion. Over a thousand years in the past. He held Jesus' hands and feet and nailed them to the cross.

Wolv remembered all of Jesus' words from the cross.

Then on his knees, Wolv screamed Jesus' words, "Father. Into your hands I commit my spirit."

Repeatedly Wolv screamed.

Each scream shook the Black Mountains.

Black-red flames spewed from Wolv's mouth and covered the sky. Wolv came out of his obsession.

IN ROSE FIRE

Everyone in Rose Fire stopped and waited for Wolv's obsessions to end.

On the battlement Warrick said to a mason, "Mix your strongest mortar. Wolv will attack with hundreds of Skinwalkers."

Warrick pointed to the peaks of the Black Mountains and said, "Look up there. That is the darkest, biggest, densest red-fog I have ever seen. The AntiChrist has millions of Things in that red fog. He will conquer Wales then spread throughout the world."

From the battlement, Warrick directed the construction and renovation of Rose Fire. He watched Marian walk across the drawbridge, out of the castle to the smelter door. He motioned to his six armored mounted knights to watch and protect Marian.

TRAITORS IN ROSE FIRE.

Lord Warrick shouted and pointed, "Drayton. Morgan. Make sure that everyone does their hour of Perpetual Adoration in Rose Fire's Chapel. Or in the Adoration wagon. Perpetual Adoration of Jesus' Real Presence in the Blessed Sacrament. Make sure everyone does weekly confession."

Morgan ran up to Warrick. Morgan said, "Warrick. We have been diligent."

Then Morgan handed Warrick a parchment and said, "Warrick. This is a list of all those that have done Adoration and confession."

Warrick said, "Assure that everyone in Rose Fire does Adoration and confession. Every servant and stable boy. Remember the disaster of Cochem, Germany. Cochem had the best trained military in Germany. Still, the red-fog turned them all into Skinwalkers. Skinwalkers that we fought. We slowed Wolv and Lilith but he always returns with his red-fog. The red-fog is our worst enemy. Never forget that only Adoration and weekly confession can keep the red fog away."

WHO MURDERED THE ADORATIONISTS?
Father Bumpus ran from the Rose Fire chapel shouting, "Disaster. Disaster. Who murdered the Adorationists?"

Warrick unsheathed Blessed Dread and ran to the chapel. He saw a chapel full of dead Adorationists. Men and women from the town. Also, nuns and priests from the local monasteries.

Warrick stopped in the doorway and said, "Who?"

Six of Warrick's knights said, "Us. We have decided to join Wolv and kill you. Lilith came into our dreams and gave us great promises. Promises of great rewards."

They turned into Boars-head Skinwalkers and attacked Warrick

Warrick said, "These are your great rewards."

Warrick beheaded all of Skinwalkers. Then he carried their heads to the bailey-andiron fire. To put them into the fire.

One Skinwalker detached head said, "Warrick. I beg of you. Exorcize me."

Warrick said to the Boar-hog Skinwalker's head, "Ask mercy from Jesus."

All six detached Skinwalker heads chanted, "Jesus. Have mercy on us. Jesus, I trust in you." All six chanted in unison.

The demons came out of them as long black-dust streams. The black dust descended into the cracks of the bailey floor.

As their heads turned back into humans, they said in unison, "Warrick. You have saved our souls."

Then they died.

Morgan ran from the chapel and said, "Warrick. You beheaded them so quickly."

Warrick said, "These six had been loyal knights for years. Lilith is extremely powerful to have used their dreams to possess them."

Warrick shouted, "Morgan. Knights. Clean the chapel and get Adoration started right now. Look at the floor. The red-fog begins to fill the floor, start Adoration this second. Otherwise, the red-fog will eat us. The red-fog comes up out of the ground."

ADORATION OF JESUS' REAL PRESENCE.

Knights ran to the chapel and began Adoration of Jesus' Real Presence. Real Presence of Jesus in the Blessed Sacrament.

The Adoration immediately pushed the red-fog back into the cracks of the bailey floor.

Warrick said, "Morgan. Wolv and Lilith know that we are defenseless without Adoration. They will do anything to kill those in Adoration."

IN THE SMELTER OUT ON THE PRACTICE FIELD

Marian directed the smith, "To open the door, we need to decrease the smelter's pressure. Now you must reverse the mortar board. Reverse the board that sends the lower fire's flames through the spaced tiles. I want you to pull all the charcoal out of the lower fire."

Marian remembered Ross-Templar' words. She thought, "Perhaps, if Ross-Templar is correct that I am the center of Warrick's thoughts. Perhaps I can approach Warrick."

The smith used long tongs to slide the mortar board out of the chimney. Then the first fire's flames roared straight up the chimney. She read from the Arabic tome, "Open the hearth door."

With a long pair of iron tongs, the smith pulled open the hearth door.

On the battlement, Warrick had an anxious feeling. He ran from the battlement out to the smelter. He stood behind Marian and waited.

Marian said, "Now that the hearth is open, use the longest tongs. You must lift the crucible from the hearth. First, put it into the larger hot clay pot so it will not break."

The smith obeyed.

Warrick felt a bit more anxious. His followed his intuition. He walked up closer behind Marian. She had no idea he stood behind her.

She said, "Now take off the lid. Pour the molten iron into the molds in the cooling oven."

With the tongs the smith flipped off the lid. Then he used the long tongs to pour the white-hot molten iron into molds. Molds of many swords and nails. The molds were in another heated clay hearth meant for slow cooling.

Marian smiled and thought, "Ross-Templar said that I am the center of Warrick's thoughts. Maybe, maybe this is some chance that Warrick could learn to love me. Learn to love me, though he wanted to give me to another lord?"

WICKEDNESS.
Then Blanche's wickedness came to fruition. The excess speed of the water wheel broke the braces. Broke the braces that held the bellows in place.
Marian yelled, "Run, the bellows has broken away from the crucible oven. The bellows will blow fire everywhere."
Then the bellows blew into the cooling oven. When the bellows broke, Warrick ripped his leather cloak off. He wrapped Marian in his cloak. With Marian in his arms, he dashed from the smelter.
The molten iron in the molds began to pop and mysteriously burst into flame. Where Marian had stood, flames and slag roared out of the cooling oven's door.
Molten slag exploded from the white-hot molten iron in the molds. Quickly the slag-fire spread to the thatch roof.
-
-
-

CHAPTER, Now in Rose Fire, Wales, Year @ 1250s A.D.

TRAITOR'S FRUITION.
Then the smelter's thatch-roof burned like a torch. The thatch fire sent fire brands high into the air.
Warrick thought, "What foolishness has Marian done now?"
In Warrick's arms, Marian thought, "Ross-Templar is correct. Warrick carries me tenderly. Perhaps I am the center of his actions. Perhaps I am the focus of his thoughts."
Wrapped in his cloak, Warrick held her in his arms. She smiled at him.
She thought, "I was so wrong. Warrick does love me."
She smiled and winked. With a hint of teasing in her voice, "Put me down now. You did not need to come out here and watch over me."

He put her on her feet. Soot covered her. Marian shook the soot from her hair.

Suddenly the fire spread from the smelter's thatch roof. Spread to both the carpenters' hut and the stone cutters' tool hut.

TRAITOR.

Blanche watched from atop the outer wall battlement and smiled.

She thought, "This is better than I could have imagined. The fire spreads."

Flames shot into the air. In Rose Fire, fire brands settled on the pink marble bailey floor.

Blanche saw the firebrands on the bailey floor. With weasel-like squinted eyes, she walked from the battlement walkway to the bailey. Then she looked in every direction as she walked to the stables. She noticed a firebrand on the bailey floor near the stable hay. Again she squinted weasel-like and looked around.

Everyone ran outside Rose Fire to throw water on the blaze. They were desperate to save the lumber and stone masons' tools.

No one saw Blanche.

Blanche thought, "Wolv will attack now if I make a fire in Rose Fire. Yes, Marian is not yet in enough trouble. Now I will make her responsible for a fire within Rose Fire. I will make her responsible for Wolv's attack. Then surely Warrick will send her away."

Blanche kicked a firebrand into the stable hay. The dry hay in the stables instantly burst into flame. She waited to scream until the flames engulfed the stable's hayloft.

A stable boy yelled, "The fire in the smelter has spread to the stables. The whole castle will burn."

In the solar, Father Malachi Martin said, "Nicola. I thought a storm was brewing. My knees ached like someone was drawing and quartering me."

Marian ran and shouted, "Nicola! Come quick. We need everyone to put out the fire in the stables."

Father Malachi ran to help with the fire.

Marian and Nicola threw buckets of water on the stable's flames. Warrick and his knights led the stable's horses to safety.

After many hours, Compline bells rang in bedtime. Marian stood in the bailey. Ash covered her hair and gown.

Otan walked up to Marian and said, "The fire is out. I do not know how this happened. Yet, Lord Warrick is sure to kill whoever did. We lost a fourth of the battlement walkway and much of the stables."

Marian walked with her head down. She breathed heavily, exhausted. With one hand she held up her skirt's gown. With her other hand, as smoke of embers stung her eyes, she wiped her eyes. She walked across the bailey and through the inner portcullises. Lady Marian hung her head in exhaustion and disappointment. She climbed the steps to the great hall's door. Then she climbed the spiral stairs to her chamber. In her chamber she leaned on Nicola and said, "I caused the fire. Oh, I must go back to mother and run my father's estate. I do not belong here."

MY LADY, YOU MUST HIDE.

Seven-year-old Luchas ran up the steps and shouted, "My lady! My lady! We have trouble! You must hide from the king's champion. His anger is fierce."

Then Luchas turned to see Lord Warrick in the doorway of Marian's chambers. Luchas put his hand over his mouth. Warrick's cheeks ballooned as if he were holding in words. Words that he wanted to blow out of his mouth. Lord Warrick's expression was blacker than storm clouds. His jaw muscles bulged tight and his leather gloves squeaked as he tightened his fists. All Warrick's muscles bulged. Then his muscles stretched his black leathers. His emerald eyes glared. Then Warrick peered out the window.

Marian thought, "Warrick counts in ancient Greek. He counts to calm himself."

Lord Warrick stood and looked out the window. An unaccustomed sensation of defeat overcame him. He sighed.

Warrick thought, "I failed my duty to protect my charge. I should have foreseen this fire."

Silence racked the chambers. Warrick did not say a word. Fear paled their faces.

As he examined each white, waxen face, he thought, "I failed Marian. Yes, somehow I should have foreseen the fire. Thatch. . .

. I should have forbidden thatches. Marian had the thatch put on the smelter which would eventually burn. She obviously has a severe lack of wisdom. Yes, I failed Marian. I should have supervised Marian since I knew that she lacked wisdom."

Lord Warrick should have told her that he thought that he had failed her. Yet, Warrick never explained and never apologized. He was angry with himself, but he seemed furious with Marian.

Warrick thought, "I have already told Marian that her beauty has defeated me. Her only response was to throw her glass figurines at me. As before, I will only have the lesser happiness that duty gives. As before I will have the greater misery that a bad marriage gives."

Marian thought, "Because of the enormous damage, Warrick has the right to cleave me, now."

As he looked out the window, Warrick thought, "Women bring me misery. What I truly want is to start this day over, to have a different day."

He drove a hand impatiently through his ash-covered hair.

Marian glanced at a wall-torch.

Suddenly Warrick was gone, so fast that she did not see him walk away.

Nicola said, "Hurry, let us close the door to the chambers before Warrick returns."

They shut the door. Nicola asked, "Marian, is it true, you cause the fires?"

Marian said, "Yes, but it was an accident."

Nicola said, "How?"

Marian said, "The bellows broke and blew sparks everywhere."

LOCKED IN HER KEEP.

"Shhhhh, Marian," Nicola said, "Listen. Someone locked your chamber doors from the outside."

Without success, Marian tried to open both doors.

Marian turned. "Nicola, someone locked both the keep-steps door and the solar door," Marian said.

Teenager Nicola said, "Marian. Warrick ordered our chambers locked. Why would they lock us in your keep?"

Marian said, "Nicola. I have heard that lords lock their wives in their chambers to prevent themselves. To prevent themselves from beating their own wives."

Marian thought, "Ross-Templar is completely wrong. I am not the center of Warrick's thoughts. His actions are not done for me. The parchment is the only truth. Warrick wants to give me to another lord. I must escape. Warrick and I can never be together."

At Prime bells Marian sat at an arrow slot.

PRIME BELLS IN THE BLACK MOUNTAINS.

At Prime bells, again Wolv's growls shook the Black Mountains. Wolv's Resurrection obsession conquered him. In the Black Mountains' heights, Wolv walked in a cave. When Wolv heard the Prime bells, his eyes glazed over black.

He screamed, "Not again. Jesus, release me from these chains." He turned into black pure carbon dust and sunk deep into the mountains. He stopped in an underground cavern covered with luminescent mushrooms.

In Wolv's memories the ground shook as the stone of Jesus' grave rolled aside. As at every Prime, Wolv watched Jesus walk from his tomb.

The AntiChrist begged on his knees, "Please. Please Jesus. Raise Pamia from the dead. Pamia is my heart."

In Wolv's memories, Jesus disappeared.

Deep under the Black Mountains, in the cavern, Wolv repeatedly growled, "Please Jesus, please. Raise Pamia from the dead for me."

Black-red flames exploded from Wolv's mouth and filled the cavern.

Wolv's repeated growls shook the Black Mountains. Exhausted, Wolv turned back again into pure carbon dust and ascended up through the earth.

IN ROSE FIRE.

In her chambers, Marian said, "I almost feel sorry for Wolv. Being the AntiChrist is a tormenting curse. His obsessions torment the Black Mountains, torment Rose Fire and torment Wolv"

Through an arrow slot, Marian watched the red Prime sun. It spread a pink hue over the Wye River Valley's grey fog. To pass the time Nicola and Marian read to one another. The only constant sounds were the smith's hammer and the canonical bells. Ting-ting-ting of the smith's hammer. Prime bells announced the day. Terse bells. Sext bells. Nones' bells. Vespers' bells. Compline bells announced the time of rest. Vigils' bells. Matins' bells. Then again Prime bells and Wolv's obsessions. All day, all night, the smith's tatating, tatating. The smith's hammer banged from before Prime, Terce, Sext, None, Vespers and after Compline bells.

All day they heard the smith's hammer. Ting-ta-ting. Ting-ta-ting. They woke to the smith's endless ting-ta-ting hammer. Marian and Nicola continued to read aloud to one another.

Then Marian closed the tome.

She asked, "Nicola. Listen. The smith stopped. I hear cheers and loud celebration from outside Rose Fire."

Otan unlocked her door and opened it.

He said, "My lady, please come with me."

Marian said, "Warrick wants to take my neck to the executioner's block?"

Otan said, "Warrick would have executed me, or any knight, that had caused that fire. Yet, he only locked you in your keep. My lady, you wield great power over him."

Marian said, "No one wields power over my lord, especially a woman my size. Where is my lord?"

Otan said, "My lady, he is still so angry that every knight fears him. When he is angry, every wise knight avoids him. He told me to unlock your door and take you to the smith."

"Come with me Nicola," Marian said, "Warrick. He wants the smith to clamp irons on my wrists and ankles."

In a few minutes, Marian and Nicola walked over the drawbridge. They walked out to the blacksmith's shop. Outside the smelter, the smith stood with a bright blessed sword. The brightest blessed sword Marian had ever seen. Many knights ran their hands covetously over the blade. They treated it as if it were the Holy Grail. Each knight demanded to wield the blessed sword.

Marian said, "I will not resist." Marian held out her wrists. She said, "Clamp Lord Warrick's manacles on my ankles and wrists."

The smith had round eyes of excitation, and a joy-filled, wide smile. He said, "My lady. You are a genius. My lady, you . . . you must watch. You musssssst seeeeeeee for yourself."

The smith raised the blade and struck an iron anvil. The new blessed sword sliced deep into the anvil.

Then the smith said, "Look, Lady Marian. Look at the blade's strength and sharpness, a blade you made. All other blades would have shattered on the anvil. No other known blade could cut a gash in an iron anvil."

He ran his finger along the edge and said, "And not even have a nick. My lady. Inspect the designs on the blessed sword. I did not make these designs. The swirls in the metal. They come from the smelter. From the air blown across the molten iron."

Marian said, "They are the swirls of Damascus steel. We have made Damascus steel."

The smith said, "No my lady. Not us. You. You have made Damascus steel. From ancient, crumbling, arabic tomes. You have made Damascus steel."

Drayton interrupted the smith, "Marian, you have made a wonderful discovery. Swords that can cut through any armor."

Ross-Templar interrupted Drayton, "I have had experience with smelters. When the air from the bellows blew across the white-hot molten iron, the impurities burned. The impurities in the molten iron burst into flame. Just like a campfire burns hotter when you blow on it."

With raised arms in exhilaration the smith said, "My lady. I have never seen molten iron boil until you built this smelter. As the iron boiled, the air smelled like rotten eggs."

Morgan said, "The smell of rotten eggs is sulfur when it burns."

The smith interrupted, "Yes my lady, the molten iron bubbled and boiled. The iron glowed so white that we could not watch it. I could smell sulfur. Slag bubbles burst as the iron boiled in the molds."

With round eyes of excitement, the grimy smith said, "My lady. You had us build the smelter's walls with baked clay.

Therefore, the walls did not burn. I and my assistants quickly put out the thatch fire. Therefore, we saved the water wheel and the bellows. Luckily the bellows continued to blow onto the boiling iron. After the knights extinguished the castle fire, I called for Morgan, Drayton, and Ross-Templar. We watched the molten iron burn for many hours as the bellows blew on it. The iron burned so bright that we could not look at its glow. Eventually whatever was in the iron burned away and the iron ceased to burn. All that remained was bright, pure, white hot molten iron. This is the purest iron that I have ever seen."

Ross-Templar said, "After the oven cooled we found the hardest sword blades. The hardest arrow heads, and nails we had ever touched."

As the smith ran his hand over the bright blade, he said, "My lady. Over many days I forged this blessed sword. I beat on it to fold it and then sharpen it."

In his enthusiasm the smith spoke too much from the heart. Spoke with too much enthusiasm. He said, "Lord Warrick said that if you do not burn the castle, then. Then he wants you to make more Damascus steel."

The smith placed his hand over his mouth and said, "Forgive me my lady."

The knights around Marian did not hear 'if you do not burn the castle.' All the knights were too covetous of the extremely hard, strong, sharp sword to hear.

The thought of the castle fire turned Marian's face red with embarrassment. Swiftly, the smith changed the topic. He picked up a handful of nails and said, "My lady. These nails are the strongest I have ever seen. You are a genius, my lady. We can now make the hardest steel, the hardest steel in all England."

A knight yelled, "To Lady Marian."

All the knights cheered repeatedly, "To Lady Marian."

Nicola whispered into her ear, "Marian, I told you. You are the center of the knights' thoughts and actions."

Morgan pointed to the practice field with his huge mace. He said, "Knights, it is time that you returned to practice. You need to hone your skills if you are to protect Marian."

Marian took a deep breath and whispered, "Nicola. Yet, the crown betrothed me to Warrick, not these knights."

Then Marian turned to the smith and said, "Concentrate on making nails. The town needs nails immediately."

TRAITOR.

Behind Drayton Blanche heard Marian and thought, "I failed. Marian is now their heroine. Yet, she is concerned with the town. Perhaps I can use Marian's compassion against her. Perhaps Marian's compassion will cause Warrick to send her away."

ARROWHEADS.

With the knights gone, Drayton lifted a crossbow. He said, "Marian. We did not want the others to see the power of your arrow heads yet."

He grasped an arrow tipped with Marian's bright, Damascus steel arrowhead. As he placed it into the crossbow's groove, he said, "Marian. You must see the arrowhead's strength."

Then he turned a crank to pull back the bowstring to a hook. Drayton raised the cross bow to his chin and aimed it.

He said, "That target is iron. Three times thicker and stronger than our knight's blessed armor, even Warrick's blessed armor."

Drayton fired. Excited and happy, a squire ran to the target. He hefted the iron target back to Marian.

Drayton said, "Look Marian. The blessed-arrowhead is so sharp and hard that it went through the blessed armor. You have made armor piercing arrow heads."

She touched the blessed arrow that stuck through the iron slab. The arrow head cut her finger.

Marian sucked on her cut finger.

Drayton said, "Armor can no longer protect the enemy."

Marian had a premonition and said, "Armor can no longer protect . . . Warrick."

Lord Drayton said, "Marian. Only blessed armor that you will make of your Damascus steel can protect Warrick. That is the strength of the arrow. Only your Damascus steel can stop the arrow. We, nor the enemy, will have such Damascus steel armor."

Marian turned to the smith and said, "Now. Concentrate on making blessed arrow heads and blessed armor of this Damascus steel. The knights need blessed armor that these Damascus Steel arrows cannot pierce. The nails must wait. Build another smelter and waterwheel. Train three more squires to be smiths."

Marian touched the arrow tip. In a black mood, Warrick walked out to the smelter with war planning scrolls. She watched his dark mood.

She turned to Ross-Templar and whispered, "You are wrong. I see no concern for me in Warrick's eyes."

He walked up to her and tossed the battlefield-scrolls onto the fire.

He said, "Marian. You have proven to everyone that you are a genius, an extraordinary genius. A genius rare in centuries. These and all classical war plans are now worthless because of your smelter. I want you to make more weapons. Can you do that without burning?"

Marian said, "My lord. I will finish your words, 'Without burning down Rose Fire'"

Warrick's request for her to work lifted her spirits. Plus his statement that she was a genius made her feel wanted. The mention of burning Rose Fire disheartened her too much.

Marian said, "Yes, my lord."

In Warrick's presence, Marian lowered her head, mortified over causing the fire.

Marian though, "If only Warrick would kiss me."

With a frown from no sleep, Warrick thought, "I want to kiss her. Yet, she would never accept me."

Warrick turned and walked to his war planning chambers in the Black Mood keep.

The smith said to Marian, "My lady. My lord's anger over the fire will fade away."

Marian said, "My lord's anger over the fire will fade away. Fade away in perhaps thirty or forty."

The smith said, "Days?"

"Years," Marian quipped.

Ross-Templar and Drayton laughed. Their laughter lightened her heart. Her curious, inquisitive, adventurous spirit bolstered her again.

Drayton, Morgan, and Ross-Templar walked away to their duties.

The smith said, "My lady. The carpenters finished the second water wheel."

Marian natural curiosity and compassion for Hereford distracted her from her troubles. She studied the up-down bellows movement. Then she grabbed the smith's arm and a goose quill. She dipped the goose quill in a crock of elderberry ink.

She began to draw on a wooden table top.

Marian said, "Make this saw from our two-man tree-saw. Begin work on another two-man tree-saw. I will have the carpenter design the supports. He can use wood you salvage from the fire."

Lady Marian continued to draw with elderberry ink on the table top. Then Marian said, "Study this design. Attach the saw with this wooden design to the second water wheel."

The smith said, "Yes, my lady, but my lord will not approve."

Marian remembered that Ross-Templar said that all Warrick's actions for her. Also, she remembered that Warrick called her a genius.

She said, "Rose Fire needs replacement lumber. The people in the town need our help. For the town's people, I can endure my lord's anger."

The smith said, "My lady, this is a serious problem. We have only one tree-saw. Are you sure that you want me to cut holes in it?"

Marian said, "Yes. We need a sawmill. Begin work on another two-man tree-saw. Rose Fire needs lumber. Make a two-handed saw of Damascus steel so the stonemasons can cut granite faster. The people of the town need oak lumber. Oak is too hard to cut by hand. They have no money to purchase it. Families sleep in barns with their horses and cattle."

Again compassion motivated Marian, compassion for the weak and helpless. Again, she did not understand the expediency of preparing Rose Fire for enemy siege. She simply had never lived in rebellious lands.

The smith said, "My lady. You smelted such high quality iron that my lord wants more. It is his highest praise for you. I trust my lord will also praise the holes in the tree saw."

The smith followed Marian's request and worked for three longs days with Marian.

Lord Warrick supervised the building and renovation of Rose Fire for the three days. Then Warrick approached the head carpenter.

He asked, "We have no more lumber. Why?"

The carpenter said, "My lord. For three days the smith has been working on the tree saw. For three days we have been unable to saw any trees."

Warrick walked out onto the practice field to inspect the smith's work. He thought that the smith had sharpened and repaired its teeth.

TRAITOR.

With both hands, Blanche raised the front of the skirt of her green satin gown. She walked up to Warrick. She wanted to cause trouble between Marian and Warrick.

Blanche said, "My lord. The smith of the new smelter knocked holes in your only two-man tree saw. The saw is now useless."

Anger flashed red across his face. He sighted Marian in the sawmill. As Warrick entered the sawbill, he observed the holes in the saw.

"Who destroyed our only tree-saw," Warrick said? "Marian, did you order the destruction of our only tree saw?"

Marian turned to Warrick. She turned to see Warrick's eyebrows in an angry V. Then she dropped a huge Arabic tome.

Marian said, "Yes. . . . No. . . . Yes. . . . No. . . . But. . . ."

Warrick said, "You almost burn down Rose Fire. Now you destroy my carpenters only tree-saw. Not only do you take the saw. You also knock holes in our one and only tree-saw."

Warrick thought, "We have no lumber."

Lady Marian hoped Warrick could take a second to look at her accomplishments. She did not understand that he frantically wanted to rebuild and reinforce Rose Fire first. Afterward he would let her do as she wished. As usual he had not explained. Warrick's weakness with Marian was that he never understood the importance of explaining. The importance of explaining anything to Marian. Lord Warrick had never been with a woman that took business and building initiative.

-

-

-

CHAPTER, Now in Rose Fire, Wales, Year @ 1250s A.D.

HE CRUSHES HER.
Marian felt as if a great weight pushed down onto her shoulders. A weight that she could not carry anymore.

She pointed at the saw and said, "But . . . my lord, you . . . you must watch."

She wanted Warrick to see her accomplishment. Quickly she opened the trough from the mountain stream. Water flowed down the trough and filled the water wheel's cups. The tree-saw, attached to the water wheel, began to move up and down. Up and down in long, stable strokes. The smith spread lard onto the wooden joints to ease movement.

Suddenly, the carpenter behind Lord Warrick shouted, "Lady Marian ruined our saw. She is a Satanic witch. Lady Marian is a Satanic witch. Only a diabolical witch could bring water to life to lift a saw."

The superstitious carpenter turned to run.

Lord Warrick grabbed his neck and lifted him off the ground with one arm.

He said, "Call her a witch again, by Christ's robe, I will cleave you. I will cleave you though you are my only master carpenter. The town's people will burn her because they are so superstitious. She is my future wife. Yes, she will eventually drive me insane and burn Rose Fire down around our ears. Yet, she is my ward by the king's order. Besides, I have grown fond of her."

He did not realize he had said the words "Fond of her," but Marian did.

Marian thought, "Finally. Warrick will not be so harsh with me, at least a little less harsh. Maybe Ross-Templar is right, maybe. Just maybe I am at the center of Warrick s actions and thoughts."

The smithy whispered to Marian, "I see you have a smile? Are you not afraid of my lord?"

Marian whispered, "No longer, he admitted that he is fond of me."

Warrick dropped the head carpenter on his butt. He said to Marian, "Ruin our only tree saw? How can you be so irresponsible? Get up to your chambers now."

THE CHAMPION CRUSHED HER.

She looked at Warrick in awe and trepidation. Lady Marian still did not understand the importance of reinforcing Rose Fire. Reinforcing Rose Fire as quickly as possible. She still did not understand the hard sharpness of a warlord. A warlord born of a Spartan life. She still did not fully grasp the hard consequences of lack of war preparations.

Lord Warrick's anger caused his chest to fill. His arm muscles bulged. His bronze face turned blood red around his bright emerald eyes.

Warrick said, "You are not to think or move without telling me."

Then Warrick thought, "Marian does not understand that these are desperate times. Now we have no lumber. We cannot fortify Rose Fire without lumber. We must now use our war axes to chop down trees and split logs. Weeks, it will take weeks to replenish our lumber with only war axes. Marian has endangered Rose Fire and herself."

Marian felt like a frightened mouse. A mouse in the midnight blackness caught under the paw of a hungry cat. Against all her common sense her pride made her raise her chin in defiance.   She said, "Ha."

That was too much for Warrick. With his long arm and stern face, he pointed to her chambers.

Lady Marian held her head low in humiliation and despair. Inside she wept that Warrick had chided her. Chided her in front of the lord's servants and freemen. Yet she controlled her emotions with all her will and walked. With both hands she raised the front of her gown's skirt. As she walked, she wanted to sob.

Once alone atop the spiral stair case she began to weep into her hands.

Through her sobs she thought, "I must wed a brutish man. A brute who will beat me and shame me before kin, servants, freemen, and serfs. I and my children will be the worst treated and lowest among all."

Lord Warrick glowered at the smith. The smith had grown accustomed to Warrick's angry demands. He had served Warrick for many years. Plus, the most valuable artisan in battle is the smith.

The smith smiled and leveled his jaw. He asked, "My lord, may I ask you an important question? One you must know. Yet, as you have often done, with the promise that you will count to fifty."

Lord Warrick shouted, "God's feet, do you want to anger me more?"

The smith smiled and said, "My lord, you are already angry."

Then the smith pointed at the tree-saw and said, "My lord. First, you must count fifty times that the saw goes up and down."

Lord Warrick said, "You have never failed me. For a few moments, I promise."

A GENIUS AGAIN?

Lord Warrick counted aloud in Latin. He watched the saw steadily go up and down. Without slowing, without tiring, as woodsmen do. The smith's assistant steadily shoved a log into the saw. The smith again put lard on all the joints that rubbed together.

Warrick replaced his V-shaped eyebrows of anger with level eyebrows. Then he raised his level eyebrows in awe and insight.

The smith said, "We can saw in a day, two weeks of lumber. Lumber we would take two weeks to saw. Nonstop. Water wheels turn from the Prime hour bells to Vigils back to Prime. All day. All night. I have already forged new tree-saws. This sawmill runs in every season, in rain and snow. I will add Marian's high quality steel to the battle axes' blades. Then the woodsmen can fell trees with the axes and new saws. We will have more lumber than the carpenters can use. Because of Marian, now. Now we can smelt more iron and saw more lumber than we have ever had. We soon can sell lumber and nails and make you richer."

Warrick said, "From England to Egypt and back, you have worked for me. I can trust your judgement."

Warrick ran his fingers through his long hair. He sighed and said, "On all matters, you must consult with me twice a day. As to the saw mill and the smelter, I want you to follow Marian's instructions."

Then Warrick poked his finger into the smith's grimy chest. Warrick said, "After . . . after you consult me. Remember. You must confer with me twice a day."

Lord Warrick examined the artisans' huts outside the castle. He said, "I order you to take the thatch off every building immediately. We are better not to have roofs than have thatch roofs. I will have the masons construct a kiln. Then you can use baked-clay tiles for the roofs."

The smith said, "My lord, may I speak my mind?"

Warrick said, "If I said no, you would speak your mind anyway. Perhaps that is why I continue to employ you."

The smith said, "I need Marian. I cannot read Latin, French, Arabic, ancient Greek, and that language she calls 'Chineeeeeseeessssssseee.' She reads from mysterious scrolls that I cannot understand. I need her with me. You may have frightened her away, . . . forever. You need to go to Marian and . . . and . . . perhaps . . . apologize?"

Warrick said, "I have never apologized, not even to the king."

Warrick spun on one foot to walk back to Rose Fire. He walked through the practice field that was full of sparing squires and knights. Sawdust and granite dust stuck to his boots. He walked through the carpenters and stonemasons work area. Then he had to walk through a flock of sheep. The wind blew his black neck-length hair. His black cloak waved behind him like great black wings. As he crossed the drawbridge, his heavy black boots clattered on the rutted wood.

TRAITOR, AGAIN.

Blanche tried to run as fast as Warrick walked. She raised the front of her gown's skirt with both hands and ran. She could not run as fast as he could walk.

In the bailey, Warrick hollered, "Where is Ross-Templar?"

At Warrick's loud voice, Drayton and Morgan ran to meet Warrick.

From behind the well, with mortar on his hands, Ross-Templar stuck his head up.

Ross-Templar said, "Yes, here."

Lady Blanche thought, "Warrick is about to apologize to Marian. I must spread a malicious rumor fast."

DEEPEST HUMILIATION.

Blanche ran up Marian's keep steps. Many handmaidens knitted and sewed in Marian's solar.

Blanche thought, "The solar door to Marian's chambers is open, good."

Blanche walked across the solar and entered her chambers. She cracked her own chamber door and spoke as if she were talking to someone.

She kept saying, "Lord Warrick is sleeping with the milkmaids."

All the handmaidens in the solar had gathered at Blanche's door to listen.

The handmaidens now whispered and giggled to one another, 'Warrick is sleeping with the milkmaids.'

Marian heard the whispering with Warrick's name.

She stepped into the solar and said, "What is so interesting about Lord Warrick? Why do you whisper about my lord?"

All the servants, all females, blushed and lowered their heads.

Marian said, "Tell me the truth if you wish to serve in Rose Fire."

A servant bowed her head and said, "My lady . . . my lady. Lord Warrick is sleeping with the milkmaids."

Marian's face bleached white. Her mouth fell open. Her humiliation in front of the servants was too much for her. Marian closed the door to her chambers.

Cried, she sat on her bed and cried.

In the solar, her humiliation in the face of her servants was unbearable.

IN ROSE FIRE'S BAILEY

In the bailey, Warrick walked up to Ross-Templar. Drayton and Morgan joined them.

Warrick said, "Brothers. What does a husband do? Do, when he has been short and ill tempered with his wife to be?"

Ross-Templar said, "I have never had a wife-to-be."

Lord Warrick's eyebrows formed and angry V and his jaw muscles bulged.

Ross-Templar crossed his arms. Then he leaned against the well and crossed his legs.

With a smile, he said, "Warrick. I never told you that I know the inner workings of the female mind."

Lord Warrick said, "Women have no mind. They only know how to curse my knights, burn down castles. Throw pieces of glass and irritate me to the point."

On opposite sides, Drayton and Morgan put their hands on Warrick's shoulders.

Drayton said, "Brother, all problems have solutions."

Warrick pointed to Marian's chamber and said, "If, if Marian were a knight. I would have banished her."

In jest, Drayton pushed Warrick's shoulder and said, "But Marian is not a knight. She is a beautiful, fragile, young virgin that you swore to protect. Soon she will become accustomed to knights' hard ways and life in dangerous lands. In Oxford she was a genius administrator. Eventually she will be the same in Rose Fire."

Morgan studied Lord Warrick's face, laughed and said, "Warrick. You are so upset because you are obsessed with her protection. I think that she is the lord and you are the servant. Her inventiveness constantly entertains me."

Warrick said, "Marian's inventiveness almost burned down Rose Fire."

Warrick calmed and sighed. He ran his hand through his black hair.

He said, "Brothers, do you think I was too harsh?"

Ross-Templar said, "I am sure the king heard you holler all the way to London. If you want peace with her, you must make her feel wanted. Not just feel safe and protected."

Lord Warrick said, "Ross-Templar. How can I maintain her safety if she burns down Rose Fire?"

Drayton said, "Warrick. You must let the three of us construct the castle. You must go to her and spend quiet time with her and learn about her. Warrick, you never explain. Also, you never apologize. Warrick. Your nature is just to order, which works with knights. Marian needs explanations. She needs you to apologize. Learn how to talk to her."

Warrick said, "I need to learn how to put out castle fires."

Morgan laughed and said, "Yes, and that too. However, the stable fire also showed us a terrible weakness of Rose Fire. Too much of the castle consists of wood."

Lord Warrick, Ross-Templar, Drayton, and Morgan walked into the great hall.

Ross-Templar said, "Also, Warrick. I talked to the stone masons and the architect. They agreed that her fire did us a favor. In an attack, the attacker could set fire to the battlement's walkway. Without the wooden walkway, the enemy could scale the walls without opposition. We would have no place to stand from which to fight. The stone masons want to build a stone walkway that will not burn."

Warrick said, "I wanted to replace it with stone. I did not want to burn it down first. If an enemy attacked now, part of the battlement would be indefensible. Morgan, I want you to find more stonemasons in the valley. We must have the stone masons repair the burned section immediately. They must not take down the remaining lumber walkway until they replace it with stone."

Drayton asked, "Warrick. Do you know how to apologize?"

Warrick said, "No. Never. I only apologize to my mother because I did not stop Wolv from killing her. No one else. I do not apologize. I conquer."

Ross-Templar said, "Marian is not an enemy to conquer. Go to her and learn to apologize. Practice saying 'I am sorry, Marian' as you walk up Marian's keep steps. Go now."

Lord Warrick climbed the stairs toward Marian's chamber. In a whisper, he practiced, "I am sorry, Marian."

His apology grated against his warrior spirit. Years of war had hardened him against the softer human emotions.

SHE PACKS TO ESCAPE.

Marian wept on her bed and told Nicola everything that happened. Marian said, "I thought I had softened his heart. He said he was fond of me. Yet, then he shouted at me like I was . . . a traitor to the king. He shouted at me as if I were a fool or his worst enemy. Just now I learn that he is sleeping with the milkmaids."

Marian got up off her bed. She opened her chests and began to pack.

She said, "I am going back to mother. Warrick is too brutish and unfaithful.

Her eyes were so full with tears she could barely see. She packed as her tears landed on her clothes.

Warrick walked up the keep steps to Marian's chamber and in a whisper, "I apologize. I apologize."

Out of frustration Marian picked up a thick cast-iron platter. Then she threw it out her open chamber door.

Warrick stepped on the landing to her chamber room. The heavy iron platter sailed through her open door and crashed on his forehead.

-

-

-

CHAPTER, Now Not Safe in Rose Fire, Wales, When: Around 1250s A.D.

RUN AWAY BRIDE.

Lord Warrick collapsed backward like a felled tree. His head bounced off the granite floor.

Marian did not see that she had hit Warrick with the iron platter. She picked up some belongings to carry down the keep steps. To prepare to leave.

As she stepped from her chamber, she slipped on a pool of Lord Warrick's blood.

Marian screamed, "I killed my betrothed."

Warrick said, "Not dead yet. Lady Hairy, horse-faced. A twelve-feet-tall, twelve-toed, sixteen-fingered bride. Though again, Marian, a good try, worthy of any Skinwalker."

At Marian's scream, Ross-Templar, Drayton and Morgan ran up the steps. They tore sheets and tightly bandaged Warrick's bleeding head wound.

Then they lifted Lord Warrick onto Marian's bed. Blood still flowed from his head. Morgan took a pouch of unguents from his belt. He took the bandage off. Then he rubbed the unguents into Warrick's head wounds. The unguents caused the blood to clot.

Warrick coughed and opened his eyes.

Marian cried, "My lord, my lord, I thought I killed you."

Warrick sarcastically said, "Not dead, yet. Another praiseworthy attempt. I am sure that you will soon succeed."

Morgan, Drayton, and Ross-Templar helped Warrick to his feet. Marian said, "I heard you say that you were fond of me."

Warrick's sarcasm overcame his reason. He said, "Yes, I am fond you pushing me out of third story windows. Fond of you burning down the castle. Fond of glass falling on me. Also, fond of you slicing my head open with iron platters. We will have a short marriage. I am sure you will very quickly kill me. I won all the battles of Europe and England. Even the battles of the Middle East trade routes could not kill me. You will soon kill me with fire, falling out of windows, platters or glass figurines."

In defiance, Marian raised her chin and looked Warrick straight in the eye.

Drayton recognized the extreme hurt in Marian.

FROM THE BLACK MOUNTAINS.

In the Black Mountains, Wolv seated himself beside Pamia's wax and plaster corpse. In Wolv's wedding-reception cavern. Wolv said to Pamia's corpse, "See, Pamia. I begged Jesus to raise you from the dead, and Jesus did. I have you now."

Then Wolv stood and held his head with both hands. Wolv growled, "Holy Mary. Leave me alone."

Wolv fell to his knees on the cavern floor. His eyes glazed over black.

In his memory Wolv was on Golgotha. He watched his half brother place Jesus' dead body across Holy Mary's lap.

Mary Magdalene cleaned Jesus' feet with her tears and hair and kissed Jesus' pierced feet.

Suddenly in Wolv's memory he was back in Egypt as a tormented six-year-old. Egyptian children danced around little Wolv and called him Ugly Eyes.

Little Jesus, also six-years-old, took Wolv's little hand and led him to Holy Mary. Jesus' mother, Holy Mary, picked Wolv up and walked with him. She carried Wolv and said, "Little Wolv. You are beautiful and intelligent. Little Wolv. I will always love you."

Wolv was on his knees in his Wales' wedding-reception cavern. High in the Wales Black Mountains.

Wolv repeatedly growled, "Little Wolv. I will always love you." His Egyptian 'Holy-Mary' obsession.

Wolv's growls shook the Black Mountains and shook Rose Fire.

The AntiChrist's hatred and rage burst from his mouth as black-red flames. The flames covered the sky and blocked out all light. Blocked out all light until the wind blew the black smoke away.

Slowly Wolv came out of his Holy-Mary obsession. His eyes lost their black glaze. He raised both fists over his head and shouted, "Holy Mary. Leave me alone. Leave me alone."

INSIDE ROSE FIRE.

Warrick did not see Marian's pain and despair.

Drayton thought, "I must prevent Warrick's sarcasm from hurting Marian more. I must take Warrick away from Marian, for now."

Drayton slung his arm around Warrick's torso. Quickly, Drayton helped Warrick from the room. He forgot to shut Marian's door. Marian could hear their loud conversation as they walked down her keep steps. Then Marian cried in Nicola's arms. She was unconsolable.

As they went down the steps, Drayton said, "Warrick. Did you tell her you were sorry?"

Marian could not hear Drayton.

Warrick talked so loud Marian could hear him. He said, "Yes, I am sorry. I am sorry that I am fond of Marian burning down Rose Fire. Plus, I am sorry that I am fond of Marian ruining our tree saw. Yes. I am sorry that I am fond of Marian scaring artisans until they. They call her a witch. Yes, I am sorry. Sorry that I am fond of Marian hitting me with iron platters. Yes, I am sorry. Sorry I am fond of a probable marriage that will cause my death."

Marian could not hear Ross-Templar.

Ross-Templar put Warrick's other arm around his neck to help Warrick. He tried to humor him and said, "You have a terrible disease. I think that you are in love with Marian. Yet, you do not know or admit it. Surely you are in love, something I have avoided at all costs. I failed. Now I must pay with a lifetime of prayer and penance."

Marian could not hear Ross-Templar.

Warrick grimaced as his head pained him.

Marian's bedchamber door and the keep door to the battlement were open. Inside her bedchamber, Marian heard the brothers.

PROBABLE MARRIAGE.

Marian said, "Nicola. Did you hear, Warrick? He said a 'probable' marriage?"

Nicola said, "Yes, Marian, they laugh about marriage. All men do that. It is nothing."

Marian's eyebrows formed an angry V. She balled her hands into fists. Then she held her arms rigid, down at her sides as she paced. "Nicola? Nothing?"

Marian stomped her foot and said, "Then. Then in Warrick's eyes I am just another 'probably'."

-

-

-

CHAPTER, Now in Rose Fire, Wales, Year @ 1250s A.D.

RUN AWAY BRIDE.

In the bed chamber, Marian said, "Nicola, Warrick hates me. He hates me."

She picked up a clay pot of water and bashed it against the wall.

Marian shouted, "Warrick brought me to this God Forsaken place just to humiliate me."

ON THE SPIRAL KEEP STEPS.

His brothers helped Warrick down Marian's spiral keep steps.

Warrick said, "The king. The king has engaged me to a fury. My honor and duty bind me to protect her. Yet, by God's sandals, who will protect me from her."

IN THE BED CHAMBER.

Marian said, "Nicola, did you just hear Warrick. He called me a fury. I am only a burden to Warrick. I must leave and return to Oxford.

Compline bells rang. The Compline hours had a strange, dry, night fog over the Wye Valley. Under the moon, the fog settled on the guard's skin and blessed armor in droplets. Droplets ran down in streams.

The Wye Valley had now had weeks of dry lightening.

Drought plagued the valley up to the Black Mountain's snow line. The fog seemed to spite the desiccated earth. Fog droplets had not settled on the mountainside's dead grass or trees.

Normally fog left thick dew on the grass. This strange fog left no moisture on the browned field grasses or trees. Snow-melt of the mountain's snow cap filled the mountain streams. Yet, night and day, whirlwinds blew dust, dead leaves, and grass. The dust stung the eyes and choked the lungs.

Midnight Vigils bells rang at the witch's hour.

As the latest Vigils bells rang, Marian heard all the knights downstairs. Down stairs in the Great Hall they shouted her name.

Marian said, "Listen to them. Warrick and his knights are making fun of me."

Nicola said, "The opposite is true. Warrick is an honorable man. He would never make fun of you behind your back. I think that they are toasting you and celebrating your upcoming wedding."

Marian said, "They are using me as the butt of their jokes. Just as they laugh about their mistresses and trollops."

Nicola was correct.

Marian was wrong. Below in the Great Hall the knights were drinking mead and toasting Marian. They cheered Marian and toasted Marian's discovery of harder steel and building sawmills. With wide eyes of admiration, they were 'oohing' and 'ahhing,' at Marian's wedding gifts. Warrick had purchased Marian's wedding gifts from London. Just this day they arrived in a cavalcade of merchants' wagons.

Upstairs she heard her name amid all the laughter from the hall.

"Nicola," Marian said, "they are making fun of me. Oafs and brutes surround me. I must marry such a brute."

Her sister said, "Marian, he is a warlord. He is behaving exactly as a warlord. He is a son of war. His father was a warlord, and Wolv murdered his mother."

Marian said, "I do not care. I am going back to our mother. War can have its own son, Warrick. I am going back to our father's estate.

Marian asked, "Nicola, are you coming with me?"

Nicola said, "No, I am wise enough to stay with Warrick, where we are safe. Besides, the guards would never let you across the drawbridge."

Marian said, "Nicola, then you can stay. I cannot stay any longer."

Nicola repeated, "The guards will never let you across the drawbridge."

Marian grabbed her coats and a few clothes and a bag of gold coins. She threw an old cloak over her self so that she looked like a merchant. She walked from her chambers. Across the outer wall battlement and down the battlement steps. In her merchant's disguise she motioned to a stable boy. To harness two work horses to a merchant's wagon.

He did. He obeyed.

Dressed as a merchant, she stole the merchant's horses and wagon. Before her sister knew, the guards had lowered the drawbridge. She sat on the wagon and slapped the reins across the two work horses' backs. They broke into a gallop and pulled the wagon across the drawbridge. In the black of night, the wooden wagon rattled on the clay and rock road.

ALONE, ALONE, AND MORE ALONE.

Marian wept over her broken heart as she held the reins of the two horses. They pulled her small wooden wagon in a steady gallop. She was alone and she felt more alone that she had ever in her life.

She did not know that Skinwalkers slept along the sandstone and grey clay road. Marian was just the succulent morsel that they prized the most.

The pounding of the horses' hooves and the wagon wheels awakened several Skinwalkers. They mounted and galloped behind her from a distance. The Skinwalkers knew exactly where they wanted to ambush her. With patience, they followed her. In an hour the road became sandstone and black clay. Her two horses galloped around a small pond. The wagon wheels slid sideways on wet black clay. She glanced back. Behind her, in the moonlight, she saw the dark figures in a gallop. She recognized the boar's head helms and knew they were Wolv's Skinwalkers. She screamed, "Murderers," and shook the reins for the horses to run faster. Her two work horses were already very tired. Then she made her next mistake. Her hands were tired. To hold the reins, she wrapped the reins around her hands. Marian did the most deadly mistake. Marian tied the reins to her wrists.

Lady Marian yelled, "Warrick, my champion, Warrick, where are you? I need you. My champion, I need you. God, God, please God, send my champion."

IN ROSE FIRE.

Back in Rose Fire, as the knights toasted Marian, Morgan turned to Lord Warrick. He said, "Warrick. You better go up there and practice saying 'I am sorry.'"

Lord Warrick set his tankard down on the table. He stood and took a deep breath. He smiled at Morgan and said, "Brothers, back into the lioness' den. If you hear an iron platter crash on the stone floor, come running."

Morgan laughed. "Go, you must go up to Marian," Morgan said.

Ross-Templar said, "Warrick. You must bring Marian down to celebrate. Go, bring her down here so we can toast her success. Her success with the saw mill and the smelter.

Six steps at a time, Warrick bounded up the spiral steps. He opened Marian's bedchamber door. Marian was not in the chamber. He walked to Nicola's chambers and unlocked the door. Nicola startled to see Warrick so tall in front of her door.

Warrick asked, "Nicola, where is Marian?"

Nicola said, "Where? Marian is in her chambers?"

Warrick asked, "No. Nicola. Where is she?"

Then Nicola said, "She took some gold coins, her coats, some clothes."

"Marian said that she would take a wagon to Oxford. To mother, many canonical bells ago in the night. I knew that the guards would not let her go. The night is old. I can hear Matins and very early weak Prime bells. I was sure that the guards at the drawbridge would not let her go. God, no, did they?"

Warrick ran down Marian's keep steps and shouted, "Everyone search for Marian."

He ran onto the battlement to the drawbridge guards. Warrick asked, "Did you let someone out of Rose Fire a few hours ago?"

The guard said, "Yes, after Vigils bells, in the tree Witches' hours. A merchant. We now know that someone stole a merchant's wagon with two draft horses. Whoever it was, he galloped away into a dangerous night."

Nicola stood beside Warrick. She said, "I believe that Marian dressed as a merchant. Therefore, they let her out of the castle."

Warrick turned to the guard and said, "Tell me quickly. Did the merchant take anybody for protection?"

The guard said, "None, the merchant went alone."

Warrick thought, "I have driven my bride into the claws of murders. She is alone."

Warrick shouted, "Come. Warriors. Marian is somewhere outside Rose Fire and she is alone, with no protection."

The word "alone" rang in his head. Drayton, Ross-Templar, Morgan and the other knights knew the look on his face. They knew the meaning of his stride. Skinwalkers were about or already had murdered or worse, kidnaped, Marian. They grabbed their weapons. The Pendragon brothers and knights mounted their warhorses. Still dressed from yesterday's practice, they wore their battle mail. They had no time to dress in their blessed armor.

The drawbridge guard shouted, "The wagon had a bad wheel, not perfectly round. Lord Warrick. You must follow the irregular wagon-wheel tracks."

Without blessed-armor and few weapons, they mounted their warhorses and stormed across Rose Fire's drawbridge. To the guard, Warrick waved that he had heard his words. The guard's words of the irregular wheel.

Yet, the other knights did not hear the guard's advice about the irregular wheel track.

THE WRONG-FORK IN THE ROAD.

Far away from Rose Fire, Marian's hands were so tired. She could barely rein the horses. She glanced back and saw the Skinwalkers at full run. At a fork in the road, she took the wrong fork.

-

-

-

CHAPTER, Now in Rose Fire, Wales, Year @ 1250s A.D.

PANIC, DEADLY PANIC. THE WRONG DIRECTION.

In Marian's panic she took the hard-packed grey clay road. The wrong road. Marian thought it would take her into England toward Oxford. Oxford was half way across England in the other direction. She sped into the wrong direction. Deeper westward into Wolv's rebellious Wales.

She was still slightly ahead of the Skinwalkers. The night's late matins bells gave way to extremely early Prime bells. Then yellow sun beams hinted of morning. The black night grew dark grey.

Her hands ached from exhaustion. They were almost useless. Marian had not realized how hard it was to rein in two large work horses.

She could now hear the Skinwalkers' horses' hoof behind her. Marian's wagon sped on the now blood-red clay road. Her wagon bumped high on sandstones.

"Warrick, Oh Warrick, where are you? My champion. Where are you?" she cried. "My champion. Where are you? Jesus, send my champion to me."

Her horses breathed hard. White lather in sheets dropped from the work horses' shoulders and hindquarters. Marian knew that her horses would not last much longer. The sun beams shown behind her. Terror filled her breast as she realized that she was running to the west.

She shouted, "I should be running toward the sun in the east. The wrong direction, I am running in the wrong direction. The sun is at my back. O Jesus, help me. Please Jesus, send my champion to save me. I am going to the west, not east. I am far into the land of our enemy, Wolv's land."

Marian cried, "Warrick. My champion, Warrick. Please. Jesus, please send my champion to save me."

HER CHAMPION WAS TOO FAR AWAY.

Far, far behind Marian, Warrick and his knights raced to save Marian.

They charged at the most dangerous speed. Their war horses' spiked horseshoes exploded the road's cobblestones and sandstone. Their horses' hooves threw chunks of clay and rock into the air. As they thundered down the rock strewn road, they leaned and slid around curves. Their enormous, young warhorses ran much faster than Marian's work horses.

Lord Warrick's warhorse, Zeus, gloried in a run of full attack speed. Warrick bred him for attack, born and trained for attack. Zeus exhaled blasts out his nostrils as if they were great eruptions of fire. His breath was the hot moisture of Zeus' lungs blown out into cool air. In the cold morn air, Zeus' breath condensed into droplets and looked like smoke. Lord Warrick leaned forward and held the reins with one hand. The wind flagged his long, midnight-black hair and his black, leather cloak. Warrick kept his eyes on the distorted wagon-wheel track.

THE WRONG WAY.

Warrick was so far ahead of his knights that they could not see him. He came to a fork in the road and turned the wrong way.
-

CHAPTER, Now in Rose Fire, Wales, Year @ 1250s A.D.

ON THE WRONG ROAD.
On the wrong fork in the road, he reined in Zeus. In the rocks and clay, Zeus locked his legs and slid to a stop. Warrick said aloud, "I cannot find the warped wheel track."

He turned Zeus around. Then he slowed Zeus to a prance back toward Rose Fire.

Lord Warrick was too far ahead of his men. At the fork in the road, Warrick dismounted. As he walked the road, he said aloud, "The irregular track. Where is the irregular wagon-wheel track?"

ENEMY TERRITORY.
Warrick squatted on the balls of his feet. He said, "Yes, yes, I found the track." He ran his finger in the track and said, "Oh no. Marian went into Wolv's territory. Wolv could have already killed her, . . . or worse."

As he glanced around to find his knights he thought, "I cannot wait for them."

He mounted Zeus and raced at attack speed down the sandstone and grey clay road. Without hesitation, he raced deeper into Wales into Wolv's stronghold.

Warrick said, "Marian is in the heart of Wolv's territory."

To himself, he said aloud, "Stretched hoof prints with two spikes. They cover over Marian's wagon tracks. The horses have galloped so fast that they slid on the clay. Wolv's Skinwalkers, these are the two-spike hoof prints of Wolv's Skinwalkers. Oh God, Wolv's Skinwalkers have found Marian, my love."

He spurred Zeus to a greater attack speed. Warrick said aloud, "Murderous Skinwalkers."

He held his reins in his clenched teeth. Then he held his blessed sword in one hand. He swung Blessed Dread in the other.

Far behind Warrick, his knights came to the same fork in the road. They did know that one wheel on Marian's wagon made a different rut. Different because it was out of round. They charged down the wrong fork. The fork that Marian did not take. The fork that led to London to the east.

ALONE, SO ALONE.

Marian was alone on the road that led deeper into Skinwalkers lands. Her wagon hit a large rock in the road. It flew high in the air. The stress broke the wagon's tongue. With her hands tied to the reins, the horses jerked her off the seat. She landed in tall grass. Behind her, the unguided wagon smashed against a tree. Then the two horses pulled her in a circle in a grassy field. White foam covered both horses. Exhaustion overcame them, both work horses neighed and fell to their knees. Then both work horses fell sideways, dead from exhaustion.

The Skinwalkers reigned in around her. They jumped off their horses and knelt beside her.

As a flock of black crows, Wolv lighted. The crows gathered atop one another. They turned into his horse and his charcoal-black human form atop his horse.

As crumbling charcoal, Wolv got off his horse. He turned Marian on her back.

Wolv said, "Such luck, you are Marian Moray of Oxford.

He bent down and smelled her neck. He licked her hands and face.

Then he said, "Yes, just as I traced. You are of Pamia's blood line. I can taste Pamia's blood. I can smell Pamia's blood. Exactly as I have traced during centuries. You are a descendant of Pamia's daughter by her first husband. Her first husband was of the Cyrene Pendragon blood line, like Warrick. I know because over a thousand years ago I killed him to have Pamia. First, I will test you to see if you are Pamia reborn. If you are Pamia reborn, you will live as my bride. If you are not Pamia reborn, then, I will use you to trap Warrick. Then after I murder Warrick, I will let my Skinwalkers will eat you, alive. Your only hope is if you are Pamia, Pamia reborn."

Marian had no strength to shove him away, nor breath to scream. She spit in his face. Two Skinwalkers held her arms to the ground.

Suddenly, Marian heard a growl that shook the earth. The growl was full of hellish anger, full of vengeance, full of fire and brimstone. She looked up to see Lord Warrick on the back of his warhorse Zeus. To Marian he seemed to move in slow motion. Warrick held the reins in his gritted teeth. He wielded his blessed sword in one hand. In his other hand he swung Blessed Dread in a wide circle. He bared his teeth and growled through his clenched, white teeth.

EMERALD-EYES.

His emerald eyes, framed in his granite hard bronze face, glared like lanterns. She thought that Zeus' hot breath bursts from his wide nostrils looked like white flames.

To Marian, the wind seemed to blow Warrick's cloak in slow motion. Like great black angel wings. His green eyes glowed in his angry bronze face. His gritted teeth gleamed.

Marian thought, "My champion, God has sent my champion, 'Blessed Dread, God's Angel of Death'."

To the Skinwalkers Warrick was an angel of death. Warrick had the advantage of surprise.

As Wolv lay on Marian, he looked up just as Warrick swung Blessed Dread.

Blessed Dread cleaved Wolv's head from his body.

At the sight of Wolv's headless body, Skinwalkers screamed, "Wolv is dead. Run from Warrick. We must run from God's Angel of Death."

Zeus ran through the Skinwalkers and jumped over Marian. As Warrick had trained him, Zeus trampled the enemy. Bright, wet, red blood flipped from Warrick's ax and his blessed sword. From his ax and blessed sword, wet red drops arched high in the air.

The red drops shimmered in the early Prime bells sunbeams. As the drops splashed on the dewy grass, they looked like momentary red roses.

Warrick cleaved the enemy. Zeus trampled the enemy. Skinwalkers dropped their weapons and ran. Lord Warrick had forged Blessed Dread to cleave through armor, men, and horse.

Blessed Dread did.

Red drops arched and sparkled in the faint morn sun. Extremely early Prime bells called monks and nuns to prayer.

More red droplets splashed on the thick grass as monks sang Jesus' praises.

Warrick circled within the Skinwalkers, around Marian.

From years of training, Zeus knew exactly where to step. Zeus' spiked-horseshoes landed inches from her. The ground was full of headless Skinwalkers.

Warrick jumped off his horse. He swung Blessed Dread. The last of the enemy, fell lifeless. He beheaded the wounded Skinwalkers. Then he threw their heads far from their bodies. So they could not easily find their heads and return to life.

Lord Warrick knelt beside Marian. For few times that he could remember, tears began to well in his eyes.

He said, "Marian, I have failed you. You are my charge to protect and I have failed."

After he pulled off his gloves, he flipped off his large, black cloak. Then Warrick wrapped Marian like a cocoon in his cloak. He carried her in one arm and Blessed Dread in his other hand. He dashed to Zeus.

With her last ounce of strength, Marian whispered, "Look, Wolv lives. I saw you cleave his head from his shoulders. Wolv is not human. You knew that Wolv was not human. Oh God, I was in the grip of a monster, a true monster."

Then Marian smelled the strong, pungent scent of bay leaf Neets' foot oil. The Neets' oil on his leathers. The bay leaf made her feel safe and warm, protected and loved. As when he defended her beside the lake in Oxford. Hundreds of miles to the east.

Zeus knelt. Lord Warrick threw his leg over the saddle. Zeus stood. He held Blessed Dread in one hand and Marian in the other arm. On Zeus, Warrick squeezed his thighs. Zeus reared and burst into an attack speed run. His iron-spiked hooves exploded sandstones. Warrick steered Zeus with his thighs.

Drayton, Ross-Templar, Morgan and Warrick's other knights raced toward them. They parted as Zeus thundered through them. The huge war horse had not expended much of his energy or nervousness. His stride lengthened until only one foot touched the ground at a time. The most dangerous speed. Though exhausted, for a brief second Marian marveled. Marveled at how Warrick could steer his horse with only his thighs. Zeus moved as if the horse could read Lord Warrick's mind. Warrick had trained Zeus until Zeus knew Warrick's every sound, every touch.

Marian tried to say, "I love you." Her throat was raw and Zeus' hooves sounded like thunderclaps.

She looked up to see tears drain down from Lord Warrick's eyes. Skinwalkers had camped on each side of the now red clay road. Warrick roared a hellish war cry and raised Blessed Dread high in the air. All the Skinwalkers ran into the forest. In what seemed seconds, Zeus pounded across the drawbridge. Zeus locked all four legs. The huge horse slid to a stop on the glistening marble bailey floor.

Marian thought, "Warrick's eyes have tears for me. He previously said that he was fond of me. Now again, he has fought unto death for me."

Marian could only whisper, "You do care for me in your own way. The honorable way of a war lord. You do love me in a warrior's hard way. My champion, you do love me. The champion in you fights for me."

Warrick could not hear her whispers. He said, "Marian, you feel as cold as snow. We must warm you fast, before you sleep."

In the bailey, Lord Warrick did not hear Marian because he roared, "Otan. Servants. Hot water. Clean cloth. Thick soup. Hot rocks from the andiron. Marian needs you, where are you?"

He yelled all this as he carried Marian up to her chambers.

On Marian's bed, Father Malachi Martin wrapped Marian's hands in poultices. The reins had blistered her hands. Lord Warrick quickly undressed her. He wrapped hot stones in thick deer-fur and spaced the wrapped stones around her. He and Father Malachi wiped Marian with warm water. Then Warrick covered her with a large sheepskin blanket.

Lord Warrick thought, "Marian hates me. I wish she would stay, but she is determined to leave."

Marian needed to hear Warrick say that he wanted her to stay. Yet, as always, he expressed himself in actions, not words.

She smiled at him and inaudibly whispered, "I love you."

He did not hear her weak voice.

Warrick said, "Marian. I know you hate me. I know you want to go back to your Oxford estate. When you are well, I will have many knights take you to Oxford. In Oxford you can administer your father's large estate. In Oxford you will find a man that you can love."

At his words of misunderstanding, Marian fell into deep sadness. Deeper depression.

Marian and Warrick made the same mistake. Too often they did not say their most intimate thoughts to each other.

Marian thought, "Just as in the parchment, he wants me gone? Yes, he said that he wanted me gone just now. My champion said. Said that he will send his knights with me to take me to Oxford. He wants me gone. He will send me back to Oxford in shame, unwanted by my betrothed. Warrick does not love me."

Father Malachi gave her something to drink to help Marian sleep. She fell asleep.

Father Malachi said, "My lord, I can find no broken bones. She must have damage inside her. Perhaps she is bleeding inside since she is so pale. She has many deep bruises."

Then Father Malachi again touched Marian's forehead and said, "My lord. I feel something very ominous. The Pendragon curse is strong in her. Perhaps Marian does not want to live. If she does not want to live, perhaps I cannot help her."

Lord Warrick waved all out of room, "Perhaps, perhaps, perhaps . . . I want answers, not perhaps."

An unseasonable, freakish, dry and freezing wind began to blow down the mountain side.

Warrick put his big hand onto the stone walls. He said, "Ice, I feel ice crystals on the walls. It seems as if the Pendragon curse is attempting to freeze Rose Fire. Freeze Rose Fire until it crumbles."

The chamber grew colder. He stoked a large fire in the andiron. The fire crackled and flames licked high.

He opened the chamber door and yelled down the spiral staircase, "Drayton. I want you to bring the Great Hall andiron to a high blaze. Then the warmth will drift up the keep steps."

Drayton did. The frozen wind howled from Prime, Terce, to Sext.

SEXT OBSESSIONS.

Wolv was as a flock of crows, eating a live, disobedient Skinwalker. The Skinwalker screamed as the crows ate him. High in the Black Mountains, in the snow.

Sext bells echoed off the Black Mountains. In unison the crows shouted, "Jesus, not again. Every day, three times a day, Jesus, you torture me. Prime, Jesus, you torture me. Sext, Jesus, you torture me. Nones, Jesus, you torture me."

The crows came together and formed Wolv's black charcoal form. Cracked black charcoal with an interior of red flame.

Then Wolv fell to his knees. His eyes glazed over. Wolv relived what he did at zenith sun, sext bells, in Jerusalem. On Golgotha, at zenith sun, Wolv nailed Jesus' hands and feet to the cross. He whispered into Jesus' ear. "Raise Pamia from the dead for me, and I will end this torture."

Then Wolv heard Jesus say from the cross, "I Thirst."

With Wolv's eyes glazed black Wolv repeatedly screamed, "I thirst."

Wolv's screams shook the Black Mountain range.

As Wolv screamed red-black flames shot from his mouth and filled the sky.

The AntiChrist had no relief from the Sext Zenith sun bells. For before Wolv came out of his Sext Crucifixion obsession, the Nones bells began. The Nones' bells, Jesus' Death on the Cross bells.

The Sext bells became Nones bells.

On his knees, in his memory, he looked up at Jesus on the Cross. He relived Jesus' saying, "Father. Into your hands I commit my spirit."

Wolv repeatedly shouted, "Father. Into your hands I commit my spirit."

High in the Black Mountains, at Nones bells Wolv remained on his knees. No relief for Wolv. Wolv's relived ramming a spear up into Jesus' right side. Up through and deep into Jesus' heart.

Wolv's eyes remained glazed over black as his Crucifixion obsessions continued to conquer him. The AntiChrist continued to growl, "Into your hands I commit my spirit."

The torment caused tears to run from his eyes.

Red-black flames continued to shoot from his mouth and fill the sky. The black flames and smoke continued to block out all light.

Slowly Wolv's eyes lost their black glaze.

Then Wolv roared, "Jesus. When will you end my torture? Jesus, please end my obsessions. My obsessions about you."

Slowly Wolv got up off his knees and again burst into a flock of crows. The crows attacked the live disobedient Skinwalker and ate it alive.

IN ROSE FIRE

In Rose Fire, Nones bells became Vespers bells. Then Compline bells, then Vigils bells, midnight, the three hours of Witches. Matins' bells ended the three hours of Witches. Distant Prime bells began.

RESURRECTION OBSESSION.

In a cave high in the Black Mountains, Wolv growled, "Candlekeeper. Is it a safe hour?"

The Candlekeeper walked backward away from Wolf and said, "Listen. In the distance the Prime Resurrection bells ring. Master Wolv. Your most painful hours approach, the Resurrection hours.

As always in his obsessions, Wolv's eyes glazed over black. Wolv growled, "Jesus, you give me no rest."

He turned into black, pure, carbon dust and dissolved into the earth. He sank into the earth until he reached another cavern. Another cavern beside a fast flowing underground river. On a ledge beside the rapid river, Wolv stopped.

Luminescent mold and mushrooms lit up the underground cavern.

In his memory the ground shook. Shook as Wolv watched the stone over Jesus' tomb move aside. No one visible moved the stone.

With black glazed eyes, Wolv watched Jesus walk from his tomb.

Wolv screamed, "How? I rammed a spear into your side up into your heart. As you hung on the cross, I speared your right side. I rammed the spear all the way up into your heart. Half the spear handle was in your chest. You cannot be alive. I nailed you to the cross. The hole, I can see the hole in you side. Also, the holes in your hands and feet. How? Teach me this magic so I can raise Pamia from the dead. Pamia is my heart. My heart is so empty. Jesus, please teach me this magic."

Jesus looked down at him and said, "You will always be my beloved childhood friend. To be with Pamia you have only to ask me for forgiveness of you sins. Then if you live in repentance, you will one day be with Pamia in Heaven."

Wolv growled, "Never will I ask for forgiveness. Never will I live in repentance, never, never."

Wolv's growls of 'Never, never' shook the Black Mountains.

Red-black flames shot from Wolv's mouth and filled the cavern. Flames born of rage, madness, hatred and anger.

Slowly Wolv came out of his Prime bells Resurrection obsession. He turned into black pure charcoal dust and rose up out through the earth. He rose until he was again in the snow atop the Black Mountain.

IN ROSE FIFE.

As the wind froze Rose Fire, the water in the well froze over. The sun did not warm the wind. As usual the weather on the mountain was not the weather in the Wye Valley. The valley was warm and sunny. The mountain froze, and the mountain rain-drought continued.

Marian began to shiver. Warrick called for more thickly wrapped hot stones. Servants carried them from the downstairs andiron. He wrapped them in thick, deer-fur and placed them around her. Her teeth began to chatter in her sleep.

Warrick opened the door of the chamber and hollered, "Father Malachi."

Father Malachi Martin touched Marian's face and said, "Lord Warrick. We can do nothing. For some reason Marian does not want to live."

In convulsions, Marian shouted, "Wolv is going to eat me. Where is my champion?"

Warrick said "Here," he shouted, "Marian, I am here."

In convulsions Marian screamed repeatedly, "Where is my champion?"

Father Malachi Martin said, "The Pendragon love curse is too strong with Marian. The Pendragon curse is too strong with her."

Warrick said, "Drayton. Morgan. Check Adoration again. Put little children in the Chapel to do Adoration for Marian. The Adoration of a Child's pure heart is very powerful. Make sure that everyone does their hour of Perpetual Adoration in Rose Fire's Chapel. Or else in the Adoration wagon. Perpetual Adoration of Jesus' Real Presence in the Blessed Sacrament. Make sure everyone does weekly confession. Contemplate our great victory in Saint Paul de Vence, France. That was when we began Adoration when Wolv attacked. We drove off the red-fog and beheaded the Skinwalkers before they could harm anyone. We exorcized many. Without his Skinwalkers and red-fog, Lilith and Wolv abandoned St Paul de Vence. Never forget. Our strength is spiritual strength. Jesus' Presence in our hearts through Adoration and weekly confession. Now go. Gather children to do Adoration for Marian. The prayer of their pure hearts is very powerful."

HER NIGHTMARE.

Lord Warrick asked, "Father Malachi. Then what can we do for Marian?"

Father Malachi said, "We can do nothing! The Pendragon curse is too strong in her. Wolv's Pendragon curse has condemned her to a death wish. In her nightmare she wants to die to escape her despair caused by her capture. Her death wish is so strong that she is dying. It sucks the warmth from her body. We cannot defeat this death wish. You cannot defeat this enemy."

Warrick's jaw muscles bulged. He said, "I always defeat my enemy. I always find a way. Morgan. Put our Holiest knights to do Adoration for Marian. Have them do confession then do Adoration. We need pure hearts to do Adoration. Get children to do Adoration for Marian. No faith is stronger than the pure heart of a child."

Father Malachi said, "Marian needs a champion in her nightmare. I can help you change nightmares caused by Satanic witches. I cannot help you change ordinary nightmares. She must find a memory that is more powerful than her nightmare. A memory about her champion, you."

Warrick said, "This is the horror of Marian's nightmare. What unbearable pain. She sees and feels Wolv and Skinwalkers hold her down. She is repeatedly reliving the horror of the capture. The pain, shock, and horror are too much for her. Do something for her."

Father Malachi said, "My lord, I cannot. Within her dream she needs to feel loved."

Lord Warrick said, "Father Malachi. You said that you were powerful."

Father Malachi said, "My lord, I am not omnipotent. I cannot cure all ill humors. I am not powerful enough to cure a death wish. Only her champion, you, can help her now. You must do the impossible. My lord, you must enter her nightmare as a memory. You must find some means to control her nightmares."

Warrick said, "You speak nonsense. Only a memory of me can save her? Nonsense."

Father Malachi said, "My lord, it is the Pendragon curse. The curse is very strong in her."

Marian began to convulse.

Warrick said, "Out, at least I can help control her convulsions."

Lord Warrick, in his bay-leaf oiled leathers, climbed in her bed with her. To prevent her from biting her tongue he put his calloused finger between her teeth. He pulled her small body to his. To keep Marian's legs from convulsing, he held her legs with one of his legs. He wrapped a long arm around her to control her back from arching. Also, to keep her arms still. Warrick held her tight.

Then something happened to her. Something that Warrick did not notice, an unconscious strong reflex. His skin, hair and leathers had the aroma of his bay leaf oil. The residue's pungent, bay leaf aroma stung and penetrated her nose. The bay leaf aroma was so strong, so memorable that it entered her nightmare.

In her nightmare she ran from the Skinwalkers and cried, "Where is my champion."

Without waking she screamed aloud, "Where is my champion?"

Warrick said aloud, "Here. Right here holding you."

Then, in her nightmare, at the sound of Warrick's 'here', the Skinwalkers ran from her. In her dream, she stood and ran toward Warrick. In her dream she ran into the arms of Warrick. She dreamed that he hugged and kissed her and unsheathed Blessed Dread to protect her. Her nightmare of the capture suddenly changed to when he first saved her. Also, to when he dispatched the Skinwalkers in Wales. When he wrapped her up in his black cloak and carried her on Zeus.

Then in her nightmare, the sight of Warrick terrified the Skinwalkers. They ran far away to where they were barely visible to her in her nightmare. She could hear them whisper to each other, "Warrick is here. We must avoid Warrick. He can kill us."

In her bed Warrick felt her convulsions stop.

Her body slowly warmed.

He did not know it, nor did she know it. The bay leaf aroma calmed her. The bay leaf aroma unconsciously revived the loving memory. A memory that she was with her champion, safe, warm, and loved. She would never completely realize the impact of his bay leaf fragrance on her. She smiled and slept.

Then he turned her on her side so she faced him. He put her head on his arm.

She dreamed of the first day that they met. When he saved her from the Skinwalkers. When Warrick wrapped her in his black cloak. As she slept, he hugged her.

In her dream they kissed. Again, far in the background, she saw the Skinwalkers. Warrick's presence in her dream terrified the Skinwalkers. Far away, with their heads cast down, they cringed.

In the bed, he hugged her close. He hugged her in what he thought was a vein attempt to save her. In his attempt to comfort her, he grew to love her more.

Warrick lay awake. He kept vigil lest she became sicker. The shadows on the floor grew long. The room grew colder.

He stepped out of bed to stoke the fire.

Without him in her bed, she could no longer smell the bay leaf aroma. In her nightmare, Warrick faded into a mist as the aroma faded from her nose. She reached out for him but could not find him.

Without waking, Marian cried out, "Where is my champion."

Warrick shouted, "Here, Marian. I am here."

She began to convulse, again as she ran from the imagined Skinwalkers.

He quickly lay back beside her and held her as he did before.

Again, without waking, Marian yelled, "Where is my champion?"

"Here," Warrick said, "Here, beside you."

As he lay beside her in bed, Warrick did not, could not, know. Warrick did not know that he was now in her dream. From the Skinwalkers, she ran to him.

In the bed, he wrapped her in his long black cloak. The bay leaf aroma on the cloak stung her nose and eyes.

Unconsciously she calmed as the pungent aroma stung her nose. In the bed, she smiled and slept.

Father Malachi opened the chamber door and entered with a bowl of broth. He used a spoon and dripped the broth into her mouth.

Father Malachi said, "My lord, Marian is much better, she swallows. Her face is warm."

Warrick said, "Father Malachi. You were correct when you said that you were fallible. Her body grows warmer. You said that Marian would die."

Father Malachi said, "Yes, my lord. Somehow you have entered her nightmare. Somehow you protected her from her Pendragon curse nightmare. You did the impossible, something far beyond my power. My lord, true love conquers all."

Father Malachi said, "Warrick. I have seen it often before, yes, true love conquers all."

Warrick said, "Leave us."

Father Malachi closed the door behind himself.

Lord Warrick ran his hand over her face and cupped her blond hair. Her beauty was an opium to him, an addiction. He hugged her. He knew that he must have her totally. Never could he hold back his instinct to protect her. His duty to protect her was becoming an uncontrollable, vulnerable love for her.

For days, Marian did not awaken. Each day at each canonical bell, Father Malachi dripped broth into Marian's mouth. If she were in Warrick's arms, she would swallow. The instant that he would leave the bed she would gag. Gag on the broth and convulse.

Father Malachi said, "My Lord. I do not know what your love did, but she will live. She will grow strong."

Warrick stood out of bed, stretched. Warrick put more logs onto the andiron. Suddenly Marian's eyes opened. She screamed long and loud. Then she fainted. He lay and hugged her tight. Her scream still rang in his ears, rang in his heart.

Days passed. Marian did not awaken. Warrick no longer tried to distinguish the canonical hour bells of day and night.

Father Malachi fed her broth at all canonical hours.

The wind howled loud in the Black Mountains. So loud no one could hear Wolv's obsessions.

IN THE BLACK MOUNTAINS.

Then Nones Bells rang.

Wolv was high in the snow capped Black Mountains, in his camp.

Then Wolv heard the Nones bells.

The AntiChrist growled, "Jesus, no. Leave me, Jesus. Stop torturing me, Jesus. Not more Crucifixion obsessions."

In the snow, Wolv fell to his knees in his war camp. His eyes glazed black as he looked up. His memory saw Jesus hanging from the Cross.

In his memory he watched and heard Jesus say to the Good Thief. "Today you will be with me in paradise."

Wolv's Nones Golgotha obsession shook the Black Mountains. He howled repeatedly, "Today you will be with me in paradise."

His howls caused avalanches high in the Black Mountains.

Wolv's raging obsession of hatred caused red-black flames to shoot from his mouth. The AntiChrist's raging fire filled the sky with black smoke and blocked out all light. Lilith, as a dragon, flew in the black fire.

As Wolv's obsession ended, the wind blew away the smoke and let in light.

IN ROSE FIRE.

Warrick said, "Father Malachi. Listen. Words that Jesus said to the Good Thief as Jesus hung on the Cross. Wolv again shakes the Black Mountains."

Lord Warrick kept the blaze in the andiron. Every time he got out of bed Marian convulsed. He again put her head on his arm and hugged her. She smelled the bay leaf and unconsciously smiled. She slept.

At Compline bells Marian awoke and felt his hairy chest on her face. She thought that it was a Skinwalker's chest.

"Get out of my bed," she shouted. "Get out of my bed."

Then she shoved on him and shouted, "Get out of my bed." Lord Warrick obliged her and stood clad only in black leathers.

Marian could no longer smell the bay leaf fragrance. Terror filled her. Her head darted about as she scanned the chamber for what frightened her. Terrified she dashed out of bed and into Lord Warrick's arms. She unconsciously smiled and breathed deep of his bay leaf flagrance. She felt safe only in his arms.

Marian could not remember Wolv's assault on her. The pain and shock were too much for her.

Lady Marian shivered from the cold and fear. The bay leaf aroma made her feel safe and warm.

Then she shoved him, "Get back in my bed. Get back in my bed." In the bed, in his arms, she fell asleep.

Several hours after asking him to get back into her bed, Marian awoke. She startled.

As she sat up in bed, she turned in bed. She searched for some unknown threat. Then she relaxed when she realized she was in her chambers.

Lady Marian put her hand on Warrick's chest. She felt a deep sense of peace and well being. He smiled at her. Then she hugged his neck. Marian fell asleep. After an hour she woke and said, "I am hungry."

He stood and opened the chamber door. Then he shouted down the spiral keep steps. "Send up much food, whatever is available and wine."

The cook and servants brought up baked duck, goose, and pork ribs in mint sauce. Next they brought in fresh rye bread, butter, cheeses, a dark beef broth, and wine. Then he opened her tall dresser and searched for a gown.

Lady Marian felt anxious. She did not know why, but her unconscious answered her problem. "I do not want a gown," Marian said. "I want your cloak."

She dashed across the floor. Marian lifted his long black cloak from the back of a chair. She wrapped it around herself.

Warrick said, "Wear this gown. It is beautiful with your blond hair and blue eyes."

Marian tightly pulled Warrick's black cloak around herself. While she breathed deep of its bay-leaf aroma, she shook her head 'no'. Marian shook her head so violently that her blond hair flipped in a flurry.

"Just your cloak, only your cloak," Marian said.

She pulled Warrick's black leather cloak up around herself and smiled. Again, unconsciously, she put it to her nose and breathed deep of its aroma. Then she plummeted into the pork ribs. Her hands hurt so she held the ribs between with her palms.

In Marian's chambers, Warrick stood in his leathers. Then he tore a leg off the roasted duck and ate it. He sat on the edge of the bed.

Warrick thought, "She has never really known danger. Marian has known tomes and all the wisdom they can impart. She knows engineering and architecture and the healing arts. All from tomes and parchments. She even knows metallurgy. She has never known danger. Outside Rose Fire's walls are only perils, with Wolv around us. Marian does not think about danger. Marian thinks about compassion. Compassion gives her stubborn courage."

Marian's beauty shoved all other thoughts out of his mind. He marveled at the deep blue of her eyes. Her curves, and her long, light golden hair. He put down his food and feasted his eyes on Marian's beauty.

Suddenly Marian's eyes darted around the chambers as if someone had startled her.

A memory of the capture and attempted murder raced back upon her. She hugged his neck and pulled him back in bed with her.

Marian asked, "Warrick. Will those horrible things ever harm me again?"

Marian had blocked out the memory of Warrick beheading Wolv.

Warrick said, "Marian. They the can only harm others in Hell."

Warrick did not tell her that the Skinwalkers would have found the heads. Then like Wolv, they would live again.

Warrick said, "Marian. I want to examine your hands."

She released her hug around his neck. He sat up in the bed and unwrapped the bandages on her hands.

He said, "The bruises healed, but your hands will be sore."

Her tender hands traveled gently up and down his back. Then through his long black hair. Marian ran her hands over him. As if she were desperately searching for some important secret, some hidden treasure. She seemed to search for some treasure without which she could not live. The secret was the bay leaf fragrance that meant that she was safe. Unconsciously she breathed deep of his bay leaf fragrance. She traced her finger along his face.

Marian said, "Warrick. Just do not move. Stay here in my chambers and do not go anywhere."

Then Marian thought, *"I remember seeing Warrick. As an angel in long black hair and great black wings. His roar shook the earth. Framed by his hard bronze face, his emerald eyes frightened his enemies, even Wolv. His eyes seem to bare peoples' secrets to him. Warrick was like death. A winged warrior astride a horse that breathed hell fire. Though his parchment stabbed my heart, I must hug my champion. Though he is like a fearsome angel of death, I must be. I must be in my champion's arms."*

As she gazed into his emerald eyes, she felt safe with him. Then Marian put her hands to her cheeks. With round eyes of surprise, she said, "Warrick. I remember now. I saw you behead Wolv. Yet, within moments I saw Wolv alive. What is Wolv?"

Warrick told Marian about Wolv's history. Then Warrick ended Wolv's thousand-year story.

Marian asked, "Such a long story, then no one can kill Wolv?"

"No one," Warrick said, "We can only temporarily stop him. The thousands of demons that possess him always heal him."

Exhaustion again overwhelmed her.

As she hugged his neck she said, "Oh God, help us."

While they lay on the bed, Marian fell asleep in Warrick's arms.

-

-

-

CHAPTER, Now in Rose Fire, Wales, Year @ 1250s A.D.

THE ENEMY AMASSES IN THE BLACK MOUNTAINS.

Three days later, in Marian's chamber, Collette brushed Marian's hair. On the battlement a stiff wind blew Warrick long black hair and cloak. He traced his finger along castle designs on a deerskin velum.

Then Warrick said, "Masons. Look high in the Black Mountains. The greatest danger. The Red Fog does not allow sunlight on the Black Mountains. You can even see the Things in the red fog from here. Remember this danger as you do your work. Be long-suffering. Use Wye river sand. Wash the sand in the Wye river. Be busy, careful, exacting. We need the best mortar. Go, and you must follow this design on this velum. Also, tell the other masons to use the Wye River sand."

The masons said in unison, "Yes, my lord," and walked down the battlement steps.

Warrick motioned for his brothers to climb the battlement steps to him.

SHE MESMERIZES HIM.

He asked, "Ross-Templar, how can one small woman have such a hold on me. Everywhere I look, I still see her beautiful face. Even with the world's greatest evil about to attack, Marian mesmerizes me. I see her petite straight back and her prideful tilt of her head everywhere. I see her long, thick, blond hair everywhere. Her hair so beautifully hangs down her back. Like a golden wheat field, her hair waves in the wind."

From the battlement, Warrick pointed to a mounted squire and shouted a command. The squire began correctly to bend his knees as the horse galloped under him.

Warrick said, "Morgan. Marian and I have been in confrontation since the first time we met. We rode directly into one another. Then both of us with our horses fell into a lake. Constant confrontation."

Morgan said, "Yes, I can guess what happened then. The very first sight of her beauty caused your reason to fly away. She curled her lower lip in a pout. The power of her curled lower lip defeated you. Am I correct?"

THE ALL-POWERFUL POUT.

Warrick rolled his eyes upward and said, "Yes. That all-powerful pout."

Drayton said, "The king demands that you protect Marian."

Warrick said, "Hold Drayton. Wolv is in one of his obsessions. The Black Mountains shake. He shouts his 'Holy-Mary' obsession.

On the battlement they could hear Wolv repeatedly growl, "Little Wolv. I will always love you."

Lord Warrick said, "Drayton. Look at the sky. The AntiChrist's hatred is so great that his mouth fills the sky with red-black flame. I have seen this flame shoot out of his mouth more than once."

Slowly the growls faded away.

Then Warrick said, "Listen now to Wolv."

High in the Black Mountains, with his fists held high Wolv growled, "Holy Mary. Leave me alone. Jesus. Stop torturing me."

Warrick said, "Torturing. Yes. Torturing Marian. What is torturing Marian to the extent that she would run?'

Warrick suddenly remembered the parchment and said, "Yes, me and me alone. Yes, the king would not allow me to send Marian back to Oxford. I asked the king to send knights to take Marian back to Oxford. I also asked the king to assign her to another lord. He would do neither."

Drayton and Morgan's eyes became round with surprise.

Ross-Templar grabbed Warrick by the shoulders. He shouted, "Warrick. You asked the king to send knights to take Marian back to Oxford. Does Marian know? When did you do that?"

Warrick said, "After I heard that Marian threatened to curse my knights. When my knights said that they would leave my service. Who would protect Marian in this war between the AntiChrist and England? Without my knights, Wolv would capture her or worse on the battlefield."

Drayton said, "Could that be why she is so angry? The two of you were progressing very well. When did she begin to avoid you?"

Warrick said, "When Lord Thedford brought the king's reply parchment. The king refused to send knights temporarily to take Marian back to Oxford."

Morgan said, "Marian may have read it. Warrick. What did the king say in his reply, exactly?"

Warrick said, "Exactly? The last two lines: *'I will not honor your request to send Marian back to Oxford. Nor will I honor your request to assign Marian to the protection of another lord.'*"

Morgan said, "Warrick. Marian must have read the king's reply."

"Yes. Morgan, Marian must have read the king's reply," Warrick said. "That is the only explanation for her negative behavior to me. This is why she is so volatile."

Ross-Templar asked, "How will you explain to Marian. Explain your request for the king to assign her to another lord?"

Warrick said, "I requested that the king send knights to take Marian to Oxford. Just to keep her safe."

Ross-Templar was quiet for a moment. Then he said, "The Pendragon curse is very strong with Marian."

Lord Warrick said, "Marian and I will never find peace."

On the battlement, Warrick walked to Marian's bedchamber door and unlocked the door.

As he entered, Marian sat at her desk and read a tome. The servant, Collette, brushed her hair. Marian glanced at Warrick then she remembered the parchment. The pain of her broken heart did not allow her to look at him.

"Marian, I must speak to you privately," Warrick said, "Collette, leave us."

Quickly, Collette scampered out the solar door into the solar. Warrick shut the solar door behind Collette.

Lord Warrick said, "You read the parchment from the king. The parchment that he would not assign you to another lord."

Marian crossed her arms on the desk and lowered her head to her arms. She wiped tears from her cheeks.

As Warrick stood beside her, he said, "I wrote that because, you remember. You threatened to curse my knights. They almost left my service. Who would protect you if my knights left me?"

-

-

-

CHAPTER, Now in Rose Fire, Wales, Year @ 1250s A.D.

EUCHARIST OBSESSION.

Marian's tears dripped onto the table. As he stood beside her, Warrick said, "Sometimes the king's reason is beyond understanding. I do not understand why the king would not temporarily assign you. Assign you temporarily to the protection of Oxford's Lord Protllyy."

EUCHARIST OBSESSION.

Church bells began to ring.

Marian froze in place as Wolv, high in the Mountains, growled, "Jesus. Leave me alone."

Wolv's growls shook the earth.

In a cavern, Wolv walked over to a Skinwalker and demanded, "You. Begin the chant 'Jesus. Have mercy on me.' With sincerity."

Wolv held his head and growled, "Jesus. Leave me alone, or I will kill all Christians.'

In the cavern the Skinwalker, in terror and sincerity, chanted, "Jesus. Have mercy on me."

The Skinwalker fell on his side. A long line of black charcoal dust came out of the Skinwalker's mouth.

Then the Skinwalker changed back into a long-ago possessed Catholic priest. Possessed in the year 300 A.D. because

Wolv threatened to burn him. Burn him if he did not sell his soul to Satan.

Now the terrified Catholic priest stood.

Wolv said, "Say Mass, the Eucharistic prayer, over this bread on that altar. I want to touch the Real Presence of Jesus in the Consecrated bread. To beg him to raise Pamia from the dead. I can torment Jesus. He torments me, so I will torment Jesus, unless he gives Pamia back to me."

Wolv stood as the priest said the Eucharistic prayer. The Catholic priest consecrated the bread and wine.

Then Wolv walked up and took the consecrated Host into his hand.

Wolv burst into red-and-yellow flame as he touched the Consecrated host. Then Wolv growled, "Jesus, you cannot escape me. I can always feel you in Consecrated bread. The same as when we played with Pamia and Symon. Children in Egypt. The same as when I nailed your hands and feet to the cross. As when, your blood poured out of your side onto me. Just after I speared you on the cross. I have the curse of certitude. Everyone else needs faith. Take away this curse of certitude."

In red-and-yellow flames Wolv growled, "Jesus. Please raise Pamia from the dead for me. Please Jesus, Pamia is my heart. I am so alone. So alone."

In Wolv's heart Wolv heard Jesus' Words, "My Beloved Childhood friend. You have only to ask me to forgive you your sins. Then eventually you can be in Heaven with Pamia forever. Ask for forgiveness."

Then Wolv burst into black flame and black smoke. He repeatedly shouted Jesus' words, "Ask for forgiveness."

Red-black flames poured from Wolv's mouth and filled the cave.

As always, his repeated growls shook the Black Mountains.

Wolv howled, "Raise Pamia from the dead for me." He came out of his obsession. Then Wolv changed into a flock of crows and ate the Catholic priest, alive.

IN ROSE FIRE.
Marian said, "Wolv gives me such a headache."

Warrick said, "The AntiChrist is the world's eternal headache."

Marian raised her tear streaked face and said, "Warrick. You said Temporary? Temporary?"

Lord Warrick said, "Of course temporary. I asked the king to send many knights to take you to Oxford temporarily."

Marian said, "You wrote to assign, to betroth, me to another lord?"

Warrick said, "No, how could you believe that. To assign is not to betroth. That the parchment said I wanted to betroth you to another? You misunderstood the parchment. Assigning to another is not betrothing to another. I wanted temporarily to assign you to an Oxford lord for your safety. I planned to call for you after I drove Wolv from Rose Fire."

Warrick hit his chest with a loud thump and said, "You are mine. You are my betrothed. No one will take you from me."

At his words, Marian jumped to her feet. She tiptoed and threw her arms around Warrick's neck.

Warrick hugged her and said, "Marian. Now why do you cry?"

Marian said, "Happiness. Such wonderful happiness."

-

-

-

CHAPTER, Now in Rose Fire, Wales, Year @ 1250s A.D.

TRAITOR. NO KISSES.

Suddenly Marian's keep shook with a great crash. A worker shouted, "My lord, help, the rose clay tiles fell off the keep roof. They landed on many workers. Help."

Warrick jumped. In frustration, Marian threw herself onto the bed. She beat her fist into her pillow.

Warrick dashed from Marian's chambers.

Marian said, "Not even a kiss."

Blanche watched Marian through a crack in the solar door. Blanche smiled. She held the pole that she used to push the tiles from the keep roof.

THE DANGEROUS ARTESIAN WELL SCENE.

All day and night Marian helped the injured. Warrick directed work on the damaged roof.

The next day the sun reflected off Warrick's black leathers and hair. He stood beside the bailey well.

Warrick said to his stone masons, "To protect Marian, we need an artesian well. This seepage well provides too little water. An artesian well will be similar to a small mountain stream within Rose Fire. I want you to dig a level, horizontal shaft back into the mountain. I know this mountain's rock structure. Ground water is close to us in the porous stone. An old map shows an underground river under Rose Fire."

For two days the stone masons dug the horizontal well shaft.

NONES OBSESSIONS HIGH IN THE BLACK MOUNTAINS

Late Nones bells rang. Again Wolv's repeated growls shook the Black Mountains. "Woman. Behold your son, behold your mother."

High on the mountains Wolv was on his knees. With fists to his eyes, Wolv saw only in memory.

He looked in memory to see Jesus hang on the Cross. Jesus looked down at Holy Mary and John, the Apostle. Jesus said, "Woman. Behold your son, behold your mother."

Wolv's rage poured out of his mouth as black-red flame and filled the sky.

IN ROSE FIRE

Warrick said, "Wolv's obsessions will one day collapse Rose Fire. Jesus' words to his mother and St John as Jesus hung on the Cross. No one is closer to Jesus than Wolv. Yet, no one hates Jesus more than Wolv."

Then Warrick said, "Listen. Wolv's Nones obsession fades."

As the late Nones bells rang, the stone masons climbed from the well. They lay on the bailey floor. Sweat streaked through the granite dust on their faces. Their chests heaved with the effort to catch their breath.

Warrick walked up and said, "What is wrong?"

Exhausted, on their backs, the master stone mason gasped, "The tunnel. The tunnel has tired us, my lord. We cannot breathe the torch smoke and we cannot see without the torches."

Lord Warrick said, "To protect Marian, we must have this well."

Then he picked up a torch, a long chisel, and a large sledge hammer.

He said, "Follow me down and carry out the stone that I break."

He glanced over to see Marian. Marian ran to him and grasped his arm.

She frowned and said, "Warrick. Please do not descend into the well. I fear for you. In Oxford I buried expert well diggers when a well collapsed. My lord, you are not an expert well digger."

Warrick smiled.

To comfort her, he lied, "Wells carved in stone do not collapse."

She tightened her grip on his arm. Then she whispered in his ear, "I saw your right eyebrow raise. You always raise your eyebrow when you lie. The well can collapse."

While Warrick climbed the latter down into the well, he laughed and said, "Marian. Some day I must shave my eyebrows."

Marian frowned, stomped and tightly crossed her arms.

Marian paced.

She demanded, "Father Malachi Martin. Warrick is a Catholic priest and you are his religious superior. Call Warrick out of the well. He is supposed to obey you."

Father Malachi said, "Marian, what must be, must be. Warrick must descend into this danger. This well is indispensable to your survival. Ancient tomes record that England's survival is your survival, through your children. Your descendants will have your genius and become great generals and politicians to fight Wolv. To fight Wolv until the end of the world. You carry the Adam-Simon-Cyrene Pendragon line."

Marian snapped, "I am not that important."

Father Malachi stared into Marian's eyes and said, "My lady. You are that important. You are the center, the reason for all Warrick's actions. Fate needs your love of Warrick and Warrick's love of you. My lady, I have said it often but you have not listened. Some loves must be. My Lady. I have listened to Wolv's bone throwers. Also, buried in many monasteries are predictions about Pamia's descendants. You are one of Pamia's descendants. In tomes, Catholic mystics mention you often by place and date of birth. This is how Wolv knew of you. From you will eventually be born two powerful Pendragon progenies. It will take centuries. Catholic mystics call them Winstosom Church de hill and Frankish Ruoos de Velt. Both of Able-Simon-Cyrene Pendragon blood, of your blood. They will lead great armies against Wolv in the next thousand years. The Catholic mystics have written. Written that Winstosom Church de hill and Frankish Ruoos de Velt will battle Wolv. Without your two descendants Wolv will destroy the world. Destroy the world with bombs that part the highest clouds. Your genius must live. You must pass on your genius through Warrick's mighty Pendragon children."

DEEP IN THE WELL

Deep under the bailey floor, Warrick crawled on hands and knees to the tunnel's end. He gave his torch to a worker behind him. Then he sat on his feet and placed the chisel against the stone. As he hit the chisel with the hammer, slabs broke from the tunnel end. For an hour, Warrick pounded the chisels into the tunnel's face. Water now seeped up to his ankles.

One mason said, "I have dug many wells. This flow of water could cause the well to collapse upon us."

Warrick said, "You must not allow your fear to overcome your reason."

Marian looked down into the well. She shouted, "Otan, the well is filling faster. You must go down in the well and pull my lord out."

Lord Warrick's squire began to descend the latter. Then the masons in the tunnel climbed up the latter. As they climbed, they pushed Otan up and out of the well. Exhausted, they collapsed on their backs to the bailey floor.

The master mason said, "Fresh air. Thank God. Fresh air."

In the tunnel, Warrick's hammer blows thudded throughout Rose Fire's bailey floor. His hammer thudded as if he were a woodsman far up the mountain.

Otan then crawled on his hands and knees down into the well. He crawled up to Warrick.

He said, "My lord, my lady is afraid the well will collapse upon you."

Warrick said, "She should fear Wolv. Fear if we do not have an adequate water supply when he sieges us. Send for my knights to empty the water from the well. We need the water level to be kept low so we can work. We need more buckets. Send for my knights to empty the well."

Otan crawled out and said, "My lady, my lord is obsessed with your safety. He will endure great danger to assure that you are safe. Warrick knows for your safety we need an artesian well's large flow.

Then Otan yelled, "Knights, all of you. Empty the well, now. Or Warrick will drown."

Marian said, "Warrick cannot assure my safety, anyone's safety, if the well collapses. If it collapses and he drowns."

Knights used buckets to empty the well.

In the fresh air, the stone masons regained their strength. Again, they descended into the tunnel. From the tunnel, hand to hand, the masons transferred stones up to the bailey floor.

The latest Nones bells ended. In the bailey, Marian paced with her arms crossed. As she paced, the bailey shadows lengthened to the east.

With muffled thuds, Warrick busted layer after layer off the tunnel. Piles of broken stones filled the bailey. As Warrick sat on his legs, the water now covered him up to his belt.

He shouted, "Get more servants to take water from the well."

Marian paced on the bailey floor and said, "The well is filling too fast."

She turned to Morgan and said, "You must get down there and pull Warrick out."

Morgan said, "Impossible, too many workers block the way."

In the bailey, everyone handed buckets to each other to empty the well. They threw the water into the moat. Blisters formed on their hands. They threw water into the moat. Their blisters broke. They carried buckets. Their hands bled.

Marian shouted, "My lord, you must get out of the well. I can feel it. Something horrible is about to happen."

Warrick could not hear Marian.

Warrick said to a worker, "Hand me a torch. I think we finally made progress."

He put the torch to the face of the tunnel. He yelled, "Out, out, out of the tunnel. We hit an underground reservoir. The water sprays into my face. Out, out, everyone, I want everyone out of the tunnel. Get out. Now. I did not expect to hit a belowground reservoir. Get out or drown."

The small sprays broke into larger ones. Warrick put his hands against the large sprays. A larger hole broke. Water poured into the tunnel. Quickly the tunnel filled half way.

He yelled, "Get out or drown. Hurry. I did not expect to hit an underground stream so easily.

Warrick pushed his back against the holes. He yelled again, "Get out. I will press my back to the sprays and hold back the water. Out, out, out."

In a long line, the masons scurried from the well.

Marian asked the masons, "Where is Warrick?"

A stone mason gasped and said, "Trapped. The ceiling of the well fell on me but I wiggled free. Lord Warrick was behind me. The well collapsed on him. He is dead."

Terror gripped Marian.

Father Malachi said, "My worst fear."

Against Warrick's back the tunnel's face completely collapsed. A big hole, wide enough for a man to go through. The water rushed in and pushed Warrick through the well. Within seconds Warrick popped up out of the well. He gasped for air.

He pulled himself out. At the sight of Warrick, Father Malachi smiled and breathed a long breath of relief.

Marian hugged Warrick. She whispered into his ear, "I want to slap you. You put your life in such danger for only a well."

He whispered into Marian's ear, "Knights would gladly accept. Gladly accept a slap from such a beautiful hand."

Warrick's laugh echoed off Rose Fire's walls. Marian stomped on his foot. Again his laughter echoed from Rose Fire's walls.

HOLY-MARY OBSESSION.

Warrick said, "Listen. Wolv's obsessions about Holy Mary."

They all stopped and listened to Wolv's repeated growls. "Little Wolv. I will always love you."

Lord Warrick said, "Marian. Look at the sky. Wolv's rage spews black and red fire from his mouth. The fire covers the sky. My knights and I have stood in this black fire. It has not burned us. We call Wolv's fire 'spiritual' fire. It only burns Wolv."

They stood in place until Wolv's obsession faded, until Rose Fire stopped vibrating.

A DEAD MAN.

Then an unconscious mason floated to the well's top. Warrick grabbed him and dragged him from the well.

A mason said, "He is dead, drowned, cold as the well water. The stonemason lay unmoving on the cold bailey floor.

Drayton said, "Yes, the mason is dead. He was underwater for too many minutes."

Father Malachi said, "My lady, do what you know. You know what Italian sailors do."

Marian pushed through the knights, squires, servants and masons. Then Marian said, "He has not had time to die."

TRAITOR.

Blanche thought, "Now is my opportunity again to defame Marian."

Blanche whispered into a servant's ear. "Only a demonic witch would say that the mason has not had time to die."

The servant whispered to the other servants, "Lady Marian is a demonic witch."

ITALIAN SAILOR WISDOM.

Marian said, "Italian sailors do not give up so easily."

While Blanche defamed Marian, Marian said, "Otan. You must kneel. Push on his chest to push the water out. I will breathe into his mouth."

Otan obeyed. Water poured from the man's mouth. Repeatedly, Marian held his nose and blew air into his mouth. She turned him on his side. Water poured from his mouth. He coughed.

Everyone eyes grew round and their mouths dropped open as the stone mason coughed.

Otan asked, "My lady, how did you know to do that?"

"I read," Marian said. "I read everything and study every language and read. Read ships logs."

Marian stood and brushed bits of stone from her gown. She said, "I read. Many captains' ship logs speak of these instructions. You have only to read Italian ships logs. Every Italian sailor knows of this technique."

Blanche thought, "Now is another opportunity."

Blanche whispered behind a female servant, "Only. Only a Satanic witch can raise someone from the dead."

The servant in front of Blanche shouted in terror, "She raised him from the dead. She is a demonic witch, a Satanic witch."

Quickly Warrick shouted, "Who said that? Fifty lashes to anyone that repeats that."

The smith happened to be beside Marian. He whispered into Marian's ear, "My lady. Do you see the expression of wide-eyed respect in the knights' eyes? They recognize your wisdom in matters of healing, the harder steel, and the saw mill."

Marian whispered, "If they respect me so much, why do? Why do they still wear their red and green sashes? If they respect me so much, why do they? They still carry small flasks of Holy Water?"

Warrick had heard Marian and the smith's whispers. He whispered, "Marian, they may respect you, but . . . they are. They are more afraid of your possible curses."

Morgan rested his large mace across his shoulder. He said, "In Venice, Italy, I saw sailors do this with drowned sailors. It is not witchcraft. It is simply a healing art. Sometimes they repeatedly hit the drowned person in the chest with their fists. Whatever it takes to make them cough. Marian should create a school for any non readers."

Still the servants whispered, "Marian is a Satanic witch, a demon. Only a Satanist could bring anyone back from the dead."

The well water flowed into the bailey's rain gutter to the moat.

-

-

-

CHAPTER, Now in Rose Fire, Wales, Year @ 1250s A.D.

DECEPTION, TORCHES ON THE MOUNTAINS.

That dark night, after Vesper's sup, Warrick and Marian walked on the battlement. Warrick pointed and said, "Marian. Look up on the mountain. Do you see that line of torches as it snakes across the mountains?"

Because she loved the bay-leaf aroma, Marian wore Warrick's extra black cloak. The one with the albino rabbit lining.

She said, "Yes, my lord, I can see the torches."

Warrick said, "Do you have any ideas on what or who they are?"

Marian said, "Druids or perhaps some wild people from the mountain's caves."

Warrick waved to a guard in a guard tower. The guard ran to Warrick.

Warrick said, "Guard. Find Lord Ross-Templar, Drayton, and Morgan, bring them here."

In minutes, Warrick's three brothers ran up the outer-battlement wall steps.

Lord Warrick said, "Drayton, I want you to send twelve archers up the mountains. I do not, I repeat, I do not, want them to engage in battle. Observe only. Do not let them see you. I need to know who carries those torches. I only want to know who and why they carry them. Tell the archers not to engage in battle. Tell the archers to stay out of sight. Information, I only want information."

Drayton said, "Yes, but I want to lead them."

Drayton held the grip of his bow and bounded down the battlement steps. He ran to awaken his archers.

DESCENDED OUT OF SIGHT.

A few moments later twelve archers threw ropes over the darker side of Rose Fire. They descended out of sight of a possible enemy. Guards pulled the ropes back up.

Marian said, "My lord, are you sure that you want to risk your best archers? Even risk Drayton on the mountainside."

Warrick said, "Marian. Drayton and his archers are skillful spies. If anyone can find out who is up there with those torches, they will."

Ross-Templar, Morgan, Warrick and Marian watched. Watched Drayton and his archers run up the mountainside. They ran toward the snaking line of bright orange torches.

Marian pulled Warrick's large black cloak tighter around her shoulders. As always, the bay leaf aroma caused her to feel safe.

Marian walked with Warrick, Ross-Templar, and Morgan. She wore a warmer gown under Warrick's extra black cloak. The albino rabbit lining was soft and warm against her skin. She had clasped it around her neck and wrapped it around herself. She had to bunch the black leather in her arms. To lift it off the battlement floor. The bay leaf aroma brought her deep happiness.

Marian walked up and intertwined her arm with Warrick's arm.

Warrick asked, "Marian. Who handed you the parchment?"

Marian said, "No one, my lord. I found it on my bed."

Warrick said, "Anybody could have put it on your bed. I left it atop other parchments in the solar."

Morgan said, "Anyone. Perhaps."

Marian said, "Perhaps not. Warrick. My intuition tells me to avoid Blanche. I want you to avoid Blanche."

Lord Warrick said, "Marian, is that an order or a request?"

Marian raised her chin and said, "An order, my lord."

MY LADY, THAT I MUST ALWAYS OBEY.

Warrick embraced her. He smiled and said, "You are my lady. My lady that I must always obey."

Marian laughed. She said, "Yes. I am your lady that you must always obey."

Warrick, Ross-Templar, Morgan and Marian stayed out on the outer wall battlement. In the moon of the Vigils witches' hours they watched the archers climb the mountain. They watched them approach the line of torches.

Warrick gazed up on the mountain side. He closed his arms tighter around Marian and glanced down at her face. He whispered, "I see your beautiful countenance everywhere. All day, as I renovate Rose Fire."

Marian pointed. She said, "Look, the fires, torches, formed into a circle."

Morgan, Warrick, Ross-Templar and Marian said nothing. Not a word, for hours. Simply because they might miss some important glimpse.

The sight of the torches fascinated Marian.

Finally she pointed and whispered, "Why to they appear to dance in circles? What kind of ceremony or dance could it be?"

Lord Warrick said, "We must wait. The archers will know. We must be quiet or we will miss a vital detail. We must be quiet."

At first Marian's brow formed a V of anger as she felt insulted. Insulted that he told her to be quiet. Then she grew a little bit more in wisdom. She quieted, recognized the importance of watching every detail on the mountain. She hugged Warrick.

Then Matins bells announced the end of the three hours of Witches. The moon of Matins and very early Prime bells moved across the black sky. Deepest, coldest, darkest night before the dawn came. Thick fog blanketed the valley. The moon glowed off the fog. Wind blew the glowing fog like great ocean waves. The fog-waves crashed in slow motion against Rose Fire. Then the fog waves descended in slow motion.

Warrick said, "Wickedness, evil is in this fog. If it moves up the mountain, Ross, his archers could fall into a ravine. A fall into a ravine could kill them."

Morgan said, "We must wait."

They had stood for hours and waited for the archers to return.

Warrick said, "Marian. You are beginning to understand your important position. That is why you stay out here with us?"

Marian said, "Yes, my lord."

Stronger Prime bells rang. The frightening torches on the mountains faded. The first light of dawn rose over the valley.

Warrick pointed through the thick fog. He said, "I see Drayton and his archers."

RUNNNNNN.

Warrick roared, "Drayton, RUN. Enemy, Skinwalkers are behind you, RUN."

Then Warrick and his brothers shot crossbow-blessed-arrows at the Skinwalkers. Blessed arrows tipped with Marian's Damascus steel. Crossbows of layers of Marian's Damascus steel. Crossbows of steel, not wood.

Morgan shouted, "We felled the Skinwalkers."

Warrick said, "Marian. With your crossbows of Damascus steel layers, we can fell any enemy. Your Damascus steel crossbows shoot much further than wood or iron crossbows."

Morgan said, "Marian. Deadly, especially with your blessed arrowheads of Damascus steel."

They watched Drayton and his archers run toward the drawbridge. Guards lowered the drawbridge and raised the portcullis.

The captain of the archers shouted, "Lord Warrick. It is just a wild group of Druid worshipers. They danced naked in the high mountain snow as if the Devil's demons possessed them."

DECEPTION.

Up on the mountain Wolv said to mercenaries, "Swale. Gulum. Warrick's spies did not suspect that the Druids were really your mercenaries. We are making Warrick's knights accustomed to torches, mercenaries, on the mountain."

Wolv turned to Gulum. He said, "I want the torches to appear every night. Every night from Compline through Vigils Witches hours, Matins' bell up to Prime bells. Every night at the same hours from now until we capture Marian."

-
-
-
-

CHAPTER, Where: Rose Fire, Wales, Year @ 1250s A.D.

SKINWALKERS AFTER HER, AGAIN

Marian strode with her head high, out to where Lord Warrick had been. Out through the bailey, out over the drawbridge and into the artisans work benches.

She asked, "Where is Lord Warrick?"

A stonemason said, "He wanted to discuss something with you. I know not what. He has gone to the quarry with the master mason to find better stone."

She turned to a stable boy and said, "Saddle my horse. I want to visit the quarry. It is very close."

The stable boy said, "Yes, my lady. The pink-white marble quarry is very close. Just a short ride."

He led Marian's horse across the drawbridge and said, "My lady. Fourteen knights are putting on their blessed-armor to protect you. They are coming. It is such a short ride to the quarry."

Marian said, "Help me up."

He cupped his hands. She put a foot in his hands and mounted her horse. She sat sidesaddle with her right knee locked around a lady's horn. Then she rubbed her heel against the horse's ribs. Her horse galloped down the red-clay mountain-road. Marian winded down the road, out of view.

She thought that her escorts of fourteen armored knights were directly behind her. They were not.

The squire shouted, "Oh My God, Lady Marian. You have no protection. You need knights with you. Wait for your escort of knights."

She did not hear. She galloped down the twisted road, beyond their sight and protection.

In seconds, the stable boy ran back to the stables and shouted, "Marian. Marian took a horse to the quarry by herself. Hurry. Hurry."

Ross-Templar shouted, "Morgan, Drayton, hurry, Marian is in danger. The sprite is in danger."

THE ANTICHRIST ATTACKS.

From far off, below the castle, Wolv saw Marian on her horse gallop. Gallop down the mountain red ribbon-like road. He shouted, "Prepare to attack, Marian will be mine today."

ALONE, AGAIN.

None of the knights with Ross-Templar, Morgan, and Drayton wore blessed-armor or mail.

Ross-Templar shouted, "Mount any horse you can find. We ride. Marian has ridden to the quarry without protection."

Ross-Templar' warhorse reared and pranced in a circle. He shouted, "We must divide and take the two roads to the quarry."

The knights pulled bridles onto their horses and rode them bareback.

Ross-Templar pointed. He said, "We must divide." He pointed to several knights and said, "You gallop down the narrow road. The rest of us will gallop down the wagon road. Pray that we have no battle, we have no blessed-armor or mail. Ride hard. Ride fast. Now ride for Marian. Speed is our best weapon.

They thundered across the drawbridge.

At a fork in the road they divided into two groups.

Ross-Templar hollered, "Without blessed-armor and even mail we are very vulnerable to attack by longbows." He repeated, "Ride hard. Ride fast. Now ride for Marian. Surprise and speed are our greatest weapons."

Their war horses shook the ground, kicked up earth, and galloped down the mountain side.

ALONE, AGAIN.

Lady Marian heard hooves pound the earth behind her. She thought that they were her fourteen knight escorts.

They were not.

They were Wolv and Skinwalkers.

She laughed and gloried in the bright morning Terce bell's sun. Very early Sext bells rang. The wind blew back her golden hair. She felt as if she were riding on her father's estate on her favorite gelding. Her long blond hair blew in the air behind her.

Marian shouted to the sky, "Like my father's fields and the days of racing. Lord Warrick will smile when he sees me."

SKINWALKERS.

Wolv and his Skinwalkers behind her grew closer. She heard their horse's hooves but she thought that they were her escorts.

Her horse galloped within sight of Lord Warrick.

Wolv immediately saw Warrick and veered off into the trees to hide. The rest of the Skinwalkers came to a stop in the now black clay road.

Lord Warrick and his knights were on their war horses. Horses and men wore full armor. They turned to the sounds of Wolv's horses. Quickly they unsheathed their blessed swords and axes.

The joy of the ride made Marian laugh. She reined in beside Lord Warrick and said, "My lord. Why do you greet me with weapons? I am no harm."

It was a very short ride. Marian thought the hooves pounding behind her were her escorts. Not Skinwalkers.

Ross-Templar and Morgan and unarmored knights on warhorses surprised the Skinwalkers from behind. They pulled their blessed swords and slashed through the Skinwalkers. They knocked many of them off their horses. The surprise was so quick that the Skinwalkers' other horses reared. The horses threw the Skinwalkers to the ground and trampled them.

Ross-Templar and his knights burst into the grassy field that lead up to the quarry.

Lord Warrick watched the wounded Skinwalkers gallop off into the forest.

Warrick shouted, "Drayton. Morgan. Make sure that everyone does their hour of Perpetual Adoration in Rose Fire's Chapel. Or in the Adoration wagon. Perpetual Adoration of Jesus' Real Presence in the Blessed Sacrament. Make sure everyone does weekly confession. Remember our great victory at Hallstatt, Austria. We brought our Adoration wagon out into the battlefield's center. A knight did Adoration in the Wagon in the battlefield. Instantly Adoration chased away the red-fog. The red-fog descended into the earth, into Hell where it belongs. Wolv did not kill even one Hallstatt soldier. Adoration kept Wolv and Lilith and the red-fog from harming anyone in Hallstatt. The Lord of Hallstatt never believed that Adoration saved him."

Morgan said, "Lord Warrick. My brother, your word is our command. We know that you know the means of great victories. You are the world's only hope against the AntiChrist and Lilith."

Warrick said, "Adoration and weekly confessions are the means of great victories. Great victories over the AntiChrist."

Warrick turned to Lord Morgan and whispered, "I just saw Wolv?"

Lord Morgan said, "Those Skinwalkers were his spy patrol."

Drayton's group of unarmored knights burst from the alternative narrow forest road. They galloped into the grassy field. Then they galloped down to the quarry.

Marian's original escort of knights thundered into the clearing.

Ross-Templar rode up to Lord Warrick where Marian could not see. Ross pulled an arrow from the heel of his boot. He put his split heel of his boot on his saddle. Then he laughed and said, "Call me the Earl of Good Omens."

Warrick saw Ross-Templar pull the arrow from his heel and smiled. He said, "Ross. Providence is surely looking over you. Though, hundreds of cuckolded husbands are surely looking for you."

Drayton reined in and whispered, "Warrick. Will you tell her of the danger?"

Lord Warrick shook his head, "No."

Drayton knew what Warrick meant. That he did not want Marian to know that she was seconds from death. Death or worse.

Warrick sat on his war horse and pulled off his helmet. He gave it to his squire. Then he reached over and grabbed Marian's saddle and bridle. He pulled her horse to himself.

He held Blessed Dread in one hand. Then he leaned over to her and said, "Hug my neck."

She did.

With one arm around her waist, Warrick lifted Marian off her horse. Warrick placed her on his saddle, behind his shield.

Warrick remembered the horror that Wolv put her through in the attempted capture. His teeth ground and he vibrated in rage.

He thought of the words that he shouted to Wolv. Deeper in Wales, when Wolv tried to capture her. 'Wolv. You will pay for this.'

Then he turned his eyes to Marian. Her beauty filled him with joy, and happiness. The overwhelming joy that fills a man with wonderful peace. With comfort when he gazes into her beautiful eyes. The joy when her beauty fulfills him. Beauty that gives his life meaning, purpose, and happiness. All because he cherishes her beauty. All because he adores her beauty, because he loves her.

A tear filled Warrick's eye.

He knew he had almost lost his spry, happy, impetuous sprite. He had almost lost his happiness.

She touched his eyelid and asked, "Why the tear?"

Warrick lied, "Just a chip of quarry stone in my eye."

Lord Warrick said, "Marian. You have all the exuberant foolishness of youth."

She turned to her many escorts that had galloped from Rose Fire. Galloped crucial minutes too late after she did.

She said, "I was not foolish this time. See all my escorts, and it was such a short ride."

Morgan's horse reared. He said, "It is time to return to the safety of Rose Fire."

Marian said, "My lord, it is not a stone in your eye. You are happy to see me. Why? One moment you turn my winepress hut into an arrow maker's hut. The next moment you shed a tear for me. You are an enigma to me."

Warrick said, "You are an enigma to me."

All but lady Marian knew what had happened. All but lady Marian knew that Wolv almost captured her . . . again.

She beamed innocent happiness. Her eyes reflected the sunlight. Her smiling lips were rosy.

She thought, "He is beginning to need me more each day. I pray he is loving me. Loving me beyond his sense of duty and honor."

SEXT OBSESSIONS.

Suddenly, off in the thick forest, Wolv howled. " My God, my God, why have you forsaken me?"

Marian said, "My God. Wolv was behind me?"

Warrick said, "Yes, Marian. The AntiChrist is in the forest captured by his Sext obsessions. My love. Wolv almost captured you again. My knights just happen to ambush his Skinwalkers from behind. Or, my Love, Wolv would have captured you. Please temper your youthful enthusiasm with wisdom."

Black flame shot out of Wolv's mouth and ascended into the sky. The black flame covered the sky and blocked out the light.

The AntiChrist came out of his Sext obsessions too late to attack them.

He stalked them from the dark shadowy forest. Saliva born of hatred dripped from Wolv's lip.

Wolv thought, "I will find out if Marian is Pamia. I do not care how much blood that I must spill. If she is not Marian, I will use her to trap Warrick. Then in revenge on Warrick I will eat Marian alive in front of Warrick."

-

-

-

CHAPTER, Where: Rose Fire Castle, Wales, When: Around 1250s A.D.

HE WILL DIE IF YOU DO NOT OBEY HIM.

The next day Marian was with Warrick. They stood at a stonemason's table. He opened large scrolls of proposed building plans. He studied them, then he pointed at sections of Rose Fire. Warrick said, "I want you to heighten the tops of the outer walls. Make the inner wall taller. I want you to make the inner wall slope. Slope like Syria's Castle Krak des Chevaliers' talus."

A stone mason ran to him with drawings and said, "My lord. You must choose the type of mortar. We are late shaping the slope of the inner wall's talus."

Warrick waved the stonemason aside. He said, "Marian. I must return to the bailey to continue refurbishing the castle."

Warrick returned to the bailey.

Marian walked with Warrick. She walked across the bailey up to Warrick and twined her arm on his forearm.

Warrick said, "Marian. Look around at my knight's expressions. Expressions as they look at you."

Marian said, "I see no change. They still wear their red and green sashes and flasks of holy water."

IN THE BLACK MOUNTAINS.

High in the Black Mountains, Swale said. "If God existed, I would pray that Wolv completely fulfills Wolv's wishes."

A flock of crows appeared beside Swale. The crows came together and formed Wolv. Wolv said, "Swale. I can assure you that God does exist. He does exist and that he does not listen to your prayers. Unless you repent your sins, then I will kill you. Give your soul to Satan. Satan will give you your wishes."

IN ROSE FIRE
In Rose Fire's bailey, Warrick held Marian's hand and led her to Father Malachi Martin. Father Malachi put his hand on Marian's arm.

Then Father Malachi's hand jumped from Marian's arm as if someone had hit him.

Father Malachi grimaced and held his hand. He said, "Marian. The Pendragon curse is too strong in you. The curse is so strong in you that it almost broke my hand and wrist. Beware my lady. The Pendragon curse is strong in you. I felt it in you as if a spear pierced my hand."

Father Malachi sighed. He said, "Remember, I am weak. I can help you or Warrick very little."

Marian sat beside Father Malachi and said, "You told us that already, we know."

Malachi warned, "I cannot help. Remember. Some loves must be. Warrick will die if . . ."

Malachi's head fell forward as he fell asleep.

Marian went to the infirmarian to help the injured.

Father Malachi woke and whispered, "Marian. Lord Warrick will die if you do not obey him."

-

-

-

CHAPTER, Now in Rose Fire, Wales, Year @ 1250s A.D.

TRAITOR.
Later Warrick and Marian walked into Father Malachi's chambers.

Marian asked, "Warrick. You and your brothers do not wear the red-green sash and flasks of holy water? Why?"

Warrick said, "Ross-Templar spends his free time saying the Rosary for Lady Innocence. He has no time to worry about curses and witches. Morgan and Drayton spend too much time in war-practice to worry."

Father Malachi pointed at Marian and said, "My lady. Witches and warlocks know who to fear. They fear Lord Warrick. They know that Lord Warrick's honor, love, and courage are stronger than witches or warlocks."

Then Father Malachi said, "My lord, my lady, I must sleep."

Warrick and Marian stepped outside Father Malachi Martin's chambers. Into Marian's solar, they closed Father Malachi's door. Then they walked down to the baileys' well.

At the well, Warrick took off his cloak, leather blouse, and boots. He emptied a full bucket of cold water over his head. He filled it again. Warrick drank from the bucket as water ran from the sides of his mouth. It ran into his leggings. He poured another bucket of water over his head. Then he lowered his head forward and threw it back. His long wet black hair flung water in high sparkling arcs across the bailey. Onto Marian.

Marian stood soaked with her arms out. The cold water shocked her. She stood with her eyes round and her mouth wide open. The water from Warrick's hair had soaked her hair and gown. Water ran down her hair, face and arms. The cold water chilled her so that she could not breathe. Water ran down her blond hair over her eyes, nose, and mouth.

Marian shouted, "You . . . you . . . you."

Warrick said, "Me . . . me . . . me . . . what?"

Warrick threw back his head and laughed.

She held out her hands and shook water from them.

He grabbed his big black cloak. The one lined with brown squirrel and threw it around Marian's shoulders.

Marian blew hair from her lips. She kicked his chin.

He laughed all the louder. He pulled his leather blouse on and pulled on his boots.

Marian attempted without success to blow her wet blond hair away from her lips. She wiped hair away from her eyes.

Warrick's thick black cloak warmed her.

She sighed and calmed herself.

Then she whispered, "Lord of Cold Water, when we first met, why?"

He laughed and said, "You look like you just fell into a lake."

Then Marian pulled his cloak tighter around her shoulders. Quickly she reached up and grabbed a fistful of hair on his chest. She said, "Stop laughing at me or . . ."

Warrick could not stop his laughter.

Marian pulled out a fistful of his chest hair.

Warrick grimaced and roared in laughter.

Marian blew water drops from her lips and marched to her chambers. Warrick followed, in laughter. Marian slammed her chamber door in Warrick's face.

He opened the door and dried Marian's hair with a large towel. He could not stop his laughter.

In her chambers she pivoted and hit him in the belly. He only laughed. His laughter was too contagious.

She glanced up at him. She smiled and giggled. His laughter was so contagious that she hugged him and began to laugh.

Warrick dried her hair.

She stood behind a screen and changed into a dry gown. Again, she wrapped his black cloak with the albino fur lining around herself.

HOLY-MARY OBSESSION.

Warrick said, "Listen. Again Wolv shakes the Black Mountains. Wolv screams, "Little Wolv. I will always love you."

IN THE BLACK MOUNTAINS.

Black-red flames shot out of Wolv's mouth and covered the sky.

IN ROSE FIRE.

Lord Warrick said, "Marian. Ancient Symon of Cyrene recorded when Wolv was six-years-old he always ran to Holy Mary. Ran to Holy Mary when the Egyptian children called him Ugly Eyes. Wolv was born with a multiple-pupil eye. In Egypt, Wolv came to love Holy Mary. Guilt eats at Wolv because he Crucified Jesus, Holy Mary's son. Wolv saw Holy Mary watch Wolv Crucify Jesus. The AntiChrist's love for Holy Mary tortures him."

Warrick put his other cloak on his shoulders. He held out his arm and said, "Come with me to the bailey. I must supervise the artisans."

Marian twined her arm on Warrick's arm. They walked to the bailey.

In the bailey Marian held Warrick's arm.

Warrick took Marian by the upper arms. He looked around to assure that no one would hear him. He said, "Marian. The truth is. In the peace of Oxford I could trust you with the truth. Here in this battlefield, I must be very careful with what I tell you. You will act upon what I tell you as if you lived in Oxford. You are sincere so you are learning fast. Soon I will tell you everything. Soon you will have the wisdom to be the lady of Rose Fire."

IN THE BLACK MOUNTAINS HIGH ABOVE ROSE FIRE.

From high above Rose Fire, Wolv gritted his teeth in hatred. He looked down into Rose Fire and watched Marian take Warrick's arm.

He said, "Gulum. I will destroy the world to have Marian. I will have Marian."

IN ROSE FIRE. MUCH LATER.

Marian looked out her window and said, "Collette. Compline bells. More night torches on the mountains. The lines of torches are longer."

Collette said, "My lady. Drayton believes that the Black Mountains are full of Druids. Wales is full of Druids. Druids live in thousands of caves. Caves in the Black Mountains. Drayton believes the Druids are celebrating the changing of seasons. Also, worshiping their tree-gods."

Marian said, "My intuition tells me Wolv is planning. The torches are Wolv's tricks to gather Skinwalkers closer to Rose Fire."

As Compline bells rang, Marian eased herself into a tub of hot water. Servants poured more hot water into the tub. She sighed and breathed in the steam. She wet a towel in the water and put it over her face. Then she fell asleep.

She heard, "My lady. Warrick's life depends on your obedience."

Marian took the towel from her face and said, "Father Malachi. How did you get in here? I locked the doors."

Father Malachi looked at her eyes and said, "My lady. I am not here."

Lady Marian blinked and no longer saw Father Malachi.

Then Marian spoke aloud, "Just a dream."

Then she heard Father Malachi, "Not a dream. Marian, I am always with you. Seen or unseen. Awake or asleep."

Marian put a towel over her breasts and shouted, "Get out. Get out."

Collette said, "You want me out. Wake, My lady. Take the towel from your face. My lady, wake."

Marian woke. She took the towel from her face and said, "Father Malachi was here."

Collette said, "No one was here. You were asleep in your tub. With that towel over your face.

Marian sighed and said, "Father Malachi. He is a spooky creature."

Collette carried an arm load of towels and said, "My lady. It is time for me to rinse you. I just came from Father Malachi's chamber off your solar. He is still asleep."

Collette rinsed, dried and helped Marian dress.

Then Warrick opened Marian's door and stepped inside.

Warrick said, "Finally, you have dressed. We will have some quiet time together."

TRAITOR.

The head mason banged on Marian's door and shouted, "My lord. The mortar is hardening in the buckets. A pin is missing from our hoist. The hoist on the top of the talus battlement. We need everyone to carry the buckets to the top of the talus battlement."

Blanche stood in the solar. She smiled and had the hoist-pin in her hand.

NO KISSES.

Warrick said, "Fate will not allow us to have any private time."

Marian hit her fist into a pillow.

Warrick ran out to the bailey. Collette reentered.

Servant, Collette brushed lavender into Marian's hair.

The latest Compline bells and the earliest Vigils bells rang.

Marian looked out her window and said, "Collette. I see more torches on the mountains. They might be closer. Even lower down the mountains."

Then Collette said, "My lady. I hear Vigils bells. Midnight. The dangerous three hours of Witches are about to begin. Lilith, the most powerful of all witches, is strongest in the Vigils hours. Servants have told me to stay inside at night. Some of them have seen Lilith fly as a dragon high above Rose Fire. Servants have said that she captures children and eats them."

Marian said, "Collette. My tomes record that Wolv can change into crows and eats people alive."

NOT EVEN A KISS.

Lord Warrick knocked on the chamber door. He said through the door, "Marian. We might have a quiet time together."

Marian said, "Collette. Leave me now Collette."

"Yes, my lady," Collette curtsied and walked out by way of the solar door.

Warrick entered.

She said, "Finally. She ran her palms along his face. As if she had never touched him until now. She glowed with happiness."

Marian felt that enormous peace and serenity that she felt when she first met him. The confidence and peace that she felt when he first hugged her.

NO KISSES.

-

-

-

CHAPTER, Now in Rose Fire, Wales, Year @ 1250s A.D.

NOT EVEN A KISS. TRAITOR.

Warrick tickled her ribs.

She laughed loud. Like a woman laughs when she knows that her lover cherishes her. Like when her lover teases her. It was a laugh from her belly and her soul.

She pulled his hand up and said, "Warrick. How I love your rough hands and calloused fingers."

TRAITOR.

Blanche stood in her solar outside Marian's chambers and listened.

Blanche thought, "I must stop this. Marian must not become pregnant with Warrick's child. Wolv will kill me if Marian becomes pregnant with Warrick's child. Wolv has warned me that Marian's progeny will change history."

Blanche turned to a servant and said, "Come, look out the window. You must get Nicola. Marian will want to see this. Marian must see this. You must get Nicola and take her to the battlement."

The servant entered Nicola's chambers and pulled Nicola and Collette to the outer battlement. The servant repeated, "Look, Marian must see this."

Nicola said, "Collette. You must go get Marian. She will want to see."

Collette banged the door and said, "I am sorry. My lady, my lord, but . . . Nicola is calling you, I think something is wrong. Forgive me . . . Nicola wants you to come to her. I think that she is in trouble."

Marian said, "Warrick, we are cursed to have no private time. If Nicola is not in trouble, I will make sure she is in trouble. In trouble with me."

Warrick laughed and said, "Fate will not allow us quiet time."

Warrick and Marian walked out onto the battlement where Nicola stood.

On the battlement a stonemason walked up to Warrick and said, "My lord. We need your permission to use the new tiles on the keep floors. You must approve them first."

Marian asked, "Nicola, what is so important?"

Nicola pointed and said, "Look. Look what is in that wagon."

Marian said, "I can barely see through the Witches hours' midnight fog."

Nicola said, "The wagon has the largest andiron I have ever seen. It is the wagon's full length and width with a huge matching iron-pot."

Marian seethed with anger at love's lost kiss. She gently smacked Nicola in the back of the head.

She said, "Nicola, if . . . if I had a pot, I would smack you with it."

FAR UP ON THE MOUNTAIN SIDE, THE ENEMY'S CAMP.

Far up on the mountain side Wolv drew maps in the snow for his Skinwalkers. He said, "This is how we will storm Rose Fire and capture Marian."

Wales' Lord David de Gruffydd, the head mercenary, said, "Wolv. I and many others pay you to capture castles. I do not pay you to run after a woman called Marian. You must give up this obsession over Marian."

Wolv could barely hold himself back from cleaving Lord Ap. Gruffydd. His face turned red and tight in anger and his jaw muscles bulged. He would have cleaved Gruffydd. Yet, he needed Gruffydd because the mercenaries were loyal to Gruffydd.

IN ROSE FIRE ON TH BATTLEMENT.

Marian said, "My lord, It seems so unfair. How come Father Malachi Martin can walk outside Rose Fire whenever and wherever he wants?"

Lord Warrick grinned, "Rumor. How come? Because people believe that anyone that harms a druid has a curse on him. Father Malachi dresses like a druid."

Marian asked, "What?"

Warrick said, "Anyone that harms a druid has a curse on him."

Marian said, "My lord, who started that rumor?"

Then Warrick looked at Marian and grinned, "Long ago Father Malachi started that rumor."

Lady Marian grinned and said, "My lord, Father Malachi and you tell many lies."

Warrick said, "Part of the art of war and leadership is deception. A hundred warriors will run away from one warrior. One warrior, if they think he has some superstitious power. Or a mysterious weapon. Get a witch to lay a useless spell on the enemy. Then many of them will scatter in every direction."

Marian asked, "I suppose you also continue to lie to me?"

Warrick wanted to tease her and said, "Yes."

Marian said, "About what?"

He decided again to tease her.

He smiled and said, "So far, most everything."

Marian smiled. She said, "I am now accustomed to your sense of humor."

Lady Marian asked, "How do you obtain information about Wales so quickly?"

Warrick said, "I pay people to get information to me very quickly. The quicker the more I pay spies. From hilltop to hilltop, they used the identical flag symbols on merchant ships. They tell me information from every direction. Also, every mountain top has a signal fire for emergencies."

Warrick's eyebrows formed an angry V.

He said, "Marian, your safety depends upon your obedience."

Marian said, "Obedience, obedience, obedience. Obedience cannot solve all problems."

Warrick ran his hand through his hair as he always did when women baffled him. Marian and only Marian baffled him.

HIGH UP IN THE BLACK MOUNTAINS.

Up on the mountain in a cave Wolv sat with some of his Skinwalkers.

He said, "Gulum, Marian's weakness is compassion. She will disobey Warrick if her compassion demands it. I plan to use her compassion."
-
-
-

CHAPTER, Now in Rose Fire, Wales, Year @ 1250s A.D.

IN ROSE FIRE. MARIAN'S CHAMBER.

Father Malachi said, "Marian, you must be obedient to Warrick. Please learn from my lord's wisdom."

A tear formed in Marian's eye. Then she straightened her back and leveled her jaw.

She thought, "I have felt enough pain. I have shed enough tears. I will be strong. No one will cause me to cry again. I can take Nicola anywhere and create businesses."

Malachi said, "You have felt enough pain. You have shed enough tears. You can be strong. No one will cause you to cry again. You can take Nicola anywhere and create businesses."

Marian snapped, "You read my thoughts? Father Malachi, you are a wraith?"

Father Malachi said, "Finally, You are again the strong twenty-some-year-old woman. That administered the largest, wealthiest estate from Oxford to London."

Marian said, "Yes. Father Malachi."

Marian went to her room to change her gown for the Nones bell's prayers.

Lord Warrick knocked on her chamber door.

She said, "Enter if you have praise, leave if you have criticism."

Lord Warrick smiled. He opened the door of Marian's chambers. He saw Marian stand in her royal red velvet gown. She wore a silver waist chain. It had an emerald encrusted sheath and dagger between her thighs.

Warrick said, "You are magnificent, beautiful. Marian, something outside waits for you."

-

-

-

CHAPTER, Now in Rose Fire, Wales, Year @ 1250s A.D.

WEALTH TO SHARE WITH THE POOR. CALM BEFORE THE STORM.

Marian looked out her window, the highest window in Rose Fire. She saw a line of wagons and knights climbing the mountains toward the castle.

She said to herself, "What could be in all that cavalcade?"

Collette dashed through the door and said, "Lady Marian. Wonderful news, heavenly news, your bride price has arrived."

Collette opened the door. She said, "Come my lady. Look down the stairs. They are bringing much of your bride price up to your chamber."

Marian said, "Collette, find Nicola, this is so exciting, bring Nicola."

Surprise rounded Marian's eyes. She put her hands to her cheeks in disbelief. Servants from the cavalcade wore brightly colored and puffed clothes. They filled the floor of her chambers and the adjoining solar. They carried sundry silver bowls, large and small jeweled chests, golden cups and saucers. Servants brought in oak chairs inlaid with silver. Also, a matching table. Upon it they put golden bowls and thick golden plates.

Marian opened chests of bright multicolored silk cloth. The cloth shone like jewels in the torch light. She pulled a handful to her cheek and smiled that it felt so smooth. The silk reflected rays of red, green, blue, and pink shades against her walls. She pushed on rolled rugs. They were Oriental rugs and tapestries. Of the most beautiful and exotic designs. She pushed one rolled rug. It hit a huge bejeweled box and turned it over.

Then Marian held her breath and put her hands to her mouth. A flood of colored sparkles poured from it. Emeralds, sapphires, amber, and rubies tumbled across the floor.

Marian said, "I had prayed to Jesus for wealth to help Wolv's victims. Finally I have the wealth to rebuild their homes and businesses. To rebuild Jesus' Churches that Wolv burned. Charity on earth will build us castles in Heaven in Jesus' Heart. Also, to make more Damascus steel to kill Wolv and his Skinwalkers."

Servants carried more Oriental rugs. With birds in flight and winged horses. She unrolled a large Flemish tapestry on the solar floor.

She opened the lid of a large coffer full of silver and gold waist-chains. They had silver and gold daggers hanging from the end. She pulled out the top layer of the coffer. A mound of gold coins.

Then she put her hand on the gold coins and she said, "Nicola. How could I have disobeyed such a wonderful man as

Warrick? How could I disobey my champion when he has so much love for me?"

Nicola said, "Marian Too often you open your mouth and shut your ears?"

Marian laughed. She shoved Nicola back onto the bed.

From a chest Marian pulled out bright pink, green, and yellow silk pillows. Pillows filled with goose-down.

Her eyes widened as she moved to a fragrant, tall Lebanon cedar chest. She reached in and unfolded linen bed sheets. Finer, softer, and whiter than she had ever seen.

Collette said, "My lady, this cloth is brighter than the Vigils' full moon. Brighter than the Vigil's bell, three hours of Witches, full moon."

Marian ran her hand across an ornately carved cedar bench. From underneath of it she slid out a cedar bed. A bed with a tick of wool and goose down. Covered with emerald green silk.

Then Marian pulled out another drawer of the cedar chest. She saw one of her favorite pastimes, collecting glass figurines for her menagerie. She ran her hands over dozens of molded solid glass figurines. Glass figurines of lions, bears, animals of all types. Marian pulled back a cloth and saw glass figurines of cats of all kinds. Warrick had them made because she loved cats. She pulled back another cloth to see glass figurines. Glass figurines of her father's Oxford Manor, Rose Fire, and the King's castles. Then she opened a small box and lifted silk. Under the silk was glass yellow and white crocuses with the thinnest petals.

Lady Marian opened the lid on another Lebanon cedar chest. She pulled out cowled coats and cowled cloaks of black squirrel. Red fox, grey fox, white squirrel, white rabbit, and white fox. The colors glowed in the sunbeams.

In the corner were many different sizes of golden harps. Lutes, different sizes and types of musical instruments.

Marian opened a large rosewood scribe's desk with a matching chair. Both with gold lines. Gold inlaid in the flow of the grain. The daylight reflected off the polished gold. It lit the room as if it were a torch.

She opened the desk top to see deer-hide vellums. Also, snow boots with white rabbit fur lining. The boots were heavy to her touch. Therefore, she emptied them into the desk. Rolls of transparent Egyptian papyrus and quill pins fell out. Also, a sealed jar of ink. Jewelry fell out, necklaces, ankle bracelets, prayer beads. All with diamonds, emeralds, amber, and sapphires.

Marian said, "For us Warrick has laid up treasure on earth. Now. Now we will lay up treasure in Heaven. Through charity. First, we defeat Wolv. Then, we will use this wealth to rebuild the towns Wolv destroyed. Rebuild warm homes. Rebuild successful businesses. First, we must defeat Wolv."

HOLY-MARY OBSESSIONS.

Marian said, "With all the echoes I cannot tell where Wolv is screaming. Wolv is screaming his Egyptian-Holy-Mary obsessions.

Wolv repeatedly screamed, "Little Wolv. I will always love you." Each scream shook the Black Mountains and vibrated Rose Fire Castle.

Marian said, "Nicola. Wolv is always near, always dangerous, always deadly. Look at the sky. See that Wolv's rage has filled the sky with his black flame."

MORE WEALTH TO SHARE WITH THE POOR.

Six male servants carried another large chest through her open chamber door. They placed it on her chamber floor beside her bed. They bowed. One asked, "My lady, we must return to the wagons. We must retrieve the rest of your bride price."

Marian said, "There is more?"

A servant said, "Yes, my lady, much More."

The servants walked out of Marian's chambers.

Marian opened the large chest to see a sea of emeralds and diamonds.

Nicola said, "Marian, you know that these are gifts, a bride price. You and Lord Warrick know that our father never required a bride price. You made him so wealthy that he could provide for us. Even if we married a man without much wealth. Lord Warrick has made you a wealthier woman."

Marian could only sigh.

She threw Warrick's extra great black cloak, the albino deer-fur lining, over her shoulders. Usually this was the only cloak that she wore. She ran barefoot from her chambers. She asked everyone she saw, "Where is my lord? Where is Warrick?" Marian stood on the cold pink -white granite outer-wall-battlement. The ice on the battlement sucked the warmth from her feet. Lady Marian was too happy and anxious to find Warrick. So happy that she did not notice the extreme pain of cold in her feet.

Morgan was on the battlement on Rose Fire's other side. He pointed down from the battlement to a stonemason. He shouted, "Because the wagons will hit them, stack the tiles away from the wagons."

Yards from Morgan, Drayton pushed torches' wooden handles into their circular iron holders.

Nearer to Marian, Ross-Templar gave orders to guards. He pointed to them to where he wanted them stationed.

Morgan and Drayton walked over to Ross-Templar.

Marian ran on the battlement around to the other side of Rose Fire. To the three brothers.

She said, "Where is my lord? Where is the Lord Warrick?"

Ross-Templar turned to her. He said, "My lady, you are barefoot. You will catch a lung humor. Run to your chambers and warm your feet."

Marian pulled Warrick's black cloak tighter around her legs. She said, "Where is my lord? Where is Warrick?"

Ross pointed down to the bailey. He said, "There with the stone masons."

Marian ran down the steps and ran across the bailey floor. She jumped and landed on Warrick.

WORTHY OF EVIL'S EFFORT.

Warrick fell backward against the wall of the well. It collapsed. Warrick fell into the artesian well and sank. The stone of the well's wall fell in open him.

He sank, unconscious.

Ross-Templar jumped off the battlement to the bailey. He landed with bent knees and on his hands. Then Ross ran to the well and dove in.

Precious moments passed. Ross came up and gasped. I need help. Morgan. Dive in and help me take rocks off Warrick."

Morgan dove into the well.

More precious time passed.

Ross and Morgan pulled Warrick out of the well.

Ross said, "Stones had covered Warrick. Warrick is not breathing."

Marian turned Warrick on his back and pushed on his chest. She said, "Ross. Push on Warrick's chest as I blow into his mouth."

They did.

BLOOD FLOWS FROM HIS HEAD.

Then Marian screamed, "Blood flows from his head."

Ross said, "Marian. Do not stop. Scalp wounds always bleed."

Marian breathed in Warrick's mouth. Ross shoved hard on Warrick's chest.

Water flowed from Warrick's mouth.

Warrick lay, drowned, bleeding heavily from his head.

Marian screamed, "I killed my betrothed."

"Not yet," Warrick coughed. He turned on his side and said, "No yet, Lady Bad Luck. Lady Hairy, horse-faced. A twelve-feet-tall, twelve-toed, sixteen-fingered bride. Though again, a good try, worthy of any Skinwalker."

Marian hugged him and wept.

His brothers helped him into the Great Hall. They placed him in a chair beside the flaming andiron. They put more logs into the andiron. Then they wrapped him in their own leather cloaks.

Marian brought him bowls of hot, thick, venison broth.

Warrick drank them and said, "Marian. Sit on my lap."

Marian sat on his lap. She wrapped his cut head.

Warrick said, "Marian. If I can survive your happiness, I can survive anything. Now put your bare feet to the andiron to warm them. Your feet are ice cold."

Marian cried herself to sleep in Warrick's hug and warmth.

Later Marian woke in her bed. She dressed in Warrick's cowled cloak and walked out onto the battlement.

Marian asked, "How did I get into my bed."

Ross said, "Marian. You fell asleep in Warrick's arms. He carried you up the keep steps and put you to bed."

Marian said, "Where is Lord Warrick?"

DANGEROUS PATROL.

Lord Ross-Templar said, "Marian. He and many of his knights galloped off to patrol the Wye valley. They hope to find the Skinwalkers camps."

Ross said, "Lady Marian. Why are you barefoot again? You know better than to be barefoot in this frozen castle."

Marian again wrapped Warrick's cloak tighter around her shoulders. She asked, "When will he return?"

Drayton pushed another torch into a circular iron wall fitting. Drayton said, "Warrick's return time is unknown. We do not know. Maybe sometime after Prime, after Wolv's Resurrection obsession. Perhaps even Sext bells with Wolv's first Crucifixion obsession. Or Nones Bells with Wolv's Crucifixion obsession, when Wolv speared Jesus in the side."

Marian said, "Drayton. You tell time by Wolv's obsessions."

Then Drayton said, "Marian, Wolv's obsessions are reliable. Wolv's, first, Resurrection, second, Nailing-to-the-Cross and, third, Jesus'-time-of-Death obsessions are reliable. When Wolv witnessed the Resurrection, Wolv's obsession at Resurrection-Prime. The nailing-to-the-cross at Sext bells, zenith sun, Wolv's Sext obsessions. Jesus' time-of-death, when Wolv speared Jesus' right side, at Nones bells. The canonical bells overlap and the monasteries use them for celebrations. Yet, Wolv's obsessions are much more consistent."

Morgan turned to a guard and said, "Give your boots to Marian. Then go to the leathery and find another pair for yourself."

The guard gazed at Morgan with surprised wide eyes and pulled his boots off.

Morgan knelt and pulled the huge boots onto Marian's small feet.

He said, "Marian. Please. Now return to your chambers while the boots are still warm. When Warrick returns and learns that you were barefoot, bad for us. Barefoot on the frozen battlement he will be very angry with you, . . . and us.

With each of her steps the huge boots clip-clopped on the pink granite. She returned to her chambers. She sat on the bed and looked at many chests she had not opened. Marian had no more room on the floor for her treasures.

Nicola pointed at the boots Marian wore and laughed.

Marian said, "Do not laugh, they are warm."

Marian looked comical in the large boots. She said, "Nicola, I can open no more gifts."

FOR THE POOR.

Lady Marian said, "After Warrick conquers Wolv, I have plenty of wealth. Wealth to hire artisans. We can make all the lumber and nails necessary to rebuild the valley's homes."

READ, READ, READ.

Nicola said, "Why did you have all the tomes brought to your bedchamber?"

Marian said, "Knowledge. I will help Warrick destroy or control Wolv with knowledge. Wolv has weaknesses that my creativity can exploit. Reading in all these ancient languages is our strongest weapon against Wolv. First, I must read everything about Wolv in all these tomes. Tomes in every language. The Chinese tomes have many secrets about Wolv. Tomes stacked high to the ceiling."

FOR THE POOR.

Nicola said, "My lord has made you a very wealthy lady. All of this is a gift to you."

Lady Marian said, "Yes. I had not expected or prepared for such riches or so much. We do not even have room for everything. I want to build schools for the children in Wye Valley."

Collette said, "The tears on your face show that my lord has taken your heart."

Marian said, "Yes. He did not have to give me such wealth. The king simply demanded this marriage. The marriage would have happened with or without a bride price. This is not a bride price. Nicola, this is a gift of wealth."

Nicola said, "I have seen him when he looks at you. Your beauty won his heart. He has sealed his love with these gifts."

A loud knock at the door attracted their attention.

Marian said, "Warrick has returned."

Marian opened it to see Drayton and eleven knights."

Lady Marian said, "I thought that you were Warrick?"

Drayton said, "No my lady. Warrick is still out on patrol."

The knights carried a heavy chest between two iron poles. They put the chest on the floor. Then they slid the heavy iron bars from the handles of the chest.

Drayton said, "My lady, may we take our leave."

Marian said, "Yes."

They turned and walked out.

She opened the chest. Here mouth fell open at the shine of uncountable gold coins.

Tears ran down her cheeks as she picked up a figurine in gold. The figurine was a replica of her precise likeness in a wedding gown.

That night Marian could not sleep. She walked the outer battlement. This time Marian wore rabbit-fur-lined boots. She walked the outer battlement and looked for Warrick to return. With Marian, on the outer battlement, Ross-Templar and Morgan walked the battlement all night. Marian stood in the black night darkness. The wind swirled unseasonable snowflakes from atop the Black Mountains. Her long, blond hair blew out over the battlement. Snowflakes settled in her hair.

Morgan elbowed Ross-Templar and said, "Now. You must have Marian return to her chambers. She will catch a deadly, breath humor if she stays out here with us."

Ross-Templar held the hilt of his blessed sword to steady it. He walked up to Marian and said, "My lady, you need not fear. My brother always returns. Warrick never fails. You must return to your chambers where it is warm."

Marian said, "I want to stay here."

Ross-Templar bowed low. He said, "My lady. When Warrick returns he will want to see you safe and warm. Think of him, it would break his heart if you were chilled and fevered. You do not want to break his heart, do you?"

Marian smiled. She said, "Ross-Templar, you are a man of too many soft words. No wonder women swooned at your words."

He held out his arm. She twined her arm around his. Together they walked back to her chambers.

A huge owl burst from the roof of Marian's keep. It snatched a mole on the red clay, stone-road that led to Rose Fire.

Ross-Templar said, "An owl, it is a good omen. According to Greek mythology, wise people always attract owls."

He pointed up, "Look, it nests in the roof of your keep. That means that you will soon accumulate wisdom."

Marian said, "Ross. So the Greek goddess of Wisdom, Athena, will bless me with wisdom?"

Ross led Marian to her bed chamber.

In her bedchamber, Ross-Templar put more logs onto the andiron. He pulled the tall mail curtain shut around the andiron.

Ross-Templar said, "My lady, may I have my leave to administer Rose Fire?"

Marian said, "You do not have to ask permission to leave my presence?"

Ross-Templar said, "My lady, you are to be the lady of Rose Fire. All but the Lord of Rose Fire must ask for permission to leave your presence. You are about to have a great and important position."

Marian said, "I have much to learn."

She raised her eyebrows in thought. She said, "Ross-Templar. I am beginning to understand my lord. Understand Warrick as himself, not as I wish him to be. I am beginning to understand Rose Fire as it is. Not as I imagined my life to be."

He bowed and said, "It is the beginning of wisdom."

He asked again, "My lady, may I have my leave to administer Rose Fire?"

Ross-Templar' constant formalisms helped her to understand her position. The lady of the castle, the love of the lord. She began to understand the formalisms. They were signs of the love from afar. Signs of respect all the knights had for her.

She said, "Yes, Lord Ross-Templar. You may go."

HOLY-MARY OBSESSION.

Ross said, "Marian. Listen. Wolv's obsessions constantly torment him."

Wolv repeatedly screamed Holy Mary's words in Egypt. "Little Wolv. I will always love you."

As always, Wolv obsessions shook the Black Mountains.

Ross said, "Danger is near. Death is always near, because Wolv is always near. Look at the sky. Wolv's black and red flames cover the sky and block out the light."

Marian said, "Ross-Templar. I am reading about Wolv's weaknesses. Can you find more tomes for me?"

Ross said, "I will send knights out. They will gather tomes from the surrounding monasteries. Monks and nuns in the monasteries spend their time copying manuscripts. They copy Vatican manuscripts. They will trust you with everything."

Slowly Wolv's Holy-Mary obsession faded away.

Marian said, "Ross-Templar. Though we cannot kill Wolv, I will read of a way to contain him."

Ross said, "My lady, may I have my leave?"

Marian said, "Yes."

Ross-Templar walked out again onto the battlement up to Morgan.

Morgan asked, "Ross. Will Marian sleep or will she be back out here again in the frost?"

Ross-Templar said, "She will be back out."

As Ross-Templar predicted, Marian came back out on the frozen battlement. Through the night she paced on the battlement. Through late Compline bells.

Marian said, "Ross. The torches' lines on the mountains grow longer each night. I fear that Wolv is amassing forces under the guise of Druid ceremonies."

Marian paced three hours on the battlement through the Vigils' Witches hours' bells. Then stiff unseasonable snow blew at Matins bells. She paced on the battlement. Snow gathered on her blond hair. Periodically, Marian walked back to her chambers to warm herself at her andiron. All night she paced and yearned and feared for Warrick.

The moon moved over the sky. She paced in worry and anticipation. The Prime bells rang in the first rays of the rising sun. As the Prime bells rang, the lines of torches on the mountains faded.

Marian said, "How beautiful the Wye Valley is in the early Prime sun."

IN THE BLACK MOUNTAINS, THE ENEMY'S CAMP.

High in the Black Mountains the Candlekeeper ran over to Wolv. He said, "Master. It is seconds from the Resurrection hour, the Prime bell's hour. You must seek safety deep in the earth.

The Wye Valley's Prime bells began to echo off the mountains.

Wolv fell sideways from his horse. On his knees, in snow, he yelled, "Jesus. Why can you not leave me alone?" His eyes glazed over black.

Then Wolv turned into black, pure, carbon dust and sunk into the Black Mountains. Deeper. He came to rest at the foot of an underground waterfall. He changed his form from black, pure, carbon dust to his original Roman uniform general.

Trapped in his memory, he watched again the stone roll from Jesus' tomb.

He fell to his knees and put his hands over his eyes. Over his eyes to try to block out the memory.

Still he saw Jesus walk from the tomb, brighter than the sun. Dressed in a white gown.

On his knees, Wolv held out his hands and begged, "Jesus. Leave me alone."

Jesus stood and looked at Wolv.

Wolv begged, "Jesus. Raise Pamia from the dead for me. Please Jesus. Please. My heart is empty. I am so alone. Pamia is my heart."

Pamia appeared before Wolv. She said, "My beloved. You have only to ask Jesus for forgiveness for your sins."

Wolv growled, "Never, never. I serve Satan. Satan has given me castles all over the world. Come with me Pamia and serve Satan with me. Serve Satan with me and live in my many castles."

Jesus and Pamia disappeared.

At the foot of the underground waterfall Wolv growled, "Pamia, Pamia. Please return to me, Pamia."

Wolv's rage turned into black-red flames that filled the cavern.

Wolv came out of his Resurrection obsession. He changed into pure charcoal dust and ascended through the earth.

IN ROSE FIRE

Morgan said, "Feel the Black Mountains rumble. Wolv in his Resurrection hour obsessions. Marian. Listen to how Wolv's obsessions for Pamia shake the mountains. Shake Rose Fire. He shouts Pamia repeatedly. The AntiChrist's obsession over Pamia convinces me that Wolv's love for Pamia will defeat him. Pure love will defeat Wolv one day."

The ground ceased to shake as Wolv's Resurrection obsession faded.

Marian said, "How beautiful Rose Fire and the Wye Valley are. Especially in the early morning Prime prayer bells.

Marian said, "Morgan. Even with Wolv's howling, I begin to feel at home at Rose Fire."

The Wye Valley was lush and warm. Yet, frost sparkled on Rose Fire's stones and the mountains above Rose Fire. Wye Valley was lush and green. Yet, the mountains from Rose Fire up to the peak's snow line were brown. Brown with lifeless trees and withered shrubs. For weeks, the mountains had not had enough rain.

So she stood on the battlement and walked. She watched the guards walk back and forth. She felt protected and safe. More than any other time, she appreciated the beauty of the early morning Wye valley. The splendor of Rose Fire.

She walked back and forth and anxiously waited for Warrick to come home.

THE ENEMY AT THE TREE LINE.

No one noticed Wolv at the practice field's tree line. Wolv and some of his Skinwalkers walked around Rose Fire. They searched for military weaknesses.

Wolv looked up to the battlement and spotted Marian. Spittle dripped from his lower lip. His eyes turned blood shot from hatred of Warrick.

Wolv pointed at a section of Rose Fire. He growled, "Rose Fire is weak at that spot. When we use it, we will capture Marian."

The full day grew long. Morning Prime shadows shortened into Terse shadows, as the sun higher. Slowly shadows disappeared in the zenith sun's Sext's bells. Hours past, shadows grew on the eastern sides of trees. The Nones bells began to ring.

With early Vespers bells the shadows extended far to the east. Shadows far to the east as the sun set in the west. All day Marian still walked the battlement and waited for Warrick.

Then bedtime Compline bells chimed.

Marian said, "Knight, more lines of torches on the mountains. They form at Compline bells. I fear the regularity of the appearance of the torches. Every day they descend the Black Mountains. A little each day."

A young knight beside Marian said, "My lady. We have investigated. They are harmless druids gathering for religious ceremonies."

The Black Mountains evening shadows spread across the valley like a great coverlet. The Black Mountains shadows put the valley to sleep. Like a father that spreads covers over his children's bed.

In the dusk, Warrick rode with his patrol up the mountain. Teams of horses pulled four wagons behind them.

Marian saw them and beamed with happiness.

THE CHAMPION. DYING.

When they rode close, Marian waved from the battlement and shouted, "My lord."

The earl waved and smiled said, "Marian, . . ."

Warrick tried to say 'my love.'

He collapsed and fell from the back of Zeus.

A pool of blood formed on the ground around Warrick.

-

-

-

CHAPTER, Now in Rose Fire, Wales, Year @ 1250s A.D.

WARRICK INJURED DYING.

Marian put her hands to her cheeks and screamed. She ran down to the drawbridge.

A knight yelled, "My lord has lost too much blood."

Ross-Templar grabbed Warrick's shoulders.

Drayton and Morgan clasped their arms together under Warrick.

Ross-Templar said, "Carry him to the best chambers, Lady Marian's chambers."

A knight followed Warrick.

Ross-Templar said, "What happened?"

A knight said, "We finished our patrol. Then my lord purchased thyme honey and potted daisy plants for the wedding. Suddenly, Wolv's Skinwalkers attacked us as we crossed a bridge. We were on one end of the bridge. Lord Warrick was on the other end. The lord would not abandon the wagons of thyme honey and potted daisy plants. Skinwalkers divided Warrick from us and beat on him. My lord cleaved them with Blessed Dread and Zeus trampled the rest."

Another knight said, "My lady. My lord must really love you. To be willing to die for just thyme honey and daisy plants."

Another knight said, "After the fight, the bank along the Wye River collapsed under Zeus. My lord was under the cold murky water for too long. His blessed-armor held him under. The current pushed him downstream. An older woman that lived in a hut pulled him from the river. Or he would have drowned."

They laid Warrick on Marian's bed.

TRAITOR.

Blanche untied the strips of bandages around Warrick's wound. Blood spurted out with each beat of his heart.

At the sight of the new blood, Marian's anger rose. She quickly realized that she was the only one trained in the healing arts. Not Blanche.

She pushed Blanche out of the way and retied the wounds. The bleeding stopped.

Blanche pushed Marian aside and untied Warrick's bandages.

Warrick bled again.

Then Marian grabbed Blanche by the hair and flung Blanche against the pink granite wall.

Blanche's head bounced off the wall. She fell unconscious. Her head bounced off the floor.

Marian tightened Warrick's bandages. The bleeding stopped.

Blanche tried to sit up. She supported herself with her arms.

Marian kicked Blanche's arms away.

Then for the second time, Blanche's bounced on the granite floor with a thud. Blanche lay crumbled unconscious.

After several minutes, Blanche held her head. The Traitor, Blanche sat on the floor and leaned against the wall.

Blanche thought, "When Marian protects Warrick, Marian is a tigress, a dangerous tigress."

Marian held Warrick's wounds with one hand. With the other hand she pointed to the door and shouted, "Blanche. I will not allow your stupidity to harm Warrick. You know nothing of healing. Get out. Run. I swear by God's Robe. I will grab your hair and throw you off the battlement to your death."

Blanche stumbled to her feet. Her eyes grew round in fear. She said, "Yes, and I know you would throw me off the battlement."

Blanche ran from Marian's room to her own chambers."

Marian said, "Reque. You must heat a dagger in the brazier, quickly. Collette. Find Father Malachi. You must bring him here now. Otan, I want you to bring the tomes from Nicola's room."

Warrick opened his eyes and whispered, "Marian, I love you. I love you and I love no other."

Marian was too busy to hear him.

His head fell to the side, unconscious.

Tears streamed down Marian's cheeks.

She said, "I love you. I need you, my lord. I love you more than I want life itself."

Marian held the red-hot dagger. She raised her eyebrows in an inverted V of compassion and worry. Intensity thinned and widened her lips.

Ross-Templar and Drayton held Warrick down.

Marian said, "I cannot harm him more."

Ross-Templar said, "You must, you must, hurry, stop the bleeding."

Drayton said, "Quick, press the dagger to the wounds until they stop bleeding."

To concentrate she squinted. She pressed the hot dagger to his flesh. The dagger steamed against his skin. She untied each strip and with each strip the dagger steamed against his skin. The earl was unconscious.

Marian saw Father Malachi and said, "We need unguents to pour on the wounds. Just, if they open again."

Father Malachi Martin leaned on his staff. He hobbled and sat in a chair. He opened a pouch, leaned forward on the chair. Then he poured unguents onto the wounds on Warrick's arm.

Ross-Templar, Morgan and Otan pulled the blessed-armor and mail from Warrick. Then they pulled off his padded leggings and padded blouse. He lay in only his loin cloth.

Marian threw a linen sheet over him and then a large sheepskin blanket.

-

-

-

CHAPTER, Now in Rose Fire, Wales, Year @ 1250s A.D.

WARRICK SICK RECOVERING?

Father Malachi again sat on a chair. He pointed at Warrick and said, "White as chalk, he is as white as chalk. Lost too much, he has lost much blood."

Marian said, "I have been so wicked. Warrick is such a good man, my love, my champion. Again, because of me, he could now die. Just to bring me thyme honey and yellow and white crocuses."

Father Malachi said, "Bring today's Boar stew broth. Any meat broth. We must put meat broth in his mouth. If he can swallow thick meat broth, he might live."

Warrick's brothers brought up bowls of meat broth. Marian dripped the broth into Warrick's mouth."

Marian cried, "My lord, my love, is swallowing."

Father Malachi said, "It is not just thyme-honey. It is love. The honey is a symbol of his love for you, another bride price. The flowers and honey are symbols of his love that he knows that you need."

Father Malachi leaned even harder on his staff. He put both hands on his cane and rested his head on his hands.

Old Father Malachi said, "Warrick fought to prove to you that he loves you. He knew how important the honey and yellow and white crocuses were to you."

Marian asked, "How can I help him now?"

Father Malachi said, "Stay with him. Place cold wet cloths under his armpits so he does not burn from fever."

Father Malachi pulled his chair over to the bed. He said, "Lord Morgan. Put all the tomes here on the bed so I can read them."

The tomes were in many languages from around the known world.

Father Malachi said, "Marian. Let Reque drip broth into Warrick's mouth. I want you to wash his body with warm water. I will read to see what the ancients would do for him."

A doctor from Hereford walked into Marian's chambers. He said, "We must bleed the illness out of him."

He took out his scalpel and turned the earl's wrist over.

Marian put a dagger to the doctor's throat and said, "You bleed him. Then I will cut your throat. I want you out of Rose Fire. You are a superstitious charlatan."

She yelled, "Morgan."

Morgan said, "My lady. You need not have yelled."

Morgan stood behind her in the chamber.

She held her dagger to the doctor's throat and said, "Morgan. Take this pretender of medicine and escort him out of Rose Fire."

She wanted to make sure that the doctor did not return. Therefore, she said, "Morgan. If it pleases you, drown him in the moat . . . as we do with all charlatans."

The doctor bolted from the room. He dashed down Marian's keep steps and sprinted across the bailey. He shouted, "Lower the drawbridge," repeatedly until he ran across it.

Drayton said, "He will not stop running until he is in the town of Hereford."

Morgan was quiet for a moment then he asked, "My lady, may I speak frankly?"

Marian said, "Yes."

Morgan said, "Marian. The threat that you just spoke, the threat to drown him in the moat. That was the type that comes from wisdom. Just the right threat to cause him to run."

Marian rubbed unguents on Warrick's arm and said, "It was not a threat."

Morgan said, "Drayton. Make sure that everyone does their hour of Perpetual Adoration in Rose Fire's Chapel. Or else in the Adoration wagon. I can never repeat enough. Perpetual Adoration of Jesus' Real Presence in the Blessed Sacrament. Make sure everyone does weekly confession. Remember Wolv's horrific victory in Sighisoara, Romania. We got there in time for Adoration to drive away Wolv. We exorcized the Skinwalkers that asked for Jesus' mercy. Then we had to behead the remaining Skinwalkers and burn their heads. Yet, Wolv's red-fog had changed every man, woman, child and animal into Skinwalkers. Wolv and Lilith had time to burn every building in Sighisoara. Every time Wolv burns a town, he sees it is as victory for himself. Again, like armies Wolv defeats, Sighisoara's army refused to do Adoration and confession."

She dressed Warrick's arm and said, "I must grow in wisdom fast."

From his chair, Father Malachi looked at Marian and said, "My lady. Your words prove you are wiser than we had expected."

Marian said, "Nicola. Tell the cook to send up venison mashed into broth."

Tears blocked Marian's vision. She kept her back straight and her chin level and did her duties. Her chin quivered but she did not break her concentration. She silently cried as she wrapped Warrick's arm and side.

Father Malachi said, "Yes, Warrick needs meat. If he can swallow mashed meat, he will surely heal."

A few moments later Marian dripped a small amount of broth into Warrick's mouth.

Warrick choked and could not swallow the thick broth.

Father Malachi pointed at Warrick. He signed and said, "Try again."

Lord Warrick choked again.

Old Father Malachi put his hand on Warrick's hand. He pulled it back as if someone hit her hand.

Father Malachi said, "The Pendragon's curse is very strong with Lord Warrick. It hurt my hand. Now we can only wait. The curse will not let him eat. His body alone, from its own reserves must create the blood he needs."

Marian asked, "Do many recover from so much blood loss?"

Morgan said, "None, my lady. I have seen this many times in battle, my lady. They all died. If any could survive, Warrick could survive."

Drayton and Ross-Templar shook their heads.

Ross-Templar said, "My lady, you must prepare yourself. No one recovers from such a large blood loss."

Marian looked at Drayton for a comforting word.

LITTLE HOPE OF LIVING.

Drayton said, "My lady, we must tell you the truth. Warrick has little hope of living."

Marian said, "Drayton. Bring me the thinnest broth. Broth with melted fat on top, and find a baby's spoon. I will not stop feeding Warrick."

-

-

-

CHAPTER, Now in Rose Fire, Wales, Year @ 1250s A.D.

WARRICK SICK RECOVERING?

That evening, during Vespers, Marian knelt beside Warrick's bed. She prayed, "Jesus. Let Warrick live. Please do not take him. Take me if you must, but let him live."

Marian lay on the bed beside Warrick, but did not sleep.

She dripped broth into Warrick's mouth. Warrick swallowed thin broth. Then she put logs into the andiron, and water in the boiling pot.

Lady Marian heard the Compline bells ring in bedtime. She watched the candles burn down. One after the other, she burned many tall candles.

Vigil's bells announced the three hours of Witches. Marian put logs on the andiron, water in the pot and paced in her chambers.

Matins' bells announced the end of the three midnight Witches' hours.

Marian whispered, "Wolv's Resurrection Prime hour is three hours away. In battle or out of battle, Wolv gives us no peace."

NO PEACE. RESURRECTION OBSESSION HOUR.
Extremely early, faint Prime bells began to ring. Prime bells far away to the east.

Wolv had not seen the morning sun for over a thousand years. In form of crows, Wolv was eating a disobedient Skinwalker Candlekeeper. . . . Alive. On the peak of the Black Mountains.

Wolv screamed, "Candlekeeper. Is it a safe hour? Do not make a mistake as did this Skinwalker."

Wolv's Hog-Head Skinwalker said, "Master Wolv. You have only moments before Jesus' Resurrection hour. Now, before your Resurrection obsession obliterates you. You must descend into the earth for protection. Look to the east. The Resurrection sun peaks over the far horizon."

Wolv said, "You have been slow. When I return, I will also eat you. . . . Alive."

Wolv turned into black, pure carbon dust and disappeared into the snow. He descended into the Black Mountains.

The half-eaten, crippled Deer-head Skinwalker jumped up. The crippled Skinwalker ran down the mountain.

Wolv descended into the Black Mountains. Then he became entangled in an underground river. Down he went. Dissolved like dust in rapids. One waterfall after another.

He came to rest in a pool and turned into his original Roman general form. Luminescent mushrooms and luminescent mold lighted the pool.

With his fists over his eyes, his eyes glazed black, his memory tortured him. He watched Jesus walk from the Tomb. Jesus brighter than the sun.

Wolv said, "Jesus. Stop torturing me. Just raise Pamia from the dead for me."

Jesus and Pamia and Saint John the Apostle and Jesus', Mother, Mary, turned to Wolv.

Holy Mary said, "Little Beloved Wolv. You have only to ask my son for forgiveness of your sins."

Pamia said, "My beloved. Ask Jesus for forgiveness of your sins. Then you and I can one day be together in Heaven."

Wolv growled, "Never in Heaven. Never in Heaven. I serve Satan. I will never give up the castles Satan has given me. Castles all over the world."

He fell to his knees in the pool and growled, "I serve Satan." He repeatedly growled, "Pamia. Pamia." His growls made the Black Mountains rumble. Red and black flames burst from Wolv's mouth and filled the cavern.

IN ROSE FIRE.

In Rose Fire Marian said, "I hear Wolv's growls of 'Pamia'. Whether in battle or not, Wolv gives us no peace. Wolv chooses to fight Jesus, and us. He shakes himself, the mountains and Rose Fire."

WOLV IN HIS RESURRECTION OBSESSION.

Deep under the Black Mountains Wolv came out of his Resurrection obsession.

The AntiChrist turned again into black, carbon dust and rose through the rushing water. Finally he came to the peak. He turned back into crows. Then he flew down the mountain to the living, half-eaten Skinwalker and devoured it.

IN ROSE FIRE.

As the Prime bells rang, the fire-red sun moved higher. Red sunbeams moved down Marian's chamber wall and lit up her chamber floor.

Almost continuously, Marian dripped warm, thin broth into Warrick's mouth. Warrick swallowed.

Warrick began to shake and gasp.

Marian yelled out her door, "Father Malachi. Ross-Templar, Drayton, Morgan. My lord is in his death throes."

Father Malachi hobbled in. He said, "I must see."

Morgan and his two brothers stepped aside for Father Malachi.

Then Malachi said, "It is not the death throe. It is the strongest humor chills I have ever seen."

Father Malachi put his ear to Warrick's chest and said, "He has breath-vapors. The cold water in the Wye River chilled him. Now he gurgles and rattles when he breathes. Otan, you must stoke the andiron to a blaze. You, Collette. Go to the buttery and find a large pot to hang over the andiron. The pot must always be full of boiling water. The room must be like a Roman steam bath. Nicola, have the servants bring up buckets of water to put into the pot. Marian's room must always be steamy so his throat will not dry out."

Father Malachi pointed, "Always leave this window cracked open to circulate fresh air."

The andiron heated the stone walls of Marian's chambers warm to the touch. Steam from the boiling water filled the room. Marian poured buckets of water into the pot as the water boiled away.

Marian fed Warrick thin but nourishing broth.

Flames in the andiron roared. She was so tired that as she watched the water boil. It almost mesmerized her for a few moments.

She rested her elbows on the seal of her open window. Marian gazed out at the Wye valley's foggy morning Prime bells haze.

Lady Marian spoke aloud, "The lines of torches on the mountains grow thicker. Now, as at every Prime, they fade away. If a Skinwalker holds each torch, it is a mighty army of demons."

The Prime bells rang in another worrisome day for Marian. She did not know the day of the week.

Lady Marian paced and dripped broth into Warrick's mouth. Worried, she glanced out the window to see the sun at its zenith. The Sext bell's sun. The zenith sun had burned off the fog. She fed Warrick broth. He gagged when she dripped any thick broth into his mouth. He could only swallow the thinnest broth.

Next time Marian glanced out the window, it was a cold, moonless night. Solid black, the black night of Vigil's bells, the three hours of Witches. Not a star shone through a haze of black clouds.

Marian spoke aloud as she looked out the window. "Torches completely line the Black mountains. Am I the only one that fears that Wolv is amassing a mighty army? Does Wales have so many druids?"

Hereford and the Wye valley were noticeable. Only by the cooking fires visible through windows. Then the watch guard blew his horn and yelled, "All is well."

She cried into her hands and said, "All is not well, my love is dying."

She could see the bailey through the flickering flames of torches. Torches mounted on the talus battlements.

Every hour she wiped his brow. She dripped thin broth into his mouth. Also, she kept cold cloths in his armpits to cool his fire. Just as Father Malachi had said.

Marian sat by the bed, her head slumped. Then she stood and paced. The Vigils bells came, the three hours of Witches. Then Matins' bells ended the three hours of Witches. Marian paced.

Lady Marian stood and said, "Prime bells. Wolv's Resurrection obsession again. He shakes Rose Fire and the Mountains with his roar of Pamia. Wolv has an eternal love of Pamia. An eternal love of Pamia. An eternal hatred of Jesus."

The bright morning sun reflected off a silver platter. One Marian had hung on the wall to use as a mirror. The glare off the platter shone into her eyes. She filled a basin full of water.

Father Malachi came in. He sat on the bed and put his ear to Warrick's chest.

UNCONSCIOUS FOR TOO MANY DAYS.

Malachi said, "I do not hear the rattle of breath humors. Warrick's arm is healing. He has his color back. The thin broth and his reserve of strength made the blood that he needed. Yet, he must awake soon. Too many days, he is completely unconscious, for too many days. If he does not wake soon and take solid food and water, Warrick will die."

Marian pulled back the sheepskin cover and the sheet. She wiped perspiration off Warrick's body in long strokes. Then she untied his loincloth and washed his legs.

She lay beside him and hugged him. She whispered into his ear and cried, "My love. You must please awaken. Please awake. I need you. My love, you are my champion. I need you, my love. I cannot live without you."

She glanced at his face to see his emerald eyes open and startled. Overjoyed she said, "You live."

Marian smiled. She put her lips to his and said, "Kiss me. Obey me and kiss me."

He wrapped his good arm around her and fell back asleep.

Though he was asleep, Marian dripped more broth into his mouth. He unconsciously swallowed. Marian did not stop. As fast as he unconsciously swallowed, she dripped more broth into his mouth.

She smiled and quipped, "Warrick. When you wake, I promise that I will always obey. Yet, only in the bed chambers."

Marian whispered to unconscious Warrick, "My lord. You foolishly risked your life for honey and daisies."

Warrick smiled. He whispered, "Water."

Then he tried to sit. He fell back onto the bed and whispered, "Dizzy, I am very dizzy."

Marian opened the door and yelled, "Father Malachi."

Marian heard, "Yes." She turned around to see Father Malachi in the corner.

Lady Marian asked, "How did you get in here?"

Father Malachi said, "I have always been with you. I will always be with you. Now put Warrick's head up with pillows. Then he can eat and drink."

Lady Marian yelled down the keep steps, "Reque. Bring well water and roast boar and roast venison. Now"

Reque entered with a bucket of well water and a ladle. Servants followed with large slices of roast boar and venison.

Father Malachi hobbled out the door and closed it behind herself.

The cycle from Prime bells to midnight Vigils bells continued. For several days. Each day Warrick sat up in Marian's bed and drank and ate. He got his strength back.

Marian rested beside him and asked, "Warrick. Why did you risk your life for honey and lilies?"

Warrick lay on his side and looked into her blue eyes.

He touched her nose and said, "For that little nose and those beautiful blue eyes."

Then he said, "Yes, I remember. The wagon had potted daisy plants and honey. A bride cannot marry without a chapel sanctuary full of yellow and white crocuses. Her wedding celebration must have honey mead. The mead to bless our marriage with passion. Yellow-white crocuses. To bless us with cheer and gladness. I remember. Skinwalkers and I danced a tune until they could not dance any more."

Marian said, "Why do you jest? You could have died in that fight?"

Tears dripped from her eyelashes. She wiped them with the back of her hand.

Warrick said, "We are knights, warriors, Marian. You must become accustomed to a life with a warrior."

Marian said, "The wound on your arm was a problem at first. Then worse, you contracted breath-vapors from the chill in the cold Wye River. I put my ear to your chest and heard a great gurgle with each breath."

She paused for a moment and said, "My lord. May I speak my mind for a moment?"

Warrick said, "Yes."

Marian said, "You need a bath."

Warrick laughed. He said, "So you disobey me and now you tell me that I stink."

She laughed and hugged him. She said, "Yes, it is so wonderful that you are alive. Alive so that I can disobey you and smell your stink."

Lady Marian lay beside him and smiled. Then she ran her hands through his thick black hair. She said, "After all, who else can I disobey and insult? Would you deprive me of such pleasures?"

DANGER APPROACHES. THE DRAGON COMES.

Warrick felt a presence.

He said, "Who is here?"

Warrick wiped water from his emerald eyes to see Malachi.

Marian said, "Father Malachi. How did you get in my chambers?"

Father Malachi held a thick linen robe in each hand.

Marian glanced at the doors and said, "Father Malachi. I locked the doors. How did you get into my chambers?"

Father Malachi said, "Marian, I am with you always. Evil lurks around Rose Fire. My lord, I have come to protect Marian, to protect your love for each other. I have been with you. Drink this and it will strengthen you. The dragon Lilith is in the air. The great evil Lilith grows impatient with Wolv. She comes as a dragon to carry Marian away."

Father Malachi paused, "Warrick, my lord. You are Marian's only hope. Warrick, you are the world's only hope."

Warrick drank the liquid. He said, "You could pour this drink into an enemy's well. They would die of thirst before they would drink from it a second time."

Warrick and Marian took the robes and put them on.

Father Malachi said, "My lord, you will find that you will need great strength. The many days that you slept gave time for evil to gather its forces. To gather its forces to descend on Rose Fire and take Marian from you."

Marian said, "Father Malachi. You make my spine chill. You never cease to frighten me."

Warrick said, "Marian. You should not worry about Father Malachi. Just become accustomed to his ways."

Father Malachi said, "My lord, you must dress my lord. Great evil surrounds Rose Fire. Dress my lord, it is time for you to come downstairs and break your fast. Warrick, you will find no reprieve from evil until Wolv is cast into Hell. He can even escape from Hell."

IN ROSE FIRE'S GREAT HALL. A WARRIOR'S DUTIES.

Flames from the Great Hall's andiron licked halfway to the roof. Unseasonable thick snow blew in the roof's smoke-apertures.

At the table in the great hall Warrick found no respite from his duties. While he ate, the carpenters and masons laid design scrolls on the table before him.

Marian sat beside him. She ate butter and wild strawberries on fresh baked bread and admired her champion.

Marian shivered and hugged her shoulders.

She whispered to Nicola, "A chill ran up my spine. Death, as if death itself touched me. Warrick could die in any battle on any day. Battle could take Warrick from me anytime."

Marian heard Father Malachi's words, "Marian. Love will protect the two of you."

She turned to search for Father Malachi, but she could not see him.

Marian said, "Nicola. Father Malachi is an eerie creature. Is he in this Great Hall?"

Nicola said, "Marian. I do not see him."

Marian put her hand on Warrick's back and rested her head on his shoulder.

He took the master carpenter by the arm and said, "Grease. Grease the water wheel that Marian designed. I want you also to make other water wheels on the mountain stream. We will have one for the ironworks bellows. Also, one for the sawmill, and one to mill grain into flour."

Warrick's words shocked Marian. She put her hand to her breasts. Her mouth fell open. She could not breathe or move for a moment. Her bright blue eyes were round with surprise. She could only look at his emerald eyes. Warrick's use of his artisans to advance her ironworks and sawmill astonished her.

Warrick continued, "And you must consult with Marian on any changes. Also, measure the dimensions of the dungeon. Use part of it for Marian's wine press, wine barrels, and thyme-honey mead."

IN THE BLACK MOUNTAIN SNOW CAPPED PEAKS
High in the Black Mountains Wolv entered a thatch hut. He sat on an irregular ax-hewn bench. The AntiChrist used his knife to carve his plans. Carve his plans to capture Marian on a split log tabletop.

Beside him Lilith, black wraith form, pointed with a dagger-like fingernail.

Lilith said, "I have a means to put you inside Rose Fire. Some loves must not be. The love between Marian and Warrick must not be. Marian must not have Warrick's children."

IN ROSE FIRE. NO PEACE.

Marian woke and rolled over in bed to see Warrick.
She sat up. Her many cats jumped off her bed covers.
She rubbed the sleep from her eyes.
Marian stepped from her bed and pulled off Warrick's
black leather blouse. Then she examined his arm.
He said, "It is healing."

NO PEACE
Marian said, "Listen. Wolv gives us no peace. He again
shakes the Black Mountains. With his Egyptian Holy-Mary-
obsession."

IN THE BLACK MOUNTAINS.
High in the mountains, on his knees. In the snow, as a black,
crumbling charcoal wraith, Wolv repeatedly screamed Holy
Mary's words. "Little Wolv. I will always love you."
Warrick said, "Wolv's guilt will not leave him alone. As a
six-year-old, he came deeply to love Holy Mary in Egypt. Yet, he
obeyed Rome and crucified Jesus as Holy Mary watched. Wolv's
guilty conscious gives him no peace."

IN THE MOUNTAINS.
Black and red flames spewed from Wolv's mouth and filled
the sky. The smoke temporarily blocked all light.

IN ROSE FIRE.
Marian said, "Finally, Wolv's fades."
Warrick said, "War with Wolv gives us no piece. The
AntiChrist's obsessions give us no peace. His obsessions give
Wolv no peace."

READ, READ, READ, READ.
Marian said, "Warrick, about Wolv's weaknesses. I am
reading hundreds of tomes in ancient languages. The language of
the Huns, Chinese, Japanese, Namibian and other African tongues.
The monasteries have tomes about Wolv in every language.
Warrick. I will find a way to contain Wolv. Wolv has never
battled a person that reads as widely as I read. That studies as hard
as I study."

Then Marian inspected his wound.

Lady Marian said, "Your body is a mass of scars."

Warrick said, "Each a metal of honor. For Jesus and king."

Marian lowered her head in shame and her arms hung at her side. She felt his latest wound was her fault. She said, "Because I wanted thyme-honey and yellow and white crocuses. I almost caused your death."

He put his black leather blouse on and laughed, "Yes. It is a superstition among knights. That it takes a lover to kill a knight quickest."

Marian said, "So a woman is a curse to a knight?"

Warrick laughed and said, "Yes, of course."

Marian said, "Warrick. Now I know your sense of humor. That you are only trying to tease me. Yet, I am worried about the many battles to come. Your quips and jokes do not put me into a laughing mood. How can you look so happy when you came so close to death?"

He smiled and said, "Marian. Because I have seen and been through much worse."

She said, "I have seen the scars all over your body. How Jesus must have looked after the scourging?"

He said, "Wolv scourged Jesus. Also, Wolv scourged me more than once. He wanted to beat hate into me. Wolv scourges the Able-Symon-Pendragons to try to make us hate."

Marian said, "Wolv has captured you?"

Warrick said, "The best way to conquer an enemy is to let him capture you."

Marian said, "How did you escape?"

Warrick said, "Superstition, wit, wisdom, bribes, deception. Quickest escape is to burn down his castles from the dungeon."

He decided to tease her and said, "Besides, as I and my knights know. I tell death who to touch. Also, I will die when I choose."

Marian sat on the bed. Now sad, she bowed her head and said, "How? How can I marry someone who is so reckless? You do not really feel indestructible?"

He smiled wide. He was pleased that he had pinched her emotions and said, "Your emotions obey me. See how I changed your emotions with just a few simple words."

Marian said, "You think so little of me?"

Warrick said, "No the opposite. I think so much about you that I have figured you out."

She crossed her arms, stomped and turned her back.

He threw water on his face. Then he said, "All knights in their youthful years feel invincible?"

Marian snapped, "You should train them that they are not!"

He laughed and said, "You take life too seriously."

Marian said, "My lord, you are not serious enough. How can you be so foolishly confident?"

Warrick said, "I have never lost a joust or a tournament. Never lost a war or a battle or even a fight. Never have I lost at chess. I killed the Skinwalkers that attacked me. I bleed. Yet, I always defeat my enemy."

She stomped and said, "OOOhhhhhhhhhh, how can you be so irresponsible with your life?"

Warrick said, "My dear beautiful lady. My irresponsible actions with my life got me the greatest of rewards, . . . you."

She smiled and put her finger to her lips as she did when she flirted. Marian said, "Yes. It is true."

Warrick said, "Again, I made your emotions obey me. You are now happy and flirting."

Marian frowned and said, "You must think that the birds of the air obey you?"

Lord Warrick said, "Yes, when I tell them to fly away, they obey. When I send my falcon, he obeys and catches them. Then he brings them back to me? When I throw grain on the ground, birds come, they obey."

Marian said, "Obey, obey, obey, that is all you think about?"

He said, "Yes, I command your hair to fall on your face."

-

-

-

CHAPTER, Now in Rose Fire, Wales, Year @ 1250s A.D.

NO PEACE. PREMONITIONS OF EVIL.

He splashed water on her head so her hair fell wet across her face.

He pointed and grinned, "See, your hair obeys my every command."

She sat on her bed and said, "You frighten me."

IRREGULAR SEXT BELLS. NO PEACE.

Warrick said, "A Cistercian Monastery is using Sext bells to celebrate a saint's day. Listen. The Sext bells will cause Wolv's Sext obsessions."

IN THE MOUNTAINS.

Wolv repeatedly screamed, "Father. Forgive them, for they know not what they do." His repeated screams shook the mountains.

Warrick said, "Look out the window. The AntiChrist's rage covers the sky again with black and red flame."

Marian said, "No peace. We will have no peace until we somehow do the impossible. Capture Wolv."

Warrick said, "I have always found a means to chase Wolv away, temporarily."

Marian said, "But, the scars on your body. No one can kill Wolv. Warrick. The AntiChrist can kill you."

Lord Warrick said, "Warriors live until they die. Die in battle. Love me until I die. Love me after I die. That is the best fate of warriors. We will be together in Heaven."

She cried into her hands and said, "I have grown to love you. Then you almost died for just honey and flowers. Are you not afraid of death? You are so cavalier. You almost died. What of Nicola and my mother at Oxford, if you were to die?"

Warrick smiled and said, "The king would betroth you to another lord to torment. I am sure."

She cried hard into her hands.

Warrick frowned and said, "I am sorry. I teased you too much."

He stood, wrapped her in his black cloak and sat beside her. He put his arm around her and said, "Marian. I did not mean to make you cry."

She jumped up and laughed. She quipped, "Your emotions obey me. See how I changed your emotions, with just a few simple words."

Marian crossed her arms tight and paced the room. He grabbed her and pulled her onto the bed.

Lady Marian laughed and hit his chest for him to let her up.

Warrick said, "I once had a conversation with another knight. I told him that I did not care about the appearance of my future wife. I told him that I would just obey the king. Obey and marry any horse-faced woman he told me to marry."

She pushed on him and said, "So I am a horse faced woman. Will your insults never stop?"

He held her tight and would not let her go, "Marian. Yes, it is what I told him, but is not what I feel now. Your beauty has changed me. Marian, I see you face in every cloud on a sunny day. I see your eyes in the bright blue sky. I see your hair when the wind blows through fields of golden wheat. Or in whirl winds of golden autumn leaves."

He ran his thumb along her eyebrows and said, "Your high eyebrows engulf me. They make me feel helpless. As helpless as when the great sand storms of Egypt engulfed me."

He stroked her cheeks and said, "Your high cheekbones are my worst weakness. They crush the hardness from my heart. Your delicate jaw gives men the joy that they feel when they contemplate beauty. Your ruby lips are more pleasing to the eyes than rubies."

Then he felt love, the power of which he could no longer express. It was only expressible by long embraces.

She felt that he cherished her. It was then that they were bound tighter together as one. It was then that they felt like a pair of souls. Souls that soared to the heavens. Soared on one set of wings. To the sight of others they were two bodies. To their souls, only one body.

They did not move, or talk. They just hugged each other.

Warrick said, "Marian. You just shivered. You are cold as ice."

Then Marian said, "Look. The shadows of the flames on the wall. In the shadows you fight with Wolv atop my keep, on the roof. You broke your sword against Wolv's sword. I lay at your feet. An arrow in my back. My premonitions of evil have always come true."

Warrick said, "Just your imagination, Marian."

Marian said, "I saw your right eyebrow raise. You are lying."
-

-

-

CHAPTER, Now in Rose Fire, Wales, Year @ 1250s A.D.

PREMONITIONS OF EVIL.
Warrick laughed.
He said, "I cannot control what you have done to my mind and body. You are so beautiful."
Marian said, "You only change the subject."
Warrick said, "Which do you want me to contemplate? Wolv's ugliness, or contemplate your astounding beauty."

NO KISSES.
Morgan knocked on the chamber door and said through the door, "Warrick. It is time for you to patrol the Wye Valley."
Lord Warrick ran his fingers through his hair as he did when Marian befuddled him. He stood and pulled on his black, leather blouse.
Marian gritted her teeth and beat her pillow.
She silently thought, "I wasted my precious time with Warrick talking about Wolv."
Warrick said, "Yes, You did waste out precious time talking about Wolv."
Marian said, "Warrick. You read my thoughts?"
Warrick said, "No Marian. You spoke aloud."

MARIAN WAITS FOR HIS RETURN
Within an hour, from the outer wall battlement, Marian watched Warrick. Warrick and many knights gallop down the mountain's red-clay road on another patrol.
Marian asked Morgan, "Squires come from Germany, France, England. Even as far away as Jerusalem to train under my lord. Why is that?"
A squire from Jerusalem stated, "My lady, may I answer that?"
Marian said, "Yes."

The squire said, "My lady, Lord Warrick's reputation is worldwide. Renowned and celebrated. The longer you train to be a knight the more you hear legends about him. Then, you must see the real man. Those who train with him are the first to become the king's personal guard."

PREMONITIONS OF EVIL.
Marian could not get out of her mind the image of Warrick on his back. Warrick battling Wolv atop Marian's keep roof. Warrick on his back with a broken sword. The AntiChrist standing over Warrick to cleave him with a sword. Marian at Warrick's feet, an arrow through her back."

Lord Morgan' squire said, "My lady. Lord Warrick also teaches something few can. Like no other, he teaches how to command, to lead, to delegate authority. If you can survive under his training, you know. You know that the king will eventually give you your own lordship. After other knights have given up, he works us. He works with us, midnight to sunup Prime. We learn in the dark hours of night, Vigils bells, Matins bells and Prime bells. When our exhausted minds are too tired to think, our bodies practice by reflex. We then begin to do battle duties by reflex, without thought. Also, he teaches everything else: Repair of armor, surgery on horses and warriors. Horsemanship, jousting, swordsmanship, weapons repair, and leather work. He thinks battle. He lives battle. Warrick is battle. Lord Warrick is only battle. This is why pages to knights come from every country to train. To train and serve with him."

Lord Morgan said, "He has something else, something inexplicable that makes a great leader. He has a mystique about him that exudes confidence. A clarity of his vision, and the coherence of his thought. That every knight seeks to attain. You will only find these leadership qualities in one or two warriors in each generation. Wolv has all the same qualities and abilities, but he uses them for evil."

The Compline bells rang from the far away Wye Valley Abbey. Rose Fire's chapel bells began to ring. Both echoed off the Black Mountains in a planned harmony. The echoes announced the close of the day. Time to sleep. The arrival of the Black Mountains' shadows. Black Mountain shadows blanket the

Wye valley and put it to sleep. It was as if the shadows themselves spread a magic sleeping mist.

As a flock of crows, Wolv flew high above Rose Fire. Wolv spoke through the crows. "Marian is beside Warrick's brothers. Otherwise, I would swoop down and carry Marian to my wedding reception cave.

IN ROSE FIRE.

In the dusk, Marian walked the outer battlement.

Lonely hours of frightful thoughts tormented her. In the fog, in an endless cycle she walked the battlement. Then stood by her campfire-like-andiron in her chambers. To warm herself. The fog settled on her long blond hair. It dripped down Warrick's extra black leather cloak that she always wore. She walked around the andiron only to walk back on the battlement again. The fog would again soak her hair until it dripped down her cloak. She strained to see through the black foggy night. To find any hint of Warrick on the mountain-switchback road.

Often she walked to her bedchamber to dry her hair.

WARRICK RETURNS.

Warrick finally opened the door to her bedchamber.

She ran to her beloved and hugged him. The fog had wetted her face and dripped from her hair.

His work exhausted him.

In her bed chamber, Warrick and Marian sat. Sat on a huge couch-like chair covered with pillows. They sat warmed beside the andiron fire. Placed in the center of her bedchamber. With his feet, he pushed his tall black leather boots off and stretched. He put his huge arm around her. She pulled her feet up on the pillows on the couch-like chair. Then she leaned against him. She ran her hand across his chest.

PREMONITIONS OF EVIL.

Marian began to weep.

Warrick said, "Why cry now?"

Marian said, "Warrick. A premonition of evil. My love. I cannot get out of my mind the image of you on your back. You are battling Wolv atop my keep roof. You broke your sword on

Wolv's sword. A broken sword, you had only a broken sword. The AntiChrist standing over you to cleave you with a sword. I am at your feet, an arrow through my back."

Warrick said, "If your premonition has substance, I will use it as forewarning."

They sat very still in the light of the flames. In the warmth of the andiron fire. The oak logs burned clean. As the fire boiled the logs' sap, the sap turned to steam. Then as the steam whistled out small cracks, the logs cracked and split lengthways. Sparks burst from the logs to explode like tiny red clouds. Explode against the andiron's tall, mail curtain. The little smoke from it drifted up and out smoke-holes in the high roof. Servants had opened the holes to draft the smoke from the Great Hall.

The andiron gave the atmosphere of a campfire in the wild.

Warrick hugged Marian close to him. Her wet hair rested against his cheek. As he breathed deep and his chest expanded with each breath, his thoughts preoccupied him.

She faced the fire and felt the warmth on her face and wet hair. The light of the andiron and candle flames flickered. Flickered off the cameo smoothness of her face and arms. Reflected off the droplets in her hair. Her blue eyes sparkled bright in the flicker of the andiron's tall flames. Behind her great shadows leapt high on the thirty-foot-high walls. The tall shadows danced like ghosts that flew around the thick stone walls.

Marian said, "Look at the shadows on the walls. They dance from the floor to the ceiling. Like scenes of great battles. Battles between spectral armies. The shadows look like a battle between the evil shadows and the flame's bright light."

Lord Warrick held her hand and pointed, "Marian. On the wall, in the shadows, I see our first son. Tall like me and blonde like you, with your blue eyes. He is a great and renowned scholar. Even in his youth he is renowned for his wisdom. He holds a great arm load of tomes. Tomes written by you. Around him I see many students sit and listen to him. With wide eyes they absorb every word he speaks. They know that he points them in the direction of truth. They know that your tomes point them to truth. Behind him in Oxford I see a great school at which he teaches."

Marian said, "And I see our daughter as she sits with her husband. Her hair is wet and her husband will not dry and comb it."

Warrick laughed. He ran his hands over her wet hair. He picked up a towel and gently dried her hair. Then he combed it. In the flashes of andiron flames her hair reflected like strands of spun gold. He started the comb at the ends of her hair. To work out the tangles. Warrick worked up. Up to her scalp and combed her hair in long smooth strokes. The comb tingled and gave her goosebumps as it brushed smoothly along her back. The only sound was the crackle of the fire and their breathing.

Marian said, "Collette always pulls so hard she breaks my hair. I think she is trying to make me bald as our cook. Warrick, you have always seemed to me to be all dangerous battle. Harsh commands, strict obedience and harsher punishment. I did not realize that you could be so gentle. Where did you learn to brush hair so gently?"

Warrick said, "You do not want me to tell. Tell you where I learned to comb hair, not really."

PREMONITIONS OF EVIL.

Marian said, "My love. Again I see that frightening forewarning. Warrick, you, on your back. Battling Wolv atop my keep's roof. My love, you have only a broken sword. The AntiChrist stands over you, Warrick, to cleave you with a sword. My lord, I am at Wolv's feet, an arrow through my back."

Warrick said, "Marian. You are battle-weary. Many of your thoughts and dreams are about battle. My love, I have solved many battle strategies in my dreams."

Marian said, "My love? You called me 'my-love'."

Warrick said, "I have grown accustomed to your hairy-horse face. My twelve feet tall, one eyebrow-from-temple-to-temple bride-to-be."

Marian laughed.

Marian said, "Now tell me how you learned to brush hair. Then I can teach Collette how to do it."

Warrick said, "You will think that I am insulting you again."

Lady Marian said, "I promise, I will not."

Lord Warrick said, "Marian. Taking the burs and tangles out of a horse's mane and tail."

Marian said, "So. The truth. You do think that I am a horse?"

Warrick laughed and said, "For safety, you must start at the ends and work up. If you brush from the top, the tangles become knots. You must be gentle or the horse will kick you and break your bones. I would not pull tangles in your hair. Or you would kick and break my bones."

Marian wanted to tease him. She rolled her lower lip in a pout and she said, "Warrick. So you are to treat me like a horse? I knew that you would take the opportunity to insult me."

Lord Warrick laughed, "You never give up. Always ready with a quip. Why do you always think that I am attacking you with my words?"

She wanted to tease him again as he often teased her. She raised her chin in the air and said, "It is very simple. Men are much better with horses than they are with women."

Warrick said, "Horses are easier to understand."

He kissed her bare shoulder, "Surely. Horses do not taste as good as your shoulder."

She turned her head from him to hide her smile from him. Then she tried to pull away from him. Marian said, "Compare me to a horse."

He turned her around.

He said, "Compare your eyes to the brightness of the full Vigils bells moon. Or compare your hair to Sext zenith-sun flashes on the mountain streams. Compare your breath to the breeze through an evergreen forest. Or compare your lips to ruby red wine."

She hugged his neck tight, then she became limp in abandonment in his arms.

She ran her hands over his face and said, "You appear too hard. Now I love those hard features. Your presence, your touch does not frighten me so much."

She ran her fingers across his dark eyebrows and bright emerald eyes. Then down his jaw muscles that bulged when he was angry or worried. Across his dark whiskered cheeks with the hint of laugh lines. His wide mouth always thinned because of his intensity at everything that he did.

Marian said, "You make me feel emotions, tingles. Feelings that I never knew existed before I met you."

Marian startled. In the shadows on the walls she saw a great arrow. A great arrow in her chest. Above her, Lord Warrick and Wolv in mortal combat.

Warrick said, "Marian, why did you suddenly shiver? You have goose bumps and are as cold as the mountain streams."

Marian said, "Hug me, hug me, Warrick."

He wrapped his huge arms around her. His hot chest and belly instantly warmed her. His arms enwrapped her like a huge heated blanket. They gave her a feeling of protection. Protection and warmth from head to toe.

She kissed his hand, "Tell me everything will be all right. Tell me that Wolv will go away forever and never bother us again."

His right eyebrow raised and he lied, "Wolv will go away."

She said, "I see your right eyebrow raise every time you lie."

-

-

-

CHAPTER, Now in Rose Fire, Wales, Year @ 1250s A.D.

EVIL NEVER WENT AWAY.

He hugged her tight. Then he thought of years of battles. Battles with Wolv. Wolv never went away. Evil Wolv never went away. Evil's face only grew redder with rage, his eyes more bloodshot with hate and drunkenness. Wolv never went away. Wicked Wolv could always find henchmen to follow him. For Wolv promised them that they could enslave and sale the people they captured. He promised that they could take their buildings, land and belongings.

Warrick hugged Marian tight.

Then Warrick lied again, this time to himself.

His right eyebrow raised and he repeated to convince himself, "Wolv will go away."

Warrick hugged Marian and was quiet for some time. He picked her up and put her on his lap.

The day had exhausted them. On the couch, both fell asleep in each another's arms.

They slept through late Midnight Vigils bells.

As a dragon, Lilith flew above Rose Fire. The three Hours of Witches ended with Matins bells. Marian slept in Warrick's arms on the couch. The Matin's bells announced the three hours from Wolv's Resurrection obsessions.

PRIME BELLS.

Hours later the morning Prime red sunbeams shone in their eyes and awakened them.

As the Prime bells rang, a stone mason knocked on Marian's door. Through the door the mason said, "My lord. You must choose the tiles to use before we can mix the mortar."

RESURRECTION OBSESSIONS.

Warrick said, "Marian. Listen. Wolv's Prime Resurrection obsessions grow stronger."

Marian said, "Yes. He shakes the Black Mountains and Rose Fire with his screams of Pamia. His roars are louder."

Warrick said, "At Prime bells he disappears deep into the earth. He is vulnerable at the Resurrection hour. If we caught him before he descended into the earth, we could dismember him. At the Prime bells, Wolv is deep in the mountain. He believes that he can convince Jesus to raise Pamia from the dead. No one has ever been closer to Jesus. No one hates Jesus more than Wolv."

HER WEDDING.

Lord Warrick stood in the morning sunbeams. He ran his hands through his hair.

Warrick said, "Marian. Tomorrow is a big day for Rose Fire. The most enjoyable event the lord and lady of a castle can hold."

Marian said, "What in the world is that?"

Lord Warrick said, "Tomorrow we will have the beginning of days of a great carnival. We will compete in jousting, sword play, archery and all the military arts. We will have acrobats, magicians, clowns and other entertainments?"

Marian's eyes grew round with surprise and said, "Why?"
Warrick said, "The king is coming here tomorrow."
Marian jumped up off the bed. She put her hands on her
hips. She leaned forward at him and shouted, "What! What! How
come you did not tell me?"

Lord Warrick stood in the open door way and said,
"Marian. I have things that I must do. I repeated to you that the
king was coming."

He sheathed Blessed Dread and his blessed sword. He
walked down the spiral stair case.

Nicola ran in and sat on the bed beside her, "I heard. What
will you do? You have never prepared to comfort the king and
queen. You have only been in the king's court for a short time.
Instead, you would sneak into the church's libraries and steal their
tomes. You are good at sneaking and stealing. Marian, you are
not good at comforting the king?"

Marian snapped, "Yes, I am good at sneaking and stealing.
I have those Arabic tomes."

Marian shoved Nicola's shoulders. Then she cried into the
large cover on the bed and said, "Nicola. My wedding will be a
shameful display of my lack of preparation."

Collette, Marian's handmaiden, clasped her hands together.
She said, "Fear not my lady, I have helped to prepare many
weddings for lords. The king's court trained me. Your wedding
day and night will be glorious."

Collette said, "We have very few hours. I will bring all the
servants up here to prepare for the king and queen."

Then it hit her, "Oh my God. The king, the king is coming
here for my wedding tomorrow? Why would he want to come here
when he has such a glorious castle? I am to be wed tomorrow?
Why is the king coming?"

Collette said, "He always comes to the dedication or
rededication of a castle. He also always comes to the marriages of
his favorite lords."

Servants of all types ran into the room. Collette told each
exactly what to do and sent them to their duties. Some servants
stayed in Marian's chambers and followed her. They took
measurements for her wedding gown. Though Marian nervously
walked back and forth.

Marian said, "We do not have the proper silk for a wedding gown." She put her hands to her cheeks and said, "Lord Warrick wants the king here."

Collette said, "No, my lady. Warrick did not request the king to come, but they are the closest of friends. As I said, the king shows up for all weddings of his favorite lords. For all dedications of castles. Warrick is one of the king's closest friends."

Marian paced. She said, "For what reason would my lord request the king's presence at my wedding? Just to embarrass me?"

Handmaiden Collette patiently repeated, "No my lady. The king always comes to castle dedications and his lord's weddings. Lord Warrick did not ask for the king to come to your wedding. The king always does this."

Marian did not listen. She said, "My lord is mad to invite the king. The king and all his court to our wedding, absolutely insane. A king at Rose Fire, Rose Fire is too small. My lord should have repeated to me. Repeated to me that he asked the king to come to our wedding."

Warrick strode back into her chambers.

In front of everyone Marian asked, "Warrick. You should have repeated that you asked the king to come to our wedding? How could you have hidden such a thing from me? The king?"

Warrick examined the bee hive of servant activity in Marian's chambers and said, "Marian. Someone knows how to prepare for the king's presence."

Marian's face turned red and she said, "Warrick. If my anger were a fire, you would be a cinder."

He said, "Then I am lucky that you are among the most beautiful women ever. Not a fire."

Marian stomped her foot. She said, "Among? Among? Just among?" She crossed her arms and fumed.

Warrick said, "I meant to say, 'That you are the . . . the most beautiful woman ever.'"

She turned her back to him and smiled. Marian did not want him to see her blush.

Then Marian wrinkled her brow on purpose. To hide the pleasing effect of his flattery and said, "Warrick. You should have repeated to me that the king was coming."

Lord Warrick called, "Collette."

The handmaiden turned to him and said, "My lord."

Warrick said, "Collette. Tell the truth or I will find another use for your tongue."

Collette put her hand over her mouth.

Warrick said, "Collette. Did you not overhear me tell Marian often to prepare for the king?"

Handmaiden Collette held both hands over her mouth and turned bright red. She said, "My lord, may I speak?"

Lord Warrick said, "Yes."

Then Collette said, "If I say 'yes,' my lady will banish me. If I say 'no,' you will banish me."

Marian tapped her toe and crossed her arms and said, "Collette. I promise. We will not banish you."

Servant Collette said, "Then my lord. You did repeat often to my lady that the king was coming."

Marian waved her arm and shouted, "I banish you. I banish you."

Warrick put his hand on Collette's shoulder and said, "Marian is only in jest." He reached over and touched Marian's cheek. He said, "Marian. Besides, Collette is the only servant that knows how to prepare for the king."

Marian said, "Oh, all right, of course, I will not banish you."

Collette curtsied to her and went behind her to work with bolts of cloth.

Nicola laughed. She said, "Marian. I also heard Lord Warrick tell you often to prepare for the king's visit.

Marian turned her back to Warrick. She whispered, "Nicola, you are to side with me when I argue with my lord. I have no one else."

Nicola grinned wide to tease Marian and said, "Marian. Nevertheless, I heard my lord tell you often that the king was coming."

Marian threw a pillow at Nicola and said, "Traitor."

Nicola laughed and said, "Yes, my lord. The day you triumphantly entered Rose Fire was the first time you told Marian."

Marian turned to Collette and hugged her, "Collette. I would never banish you, but I would banish him."

She pointed at Warrick.

Collette raised the front of her gown with both fists. She darted for the door, "My lord. May I take my leave to guide the other servants in the buttery?"

Warrick said, "Yes."

Collette flew, escaped, out the door. She caught a buttery maid by the arm. Then she said, "Listen carefully, tell everyone not to go into Marian's chambers. Unless they want to find themselves banished to another castle or . . . country."

In her chambers, Marian stomped, "So I must be ready to wed tomorrow. So be it."

A seamstress held up a bolt of silk and said, "Marian. With this cloth, we can have your wedding dress, plenty of time for the wedding."

Marian said "The servants know the date of my wedding and I do not?"

Warrick smiled and said, "Yes."

Marian said, "But, but, I am the bride."

Warrick said, "Marian, you did not concern yourself with bridal matters. You worked on wine presses and sawmills and casting iron and water wheels. You struggled with curses and wine and black-cats and Father Malachi's noises."

Lady Marian said, "You . . . you did not tell me when I was to be wed."

Lord Warrick laughed and shouted down the spiral staircase, "Collette, Collette."

Marian sat in a chair and put her face into her hands and cried, "No. No, no, please, not Collette. She knows more than I do."

Warrick said, "Why do you cry?"

Marian said, "What is supposed to be the happiest day of my life. It will be a day of shame before the king's court. We will not be ready."

Warrick said, "Rose Fire and our readiness will not shame you. He is just the king. An old friend of jousting and days of too much ale."

Marian shouted. She threw her arms into the air, "Just the king, just the king! How can you say, It is just the king?'"

Warrick said, "He is only a man like every other man. Perhaps my closest confident, but with more authority. Beside you will also enjoy the presence of the queen. You will entertain her."

She gazed up at him with round eyes and an open mouth.

She shouted, "I must entertain the queen? I feel like all my muscles have lost their strength. I wish to turn to water and flow into the cracks of the floor. How can I entertain the queen and the king? All I really know to do is command. Command servants to do their duties. I know how to hide under a cowl and sneak into seminaries and steal tomes. Do not know how, I cannot entertain."

Warrick said, "Then do not entertain, do better than entertain. Listen and they will think you are a saint and a genius. Only saints and geniuses know how to listen. Listen with the same intensity that you read those stolen tomes. If you listen to them, the queen and her courtiers will be good camaraderie."

Marian said, "How many courtiers?"

He decided to tease her and said, "Enough that many must sleep in the stables."

Marian shouted, "The stables!" She stopped breathing then said, "My wedding guests sleep in the stables."

Again she stopped breathing. As she stood, she gazed at him with big round eyes. Her lower lip rolled out as if she were about to cry.

Warrick said, "I should not have teased you. I had no idea how important this was to you. My first wedding was just three, a traitor, myself, and a priest."

Marian said, "No wonder your first wife became a traitor to you."

Warrick just sighed. He said, "I promise, Marian. Everyone in Rose Fire will help you prepare for your wedding. You should be very happy, the archbishop himself will marry us. If it were up to me, I want just you, me and a priest. Our wedding is a lord's wedding and a castle rededication to the king. The king always comes to these weddings."

Marian said, "The king? The queen? The complete court? Also, the archbishop? Why not try to feed all of London?"

She threw her arms in the air and said, "Bring in all of London. No bring in all of England. We can feed all of England."

Warrick said, "The king's cavalcade will bring enough food. The king's arrival is nothing to cause a distraction. They are just like us. They are not Mount Olympus Gods."

Marian said, "You do not know anything about a woman's feelings. About their wedding. Do you not understand anything about women? I have no control over my own wedding."

She again began to cry.

Warrick said, "Your crying, crying again! You leave me totally dumbfounded."

She sobbed, "How. . . . Could? . . . . You. . . . Do. . . . This?"

He raised his voice, "God's shoes. You turn a great honor. The presence of the king and queen at your wedding. Marian, you turn their presence into a shameful event. Your world is upside down. I suppose you will want to turn shame into honor?"

Marian cried, "I have not prepared Rose Fire for a royal visit. The ladies of the king's court will laugh at me and our children forever."

Warrick said, "If anyone in the king's court questions your honor. I will challenge them or their champion by holy right of combat."

Tears ran down her cheeks and she said, "The sword cannot restore everything. You cannot fight all of them."

Warrick said, "Yes, I can and will for you."

She hugged his arm and said, "I know you would. No, I could not bear to see your life at such a risk. I would not let you."

Lord Warrick said, "You could not stop me."

She wiped the tears from her cheeks. She said, "Lack of preparation for my wedding will shame me. Then worse, my shame will put our family and our children at risk. I cannot allow the women of the king's court to shame me. The women of the court have great power. You do not understand a woman's shame. A man can regain his honor with his sword, but a woman, a wife?

A champion's blessed sword can only quiet the dishonor among women. Women can never regain honor among women. They will shame me and our children. Gossips among the courtiers assure that shame lives forever. The gossips are only a few women. Yet, they destroy reputations to maintain their positions close to the king. Those few gossips will say that I am incompetent. Our children will have a reputation for incompetence even before they are born."

Warrick said, "Who are these gossips?"

Marian said, "They change as fast as the courtier changes."

Warrick said, "If Rose Fire were completely ready, would everything be all right?"

Marian said, "Yes."

Lord Warrick said, "Rose Fire is ready. We strengthened the towers and deepened and widened the moat. Like the most secure castles of the known world. We have outer walls. Also, an inner talus wall with the best constructed slope of any castle. We have barbicans on both sides of the talus' battlement portcullis. Rose Fire now has barbicans on the drawbridge's sides on the outer battlement walls. The drawbridge also had a thick iron portcullis. I have the best knights of all England and the continent. The best horseman, the best longbow men, the best infantry. All dedicated and sworn to protect. No harm will possibly come to the court here in Rose Fire. Be happy and be proud, woman. Stop this blithering."

Marian clinched her fists and snapped, "Blithering? Will your insults never stop?"

She said through tears. "Warrick. How could you not tell me often that the king and queen were coming?"

-

-

-

CHAPTER, Now in Rose Fire, Wales, Year @ 1250s A.D.

CONFUSION IN ROSE FIRE.

Warrick said, "I told you often that the king was coming to Rose Fire. I tell my soldiers once and they do it or else."

She threw a glass figurine at him and shouted, "I am not a soldier."

UPON THE BLACK MOUNTAINS.

As crows, Wolv was far up on the Black Mountain. He could not hear the words. Yet, he could hear the tone of Warrick and Marian's conversation. He said, "Gulum. The more discord between Warrick and Marian, the easier it will be to capture Marian."

IN ROSE FIRE.

Marian worked in the buttery all night. Everyone worked all night. Through Compline bells, then the Vigils' bells' three hours of Witches. Then Matins' bells that ended the three hours of Witches. Three hours later Prime bells rang.

HIGH ON THE BLACK MOUNTAINS.
RESURRECTION OBSESSION.

As a flock of crows, Wolv heard the faint Prime bells. The crows fell to the ground and formed his burning charcoal form. With flames from the charcoal, he fell to his knees and howled, "Jesus. Stop torturing me. Please raise Pamia from the dead for me."

His eyes glazed over black. Wolv's resurrection obsession overcame him. He changed from burning charcoal to black, pure, carbon dust. Then as with every Prime, Wolv sunk into the earth. Sunk into the earth to avoid his vulnerable Resurrection hours.

Down he sank into underground rivers. Into fast flowing pools. Over underground crashing waterfalls. He came to an underground cavern lighted with luminescent mushrooms. Wolv knelt and said, "Please Jesus, stop this torture."

In his memory, as always, the ground shook. Shook as the stone over Jesus's tomb rolled aside.

Jesus stepped forth from the tomb, bright as the sun.

Then Jesus said, "My Beloved childhood friend. I do not torture you. Your hatred of me tortures you. Like all people, you, Wolv, are one of my Father's beloved children. You know me better than anyone. Ask me for forgiveness of you sins. Then one day you will be with Pamia in Heaven."

Holy Mary appeared beside Jesus and said, "Beautiful little Wolv. In Egypt I told you not to hate. Your soul still has a tiny beautiful spark. That spark is your love for Pamia. Ask my son for forgiveness and then you can join Pamia in Heaven."

Wolv growled, "Heaven. Never. Hell is my home. Satan is my master. Give me Pamia. Pamia is my heart."

Holy Mary said, "One day, Little Wolv, your love for Pamia, will save your soul. Love will save the world."

Holy Mary's words obsessed him. Wolv repeatedly growled, "Love will save the world."

Wolv's growl that 'love will save the world' shook the Black Mountains.

The AntiChrist's rage and hatred spewed from his mouth as red and black flames. The flames filled the cavern. As Wolv's obsession faded, he found himself alone in the cavern. He turned into pure carbon dust and rose up through the earth.

IN ROSE FIRE

Everyone in Rose Fire had worked the whole night.

In Rose Fire everyone froze. Froze as Wolv's repeated roars filled the air. Vibrated Rose Fire.

"Love will save the world," Wolv growled incessantly.

Slowly Wolv's growls faded away. Faded away as the Wye valley's Terce Bells announced midmorning. Announced the end of Wolv's agonizing Resurrection hours.

Marian said, "Nicola. No peace. The AntiChrist gives us no peace. War. The threat of war. Quaking the earth. Wolv has no peace. We have no peace. I will find a way to capture and hold Wolv. Yes. I will find a way to capture and hold Wolv. I will read every ancient tome. Yes, will find a way to contain Wolv, to capture Wolv."

Marian had worked in the buttery for everyone knew the food must be perfect.

She heard roosters crow. She rubbed her forehead and closed the buttery door behind herself. Then she walked into the great hall. She sat at a knight's seat. Then she rested her head on her arms on the table. Marian slipped off her shoes and stretched her toes. Then she put her bare toes onto the floor. Surprised, she did not feel cold pink marble.

HOLY-MARY OBSESSIONS.

High in the Black Mountains Wolv fell to his knees and screamed, "Holy Mary. Go away. Leave me alone. Not so soon, not again, not so soon, Holy Mary, stop torturing me."

On his knees, Wolv began to scream repeatedly, "Little Wolv. I will always love you."

His screams shook the Black Mountains and vibrated Rose Fire.

Wolv's rage and hatred spewed from his mouth as black and red flames. The flames filled the sky and blocked out all light, temporarily.

Slowly Wolv's Holy-Mary-obsession faded.

IN ROSE FIRE

Everyone in Rose Fire stood still until Wolv's obsessions stopped.

Marian said, "Nicola. Wolv gives me chills."

Wolv shook the Black Mountains again with a scream. "Holy Mary. Leave me alone."

Marian sighed and said, "Nicola. We will have a few hours until Wolv's Sext obsessions. When Wolv nailed Jesus to the cross at zenith sun."

Then Marian glanced down to see fabulous Persian rugs on top of many thick pads. The rugs had red, yellow, blue, sand-gold and purple scenes of the sunsets. Sunrises over mountains and seas. The Persian rugs had scenes of sea monsters. Ships cast about in greats storms at sea. Flying horses, magical genies, knights in shining armor. Sultans in their finery. The rugs laid out scenes of great battles. She saw scenes of warriors and great armies of every country. Depicted warriors raised axes and swords against each other. She gazed at scenes of mounted knight armies charge against a Great Sultan's mounted minions.

She glanced up to see the walls. Now full of the most beautiful Flemish tapestries. They hung from the great rafter beams. Like innumerable pennants and from spikes driven into the walls. The tapestries had scenes of all the fairytales. Tapestry scenes in such colorful, emotional sequence that she grew dizzy and had to sit.

Tapestries of Rome's ancient wars in Carthage and Gaul. Gigantic tapestries of the naval battle between Cleopatra and Rome.

Never had she seen such color. She sat in the King's great chair. Above the Great Hall door was a tapestry of the king and his queen. On all the walls were tapestries of the previous kings and queens.

She shouted, "Nicola! Come quick!"

Nicola did not respond.

Marian ran up the spiral stairs of her keep. Then she saw the keep's staircase wall covered with a serpentine tapestry. It wound its way up the steps. At the bottom it showed scenes of the king as a babe, then a boy. Then a young man. The tapestries showed his coronation, and finally, his adulthood as he is today.

Royal red carpets lay on her keep steps. From the Great Hall to her chamber door. Bright blue tapestries with gold crowns embossed on them. On the foyer walls to the chambers and the solar. They hung from the rafters to the floor. Royal blue carpet covered the floor of the foyer to her chambers. All the chambers and the solar had the same carpet and tapestries, all new. All sparkling in the sun, all royal blue and royal red.

Out her chamber window she saw great tapestries of the king hang inside the bailey. From the talus battlement, and from the outer battlement. Her eyes grew round at the sight of the king's colors. Flying from every roof peak, arrow slot, and top blocks of the two battlement walls. The King's color's flew anywhere they could brace a flag pole. A great flag of England blew in the wind from a newly replaced flag pole. Warrick had the pole placed in the middle of the bailey.

In the bailey, the wind waved every tapestry that hung inside the battlement. The wind flapped the many pendants and the great English flag. Rose Fire was alive with moving colors that flashed in the bright morning Terce sun. Then she glanced at the bed in her chambers that the king would sleep in. It now had a great head board with the king's pendant. A crown in inlaid gold. A new mattress and pillows of down. Covers were of the softest white rabbit pelts.

She turned to see Warrick at the door of her chambers.

Warrick commanded, "Drayton. Morgan. I endlessly repeat. Make sure that everyone does their hour of Perpetual Adoration in Rose Fire's Chapel. Or else in the Adoration wagon. In the Adoration wagon, Perpetual Adoration of Jesus' Real Presence in the Blessed Sacrament. Make sure everyone does weekly confession. Every minute of every day you must contemplate our victories and defeats. Contemplate the defeat of the army of Cinque Terre, Italy. They also refused to do Adoration and Weekly confession. Wolv and Lilith changed everyone into Skinwalkers and took them away to burn more towns. Wolv burned Cinque. We chased Wolv's Cinque Skinwalkers for a month and defeated them. Defeated then with the Scipio Africanus technique. We encircled them and beheaded them. Our great loss was that not one Skinwalker asked for exorcism. Each choose to die as Satan's warriors. Not only did their bodies die, we also lost their souls. Kings have never learned that only Adoration and weekly confession can improve their countries. Protect their countries against Satan. Now go. Bring me a written report of everyone that has done Adoration and weekly confession."

Then Warrick turned to Marian said, "Marian. Are you ashamed to show the king and queen your home now?"

She threw her self into his arms, too happy to say anything. Marian choked back her tears. She glowed with happiness and smiled. Marian said, "Warrick. You, . . . you do, you do understand a woman's shame. The castle had to be more than prepared. It had to be beautifully prepared for a celebration."

Warrick decided to tease her. He smiled and said, "No. No, I will never understand life from a woman's point of view."

She pushed herself away from him and said, "Warrick. You still do not understand me after all this time."

Warrick smiled and again decided to tease her and said, "I will never understand you."

Marian rolled her lower lip in a pout. Then she again looked at all the color and beauty. Her spirits lifted.

She smiled. Then she pointed around the room, "My lord. Earl of teasing and bedevilment. From where did all these tapestries and carpets come, and the furniture?"

Warrick said, "Marian. Do you think that I would travel the world and not buy anything? The Pendragon Castle on Swansea has many timeless treasures."

Marian said, "Where did you store them?"

Warrick said, "In the many locked floors of the twelve keeps. Especially the floors of my Black Mood keep. Black Mood Keep, where everyone else is afraid to go."

She hugged him and said, "Rose Fire is now more than a fairytale castle. Walls and floors and ceilings are full of legends and stories of all time. I can look at one tapestry. Then dream of the story behind it all day."

Warrick said, "When you said that you would be ashamed. Shamed before the women of the court I tried to imagine what you meant. So last night my warriors rolled out the rugs and hung the tapestries. We thought that if we could fill Rose Fire with manly art. Do you think the ladies will like the manly art? The art I purchased from all over the world?"

She laughed, "Envy will make them eat their livers. Especially when they see the beauty of your tapestries and rugs."

She hugged him tight and said, "Also, your handsomeness will turn them green with jealousy. Covetous feelings for you will overcome their reason."

IN THE BLACK MOUNTAINS.

Far up on the mountain more Skinwalkers joined Wolv on a plateau. He pulled out drawings of the castle and said, "Here. This is how we will weaken the protection of the castle to capture Marian."

He pointed to Gulum and said, "Go. Find more mercenaries and Skinwalkers. Tell them that I will pay them well if they help me capture Marian."

-

-

-

CHAPTER, Now in Rose Fire, Wales, Year @ 1250s A.D.

SHE MUST NOT GIVE BIRTH TO HER CHAMPION'S CHILDREN.

ARRIVAL OF THE KING. WEDDING. ANOTHER RUSE OF BATTLE.
Faint, distant Sext bells began to ring.

IN THE BLACK MOUNTAINS, SEXT BELLS OBSESSIONS.
Wolv walked back into a cave to a kidnaped Catholic priest. He said, "You have said Mass and consecrated the bread?"
The priest said, "Yes. I am about to eat the consecrated bread."
Wolv snatched the consecrated host from the rough wooden altar.
As he touched the consecrated host, Wolv burst into red-yellow flame.
Wolv howled, "Priest. You are to call me master."
The priest answered, "Only Jesus is my master."
The AntiChrist growled, "Then out of the cave while I talk with your master. You will live since you say Mass for me. I must have Jesus' Presence in the Eucharist."
Then the priest said, "It is a dream of every catholic priest. Every priest to feel Jesus in the Eucharist as you do. Without faith, but with certitude."
Wolv growled, "Not a dream, a nightmare, a curse. The curse of certitude. To know Jesus intimately, to touch him. In Egypt to play with him as a child. In Jerusalem, to scourge him. To nail him to the cross in Jerusalem. A spear, to thrust a spear into his side up into his heart in Jerusalem. The only mercy I ever showed Jesus."
The priest said, "How could you give Jesus mercy?"
Wolv said, "I thrust a spear into his side up into his heart. Not break his legs and arms. We broke the legs and arms of the two thieves. Priest. Run from me out of this cave before I eat you. Alive."
Then the kidnaped priest ran from the cave out into the Black Mountains' snow.
Wye Valley Sext Bells grew louder.
In the cave Wolv fell to his knees and begged. "Please take from me this Sext torture. Jesus, I can feel you in the consecrated host the same. The same as when I nailed you to the cross at Sext

bells. I know you are here in my palm. Jesus, please end my misery. Please give me Pamia. Please raise Pamia from the dead for me."

Wolv's Sext growls of 'Pamia' again shook the mountains.

OUTSIDE ROSE FIRE.

When the Sext sun was at its zenith, the king's heralds pranced outside Rose Fire.

Warrick said, "Marian. The king arrives in the middle of Wolv's Crucifixion obsessions. He chooses to ignore Wolv's dangers. King Edward is well aware of Wolv's power and danger."

IN A CAVE ATOP THE BLACK MOUNTAINS.

Wolv heard Jesus' words, "My beloved childhood friend. Ask for forgiveness of your sins and you can be with Pamia."

The AntiChrist shook the mountains with his repeated growls, "Never, forgiveness. Never."

Then Wolv's anger, rage and hatred shot from his mouth as black-red flames. The flames filled the cavern.

Then Wolv's Sext's obsessions faded.

IN ROSE FIRE. WEDDING IS A RUSE FOR BATTLE PREPARATION.

Lord Warrick ordered the lowering of the drawbridge. The king's heralds stormed in and mounted the outer wall battlement. From the battlement they blew their trumpets to announce the arrival of the king.

Their music echoed between the clefts in the Black Mountains. It mixed with the bells in Rose Fire and the Wye River Valley Sext bells.

ON THE BLACK MOUNTAINS.

Far up on the mountain Wolv said, "Gulum. If we knew King Edward was coming we could have laid a trap for him. Warrick would have charged from Rose Fire to save his king. With Warrick and his knights gone, we would have invaded Rose Fire and captured Marian."

IN ROSE FIRE.

In the castle, Marian and Nicola ran out onto the battlement.

Next over the drawbridge, rode the king's guard. Just in front of the king and queen. All in the king's guard wore polished armor. Their horses pranced. All the king's guard knew Warrick. He trained every one of them. King Edward only trusted Warrick's knights.

Edward the First and Queen Eleanor rode on prancing horses. Across Rose Fire's drawbridge. From the horses' halters, braided with golden strands, golden bells. They rang with each prance of the horses. Royal red thick linen riding blankets covered the horses. From around their necks to their haunches. Down to their ankles. Both mounts held their heads high as if with the greatest of pride.

The king and queen wore the same gold braid linen. His queen wore a royal red cloak over a royal red gown. The king wore a thick padded cloak and padded leggings. Of the same texture and color, royal red. Both wore mail and armor under their clothes.

Next came the king's rear royal guard, all in polished silver-plated armor. Then mounted pages held high the church's pennants of a cross upon a red field.

Behind the pages the archbishop, with a great white fur coat lined in red. His cloak's lining was royal red fur. His guards wore armor with red crosses on their breast plates. Each guard carried the church pennants high on the tips of their jousting lances.

Nicola pointed, "There, behind the archbishop, is the fun. See the many bright red wagons. They are full of giant pavilions where the entertainers will sleep and eat. The wagons are full of clowns and acrobats and good candies to eat."

Marian said, "The courtier will sleep in pavilions? Warrick said that the courtier would sleep in the stables."

Nicola said, "You are so easy to tease. You need to learn Warrick's sense of humor. They will put the pavilions up in the bailey."

Marian formed two fists. She said, "I am so angry with him. I will find a way to get him back."

Nicola said, "Marian. He plays your emotions like a musician plays a lute."

Nicola pointed and said, "Marian. Jewels on the long train of nobles and their ladies. What bright shades of amber and emerald and crimson."

Nicola pointed, "What is the name of that blue color?"

Marian said, "Sapphire blue."

Then Nicola said, "Marian, look, more wagons, way down the mountain. Ox wagons."

Teenage Nicola jumped up and down and clapped her hands. She said, "The gossip is that they carry gifts for you and Warrick."

Warrick ran up the steps on the outer battlement and said, "Hurry. Marian, Nicola, run down to the bailey, hurry."

Warrick waved his hand. He said, "Hurry, the king is about to dismount."

Warrick, Marian, and Nicola ran up to and beside the king.

One of the king's guards brought a stool to the king. A stool he used to dismount while another did the same for the queen.

The king shouted "Warrick" and stepped forward. He gave Warrick a hug as if he were hugging a long lost brother. Then he held him by the shoulders and said, "How are you? My closest friend, England's greatest warrior, and my champion?"

WEDDING AS A GUISE FOR A MILITARY BUILD UP.

King Edward put his arm around Warrick's neck and led him over to a corner. Edward said, "Warrick. You are the world's only hope. We are staging this wedding as a guise for a military buildup. Wolv's red fog is in London, Rome, Jerusalem, Germany, everywhere. Messengers bring us news that Wolv's red-fog is all over the world. You must tell me how you will defeat Wolv. Or he will spread war all over the world. Just as when Wolv was Attila. Attila the Hun. He ravaged the world. Until his new bride, his new 'Pamia', called Gudrun or Ildico, got Attila drunk. She was secretly also of your Able-Symon-Cyrene Pendragon line. Then she plunged Blessed daggers into him until the hilts were not visible. Then she poured Blessed Extreme Unction Oil down his throat. The Blessed daggers and blessed Extreme unction oil made him burn red-yellow flames. His followers thought the gods made him burn. They buried him like that. His Skinwalkers dug him up. When the Huns saw him alive, they fled in fear. They abandoned him. They did not know that no one can destroy Wolv. Only slow him. We are staging this wedding as a disguise for a military build up. Warrick, you are the world's only hope."

Marian glanced at the faces in the great crowd.

Marian whispered to Nicola, "Look at their faces. Many of them are truly happy for my lord but look at the rest."

Nicola said, "Yes Marian. Envy, the look of envy on the king's lords and ladies."

Marian said, "Yes. Everyone here knows that the king will give Warrick much more wealth and responsibility. They envy him to the extent that many would harm him if they could."

The king put one hand on Marian's shoulder and his other on Nicola's shoulder. He said, "And what would the two of you be whispering about. How to overthrow England?"

He grinned wide and gazed straight into their eyes.

Marian's eyes grew big as white saucers. White saucers with little blue dots in the center. *Her only thought was, "I can escape if I fall over and play dead. Then they will bury me."*

Nicola tried to address the king and said, "My lord, no, my lady. . . ." She put her hand over her mouth.

Warrick said, "Nicola. You curtsy and say 'Your Majesty.'"

Marian and Nicola curtsied and Nicola said, "Your Majesty. We were talking about how magnificent you looked. More wonderful than anyone told us."

He put his hands on his hips, threw his head back, and roared in laughter. His laughter echoed off Rose Fire then off the mountains. It sounded like Warrick's thunderclap-like laugh.

He bent down low and whispered, "Marian. You were saying that some of those here envy Lord Warrick."

Both Marian and Nicola put their hands over their mouths. Marian said, "Your Majesty, you heard."

The king said, "Yes, I always hear everything."

The king straightened his back. He pointed high to his heralds on the battlement. The heralds obeyed and trumpeted for all to listen to the king. All grew quiet. He bellowed, "It has come to my attention through innocent eyes that. That many of you envy my love and admiration for Lord Warrick."

Then the crowd gave a loud nervous laugh.

Edward shouted to the crowd, "Lord Warrick is my champion. Lord Warrick has defeated the greatest knights in all England in the war games. He saved my life in France. That when all others were afraid to wade into the enemy."

The king pulled Warrick's great ax from Warrick's sword belt. He held blessed Dread over his head and bellowed, "Lord Warrick. It was Lord Warrick and only Warrick. My champion pulled out this ax, blessed Dread, and charged the enemy. It was Warrick and only Warrick that sent my attackers to perdition. It was Warrick and only Warrick that bandaged me before I could bleed to death. So I say to all of you. You that envy the love that I have for Lord Warrick."

The king took in a deep breath and shouted, "Go . . . to . . . Hellllllllllllllllllllllllllllll."

The word "hell" echoed off the Black Mountains.

A great hush struck the crowd. Nobody breathed.

The head of the king's guard yelled, "To Lord Warrick and his bride Marian." Five times all yelled this phrase, five times.

Drayton whispered into Marian's ear, "Warrick had trained every knight in the king's guard. They are as loyal to Warrick as they are to the king. Warrick is loyal to the king."

Then the king bent down to Marian and Nicola. King Edward laughed and said, "Marian. Look around, now do you see envy on anyone's face."

Marian said, "No, your majesty."

Nicola said, "Only fear. Except him." She naively pointed.

The king turned. He threw his head back and laughed. He bent down to Nicola. Edward pointed and said, "He is my treasurer. It is not the face of coveting thy neighbor's goods."

King Edward pinched Marian's bottom.

Marian jumped. She held her bottom with both hands.

Edward said, "Marian. It is the face of coveting thy neighbor's wife."

The king and Warrick guffawed.

Marian blushed.

The king said, "Marian. The look on all the men's faces until we leave your beautiful presence."

She felt mortified and froze like a fawn in tall grass. Like a fawn trying to hide from a lion.

Warrick said, "You are supposed to curtsy and say, thank you, your majesty."

Marian curtsied and said, "Thank you, your majesty."

Marian screwed up her courage and asked, "Your Majesty, may I speak."

Then the king said, "Please, you have opened my eyes to envy this day. What other revelations will you have?"

Marian said, "May I kick Lord Warrick's chins?"

Everyone heard and laughed.

The king said, "I hear that you do better than that." He took her hand and said, "Do what I hear that you do." He put her hand on Warrick's chest hair and said, "Marian. Grasp a great handful and pull."

The king and Warrick and all laughed. They knew she would not.

She did. She blew his chest hair from her hand.

Warrick grimaced.

The king roared in laughter and said, "Not only is Marian England's fairest child. She has courage. Warrick. I love her."

Jealously and envy ran through the courtier ladies. Jealously that the king considered Marian the fairest child of all. Deep, dangerous jealously shocked the ladies of the court. Many could not breathe. Some put their hands over their mouths. Some of them looked around nervously but avoided everyone's eyes. Their gaze circled the faces of others. They did not give an honest gaze to anyone. Intense jealously crippled them. Jealously shocked them so much that it bleached all the color from their faces. Bleached as white as summer clouds.

The king said, "Marian has wisdom, genius, and courage . . . and . . . beauty. I may just steal her for my self."

Suddenly the king made big eyes of expectation of trouble. Trouble with the queen. He looked at the queen with a worrisome look.

The queen just rolled her eyes high. She knew he was always bombastic and humorous like this.

The king raised his eyebrows and furrowed his brow. He knew that when he was in their private chambers, the queen would chide him. Chide him for his word that he would take Marian for himself.

He glanced at the queen.

Marian curtsied and said, "Your Majesty. A meal is awaiting you that anyone would serve in the greatest castles in Heaven."

The king commanded, "Then lead on."

As they walked in the great hall, Marian whispered to Warrick, "Warrick. You embarrassed me. I knew to curtsy."

Warrick whispered, "Marian. I am sure you would have curtsied in a day or two."

HIGH ON THE BLACK MOUNTAINS.

From high on the mountain Wolv surveyed the number of armored knights. All to quarter inside and outside the castle. Wolv said, "Gulum. With the king at Rose Fire Warrick will become over confident. He will think that he is safe. He will be easier to trick."

From a red dragon Lilith changed into a feminine wraith beside Wolv. Lilith said, "Wolv. You will capture Marian, and change her destiny. Remember Wolv. Warrick and Marian must not be together. Some loves must not be. Marian must not give birth to Warrick's children."

-

-

-

CHAPTER, Now in Rose Fire, Wales, Year @ 1250s A.D.

YOU ARE DESTINED TO FILL HELL WITH SOULS, SOULS FULL OF HATE.

As they walked, the king said, "Warrick. Gwynedd Llewellyn, Prince of Wales, and Llewellyn's brother, David Ap. Gruffydd, and Wolv are the cause of the Wales rebellion. Wolv is using the Gruffydd clan and Llewellyn's clan to conquer Wales. Then he will take Skinwalkers and invade England."

Warrick said, "Yes, Llewellyn is a source of trouble here. He combined with Wolv to gain castles, wealth and power. The AntiChrist will kill all the Welsh when he finishes. We must save the Welsh from Wolv."

The king said, "We must reinforce a circle of castle fortifications around Wales. Fortifications from the Wye River's Builth to north Wales Beaumaris. Then back down to south Wales Dryslwyn."

Lord Warrick said, "Yes. My king. We need to build many new castles to encircle Wales. Or the Skinwalkers will burn a swath to London, after they burn all Wales."

The king walked and said, "Warrick. The prisoners you sent danced a tune and sang a song. We learned much from them. We brought battle plans with us."

TRAITOR.

Lord Warrick stopped short. He whispered, "My king. You have a traitor, a viper in your bosom. He or she gives secrets to the enemy. Throw out those battle plans. They are already in enemy hands."

The king said, "You wrote me that I have a viper in my court. It is why you took the initiative? The initiative to take Rose Fire at a date without my knowledge?"

Warrick said, "Yes, my king. From Cheshire to Newport, the enemy has attacked your armies in strategic mountain passes. They had such precise information of where and when. They had time to build great landslides in front and behind your armies. These tactical landslides take weeks to build and plan. The ambushes happened too often to be accidental."

Edward said, "If all my lords were of your initiative, England would be peaceful. Peaceful like a babe in its mother's arms."

IN THE BLACK MOUNTAINS.

Wolv said, "Now my destiny is to have Marian. All I want is Marian. Marian has Pamia's soul. I will have Marian and Rose Fire as Marian's gilded cage. I care not for Wales or England, all I want is Marian. Yes, I will have her no matter how much blood I must spill."

Lilith appeared and said, "We have our means, Wolv, Marian will soon be yours. After you fulfill your obsession over Marian, you must do as Satan wishes. Turn men from Holiness to Haters-of-Jesus, just like you. You are to lead men into evil and from evil into Hell. Your destiny is to fill Hell with souls. Souls that dedicate themselves to evil."

-

-

-

CHAPTER, Now in Rose Fire, Wales, Year @ 1250s A.D.

COLNE THE TRAITOR.

In the shelter of the great hall the king put his hand on Warrick's shoulder. The king walked with Warrick over to a tall thin man in green leathers. Green, the color of greed and envy. A thin man of hungry-build.

The king said, "Warrick. Meet Lord Colne of Sudbury."

Warrick looked into Colne's cold eyes, then put his hand on Blessed Dread's hilt. Colne's caved in cheeks gave the appearance of a hungry hyena.

Suddenly Colne's eyes glanced down to the hilt. Then up into Lord Warrick's now burning emerald eyes.

Colne stepped back and grimaced. Somehow he knew Lord Warrick could see through to his traitorous heart.

The king said, "My trusted friends, you should not take a dislike to each other. Treasurer Colne has done an exemplary service on England's finances. He has improved trade so that tariffs have brought in much more taxes."

Treasurer Colne walked on one side of the king. Lord Warrick and Marian on the other.

Lord Warrick walked backwards and motioned Drayton to himself.

Warrick whispered to Drayton, "Follow Colne. Tell me everything he does and sees. Everyone to whom he speaks."

The king reached over and took Marian's hand. He had a merry smile on his tanned face.

Marian's knees grew weak. She stopped walking, curtsied and bowed her head low. She became dizzy and thought she would faint at his feet.

The king said, "Marian, no young maidens in England are more beautiful than you."

Marian blushed.

They sat at the great horseshoe-shaped table. The smells from the buttery were heavenly. Rose Fire's great hall was full of royalty, lords, ladies, clergy and servants. The archbishop said a prayer. Then the king sat in a great high back chair. After he sat, all the others sat.

Warrick held out a great key and said, "My king, with your leave. I go to bring the wine, mead and ale."

The king said, "Yes, make haste."

Warrick and servants came out of the converted dungeon. They carried caskets of wine, mead and ale. They knocked the corks from them and pushed in turn-stoppers. The servants quickly filled mugs for all the guests. They returned for more barrels.

The king quaffed down three tankards of mead and said, "Warrick. It is the strongest, sweetest mead I have ever tasted. Who is responsible for this brew?"

Warrick said, "Marian, my king, Marian."

The king said, "What causes the castle to vibrate?"

Warrick said, "That is Wolv in his Holy-Mary-obsession. Guilt causes him to scream Holy Mary's words to him, 'Little Wolv. I will always love you'."

The king said, "Wolv is strong. Warrick, you are the world's only hope against the AntiChrist."

Lord Warrick said, "My king. I have chased him away several times. I will chase him away again. While I have life, I will chase Wolv across the earth. No peace to Evil, I will give Wolv no peace."

Then the king said, "Mead, food for the body and happiness for the soul." He raised his pewter-mug high and said, "To Marian, the provider of the feast. To Marian the brew master."

Everyone by this time had drunk at least one tankard of mead. They shouted the same words as the king. "To Marian the brew master."

The cooks lined up to present the king with each dish for his approval. First the cooks carried platters of roasted venison. Then wild-boar, then platters filled with rabbit in many different spices. The king nodded approval to them all. Then he waved to the cooks and said, "Serve everything."

Servants carried flaming capons and boiled eggs. Then they brought out roasted peacocks stuffed with honey sauce-covered apples and raisins.

The servants carried baked apples and hams stuffed with cumin and bay leaf. They brought in vegetable dishes of spinach greens and leeks. Servants poured ladles of honey sauce over them. They brought out chicken pies, beef and venison pies. Breads of every variety. They placed shakers of precious salt and even more precious pepper on the tables.

Servants did not stop piling the tables high with food. As everyone ate, they carried out cakes of fruits, figs and raisins, and custard tarts. The servants laid bowls of cherry pottage and bacon pudding around the tables.

The guests raved about the mead and wine. It was the mead that they consumed the most.

IN THE BLACK MOUNTAINS.

A spy climbed the mountain to Wolv and said, "Lord Wolv."

As a flock of crows, Wolv alighted around the spy. Wolv, as crows, said in unison, "Speak."

The spy said, "My lord. Bad news, all in the castle are in good spirits my lord. They will be very hard to defeat."

As crows, Wolv said, "I can hear their revelry. We will defeat them. I and I alone will have Marian."

-

-

-

CHAPTER, Now in Rose Fire, Wales, Year @ 1250s A.D.

CREAL THE SPY

Marian looked out on the outer wall battlement and saw Collette with Creal. Creal was a red haired, freckled, six-foot young man, one of the king's squires.

Marian said, "Nicola, look, Collette has found a sweat heart."

Nicola said, "Yes."

Collette ran from the battlement to Marian and curtsied. She said, "My lady, I beg you. Would you intervene with Lord Warrick so Creal can train with him as a knight?"

Marian lead Creal to Warrick out on the training field. Warrick stood with Ross-Templar, Morgan, and Drayton.

Lady Marian said, "My lord, this is Creal, a squire in the king's court."

Marian turned to Creal and said, "Ask my lord what you will."

The young freckled red-haired squire, Creal said, "My lord. I am a squire from the king's court. I wish to train under you as a knight, may I?"

Warrick turned to Creal and said, "You dare disturb me on the practice field?"

Creal said, "My lord, it is where warriors belong."

Suddenly, Warrick raised his arm to punch the squire.

Marian gasped. She put her hands over her mouth that Warrick would be so cruel.

The squire stood firm.

Then Warrick said, "If you had backed away, I would have said no. You stood your ground. It is the first test of a good knight. You were a squire in the king's court, but with me you are a page."

Warrick pointed, "Lord Morgan will assign you to a knight. Assign to practice for the king's tournament games, be off."

The freckle faced squire-now-page, Creal, stood in stunned silence. He said, "But my lord, you have reduced me from a squire to a page. It took me five years of hard work to become a squire."

Warrick said, "Page, you just failed a test. You are supposed to obey orders without question. You will now take six years to become a squire. Now start with one year as a stable boy and quarry worker. You are to follow the orders of the other stable boys without question. At night you will work in the quarry. From Compline bells to morn Prime bells, you will carry granite from the quarry."

The freckle-faced red-haired Creal, hung his head. He walked toward Rose Fire's stables.

Once Creal was too far away to hear, Marian put her fists to her chest. She said, "Warrick. Never have I seen such a heartless man as you."

Warrick said, "Marian. Obedience, strict obedience is at the very heart of knighthood. Only an obedient knight survives battle."

Marian whispered, "Obey, obey, obey, you only think about obedience."

Creal walked over to the drawbridge guard. He said, "Sire, I am to spend a year in the stables. Then at night carry granite in the quarry. That before I can test for a page position."

The guard pointed to the stables inside Rose Fire.

ON THE PRACTICE FIELD.

Marian said, "My lord, your hard ways constantly astound me. They infuriate me."

Marian pivoted. Her brow formed and angry V. She leveled her jaw and walked back into Rose Fire.

DOUBTS ABOUT CREAL.

Warrick and his tree brothers stood together. All four brothers had heard Marian's words. All four brothers had observed Creal.

Warrick said, "Drayton. We will test Creal's obedience and his instinct to follow orders. Morgan. If he works obediently for thirty days, make him a page. If he does his duties as a page for thirty days make him a squire."

Morgan said, "Should you not explain that to Marian?"

Warrick said, "No. Marian would only tell Creal and comfort him. That would ruin the test. Creal has to believe he is a stable boy for a long time."

Ross-Templar put his thumbs in his sword belt. He said, "Warrick. You never agree to train other squires. You demand that you train everyone from page to knight. Why did you say that you would train him?"

Lord Warrick said, "Only as a favor to Marian. I fear, an unwise favor to Marian."

Warrick asked, "Brothers. Did any of you have an uneasiness toward Creal?"

Drayton held his bow in his crossed arms. He said, "He lowers his head and shifts his eyes too much. Like a weasel that searches for prey."

Warrick said, "I noticed that too. Yet, I did not want to break Marian's heart again. I will work him hard and melt that shiftiness out of him."

Morgan held his mace over his shoulder and said, "Warrick. An emotional gulf still exists between you and Marian."

Warrick said, "Yes. The only thing Marian and I have in common are our misunderstanding of each other. We argue like an old married couple."

TRAITOR CREAL.

Inside the stables, Creal climbed into the upper loft. He pulled velum parchments from under the hay. Then he wrote the same message on all vellums.

To Lord David Ap. Gruffydd of Wales and Lord Llewellyn Ap. Gruffydd of Wales, Wolv, and Colne.

I am inside Rose Fire as a permanent worker. I will kidnap Marian when you request. *Creal, your loyal servant.*

Then Creal stuffed the vellums underneath a haystack. Slowly he climbed down to the horses. Then, Creal began to shovel horse manure into a wagon. A wicked grin formed on his face.

He began to shovel horse manure into a wagon. He lowered his head and shifted his eyes to see if anyone noticed him.

The head stable boy yelled, "Hey, you with the shifty eyes, shovel here first. I will call you 'shifty eyes,' yes your name is now 'Shifty Eyes.'"

Creal led the horse and wagon to where the head stable boy stood.

COLNE, THE TRAITOR.

In the upper loft of the stables, Colne, the king's treasurer, appeared. Appeared from out of the shadows. He reached deep under the hay and pulled out the vellums.

-

-

-

CHAPTER, Now in Rose Fire, Wales, Year @ 1250s A.D.

SKINWALKERS WITHIN ROSE FIRE.

Handmaiden, Collette arranged Marian's wedding dress on her. The dress did not fit well.

Marian raised her chin and said, "This dress must do. It is the only one that I have."

Collette whispered to a seamstress that helped with the sewing. She said, "How come Marian's waist looks so wide?"

The seamstress whispered, "Collette. No one in the castle knows how to sew this silk. The seams will not hold the curve of Marian's waist or highlight her breasts' curves. None of us understand how the silk stretches or folds."

Then the seamstress again whispered to Collette, "Marian will always be disappointed. Disappointed that her wedding dress was not adequate."

Queen Eleanor and Nicola entered the solar. Behind Nicola a servant carried something long. Whatever it was, someone had wrapped it in beautiful white satin. The long item stretched across both the servants' arms. It reached down to the floor from both their arms.

Marian asked, "My queen, whatever could that be? It is twice your height."

Behind Nicola two servants carried a large oak box. Behind those two servants, another servant carried a smaller oak box.

Eleanor said, "Marian. Let us help you take off that wedding gown and put on this one."

They helped her take off the defective gown. The one she did not want to wear, the one that did not fit.

The servant placed the long wrap of satin on the bed and straightened it. She unwrapped it. The shine of gold and silver threads struck Marian's eyes. She clasped her hands and gasped, "A wedding gown. A gold and silver threaded wedding gown, of the finest silk."

Eleanor said, "Yes. Its many layers of satin silk are so thin they are transparent. A wedding gown fit for any queen."

Marian asked, "Who?"

Eleanor answered, "Lord Warrick. He ordered it made in London and shipped it with us to you."

Eleanor said, "No tears of happiness now. Your tears will stain the dress."

Marian dabbed a cloth to her eyes. She said, "He does have a soft heart. He loves me. He does love me and have a soft heart. Where is he? I must go to him."

Queen Eleanor said, "Not now, we have many things to do."

They pulled the wedding gown over her head. Eleanor said, "Marian, you must stop dripping tears, they will stain the satin."

Eleanor opened the smaller box. She pulled out a diamond studded gold link belt with a dagger and sheath. That hung from the last link. Polished, cut white diamonds covered the dagger and sheath.

Eleanor said, "Warrick brought these diamonds and rubies from Jordan. He gave them to the royal jeweler to make you this belt and dagger."

Torchlight glistened off the diamonds on the dagger handle and sheath.

Collette knelt and put silk shoes on Marian.

Queen Eleanor took a gold circlet from the longer box. She placed it on Marian's head. Then she pulled out a long train from the larger box.

She said, "We attach this long train to your gold circlet. Warrick had it made with transparent satin silk and gold thread. The train is equal in length to the chapel."

She attached the train to the gold circlet on Marian's head.

Then Eleanor said, "And this," she pulled out a golden ringlet of emeralds. "It snaps inside the other ringlet to hold the train to your head."

Collette said, "The emeralds are almost as bright as Warrick's eyes."

Eleanor said, "Yes. Never have I seen such handsome eyes as Warrick's emerald eyes." She grinned and whispered low in Marian's ear, "Not even in Edward."

Eleanor placed the emerald ringlet inside the outer gold ring. With a slight push they snapped together and held her train on her head.

Eleanor pulled Marian's golden hair forward so it cascaded over her shoulders.

Queen Eleanor said, "Every man will envy Warrick tonight."

Marian blushed.

Collette said, "Marian. My lady, you are stunning, so stunning."

Nicola said, "Yes. Dazzling."

Eleanor said, "Today is your special day, today you are a bride. It is a day every girl plans a thousand times in her happiest dreams."

HIGH IN THE BLACK MOUNTAINS SKINWALKERS GATHER.

Far up on the mountainside, on a plateau, Wolv said, "Gulum. Soon Marian will be mine."

In a black, feminine specter form, Lilith appeared beside Wolv.

Lilith said, "Creal is within the castle. Wolv. Marian will soon be yours. Then you can do Satan's work, with your Marian-obsession ended. Satan demands that you turn souls to evil. Just as your soul is evil."

Wolv said, "Lilith. Have you prepared Rose Fire?"

Lilith said, "I have threatened many Rose Fire servants with death. To escape death they chose to be possessed. They sold their souls to Satan as you did. They are Skinwalkers in disguise. Wolv. They will be loyal to you when we attack."

-

-

-

CHAPTER, Now in Rose Fire, Wales, Year @ 1250s A.D.

THE WEDDING. A MILITARY RUSE.

In her wedding gown, Marian waited at the entrance of the chapel, in an alcove. She moved to a room off the chapel vestibule. There she waited for the wedding to start. Those in the wedding procession waited with her for the music to begin.

Warrick had ordered the chapel filled with yellow and white crocuses in full bloom. The sun beamed through the colored glass of the chapel windows.

The chapel's pink granite and polished oak reflected the stained glass windows' colors. Colored sunbeams sparkled off the bright gowns and knight's polished armor.

In the first pew, the king and queen sat, both in royal red. The king wore his crown and a royal red blouse. Red leggings. He had a long royal red cape over his shoulders. Edward's queen wore her crown and a royal red gown. A royal red cloak identical in color and texture to the king.

Lords and ladies filled the rest of the chapel. Edward's lords wore fine leathers and polished armor. Their ladies wore brightly colored beautiful gowns. They filled all the chapel pews. Their gowns and armor glistened in the sunbeams through the colored glass window.

Warrick's knights in shining blessed-armor stood at attention. They lined the sides of the chapel. From the chapel's entrance to the chapel's sanctuary rail.

In front, at the sanctuary rail, Warrick and the Archbishop stood. They waited for Marian to walk up the aisle.

Warrick and the Archbishop stood before the altar at the sanctuary rail.

Four altar boys knelt around the altar with hand-rung silver bells. Altar boys waited to ring to announce the presence of Marian.

England's bishops lined the chapel sanctuary.

Warrick's black hair glistened down his head and neck. It settled on his golden blessed-armor yolk on his shoulders. He stood in polished gold-plated blessed-armor before the archbishop. His helm and gauntlets lay on the altar behind the archbishop.

The altar boy rang the silver bells to announce the bride. The king's heralds blew the wedding songs.

Small boys sang in the choir loft. The church filled with heavenly music.

Flower children threw daisy pedals before Marian. She walked into view. Everyone turned around in their seats to see her. They gasped at the sight of her beauty. A great hush rolled over the crowd. They saw her in the beautiful silver-gold embossed gown Warrick had ordered made for her. Her train was the length of the chapel.

Monks from the village friary sang with the boys' choir.

Joy filled the air.

It was as if Warrick were in a trance. He could only look into her blue eyes and drink in her beauty. Her beauty brought him peace, fulfillment, rapture, happiness.

Marian's beauty filled him with happiness and love. A love that creates the most wonderful tender heartfelt marriages.

The ceremony seemed to go so fast for him. Suddenly he heard, "You may kiss the bride."

They kissed as if for the first time.

Marian felt his love pour into her. She felt an unbounded love from him.

The altar boys rang silver bells in the chapel. Boys pulled the ropes of the great bells of the Rose Fire chapel. The bells pulled the boys up and down off the floor.

Then the great bells rang of all the Monasteries, Nunneries and Chapels. Wye River Valley now had a Lady for their Lord.

Joy filled their hearts.

HIGH IN THE BLACK MOUNTAINS.

High on the mountain above Rose Fire Wolv heard the marital music. Wolv clenched his fists and spit.

He thought, "I will have Marian all to my self. No matter how many bodies I must cleave."

Wolv thought of what he knew about Marian.

He thought, "Marian's compassion is the key to capturing Rose Fire. Thus, capturing her. I will have her to myself."

Wolv sat on his wraith horse.

Lilith floated in the air beside him and said, "We have Creal within Rose Fire. I have threatened other servants in Rose Fire. They have sold their souls to Satan rather than have me kill them. Remember. The love of Marian and Warrick must not be. Some loves must not be. Marian must not bear Warrick's children. Through future centuries, their progeny will defeat you, Wolv."

-

-

-

CHAPTER, Now in Rose Fire, Wales, Year @ 1250s A.D.

EVIL BURNS THE WYE VALLEY.

High up on the mountain above the snow line, Wolv raged. Wolv swore all night because Marian was this night in Warrick's arms. He shouted curse words and spit with each curse. He stomped deep footprints in the earth. Hatred caused saliva to flow down his chin. With each turn of his head he flung the saliva from his chin. His red bloodshot eyes glowed. He growled and threw his arms into the air.

NO PEACE FOR EVIL.
Wolv fell to his knees and growled, "Holy Mary. Leave me alone."

His eye glazed over black as his ancient Holy-Mary-obsession overcame him. On his knees, Wolv repeatedly howled Holy Mary's words, "Little Wolv. I will always love you." Each howl shook the Black Mountains.

Wolv's rage shot from his mouth as black-red flame and filled the sky. The black smoke blocked out all light, until the wind blew it away.

Slowly Wolv came out of his obsessions. On his knees in the snow, Wolv raised his fists to the night sky. He growled, "Holy Mary. Leave me alone, stop torturing me."

IN THE WYE RIVER VALLEY
Wolv descended into the Wye River Valley.

Down in the Wye River Valley, Wolv surveyed the valley. Wolv said, "Gulum. I know how to trick Warrick's knights to leave Rose Fire defenseless. Then I can capture Marian."

Wolv dug his heels into his steed. He galloped and said, "Yes, Gulum, Marian will be mine and mine alone."

Then Wolv burst into black crows and flew high into the Black Mountains.

Then the AntiChrist formed into his black wraith form with his charcoal horse. He spoke aloud, "Skinwalkers. From here I can see the necessary signals."
-

-

-

CHAPTER, Now in Rose Fire, Wales, Year @ 1250s A.D.

A PERFECT NIGHT FOR EVIL. RED-FOG ROLLS DOWN
FROM THE BLACK MOUNTAINS.

Marian held Warrick's arm and said, "My love. Must you patrol, so close to our wedding day? We were just married."

Warrick said, "Marian. The red-fog rolls down from the mountain peaks. Wolv prepares to attack."

Lord Warrick stood on the outer wall battlement in his black leathers. He put both his big calloused hands on the battlement ramparts. They looked out over his protectorate. The wind blew his black cloak as if he had great black eagle wings. The mountain wind blew his hair back.

Marian wore his other black cloak with the white deer-fur lining. She hugged his huge strong arm between her breasts.

She said, "In the moonlight, I can see the valley children in the apple trees. They sit high in the branches and bite into big round tangy apples."

Warrick said, "The valley smells of bubbling pots of apple butter and apple dumplings."

Marian said, "This fall the Wye Valley is green and lush from the blessed rain."

Warrick said, "Marian. This fall the Black Mountains below the snow line are arid from the mountain drought.

Lord Warrick said, "Lilith and Wolv have brought death to the Black Mountains. Evil, death and drought. The AntiChrist wants to destroy all life, everywhere."

Warrick pointed into the Black Mountains and said, "Marian. Look. In the mountains above Rose Fire, the trees already stand black. Bare, dry, their dead leaves piled on the brittle bushes under the trees. The only moisture in the soil is in the high snow line atop the mountains. Rabbits, deer and other forest creatures migrated from the dry mountains down. Migrated into the Wye valley. The presence of Wolv and Lilith has cursed the Black Mountains. Death. No life in the snow cap. No life below the snow cap on the mountainside."

Marian said, "In the valley, the leaves have turned to brilliant red, pink, and yellow."

Warrick said, "Look at the whirlwinds. In the valley, whirlwinds blow red, purple and yellow leaves in circles."

Marian said, "On the mountain's sides whirlwinds blow only black leaves and dust."

In the moonlight, geese flew overhead south as they honked to one another.

The andiron blazed within Rose Fire and warmed everyone.

Warrick said, "All summer no rain has fallen on the mountains. They are so deep in drought. Wolv has brought a blanket of death upon the mountains. Nothing lives on the mountains below or above the snow line. The trees are dry, brown, and brittle. The mountain grasses and forests could easily burn. Summer rain has blessed the valley. Wolv has cursed the mountains."

Silently, grey fog rolled from the Wye River. The fog settled on the Valley grasses and trees, not on the mountains. Nothing watered the mountains. Darkness as black and opaque as coal encased Rose Fire. A perfect night for evil.

SPY CREAL IN ROSE FIRE.

In the Rose Fire stables *Creal thought, "Tonight Wolv will capture Marian and Rose Fire. I will receive a great reward."*

ON PATROL.

Inside Rose Fire, in Marian's chambers, Warrick took Marian by the shoulders. He said, "Tonight I must go on patrol. I can feel evil in the wind. No matter what happens, do not leave the castle while I am gone. Do not allow any of the knights to leave no matter what happens. Wolv is ruthless and crafty. He has spies in the forests above us. He will know when we leave. This is why we are leaving to patrol on a moonless night. We will be many miles away. We will not be back until morning. If anyone leaves the castle, we will be too far away to help. Do not allow anyone to leave the castle during the night."

Warrick raised Marian by the shoulders and kissed her.

Warrick and his knights walked. They led their horses over the drawbridge as quietly as possible. Once they were well down the mountain, they mounted their steeds. Then they galloped on their patrol.

TRAITOR.

Creal went to the back of Rose Fire. To a section of the outer battlement wall hidden behind a keep tower. Then Creal lit a torch and waved it. He waved the torch to signal to Wolv, higher on the mountain. Signal that Warrick and most of his knights had left Rose Fire.

High on the mountain Wolv waved his torch to tell Creal he saw his message.

In her Chambers Marian glanced out the window. She said, "Nicola. Look, high on the mountain, the Druid worshipers are dancing again."

The full moon moved across the sky.

Warrick was far below in the Wye Valley, far beyond the view of Hereford. No one in Rose Fire could see Warrick. He galloped with his knight north along the Wye River.

A spy in Hereford had watched Warrick ride out of sight. Beyond the sight of the castle. Beyond the sight of Hereford. The spy in Hereford climbed upon a roof. He lit a torch and waved the torch.

High up on the mountains, above the castle, Wolv saw the torch. The torch moved back and forth on the roof of the Hereford building.

Wolv said, "Gulum, Warrick is too far away from Hereford to see Hereford burn. Tonight I capture Marian. Tonight Marian's compassion conquers her."

Wolv waved his own torch to signal to his Skinwalkers. To signal his Skinwalkers around Hereford to burn Hereford.

INSIDE ROSE FIRE.

In the night, inside Rose Fire a bright light attracted Marian to her chamber window. She looked out her window to see Hereford burning in the night like a fireball. The thatch roofs burned so fast that their heat formed their own tornado whirlwinds. The whirlwinds spread sparks through the whole valley.

Marian ran out onto the outer wall battlement. She ran up to the guards on duty and said, "Now. We must help the town's people. Now."

A guard said, "My lady. I am sure the fire is a trick to draw the knights from Rose Fire. Lord Warrick told us not to leave the castle for any reason. Rose Fire would be left with too few knights."

Marian said, "We cannot just let the town burn. Who is the duty knight until Lord Warrick?"

The guard said, "Sir Thetford. He is in the garrison above the first portcullis."

She ran across the outer wall battlement to the garrison. She threw open the door.

In the garrison above the outer wall's portcullis Sir Thetford stood as Marian entered.

Marian said, "Sir Thetford. Should we not help with the Hereford fire?"

Thetford said, "No, my lady, we will not help them. My lord ordered us not to leave Rose Fire until he returns from patrol."

Thetford stood with his other knights, and watched the whole town of Hereford burning. Yellow and red flames whipped into the black night. A tall black column of sparks and smoke swirled out over the valley.

Wolv's Skinwalkers now began to torch the barns around Hereford.

Marian yelled, "Look. Fire on other buildings in the valley. The whole valley could burn. Go. We need some knights to go down there and help them with the flames. Go. Their barns of grain and corn are on fire. They will have no food. Everyone will starve this winter."

A knight said, "Lord Warrick could not have foreseen that the valley would burn. He would want some of us to help with the fires. No matter the danger to Rose Fire."

THE TRAITOR.

Creal wanted more knights to go to Hereford so the castle would be defenseless. So Creal insulted everyone, "Cowards. We would be cowards if we do not help them with the flames."

Sir Thetford turned his head to the town and said, "Remember Lord Warrick. He ordered us not to leave the castle for any reason. If the castle falls to the Skinwalkers, they will still kill everyone in the valley."

Marian said, "Look, the Skinwalkers tonight will leave no one alive. We are here to protect the innocent. Some knights must go to protect the innocent."

TRAITOR.

Creal wanted Warrick's knights to leave Rose Fire unprotected so he shouted, "Cowards. We who are not cowards will go."

Sir Thetford said, "Hold your tongue Creal. Warrick will banish you from his service."

Sir Thetford studied the fires across the valley and frowned. He lowered his head. He sighed and said, "Lady Marian. It is against my lord's orders. Yet, he could not have foreseen that fire would spread across the valley. My best judgement says that the fires are one of Wolv's tricks. We cannot just sit here safely and let the town and valley burn?"

He pointed to a knight and said, "You. Take half the knights to the valley and town. Help with the fires."

They lowered the drawbridge. Half Rose Fire's knights galloped on war horses to help with the valley's fires.

All the remaining knights stood on the outer wall battlement above the drawbridge. The fires in the valley mesmerized them.

TRAITOR.

For this short moment no knights or guards stood at the back of Rose Fire.

Creal crept away from them. He went behind the castle, behind a keep tower. Then Creal waved a torch three times and lowered a rope down over the battlement.

Wolv waved his Skinwalkers forward out of the blackness from under the trees. Silently, one by one they climbed the rope. They themselves lowered other ropes to their waiting Skinwalkers. With many ropes over the side, the Skinwalkers swarmed up the castle wall. They looked like bees on a hive. They covered the backside of Rose Fire. Ropes dangled and swung and snapped tight with their weight. Many Skinwalkers walked through the inner wall's open portcullis. The enemy occupied the battlement of the slanted inner wall, the talus. Also, Skinwalkers captured the talus' garrison above the talus' portcullis.

In a few minutes all the murderous Skinwalkers rushed across the battlement.

Marian and Sir Thetford turned around to see Skinwalker swords at their throats. A hoard of Skinwalkers filled the battlement in both directions.

Wolv grasped Marian by the upper arms.

Sir Thetford, "It is futile. We are too few. If we fight, they will harm Lady Marian. It is best we surrender and fight another day. Lads, lay down your weapons."

They put their weapons down.

Marian thought, "Warrick and Father Malachi told me my compassion was my weakness. Now my own compassion may cost us Rose Fire and . . . Everyone's lives."

Lord Wolv yelled, "Kill every male, adult and child. Sale the females as slaves. I have what I want, Marian. Marian is now mine."

Marian yelled, "No, for God's love, no. If you harm anyone, I will never give myself to you. Spare everyone and . . . and at the end of this disaster. I will give myself to you willingly. Without my cooperation you will never know if I am Pamia. Pamia would never allow you to kill. She tried to stop you from Crucifying Jesus."

Marian thought, "Wolv's weakness is his Pamia obsession. I have read every ancient parchment about Pamia. I will use my knowledge of Pamia to convince Wolv that I am Pamia."

Marian said, "I tried to stop you from Crucifying Jesus. Through tears, I told you that I loved Jesus. That was when you knocked me off Mount Masada."

Wolv said, "Pamia. You said 'knocked 'me' off Mount Masada'."

Marian said, "Wolv. I told you that I loved Jesus and you shouted, 'You only love me'. Then you backhanded my face. I fell backward over the railing. You caught my hand, but my tears on my hand kept you from gripping me. I fell the longest time. Wolv. Harm no one or you will not have me."

Wolv fell to his knees and wept, "Marian. You are Pamia. Only Pamia would know these details."

Marian thought, "Good. My study of Wolv's history is working. He begins to believe that I am Pamia."

Then Wolv stood. Saliva born of the obsession over Pamia dribbled down Wolv's chin. He said, "Skinwalkers. Stay their swords. I have what I want. I have Marian. She is Pamia. Only Pamia would have these memories."

Wolv turned to Marian and said, "Pamia. You must willingly do what I say. Otherwise, you will never see Nicola again."

Marian shouted, "Oh, Warrick. My champion. Where are you?"

Wolv said, "Marian. Pamia. Do not confuse yourself. You see that Pamia has not had time to come forward in you. You must allow Pamia to come out completely. As to Warrick, he will soon be dead. We have laid a trap for him, a trap that no man can survive."

Marian said, "Wolv. If you harm Nicola or any in Rose Fire, you will never have me. I will not allow Pamia to show herself."

Wolv twisted her arm and said, "A little torture will loosen your will."

Marian said, "I will only fall unconscious or die. You killed me when you backhanded me from your Mount Masada castle. Either way you will not have me. Not willingly. Pamia wants to come forth and be with you. Yet, Pamia is like me. She will not accept your evil."

Lord David Ap. Gruffydd and Lord Llewellyn Ap. Gruffydd, stepped forward. Traitor Creal stepped from behind them.

Marian slapped Creal and said, "Warrick was training you. Your affections for Collette were only ruses."

The AntiChrist said, "Effective and planned ruses. Down to your bending your lord's will to let Creal into Rose Fire. Your compassion for all, including Creal, is your weakness."

Wolv pulled out a dagger and plunged it deep into Creal's belly.

He wiped his dagger on his sleeve and said, "Never, never trust a traitor."

Marian shouted, "No more killing. Or you will never see Pamia. No more killing."

Wolv walked away from Marian and said, "Gulum. Swale. I do not want Marian to hear or know. Make sure that you kill all Adorationists. Go into the chapel. Kill anyone that tries to do

Adoration. Then Gulum, come back to me and tell me what you found."

Within moments Gulum returned and said, "Wolv. We killed all the Adorationists in the Chapel. No one in Rose Fire does Adoration. In the chapel, only an insane little female, a girl. The insane child dances barefoot and talks to her doll."

Wolv said, "An insane girl, good, she will be a burden to Warrick's knights. Therefore, let her live. Any burden to Warrick's knights is a help for us."

OBSESSION WITH THE EUCHARIST.

Then Wolv growled, "Candlekeeper. Is it a safe candle hour?"

The candle keeper held up his candle-lantern and said, "Master Wolv. In the rush, I knocked over the candle and put it out. I do not know if it is a safe candle hour. Yet, I think that I hear irregular Prime bells, Resurrection hour bells from the valley. I am not sure of the candle hour."

Wolv pulled his sword to cleave the Candlekeeper, but the Candlekeeper was too far away.

Wolv howled, "Jesus. Stop torturing me. Every Prime, every Sext, every Nones you torture me."

Wolv's eyes glazed over black as his obsessive memories seized him.

Marian watched Wolv's changes. Change into pure, black, carbon dust. She watched Wolv descend into Rose Fire's cracks. Descend into Rose Fire's bailey floor.

Then Marian whispered to her sister, "Nicola. Wolv has just revealed to me a way to capture him."

As pure, carbon dust, Wolv descended through solid stone, through the earth. Then he stood in a lake up to his knees, full of light. Glowing mold, glowing mushrooms, glowing fungus grew on the cavern walls.

Wolv walked to an underground bank and begged, "Jesus. You withhold Pamia from me. Why do you withhold my only love from me?"

Wolv's memories seized him as he saw the Resurrection. Just as he originally saw it in Jerusalem. He watched the huge stone before Jesus' tomb move aside. As bright as the sun, Jesus stepped forth from his tomb.

Wolv fell to his knees and begged, "Jesus. Every morning you make me beg you for you to give me Pamia. For over a thousand years I have captured and question Pendragon brides. Just to see if they are Pamia reborn. They have never been Pamia. Jesus, Pamia is my heart. I am so lonely, so empty. Please raise Pamia from the dead for me."

Jesus said, "My beloved childhood friend. All you have to do is ask for forgiveness of your sins."

Wolv growled, "Jesus. Get off my throne. Never will I repent. Jesus, you are on my throne. Raise Pamia from the dead for me. Raise Pamia from the dead for me."

Jesus disappeared.

Wolv growled, "Pamia, Pamia."

Then Wolv's growls of Pamia shook the Black Mountains. His growls shook stones from Rose Fire's battlements.

As pure, carbon dust, Wolv rose from the cracks in Rose Fire's bailey floor.

Wolv congealed on the bailey floor and growled, "Jesus. I will not let you get away. Yes, I know where to find you, to hound you as you hound me."

The AntiChrist walked into the Rose Fire chapel.

Marian leaned over and whispered, "Nicola. Wolv just showed me his nature. I now have the information I need to capture Wolv."

As Wolv stepped on the blessed Chapel floor, he burst into red-yellow flame. He walked over dead knights and grasped the Tabernacle. Then he crashed the Tabernacle on the Altar.

Some unconsecrated hosts, bread, had fallen upon the consecrated hosts. Wolv searched through the bread and growled, "Jesus. I will find you. You are not the unconsecrated hosts."

Then Wolv growled, "Jesus. I have found you." Wolv picked up a consecrated host, from among the scattered unconsecrated hosts.

As Wolv picked up the consecrated bread, he said, "Jesus. You have cursed me with the certitude of your Real Presence. Cursed me with your Real presence in Consecrated bread. The Blessed Sacrament. You cannot escape me. I can feel you in this

Consecrated Bread. The same as when I felt your hands and feet when I killed you. When I nailed your hands and feet to the cross. The same as when I scourged you. Just as when I pounded the Crown of Thorns on your head. You cannot escape me. I have a Catholic priest captive to say Mass every day. So that I can feel your presence in the Eucharist and hound you."

Wolv held the consecrated host and growled, "Give me Pamia. Raise Pamia from the dead for me."

From the back of the chapel Wolv heard a tiny female voice, "You. You also see the beautiful man? I thought that only I could see him. I love him?"

Wolv howled and swung his hand to backhand someone and growled, "Pamia. You love only me."

Instead, Wolv had thought that he heard Pamia's long ago voice, "But I love Jesus."

At those words, a thousand years ago, was when Wolv growled, "Pamia. You only love me." Then, originally, Wolv backhanded Pamia to her death off the Masada cliff.

Wolv's spiritual flames turned from red-yellow to black with billowing black smoke. The AntiChrist's spiritual flames burned nothing but Wolv. The AntiChrist's spiritual flames never burned anything but himself.

Then Wolv's eyes glazed over black and he wept, "Pamia. In my rage, I have again knocked you off Masada. Pamia, again, I have killed you."

Wolv did not comprehend the tiny voice say, "Only I am here. Only me."

Then Wolv's eyes lost their glaze. He could not see the little girl in the far corner behind a pew. The AntiChrist only thought about his murder of Pamia.

Wolv wept, "Pamia. Again I have knocked you off the Masada cliff."

Then Wolv turned to the broken Tabernacle and growled, "Jesus. I will hound you just as you hound me."

Then Wolv turned and said, "Pamia. Oh Pamia, I murdered you." He walked from the chapel.

As Wolv stepped off the Chapel's blessed ground, the flames on him ceased. The spiritual flames on Wolv never burned anything around him.

Then Wolv ran to Marian and ripped Marian's gown off her. Marian stood in only her shift. He said, "Pamia. I need your gown."

-

-

-

CHAPTER, Now in Rose Fire, Wales, Year @ 1250s A.D.

EVIL LICKED HER FACE FROM CHIN TO FOREHEAD. "YOU TASTE OF HER. SMELL OF HER. YOU HAVE HER MEMORIES. LET HER COME FORTH. OR I WILL EAT YOU ALIVE."

Creal lay dead at Wolv's feet. Wolv soaked Marian's gown in Creal's blood.

Marian said, "Warrick will send all of you to Hades."

Wolv said, "It is not the same Warrick that took Rose Fire from me. Now, as with Ogina, love weakens him. Love weakens his reason. Just as when I turned Ogina against Warrick. Lord Warrick will see your bloody gown and think that you are dead, or worse. He will think you are dead because of him and mourn. His rage and grief will consume his reason."

Wolv pointed at the body of Creal and said, "Now. Throw Creal over the side of the moat. When Warrick arrives he will think that we are executing his knights."

He then tore the gown off Nicola and soaked it in Creal's blood.

Wolv said, "Warrick is to rage. Let him rage over more innocent blood."

Then Wolv grabbed a young page by the hair and bent the page's head back. Then he pulled out his dagger. Wolv said, "Skinwalkers. Again I say, kill all the males. Throw them over Rose Fire's walls."

Marian grabbed Wolv's dagger hand. She said, "You know that I am Pamia. If you harm anyone in the castle, I will never give myself to you willingly. I will never love you."

Wolv bared his teeth and growled at Marian.

Marian did the same thing that Pamia did a thousand years ago. Marian put her forefinger over Wolv's lips and said, "Shush."

Wolv said, "Only Pamia has had the courage to put her finger to my lips. You are truly Pamia."

Lady Marian said, "I have met you hundreds of times over this thousand years. Met you and seen your rages destroy you. Destroy others. Destroy me hundreds of times, just like when you knocked me off Mount Masada."

Marian straightened her back, leveled her jaw and drew on her endless courage. Endless courage born of her compassion.

Pukal, Swale's brother, stepped forward. He grasped Wolv's arm.

Pukal said, "Wolv. No, no, I know of Marian. She will have nothing to do with you if you kill anyone in the castle. She has too much courage."

Wolv pulled his dagger from the page's throat and said, "Swale. Lock all the males in the dungeons."

The AntiChrist said, "Pukal. Tell me why I should not run you through for your interference."

Pukal said, "Who financed this foray? Who will finance your future forays?"

Wolv sheathed his dagger and said, "Pukal. You will soon clash with me once too often."

The AntiChrist said, "I want you, Marian. Or else something could happen to Nicola."

Marian stomped on the foot of the Skinwalker that held her. She dashed forward and smacked Wolv's face with her fist.

She stood before Nicola and shouted, "To my last breath I will defend Nicola."

Marian asked, "Why does Lilith demand that I not have Warrick's children."

Too much rage, ale and wine had loosened Wolv's tongue. Wolv said, "Ancient Catholic tomes written by Catholic mystics say some loves must be. I and Lilith have watched our bone throwers. I have listened to them. Ancient Catholic tomes buried in monasteries have predictions about Pamia's descendants. You are one of Pamia's predicted descendants. In tomes Catholic mystics mentioned you often by place and date of birth. This is how I knew of you. The Catholic mystics wrote that in centuries you will have two powerful Pendragon progenies. It will take centuries. Catholic mystics call them Winstosom Church de hill and Frankish Ruoos de Velt. Both of Pendragon blood, of your blood. They will lead great armies against me in the next thousand years. The Catholic mystics have written. Written that Winstosom Church de hill and Frankish Ruoos de Velt will battle me. Without your two descendants I will destroy the world. Destroy the world with bombs that part the highest clouds. Your genius must not live in Warrick's progeny. You must not pass on your genius through Warrick's mighty Pendragon children."

The AntiChrist said, "Lock the women in their chambers. Lock Nicola in Marian's chambers along with her chambermaid. Marian is mine and mine alone."

Marian stood before Nicola to protect her.

Wolv looked Marian up and down.

She stood defiant, back straight, chin level, in only her shift.

Then Wolv said, "Pamia. You are mine in all your beauty."

Wolv licked Marian's face from chin to forehead and said, "Marian. You taste of Pamia. You smell of Pamia. I will test if you have all Pamia's memories. I you are Pamia, then you will live. If you are not Pamia, I will eat you, alive."

-

-

-

CHAPTER, Now in Rose Fire, Wales, Year @ 1250s A.D.

NO ESCAPE. INTO THE JAWS OF DEATH.

Warrick was far away on the Wye River, out of sight of Rose Fire. He watched a dry thunderstorm. Lightening with no rain streak the sky. Thunder shook the earth. It made the sky look like a shattered glass window. Just as if an arrow shattered it in firelight. He felt the thunder shake the earth under Zeus. Thunder pounded into his eardrums.

The lightening hit the earth. Their horses reared.

A knight said, "This is a black fall season in the mountains. If we do not have rain soon, this dry lightening will cause forest fires. The dry grasses and trees on the mountain sides will burn."

Warrick said, "Yes. The low fog and rain in the valley kept the Wye Valley green. Yet, the Black Mountains live up to their name, black, dead. Except snow on the peaks, no moisture has fallen on the Black Mountains. No rain. No dew. The trees and grass on the mountain are brown, brittle and the driest of firewood."

Warrick said, "Drayton. Morgan. Marian's life depends on Adoration and weekly confession. Make sure that everyone does their hour of Perpetual Adoration in Rose Fire's Chapel. Or in the Adoration wagon. Perpetual Adoration of Jesus' Real Presence in the Blessed Sacrament. Make sure everyone does weekly confession. Remember our great victory at San Gimignano, Italy. Wolv and Lilith arrived to burn the town. We arrived with the Adoration wagon. Adoration by a small innocent child chased away the red fog. That tiny boy's purity, trust in Jesus was so great that every Skinwalker knelt. All the Skinwalkers chanted, 'Jesus. Have mercy on me. Jesus, I trust in you.' That day we exorcized a thousand Skinwalkers. We saved a thousand souls. Our greatest victory is in saving souls from Hell. We saved the souls of a thousand Catholic priests that day. Remember. Only Adoration and weekly confession can drive Wolv's red-fog back to Hell. Only Perpetual Adoration and weekly confession can defeat the AntiChrist."

Warrick said, "Listen. Wolv has his Holy-Mary-Egyptian obsession.

FAR AWAY, INSIDE ROSE FIRE.

Far away from Warrick, on Rose Fire's bailey floor, Wolv fell to his knees. His eyes glazed over black.

He howled, "Holy Mary. Leave me alone. Not now, not now."

On his knees, on the bailey floor, eyes glazed black, Wolv repeatedly growled, "Little Wolv. I will always love you."

As always, each growl shook the Black Mountains. With each growl Wolv flung long gobs of red froth from his gaping mouth.

Red fog poured off Wolv.

Black-red flames, born of rage and hatred, spewed from Wolv's mouth. The flames filled the sky and blocked out all light from the sky. The wind blew away the black smoke.

Slowly Wolv came out of his Holy-Mary-obsession. He wiped the thick red froth from his mouth with his sleeve.

Then Wolv growled. "Holy Mary, leave me alone."

Lilith, as a black, floating wraith, appeared beside Wolv. Lilith said, "Look at the floor. Your red-froth and red-fog disappeared into the ground. Someone in Rose Fire is doing Adoration of Jesus' Real Presence. Rose Fire should be full of red-fog. We need the red fog to conquer Warrick."

Wolv turned to two Skinwalkers and said, "You two. Go back into the chapel and kill anyone doing Adoration of the Blessed Sacrament."

Moments later the two Skinwalkers returned. One said, "No one is doing Adoration. Only a silly, tiny girl talking to herself. She spins and talks to a doll. She is addlebrained."

Wolv said, "She will soon die of hunger and thirst. Leave her alone. Perhaps I will eat the little girl as a tasty supper."

ON PATROL.

They began again to gallop on patrol beside the Wye River.

From behind, Warrick heard a shout.

Warrick reined in Zeus and drew his blessed sword.

A knight yelled, "It is just a mounted unarmed lad. He has no bridle or saddle."

The horse dashed up to them. A small boy on the back.

Zeus lurched forward and Warrick reached out and grabbed the horse's mane.

As Warrick held the horse's mane, it tried to run in a circle around Zeus. The horse could not escape Warrick's iron grip. It stiffened its legs and slid to a halt. A small lad hung onto the horse's mane.

Lord Warrick said, "It is seven-year-old Luchas."

Luchas's aged horse began to shake and convulse. Warrick said, "Luchas, your old horse is about to die. Its heart has burst."

Warrick wrapped his huge arm around Luchas and pulled him onto Zeus.

The aged horse's heart burst. It fell dead.

Little Luchas fought for breath and blinked. Looking up at Warrick, he gasped, "Lord Warrick?"

Lord Warrick said, "Yes, what is wrong?"

Little Luchas breathed hard and gasped between words, "Wolv . . . captured . . . Marian . . . and . . . Rose . . . Fire."

Lord Warrick froze and remembered his first wife, Ogina, burned to ashes. Burned to ashes because of Wolv.

Warrick said, "How can I believe you? How did you escape?"

Luchas took a long deep breath and said, "My lord, . . . promise first. Promise . . . that you will not . . . beat me."

"Yes," Warrick said.

Luchas said, "My lord, you know that I am a thief. Forgive me my lord. You know that I can climb down the castle walls. I had snuck outside during the day to steal honey from the hives. Also, to explore the mountains with this old mare that you put out to pasture."

Warrick noticed that his own hand was now full of honey from Luchas's blouse.

Then Luchas said, "I stayed out all day and into the night. I started back to Rose Fire, from the tree line. Then I saw Wolv on the outer battlement. I heard him shout that he is using Marian to lead you into a trap."

Lord Warrick said, "Then they have succeeded. Yes, I will ride into any trap for Ogina. How did you find us?"

Luchas said, "My lord. You call Marian, Ogina. Why?"

Warrick said, "I repeat. How did you find us?"

Lucas said, "Lord Warrick. I only thought as you would, only I rode only. Only, where nobody would ride. Just like you. You do the unexpected. I imitated you and did the unexpected. I spurred this horse bareback as fast as it could take me."

Warrick pointed to a knight and said, "Take the lad on your saddle."

Lord Warrick could not get the image of Ogina burned to ash from his mind.

Warrick shouted to his knights, "I ride into a trap Wolv has laid for me. He has Ogina in Rose Fire. They use her for bait to lure me into a trap. Who is with me to ride into the jaws of a trap? To save Marian."

His knights looked at each other quizzically. They understood that grief caused Warrick to call Marian Ogina.

Beside the sparkling Wye River, all raised their weapons and looked toward the castle. In unison, from years of practice, they shouted, "To War, for Marian."

Far away, up the mountain side, in Rose Fire, Wolv heard their war cry.

Wolv said, "Stop. Listen. Was that thunder? Sometimes I think that I can hear Warrick's roar. No matter where he is in the world."

Lord Warrick's war cry echoed off the mountains. He commanded, "We ride to battle!"

His fists shook, his jaw muscles bulged. His shoulders and chest grew wider and thicker.

They all raised their blessed swords into the air.

Dry thunder shook the earth. Lightening with no rain exploded trees. They raised their faces to the heavens. In unison they prayed a battle-cry prayer. A prayer that they had prayed from England to Egypt. They said Marian's name in the prayer, "Oh God. We swear with our lives that we will defend Lady Marian unto death."

Warrick rode fast with his knights to Hereford. Smoke rose over the ashes of the valley and Hereford. The fires were out.

The residents yelled to Warrick, "Wolv did this evil, Wolv."

Warrick waved to the knights that had rode from Rose Fire. The ones that Thetford sent from Rose Fire to help with the fire.

He commanded, "We can do nothing more for the town or the valley. Come with us. We battle Wolv."

A knight reined in his horse and asked, "Why would Wolv destroy a whole town?"

Warrick said, "To draw knights from Rose Fire. So he could storm the walls with little opposition. He did draw many knights from the castle to the town, which was his purpose."

Warrick put his gauntlet-covered hand to the forehead of his helm. He hung his head low.

Then he said, "Ross-Templar, Drayton, Morgan, I need you. Come to me."

Their horses reared and they reined in around Warrick.

He said, "My skin just crawled, Ogina is in great danger. She will not submit to Wolv's demands. I feel helpless. I do not think that I can lead the fight. Not with the thought that Marian is in Wolv's hands. My rage and fear for Ogina are too overwhelming."

Morgan's horse reared.

Then Morgan said, "Warrick. You are the world's only hope against the AntiChrist. You have fought him from the time you were six years old. Your infinite courage, reason, your wisdom, your battle genius is Marian's only recourse. You are the world's only hope. Yes, you, Warrick, are Marian's only hope. The king is correct. Warrick, you are the world's only hope. Soon the AntiChrist's red-fog will cover the earth and he will be strong. Just like when he was Attila, the Hun."

Dayton's horse pranced and spun in nervous energy.

Drayton said, "Warrick, you must push your emotions aside. Now you must withdrawal into reason, into logic now. You are the world's only hope."

Ross-Templar' horse pranced in place.

Then Ross said, "Warrick, only your logic, reason and experience can defeat the AntiChrist. The enemy greatly outnumbers us. You must lead us in the most unexpected tactics. Warrick, the king is correct, you are the world's only hope."

Morgan's horse pranced sideways. He said. "Warrick. You must set your emotions aside."

Warrick relaxed. Zeus felt Warrick calm down. Zeus knew to stand calmly and did. Lord Warrick breathed deep. He pulled off his helm. He rested his helm and his gauntlet hands on the blessed-armor of his thighs. Then he leveled his chin.

Drayton leaned over to Ross-Templar and whispered, "I have never seen Warrick so intense. His jaw muscles flexed so massively that I can see them. See them move through his mail hood."

Warrick withdrew from his emotions, from his fears into a warrior's logic and reason. He concentrated on his thousands of memorized historical battles and battle plans. From the ancient Romans and Greeks to today's Skinwalker battles. His emerald eyes regained their battle glow. Framed by his bronze face, his lips and eyes narrowed with determination.

Warrick said, "I am ready to save Ogina."

Drayton leaned over to Morgan and whispered, "Is Warrick able to overcome his grief? Can he lead us against this world of demons? Thoughts of Ogina cripple him."

Morgan said, "We have no choice. The world has no choice. He must."

Warrick pointed to an able knight on a much swifter Arabian stallion and said, "You. Run ahead of us as fast as you are able. You must be ready to dodge arrows. Ride hard to the practice field. Do not stop. I want you to ride hard back to me and tell me what you see."

The knight's Arabian instantly broke into a full run.

The horses of all the knights reared and pranced in circles. They walked sideways out of nervousness. Warrick said, "Rein in your horses. Let the knight on the Arabian get a lead on us. Wolv could have a group ready to ambush us. The Arabian is swift enough to avoid their arrows."

Warrick pointed to a knight and said, "You. Take half the knights and half the archers. Hide yourselves and your horses behind the burned town. Hide well because more Skinwalkers might ride up this road. They could attack us from behind up to Rose Fire. If they do, do not fight them. Under no circumstances show your selves until you hear my war horn. Now, dismount and lead your horses as quietly as possible and hide."

The group of knights disappeared behind the burned structures of Hereford.

Zeus reared. Warrick raised an arm and shouted, "To the castle to save Marian."

The ground shook under the hooves of Warrick's war horses.

Far behind the knight on the Arabian, they galloped up the mountains' switchback road. Warrick saw the knight on the Arabian gallop back to them. Then He raised his hand to signal for the column to stop.

The knight on the Arabian bolted back to them. He was out of breath but managed to say, "Rose Fire. Rose Fire and the forest are too quiet. What kind of trap could they have the set for us?"

Warrick thought, "With Marian, with my love, Wolv has the worst kind of trap."

The knight could not calm his Arabian. It circled Zeus and continued to rear.

Warrick said, "We know that they heard our horses hooves pound the road."

Ross-Templar said, "From where do you think they plan to attack us?"

Lord Warrick said, "From the high ground."

Then Warrick pointed up the road and said, "Ross-Templar. The AntiChrist probably has half his Skinwalkers in the trees. Trees that line our practice field. He probably has the other half inside Rose Fire. He could have a third in the trees, a third in the castle. Even another third to attack us from the rear. I know Wolv. Now he and his Skinwalkers feel secure. So secure in Rose Fire that they are drunk on Ogina's wine, ale, and mead. Perhaps her strong mead will be a weapon against the Skinwalkers."

Ross said, "You keep calling Marian, Ogina."

Drayton asked, "What shall you do?"

Warrick said, "The same thing that you would do. We will use Wolv's strength against them."

Warrick silently prayed, "Dear God, please protect Marian."

INSIDE ROSE FIRE.

Inside Rose Fire in her chambers, Marian knelt and silently prayed, "Dear God. Please protect Warrick."

ON THE ROAD OUTSIDE ROSE FIRE.

On the mountain road up to Rose Fire, Warrick pointed to five of the archers.

Then Warrick said, "Drayton. Bring the five archers and come with me."

Lord Warrick turned in his saddle.

He said, "Ross-Templar, Morgan. I want you to hold everyone else here. Unless Skinwalkers attack us from Rose Fire or from the town."

Warrick galloped with his archers up the mountain road and said, "Drayton. Stop and dismount."

Drayton said, "Warrick. We are too far away from the enemy to hit the castle with arrows."

Warrick said, "Drayton. Obey."

In unison the archers said, "Yes. My lord."

Warrick said, "Use your flints, make a fire of dry grass and twigs."

They did.

Lord Warrick thought, "Where in the castle would Wolv imprison Marian."

"Take out your oil-soaked cloths," Warrick commanded. "Now I want you to rip them into twenty small strips. Tie them to the tips of twenty separate arrows."

They each tied a strip of oil cloth to arrows.

"Now light them all in the fire," Warrick commanded. "Quickly shoot them into the tall dead grass on the mountain."

They shot their burning arrows into the dry grass. The fire quickly spread through the grass and up into the trees. The lack of rain and early frost had lowered the trees' sap into the roots. Quickly, the trees burned like kindling. The dehydrated leaves and very thick dry brush under the trees caught fire. Flames jumped into the brittle branches of the trees.

Drayton said, "Warrick, you said that you would use the high ground against them."

Warrick said, "Yes."

Drayton said, "The fire will climb the mountain. Climb all the way up to the snow line. If Skinwalkers are in the forest, they will burn."

Warrick said, "Saving Ogina will not be so easy."

Warrick waved the rest of Warrick's warriors to ride up to him.

The Skinwalkers' yells of 'run' rose from the mountain side. The demons ran up the mountain to escape the fire.

Morgan dismounted beside Warrick and said, "The Skinwalkers cannot outrun the fire."

Lord Warrick put his hand on the hilt of his blessed sword and said, "Now. Now for the Skinwalkers in Rose Fire. Now for the impossible, to save Marian."

Then Ross-Templar said, "What is that howl coming from the castle?"

Outside Rose Fire, on the Rose Fire road, Warrick said, "Ross-Templar. Wolv howls. He howls because he is angry that we discovered his men in the trees. By the sound of it he is full of too much mead. If we are lucky, his Skinwalkers are drunk on Marian's wine and mead."

IN ROSE FIRE.

On the outer battlement, Lord David Ap. Gruffydd walked over to Wolv. He demanded, "Tell your Skinwalkers to stop drinking ale. It will weaken them."

Wolv said, "We celebrate because I have captured Marian. The same as when I captured Warrick's first wife, Ogina. It is impossible to separate Skinwalkers from ale. Impossible. Besides, look at Rose Fire. Warrick made it impenetrable to anything except traitors, treachery. Or ill-conceived compassion. Leave my Skinwalkers alone. I will let them drink all the ale they want. We only need to stay in the castle. Defend the walls and celebrate the capture of Marian."

David Gruffydd gritted his teeth, and made a fist. He walked away from Wolv.

OUTSIDE ROSE FIRE.

Warrick lead his knights slowly, cautiously. They climbed the road up to the practice field that would now be a battleground.

Warrick said, "Where is the Adoration wagon?"

Drayton said, "Here."

Warrick said, "Cover the Adoration wagon with branches. Make the Adoration wagon look like a trash-heap of branches. Adoration will keep the red-fog away. Take off its wheels so the Adoration wagon looks like broken down junk. In it, keep three knights to do Adoration in eight hour shifts. We must always have Adoration on the battlefield. If it looks like junk, under a trash heap, the Skinwalkers will leave it alone. Adoration is our strongest defense against the AntiChrist. Adoration will keep the red-fog away from the battlefield, otherwise the red-fog will eat us. Also, find the tiny monstrance that contains the Eucharist. The little monstrance we sealed in wax. The little monstrance that I carry into battle in my blouse pocket."

Drayton said, "Warrick, here. I have the little monstrance in my breast pocket."

Warrick said, "Drayton. Let me have it. I will take it into battle with me. It will keep the red-fog away. If I die in battle, take it from me and give it to another."

Warrick took the small, wax-covered Monstrance and put it into his breast pocket.

Then Warrick said, "Brothers. I stocked Rose Fire with a three-year supply of smoked meat. With an artesian well, the enemy has plenty of free flowing water. We dug the moat down to bed rock so we cannot tunnel under it. We made the walls taller and stronger. If Wolv defends the battlement, they are impossible to scale. Even if we scale the outer wall, we must scale the even taller inner wall. That up the slope of the talus. Except a traitor, Rose Fire is almost impregnable."

He raised a hand and said, "We will camp here. Out of range of their arrows. Ross-Templar. Have the knights form lines of tents. Put the tents close together so the tent ropes overlap. That way they will also serve as trip lines against the enemy.

Drayton said, "Warrick. Here we are again, in a siege of the same castle."

Warrick said, "No, Drayton. Rose Fire is different. It is too strong to siege. Besides, if we siege, they would only threaten Marian, or worse. On our first siege, Wolv ran out of food, water and fire wood. It is not cold enough for them to run out of firewood. Wolv will not make the same mistake twice. He has plenty of food, and the artesian well will supply him with enough water."

That night Lord Warrick walked from each guard around the battlefield. They all stood, obedient to his command.

He gazed into the black night at Marian's keep. He saw her silhouette in her window. With the light of candles, the fireplace, and oil lamps behind her.

Warrick tightened his fists and gritted his teeth in rage. In rage that Marian was now at the mercy of Wolv.

INSIDE ROSE FIRE. HER BEDCHAMBER.

In her Rose Fire' chambers from her window Marian could see. Marian could see the dark fields around the castle.

She knelt by her bed and prayed, "Oh God, protect Warrick from all danger."

She silently prayed, "Lord God. Would you please help me to open the drawbridge and save Nicola."

She did not want to burden her sister but *she thought,* *"Warrick. Warrick will never trust me again. Not after I begged that the knights go to the fire in the town. He is my life, my world.*

He will cease to love me now that he will not trust me. How can I show him that I love him?"

Marian said, "Nicola. How can I escape these chambers and hide? Hide until I can open the drawbridge before Wolv catches us."

INSIDE ROSE FIRE.

Wolv slammed open the chamber door, "Marian. Just like Ogina, you want to escape. You cannot escape. Warrick will never get inside unless he has help from you. He will fight to his death before he will let anyone harm you. You will be his downfall and then you will be mine and mine alone. Then, to save Nicola, you will allow Pamia out of yourself."

Lightening with no rain smacked her keep roof and splintered trees in the forest. The trees caught fire. Dry wind slammed against Rose Fire.

-

-

-

CHAPTER, Now in Rose Fire, Wales, Year @ 1250s A.D.

OUTSIDE ROSE FIRE ON THE BATTLE FIELD.

Outside in Warrick's war camp, a page opened the flap of Warrick's tent. He said, "My lord?"

Warrick said, "Enter."

The page stepped in. He carried a plate of roasted venison and a tankard of spring water.

He said, "My lord, you must eat and sleep."

Warrick waved the page aside and stood. That Wolv captured Marian caused Warrick to dry-retch his empty stomach.

Morgan and Ross-Templar appeared at the door of the tent. Morgan said, "David Ap. Gruffydd has to be behind this."

Lord Warrick said, "Yes, he had made peaceful agreements with King Edward. Then David Ap. broke his oath to Edward. He gave his allegiance to his brother, Llewellyn Ap. Both the grandsons of the Great Llewellyn. Their plans are to use Wolv's Skinwalkers to capture key castles from England. Then to combine with other traitorous English lords to invade London.

Wolv will destroy his Welsh allies, David and Llewellyn. Wolv always destroys his human allies."

Drayton walked up with his bow in his hand. He elbowed his way between Ross-Templar and Morgan.

Ross-Templar asked, "Traitors in the king's court planned this? What does your gut tell you?"

Lord Warrick said, "What did you think of Colne, the king's treasurer?"

Drayton snapped, "A brilliant, shifty-eyed, deadly weasel."

"Yes, brothers," Warrick said. "I make it a point to know all those in the king's court."

Warrick reached into his blouse and pulled out a scroll. He handed it to Ross-Templar. He said, "Ross. Read it."

To Lord Warrick, earl of Rose Fire,

"The full name of Colne, is not Colne Wassan as he calls himself. He is Colne Ap. Gruffydd."

Lord Ross-Templar asked, "How in the world did you learn this?"

Lord Warrick said, "The first rule of victory is 'to know thy enemy.' I have friends in the Ap. Gruffydd family. Colne, the king's treasurer wants the Gruffydd family to control Wales. Then with traitorous English lords, Colne wants to form a revolution against the king. London itself, Colne wants to take control of London itself. He plans to help Wolv capture Welsh strongholds at key positions. One of those positions is Rose Fire. Treasurer, Colne, thinks that the AntiChrist will give him control of London."

Morgan said, "You will soon retake Rose Fire and Marian will be safe."

Lord Warrick made a fist and said, "Yes, I must. I must. I will take Ogina from Wolv's grasp. Not Ogina, I meant Marian from Wolv's grasp. I failed Ogina."

INSIDE ROSE FIRE.

Wolv stepped from Marian's chambers and locked the door.

Inside the castle Marian listened at the door of her chambers. She heard David Ap. Gruffydd and Wolv. Wolv shouted, "We will never relinquish Rose Fire. Rose Fire is critical in a long line of castles. Castles that we have sieged and taken from the English. The English will not defeat us. My Skinwalkers will rule England even if we must reduce England to ash."

Marian's chills of fear were so strong she hugged herself and shook.

Nicola sat on the bed and cried. Marian knelt before her and said, "Nicola. I will not allow any harm to come to you. Warrick is just outside the walls."

Nicola said, "Warrick has designed Rose Fire that if Wolv guards it, it is impregnable?"

Marian said, "Warrick has endless inventive imagination. Take heart. Did you see Warrick burn half Wolv's Skinwalkers when he ignited the mountains? The fire will burn all the way up to the snow line. Warrick knows how to save us."

-

-

-

CHAPTER, Now in Rose Fire, Wales, Year @ 1250s A.D.

ON THE BATTLEFIELD.

Planning for the attack of Rose Fire consumed Lord Warrick's evening. He and his brothers stood and argued about the best way to siege.

Lord Warrick made a fist and said, "Morgan. The only way to rescue Ogina is with a siege. A siege with enormous loss of life."

Then Warrick turned and said, "Ross. I feel like I am losing my mind. Like I did when I watched Ogina burn to ash. I could not save Ogina. I failed my Pendragon curse trial by fire with Ogina."

Morgan said, "That was not the trial by fire of the curse. Remember that you found the secret of Greek fire and used it. That was Greek Fire that burns water. The fire was only on her gown. She had only to take off her gown and throw it away. Instead she threw water on herself."

Warrick said, "My Greek Fire burned Ogina. I killed Ogina."

Morgan said, "No Warrick. Ogina sided with Wolv."

Ross-Templar said, "Warrick. Every knight here will give his life for Marian."

Lord Warrick lowered his head and said, "Morgan. We ourselves constructed an impregnable castle."

He smashed one gauntlet fist into the palm of the other. He said, "We have no alternative. We must construct a trebuchet to throw stones against the walls. Throw stones until we bash a hole through them."

Drayton said, "I will have many knights start building a belfry. A belfry as tall as the wall. We will build it on wooden wheels. Then can push it up to the walls."

Morgan said, "We will make a covered casing. A casing that we can use to protect us as we fill the moat. Then we can use the casing to cover a battering ram."

Lord Warrick said, "Do it, do it. This will be a long siege. Nothing is promising to be a quick method. What time is it?"

Otan said, "I heard distant Vigils bells from some monasteries. Vigils Bells, Midnight, the three hours of Witches. Lilith's strongest hours."

Lord Warrick pointed at the forest line, "It is midnight. Let us build our siege weapons."

He pointed and said, "Begin by cutting down those trees. We already burned the tree's exterior, so Wolv cannot burn them. Cannot burn them with flaming arrows."

Otan again decided to try to get Warrick to eat. He walked over to a boiling pot. Then he filled a bowl full of venison stew, a tankard of spring water. He carried both to Lord Warrick.

The thought of Marian under Wolv's control wretched Warrick's stomach. Warrick bent over and spilled his empty stomach. Lord Warrick was too enraged to eat.

He waved Otan and the food away. Warrick pulled off his helm and mail cowl. Then He lowered his head and poured a bucket of water over his head. Lord Warrick threw his head back to flip his hair back. He straightened his back and rose to his full huge height.

Lord Warrick confided to Ross-Templar, "I feel paralyzed. I cannot lift my arms. What good is all my strength and skill. I can crash an ax through the hardest armor. Use blessed sword and mace as the king's champion. It is all for naught because I cannot even protect Ogina, my love. The failed duty that my king has entrusted to me."

Lord Warrick placed his hands on his hips. He began involuntarily to breathe too deep and too fast.

Otan said, "Lord Ross-Templar. I saw this when raiders killed my mother before my own father's eyes. My father stood with his hands and feet bound. He began to breathe fast and hard. He grew weaker and began to collapse. This is the helpless reaction when harm comes to loved ones. The shock was so great that my father fell over dead."

Lord Warrick held his throat and could not catch his breath. His chest began to quiver.

Ross-Templar stepped up to Warrick and shouted, "Otan. He is having a seizure. Help me lower him to the ground."

Lord Warrick waved Otan and Ross-Templar away. He stood and his chest began to quake.

He held his throat and said, "My heart beats too fast, too hard. It is going to burst. Like a horse ridden too hard. Helplessness is pulling the life from me."

Morgan ran up and said, "It is your anger, your fury. You need to let it out. You need to act. Now. Build with us. Yell, roar."

Tears filled his eyes and he roared, "Marian, we are coming for you."

Where they stood, his men raised their voices and roared, "Marian. We are coming for you."

INSIDE ROSE FIRE.

Inside Rose Fire, tears welled in Marian's eyes. She heard Warrick's men shout her name. Though she was Wolv's captive, she felt hopeful and loved.

Wolv unlocked Marian's chamber door, jerked it open, ran in and grabbed Marian's wrists.

He swore, "You make the most delicious bait. Hear them out there. They have come. Warrick and his knights have come. Come for us to slaughter them. Soon they will try to climb the walls of Rose Fire. We will slaughter them."

Suddenly Wolv froze as he heard Warrick's roar, 'Wolv, you will suffer for this.' Wolv's face turned white from shock. He feared Warrick.

Only his hatred of Warrick was stronger than his fear of Warrick.

Wolv cursed, "Lord Warrick," and spit. He grabbed the eye that six-year-old Warrick had stabbed. The eye that had not healed for over twenty years. The same as Wolv's palm had not healed that King Arthur stabbed. Stabbed centuries ago with Excalibur.

OUTSIDE ROSE FIRE.

Lord Warrick's men roared in unison, "Wolv, you will suffer for this."

INSIDE ROSE FIRE. INSIDE HER CHAMBER.

Wolv swore and walked from Marian's chamber. He locked Marian in her chamber.

OUTSIDE ROSE FIRE.

On the battlefield, Drayton took Warrick by the shoulders. He said, "You must act. Now. You cannot just stand and let grief and worry overcome you. Throw yourself into physical labor. Now."

Lord Warrick poured himself into chopping, hewing, roping. Knotting, nailing, sawing and building war machines. Ogina's burned body popped up in his imagination and haunted him. Then Marian's happy smile when she was pleased and content. Marian's laugh when a joke caught her off guard. His mind was more unmerciful to him than any enemy could ever be. For Warrick imagined Marian suffering at the hands of Wolv. Then he threw himself even harder into building war machines to climb Rose Fire's walls.

Lord Warrick told himself, "Warrick you must wake. Wake up. This is just an awful nightmare."

He did not wake up. The nightmare was real. All he saw and felt was horrible reality. Sweat of worry and terror dripped off his nose and chin.

He glanced up and saw Marian in the towering keep window. In the flickering chamber's torch light surrounded by the blackness of night. Late Vigils' and early Matins' bells blackness. He felt so helpless.

Ross-Templar shouted, "Chop. Chop, Warrick, or worry will weaken you."

Helplessness began to paralyze his arms. She was so close, but infinitely far away. He felt so powerless.

Warrick took Ross-Templar' admonishment. He chopped as fast and as hard as he could. Wood chips flew. Lord Warrick quickly chopped and notched the logs for the trebuchet catapult.

IN ROSE FIRE.

The candle light burned out behind Marian. Warrick could no longer see her. All he could see was the tall pink-white marble tower against the black sky.

Then Warrick clinched his fists and held his eyes shut. Shut to prevent his emotions from crippling him again. His emotions of helplessness welled within him. He lowered his head and dropped his arms as if defeated.

Lord Warrick raised his eyes to the Heavens. He prayed, "Jesus, let me trade my soul for Marian's life. She means more to me than my life, my breath, my soul, my mind. Jesus, give me the strength to save Marian."

INSIDE ROSE FIRE.

Inside Rose Fire, Wolv had a catapult built. He tied Marian and Nicola's bloody gowns to a large stone. Then he put the bound gowns into the catapult's spoon and tripped the catapult. The stone with its gowns flew high into the air. It pounded into a tent in Warrick's camp.

Warrick ran to the tent and pulled it aside and saw no one was hurt. Then he picked up the ball of two bloody gowns and gasped. He immediately recognized Marian's gown. It was the gown she wore most often. When they walked the talus and outer battlements. When they kissed in the moonlight. In those nights it had reflected the moonlight in the Vigils bells. He remembered that it felt so silky, so cool to his touch on her curves.

He said, "I caused Marian's death. I caused Marian's death."

Warrick fell to his knees and shook in grief and rage.

IN ROSE FIRE.

Inside Rose Fire, Marian peered out the window of her chambers. Marian said, "Nicola, I see my lord on his knees. On his knees among the tents."

Nicola asked, "Why is he on his knees?"

She moved next to Marian and watched Warrick.

ON THE BATTLEFIELD.

On his knees, outside Rose Fire, Warrick held Marian's gown. The gown had dried, red, crusted blood all over it.

He yelled, "Life cannot be such hell. Life cannot be just fighting endlessly with demons. I have tasted love. I have tasted peace and love. God, you cannot be so cruel. First Ogina, and now my love, Marian."

Lord Warrick said, "Marian is dead. God has forsaken her. Marian is dead. The Pendragon curse continues."

He lifted the gown to his lips. He shook and convulsed in rage, despair and grief. His heart stopped. Warrick hugged the gowns to the chest of his blessed-armor. Then he fell face first like a felled tree onto the battlefield. He was in a state of shock. Shock with the grief and unfathomable rage.

Otan ran to him.

Drayton commanded, "Do not touch Lord Warrick. If Warrick is dead, then he is dead. If he is still alive, do not disturb his sleep, let him sleep."

-

-

-

CHAPTER, Now in Rose Fire, Wales, Year @ 1250s A.D.

NOW, I WILL DROWN.

From Marian's chambers, Nicola watched Warrick from a window and shouted, "Marian. He fell. Lord Warrick fell. He is not moving. He is dead. Poor Lord Warrick, he is a man of virtue and valiant. Lord Warrick has suffered and now he dies in a battlefield."

Marian looked out the window and cried.

She said, "Yes, my love is dead. Warrick is dead."

Marian wept so hard she could only sit on the bed and hold Nicola.

Warrick's other knights approached him. Drayton stretched out his arms and held them back and said, "Move back. Back, back away from my brother."

Drayton pushed them back far enough so Warrick could not possibly hear.

Then Drayton said, "All of you must know. Your lord has Nicola and Marian's gowns, covered with blood. Wolv killed them to defeat Warrick emotionally. Now is the time to let my lord sleep, hopefully for hours. If he is dead, he is dead, but if he is asleep, let him sleep."

Warrick lay unconscious on the ground as still as a corpse. Drayton threw a deer-hide cape over him.

Drayton said, "To keep him warm, in case he was not dead. Now, everyone, return to your duties."

Suddenly, a guard lowered his pike and shouted, "Who goes there?"

A shaky voice said, "Father Malachi Martin."

Then four guards thrust their pikes forward. One shouted, "Show yourself."

Father Malachi, in the antlered-skull of a stag and deer hides, hobbled down the mountain. He held his chin high, leaned on his cane, and hobbled across the camp. He walked over to Warrick and knelt beside him.

Then Father Malachi stood and asked, "Morgan, what is wrong? Why is he despondent?"

Morgan replied, "Marian is dead."

Father Malachi Martin demanded, "Help me to help Warrick to stand. Give me the evidence that Marian is dead."

Several knights in full blessed-armor grabbed Warrick's arms and pulled him to his feet.

Old Father Malachi said, "My lord, we will see what has happened to Marian. Let me have her bloody gown."

Father Malachi smelled all parts of the gown. Then Father Malachi said, "Dried blood, thick dried and decayed blood. Thick globs of blood, just like someone scooped up blood on the gown. The blood smells of decay. Maggots are already on the blood. You said that you saw Marian in the tower window not an hour ago. If Wolv killed her just now, maggots would not be on the gowns. The gown has the thick smell of horse sweat. I see kernels of hay seed. Smells of house manure. Also, the smell of the stable's fresh pine-tar timbers. Wolv has not had time to figure out if Marian is Pamia. He would never kill Marian before he proved she is or is not Pamia. Wolv killed a stable boy then smeared Marian's gown in the boy's blood. That is why I smell the horse sweat, horse manure and the stable's pine tar. Marian and Nicola are alive, probably in their chambers."

Warrick gasped and said, "Marian. She is alive with Nicola in her chambers. She is alive."

Drayton whispered, "Father Malachi. Now, over here where no one can hear us. You think that the blood on the gown is not Marian's blood."

Father Malachi said, "False hope and lies win wars. If Marian is dead, she is dead. If she is alive, let us go save her. In the best case, Wolv is still close to killing her. Wolv will know in hours that Marian is not Pamia, then Wolv will kill Marian."

Drayton said, "So you lied to Warrick?"

Father Malachi said, "Drayton. Of course. Now keep your mouth shut and follow Warrick. Lord Warrick is the world's only hope."

BACK TO THE CHAMPION.

Old Father Malachi walked back to Warrick.

Father Malachi said, "Warrick. For now Marian is alive. If you attack the castle, you will all die at the base of the drawbridge."

Then Father Malachi said, "Warrick. That is the future. Unless you obey me no matter the pain, no matter the danger. Obey me or all will be lost. Marian has read secrets that can capture Wolv for centuries. Marian is a linguistic genius of once in a century."

Old Father Malachi said, "Warrick. We must hurry. Now, while it is still dark. You and half your knights must come up the mountain with me. Burn many fires. Then it will seem like all the knights are in the camp."

Warrick turned to a trusted knight seasoned in many wars and said, "You. I put the camp into your knowledgeable hands. Do as Old Father Malachi requested. Every campfire must burn high. The camp must appear that it has the same number of warriors.

Yet, if the Skinwalkers attack you, immediately retreat up the mountain and follow us. For now, station your archers high up behind the burned trees. The archers are to protect your retreat up the mountain. It is important that we not fight with too few knights. It is important that we fight together as one. Send a knight down to Hereford to retrieve the knights that I left there. They will stay with you."

Old Father Malachi said, "Warrick. I can feel the coming of death. Death is coming for Marian if you do not act now. Marian is in grave danger. Wolv is beginning to know that she is not Pamia."

Old Father Malachi stood silent and gazed at Warrick's emerald eyes.

Father Malachi said, "Beware my lord, take great care my lord. To save Marian, you must prepare for a trial by fire. My lord, evil, Lilith, will test your love in fire. Remember, the Pendragon curse. Only burning love can defeat burning hate."

Warrick said, "Father Malachi. Yes. Lead on."

IN ROSE FIRE.

Inside Rose Fire, in the Great Hall, Wolv sat and swilled ale, wine, and mead. With his Skinwalkers to celebrate their capture of such a strong castle.

OUTSIDE ROSE FIRE ASCENDING THE BLACK MOUNTAINS.

Outside the castle, in the blackest of night, the darkness before dawn. Father Malachi Martin led Warrick and half Warrick's knights high into Black Mountains' snow cap. At the top of the mountain, they trudged in their blessed-armor in deep snow. Ice formed on their armor.

A knight asked, "Warrick. Did you bring us up here just to freeze?"

Old Father Malachi said, "Only the determined will survive. The rest will die. Climb or Wolv will kill Marian or worse."

One knight fell unconscious into the snow. The knights looked at each other. They expected to freeze, but they followed Warrick. They had complete and unending confidence in him.

Warrick said, "Carry him."

Old Father Malachi said, "Today's trials will sorely test lesser knights."

Two knights shivered and carried the unconscious knight. The very early Prime bells began in the Wye Valley. The sun peaked over the horizon onto the frozen mountain peaks.

Warrick said, "Father Malachi. Wolv's obsessions shake the ground. Look at the sky. The red-black flames have shot up from Wolv's mouth and covered the sky."

Father Malachi said, "Warrick. Wolv's black smoke will block the light, until the wind blows away the smoke."

When the Terce bells rang and the morn sun was higher, only Warrick stood tall. All the knights entered a cavern, a monstrous cavern. The opening was full of stalactites and stalagmites like jagged teeth of a monster's mouth. Above the mouth were two large holes through which a red fire glowed. They looked like evil red eyes. Father Malachi's students, exorcism Catholic priests, came to help the half-frozen knights.

Old Father Malachi said, "Put them beside the fire. Put more wood on until it blazes."

Smoke rose through a natural chimney in the caverns. The floor and walls were warm from the fire. The knights shed their armor and shivered before the fire.

Old Father Malachi said, "Come, you can enjoy pleasures after the battle."

A knight said, "Pleasures? My fingernails are near black from frostbite."

Malachi said, "Shed the rest of your armor and mail. They will only drown you."

In unison they all said, "Drown?"

"Yes," Father Malachi said. "With armor, you would drown. You must go through much danger before we can save Marian."

Warrick said, "Obey Father Malachi. Take off your armor, down to your blouse and leggings."

They obeyed.

Old Father Malachi Martin said, "Eat." He gave them ale and venison jerky. "Jerky and ale will give you strength."

They had taken a moment to eat. Father Malachi said, "Now hurry. Each of you is to carry a bundle of rope. Take all the rope. Then follow me."

One knight said, "These are not bundles, each of these is a mountain of rope."

Old Father Malachi said, "Knights. We will need every foot and still it may not be enough."

They followed Father Malachi into the cavern deep inside the Black Mountains.

Warrick said, "Each of you is to take out your blessed sword. Score the floor with the points. So that we can find our way back if we must."

A wet wind from inside the mountain blew against their faces. The flames of their torches flagged in the wind. Droplets of water formed on their clothes. The walls became wetter and wetter until water dripped off them. It flowed in small separate streams. Their torches highlighted rainbows of color. They snaked their way around stalagmites and stalactites. They had stripes of yellow, red, blue and green. The multicolors reflected on the ceiling, on the floor, on the stalagmites and stalactites. They were in endless rainbow-colored mazes in all directions. Rainbow-colored walls reflected the light of the torches.

Suddenly a strange luminescent light surrounded them.

Old Father Malachi said, "We no longer need the torches."

Ross-Templar asked, "What is this curious light?"

Father Malachi said, "A rare luminescent mold on everything. I have seen this type of light in cellars. I planted it here and it has spread through the underground rivers."

Old Father Malachi pointed at them and said, "Beware. The mold on the walls of the cavern will cling to you. It will make you glow. The Skinwalkers can see you at night and shoot their arrows into you."

Drayton said, "So be it."

Wind blew droplets against their faces. Now they were soaked and chilled. In an hour they also glowed because, they had brushed against the mold.

They turned a corner to see a fast flowing underground river. It reflected the cavern ceiling's pink, orange and red glow.

They came to four boats. Tied on the edge of the river. Each boat glowed with the mold and had a high dragon head on the front.

Old Father Malachi said, "This is where we need to be. Everyone into the boats and row hard. We have far to go before we can help Marian."

Old Father Malachi pointed at everyone and said, "Danger. Great danger. Under no circumstances look over the side of the boats. Do not extend a hand over the side. Wolv has put demons in the water. Mysterious demon-things in the river will grab you and eat you. These scaly things lay asleep for years until movements awaken them. They can even turn the boats over and eat us all."

The boats had rows of oars that the knights sat at and rowed. They rowed hard against the rapid river. Water dripped and ran from bright and multicolored stalactites on the ceiling. Water from snow-melt on the mountains. Their sweat glowed and dripped off their noses and chins from the effort. The boats moved swiftly through the endless lake.

Enormous florescent fins of mysterious creatures broke the surface. The knights' eyes grew round. They rowed faster. Gigantic incandescence snakelike scaled fish formed waves. The waves rocked the boats. One demon raised its head from the water. They saw that it had teeth like swords. At the sight, they rowed so hard that their hair blew in the air.

Old Father Malachi pointed and said, "Row up onto this island."

He said, "Remember, you will glow because you brushed against the florescent mold. The enemy can see you to shoot arrows at you."

They rowed hard. The boats scraped onto the small rock stalagmite island.

Father Malachi Martin said, "Pull the boats up onto the island."

Sweat glowed and dripped from their noses and chins. With great heaves they pulled the boats out of the lake.

Old Father Malachi said, "If we are to save Marian, we must be quiet. If the demons in the water sense us, they will eat us."

Father Malachi said, "Now tie all the ropes end to end. We will need every inch of rope if we are to save Marian. Take off your shoes and tie them to your waist. All but the first to go, must secure their weapons to their waists."

Malachi stood on the highest spot of the small island and said, "To save Marian. Now, we must do the most dangerous actions. Fishermen have fallen in here and come out, some alive in the Wye River. Most dead and eaten by creatures in the water. Some have come out the springs on the mountain sides and lived. The underground rivers are full of glowing mold and glowing mushrooms. The underground river has many, many adequate air pockets. When you think that your lungs will burst, take heart. Know that you are coming to an air pocket. Waterfalls end in large pools with air pockets and florescent light. Do not panic. Be patient. Hold your breath and the current will bring you to another air pocket."

She pointed to a whirlpool, "Warrick. The strongest swimmer among you must descend into this fast whirlpool. Into the undertow with the rope tied around his waist. He must find the entrance to the well within the castle. Then he must enter it and tie off the rope. The well has a strong underwater crossbeam."

Every knight shouted, "I will go for Marian."

Old Father Malachi said, "Quiet." He pointed. A creature made a large wave in the water.

Old Father Malachi raised a long bony arm covered with deer hides.

He whispered, "Only Warrick is strong enough to swim in this rapid current. The rest of you can follow on the rope. Only after he secures it to timbers in Rose Fire's well. Only Warrick has a chance to swim without directions to find the artesian-well's entrance. The well has a massive flow. Thus we know that it has a large enough entrance. The well flows out of the bailey, fills the moat and flows down the mountain. That artesian-well is like a natural rushing spring. Let the well's flow push your weight to the top of the well."

Father Malachi Martin said, "My lord, Warrick. You must not swim with even the weight of a dagger. You can take no weapons because they will carry you down in the water."

Old Father Malachi turned to the other knights. He said, "Once Lord Warrick secures the rope to the well. Then the rest of you can take your blessed swords. Since now, the rope will support them."

Old Father Malachi turned to Warrick and said, "My lord. If you come out of the well, you must fight without a weapon."

Warrick said, "What must be to save Marian, must be." He tied one end of the rope to his waist.

From the back, a knight said, "Father Malachi. We cannot let our lord die. He is our leader. He is our tactician. Without him we could not recapture Rose Fire. Without him we could not save Marian."

Old Father Malachi said, "Lord Warrick must swim underwater in this dangerous whirlpool. If not, you will not enter the castle. Wolv will continue to dominate Rose Fire and Marian, . . . and Wales. From Wales, Wolv will conquer England. Then just like when he was Attila, the Hun, Wolv will dominate the world."

Warrick said, "I am ready. If I want you to pull me backwards, I will jerk twice on the rope."

Father Malachi said, "My lord. Backward does not exist. Backward is to drown. Forward is possible life."

Lord Warrick said, "If I find my way into Rose Fire, then. Then I will tie it off and jerk four times. . . . If you pull and I do not pull back, assume that I drowned. Do not wait too long to send the next volunteer."

Old Father Malachi said, "Marian has very little time. I can feel Wolv's rage build. My lord, you must swim close to that whirlpool. Then say a prayer to God to save your soul. At that, swim down into the center of the whirlpool. We are not sure of its course. We do know that it runs under the castle. This is the most dangerous act I have ever asked any to do."

One knight said, "We have a mountain of rope. Surely this is enough?"

Old Father Malachi Martin said, "Perhaps a mountain is not enough. This underground current has many twists and turns. Many that have fallen into it have never been found."

Warrick swam to the whirlpool, said a prayer. With long strong strokes of his thick arms he swam down into the whirlpool. *He thought, "Marian, I am coming."*

One knight, by instinct pulled back hard on the rope.

Old Father Malachi shouted, "You must let the rope run freely through your hands. Or, you will drown Lord Warrick."

Malachi tied the back end of the rope to a thick stalagmite.

Warrick swam with great long strokes. His head hit the top of the cavern. He could see in the mold's glow on the river's sides. His lungs burned for air. He exhaled a little and begged God for air. The current turned him backward and crashed him against stones.

He prayed, "God, give me strength to save Ogina."

Suddenly he popped to the top of the water. In an air pocket, he breathed out and in only to inhale much water. Then his head popped up above the water again. Again, he spread his arms to catch anything to hold him in the air pocket. Luckily, he caught a thin ledge and breathed.

Then he thought, "Marian, we must be patient, I will soon rescue you. God, please, you must protect Marian."

In the light of the mold Warrick saw the mouth of a great creature. It opened behind him to swallow him.

The ledge broke. The current suddenly descended. As if through a great pipe and knocked Warrick against jagged edges. Then he hit a barrier of small thin stalactites and stalagmites with small pillars. They barred his progress and held him underwater.

He glanced back to see the mouth of the giant creature. Open again to eat him.

He pulled against the prison-bar-like barrier. They broke. The current pushed him through. The creature could not squeeze through the opening.

Suddenly the current caught him again. It pushed him through a narrow opening. He saw a brighter light above him and swam for it. A bright light as if a torch flickering.

He thought, "The well. Marian, I am coming to save you."

He swam hard to the brighter light. The current shoved him out of a spring. In great disappointment, it was not the well. So he lay only on the side of a cold spring. Slowly he caught his breath. Lord Warrick looked up and said aloud, "The light is the full moon. It is night. The whole day is gone."

He turned his head and gasped to see Rose Fire far below him. In the night, he glimpsed Marian in the torch light of her chamber window.

He thought, *"Marian is truly alive. My love is truly alive. I must save my love."*

Then he took a deep breath and immersed himself back into the cold water. Back into the eerie florescent glow. The current bashed him against the walls.

Far ahead he saw another brighter light. He swam for it as hard as he could.

He thought, *"It must be the moonlight also."*

Finally, he reached the opening. It was too small for his shoulders.

He thought, *"Now. I will drown."*

-

-

-

CHAPTER, Now in Rose Fire, Wales, Year @ 1250s A.D.

SKINWALKERS HELD THE CHAMPION'S HEAD UNDERWATER.

Warrick turned to see the creature, teeth like swords, open its mouth to swallow him.

The current tore at Warrick's leathers. He held one edge of the opening and kicked other edges away. He tried to enter and could not. Then he pulled on the edges. Another piece cracked off. Through the cracked-off hole, the current rushed him through the well.

The creature crashed into the opening. It could not enter, so it swam away.

Warrick's head popped up out of the water. Into the night. He got his breath and descended back into the well.

He untied the rope from his belt. Then he tied it to a wooden well beam that extended under the water. He pulled on it to test it. The beam broke. Warrick rose to the top and breathed in again and descended into the water. Then he tied it to a very long and very thick beam and tested it. Against his huge muscles, the beam did not break. Then he pulled on the rope four times. Four times to tell those in the cavern that they could follow. They could follow the rope to the well.

IN ROSE FIRE.
Wolv walked over to the well and dipped in a ladle. He drank the clear cold water. Water ran down the sides of his mouth. From under the water Warrick could see him.

Warrick thought, "Wolv, you will suffer for this. You will suffer for this."

Wolv said, "I swear that I can see the reflection of Warrick in this water."

His lieutenant said, "You are just too obsessed with him."

The AntiChrist pulled his sword and beheaded his Skinwalker lieutenant. Then he threw the Skinwalker's head in the bailey-andiron fire. He wiped his sword on his arm. He pointed his sword to the Skinwalkers standing around him. Then he said, "With his head burned to ash, he cannot come back to life. Never. Never criticize me, never."

Warrick could not hold his anger that Wolv had Marian. He swam for the top of the well. His arms broke the surface of the well into the moonlight. Then he grabbed Wolv by the neck and dragged him into the water. A Skinwalker hit Warrick in the head with a club. Warrick floated unconscious on the top of the water.

Wolv climbed out of the well and said, "Drown him."

The Skinwalker held Warrick's head under the water.

-

-

-

CHAPTER, Now in Rose Fire, Wales, Year @ 1250s A.D.

THE ROPE BROKE.
Back in the cavern Father Malachi said, "That was the signal. The signal that others are to follow. Pull hard to straighten the rope. Warrick is now at the well, close to Marian."

All of them pulled. Then the well-timber, to which Warrick had tied the rope, broke. They all fell backward. Then the rope pulled tight.

Old Father Malachi said, "Death is very close to Marian."

He clasped his hands and said, "It broke. The rope obviously broke off from where my lord first tied it. Perhaps the rope lodged in a crevice or in the well. Perhaps Warrick did not make it and is dead."

-

-

-

CHAPTER, Now in Rose Fire, Wales, Year @ 1250s A.D.

SHE HAS NO HOPE.
Wolv held Warrick's head underwater.

Wolv said, "Little Warrick. Now I will finish the drowning I began when you were six years old. Your drowning, just after I killed your mother."

A Skinwalker high on the talus battlement yelled, "Warrick. Glows in the night. Satan works against us. What witchcraft is this? What evil is upon us? Warrick has doomed us. Drown Warrick. He glows."

Warrick had brushed against the sides of the cavern. The florescent moss and mold had permeated his clothes, hair, and settled on his skin.

The other Skinwalkers looked at the glow on Warrick. Their eyes grew round from fear. One shouted, "Warrick is too strong for us. He is so strong that he glows in the night. In the Matins bells blackness. He has come bewitched with power. Drown Warrick."

Wolv ignored the glow. He pulled Warrick's head out of the water and said, "No. I want Warrick to suffer. Pull him out and drop him on the floor. Marian will give herself to me freely. I will imprison Warrick and threaten to kill him, if she does not."

They dropped Warrick onto the cold pink-white marble bailey floor.

In the black night, late Vigils and Matins bells, Warrick glowed and coughed. He regained consciousness. Skinwalkers wrenched the knots tight on Warrick's feet and on his hands.

Wolv shouted, "Somehow Warrick entered Rose Fire. Others must be in the castle. Guards, find them, find them now and kill them. If they glow like him in the Matins bells night, you can see them. Kill them."

HOLY-MARY OBSESSION.

Wolv grasped his head with both hands and shouted, "Not now, Holy Mary. Not now when I have my victory."

The AntiChrist fell to his knees. His eyes glazed over black. His memories went back to Egypt when he was six-years-old, crying. Crying because the Egyptian children called him ugly-eyes.

He remembered Holy Mary picking him up saying to him, "Little Wolv. You are beautiful and intelligent. Little Wolv, I will always love you."

On his knees on the bailey floor, Wolv screamed repeatedly, "Little Wolv. I will always love you."

Black-red flames shot from Wolv's mouth and filled the sky.

Wolv's eyes lost their black glaze and he raised his fists to the sky. He growled, "Holy Mary. Get out of my head."

At the glow on their strongest enemy, Warrick, Wolv's drunken Skinwalkers lost their confidence. They also staggered with drunkenness. They had drunk too much of Marian's delicious ale, mead, and wine.

Wolv looked down at Warrick and said, "Warrick. I do not know how you entered Rose Fire. Nor do I know how you hid in the well. Yet, it did you no good."

Wolv had humiliated Blanche. He had put Blanche to work and sleep in the wash room.

Blanche saw her only hope of escaping this humiliation. Somehow to keep Warrick alive. She knew Wolv would probably kill her also. She saw Warrick, knelt beside him, and hugged him. Then she begged, "Wolv. Do not harm Warrick. Please."

Wolv said, "Useless woman."

He grabbed Blanche's upper arms. He threw her across the bailey. Then Wolv said, "Go back to the wash room worthless woman."

Warrick, though tied up on the bailey floor, yelled, "Marian, I am here. Your hero."

Wolv kicked him in the ribs. He said, "In this night of Matins bells you cannot hide. Not with that accursed glow?"

Lord Warrick pulled against the wet ropes on his feet and on his hands. Then he shouted a lie to dishearten Wolv's

Skinwalkers. "The glow is a sign of a curse. A curse on all of you. A sign of your defeat. It is a sign that Satan will wreck havoc upon you for taking Marian."

Wolv laughed and said, "Satan is an ally of mine."

Wolv again kicked Warrick in the ribs. He said to a guard, "You. Take Skinwalkers. Find and kill any of Warrick's men in Rose Fire, not in the dungeon."

Wolv pointed up to a guard atop the talus wall. He said, "Watch Warrick from the battlement. Do not take your eyes off Warrick's men outside the castle and on Warrick here. I want to eat and think of a proper torture for Warrick."

Lord Warrick thought, "I smell ale on all of the Skinwalkers. They have been celebrating their capture of the castle. We still have a chance if they are drunk."

Within minutes Blanche appeared from behind a wagon.

She deviously thought, "To survive I cannot join Wolv. He kills traitors, English traitors or Skinwalker traitors. Creal, Wolv killed Creal. I must appear loyal to Warrick. That is my only chance. Appear not to be a traitor to Warrick."

She whispered, "Quiet, Lord Warrick. Quiet. Why do you glow in the night?"

The water that ran off Warrick also glowed.

She thought, "I must appear loyal to Warrick."

Blanche began to untie his hands and said, "I can bring weapons. Where do you want them? My lord, why do you glow?"

Warrick said, "Blanche, we need weapons. Find weapons and put them against the well."

Blanche untied Warrick.

Warrick threw off the ropes and asked, "Where is Marian?"

Then he grabbed a torch off a wall and threw it into the stable's hayloft.

The hayloft burst into flame.

At the words 'where is Marian' Blanche turned her face away from Warrick. Jealously turned her face red. Her forehead wrinkled in anger. Blanche's eyebrows formed a deep angry V of jealously.

Wolv yelled, "Blanche!" He backhanded Blanche's face. She fell to the bailey floor and pretended to be unconscious.

Dozens of Skinwalkers put their sword tips to Warrick's chest. Others grabbed him and tied him again. Still, other Skinwalkers fought the fire in the hay loft.

The mold on Warrick glowed on the Skinwalkers' hands as they tied Warrick.

One intoxicated Skinwalker looked at his hands and shouted, "The glow. The glow on Warrick is a curse. I have a curse on me, on my hands."

He plunged his hands into the stream of well water. Well water that flowed in a ditch on the bailey floor.

Wolv pulled his sword and cleaved the Skinwalker's head. He threw the Skinwalker's head into the bailey-andiron's fire.

Wolv shouted, "With his head burned to ash he cannot come back to life. I will kill any man or Skinwalker that shows fear. I will not tolerate weakness."

Blanche saw that Wolv was not going to kill Warrick right now. She saw Wolv slide his sword into his sheath. Greed motivated Blanche.

Blanche thought, "I will fake protecting Warrick. That way Warrick will think that I am loyal to him and England. I can only gain Rose Fire and Warrick's wealth through Warrick. The Skinwalkers will kill Marian. If Warrick lives I will wed him and have his power and wealth. If Warrick does not live, the Skinwalkers will enslave me. In Wales I will seduce my way back into a powerful position. To survive I must show loyalty to Warrick."

She threw herself onto Warrick to feign protecting him and shouted, "No. Do not kill Warrick."

Warrick yelled, "Run! Blanche! Run. Wolv will kill you."

Warrick rolled so he could push Blanche from Wolv. She calculated her risks, her quickest paths to wealth. She rolled and jumped.

The AntiChrist stepped forward and plunged his dagger at Blanche's chest.

Blanche pretended to trip and hit her head on a stone. She pretended to be unconscious.

Blanche thought, "Wolv is so obsessive about Marian that he will completely forget me."

Yet, she knew that Wolv would not harm her while she was unconscious. Blanche knew Wolv would want to question her.

Then Blanche decided to lay as if she were unconscious until the battle ended.

Gulum staggered from too much mead. He said, "Wolv. Warrick could only have come into Rose Fire one way, through the well."

Wolv said, "Nobody can come up through the well. Impossible." He paused for a moment then said, "Search the well."

An inebriated Skinwalker descended into the well and came back up. He said, "Two of the great wood beams are broken. I see no way that anyone can enter through the well."

Lord Warrick thought, "I tied the rope to the second beam. It is now broken. The second beam is broken. My knights have no chance. They will all drown if they try to follow the rope. Marian has no hope."

-

-

-

CHAPTER, Now in Rose Fire, Wales, Year @ 1250s A.D.

KICKED HER CHAMPION IN THE RIBS.

Wolv said, "Warrick. I will have Marian because I have you tied up like a pig. A pig for the butcher. When she sees you like this, she will do anything I ask, willingly."

Under the full moon, late Vigils and Matins bells, in the cold night. Lord Warrick's feet bound and his hands tied behind his back. Warrick lay helpless on his back on the pink-granite bailey floor.

Warrick said, "Wolv. For catching Marian, I will have no mercy on you."

Then Wolv laughed and kicked Warrick's face. The AntiChrist pushed his dagger back into its sheath and ordered, "Gulum. It does seem impossible that they would come up through the well. Even so, stack boards across the well. Pile heavy stones on top of the boards."

Wolv pointed to a Skinwalker and ordered, "Lock Blanche in the dungeon."

Lord Warrick looked at Blanche.

Blanche faked unconsciousness and thought, "I have deceived Warrick. He thinks that I am loyal to him and to England."

Warrick thought, "Blanche is undependable, nevertheless, I see why the king likes her. She is confused. Yet, in the end she is loyal in the face of the enemy."

Warrick did not know the depth of Blanche's conniving vixen mind. Blanche had simply weighted her opportunities. She now knew Wolv killed traitors. Wolv had killed Creal. He never trusted traitors to be loyal to him. If she had betrayed Warrick, she knew that Wolv would have chased her. Caught her, and ran her through with his dagger. She calculated that she would survive as a tart under the Skinwalkers. Or flourish again as a tart under the English. She would have betrayed Warrick if it had been to her advantage. So selfishly to save her life, she chose to appear faithful to Warrick. Still, Blanche faked unconsciousness.

A Skinwalker carried Blanche into the Great Hall. Then down below the wine cellar to the dungeon. He put Blanche onto a table. Then the Skinwalker ignored Blanche. He ran out of the dungeon to extinguish the fire in the stables.

In the bailey Warrick yelled, "Marian, I am here, your champion."

Wolv laughed and kicked Warrick in the ribs.

-

-

-

CHAPTER, Now in Rose Fire, Wales, Year @ 1250s A.D.

A SWORD AIMED FOR HIS HEAD.

Within the cavern, when the long beam broke, the knights fell backward.

Old Father Malachi said, "Pull again. We must save Marian. We must not allow Wolv to change Marian's destiny. Warrick is Marian's destiny. Marian is Warrick's destiny. Warrick's destiny is the world's destiny. Some loves must be."

They all pulled on the rope. This time the rope remained tight.

Old Father Malachi said, "We know that the rope broke away from its original tie. Perhaps it is where it should be and perhaps not. The next volunteer could easily drown. Warrick could already have drowned."

Ross-Templar stepped forward before anyone else could move. As always, his boyish smile showed his white teeth.

Old Father Malachi said, "Ross-Templar. If he has already drowned, it will be up to you. Up to you to lead the recapture of Rose Fire and save Marian."

Malachi said, "Ross. In front of you, you must cross your feet on the rope. Hold the rope with both arms. Let the current carry you as fast as it can. Put your arms around the rope and protect your head. Remember, when you arrive, pull four times to tell the rest of us to continue. Make sure that your blessed sword is secure on your side."

Ross-Templar did as Father Malachi Martin said. On the rope, through the holes that Warrick had widened. The whirlpool current swept down and knocked him against the cave's sides. In less than a minute, his feet hit the entrance to the well. Ross-Templar worked his way into the well. His lungs were ready to burst. Then his fingers felt the wooden beam that had broken. The beam had broken but it had lodged against the well's walls. Ross-Templar swam around the beam. With long strokes he swam for the surface. He found a small place under the boards and rocks to gain his breath. Ross-Templar glanced up to see a sword aimed down for his head.

-

-

-

CHAPTER, Now in Rose Fire, Wales, Year @ 1250s A.D.

THE SIDE OF THE WELL COLLAPSED.

Wolv underestimated Warrick's strength and determination to save Marian.

Warrick's wet leathers had soaked the ropes that held his wrists. He gritted his teeth and stretched the ropes on his wrists behind his back. His muscles bulged as he stretched the ropes until they fell off his wrists. His hands were free.

Four Skinwalkers came up to him. He wrapped the ropes around his hands behind his back. To pretend the ropes still held his hands. Ropes still tied Warrick's feet.

The four Skinwalkers lifted Warrick to his feet.

One said, "Wolv wants to torture you in the dungeon."

Warrick glanced back to see Ross-Templar' head pop up in the well.

A Skinwalker glanced with Warrick and saw Ross-Templar. He raised his sword to run it into Ross-Templar' head.

Warrick let the ropes drop from his hands. He grabbed the sword from the Skinwalker. With a clang on the granite floor, he cut the ropes on his feet. In one continuous motion he swung the sword in a circle three times. Droplets of glowing water arched off his hair and arms.

The four beheaded Skinwalkers fell useless. Of course, unless they could find their detached heads.

Warrick yelled, "Marian, my love, I am here. Where are you? Your champion is here?"

Within Marian's keep, a tear ran down her cheek. Marian hugged Nicola and said, "We have our champion again."

Warrick grabbed an oil-lamp off the bailey wall. Then he threw it into the hay in the bailey stables. The oil spread fire throughout the stables.

Wolv yelled, "Put out the fire. It will burn down Rose Fire."

Warrick cleaved the Skinwalkers near him. Then he threw another oil lamp into the hay in the stables.

A Skinwalker yelled, "It is the glow on Warrick. The glow has doomed us. Lord Warrick has the Devil with him."

Warrick cleaved every Skinwalker within reach. Droplets of glowing water flung off his hair and hands. He grabbed a massive mace and smacked the side of the well. The side of the well collapsed.

The Skinwalkers were too drunk to move fast.

He yelled, "My love. Marian. Where are you my love?"

-

-

-

CHAPTER, Now in Rose Fire, Wales, Year @ 1250s A.D.

DEFECTIVE WEAPONS.

Blanche cracked her eyelid and looked around in the dungeon. Torch light allowed her to see that no Skinwalkers watched her. She glanced around to see Sir Thetford and his knights behind bars. She was not behind bars.

Thetford said, "Blanche. I see the slit in your eye. Hand me one of those iron bars."

Warrick had stacked many dungeon-iron bars there. That was when Warrick turned part of the dungeon into Marian's wine cellar.

Blanche's devious mind schemed.

She thought, "I wish Thetford would not have seen me open my eye. I must appear loyal to Warrick or Wolv will kill me as he did Creal."

Blanche looked around, then she dragged a large iron bar to Thetford.

Thetford said, "Bring more of them, more of them."

Blanche dragged the iron bars to Thetford and the imprisoned knights. The knights wedged the bars against the dungeon lock and pushed. Their prison bars squealed. With a great clang, the prison lock broke.

Thetford said, "Lads. I want each of you to take an iron bar. You must use them to bash the heads of Skinwalkers."

They ran with their iron bars up the dungeon steps. Only to battle Skinwalkers on the steps. With blunt iron bars, Thetford's knights could not fight upward on the dungeon steps. The Skinwalkers had proper weapons.

-

-

-

CHAPTER, Now in Rose Fire, Wales, Year @ 1250s A.D.

HER CHAMBERS ARE ON FIRE.

Warrick again crashed the huge mace against the well's stone wall. Part of the stone side of the well crumbled. Well water rushed out onto the bailey floor.

Ross-Templar could not squeeze through the hole.

Warrick swung the mace in a great circle and crushed many Skinwalkers.

He again smashed the huge mace against the stone side of the well. This time he broke a hole through which Ross-Templar pulled himself. Lord Ross-Templar also glowed from the florescent mold.

Lord Ross-Templar crawled out onto the bailey floor to see Warrick bash Skinwalkers.

On the talus battlement a Skinwalker yelled, "Another enemy glows. He came up through the well. Like a demon from Hell. We fight demons from hell. We fight our own master, Satan. Our own master, Satan, is against us."

Warrick yelled, "My love, Marian. Where are you, my love?"

Warrick said, "Ross-Templar. Are you going to fight? Or are you going to backslide and bed three women in the hay? Come and fight and earn Lady Innocence's release from Hell."

Lord Ross-Templar said, "Warrick. You would remind me of my first shameless vocation. My sins that sent Lady Innocence to hell for her suicide."

Ross-Templar grabbed the sword of a fallen Skinwalker and cut down the enemy.

Lord Warrick said, "Ross-Templar. We have a small chance to save Marian. All the Skinwalkers have drunk too much of her ale and wine."

Morgan climbed from the well with his huge mace, then Drayton with a blessed sword. A long line of Warrick's knights climbed from the well. All with their blessed swords. They all glowed.

They fought and shouted, "For Marian, for Marian."

Warrick said, "Ross-Templar. Drayton. Morgan. Order some knights to battle their way to the Chapel. Make sure that they do Adoration. Even in the midst of this battle, set up Perpetual Adoration in Rose Fire's chapel. Adoration against these demons is Marian's only hope. Perpetual Adoration of Jesus' Real Presence in the Blessed Sacrament. Even in the midst of the battle, begin hearing confessions. Remember our horrible defeat in Chester, England. We had Adoration of the Blessed Sacrament, but outside the battle's midst. Wolv's Skinwalkers killed everyone but us. Always remember that we do not fight flesh and blood. We fight Satan's immaterial dominions and hierarchies."

Ross-Templar pointed to five knights. He shouted, "Battle your way to the chapel to do and protect Adoration. You are all priests, hear each other's confessions."

A Skinwalker on the battlement screamed, "Glowing demons from Hell fight us."

More of Warrick's knights emerged from the well. The dislodged mold glowed on all of them.

Warrick yelled, "Drayton, we need more knights to save Marian. Burn the drawbridge ropes to let in my knights. Knights that are out on the practice field."

Drayton pulled oil lamps off the talus-battlement wall. Then he threw them up into the guardhouse. The guardhouse above the drawbridge. The oil lamps landed on the drawbridge ropes.

Skinwalkers threw the oil lamps off the ropes and put out the fires.

A Skinwalker on the bailey floor screamed, "We fight glowing demons from Hell."

The danger and battle sobered the Skinwalkers. They were initially caught unaware. Now they fought with all the skill of a trained army. An army that knew they were in mortal combat.

Wolv yelled, "Away from the fire. Let the stables burn. Warrick's knights are already inside. To the well. Block the well."

Warrick's knights flung long glowing streams of water from weapons. The droplets splashed and glowed on the Skinwalkers. Also, on the pink marble bailey floor.

Lord Warrick yelled, "Marian, where are you? I am here to save you."

Drayton threw more torches into the wooden buildings attached to the guardhouse. The wooden sleeping quarters above the drawbridge. The straw mattresses in the wooden buildings burst into flame.

HOLY-MARY OBSESSION.

On the bailey floor Wolv fell to his knees and growled, "Not now, Holy Mary. Stop torturing me."

On his knees, Wolv howled, "Little Wolv. I will always love you."

Ross swung his sword and cut off Wolv's head.

Red-black flames poured out of Wolv's beheaded mouth and filled the sky.

Warrick shouted, "Ross. Throw Wolv's head into the andiron and burn Wolv's head to ash."

Drayton threw Wolv's head into the andiron. Wolv's head quickly burned to ash.

All the wooden buildings including the drawbridge guardhouse burned. Now the drawbridge ropes burned.

They burned through. They snapped. The drawbridge squeaked and groaned. It fell with a great cloud of dust. A thump that hurt every one's ears.

Warrick's knights on the practice grabbed their weapons. They shouted, "Attack for Marian. For Marian."

Along with their weapons, they picked up long wooden poles and large stones. The knights rushed across the drawbridge. With the long poles, they pried the portcullis up. Then they put the stones under it to hold it up.

They shouted, "Attack for Marian. They crawled under the portcullis and battled the Skinwalkers inside.

Then they wedged open the talus' portcullis, the inner wall portcullis. After they wedged open the portcullis, they crawled underneath it.

DOWN IN THE DUNGEON.

On the dungeon steps Thetford yelled, "Hit the enemy's weapons."

The iron bars were heavy. As the knights swung them, they knocked the weapons from the Skinwalker's hands.

Finally Sir Thetford's men fought their way up the dungeon steps. They fought with the weapons that they had knocked from the Skinwalkers. Thetford's knights stormed through the Great Hall and out into the bailey.

Warrick thought, "The fear in the enemy's eyes has overcome their drunkenness. Wolv has three times the number of warriors than us. The AntiChrist's Skinwalkers may defeat us. Wolv can change from ash and combine again with his body. Then, Wolv might keep Marian."

Lightening and thunder cracked across the sky and shook the ground.

The fire in the stables spread to the keep. To Marian's keep, where Wolv had locked her in.

Then Wolv changed himself from ash, pure carbon dust, to his Roman general head. The AntiChrist's body reached out and placed his head upon his shoulders. Then Wolv laughed and said, "Foolish Warrick. You know that I am indestructible. I am infinitely more powerful than a mere Skinwalker."

Warrick shouted, "Show us again." Then Warrick split Wolv from forehead to groin.

Wolv combined his two halves.

-

-

-

CHAPTER, Now in Rose Fire, Wales, Year @ 1250s A.D.

DYING.

After Wolv combined his two halves, Drunken Wolv ran to Marian's chambers. He kicked the door. He had lost the key. The door gave only a little. Marian's ale and wine had weakened Wolv.

He shouted, "Marian. When I get in there, I will hold a dagger to your throat. Then Warrick will do anything I ask."

Marian said, "Nicola. We must escape."

Nicola said, "Wolv does not want me. Wolv's obsession is with you, Marian. He only wants you. I can stay. You must escape."

Wind blew down the chimney. Marian grabbed Nicola by the shoulders and said, "Yes. We have a way out, up the new big chimney. Let us go up the chimney."

Marian pushed Nicola up the chimney.

Behind Nicola Marian climbed.

Wolv picked up an ax and chopped through Marian's door.

Marian pushed Nicola up the chimney and climbed herself.

Wolv grabbed Marian's shoe. She pulled. Her shoe came off in his hand. He growled like a wild dog.

The wraith Lilith appeared beside Wolv and said, "Wolv. This is another chance to change Marian's destiny. Marian must not stay with Warrick. Some loves must not be."

Lilith disappeared in a wisp of charcoal dust and red eyes.

Wolv yelled up the chimney, "Marian, you want to go up a chimney. Then I will put fire in the chimney."

He threw pillows into the fireplace and poured lamp oil on them. Then Wolv threw the brazier on the oil. The oil burst into flame and smoke.

Smoke and heat immediately engulfed Marian and Nicola. They coughed and could not climb anymore. Marian slipped.

Marian yelled, "Then you will not have Pamia. You know that I am Pamia. Again you kill me, just like at Mount Masada. Again your rage kills me, your Pamia."

Smoke clogged their lungs.

Just then another dry strong wind blew down the chimney as it did before.

Wolv though, "I want Pamia. I want Pamia alive."

He pulled the fire from the fireplace and stomped it out.

Wolv yelled up the chimney, "Pamia, I want you alive. I will kill Warrick if you do not give yourself to me."

Marian pushed Nicola out of the chimney onto the roof. Then she climbed out.

Wolv had stomped out the fire. He looked up and saw that Marian had climbed out. He began to climb it also.

Marian pulled a rose clay tile off the roof. She dropped it onto Wolv's head.

The heavy tile hit and cut Wolv's forehead. He fell to the base of the chimney. Then he crawled out onto the floor of Marian's chambers.

She pulled up another tile. Then she waited for Wolv again to show his head.

Wolv held his bloodied face and roared to his men, "Find Marian. Capture her. Now."

Wolv shouted to one of his Skinwalkers, "Give me your sword."

Marian and Nicola wore only their shifts. They clung to the parapet spike and sat on the keep's crest. Cold wind blew their hair. Their teeth chattered.

Marian saw Warrick battle in the bailey and yelled, "Warrick."

He looked up to see her on the roof, her keep on fire below her. With the distraction a club hit him on the back of the head. He staggered and blinked.

Marian screamed.

He caught his balance. Then Warrick fought his way up to the burning talus-battlement steps. From there he could go to Marian.

All Warrick's knight's were in the castle. They had either come up through the well or pushed open the two portcullises. They fought Skinwalkers throughout the interior of Rose Fire. The glow on them flew in great drops. Drops from their hair and their arms as they fought. The bright drops arched into the air and splashed in rainbows of reflected moonlight.

Wolv grasped a sword. He wiped blood from his face.

Then he walked out onto the burning battlement and yelled, "Everyone. Capture Marian. She is on the roof. I will give Rose Fire to the Skinwalkers that capture Marian alive."

From the battlement, he pointed up to Marian on the roof.

Marian pushed Nicola to the other side of the round pointed keep-roof. Arrows clunked on the clay tiles. Flames leapt around the roof.

Marian glanced around the edge to see Wolv climb onto the circular keep-roof. Suddenly he stood over them with a sword. Flames danced around them.

Marian said, "We must jump to the chapel roof."

Wolv grabbed the shoulder of Marian's shift.

Nicola put her hands to her mouth and screamed.

Nicola and Marian jumped down to the chapel roof.

The shoulder of Marian's shift tore off in Wolv's hand.

He growled and threw it away. The ripped cloth swirled in the cold night wind down to the marble bailey floor.

Marian turned to see Wolv's Skinwalkers climb on the other side of the chapel roof. They rushed her from one side. Wolv rushed at them from the other side.

Warrick suddenly jumped from Marian's keep roof. His emerald eyes blazed. The mold residue on him glowed in the black night. Two Skinwalkers shot arrows at him. He blocked their arrows with his thick blessed sword and blessed shield.

Morgan appeared behind the Skinwalkers with a blessed sword and blessed shield. He beheaded half of them.

One Skinwalker cried, "They glow, we are cursed. The devil is with them."

That Skinwalker ran.

The rest of the Skinwalkers battled Morgan with swords. Wolv stood before Warrick.

Marian screamed, "Warrick. Wolv's hand burns red-yellow flames because his sword is blessed. Wolv has the harder blessed sword, the blessed Damascus steel sword that I made. It can break your blessed sword. How did he get it?"

The flames leapt higher around them.

In the flames and moonlight, Warrick and Wolv clashed like two giants. The AntiChrist burned red-yellow because he held a blessed sword. Lord Warrick glowed. Their weight broke the rose clay tiles under their feet. They hacked at one another's blessed shields until the blessed shields fell apart. Sparks burst from their swords when they clanged together. From below Warrick and Wolv looked like great shadows against the sky. Flames leapt around them. Warrick still glowed. The glow on him still flipped from his hair, legs, and sleeves. Rose clay tiles fell off the roof to the fires below. With both hands on the hilts, they clanged swords. Fire brands flew into the air. Sweat dripped off their noses and chins. When their swords hit, sparks jumped from their swords.

Wolv's rage caused him completely to burst into red-yellow and black flames.

Warrick's blessed sword broke against the blessed sword Marian herself had designed.

Marian screamed, "Warrick. My premonition."

She hugged Nicola and said, "Nicola. My own harder Damascus sword is the cause of my love's death."

Wolv held the point of his blessed sword to Warrick's throat and said, "Little Warrick. Finally, I defeated you. I will savor this moment."

He raised his blessed sword over his own head to slice through Warrick.

Lord Warrick buried his broken blessed sword into Wolv's belly. Warrick said, "Forewarned by Marian."

Wolv howled in pain. Then Wolv dropped Marian's Damascus steel-blessed-sword and held his belly.

Then Warrick said, "Same old Wolv. You pause to hate."

Warrick grasped Wolv's throat and squeezed with an iron grip.

The AntiChrist howled in pain and growled, "Warrick. You use Jesus' Real Presence in the Eucharist against me. You carry a monstrance under your blouse."

Then Wolv's eyes glazed over black and he growled, "Jesus. I can feel your Real Presence in the monstrance. Give me Pamia. Raise Pamia from the dead for me. She is my only love. My love, Pamia, is my only happiness. Jesus. Raise Pamia from the dead for me."

Suddenly Wolv only laughed, "Warrick. You know that you cannot kill me. You can only slow me. I heal and come back."

Warrick twisted the broken blessed sword and said, "Yes. Yet, pain keeps you from changing form and escaping."

Wolv again howled in pain.

Lord Warrick pushed the broken blessed sword deeper into Wolv's belly.

Marian's blessed sword landed on the roof.

Tiles under their feet broke away. They grappled and rolled down to the side of the chapel roof.

Lord Warrick to fall to a sure death.

The glowing water flipped off Warrick's hair and leathers.

Still, in a rage of yellow-red and black flames, Wolv rolled over the side. Wolv's spiritual flames never burned any thing but himself.

Warrick rolled uncontrollably to a sure death. He grabbed at the tiles. They broke in his hands.

Marian dove for Warrick. She caught the back of Warrick's leather blouse. Her grip was just enough to stop his tumble. He did not roll over the edge.

Warrick said, "Marian. That was foolish. You could have died."

She said, "I would rather die with you than live without you."

Wolv had caught the iron water spout.

Warrick sat up on the roof and looked down at Wolv.

The AntiChrist glanced down at the fires below him. Directly under him burned a wagon of barrels of pine tar. Black pine-tar smoke and flames rose from the wagon.

The AntiChrist laughed, "Warrick. You cannot kill me. No matter what you do to me, you cannot kill me. I always heal and come back."

Warrick said, "You cannot change form if you are in pain."

Then Warrick threw Marian's blessed sword and impaled Wolv from collarbone to pelvic bone.

Warrick said, "Surrender or I will impale you with more blessed swords. More pain. Do you surrender?"

Wolv yelled, "Of course, you can only slow me. You cannot kill me. Yes, I surrender."

Lord Warrick said, "Wolv. Yell to your Skinwalkers to surrender."

Wolv yelled, "Surrender to Warrick! Surrender to Warrick! Lay down your weapons!"

All of Wolv's mercenaries and Skinwalkers dropped their weapons.

The AntiChrist yelled to his Skinwalkers, "Shoot Warrick now. Shoot him now."

A Skinwalker picked up a crossbow.

Marian shouted, "My love. The Skinwalker has the armor-piercing blessed-arrowhead that I myself designed. It will pierce any blessed shield. It will kill you."

Warrick did not hear Marian.

The archer aimed Marian's blessed-arrow at Warrick's back. A blessed shield lay at Warrick's feet.

Marian yelled again, "The archer has my armor-piercing blessed-arrow. Warrick. Protect yourself."

In the roar of the flames, Warrick did not hear her.

She despaired, "My love will die by a blessed-arrow that I myself invented. The blessed-arrow will pierce any shield and kill him."

Marian remembered the Pendragon curse. "When it is time, you will remember. If you want to love Warrick, you must give your life for Warrick."

Marian yelled, "No."

She grabbed a blessed shield and jumped between the arrow and Warrick. She knew the blessed-arrow would go through the blessed shield. Therefore, she threw herself and the shield between Warrick and the arrow.

The arrow pierced Marian's shield and Marian.

-

-

-

CHAPTER, Now in Rose Fire, Wales, Year @ 1250s A.D.

AGAIN, PAMIA IS DEAD.

Wolv laughed, "If I cannot have Marian, nobody now will have her. So the family curse of the line of Pendragon will go on. You will not find happiness until you find a pure love. Now this pure love, Marian, is dead."

Warrick turned to Wolv and said, "You will suffer for this. Now, I will burn you to ash in physical fire. Your spiritual fire may not harm you, but physical fire burns you to ash. I know that physical fire causes you pain."

Warrick scooted closer to Wolv.

The AntiChrist yelled, "NO, NO, NO more pain. Do not kick me into the tar fire. I cannot change form when I am in pain. Do not kick me into the tar fire. No more pain, no more pain." Wolv howled, "I murdered Pamia again, Pamia, Pamia."

Now on the edge of the roof, Warrick sat and said, "Wolv. I have had enough of you."

Then Warrick kicked Wolv's hands free from the gutter. From the chapel roof, the AntiChrist fell into the flaming pine-tar-wagon.

Warrick pointed at Wolv in the burning pine tar. He yelled, "Wolv is helpless. All Skinwalkers surrender. Or end like Wolv in the burning pine tar."

Wolv burning in the tar, the blessed swords through him, disheartened the Skinwalkers.

Wolv kept howling in despair, "Again, I again killed my love."

Lord Warrick picked up Marian and yelled, "Morgan. Send all those that do not surrender to perdition. Decapitate them and burn their heads."

Then Wolv's Skinwalkers surrendered.

Morgan shouted, "Skinwalkers. Do you ask Jesus for mercy? Ask Jesus for mercy and let Jesus exorcize the demons from you. Wolv is gone. He can no longer harm you. Ask Jesus for mercy and Jesus will exorcize you of your demons."

The Skinwalkers chanted, "Jesus, have mercy on me."

They fell to the bailey floor and writhed. Long lines of black dust rolled out of their mouths.

They changed into Catholic priests that centuries ago sold their souls to Satan. Sold their souls to Satan rather than die as Christian martyrs.

In unison, the exorcized Skinwalkers, now Catholic priests, chanted, "Warrick, Father Malachi Martin. You have saved our souls. We are free of Satan. We are free of Satan."

Warrick shouted, "Who is doing Adoration? Someone is doing Adoration for us to be able to defeat Wolv? Adoration has constantly weakened Wolv in this battle."

Morgan shouted, "No one is doing Adoration. Everyone in the Chapel is dead."

Warrick shouted, "Someone is doing Adoration. Extremely strong Adoration. Find them. They are powerful with pure hearts. Find out who is doing such powerful Adoration. Someone is doing Adoration or else we could not have driven Wolv and Lilith away. Go to the chapel and find the knight that did Adoration."

Morgan ran to the chapel and said, "Who is in the chapel? Who was doing Adoration during the battle?"

A tiny voice said, "Just me and these sleeping knights. Also, Him."

Morgan looked to see little Greta under the Altar. He did not tell her that the sleeping knights were dead.

Morgan asked, "Greta. What do you mean by him? Him who?"

Greta pointed to the Tabernacle and said, "Don't you see him. How beautiful he is. He told me that he is Jesus. He is beautiful. All full of light, standing before the Tabernacle. Don't you see how beautiful Jesus is?"

Morgan said, "Greta. Your Adoration of Jesus with your pure, innocent heart saved us. Can you stay here with Jesus?"

In her little dress Greta spun on one foot and said, "Oh yes. Jesus fills me with such happiness. Jesus is Sunshine. He is Beautiful."

Other knights came into the Chapel to do Adoration.

Morgan said, "Knights. Let Greta do all the Adoration she wants. Unlike us, she sees, feels, Jesus' Real Presence in the Blessed Sacrament. A blessing for her and us. The same way Wolv can see and feels Jesus. Wolv can see Jesus, feels Jesus, in the Blessed Sacrament. Yet, for Wolv it is a curse. For Greta it is a joy. Spread the word throughout Rose Fire that Greta's Adoration saved us. Only, after you yourselves do Adoration, Adoration of Thanksgiving. Wolv always returns. Keep doing Adoration. Wolv always returns."

TRYING TO HEAL HIS BELOVED.

Lord Warrick carried Marian and shouted, "Drayton. Have the exorcized priests help extinguish the fires."

Warrick carried Marian and said, "Drayton Morgan. Make sure that everyone does their hour of Perpetual Adoration in Rose Fire's Chapel. Or else in the Adoration wagon. We must keep Perpetual Adoration of Jesus' Real Presence in the Blessed Sacrament. Again. Make sure everyone does weekly confession. Remember our wonderful victory in Citta Di San Marino, San Marino. When Wolv attacked, we placed our Adoration wagon in the town's center. Wolv and Lilith left and harmed no one in the town. We exorcized demons from hundreds of Skinwalkers. All of them were possessed Catholic priests over centuries. All had made a pact with Satan to escape martyrdom by fire. We saved the souls of hundreds of possessed Catholic priests."

LILITH HELPS WOLV.

Lilith appeared beside Wolv and said, "I can be your strength. Satan has missions for your hatred. You will heal. I will heal you faster."

In despair and despondency Wolv cried, "Again my rage killed Pamia.

Lilith, with all her thousands of demons, entered Wolv's body. With Lilith's strength, Wolv rolled out of the burning pine-tar wagon. He burned like a torch and landed in the stream of well water. Spiritual fire never destroyed him. Material fire could temporarily destroy him. Burns would temporarily deform his skin. Or burn him to ash. He rolled in the water. Marian's blessed sword still extended from Wolv's collarbone to his pelvis. The other blessed sword extended from his stomach.

Wolv wept, "I killed Pamia, again, Pamia, Pamia."

With the flames extinguished on him, he lay in the stream of well water. The cold water sizzled on his blackened skin. From the two blessed swords in him, he would not change form because of pain.

Wolv hobbled across the drawbridge and jumped into the moat.

Warrick yelled, "Put out the fires. Do not waste time running after Wolv."

The AntiChrist sunk into the cold moat water. He rubbed his burns with cool mud. In the blackness of night he rolled in the moat's mud. Camouflaged under the mud and the blackest of night, he limped down the mountain.

Wolv kept weeping and saying, "I killed Pamia, again."

Beside him Wolv saw Lilith's red eyes. Lilith face appeared as charcoal dust. She said, "This way to David Ap. Gruffydd. David waits to see who won the battle."

Lilith said, "Wolv. Hate will motivate you. Hate will save you. Now hate will give your life, hatred of Warrick and Marian. That is, if Marian lives."

Wolv said, "Pamia is dead. Again, what have I done? Again I have killed Pamia? Not again, my rage has killed Pamia?"

As two red eyes in a charcoal mist Lilith said, "Wolv. Satan wants you to give up your obsessions over Pamia. She is a distraction. You are only to turn people to hatred. Hatred harvests souls for Hell. Satan only wants you to harvest souls for Hell."

David Ap. Gruffydd was where Lilith pointed, on his horse. He said, "Make a cot for Wolv. Pull the swords out of him. Wolv needs time to heal. Despondency that he killed Pamia weakens him. Wolv needs time to recover."

He pointed to four Skinwalkers and said, "The four of you carry him with us. Let no one say the Gruffydd family abandons allies in the field."

David Ap. dismounted and walked over to Wolv and said, "Wolv. You are not a pretty sight. Your obsession over Pamia has cost us this battle."

As a wisp of charcoal dust, Lilith whispered into Wolv's ear, "Wolv. Find me the most powerful witch of black magic. I need a Satanic witch, in Wales. Tell her to come quickly. For Wolv, you will give her your soul to gain your revenge. She will know that your soul and demons in you will give her great power."

-

-

-

CHAPTER, Now in Rose Fire, Wales, Year @ 1250s A.D.

TO HEAL HIS BELOVED.

Lightening, with no rain, ripped the black sky.

Suddenly Morgan shouted, "Rain, blessed rain. Torrents of blessed rain."

Tempests of rain dropped on Rose Fire and extinguished many flames.

With the torrential rain, Warrick's knights and the exorcized priests extinguished the flames.

In the driving rain Warrick carried Marian in his arms. The blessed-arrow stuck through her collarbone and out above her shoulder blade.

Marian said, "My love. You must order your knights to take wounded knights inside the great hall. They need care. Quickly."

Lord Warrick shook in grief and rage. He gritted his teeth and said, "Marian. Now that I have found you, I cannot lose you. God would not be so cruel."

Thunder rocked the mountain. Torrents of rain poured like waterfalls from the roofs. The rain filled the bailey a foot deep.

He shouted, "All you that can walk. Carry those that cannot walk into the great hall. Put out the fires. The rain will help put out the fires."

He carried Marian into the great hall and screamed, "Father Malachi Martin, where are you?"

Father Malachi said, "Yes, my lord. I and all my students are here."

Warrick said, "Father Malachi. Help me with Marian?"

Marian looked up and said, "My love. I will always love you. Remember. I will always love you."

Lord Warrick said, "Oh God, I have caused Marian's death. God, I have failed all my sworn oaths and I have failed my love."

He felt her warm blood flow over his hands. Rage that he could not protect her caused him to shake.

Old Father Malachi said, "My lord. You must bring her into the buttery. The buttery is warm. All the unguents are in the buttery. We must stop this bleeding."

Old Father Malachi hobbled with his cane and said, "Lay her here."

He pulled a bag of unguents from a buttery drawer and his belt. He took clean cloth from the buttery and put the unguents on Marian.

Father Malachi said, "Break off the blessed-arrow head, you must leave the wood."

Warrick did.

Old Father Malachi, "Char the length of the blessed-arrow with this candle. Then you must jerk the blessed-arrow out backward and hold the wounds tight. The hot charred arrow will help cauterize the wound and prevent festering."

He put his hand to the blessed-arrow and said, "Marian. I cannot cause you more pain."

Marian said, "My love, my only pain is that you mourn for me."

He said, "That I could take your wound and your pain."

She said, "I love you."

She moaned.

Tears ran down his face. He used the candle to char the blessed-arrow. Then he grasped the blessed-arrow by the feather-end. With one quick move, he jerked it out.

She moaned again.

Her blood now pumped out with each heart beat.

Old Father Malachi said, "Quickly, my lord. Press on the wounds with both your hands."

Father Malachi pointed to Otan and said, "You. Bring all the bed linens from Marian's chambers, quickly."

Old Father Malachi said, "My lord, you train your soldiers hard. Hard as a hammer on an anvil. The hard training showed its value today. I think all of your warriors will recover and grow strong."

Warrick said, "Except Marian, the very one that we were supposed to protect."

Morgan walked over to Marian and said, "Warrick. The battle was hard but we won."

Warrick said, "If Marian dies, we have lost."

Warrick held Marian's wounds. He shook and said, "Marian. For love of me, you must stay with me, please, you must not leave me. I cannot live without you."

She awakened and whispered to him. He lowered his ear to her lips, "I would never leave you. I would never be so disobedient."

He trembled with rage, compassion and love. His emotions changed so fast, so hard that he quaked.

Marian whispered, "See to your men."

Lord Warrick cried, "I do not want to lose you, I cannot live without you."

He held her wounds with his palms and whispered into her ear, "Oh God. Do not die. Do not leave me now that I have found you. You are my love."

She grew weaker and said, "I promise that I will not die. My purpose in life is to make you chase after me all over England."

He laughed and cried.

Father Malachi pulled back the bandages and said, "You must put Marian on her side."

Malachi tore a loaf of green moldy bread in half. Then Malachi said, "Green mold covers this bread. We do not know why, but it helps with infected wounds. Press half the loaf to her back wound. Press the other half to her chest wound. You must press tight to stop the bleeding. Do not let go until I say."

Lord Warrick did as Malachi told him. He bent over and pressed the moldy bread against Marian's wounds. He pushed his emotions aside.

Father Malachi made a liquid of broth and green-moldy bread. He dripped in into Marian's mouth.

Warrick said, "Can you heal her?"

Old Father Malachi said, "My lord, I have some skill. You must stop the bleeding. It is your love that will not let her die. We will know in three days. The blood flow is not great and she does not cough up blood. Her wound is high in the collar bone and above the shoulder blade. She is very lucky."

Warrick said, "Father Malachi. You have told me so often that you are wiser?"

Old Father Malachi said, "The Pendragon curse is strong in her. Perhaps too strong for me to help her. "

Marian whispered, "You have never hugged me so tight."

Tears flowed down Warrick cheeks.

His highly disciplined mind concentrated on their love. He felt each beat of her heart.

Far away prayer bells of break of fast Prime bells rang in the valley. Then it seemed to Warrick that the evening Compline bells rang within minutes. The day seemed to him to go in a second. The beat of Marian's heart had slowed.

Old Father Malachi washed Warrick's hands and Marian's body.

Then each hour Father Malachi put more green, moldy bread in Warrick hands. To push against the wounds.

Father Malachi cleaned the wounds with salt and sulfur.

Warrick's arms ached, burned. He was holding them in one position for so many hours.

The blessed-arrow had pierced under her collar bone and above her shoulder blade. A full day Warrick pressed on Marian's back and chest. His emotional discipline began to weaken.

Old Father Malachi said, "I see your face turning rage-red. Unclench your teeth. You must not allow rage to overtake you. She needs your love. Only your love can save her, if she is to live. She needs your ceaseless devotion."

Finally Father Malachi touched the wounds. He said, "Warrick. This is the third day. The wounds have not grown hotter. Evil humors have not entered the wound. The green-mold on the bread has done its effects. Always keep a large supply of old green-moldy bread. No one knows why, but green-moldy bread has healed wounds through the ages."

Father Malachi sat and put ingredients into a mortar and ground them with a pestle.

Then he put clean cloth on Warrick's hands and filled them with the unguents. Warrick pressed them against the wounds.

Old Father Malachi said, "This is good, good. Hold her tight. These unguents work wonders on infections."

Father Malachi said, "My lord, your trial by fire is not far off. I cannot stress enough, only burning love can defeat burning hate."

After many more hours Old Father Malachi said, "Warrick. Take your hands off and let me see."

Warrick slowly removed his hands.

Old Father Malachi inspected the wounds and breathed a sign of relief. He said, "Good, the bleeding has stopped. Three days as I had said. Marian has regained her color. She is not bleeding inside her body or outside. If she was bleeding inside, she would not have regained her color. Your devotion is still necessary if you are to save her life. Her wound did not become putrid. The wounds are clean and have begun to heal, but she may still die. The Pendragon curse may still kill Marian."

Warrick knelt and prayed, "Lord God. Would you please take my soul in exchange for my bride's life. Death would not be enough punishment for my failing to protect her. Satan, take my soul and heal Marian."

Old Father Malachi said, "Careful what you ask, Satan also hears your prayers. Satan may agree to the exchange."

THEN SATAN CAN HAVE MY SOUL.
Warrick said, "Then Satan can have my soul."
The room boomed, flashed red, and filled with thick red fog.

Old Father Malachi raised a Crucifix and shouted, "Satan. In the name of our Savior, Jesus Christ, be off. In the name of Jesus Christ, I exorcize you from this room. Now, in the name of Jesus Christ, I exorcize you, Satan, from Rose Fire castle."

A roar filled the room. Then the red mist, in a great roar and blast of air circled the room. The red-fog descended into the buttery floor cracks. Into the floor's cracks and down into the earth.

Father Malachi said, "Warrick. That was foolish. You yourself are an exorcist. An exorcist of the Knights of the Sorrowful Lady. The red mist was Satan. You called him and but for me, he would be here. He would have taken your soul, left you dead. Then Marian would have no hope against the Pendragon curse."

Warrick said, "You are a powerful exorcist to exorcize Satan so quickly. I did not know."

Then Father Malachi said, "I am in a secret Vatican order of Exorcists. My students are also Vatican exorcists sent to battle to AntiChrist."

Warrick said, "I did not do my duty. My duty was to protect Marian from her own foolishness. Protect her until she learned about life in troubled areas. I failed my love and my duty."

He said to Old Father Malachi, "I have seen men die. I have seen the worst of bloody wounds. Enemies have stabbed, impaled, hacked and shot me with arrows. Never have I had such pain as watching my love near death. It is a pain that I cannot bear. All my nightmares about Ogina."

Warrick could not tell how many long he held Marian. For Warrick each day ran into an endless night waiting for Marian to wake.

SHE WILL NEVER WAKE. YOU MUST GO FIND HER. TRIAL BY FIRE.

Old Father Malachi said, "My lord, she will never wake. She will not die for a long time. Yet, the Pendragon curse has her. Marian will never wake unless you go find her. Find her soul with an exorcism. Now is the time for your most difficult fight, the trial by fire. You must go fine her because Wolv and Lilith battle for her soul. For her mind. We must all exorcize the Pendragon curse from Marian. From you."

Warrick knelt by the bed and said, "I do not understand."

Old Father Malachi then said, "I feel great evil. I feel the presence of a powerful demonic witch of the greatest evil. She is in the hands of the one called Evil, the demon Lilith. I fear Marian will never awaken, unless you find her. Find her within her own mind. Prepare for your trial by fire. Wolv's Pendragon curse trial by fire. The most difficult of exorcisms. Cain Pendragon put a curse on the Able Pendragons two thousand years ago. Wolv Pendragon put another curse on the Symon Able-Pendragon line a thousand years ago. Together these two curses have rarely been broken."

      ONLY YOUR LOVE CAN SAVE HER.
      Old Father Malachi said, "Listen to me. I told you that only your love could save her. Tonight if your love fails, the one called Hate, Lilith, will doom you. Doom Marian, and doom me to Hell. If your love succeeds, you and Marian will live in marital bliss. You must not tire in this exorcism."
      Warrick said, "You are not strong enough to wake her?"
      Old Father Malachi said, "The Satanic witch has great power. Yet, your love for Jesus, for Marian, is stronger than Lilith and Wolv. Love and exorcism can take you where Wolv's hate has trapped Marian. I know how this is done. Wolv has offered his own fate to a powerful Satanic witch to take Marian's soul. Wolv thinks Marian is Pamia. He wants Pamia in Hell with him. To do this, Wolv is willing to take Marian into Hell. Now he has trapped Marian's soul at the mouth of Hell."
      Warrick said, "What must we do?"
      Old Father Malachi said, "Warrick. I can take you to her, but I cannot fight. You must be the major exorcist. All of your knights must pray the exorcism prayers in unison. Pray until Marian awakens. Your love of Marian, your love of Jesus, alone must fight. By myself, Wolv's curse can defeat me. I could not defeat this curse even at the height of my strength. Simply, because the Pendragon curse is not upon me. My lord Warrick. The Pendragon curses are upon you and Marian. You will find that your love of Jesus and Marian is stronger than Satan. Yet, you must go and find Marian. You must endure fire. The same heat that burned Ogina to ash. The same heat that you have used to reduce Wolv to ash. Yet this fire is spiritual. You will feel the pain, but it will not reduce you to ash. In the pain never forget that the fire will not really harm you."

TO THE BRINK OF HELL.
Old Father Malachi said, "My lord Warrick. Everyone in
Rose Fire will kneel and do Adoration. We will not abandon you.
In your mind I will go with you, to the brink of Hell. If you fail, I
will fall into Hell with you and Marian. Marian's wound has
healed, but her mind and her soul are under Wolv's control. Wolv
and Lilith have trapped Marian within her mind, between life and
death. They have trapped Marian at the mouth of Hell. As an
exorcist, I can take you to where she is. The burden is on you, my
lord, your love, your love of Jesus. You alone must save her."
Warrick asked, "What shall I fight?"
Old Father Malachi said, "Hate. Hate itself. You go to
fight hate, the Ones Called Hate. Satan and Lilith and Wolv,
hundreds of thousands of demons."
Warrick asked, "What shall I fight with, what weapons will
I take."
Malachi Martin said, "Holiness. You will fight with the
authority of the Pope, The Seat of Peter. Through the Pope, the
authority of Jesus to exorcize demons. Holy Mary and Jesus and
all the saints will be with you. In your dreams you will fight with
your weapons, especially Adoration. We well bless your weapons
so that they can cleave immaterial demons. Also, as you battle, do
Adoration for the demons. Jesus will give them crippling remorse
for sins."
Malachi Martin said, "Warrick. Let me spread blessed
Extreme Unction Holy Oil on you and Marian. Now kneel and
take Holy Communion."
Warrick knelt and Malachi Martin put a concentrated Host
into Warrick's mouth. A consecrated host, the Real Presence of
Jesus in the Blessed Sacrament. Malachi Martin also put a
consecrated Host into Marian's mouth.
Father Malachi and his priest-students oiled Marian's hair
and body with Extreme Unction oil. Then thy oiled Warrick's hair
and body. Also, they oiled Warrick's weapons, blessed sword and
his ax, Blessed Dread.
Then Malachi Martin pointed to three of his students and
said, "Go. Spread this Extreme unction oil on Warrick horse,

Zeus, Zeus' blessed armor and lance. Bless Zeus, and bless Zeus' armor, bless the lance, and bless Zeus' saddle and bridle.

LOVE, LOVE ITSELF, PURE LOVE.
Old Father Malachi said, "Warrick. Love. Love itself, pure love. Your love must endure. My lord, some loves must be, your love must be, forever. Sleep now. Lower your head and sleep beside Marian, hug her and sleep. You must fight at the very mouth of Hell. Beware. I am almost used up. I have almost no strength. My exorcism may not be strong enough to bring you back after you find her. Remember, only burning love can defeat burning hate. Only burning love can defeat burning hate."

Old Father Malachi hobbled to Marian's chamber door and opened it. His other exorcism students were outside the door. They had waited for him.

He said, "Come in around Marian's bed. Read the exorcism prayers with me."

They did.

He said to her students, "Come, pray with me. Today you will see the Gates of Hell."

His students, dressed like Old Father Malachi in Antlers and deer hides, gathered around. Dressed as druids to keep others from murdering them.

Warrick hugged Marian and slept beside her.

LOVE BATTLES IN HER DREAMS.
Lord Warrick's dreams became vivid, more vivid, more real that actual life. He stood in a misty ethereal dream. Warrick wore full bright silver blessed-armor. He raised his visor. Zeus walked up behind him and knelt. In his dream, Warrick mounted Zeus. Zeus had a long sharp lance attached to the saddle in an upward pointed sheath. Zeus also had a silver-blessed shield.

In the dream, the war horse pranced in the mist.

Warrick shouted through the mist, "Marian, my love, I am here for you. I am here to take you home."

In the mist, Zeus galloped and tripped. Warrick fell off Zeus and grabbed the edge of an unseen cliff. He glanced below him to see an endless canyon of boiling, bubbling red demons. The red demons burned as if they were lumps of liquid lava.

LILITH THE WINGED DRAGON.

He held onto the edge and glanced behind himself to see a great winged dragon. A winged dragon with the faces of Wolv and Lilith. The dragon's skin was transparent to reveal it was composed of screaming burning demons.

The dragon said, "Warrick. You dare to burn me to ash in pine tar. Today I will burn you and Marian in Hell."

Fire shot from the Dragons mouth and engulfed Warrick. Pain. His blessed-armor heated red. He gritted his teeth as he heard his skin sizzle. He lost his grip amid blinding pain. Suddenly he slipped to a lower ledge. He saw his blessed-armor burn, but it did not melt, searing pain. Warrick saw his gauntlets flame. Yet, the flames did not consume him, searing pain in his fingers. Pain, pain, he only had the horrible pain of burning.

His helm and mail cowl fell off into the endless canyon. Warrick yelled, "I cannot endure. The pain is too great. My skin crackles and sears like meat over a brazier."

HOLY MARY.

As Warrick clung to a ledge, a peaceful woman's face in blue appeared before him. "Call upon my Son, Jesus. Depend upon my Son, Jesus. You also are my beloved son. You can endure. My son, you have more than enough strength. Your pure, true love of Marian and Jesus is stronger than Wolv's hate."

Warrick turned his head to see a peaceful woman's face before him. A peaceful woman's face in a blue mantle. He said, "Holy Mary. Jesus' Mother, Mother of God. Please help me."

As an ethereal face in blue, Holy Mary said, "You are also my beloved son. You must save Marian. The flames are only in your mind. Wolv chooses to go to Hell. You are to send Wolv to Hell. He chooses to go to Hell. Save Marian. Remember, only burning love can defeat burning hatred. Now go, do as Jesus wants, save Marian."

Warrick gritted his teeth. His jaw muscles bulged. He repeated, "Only burning love can defeat burning hatred."

Warrick clenched his teeth and growled, "For Marian."

Though he burned like a torch, he pulled himself up. Up ledge to ledge until he reached the top. The flames exhausted him.

He fell prone, face down in the mist. Flames on his blessed-armor licked high in the air above him. His padding under the blessed-armor burned. As he lay prone, Warrick gritted his teeth and shouted, "I must save Marian. The fire does not consume me. The pain is not real. Only in my mind, the pain is only in my mind, in my dream."

PAIN IS ONLY IN MY MIND.

With tight fists and gritted teeth, he struggled to one knee. With his fists clenched, he leaned back. Like the Lion of War that he was, he shouted, "The pain is not real." He found the strength of his endless well of determination. He gritted his teeth. Then he held his breath and ignored his heated blessed-armor and burning pads. As his fists shook, he stood and faced the dragon. He held his fist high in the air and roared, "For Marian."

The enormous dragon flew backward in surprise. The dragon said, "No one has ever survived this fire."

Warrick touched Zeus. Zeus could not feel the fire. The fire only effected Warrick. He mounted Zeus. Warrick grabbed his lance with one arm and his blessed shield in the other. Searing pain of fire coursed through his brain, through his dream. He gritted his teeth to control the pain and yelled, "Marian, Marian, where are you. Your champion is here. Your hero. Marian, I love you."

In Marian's fevered dreams she saw her love in the mist. She saw Warrick on his great warhorse Zeus. Yet, on the other side of the endless canyon. She saw flames burn from Warrick. On the other side of the chasm she could hear him yell, "Marian. Where are you?"

She saw the flames on his blessed-armor change from white to yellow. Then from red to purple.

Marian screamed, "Warrick. Here Warrick, I am here. How can you withstand the pain of the fire?"

She yelled, "My love, I am here."

Warrick could not see her. Nor could Warrick hear her.

WOLV AND LILITH WERE THE GREAT WINGED-DRAGON.

Wolv and Lilith, as the great winged dragon, snapped his jaws at Marian. Marian ran from it.

The dragon growled, "Marian, if I cannot have you, no one will have you. I will drop you into Hell."

As the winged dragon hovered, it bit Marian's gown. It pulled her closer to the edge of the canyon.

She screamed, "Warrick, where are you?"

Through the volcanic like fire and smoke, Warrick and Zeus jumped the canyon. Warrick rode beside Marian.

He shouted, "Marian, where are you? Do not leave me."

In her dream she shouted, "I am here beside you. Take my hand and pull me up on Zeus with you."

Warrick could not see her for the thick mist. He could not hear here for the dragon's roar.

Marian could see and hear Warrick. Warrick and Zeus jumped across the chasm. Each time only to ride beside Marian and not see or hear her.

Marian felt herself grow lighter and begin to drift. In her dream she saw the dragon, Wolv, stand over her. She had no where to run. The dragon bit her gown and dragged her to the edge.

WHERE IS MY CHAMPION?

She screamed and tried to run, "Warrick, my love, where is my champion. Where is my champion?"

"Here," shouted Warrick. Marian could not see Warrick. As the dragon bit Marian's gown, it dragged Marian closer to the chasm. Then Marian's gown ripped away. She stood and ran.

As Marian ran, Warrick saw her. Zeus galloped after her. The dragon, with Wolv's face, flew after Zeus and blew fire. Warrick reached down from behind Marian. Then he caught Marian on the run around her waist. With one arm, he lifted her to Zeus' saddle. Just as he had done when they first met.

-

-

-

CHAPTER,   THE DRAGON.

Marian screamed, "I will burn," as his burning arm pulled her up and onto Zeus. She touched his blessed-armor and did not feel the heat. Then she realized that only Warrick felt the pain of the fire. She realized that neither she nor Zeus could feel the fire. With one arm he held Marian tight. With the other arm, he held his long lance. Warrick used his strong thighs to steer Zeus. He charged at the great Dragon, Lilith and Wolv.

The dragon attacked with a great burst of flame. Marian screamed. Zeus jumped to one side of the flames. Then Warrick steered Zeus head first into the dragon's underbelly. As the dragon hovered, Warrick ran his lance into the dragon's belly. Up to the hilt into the dragon's belly.

The dragon raised its head and blew great flames many miles into the sky. The flames turned the entire sky, horizon to horizon, red and yellow. Then the dragon clawed at the lance. Only to tear open its belly with its claws. As it clawed its belly, it circled. In rage, it blew flame in a great circle around itself. Frantically, with its claws, it tried, but could not pull the lance from its belly. As the dragon's wings slowed, it fell deep into the endless volcanic-like canyon. The demons that burned below grabbed it. They pulled it under the red molten lava river-like demons.

THE DRAGON IS DEAD.

In her dream Warrick held Marian tight and Zeus jumped the canyon. Zeus pranced in a circle in the mist.

Warrick still burned. He said, "My love, the dragon is dead. You are mine."

He looked around and shouted, "Father Malachi. Father Malachi. Malachi Martin. Where are you?"

In the mist, Marian smiled. Zeus reared.

Suddenly, the wraith Wolv appeared with a great war ax. He said, "I am not finished. You have won nothing. You will never leave here. The curse will consume both you and Marian."

On his wraith horse, Wolv jumped and pulled Marian from Warrick's arms. The Extreme Unction oil and Jesus in Marian's mouth caused Wolv to burn.

Wolv said, "I will throw Marian into Hell. If I cannot have Marian, no one will have Marian."

Warrick shouted, "Jesus. Give Wolv remorse for his sins. Give Wolv remorse for murdering Pamia."

Warrick shouted, "Wolv. You would kill Pamia again."

Then Wolv howled, "Pamia, Pamia. I love you, Pamia."

Lord Warrick still burned. He turned Zeus beside Wolv. With one burning hand, he grabbed Wolv's crumbly black crumbly, charcoal throat. Wolv's mouth opened in silent pain. The Extreme Unction oil burned Wolv. As Warrick gritted his teeth and squeezed Wolv's throat, Wolv's red eyes bulged out. Like they would pop, pop from their sockets. With his other flaming hand, Warrick pulled Marian from Wolv's arms.

Warrick seated Marian on Zeus.

Then Warrick grasped Wolv's throat with both hands. Wolv gagged his words, "Warrick. You cannot defeat me because you have not finished your trail by fire."

Then Warrick growled, "Wolv. I know that you are now in pain so you cannot change form. I can drag you into Hell with me so Marian can be safe."

Wolv yelled, "Not without Pamia. No, not eternity in Hell's flames without Pamia! I just barely escaped. Endure, and I cannot endure Hell without Pamia with me."

BOTH FELL INTO HELL.

Warrick dragged Wolv off his black charcoal horse. Both Warrick and Wolv fell into the great chasm of Hell.

Warrick said, "Wolv. With you in Hell Marian is safe. I will battle you in Hell forever to keep Marian safe."

The AntiChrist screamed, "Father Malachi Martin blessed your blessed-armor. He covered you with Extreme Unction oil. You have the Real Presence of Jesus in Your Mouth, the Eucharist. Malachi Martin and you, Warrick, have outsmarted me."

-

-

-

CHAPTER, HOLY MARY.

In Hell's flame and demons, suddenly the face of Holy Mary appeared. Under her blue mantel she said, "Warrick. You have done Jesus' will. Just as Jesus sacrificed himself on the Cross, you have sacrificed yourself."

Under the protection of Holy Mary's blue mantel, Ogina appeared. "Ogina said, "My love, Warrick. Your Rosaries for me have saved my soul. Because of your Rosaries, Holy Mary gained permission from Jesus to take me from Hell. Warrick. Your

Adoration of the Blessed Sacrament, weekly confessions and Rosaries saved my soul. Warrick, and your holiness saved my soul."

Angels appeared and carried Ogina into Heaven.

Then Holy Mary said, "Now is the time to let go of Wolv's throat. Leave Wolv in Hell where Wolv wants to be."

Lord Warrick held Wolv's throat as Wolv screamed, "Warrick. Do not let go of me. Please do not abandon me in Hell without Pamia. Please, Warrick. Do not abandon me in Hell without Pamia. I am so lonely without Pamia. She is my love. Pamia is my heart."

Under the protection of Holy Mary's blue mantle, Pamia appeared. Pamia said, "Wolv. My love. You have only to ask Jesus for mercy. Ask Jesus for forgiveness of your sins. Then we can be together in Heaven. Just ask for Forgiveness."

Wolv screamed, "Never. Never forgiveness. Remember how Jesus killed my parents. Pamia. Warrick is going to let go of me. My love, Pamia, take my hand and come into Hell with me."

Then Pamia said, "Wolv. You know that your father, General Assassio, tried to kill Jesus in Egypt. Herod of Jerusalem asked Rome to send your father, Assassio, to Egypt. To find and kill Jesus. In Assassio's foolish attempt to run over Jesus, he ran his chariot off a cliff. Your step mother died immediately of a broken heart when she saw Assassio dead. Wolv, you know the truth."

The AntiChrist shouted, "Truth. What is truth?"

Then Pamia disappeared.

Wolv howled, "Pamia. Pamia."

Then Warrick said, "Wolv. You killed my mother. When I was six-years-old, I told you that I would return and kill you."

Then Warrick released his hold on Wolv's neck.

Wolv dropped into Hell's flames.

The winds of Hell sucked Wolv into the endless lava of demons. The canyon-mouth of Hell.

Then Holy Mary said, "Warrick, my heroic son. Wake now."

-

-

CHAPTER, In Rose Fire, Wales, Around 1250s A.D.

EVIL NOT GONE.

Then in her chambers in Rose Fire, Marian woke in Warrick's arms.

Marian listened to Warrick talk in his sleep, "My love, the dragon is dead. You are mine. My love, the dragon is dead. You are mine."

Marian thought, "Warrick had the same dream as me?"

She touched his stubbled cheek and said, "My love, the dragon is dead. Warrick, and you are mine." He woke. He kissed her lips and eyes and hugged her tight to himself.

Warrick said, "Marian, my love, you are mine. Our struggle is over. You proved yourself. You gave your life for me and I have endured the test of burning love. We are free from the Pendragon curse. Wolv is in Hell."

Lord Warrick immediately said, "Drayton. Morgan. We cannot rest. Make sure that everyone does their hour of Perpetual Adoration in Rose Fire's Chapel. Or else in the Adoration wagon. My intuition tells me that Wolv will escape from Hell. Wolv always escapes from Hell. The AntiChrist has armies of Satan worshipers on earth. Set up Perpetual Adoration of Jesus' Real Presence. Real Presence in the Blessed Sacrament. Repair the Adoration wagon and bring it into Rose Fire's bailey. Make sure everyone does weekly confession. Remember in Vitre, France when we thought that we had vanquished Wolv to hell. A Satan worshiper gave his soul to Satan. So that Wolv could come from hell and possess him. Satan worshipers cover the earth."

Warrick asked, "Which knight did such powerful Adoration that we defeated Wolv?"

Drayton said, "Not a knight. Skinwalkers killed all the knights in the chapel. Little Greta, with her pure heart did the Adoration."

Then let us set up a celebration of little Greta's pure heart.

-

-

-

CHAPTER,   TRAITOR.

ESCAPING HELL.

Suddenly a student in Marina's chamber screamed. "I want Wolv's strength. Wolv, possess my body. I give you myself completely. Possess my body. Wolv, I want your strength."

The priest-exorcism student ran.

Warrick shouted, "Catch him. Run after him."

The exorcism-priest student stumbled from Rose Fire out onto the battlefield. Then he ran down the mountain road shouting, "Wolv. I give you permission to enter me. Give me your strength. Possess me completely, Wolv."

He struggled down the mountain road. His eyes turned red and his skin charcoal crumbly black. A wraith horse formed under him. Hell's flames engulfed him. Then the student turned into Wolv. In Hell's flames, Wolv howled in pain. He said, "Lilith, you are in me within this student. We have escaped from Hell through this foolish student. Satan's worshipers are everywhere."

As Hell's flames burned Wolv, Wolv howled in pain. All curses have a cost. Wolv's curse burned him in return. He rode on the wraith's red-eyed horse. The student no longer existed. Wolv had escaped Hell through him. Wolv grasped his head and screamed in pain as the curse took revenge on him. Revenge on him as Hell's flames.

He screamed, "Now. The curse will burn me. I failed to defeat Warrick, to change Warrick and Marian's fate. So the curse demands payment. Marian, Marian is still not beyond my grasp."

Then Wolv turned on his wraith horse and rode back to Rose Fire. Rode back to Rose Fire to capture Marian."

INSIDE ROSE FIRE IN HER CHAMBERS.

Inside Rose Fire, in Marian's chambers, Marian sat up and pointed. She said, "Warrick. What is that?"

They looked in the corner to see Warrick's blessed-armor, as it stood, melted, smoldering. Warrick had fulfilled his obligation of a 'burning love can only defeat a burning hate.' Marian had fulfilled her obligation of an unselfish love by taking Warrick's blessed-arrow.

-

-

-

CHAPTER, In Rose Fire, Wales, Around 1250s A.D.

EVIL. BACK FROM HELL.

Wolv was now this instant returning for revenge.

The AntiChrist, Wolv, with Lilith inside him, rode his crumbly, charcoal, wraith horse. Rode his horse into Rose Fire's bailey.

A knight range the warning bell. Everyone ran out to the bailey.

Wolv shouted, "Warrick. I can even escape from Hell. You have not defeated us, Lilith is inside me to strengthen me. We are back to take Marian and kill the rest of you. You cannot even condemn me to Hell. Satan worshipers on earth bring me back from Hell. Warrick. You cannot stop me."

"Remember me," Old bald Norwin plunged a blessed dagger into Wolv's back.

Wolv howled, frozen in pain. The blessed dagger caused him to burst into red-yellow flame.

Norwin twisted the dagger. Then Norwin said, "This. This is the same dagger you used to kill Beatrice Pendragon, Warrick's mother."

Lord Warrick shot Wolv with a blessed arrow. He commanded, "All of you. I order all of you to shoot Wolv with blessed arrows. He cannot change form when he is in pain. Shoot him more. Spear him and the charcoal horse with blessed spears. The blessing on the arrows causes him to burn in pain."

Marian ran out onto the battlement and shouted, "Wolv. You harassed the wrong woman. I know your secrets. Blacksmiths? Is the smelter hot?"

The blacksmith shouted from outside the walls, "My Lady Marian. The smelter is white hot, just as you demand that it always be."

Then Marian picked up a heavy blessed sword. She dragged it behind herself and descended the battlement steps to the bailey.

THE LADY OF THE CASTLE.

She said, "Wolv. I have had enough of you."

She swung the blessed sword and cut off one of Wolv's legs. In pain, Wolv could not move or change form.

Marian shouted, "Shoot the leg with blessed arrows. All your arrows and spears are blessed."

Wolv shouted, "Pamia, how can you do this to me."

From pain, Wolv fell from his horse.

Marian chopped off Wolv's arms.

Marian shouted, "Knights. I know how to slow Wolv for a long time. Shoot him with more blessed arrows and help me chop Wolv into pieces. Stick a blessed arrow in each piece."

Knights joined Marian. They chopped Wolv into small pieces.

Wolv's detached head said with Lilith's voice, "Marian. You know that you cannot kill us."

Marian said, "Wolv, Lilith. You do not know me. I read. Lilith, you made your worst mistake combining with Wolv and coming back. I read and I observe. The ancient Damascus tomes explain that we can harden Damascus steel with pure carbon. We have observed that you both change into black dust, carbon, pure charcoal. Your physical essence is pure carbon, pure charcoal. Now I will capture you for a long time. We will record for future generations how to capture you."

Marian shouted, "Now knights. Bring the pieces of Wolv out to the smelter."

Then Marian shouted, "Warrick. Have your knights gather all my Damascus steel weapons. Have Father Malachi Martin bless them all."

Drayton said, "Should we obey her."

Warrick said, "Absolutely. That woman just chopped both Lilith and Wolv into pieces. Marian is angry. A true angry warrior. Obey her or she may chop you into pieces."

At the smelter Marian said, "Now Father Malachi Martin. Bless all the Damascus Steel weapons. Bless the smelter continuously."

Warrick and Malachi Martin obeyed. As obedient Vatican Catholic priests, they constantly sprinkled Holy Water on the smelter. They blessed it in the name of the Father, Son and Holy Spirit.

At the smelter, Marian instructed the blacksmith. "Put a piece of Wolv in the sphere. In the sphere with a Damascus steel weapon. Then clamp the sphere shut. Now speed up the waterwheel bellows."

Within an hour white-hot metal flowed from the bottom of the sphere.

Marian said, "Warrick. Father Malachi. Continuously keep blessing this smelter as we use it."

Warrick said, "Of course I will obey."

Marian said, "Now. The molten metal has flowed into the molds. Do not blow air across the molten metal. We blow air across the molten metal to burn away impurities. The impurities are Wolv and Lilith. Here we want these impurities to remain in the blessed metal. If you blow air across the molten iron, the impurities will burn away. We want to trap these impurities. We want to trap Wolv and Lilith in carbonized Damascus steel. The hardest of Damascus steel. Damascus tomes call this steel, Damascus charcoal steel, if done with pure charcoal. Carbon steel. Keep blessing the steel and the smelter."

Marian shouted, "Warrick. Come here and bless this molten metal."

As Warrick blessed the molten iron Wolv and Lilith growled in pain.

The smith stepped back and shouted, "Run. I see both Wolv's face and Lilith's face in the steel. I see the faces of many demons trapped in the steel. They move like people trapped inside a mirror."

Marian said, "We trapped them. Fear not. When this steel cools, we will have trapped Wolv and Lilith. Trapped in it just as Damascus steel traps carbon. The blessing causes them too much pain to change form. Blessed Damascus carbon steel.

All day and all night, all the knights watched Marian and the blacksmith. They trapped pieces of Wolv-Lilith. Pieces trapped in separate pieces of carbonized, blessed Damascus steel. Trapped in many Damascus steel swords, axes, shields. All blessed steel. Now all carbonized.

The next day Warrick wiped his brow and said, "Marian. Now you have one hundred pieces of Wolv-Lilith, all trapped in this Damascus steel. What do you propose we do with them?"

Marian said, "Bury them in blessed ground. We dig up the chapel floor, deep, and bury the pieces in concrete. Blessed concrete. In blessed ground both Wolv and Lilith will be helpless. We keep Perpetual Adoration above them always."

Warrick said, "Could Wolv ever escape the Damascus steel?"

Marian said, "Of course. Just use the original process of making Damascus steel. Melt it down and blow air across the molten metal until the impurities burn off. Wolv and Lilith are the impurities. It would have to be done to all the pieces. Otherwise, Wolv and Lilith would be missing arms or legs or parts of their heads."

They buried the pieces under Rose Fires' chapel floor.

The moment they buried Wolv, gentle rain fell on the lower Black Mountains. Rain below the snow line. The drought on the mountains below the snow line was over. All was right in their world.

On the battlement, Warrick hugged Marian and said, "Drayton. Open the wine and mead caskets. Pour the ale, bake endless sweet cakes, open the honey caskets. I want you to bring everyone from the valley to celebrate. For Marian is with us again. Let the bells ring throughout the valley."

Marian said, "Warrick? Did you hear that the king devastated Blanche? He pledged Blanche in marriage to the unsightly merchant, Fragate Schaaner? Schaaner took her to sea. To sea where he will keep her out of England on the oceans. Blanche hates sea voyages."

Then Morgan said, "Has anyone seen Ross?"

Warrick said, "Find Ross. Where is Ross-Templar? Search Rose Fire. Find Ross-Templar."

Warrick shouted, "Has anyone seen Ross-Templar? Where is Ross-Templar?"

-

-

-

CHAPTER,
LADY INNOCENCE.

At the Wye river, an elder woman, a peasant dripped broth into Ross-Templar's mouth. She had dragged him out of the Wye river.

As Ross breathed, he rattled and coughed up muddy water from his lungs.

The elderly woman said, "Young Knight. If you do not wake up soon, you will die."

In Ross-Templar's night mare he saw Lady Innocence. She leapt off her farther's home-manor. Repeatedly, she jumped off the wall to her death.

In his nightmare Lady Innocence knelt beside him and said, "Look. In my arms is your son. Your Rosaries for me have gained forgiveness for me committing suicide. Your love of me has gained the Heavenly Father's forgiveness. Holy Mary's Rosaries are very powerful. Holy Mary said that this is not your time to die. I love you, Ross. I will always love you. Now, lay on your side and cough up that mud."

In the hut Ross said, "Lady Innocence. My little son."

The elder woman said, "No one is here, but me."

Ross rolled on his side and coughed up river mud.

The elder woman said, "Keep coughing until you can breathe easily. I was sure that you would die. So many people that I pull out of the river are dead."

From outside the hut Ross heard, "Ross-Temple, where are you?"

Ross-Templar coughed and said, "Warrick. With Lady Innocence, my son and this charitable woman."

Then the elder woman said, "Warrick."

Ross said, "Yes, Lord Warrick of Rose Fire."

THE CHAMPION'S MOTHER?

The elder woman leaned on a stick and stepped from her hut. She repeated, "Warrick. Not a common name."

Warrick said, "Is Ross sick, wounded?"

Then the elder woman said, "Warrick. Ross is better. Warrick, please dismount. Let me touch your face. It is impossible but you sound familiar."

The elder woman said, "My heart pounds at the sound of your voice."

Warrick dismounted. The elder woman walked to him and said, "My eyes fail me. Let me touch your face."

She reached up and touched his face and said, "Little Warrick? I am Beatrice Pendragon."

Tears formed in Warrick's eyes as he said, "Impossible. I saw Wolv. He stabbed you."

Beatrice said, "Warrick. Then I saw you stab Wolv. Stab Wolv before Wolv could shove the knife deeper into my back. Little Warrick. You saved me as you said you would. The servants nursed me back to health and brought me here. They faked my grave."

Warrick commanded, "Morgan, bring Ross."

Warrick picked up his elder mother. He wrapped her in his huge black fur lined cape. His mother in Warrick's arms, mother and son rode back to Rose Fire. A ride of Victory and tears of happiness.

46495304R00330

Made in the USA
Lexington, KY
27 July 2019